SELECT TALES

OF

TCHEHOV

SELECT TALES

OF

TCHEHOV

Translated from the Russian
by
Constance Garnett

CHATTO & WINDUS
LONDON

PUBLISHED 1927

NOTE

ANTON PAVLOVITCH TCHEHOV, the son of a grocer and one of a family of six, was born at Taganrog in Southern Russia on January 17, 1860. In 1884 he took his medical degree at the University of Moscow. He never practised regularly ; his family was poor, and he had found that he could make money by writing. His first works were humorous stories, but about 1886 he turned to stricter subjects. In 1890 he made a journey to Sahalin across Siberia and back by sea. From that year he lived mainly in Russia, at Melihovo, a small estate he had bought in the province of Moscow (1892-1898) ; and later at Yalta in the Crimea (1898-1904), where he had to go on account of pulmonary consumption. In 1901 he married the actress Olga Knipper. His two chief plays, *Three Sisters* and *The Cherry Orchard*, were first produced in 1901 and 1903. In 1904 he went abroad for a cure to Badenweiler in the Black Forest ; he died there on July 2, 1904. His body was buried in Moscow.

The most complete translation of his *Tales* is that by Constance Garnett : 13 volumes (St. Martin's Library), Chatto & Windus. It contains, with the exception of a few minor sketches, all the tales that Tchehov considered worth republishing in his lifetime ; and a selection of the best of those republished after his death. A full

NOTE

list will be found at the end of this book. His *Plays* have also been translated by Constance Garnett : 2 vols. (St. Martin's Library), Chatto & Windus ; they contain all his dramatic work, with the exception of *The Wood Demon*, translated by S. S. Koteliansky : 1 vol., Chatto & Windus.

There are two good selections of his letters : *Letters of Anton Tchehov to his Family and Friends*, translated by Constance Garnett, with an abridged version of the biographical sketch of Tchehov by his brother Mihail : 1 vol., Chatto & Windus ; and *The Life and Letters of Anton Tchekhov*, translated and edited, with interesting biographical and bibliographical material, by S. S. Koteliansky and Philip Tomlinson : 1 vol., Cassell & Co. Ltd. *The Letters of Anton Pavlovitch Tchehov to Olga Leonardovna Knipper*, translated by Constance Garnett : 1 vol., Chatto & Windus, should also be consulted.

See too *The Note-Books of Anton Tchekhov, together with Reminiscences of Tchekhov by Maxim Gorky*, translated by S. S. Koteliansky and Leonard Woolf : The Hogarth Press ; *Anton Tchekhov : Literary and Theatrical Reminiscences*, translated and edited by S. S. Koteliansky : Routledge ; and *Anton Chehov : a Critical Study* by William Gerhardi : Cobden-Sanderson.

CONTENTS

CONTENTS

The numbers after the stories are those of the volumes
in which the stories are published in the
St. Martin's Library.

THE LADY WITH THE DOG

I.

It was said that a new person had appeared on the sea-front: a lady with a little dog. Dmitri Dmitritch Gurov, who had by then been a fortnight at Yalta, and so was fairly at home there, had begun to take an interest in new arrivals. Sitting in Verney's pavilion, he saw, walking on the sea-front, a fair-haired young lady of medium height, wearing a *béret*; a white Pomeranian dog was running behind her.

And afterwards he met her in the public gardens and in the square several times a day. She was walking alone, always wearing the same *béret*, and always with the same white dog; no one knew who she was, and everyone called her simply " the lady with the dog."

" If she is here alone without a husband or friends, it wouldn't be amiss to make her acquaintance," Gurov reflected.

He was under forty, but he had a daughter already twelve years old, and two sons at school. He had been married young, when he was a student in his second year, and by now his wife seemed half as old again as he. She was a tall, erect woman with dark eyebrows, staid and dignified, and, as she said of herself, intellectual. She read a great deal, used phonetic spelling, called her husband, not Dmitri, but Dimitri, and he secretly considered her unintelligent, narrow, inelegant, was afraid of her, and did not like to be at home. He had begun being unfaithful to her long ago— had been unfaithful to her often, and, probably on that account, almost always spoke ill of women, and when they were talked about in his presence, used to call them " the lower race."

It seemed to him that he had been so schooled by bitter experience that he might call them what he liked, and yet he could not get on for two days together without " the lower race." In the society of men he was bored and not himself, .with them he was cold and uncommunicative; but when he was in the company of women he felt free, and knew what to say to them and how to behave; and he was at ease with them even when he was silent. In his appearance, in his character, in his whole nature, there was something attractive and elusive which allured women and disposed them in his favour; he knew that, and some force seemed to draw him, too, to them.

Experience often repeated, truly bitter experience, had taught him long ago that with decent people, especially Moscow people—always slow to move and irresolute—every intimacy, which at first so agreeably diversifies life and appears a light and charming adventure, inevitably grows into a regular problem of extreme intricacy, and in the long run the situation becomes unbearable.

THE LADY WITH THE DOG

But at every fresh meeting with an interesting woman this experience seemed to slip out of his memory, and he was eager for life, and everything seemed simple and amusing.

One evening he was dining in the gardens, and the lady in the *béret* came up slowly to take the next table. Her expression, her gait, her dress, and the way she did her hair told him that she was a lady, that she was married, that she was in Yalta for the first time and alone, and that she was dull there. . . . The stories told of the immorality in such places as Yalta are to a great extent untrue; he despised them, and knew that such stories were for the most part made up by persons who would themselves have been glad to sin if they had been able; but when the lady sat down at the next table three paces from him, he remembered these tales of easy conquests, of trips to the mountains, and the tempting thought of a swift, fleeting love affair, a romance with an unknown woman, whose name he did not know, suddenly took possession of him.

He beckoned coaxingly to the Pomeranian, and when the dog came up to him he shook his finger at it. The Pomeranian growled: Gurov shook his finger at it again.

The lady looked at him and at once dropped her eyes.

" He doesn't bite," she said, and blushed.

" May I give him a bone ?" he asked; and when she nodded he asked courteously, " Have you been long in Yalta ?"

" Five days."

" And I have already dragged out a fortnight here."

There was a brief silence.

" Time goes fast, and yet it is so dull here !" she said, not looking at him.

" That's only the fashion to say it is dull here. A provincial will live in Belyov or Zhidra and not be dull, and when he comes here it's ' Oh, the dulness ! Oh, the dust !' One would think he came from Grenada."

She laughed. Then both continued eating in silence, like strangers, but after dinner they walked side by side; and there sprang up between them the light jesting conversation of people who are free and satisfied, to whom it does not matter where they go or what they talk about. They walked and talked of the strange light on the sea: the water was of a soft warm lilac hue, and there was a golden streak from the moon upon it. They talked of how sultry it was after a hot day. Gurov told her that he came from Moscow, that he had taken his degree in Arts, but had a post in a bank; that he had trained as an opera-singer, but had given it up, that he owned two houses in Moscow. . . . And from her he learnt that she had grown up in Petersburg, but had lived in S—— since her marriage two years before, that she was staying another month in Yalta, and that her husband, who needed a holiday too, might perhaps come and fetch her. She was not sure whether her husband had a post in a Crown Department or under the Provincial Council—and was amused by her own ignorance.

4

And Gurov learnt, too, that she was called Anna Sergeyevna.

Afterwards he thought about her in his room at the hotel—thought she would certainly meet him next day; it would be sure to happen. As he got into bed he thought how lately she had been a girl at school, doing lessons like his own daughter; he recalled the diffidence, the angularity, that was still manifest in her laugh and her manner of talking with a stranger. This must have been the first time in her life she had been alone in surroundings in which she was followed, looked at, and spoken to merely from a secret motive which she could hardly fail to guess. He recalled her slender, delicate neck, her lovely grey eyes.

"There's something pathetic about her, anyway," he thought, and fell asleep.

II.

A week had passed since they had made acquaintance. It was a holiday. It was sultry indoors, while in the street the wind whirled the dust round and round, and blew people's hats off. It was a thirsty day, and Gurov often went into the pavilion, and pressed Anna Sergeyevna to have syrup and water or an ice. One did not know what to do with oneself.

In the evening when the wind had dropped a little, they went out on to the groyne to see the steamer come in. There were a great many people walking about the harbour; they had gathered to welcome someone, bringing bouquets. And two peculiarities of a well-dressed Yalta crowd were very conspicuous: the elderly ladies were dressed like young ones, and there were great numbers of generals.

Owing to the roughness of the sea, the steamer arrived late, after the sun had set, and it was a long time turning about before it reached the groyne. Anna Sergeyevna looked through her lorgnette at the steamer and the passengers as though looking for acquaintances, and when she turned to Gurov her eyes were shining. She talked a great deal and asked disconnected questions, forgetting next moment what she had asked; then she dropped her lorgnette in the crush.

The festive crowd began to disperse; it was too dark to see people's faces. The wind had completely dropped, but Gurov and Anna Sergeyevna still stood as though waiting to see someone else come from the steamer. Anna Sergeyevna was silent now, and sniffed the flowers without looking at Gurov.

" The weather is better this evening," he said. " Where shall we go now ? Shall we drive somewhere ?"

She made no answer.

Then he looked at her intently, and all at once put his arm round her and kissed her on the lips, and breathed in the moisture and the fragrance of the flowers; and he immediately looked round him, anxiously wondering whether anyone had seen them.

" Let us go to your hotel," he said softly. And both walked quickly.

6

THE LADY WITH THE DOG

The room was close and smelt of the scent she had bought at the Japanese shop. Gurov looked at her and thought: "What different people one meets in the world!" From the past he preserved memories of careless, good-natured women, who loved cheerfully and were grateful to him for the happiness he gave them, however brief it might be; and of women like his wife who loved without any genuine feeling, with superfluous phrases, affectedly, hysterically, with an expression that suggested that it was not love nor passion, but something more significant; and of two or three others, very beautiful, cold women, on whose faces he had caught a glimpse of a rapacious expression —an obstinate desire to snatch from life more than it could give, and these were capricious, unreflecting, domineering, unintelligent women not in their first youth, and when Gurov grew cold to them their beauty excited his hatred, and the lace on their linen seemed to him like scales.

But in this case there was still the diffidence, the angularity of inexperienced youth, an awkward feeling; and there was a sense of consternation as though someone had suddenly knocked at the door. The attitude of Anna Sergeyevna— "the lady with the dog"—to what had happened was somehow peculiar, very grave, as though it were her fall—so it seemed, and it was strange and inappropriate. Her face drooped and faded, and on both sides of it her long hair hung down mournfully; she mused in a dejected attitude like "the woman who was a sinner" in an old-fashioned picture.

7

" It's wrong," she said. " You will be the first to despise me now."

There was a water-melon on the table. Gurov cut himself a slice and began eating it without haste. There followed at least half an hour of silence.

Anna Sergeyevna was touching; there was about her the purity of a good, simple woman who had seen little of life. The solitary candle burning on the table threw a faint light on her face, yet it was clear that she was very unhappy.

" How could I despise you ?" asked Gurov. " You don't know what you are saying."

" God forgive me," she said, and her eyes filled with tears. " It's awful."

" You seem to feel you need to be forgiven."

" Forgiven ? No. I am a bad, low woman; I despise myself and don't attempt to justify myself. It's not my husband but myself I have deceived. And not only just now; I have been deceiving myself for a long time. My husband may be a good, honest man, but he is a flunkey ! I don't know what he does there, what his work is, but I know he is a flunkey ! I was twenty when I was married to him. I have been tormented by curiosity; I wanted something better. ' There must be a different sort of life,' I said to myself. I wanted to live ! To live, to live ! . . . I was fired by curiosity . . . you don't understand it, but, I swear to God, I could not control myself; something happened to me: I could not be restrained. I told my husband I was ill, and came here. . . . And here I have been walking about as though I

were dazed, like a mad creature; . . . and now I
have become a vulgar, contemptible woman whom
anyone may despise."

Gurov felt bored already, listening to her. He
was irritated by the naïve tone, by this remorse,
so unexpected and inopportune; but for the tears
in her eyes, he might have thought she was jesting
or playing a part.

"I don't understand," he said softly. "What
is it you want?"

She hid her face on his breast and pressed close
to him.

"Believe me, believe me, I beseech you . . ."
she said. "I love a pure, honest life, and sin is
loathsome to me. I don't know what I am doing.
Simple people say: ' The Evil One has beguiled
me.' And I may say of myself now that the
Evil One has beguiled me."

"Hush, hush! . . ." he muttered.

He looked at her fixed, scared eyes, kissed her,
talked softly and affectionately, and by degrees
she was comforted, and her gaiety returned; they
both began laughing.

Afterwards when they went out there was not
a soul on the sea-front. The town with its
cypresses had quite a deathlike air, but the sea
still broke noisily on the shore; a single barge
was rocking on the waves, and a lantern was blinking sleepily on it.

They found a cab and drove to Oreanda.

"I found out your surname in the hall just
now: it was written on the board—Von Diderits,"
said Gurov. "Is your husband a German?"

" No; I believe his grandfather was a German, but he is an Orthodox Russian himself."

At Oreanda they sat on a seat not far from the church, looked down at the sea, and were silent. Yalta was hardly visible through the morning mist; white clouds stood motionless on the mountain-tops. The leaves did not stir on the trees, grasshoppers chirruped, and the monotonous hollow sound of the sea, rising up from below, spoke of the peace, of the eternal sleep awaiting us. So it must have sounded when there was no Yalta, no Oreanda here; so it sounds now, and it will sound as indifferently and monotonously when we are all no more. And in this constancy, in this complete indifference to the life and death of each of us, there lies hid, perhaps, a pledge of our eternal salvation, of the unceasing movement of life upon earth, of unceasing progress towards perfection. Sitting beside a young woman who in the dawn seemed so lovely, soothed and spellbound in these magical surroundings—the sea, mountains, clouds, the open sky—Gurov thought how in reality everything is beautiful in this world when one reflects: everything except what we think or do ourselves when we forget our human dignity and the higher aims of our existence.

A man walked up to them—probably a keeper—looked at them and walked away. And this detail seemed mysterious and beautiful, too, They saw a steamer come from Theodosia, with its lights out in the glow of dawn.

" There is dew on the grass," said Anna Sergeyevna, after a silence.

" Yes. It's time to go home."

They went back to the town.

Then they met every day at twelve o'clock on the sea-front, lunched and dined together, went for walks, admired the sea. She complained that she slept badly, that her heart throbbed violently; asked the same questions, troubled now by jealousy and now by the fear that he did not respect her sufficiently. And often in the square or gardens, when there was no one near them, he suddenly drew her to him and kissed her passionately. Complete idleness, these kisses in broad daylight while he looked round in dread of someone's seeing them, the heat, the smell of the sea, and the continual passing to and fro before him of idle, well-dressed, well-fed people, made a new man of him; he told Anna Sergeyevna how beautiful she was, how fascinating. He was impatiently passionate, he would not move a step away from her, while she was often pensive and continually urged him to confess that he did not respect her, did not love her in the least, and thought of her as nothing but a common woman. Rather late almost every evening they drove somewhere out of town, to Oreanda or to the waterfall; and the expedition was always a success, the scenery invariably impressed them as grand and beautiful.

They were expecting her husband to come, but a letter came from him, saying that there was something wrong with his eyes, and he entreated his wife to come home as quickly as possible. Anna Sergeyevna made haste to go.

" It's a good thing I am going away," she said to Gurov. " It's the finger of destiny !"

She went by coach and he went with her. They were driving the whole day. When she had got into a compartment of the express, and when the second bell had rung, she said:

" Let me look at you once more . . . look at you once again. That's right."

She did not shed tears, but was so sad that she seemed ill, and her face was quivering.

" I shall remember you . . . think of you," she said. " God be with you; be happy. Don't remember evil against me. We are parting for ever—it must be so, for we ought never to have met. Well, God be with you."

The train moved off rapidly, its lights soon vanished from sight, and a minute later there was no sound of it, as though everything had conspired together to end as quickly as possible that sweet delirium, that madness. Left alone on the platform, and gazing into the dark distance, Gurov listened to the chirrup of the grasshoppers and the hum of the telegraph wires, feeling as though he had only just waked up. And he thought, musing, that there had been another episode or adventure in his life, and it, too, was at an end, and nothing was left of it but a memory. . . . He was moved, sad, and conscious of a slight remorse. This young woman whom he would never meet again had not been happy with him; he was genuinely warm and affectionate with her, but yet in his manner, his tone, and his caresses there had been a shade of light irony, the coarse condescension of a happy man who was, besides, almost twice her age. All the time she had called him kind, exceptional, lofty; obviously he had seemed to her different from what he really was, so he had unintentionally deceived her. . . .

Here at the station was already a scent of autumn; it was a cold evening.

" It's time for me to go north," thought Gurov as he left the platform. " High time !"

III.

At home in Moscow everything was in its winter routine; the stoves were heated, and in the morning it was still dark when the children were having breakfast and getting ready for school, and the nurse would light the lamp for a short time. The frosts had begun already. When the first snow has fallen, on the first day of sledge-driving it is pleasant to see the white earth, the white roofs, to draw soft, delicious breath, and the season brings back the days of one's youth. The old limes and birches, white with hoar-frost, have a good-natured expression; they are nearer to one's heart than cypresses and palms, and near them one doesn't want to be thinking of the sea and the mountains.

Gurov was Moscow born; he arrived in Moscow on a fine frosty day, and when he put on his fur coat and warm gloves, and walked along Petrovka, and when on Saturday evening he heard the ringing of the bells, his recent trip and the places he had seen lost all charm for him. Little by little

he became absorbed in Moscow life, greedily read
three newspapers a day, and declared he did not
read the Moscow papers on principle ! He already
felt a longing to go to restaurants, clubs, dinner-
parties, anniversary celebrations, and he felt
flattered at entertaining distinguished lawyers
and artists, and at playing cards with a professor
at the doctor's club. He could already eat a
whole plateful of salt fish and cabbage. . . .

In another month, he fancied, the image of
Anna Sergeyevna would be shrouded in a mist in
his memory, and only from time to time would
visit him in his dreams with a touching smile as
others did. But more than a month passed, real
winter had come, and everything was still clear
in his memory as though he had parted with Anna
Sergeyevna only the day before. And his
memories glowed more and more vividly. When
in the evening stillness he heard from his study
the voices of his children, preparing their lessons,
or when he listened to a song or the organ at the
restaurant, or the storm howled in the chimney,
suddenly everything would rise up in his memory:
what had happened on the groyne, and the early
morning with the mist on the mountains, and the
steamer coming from Theodosia, and the kisses.
He would pace a long time about his room, remembering it all and smiling; then his memories
passed into dreams, and in his fancy the past was
mingled with what was to come. Anna Sergeyevna did not visit him in dreams, but followed
him about everywhere like a shadow and haunted
him. When he shut his eyes he saw her as though

she were living before him, and she seemed to him lovelier, younger, tenderer than she was; and he imagined himself finer than he had been in Yalta. In the evenings she peeped out at him from the bookcase, from the fireplace, from the corner—he heard her breathing, the caressing rustle of her dress. In the street he watched the women, looking for someone like her.

He was tormented by an intense desire to confide his memories to someone. But in his home it was impossible to talk of his love, and he had no one outside; he could not talk to his tenants nor to anyone at the bank. And what had he to talk of? Had he been in love, then? Had there been anything beautiful, poetical, or edifying or simply interesting in his relations with Anna Sergeyevna? And there was nothing for him but to talk vaguely of love, of woman, and no one guessed what it meant; only his wife twitched her black eyebrows, and said: " The part of a lady-killer does not suit you at all, Dimitri."

One evening, coming out of the doctors' club with an official with whom he had been playing cards, he could not resist saying:

" If only you knew what a fascinating woman I made the acquaintance of in Yalta!"

The official got into his sledge and was driving away, but turned suddenly and shouted:

" Dmitri Dmitritch!"

" What?"

" You were right this evening: the sturgeon was a bit too strong!"

These words, so ordinary, for some reason

moved Gurov to indignation, and struck him as degrading and unclean. What savage manners, what people ! What senseless nights, what uninteresting, uneventful days ! The rage for card-playing, the gluttony, the drunkenness, the continual talk always about the same thing. Useless pursuits and conversations always about the same things absorb the better part of one's time, the better part of one's strength, and in the end there is left a life grovelling and curtailed, worthless and trivial, and there is no escaping or getting away from it—just as though one were in a madhouse or a prison.

Gurov did not sleep all night, and was filled with indignation. And he had a headache all next day. And the next night he slept badly; he sat up in bed, thinking, or paced up and down his room. He was sick of his children, sick of the bank; he had no desire to go anywhere or to talk of anything.

In the holidays in December he prepared for a journey, and told his wife he was going to Petersburg to do something in the interests of a young friend—and he set off for S——. What for ? He did not very well know himself. He wanted to see Anna Sergeyevna and to talk with her—to arrange a meeting, if possible.

He reached S—— in the morning, and took the best room at the hotel, in which the floor was covered with grey army cloth, and on the table was an inkstand, grey with dust and adorned with a figure on horseback, with its hat in its hand and its head broken off. The hotel porter gave

him the necessary information; Von Diderits lived
in a house of his own in Old Gontcharny Street—
it was not far from the hotel: he was rich and lived
in good style, and had his own horses; everyone
in the town knew him. The porter pronounced
the name " Dridirits."

Gurov went without haste to Old Gontcharny
Street and found the house. Just opposite the
house stretched a long grey fence adorned with
nails.

" One would run away from a fence like that,"
thought Gurov, looking from the fence to the
windows of the house and back again.

He considered: to-day was a holiday, and the
husband would probably be at home. And in
any case it would be tactless to go into the house
and upset her. If he were to send her a note it
might fall into her husband's hands, and then it
might ruin everything. The best thing was to
trust to chance. And he kept walking up and
down the street by the fence, waiting for the
chance. He saw a beggar go in at the gate and
dogs fly at him; then an hour later he heard a
piano, and the sounds were faint and indistinct.
Probably it was Anna Sergeyevna playing. The
front door suddenly opened, and an old woman
came out, followed by the familiar white Pomeranian. Gurov was on the point of calling to the
dog, but his heart began beating violently, and
in his excitement he could not remember the
dog's name.

He walked up and down, and loathed the grey
fence more and more, and by now he thought

irritably that Anna Sergeyevna had forgotten him, and was perhaps already amusing herself with someone else, and that that was very natural in a young woman who had nothing to look at from morning till night but that confounded fence. He went back to his hotel room and sat for a long while on the sofa, not knowing what to do, then he had dinner and a long nap.

" How stupid and worrying it is ! " he thought when he woke and looked at the dark windows: it was already evening. " Here I've had a good sleep for some reason. What shall I do in the night ? "

He sat on the bed, which was covered by a cheap grey blanket, such as one sees in hospitals, and he taunted himself in his vexation:

" So much for the lady with the dog . . . so much for the adventure. . . . You're in a nice fix. . . ."

That morning at the station a poster in large letters had caught his eye. " The Geisha " was to be performed for the first time. He thought of this and went to the theatre.

" It's quite possible she may go to the first performance," he thought.

The theatre was full. As in all provincial theatres, there was a fog above the chandelier, the gallery was noisy and restless; in the front row the local dandies were standing up before the beginning of the performance, with their hands behind them; in the Governor's box the Governor's daughter, wearing a boa, was sitting in the front seat, while the Governor himself lurked modestly behind the curtain with only his hands visible; the orchestra was a long time tuning up; the stage curtain swayed. All the time the audience were coming in and taking their seats Gurov looked at them eagerly.

Anna Sergeyevna, too, came in. She sat down in the third row, and when Gurov looked at her his heart contracted, and he understood clearly that for him there was in the whole world no creature so near, so precious, and so important to him; she, this little woman, in no way remarkable, lost in a provincial crowd, with a vulgar lorgnette in her hand, filled his whole life now, was his sorrow and his joy, the one happiness that he now desired for himself, and to the sounds of the inferior orchestra, of the wretched provincial violins, he thought how lovely she was. He thought and dreamed.

A young man with small side-whiskers, tall and stooping, came in with Anna Sergeyevna and sat down beside her; he bent his head at every step and seemed to be continually bowing. Most likely this was the husband whom at Yalta, in a rush of bitter feeling, she had called a flunkey. And there really was in his long figure, his side-whiskers, and the small bald patch on his head, something of the flunkey's obsequiousness; his smile was sugary, and in his buttonhole there was some badge of distinction like the number on a waiter.

During the first interval the husband went away to smoke; she remained alone in her stall. Gurov, who was sitting in the stalls, too, went up to her and said in a trembling voice, with a forced smile:

"Good-evening."

She glanced at him and turned pale, then glanced again with horror, unable to believe her eyes, and tightly gripped the fan and the lorgnette in her hands, evidently struggling with herself not to faint. Both were silent. She was sitting, he was standing, frightened by her confusion and not venturing to sit down beside her. The violins and the flute began tuning up. He felt suddenly frightened; it seemed as though all the people in the boxes were looking at them. She got up and went quickly to the door; he followed her, and both walked senselessly along passages, and up and down stairs, and figures in legal, scholastic, and civil service uniforms, all wearing badges, flitted before their eyes. They caught glimpses of ladies, of fur coats hanging on pegs; the draughts blew on them, bringing a smell of stale tobacco. And Gurov, whose heart was beating violently, thought:

"Oh, heavens! Why are these people here and this orchestra! . . ."

And at that instant he recalled how when he had seen Anna Sergeyevna off at the station he had thought that everything was over and they would never meet again. But how far they were still from the end!

On the narrow, gloomy staircase over which was written "To the Amphitheatre," she stopped.

"How you have frightened me!" she said, breathing hard, still pale and overwhelmed. "Oh,

how you have frightened me ! I am half dead.
Why have you come ? Why ?"

" But do understand, Anna, do understand . . ."
he said hastily in a low voice. " I entreat you
to understand. . . ."

She looked at him with dread, with entreaty,
with love; she looked at him intently, to keep his
features more distinctly in her memory.

" I am so unhappy," she went on, not heeding
him. " I have thought of nothing but you all
the time; I live only in the thought of you. And
I wanted to forget, to forget you; but why, oh
why, have you come ?"

On the landing above them two schoolboys were
smoking and looking down, but that was nothing
to Gurov; he drew Anna Sergeyevna to him, and
began kissing her face, her cheeks, and her hands.

" What are you doing, what are you doing !"
she cried in horror, pushing him away. " We are
mad. Go away to-day; go away at once. . . .
I beseech you by all that is sacred, I implore
you. . . . There are people coming this way !"

Someone was coming up the stairs.

" You must go away," Anna Sergeyevna went
on in a whisper. " Do you hear, Dmitri Dmitritch ? I will come and see you in Moscow. I
have never been happy; I am miserable now, and
I never, never shall be happy, never ! Don't
make me suffer still more ! I swear I'll come to
Moscow. But now let us part. My precious,
good, dear one, we must part !"

She pressed his hand and began rapidly going
downstairs, looking round at him, and from her

eyes he could see that she really was unhappy. Gurov stood for a little while, listened, then, when all sound had died away, he found his coat and left the theatre.

IV.

And Anna Sergeyevna began coming to see him in Moscow. Once in two or three months she left S——, telling her husband that she was going to consult a doctor about an internal complaint— and her husband believed her, and did not believe her. In Moscow she stayed at the Slaviansky Bazaar hotel, and at once sent a man in a red cap to Gurov. Gurov went to see her, and no one in Moscow knew of it.

Once he was going to see her in this way on a winter morning (the messenger had come the evening before when he was out). With him walked his daughter, whom he wanted to take to school: it was on the way. Snow was falling in big wet flakes.

"It's three degrees above freezing-point, and yet it is snowing," said·Gurov to his daughter. "The thaw is only on the surface of the earth; there is quite a different temperature at a greater height in the atmosphere."

"And why are there no thunderstorms in the winter, father?"

He explained that, too. He talked, thinking all the while that he was going to see *her*, and no living soul knew of it, and probably never would know. He had two lives: one, open, seen and known by all who cared to know, full of relative truth and of relative falsehood, exactly like the lives of his friends and acquaintances; and another life running its course in secret. And through some strange, perhaps accidental, conjunction of circumstances, everything that was essential, of interest and of value to him, everything in which he was sincere and did not deceive himself, everything that made the kernel of his life, was hidden from other people; and all that was false in him, the sheath in which he hid himself to conceal the truth—such, for instance, as his work in the bank, his discussions at the club, his "lower race," his presence with his wife at anniversary festivities—all that was open. And he judged of others by himself, not believing in what he saw, and always believing that every man had his real, most interesting life under the cover of secrecy and under the cover of night. All personal life rested on secrecy, and possibly it was partly on that account that civilized man was so nervously anxious that personal privacy should be respected.

After leaving his daughter at school, Gurov went on to the Slaviansky Bazaar. He took off his fur coat below, went upstairs, and softly knocked at the door. Anna Sergeyevna, wearing his favourite grey dress, exhausted by the journey and the suspense, had been expecting him since the evening before. She was pale; she looked at him, and did not smile, and he had hardly come in when she fell on his breast. Their kiss was slow and prolonged, as though they had not met for two years.

" Well, how are you getting on there ?" he asked. " What news ?"

" Wait; I'll tell you directly. . . . I can't talk."

She could not speak; she was crying. She turned away from him, and pressed her handkerchief to her eyes.

" Let her have her cry out. I'll sit down and wait," he thought, and he sat down in an armchair.

Then he rang and asked for tea to be brought him, and while he drank his tea she remained standing at the window with her back to him. She was crying from emotion, from the miserable consciousness that their life was so hard for them; they could only meet in secret, hiding themselves from people, like thieves ! Was not their life shattered ?

" Come, do stop !" he said.

It was evident to him that this love of theirs would not soon be over, that he could not see the end of it. Anna Sergeyevna grew more and more attached to him. She adored him, and it was unthinkable to say to her that it was bound to have an end some day; besides, she would not have believed it !

He went up to her and took her by the shoulders to say something affectionate and cheering, and at that moment he saw himself in the looking-glass.

His hair was already beginning to turn grey. And it seemed strange to him that he had grown so much older, so much plainer during the last few years. The shoulders on which his hands rested were warm and quivering. He felt compassion for this life, still so warm and lovely, but probably already not far from beginning to fade and wither like his own. Why did she love him so much ? He always seemed to women different from what he was, and they loved in him not himself, but the man created by their imagination, whom they had been eagerly seeking all their lives; and afterwards, when they noticed their mistake, they loved him all the same. And not one of them had been happy with him. Time passed, he had made their acquaintance, got on with them, parted, but he had never once loved; it was anything you like, but not love.

And only now when his head was grey he had fallen properly, really in love—for the first time in his life.

Anna Sergeyevna and he loved each other like people very close and akin, like husband and wife, like tender friends; it seemed to them that fate itself had meant them for one another, and they could not understand why he had a wife and she a husband; and it was as though they were a pair of birds of passage, caught and forced to live in different cages. They forgave each other for what they were ashamed of in their past, they forgave everything in the present, and felt that this love of theirs had changed them both.

In moments of depression in the past he had comforted himself with any arguments that came into his mind, but now he no longer cared for arguments; he felt profound compassion, he wanted

25

to be sincere and tender. . . .

"Don't cry, my darling," he said. "You've had your cry; that's enough. . . . Let us talk now, let us think of some plan."

Then they spent a long while taking counsel together, talked of how to avoid the necessity for secrecy, for deception, for living in different towns and not seeing each other for long at a time. How could they be free from this intolerable bondage?

"How? How?" he asked, clutching his head. "How?"

And it seemed as though in a little while the solution would be found, and then a new and splendid life would begin; and it was clear to both of them that they had still a long, long way to go, and that the most complicated and difficult part of it was only just beginning.

1899

THE HORSE-STEALERS

A HOSPITAL assistant, called Yergunov, an empty-headed fellow, known throughout the district as a great braggart and drunkard, was returning one evening in Christmas week from the hamlet of Ryepino, where he had been to make some purchases for the hospital. That he might get home in good time and not be late, the doctor had lent him his very best horse.

At first it had been a still day, but at eight o'clock a violent snow-storm came on, and when he was only about four miles from home Yergunov completely lost his way.

He did not know how to drive, he did not know the road, and he drove on at random, hoping that the horse would find the way of itself. Two hours passed; the horse was exhausted, he himself was chilled, and already began to fancy that he was not going home, but back towards Ryepino. But at last above the uproar of the storm he heard the far-away barking of a dog, and a murky red blur came into sight ahead of him: little by little, the outlines of a high gate could be discerned, then a long fence on which there were nails with their points uppermost, and beyond the fence there stood the slanting crane of a well. The wind

27

drove away the mist of snow from before the eyes, and where there had been a red blur, there sprang up a small, squat little house with a steep thatched roof. Of the three little windows one, covered on the inside with something red, was lighted up.

What sort of place was it? Yergunov remembered that to the right of the road, three and a half or four miles from the hospital, there was Andrey Tchirikov's tavern. He remembered, too, that this Tchirikov, who had been lately killed by some sledge-drivers, had left a wife and a daughter called Lyubka, who had come to the hospital two years before as a patient. The inn had a bad reputation, and to visit it late in the evening, and especially with someone else's horse, was not free from risk. But there was no help for it. Yergunov fumbled in his knapsack for his revolver, and, coughing sternly, tapped at the window-frame with his whip.

"Hey! who is within?" he cried. "Hey, granny! let me come in and get warm!"

With a hoarse bark a black dog rolled like a ball under the horse's feet, then another white one, then another black one—there must have been a dozen of them. Yergunov looked to see which was the biggest, swung his whip and lashed at it with all his might. A small, long-legged puppy turned its sharp muzzle upwards and set up a shrill, piercing howl.

Yergunov stood for a long while at the window, tapping. But at last the hoar-frost on the trees near the house glowed red, and a muffled female figure appeared with a lantern in her hands.

" Let me in to get warm, granny," said Yergunov.
" I was driving to the hospital, and I have lost my
way. It's such weather, God preserve us. Don't
be afraid; we are your own people, granny."

" All my own people are at home, and we didn't
invite strangers," said the figure grimly. " And
what are you knocking for ? The gate is not
locked."

Yergunov drove into the yard and stopped at the
steps.

" Bid your labourer take my horse out, granny,"
said he.

" I am not granny."

And indeed she was not a granny. While she
was putting out the lantern the light fell on her
face, and Yergunov saw black eyebrows, and
recognized Lyubka.

" There are no labourers about now," she said
as she went into the house. " Some are drunk and
asleep, and some have been gone to Ryepino since
the morning. It's a holiday. . . ."

As he fastened his horse up in the shed, Yergunov
heard a neigh, and distinguished in the darkness
another horse, and felt on it a Cossack saddle.
So there must be someone else in the house besides
the woman and her daughter. For greater security
Yergunov unsaddled his horse, and when he went
into the house, took with him both his purchases
and his saddle.

The first room into which he went was large and
very hot, and smelt of freshly washed floors. A
short, lean peasant of about forty, with a small,
fair beard, wearing a dark blue shirt, was sitting at

the table under the holy images. It was Kalashnikov, an arrant scoundrel and horse-stealer, whose father and uncle kept a tavern in Bogalyovka, and disposed of the stolen horses where they could. He too had been to the hospital more than once, not for medical treatment, but to see the doctor about horses—to ask whether he had not one for sale, and whether his honour would not like to swop his bay mare for a dun-coloured gelding. Now his head was pomaded and a silver ear-ring glittered in his ear, and altogether he had a holiday air. Frowning and dropping his lower lip, he was looking intently at a big dog's-eared picture-book. Another peasant lay stretched on the floor near the stove; his head, his shoulders, and his chest were covered with a sheepskin—he was probably asleep; beside his new boots, with shining bits of metal on the heels, there were two dark pools of melted snow.

Seeing the hospital assistant, Kalashnikov greeted him.

" Yes, it is weather," said Yergunov, rubbing his chilled knees with his open hands. " The snow is up to one's neck; I am soaked to the skin, I can tell you. And I believe my revolver is, too. . . ."

He took out his revolver, looked it all over, and put it back in his knapsack. But the revolver made no impression at all; the peasant went on looking at the book.

" Yes, it is weather. . . . I lost my way, and if it had not been for the dogs here, I do believe it would have been my death. There would have been a nice to-do. And where are the women ?"

" The old woman has gone to Ryepino, and the girl is getting supper ready . . ." answered Kalashnikov.

Silence followed. Yergunov, shivering and gasping, breathed on his hands, huddled up, and made a show of being very cold and exhausted. The still angry dogs could be heard howling outside. It was dreary.

" You come from Bogalyovka, don't you ?" he asked the peasant sternly.

" Yes, from Bogalyovka."

And to while away the time Yergunov began to think about Bogalyovka. It was a big village and if lay in a deep ravine, so that when one drove along the highroad on a moonlight night, and looked down into the dark ravine and then up at the sky, it seemed as though the moon were hanging over a bottomless abyss and it were the end of the world. The path going down was steep, winding, and so narrow that when one drove down to Bogalyovka on account of some epidemic or to vaccinate the people, one had to shout at the top of one's voice, or whistle all the way, for if one met a cart coming up one could not pass. The peasants of Bogalyovka had the reputation of being good gardeners and horse-stealers. They had well-stocked gardens. In spring the whole village was buried in white cherry-blossom, and in the summer they sold cherries at three kopecks a pail. One could pay three kopecks and pick as one liked. Their women were handsome and looked well-fed, they were fond of finery, and never did anything even on working-days, but spent all their time

sitting on the ledge in front of their houses and
searching in each other's heads.

But at last there was the sound of footsteps.
Lyubka, a girl of twenty, with bare feet and a red
dress, came into the room. . . . She looked sideways at Yergunov and walked twice from one end
of the room to the other. She did not move simply,
but with tiny steps, thrusting forward her bosom;
evidently she enjoyed padding about with her bare
feet on the freshly washed floor, and had taken off
her shoes on purpose.

Kalashnikov laughed at something and beckoned
her with his finger. She went up to the table, and
he showed her a picture of the Prophet Elijah,
who, driving three horses abreast, was dashing up
to the sky. Lyubka put her elbow on the table;
her plait fell across her shoulder—a long chestnut
plait tied with red ribbon at the end—and it almost
touched the floor. She, too, smiled.

" A splendid, wonderful picture," said Kalashnikov. " Wonderful," he repeated, and motioned
with his hand as though he wanted to take the reins
instead of Elijah.

The wind howled in the stove; something
growled and squeaked as though a big dog had
strangled a rat.

" Ugh ! the unclean spirits are abroad !" said
Lyubka.

" That's the wind," said Kalashnikov; and after
a pause he raised his eyes to Yergunov and asked:
" And what is your learned opinion, Osip Vas-
silyitch—are there devils in this world or not ?"

" What's one to say, brother ?" said Yergunov,

and he shrugged one shoulder. "If one reasons from science, of course there are no devils, for it's a superstition; but if one looks at it simply, as you and I do now, there are devils, to put it shortly. . . . I have seen a great deal in my life. . . . When I finished my studies I served as medical assistant in the army in a regiment of the dragoons, and I have been in the war, of course. I have a medal and a decoration from the Red Cross, but after the treaty of San Stefano I returned to Russia and went into the service of the Zemstvo. And in consequence of my enormous circulation about the world, I may say I have seen more than many another has dreamed of. It has happened to me to see devils, too; that is, not devils with horns and a tail—that is all nonsense—but just, to speak precisely, something of the sort."

"Where?" asked Kalashnikov.

"In various places. There is no need to go far. Last year I met him here—speak of him not at night—near this very inn. I was driving, I remember, to Golyshino; I was going there to vaccinate. Of course, as usual, I had the racing droshky and a horse, and all the necessary paraphernalia, and, what's more, I had a watch and all the rest of it, so I was on my guard as I drove along, for fear of some mischance. There are lots of tramps of all sorts. I came up to the Zmeinoy Ravine—damnation take it—and was just going down it, when all at once somebody comes up to me—such a fellow! Black hair, black eyes, and his whole face looked smutted with soot. . . . He comes straight up to the horse and takes hold of

B

the left rein: ' Stop !'   He looked at the horse, then at me, then dropped the reins, and without saying a bad word, ' Where are you going ?' says he.   And he showed his teeth in a grin, and his eyes were spiteful-looking. . . .   ' Ah,' thought I, ' you are a queer customer !'   ' I am going to vaccinate for the smallpox,' said I.   ' And what is that to you ?'   ' Well, if that's so,' says he, ' vaccinate me.'   He bared his arm and thrust it under my nose.   Of course, I did not bandy words with him; I just vaccinated him to get rid of him.   Afterwards I looked at my lancet and it had gone rusty."

The peasant who was asleep near the stove suddenly turned over and flung off the sheepskin; to his great surprise, Yergunov recognized the stranger he had met that day at Zmeinoy Ravine. This peasant's hair, beard, and eyes were black as soot; his face was swarthy; and, to add to the effect, there was a black spot the size of a lentil on his right cheek.   He looked mockingly at the hospital assistant and said:

" I did take hold of the left rein—that was so; but about the smallpox you are lying, sir.   And there was not a word said about the smallpox between us."

Yergunov was disconcerted.

" I'm not talking about you," he said.   " Lie down, since you are lying down."

The dark-skinned peasant had never been to the hospital, and Yergunov did not know who he was or where he came from; and now, looking at him, he made up his mind that the man must be a gypsy.

34

The peasant got up, and, stretching and yawning loudly, went up to Lyubka and Kalashnikov, and sat down beside them, and he, too, began looking at the book. His sleepy face softened, and a look of envy came into it.

"Look, Merik," Lyubka said to him; "get me such horses and I will drive to heaven."

"Sinners can't drive to heaven," said Kalashnikov. "That's for holiness."

Then Lyubka laid the table and brought in a big piece of fat bacon, salted cucumbers, a wooden platter of boiled meat cut up into little pieces, then a frying-pan, in which there were sausages and cabbage spluttering. A cut-glass decanter of vodka, which diffused a smell of orange-peel all over the room when it was poured out, was put on the table also.

Yergunov was annoyed that Kalashnikov and the dark fellow Merik talked together and took no notice of him at all, behaving exactly as though he were not in the room. And he wanted to talk to them, to brag, to drink, to have a good meal, and if possible to have a little fun with Lyubka, who sat down near him half a dozen times while they were at supper, and, as though by accident, brushed against him with her handsome shoulders and passed her hands over her broad hips. She was a healthy, active girl, always laughing and never still: she would sit down, then get up, and when she was sitting down she would keep turning first her face and then her back to her neighbour, like a fidgety child, and never failed to brush against him with her elbows or her knees.

And he was displeased, too, that the peasants drank only a glass each and no more, and it was awkward for him to drink alone. But he could not refrain from taking a second glass, all the same, then a third, and he. ate all the sausage. He brought himself to flatter the peasants, that they might accept him as one of the party instead of holding him at arm's length.

" You are a fine set of fellows in Bogalyovka !" he said, and wagged his head.

" In what way fine fellows ?" enquired Kalashnikov.

" Why, about horses, for instance. Fine fellows at stealing !"

" H'm ! fine fellows, you call them. Nothing but thieves and drunkards."

" They have had their day, but it is over," said Merik, after a pause. " But now they have only Filya left, and he is blind."

" Yes, there is no one but Filya," said Kalashnikov, with a sigh. " Reckon it up, he must be seventy; the German settlers knocked out one of his eyes, and he does not see well with the other. It is cataract. In old days the police officer would shout as soon as he saw him: ' Hey, you Shamil !' and all the peasants called him that—he was Shamil all over the place; and now his only name is One-eyed Filya. But he was a fine fellow ! Lyuba's father, Andrey Grigoritch, and he stole one night into Rozhnovo—there were cavalry regiments stationed there—and carried off nine of the soldiers' horses, the very best of them. They weren't frightened of the sentry, and in the morning they sold all the horses for twenty roubles to the gypsy Afonka. Yes! But nowadays a man contrives to carry off a horse whose rider is drunk or asleep, and has no fear of God, but will take the very boots from a drunkard, and then slinks off and goes away a hundred and fifty miles with a horse, and haggles at the market, haggles like a Jew, till the policeman catches him, the fool. There is no fun in it; it is simply a disgrace! A paltry set of people, I must say."

"What about Merik?" asked Lyubka.

"Merik is not one of us," said Kalashnikov. "He is a Harkov man from Mizhiritch. But that he is a bold fellow, that's the truth; there's no gainsaying that he is a fine fellow."

Lyubka looked slily and gleefully at Merik, and said:

"It wasn't for nothing they dipped him in a hole in the ice."

"How was that?" asked Yergunov.

"It was like this . . ." said Merik, and he laughed. "Filya carried off three horses from the Samoylenka tenants, and they pitched upon me. There were ten of the tenants at Samoylenka, and with their labourers there were thirty altogether, and all of them Molokans. . . . So one of them says to me at the market: 'Come and have a look, Merik; we have brought some new horses from the fair.' I was interested, of course. I went up to them, and the whole lot of them, thirty men, tied my hands behind me and led me to the river. 'We'll show you fine horses,' they said. One hole in the ice was there already; they cut another beside it seven feet away. Then, to be sure, they took a cord and put a noose under my armpits, and tied a crooked stick to the other end, long enough to reach both holes. They thrust the stick in and dragged it through. I went plop into the ice-hole just as I was, in my fur coat and my high boots, while they stood and shoved me, one with his foot and one with his stick, then dragged me under the ice and pulled me out of the other hole."

Lyubka shuddered and shrugged.

"At first I was in a fever from the cold," Merik went on, "but when they pulled me out I was helpless, and lay in the snow, and the Molokans stood round and hit me with sticks on my knees and my elbows. It hurt fearfully. They beat me and they went away . . . and everything on me was frozen, my clothes were covered with ice. I got up, but I couldn't move. Thank God, a woman drove by and gave me a lift."

Meanwhile Yergunov had drunk five or six glasses of vodka; his heart felt lighter, and he longed to tell some extraordinary, wonderful story too, and to show that he, too, was a bold fellow and not afraid of anything.

"I'll tell you what happened to us in Penza Province . . ." he began.

Either because he had drunk a great deal and was a little tipsy, or perhaps because he had twice been detected in a lie, the peasants took not the slightest notice of him, and even left off answering his questions. What was worse, they permitted themselves a frankness in his presence that made him feel uncomfortable and cold all over, and that meant that they took no notice of him.

Kalashnikov had the dignified manners of a sedate and sensible man; he spoke weightily, and made the sign of the cross over his mouth every time he yawned, and no one could have supposed that this was a thief, a heartless thief who had stripped poor creatures, who had already been twice in prison, and who had been sentenced by the commune to exile in Siberia, and had been bought off by his father and uncle, who were as great thieves and rogues as he was. Merik gave himself the airs of a bravo. He saw that Lyubka and Kalashnikov were admiring him, and looked upon himself as a very fine fellow, and put his arms akimbo, squared his chest, or stretched so that the bench creaked under him. . . .

After supper Kalashnikov prayed to the holy image without getting up from his seat, and shook hands with Merik; the latter prayed too, and shook Kalashnikov's hand. Lyubka cleared away the supper, shook out on the table some peppermint biscuits, dried nuts, and pumpkin seeds, and placed two bottles of sweet wine.

" The kingdom of heaven and peace everlasting to Andrey Grigoritch," said Kalashnikov, clinking glasses with Merik. " When he was alive we used to gather together here or at his brother Martin's, and—my word! my word! what men, what talks! Remarkable conversations! Martin used to be here, and Filya, and Fyodor Stukotey. . . . It was all done in style, it was all in keeping. . . .

And what fun we had ! We did have fun, we did have fun !"

Lyubka went out and soon afterwards came back wearing a green kerchief and beads.

" Look, Merik, what Kalashnikov brought me to-day," she said.

She looked at herself in the looking-glass, and tossed her head several times to make the beads jingle. And then she opened a chest and began taking out, first, a cotton dress with red and blue flowers on it, and then a red one with flounces which rustled and crackled like paper, then a new kerchief, dark blue, shot with many colours—and all these things she showed and flung up her hands, laughing as though astonished that she had such treasures.

Kalashnikov tuned the balalaika and began playing it, but Yergunov could not make out what sort of song he was singing, and whether it was gay or melancholy, because at one moment it was so mournful he wanted to cry, and at the next it would be merry. Merik suddenly jumped up and began tapping with his heels on the same spot, then, brandishing his arms, he moved on his heels from the table to the stove, from the stove to the chest, then he bounded up as though he had been stung, clicked the heels of his boots together in the air, and began going round and round in a crouching position. Lyubka waved both her arms, uttered a desperate shriek, and followed him. At first she moved sideways, like a snake, as though she wanted to steal up to someone and strike him from behind. She tapped rapidly with her bare heels as Merik had done with the heels of his boots, then she turned round and round like a top and crouched down, and her red dress was blown out like a bell. Merik, looking angrily at her, and showing his teeth in a grin, flew towards her in the same crouching posture as though he wanted to crush her with his terrible legs, while she jumped up, flung back her head, and waving her arms as a big bird does its wings, floated across the room scarcely touching the floor. . . .

"What a flame of a girl!" thought Yergunov, sitting on the chest, and from there watching the dance. "What fire! Give up everything for her, and it would be too little. . . ."

And he regretted that he was a hospital assistant, and not a simple peasant, that he wore a reefer coat and a chain with a gilt key on it instead of a blue shirt with a cord tied round the waist. Then he could boldly have sung, danced, flung both arms round Lyubka as Merik did. . . .

The sharp tapping, shouts, and whoops set the crockery ringing in the cupboard and the flame of the candle dancing.

The thread broke and the beads were scattered all over the floor, the green kerchief slipped off, and Lyubka was transformed into a red cloud flitting by and flashing black eyes, and it seemed as though in another second Merik's arms and legs would drop off.

But finally Merik stamped for the last time, and stood still as though turned to stone. Exhausted and almost breathless, Lyubka sank on to his bosom and leaned against him as against a post, and he put his arms round her, and looking into her eyes, said tenderly and caressingly, as though in jest:

" I'll find out where your old mother's money is hidden, I'll murder her and cut your little throat for you, and after that I will set fire to the inn. . . . People will think you have perished in the fire, and with your money I shall go to Kuban. I'll keep droves of horses and flocks of sheep. . . ."

Lyubka made no answer, but only looked at him with a guilty air, and asked:

" And is it nice in Kuban, Merik ?"

He said nothing, but went to the chest, sat down, and sank into thought; most likely he was dreaming of Kuban.

" It's time for me to be going," said Kalashnikov, getting up. " Filya must be waiting for me. Good-bye, Lyuba."

Yergunov went out into the yard to see that Kalashnikov did not go off with his horse. The snow-storm still persisted. White clouds were floating about the yard, their long tails clinging to the rough grass and the bushes, while on the other side of the fence in the open country huge giants in white robes with wide sleeves were whirling round and falling to the ground, and getting up again to wave their arms and fight. And the wind, the wind ! The bare birches and cherry-trees, unable to endure its rude caresses, bowed low down to the ground and wailed: " God, for what sin hast Thou bound us to the earth and will not let us go free ?"

" Wo !" said Kalashnikov sternly, and he got

on his horse; one half of the gate was opened, and by it lay a high snowdrift. "Well, get on!" shouted Kalashnikov. His little short-legged nag set off, and sank up to its stomach in the drift at once. Kalashnikov was white all over with the snow, and soon vanished from sight with his horse.

When Yergunov went back into the room, Lyubka was creeping about the floor picking up her beads; Merik was not there.

"A splendid girl!" thought Yergunov, as he lay down on the bench and put his coat under his head. "Oh, if only Merik were not here." Lyubka excited him as she crept about the floor by the bench, and he thought that if Merik had not been there he would certainly have got up and embraced her, and then one would see what would happen. It was true she was only a girl, but not likely to be chaste; and even if she were—need one stand on ceremony in a den of thieves? Lyubka collected her beads and went out. The candle burnt down and the flame caught the paper in the candlestick. Yergunov laid his revolver and matches beside him, and put out the candle. The light before the holy images flickered so much that it hurt his eyes, and patches of light danced on the ceiling, on the floor, and on the cupboard, and among them he had visions of Lyubka, buxom, full-bosomed: now she was turning round like a top, now she was exhausted and breathless. . . .

"Oh, if the devils would carry off that Merik," he thought.

The little lamp gave a last flicker, spluttered, and went out. Someone, it must have been Merik,

43

came into the room and sat down on the bench. He puffed at his pipe, and for an instant lighted up a dark cheek with a patch on it. Yergunov's throat was irritated by the horrible fumes of the tobacco smoke.

" What filthy tobacco you have got—damnation take it !" said Yergunov. " It makes me positively sick."

" I mix my tobacco with the flowers of the oats," answered Merik after a pause. " It is better for the chest."

He smoked, spat, and went out again. Half an hour passed, and all at once there was the gleam of a light in the passage. Merik appeared in a coat and cap, then Lyubka with a candle in her hand.

" Do stay, Merik," said Lyubka in an imploring voice.

" No, Lyuba, don't keep me."

" Listen, Merik," said Lyubka, and her voice grew soft and tender. " I know you will find mother's money, and will do for her and for me, and will go to Kuban and love other girls; but God be with you. I only ask you one thing, sweetheart : do stay !"

" No, I want some fun . . ." said Merik, fastening his belt.

" But you have nothing to go on. . . . You came on foot; what are you going on ?"

Merik bent down to Lyubka and whispered something in her ear; she looked towards the door and laughed through her tears.

" He is asleep, the puffed-up devil . . ." she said

44

Merik embraced her, kissed her vigorously, and went out. Yergunov thrust his revolver into his pocket, jumped up, and ran after him.

"Get out of the way!" he said to Lyubka, who hurriedly bolted the door of the entry and stood across the threshold. "Let me pass! Why are you standing here?"

"What do you want to go out for?"

"To have a look at my horse."

Lyubka gazed up at him with a sly and caressing look.

"Why look at it? You had better look at me . . ." she said, then she bent down and touched with her finger the gilt watch-key that hung on his chain.

"Let me pass, or he will go off on my horse," said Yergunov. "Let me go, you devil!" he shouted, and giving her an angry blow on the shoulder, he pressed his chest against her with all his might to push her away from the door, but she kept tight hold of the bolt, and was like iron.

"Let me go!" he shouted, exhausted; "he will go off with it, I tell you."

"Why should he? He won't." Breathing hard and rubbing her shoulder, which hurt, she looked up at him again, flushed a little and laughed. "Don't go away, dear heart," she said; "I am dull alone."

Yergunov looked into her eyes, hesitated, and put his arms round her; she did not resist.

"Come, no nonsense; let me go," he begged her. She did not speak.

45

" I heard you just now," he said, " telling Merik that you love him."

" I dare say. . . . My heart knows who it is I love."

She put her finger on the key again, and said softly: " Give me that."

Yergunov unfastened the key and gave it to her. She suddenly craned her neck and listened with a grave face, and her expression struck Yergunov as cold and cunning; he thought of his horse, and now easily pushed her aside and ran out into the yard. In the shed a sleepy pig was grunting with lazy regularity and a cow was knocking her horn. Yergunov lighted a match and saw the pig, and the cow, and the dogs, which rushed at him on all sides at seeing the light, but there was no trace of the horse. Shouting and waving his arms at the dogs, stumbling over the drifts and sticking in the snow, he ran out at the gate and fell to gazing into the darkness. He strained his eyes to the utmost, and saw only the snow flying and the snowflakes distinctly forming into all sorts of shapes: at one moment the white, laughing face of a corpse would peep out of the darkness, at the next a white horse would gallop by with an Amazon in a muslin dress upon it, at the next a string of white swans would fly overhead. . . . Shaking with anger and cold, and not knowing what to do, Yergunov fired his revolver at the dogs, and did not hit one of them; then he rushed back to the house.

When he went into the entry he distinctly heard someone scurry out of the room and bang the door

It was dark in the room. Yergunov pushed against the door; it was locked. Then, lighting match after match, he rushed back into the entry, from there into the kitchen, and from the kitchen into a little room where all the walls were hung with petticoats and dresses, where there was a smell of cornflowers and fennel, and a bedstead with a perfect mountain of pillows, standing in the corner by the stove; this must have been the old mother's room. From there he passed into another little room, and here he saw Lyubka. She was lying on a chest, covered with a gay-coloured patchwork cotton quilt, pretending to be asleep. A little ikon-lamp was burning in the corner above the pillow.

" Where is my horse ?" Yergunov asked.

Lyubka did not stir.

" Where is my horse, I am asking you ?" Yergunov repeated still more sternly, and he tore the quilt off her. " I am asking you, she-devil !" he shouted.

She jumped up on her knees, and with one hand holding her shift and with the other trying to clutch the quilt, huddled against the wall. . . . She looked at Yergunov with repulsion and terror in her eyes, and, like a wild beast in a trap, kept cunning watch on his faintest movement.

" Tell me where my horse is, or I'll knock the life out of you," shouted Yergunov.

" Get away, dirty brute !" she said in a hoarse voice.

Yergunov seized her by the shift near the neck and tore it. And then he could not restrain himself, and with all his might embraced the girl. But hissing with fury, she slipped out of his arms, and freeing one hand—the other was tangled in the torn shift—hit him a blow with her fist on the skull.

His head was dizzy with the pain, there was a ringing and rattling in his ears, he staggered back, and at that moment received another blow—this time on the temple. Reeling and clutching at the door-posts, that he might not fall, he made his way to the room where his things were, and lay down on the bench; then after lying for a little time, took the matchbox out of his pocket and began lighting match after match for no object: he lit it, blew it out, and threw it under the table, and went on till all the matches were gone.

Meanwhile the air began to turn blue outside, the cocks began to crow, but his head still ached, and there was an uproar in his ears as though he were sitting under a railway bridge and hearing the trains passing over his head. He got, somehow, into his coat and cap; the saddle and the bundle of his purchases he could not find, his knapsack was empty: it was not for nothing that someone had scurried out of the room when he came in from the yard.

He took a poker from the kitchen to keep off the dogs, and went out into the yard, leaving the door open. The snow-storm had subsided and it was calm outside. . . . When he went out at the gate, the white plain looked dead, and there was not a single bird in the morning sky. On both sides of the road and in the distance there were bluish patches of young copse.

THE HORSE-STEALERS

Yergunov began thinking how he would be greeted at the hospital and what the doctor would say to him; it was absolutely necessary to think of that, and to prepare beforehand to answer questions he would be asked, but this thought grew blurred and slipped away. He walked along thinking of nothing but Lyubka, of the peasants with whom he had passed the night; he remembered how, after Lyubka struck him the second time, she had bent down to the floor for the quilt, and how her loose hair had fallen on the floor. His mind was in a maze, and he wondered why there were in the world doctors, hospital assistants, merchants, clerks, and peasants instead of simply free men? There are, to be sure, free birds, free beasts, a free Merik, and they are not afraid of anyone, and don't need anyone! And whose idea was it, who had decreed that one must get up in the morning, dine at midday, go to bed in the evening; that a doctor takes precedence of a hospital assistant; that one must live in rooms and love only one's wife? And why not the contrary—dine at night and sleep in the day? Ah, to jump on a horse without enquiring whose it is, to ride races with the wind like a devil, over fields and forests and ravines, to make love to girls, to mock at everyone. . . .

Yergunov thrust the poker into the snow, pressed his forehead to the cold white trunk of a birch-tree, and sank into thought; and his grey, monotonous life, his wages, his subordinate position, the dispensary, the everlasting to-do with the bottles and blisters, struck him as contemptible, sickening.

" Who says it's a sin to enjoy oneself ?" he asked

himself with vexation. "Those who say that have never lived in freedom like Merik and Kalashnikov, and have never loved Lyubka; they have been beggars all their lives, have lived without any pleasure, and have only loved their wives, who are like frogs."

And he thought about himself that he had not hitherto been a thief, a swindler, or even a brigand, simply because he could not, or had not yet met with a suitable opportunity.

* * * * *

A year and a half passed. In spring, after Easter, Yergunov, who had long before been dismissed from the hospital and was hanging about without a job, came out of the tavern in Ryepino and sauntered aimlessly along the street.

He went out into the open country. Here there was the scent of spring, and a warm, caressing wind was blowing. The calm, starry night looked down from the sky on the earth. My God, how infinite the depth of the sky, and with what fathomless immensity it stretched over the world! The world is created well enough, only why and with what right do people, thought Yergunov, divide their fellows into the sober and the drunken, the employed and the dismissed, and so on? Why do the sober and well-fed sleep comfortably in their homes while the drunken and the hungry must wander about the country without a refuge? Why was it that if anyone had not a job and did not get a salary he had to go hungry, without clothes and boots? Whose idea was it? Why was it the birds and the wild beasts in the woods did not have jobs and get salaries, but lived as they pleased ?

Far away in the sky a beautiful crimson glow lay quivering, stretched wide over the horizon. Yergunov stopped, and for a long time he gazed at it, and kept wondering why was it that if he had carried off someone else's samovar the day before and sold it for drink in the taverns it would be a sin ? Why was it ?

Two carts drove by on the road; in one of them there was a woman asleep, in the other sat an old man without a cap on. . . .

" Grandfather, where is that fire ?" asked Yergunov.

" Andrey Tchirikov's inn," answered the old man.

And Yergunov recalled what had happened to him eighteen months before in the winter, in that very inn, and how Merik had boasted; and he imagined the old woman and Lyubka, with their throats cut, burning, and he envied Merik. And when he walked back to the tavern, looking at the houses of the rich publicans, cattle-dealers, and blacksmiths, he reflected how nice it would be to steal by night into some rich man's house !

1890

THE BISHOP

I.

THE evening service was being celebrated on the eve of Palm Sunday in the Old Petrovsky Convent. When they began distributing the palm it was close upon ten o'clock, the candles were burning dimly, the wicks wanted snuffing; it was all in a sort of mist. In the twilight of the church the crowd seemed heaving like the sea, and to Bishop Pyotr, who had been unwell for the last three days, it seemed that all the faces—old and young, men's and women's—were alike, that everyone who came up for the palm had the same expression in his eyes. In the mist he could not see the doors; the crowd kept moving and looked as though there were no end to it. The female choir was singing, a nun was reading the prayers for the day.

How stifling, how hot it was! How long the service went on! Bishop Pyotr was tired. His breathing was laboured and rapid, his throat was parched, his shoulders ached with weariness, his legs were trembling. And it disturbed him unpleasantly when a religious maniac uttered occasional shrieks in the gallery. And then all of a sudden, as though in a dream or delirium, it seemed to the bishop as though his own mother Marya Timofyevna, whom he had not seen for nine years, or some old woman just like his mother, came up to him out of the crowd, and, after taking a palm branch from him, walked away looking at him all the while good-humouredly with a kind, joyful smile until she was lost in the crowd. And for some reason tears flowed down his face. There was peace in his heart, everything was well, yet he kept gazing fixedly towards the left choir, where the prayers were being read, where in the dusk of evening you could not recognize anyone, and—wept. Tears glistened on his face and on his beard. Here someone close at hand was weeping, then someone else farther away, then others and still others, and little by little the church was filled with soft weeping. And a little later, within five minutes, the nuns' choir was singing; no one was weeping and everything was as before.

Soon the service was over. When the bishop got into his carriage to drive home, the gay, melodious chime of the heavy, costly bells was filling the whole garden in the moonlight. The white walls, the white crosses on the tombs, the white birch-trees and black shadows, and the far-away moon in the sky exactly over the convent, seemed now living their own life, apart and incomprehensible, yet very near to man. It was the beginning of April, and after the warm spring day it turned cool; there was a faint touch of frost, and the breath of spring could be felt in

the soft, chilly air. The road from the convent
to the town was sandy, the horses had to go at
a walking pace, and on both sides of the carriage
in the brilliant, peaceful moonlight there were
people trudging along home from church through
the sand. And all was silent, sunk in thought;
everything around seemed kindly, youthful, akin,
everything—trees and sky and even the moon,
and one longed to think that so it would be always.

At last the carriage drove into the town and
rumbled along the principal street. The shops
were already shut, but at Erakin's, the millionaire
shopkeeper's, they were trying the new electric
lights, which flickered brightly, and a crowd of
people were gathered round. Then came wide,
dark, deserted streets, one after another; then the
highroad, the open country, the fragrance of pines.
And suddenly there rose up before the bishop's
eyes a white turreted wall, and behind it a tall
belfry in the full moonlight, and beside it five
shining, golden cupolas: this was the Pankratievsky
Monastery, in which Bishop Pyotr lived. And
here, too, high above the monastery, was the
silent, dreamy moon. The carriage drove in at the
gate, crunching over the sand; here and there in
the moonlight there were glimpses of dark monastic figures, and there was the sound of footsteps
on the flag-stones. . . .

" You know, your holiness, your mamma
arrived while you were away," the lay brother
informed the bishop as he went into his cell.

" My mother ? When did she come ?"

" Before the evening service. She asked first

54

where you were and then she went to the convent."

" Then it was her I saw in the church, just now! Oh, Lord !"

And the bishop laughed with joy.

" She bade me tell your holiness," the lay brother went on, "that she would come to-morrow. She had a little girl with her—her grandchild, I suppose. They are staying at Ovsyannikov's inn."

" What time is it now ?"

" A little after eleven."

" Oh, how vexing !"

The bishop sat for a little while in the parlour, hesitating, and as it were refusing to believe it was so late. His arms and legs were stiff, his head ached. He was hot and uncomfortable. After resting a little he went into his bedroom, and there, too, he sat a little, still thinking of his mother; he could hear the lay brother going away, and Father Sisoy coughing the other side of the wall. The monastery clock struck a quarter.

The bishop changed his clothes and began reading the prayers before sleep. He read attentively those old, long familiar prayers, and at the same time thought about his mother. She had nine children and about forty grandchildren. At one time, she had lived with her husband, the deacon, in a poor village; she had lived there a very long time from the age of seventeen to sixty. The bishop remembered her from early childhood, almost from the age of three, and—how he had loved her ! Sweet, precious childhood, always fondly remembered ! Why did it, that long-past time that could never return, why did it seem brighter, fuller, and more festive than it had really been ? When in his childhood or youth he had been ill, how tender and sympathetic his mother had been ! And now his prayers mingled with the memories, which gleamed more and more brightly like a flame, and the prayers did not hinder his thinking of his mother.

When he had finished his prayers he undressed and lay down, and at once, as soon as it was dark, there rose before his mind his dead father, his mother, his native village Lesopolye . . . the creak of wheels, the bleat of sheep, the church bells on bright summer mornings, the gypsies under the window—oh, how sweet to think of it ! He remembered the priest of Lesopolye, Father Simeon—mild, gentle, kindly; he was a lean little man, while his son, a divinity student, was a huge fellow and talked in a roaring bass voice. The priest's son had flown into a rage with the cook and abused her: " Ah, you Jehud's ass !" and Father Simeon overhearing it, said not a word, and was only ashamed because he could not remember where such an ass was mentioned in the Bible. After him the priest at Lesopolye had been Father Demyan, who used to drink heavily, and at times drank till he saw green snakes, and was even nicknamed Demyan Snakeseer. The schoolmaster at Lesopolye was Matvey Nikolaitch, who had been a divinity student, a kind and intelligent man, but he, too, was a drunkard; he never beat the schoolchildren, but for some reason he always had hanging on his wall a bunch of birch-twigs, and below it an utterly meaningless inscription in Latin: " Betula kinderbalsamica secuta." He had a shaggy black dog whom he called Syntax.

And his holiness laughed. Six miles from Lesopolye was the village Obnino with a wonder-working ikon. In the summer they used to carry the ikon in procession about the neighbouring villages and ring the bells the whole day long, first in one village and then in another, and it used to seem to the bishop then that joy was quivering in the air, and he (in those days his name was Pavlusha) used to follow the ikon, bareheaded and barefoot, with naïve faith, with a naïve smile, infinitely happy. In Obnino, he remembered now, there were always a lot of people, and the priest there, Father Alexey, to save time during mass, used to make his deaf nephew Ilarion read the names of those for whose health or whose souls' peace prayers were asked. Ilarion used to read them, now and then getting a five or ten kopeck piece for the service, and only when he was grey and bald, when life was nearly over, he suddenly saw written on one of the pieces of paper: " What a fool you are, Ilarion." Up to fifteen at least Pavlusha was undeveloped and idle at his lessons, so much so that they thought of taking him away from the clerical school and putting him into a shop; one day, going to the post at Obnino for letters, he had stared a long time at the post-office clerks and asked: " Allow me to ask, how do you get your salary, every month or every day ?"

His holiness crossed himself and turned over on

the other side, trying to stop thinking and go to sleep.

"My mother has come," he remembered and laughed.

The moon peeped in at the window, the floor was lighted up, and there were shadows on it. A cricket was chirping. Through the wall Father Sisoy was snoring in the next room, and his aged snore had a sound that suggested loneliness, forlornness, even vagrancy. Sisoy had once been housekeeper to the bishop of the diocese, and was called now "the former Father Housekeeper"; he was seventy years old, he lived in a monastery twelve miles from the town and stayed sometimes in the town, too. He had come to the Pankratievsky Monastery three days before, and the bishop had kept him that he might talk to him at his leisure about matters of business, about the arrangements here. . . .

At half-past one they began ringing for matins. Father Sisoy could be heard coughing, muttering something in a discontented voice, then he got up and walked barefoot about the rooms.

"Father Sisoy," the bishop called.

Sisoy went back to his room and a little later made his appearance in his boots, with a candle; he had on his cassock over his underclothes and on his head was an old faded skull-cap.

"I can't sleep," said the bishop, sitting up. "I must be unwell. And what it is I don't know. Fever !"

"You must have caught cold, your holiness. You must be rubbed with tallow." Sisoy stood

58

a little and yawned. " O Lord, forgive me, a sinner."

" They had the electric lights on at Erakin's to-day," he said; " I don't like it !"

Father Sisoy was old, lean, bent, always dissatisfied with something, and his eyes were angry-looking and prominent as a crab's.

" I don't like it," he said, going away. " I don't like it. Bother it !"

II.

Next day, Palm Sunday, the bishop took the service in the cathedral in the town, then he visited the bishop of the diocese, then visited a very sick old lady, the widow of a general, and at last drove home. Between one and two o'clock he had welcome visitors dining with him—his mother and his niece Katya, a child of eight years old. All dinner-time the spring sunshine was streaming in at the windows, throwing bright light on the white tablecloth and on Katya's red hair. Through the double windows they could hear the noise of the rooks and the notes of the starlings in the garden.

" It is nine years since we have met," said the old lady. " And when I looked at you in the monastery yesterday, good Lord ! you've not changed a bit, except maybe you are thinner and your beard is a little longer. Holy Mother, Queen of Heaven ! Yesterday at the evening service no one could help crying. I, too, as I looked at you, suddenly began crying, though I couldn't say why. His Holy Will!"

And in spite of the affectionate tone in which she said this, he could see she was constrained as though she were uncertain whether to address him formally or familiarly, to laugh or not, and that she felt herself more a deacon's widow than his mother. And Katya gazed without blinking at her uncle, his holiness, as though trying to discover what sort of a person he was. Her hair sprang up from under the comb .and the velvet ribbon and stood out like a halo; she had a turned-up nose and sly eyes. The child had broken a glass before sitting down to dinner, and now her grandmother, as she talked, moved away from Katya first a wineglass and then a tumbler. The bishop listened to his mother and remembered how many, many years ago she used to take him and his brothers and sisters to relations whom she considered rich; in those days she was taken up with the care of her children, now with her grand-children, and she had brought Katya. . . .

" Your sister, Varenka, has four children," she told him; " Katya, here, is the eldest. And your brother-in-law Father Ivan fell sick, God knows of what, and died three days before the Assumption; and my poor Varenka is left a beggar."

" And how is Nikanor getting on ?" the bishop asked about his eldest brother.

" He is all right, thank God. Though he has nothing much, yet he can live. Only there is one thing: his son, my grandson Nikolasha, did not want to go into the Church; he has gone to the university to be a doctor. He thinks it is better; but who knows ! His Holy Will !"

" Nikolasha cuts up dead people," said Katya, spilling water over her knees.

" Sit still, child," her grandmother observed calmly, and took the glass out of her hand. " Say a prayer, and go on eating."

" How long it is since we have seen each other !" said the bishop, and he tenderly stroked his mother's hand and shoulder; " and I missed you abroad, mother, I missed you dreadfully."

" Thank you."

" I used to sit in the evenings at the open window, lonely and alone; often there was music playing, and all at once I used to be overcome with homesickness and felt as though I would give everything only to be at home and see you."

His mother smiled, beamed, but at once she made a grave face and said:

" Thank you."

His mood suddenly changed. He looked at his mother and could not understand how she had come by that respectfulness, that timid expression of face: what was it for ? And he did not recognize her. He felt sad and vexed. And then his head ached just as it had the day before; his legs felt fearfully tired, and the fish seemed to him stale and tasteless; he felt thirsty all the time. . . .

After dinner two rich ladies, landowners, arrived and sat for an hour and a half in silence with rigid countenances; the archimandrite, a silent, rather deaf man, came to see him about business.

Then they began ringing for vespers; the sun was setting behind the wood and the day was over. When he returned from church, he hurriedly said his prayers, got into bed, and wrapped himself up as warm as possible.

It was disagreeable to remember the fish he had eaten at dinner. The moonlight worried him, and then he heard talking. In an adjoining room, probably in the parlour, Father Sisoy was talking politics:

"There's war among the Japanese now. They are fighting. The Japanese, my good soul, are the same as the Montenegrins; they are the same race. They were under the Turkish yoke together."

And then he heard the voice of Marya Timofyevna:

"So, having said our prayers and drunk tea, we went, you know, to Father Yegor at Novokatnoye, so . . ."

And she kept on saying, "having had tea" or "having drunk tea," and it seemed as though the only thing she had done in her life was to drink tea.

The bishop slowly, languidly, recalled the seminary, the academy. For three years he had been Greek teacher in the seminary: by that time he could not read without spectacles. Then he had become a monk; he had been made a school inspector. Then he had defended his thesis for his degree. When he was thirty-two he had been made rector of the seminary, and consecrated archimandrite: and then his life had been so easy, so pleasant; it seemed so long, so long, no end was in sight. Then he had begun to be ill, had grown very thin and almost blind, and by the advice of the doctors had to give up everything and go abroad.

" And what then?" asked Sisoy in the next room.

" Then we drank tea . . ." answered Marya Timofyevna.

" Good gracious, you've got a green beard," said Katya suddenly in surprise, and she laughed.

The bishop remembered that the grey-headed Father Sisoy's beard really had a shade of green in it, and he laughed.

" God have mercy upon us, what we have to put up with with this girl !" said Sisoy, aloud, getting angry. " Spoilt child ! Sit quiet !"

The bishop remembered the perfectly new white church in which he had conducted the services while living abroad, he remembered the sound of the warm sea. In his flat he had five lofty light rooms; in his study he had a new writing-table, lots of books. He had read a great deal and often written. And he remembered how he had pined for his native land, how a blind beggar woman had played the guitar under his window every day and sung of love, and how, as he listened, he had always for some reason thought of the past. But eight years had passed and he had been called back to Russia, and now he was a suffragan bishop, and all the past had retreated far away into the mist as though it were a dream. . . .

Father Sisoy came into the bedroom with a candle.

" I say !" he said, wondering, " are you asleep already, your holiness ?"

"What is it?"

"Why, it's still early, ten o'clock or less. I bought a candle to-day; I wanted to rub you with tallow."

"I am in a fever . . ." said the bishop, and he sat up. "I really ought to have something. My head is bad. . . ."

Sisoy took off the bishop's shirt and began rubbing his chest and back with tallow.

"That's the way . . . that's the way . . ." he said. "Lord Jesus Christ . . . that's the way. I walked to the town to-day; I was at what's-his-name's—the chief priest Sidonsky's. . . . I had tea with him. I don't like him. Lord Jesus Christ. . . . That's the way. I don't like him."

III.

The bishop of the diocese, a very fat old man, was ill with rheumatism or gout, and had been in bed for over a month. Bishop Pyotr went to see him almost every day, and saw all who came to ask his help. And now that he was unwell he was struck by the emptiness, the triviality of everything which they asked and for which they wept; he was vexed at their ignorance, their timidity; and all this useless, petty business oppressed him by the mass of it, and it seemed to him that now he understood the diocesan bishop, who had once in his young days written on "The Doctrines of the Freedom of the Will," and now seemed to be all lost in trivialities, to have forgotten everything, and to have no thoughts of

religion. The bishop must have lost touch with
Russian life while he was abroad; he did not
find it easy; the peasants seemed to him coarse,
the women who sought his help dull and stupid,
the seminarists and their teachers uncultivated
and at times savage. And the documents coming
in and going out were reckoned by tens of thousands; and what documents they were! The
higher clergy in the whole diocese gave the priests,
young and old, and even their wives and children,
marks for their behaviour—a five, a four, and sometimes even a three; and about this he had to
talk and to read and write serious reports. And
there was positively not one minute to spare;
his soul was troubled all day long, and the bishop
was only at peace when he was in church.

He could not get used, either, to the awe which,
through no wish of his own, he inspired in people
in spite of his quiet, modest disposition. All the
people in the province seemed to him little,
scared, and guilty when he looked at them.
Everyone was timid in his presence, even the old
chief priests; everyone "flopped" at his feet,
and not long previously an old lady, a village
priest's wife who had come to consult him, was
so overcome by awe that she could not utter a
single word, and went empty away. And he, who
could never in his sermons bring himself to speak
ill of people, never reproached anyone because
he was so sorry for them, was moved to fury
with the people who came to consult him, lost his
temper and flung their petitions on the floor.
The whole time he had been here, not one person

had spoken to him genuinely, simply, as to a human being; even his old mother seemed now not the same! And why, he wondered, did she chatter away to Sisoy and laugh so much; while with him, her son, she was grave and usually silent and constrained, which did not suit her at all. The only person who behaved freely with him and said what he meant was old Sisoy, who had spent his whole life in the presence of bishops and had out-lived eleven of them. And so the bishop was at ease with him, although, of course, he was a tedious and nonsensical man.

After the service on Tuesday, his holiness Pyotr was in the diocesan bishop's house receiving petitions there; he got excited and angry, and then drove home. He was as unwell as before; he longed to be in bed, but he had hardly reached home when he was informed that a young merchant called Erakin, who subscribed liberally to charities, had come to see him about a very important matter. The bishop had to see him. Erakin stayed about an hour, talked very loud, almost shouted, and it was difficult to understand what he said.

" God grant it may," he said as he went away " Most essential! According to circumstances, your holiness! I trust it may!"

After him came the Mother Superior from a distant convent. And when she had gone they began ringing for vespers. He had to go to church.

In the evening the monks sang harmoniously, with inspiration. A young priest with a black

66

beard conducted the service; and the bishop, hearing of the Bridegroom who comes at midnight and of the Heavenly Mansion adorned for the festival, felt no repentance for his sins, no tribulation, but peace at heart and tranquillity. And he was carried back in thought to the distant past, to his childhood and youth, when, too, they used to sing of the Bridegroom and of the Heavenly Mansion; and now that past rose up before him—living, fair, and joyful as in all likelihood it never had been. And perhaps in the other world, in the life to come, we shall think of the distant past, of our life here, with the same feeling. Who knows ? The bishop was sitting near the altar. It was dark; tears flowed down his face. He thought that here he had attained everything a man in his position could attain; he had faith and yet everything was not clear, something was lacking still. He did not want to die; and he still felt that he had missed what was most important, something of which he had dimly dreamed in the past; and he was troubled by the same hopes for the future as he had felt in childhood, at the academy and abroad.

"How well they sing to-day !" he thought, listening to the singing. "How nice it is !"

IV.

On Thursday he celebrated mass in the cathedral; it was the Washing of Feet. When the service was over and the people were going home, it was sunny, warm; the water gurgled in the gutters, and the unceasing trilling of the larks, tender, telling of peace, rose from the fields outside the town. The trees were already awakening and smiling a welcome, while above them the infinite, fathomless blue sky stretched into the distance, God knows whither.

On reaching home his holiness drank some tea, then changed his clothes, lay down on his bed, and told the lay brother to close the shutters on the windows. The bedroom was darkened. But what weariness, what pain in his legs and his back, a chill heavy pain, what a noise in his ears! He had not slept for a long time—for a very long time, as it seemed to him now, and some trifling detail which haunted his brain as soon as his eyes were closed prevented him from sleeping. As on the day before, sounds reached him from the adjoining rooms through the walls, voices, the jingle of glasses and teaspoons. . . . Marya Timofyevna was gaily telling Father Sisoy some story with quaint turns of speech, while the latter answered in a grumpy, ill-humoured voice: "Bother them! Not likely! What next!" And the bishop again felt vexed and then hurt that with other people his old mother behaved in a simple, ordinary way, while with him, her son, she was shy, spoke little, and did not say what she meant, and even, as he fancied, had during all those three days kept trying in his presence to find an excuse for standing up, because she was embarrassed at sitting before him. And his father? He, too, probably, if he had been living, would not have been able to utter a word in the bishop's presence. . . .

Something fell down on the floor in the adjoining room and was broken; Katya must have dropped a cup or a saucer, for Father Sisoy suddenly spat and said angrily:

" What a regular nuisance the child is ! Lord forgive my transgressions ! One can't provide enough for her."

Then all was quiet, the only sounds came from outside. And when the bishop opened his eyes he saw Katya in his room, standing motionless, staring at him. Her red hair, as usual, stood up from under the comb like a halo.

" Is that you, Katya ?" he asked. " Who is it downstairs who keeps opening and shutting a door ?"

" I don't hear it," answered Katya; and she listened.

" There, someone has just passed by."

" But that was a noise in your stomach, uncle."

He laughed and stroked her on the head.

" So you say Cousin Nikolasha cuts up dead people ?" he asked after a pause.

" Yes, he is studying."

" And is he kind ?"

" Oh yes, he's kind. But he drinks vodka awfully."

" And what was it your father died of ?"

" Papa was weak and very, very thin, and all at once his throat was bad. I was ill then, too, and brother Fedya; we all had bad throats. Papa died, uncle, and we got well."

Her chin began quivering, and tears gleamed in her eyes and trickled down her cheeks.

"Your holiness," she said in a shrill voice, by now weeping bitterly, "uncle, mother and all of us are left very wretched. . . . Give us a little money . . . do be kind . . . uncle darling. . . ."

He, too, was moved to tears, and for a long time was too much touched to speak. Then he stroked her on the head, patted her on the shoulder and said:

"Very good, very good, my child. When the holy Easter comes, we will talk it over. . . . I will help you. . . . I will help you. . . ."

His mother came in quietly, timidly, and prayed before the ikon. Noticing that he was not sleeping, she said:

"Won't you have a drop of soup?"

"No, thank you," he answered, "I am not hungry."

"You seem to be unwell, now I look at you. I should think so; you may well be ill! The whole day on your legs, the whole day. . . . And, my goodness, it makes one's heart ache even to look at you! Well, Easter is not far off; you will rest then, please God. Then we will have a talk, too, but now I'm not going to disturb you with my chatter. Come along, Katya; let his holiness sleep a little."

And he remembered how once very long ago, when he was a boy, she had spoken exactly like that, in the same jestingly respectful tone, with a Church dignitary. . . . Only from her extraordinarily kind eyes and the timid, anxious glance

70

she stole at him as she went out of the room could one have guessed that this was his mother. He shut his eyes and seemed to sleep, but twice heard the clock strike and Father Sisoy coughing the other side of the wall. And once more his mother came in and looked timidly at him for a minute. Someone drove up to the steps, as he could hear, in a coach or in a chaise. Suddenly a knock, the door slammed, the lay brother came into the bedroom.

" Your holiness," he called.

" Well ?"

" The horses are here; it's time for the evening service."

" What o'clock is it ?"

" A quarter past seven."

He dressed and drove to the cathedral. During all the " Twelve Gospels " he had to stand in the middle of the church without moving, and the first gospel, the longest and the most beautiful, he read himself. A mood of confidence and courage came over him. That first gospel, " Now is the Son of Man glorified," he knew by heart; and as he read he raised his eyes from time to time, and saw on both sides a perfect sea of lights and heard the splutter of candles, but, as in past years, he could not see the people, and it seemed as though these were all the same people as had been round him in those days, in his childhood and his youth; that they would always be the same every year and till such time as God only knew.

His father had been a deacon, his grandfather a priest, his great-grandfather a deacon, and his whole family, perhaps from the days when Christianity had been accepted in Russia, had belonged to the priesthood; and his love for the Church services, for the priesthood, for the peal of the bells, was deep in him, ineradicable, innate. In church, particularly when he took part in the service, he felt vigorous, of good cheer, happy. So it was now. Only when the eighth gospel had been read, he felt that his voice had grown weak, even his cough was inaudible. His head had begun to ache intensely, and he was troubled by a fear that he might fall down. And his legs were indeed quite numb, so that by degrees he ceased to feel them and could not understand how or on what he was standing, and why he did not fall. . . .

It was a quarter to twelve when the service was over. When he reached home, the bishop undressed and went to bed at once without even saying his prayers. He could not speak and felt that he could not have stood up. When he had covered his head with the quilt he felt a sudden longing to be abroad, an insufferable longing! He felt that he would give his life not to see those pitiful cheap shutters, those low ceilings, not to smell that heavy monastery smell. If only there were one person to whom he could have talked, have opened his heart!

For a long while he heard footsteps in the next room and could not tell whose they were. At last the door opened, and Sisoy came in with a candle and a tea-cup in his hand.

" You are in bed already, your holiness ?" he

asked. " Here I have come to rub you with spirit and vinegar. A thorough rubbing does a great deal of good. Lord Jesus Christ ! . . . That's the way . . . that's the way. . . . I've just been in our monastery. . . . I don't like it. I'm going away from here to-morrow, your holiness; I don't want to stay longer. Lord Jesus Christ. . . . That's the way. . . ."

Sisoy could never stay long in the same place, and he felt as though he had been a whole year in the Pankratievsky Monastery. Above all, listening to him it was difficult to understand where his home was, whether he cared for anyone or anything, whether he believed in God. . . . He did not know himself why he was a monk, and, indeed, he did not think about it, and the time when he had become a monk had long passed out of his memory; it seemed as though he had been born a monk.

' I'm going away to-morrow; God be with them all."

" I should like to talk to you. . . . I can't find the time," said the bishop softly with an effort. " I don't know anything or anybody here. . . ."

" I'll stay till Sunday if you like; so be it, but I don't want to stay longer. I am sick of them !"

" I ought not to be a bishop," said the bishop softly. " I ought to have been a village priest, a deacon . . . or simply a monk. . . . All this oppresses me . . . oppresses me."

" What ? Lord Jesus Christ. . . . That's the way. Come, sleep well, your holiness ! . . .

What's the good of talking ? It's no use. Good-night !"

The bishop did not sleep all night. And at eight o'clock in the morning he began to have hæmorrhage from the bowels. The lay brother was alarmed, and ran first to the archimandrite, then for the monastery doctor, Ivan Andreyitch, who lived in the town. The doctor, a stout old man with a long grey beard, made a prolonged examination of the bishop, and kept shaking his head and frowning, then said:

" Do you know, your holiness, you have got typhoid ?"

After an hour or so of hæmorrhage the bishop looked much thinner, paler, and wasted; his face looked wrinkled, his eyes looked bigger, and he seemed older, shorter, and it seemed to him that he was thinner, weaker, more insignificant than anyone, that everything that had been had retreated far, far away and would never go on again or be repeated.

" How good," he thought, " how good !"

His old mother came. Seeing his wrinkled face and his big eyes, she was frightened, she fell on her knees by the bed and began kissing his face, his shoulders, his hands. And to her, too, it seemed that he was thinner, weaker, and more insignificant than anyone, and now she forgot that he was a bishop, and kissed him as though he were a child very near and very dear to her.

" Pavlusha, darling," she said; " my own, my darling son ! . . . Why are you like this ? Pavlusha, answer me !"

THE BISHOP

Katya, pale and severe, stood beside her, unable to understand what was the matter with her uncle, why there was such a look of suffering on her grandmother's face, why she was saying such sad and touching things. By now he could not utter a word, he could understand nothing, and he imagined he was a simple ordinary man, that he was walking quickly, cheerfully through the fields, tapping with his stick, while above him was the open sky bathed in sunshine, and that he was free now as a bird and could go where he liked !

"Pavlusha, my darling son, answer me," the old woman was saying. "What is it ? My own !"

"Don't disturb his holiness," Sisoy said angrily, walking about the room. "Let him sleep . . . what's the use . . . it's no good. . . ."

Three doctors arrived, consulted together, and went away again. The day was long, incredibly long, then the night came on and passed slowly, slowly, and towards morning on Saturday the lay brother went in to the old mother who was lying on the sofa in the parlour, and asked her to go into the bedroom: the bishop had just breathed his last.

Next day was Easter Sunday. There were forty-two churches and six monasteries in the town; the sonorous, joyful clang of the bells hung over the town from morning till night unceasingly, setting the spring air aquiver; the birds were singing, the sun was shining brightly. The big market square was noisy, swings were going, barrel organs were playing, accordions were squeaking, drunken voices were shouting. After midday people began driving up and down the principal street.

In short, all was merriment, everything was satisfactory, just as it had been the year before, and as it will be in all likelihood next year.

A month later a new suffragan bishop was appointed, and no one thought anything more of Bishop Pyotr, and afterwards he was completely forgotten. And only the dead man's old mother, who is living to-day with her son-in-law the deacon in a remote little district town, when she goes out at night to bring her cow in and meets other women at the pasture, begins talking of her children and her grandchildren, and says that she had a son a bishop, and this she says timidly, afraid that she may not be believed. . . .

And, indeed, there are some who do not believe her.

1902

IN THE RAVINE

I.

THE village of Ukleevo lay in a ravine so that only the belfry and the chimneys of the printed cottons factories could be seen from the high road and the railway-station. When visitors asked what village this was, they were told:

"That's the village where the deacon ate all the caviare at the funeral."

It had happened at the dinner at the funeral of Kostukov that the old deacon saw among the savouries some large-grained caviare and began eating it greedily; people nudged him, tugged at his arm, but he seemed petrified with enjoyment: felt nothing, and only went on eating. He ate up all the caviare, and there were four pounds in the jar. And years had passed since then, the deacon had long been dead, but the caviare was still remembered. Whether life was so poor here or people had not been clever enough to notice anything but that unimportant incident that had occurred ten years before, anyway the people had nothing else to tell about the village Ukleevo.

The village was never free from fever, and there was boggy mud there even in the summer, especially under the fences over which hung old willow-trees that gave deep shade. Here there was always a smell from the factory refuse and the acetic acid which was used in the finishing of the cotton print.

The three cotton factories and the tanyard were not in the village itself but a little way off. They were small factories, and not more than four hundred workmen were employed in all of them. The tanyard often made the water in the little river stink; the refuse contaminated the meadows, the peasants' cattle suffered from Siberian plague, and orders were given that the factory should be closed. It was considered to be closed, but went on working in secret with the connivance of the local police officer and the district doctor, who was paid ten roubles a month by the owner. In the whole village there were only two decent houses built of brick with iron roofs; one of them was the local court, in the other, a two-storied house just opposite the church, there lived a shopkeeper from Epifan called Grigory Petrovitch Tsybukin.

Grigory kept a grocer's shop, but that was only for appearance' sake: in reality he sold vodka, cattle, hides, grain, and pigs; he traded in anything that came to hand, and when, for instance, magpies were wanted abroad for ladies' hats, he made some thirty kopeks on every pair of birds; he bought timber for felling, lent money at interest, and altogether was a sharp old man, full of resources.

He had two sons. The elder, Anisim, was in the police in the detective department and was rarely at home. The younger, Stepan, had gone in for trade and helped his father: but no great help was expected from him as he was weak in health and deaf; his wife Aksinya, a handsome woman with a good figure, who wore a hat and carried a parasol on holidays, got up early and went to bed late, and ran about all day long, picking up her skirts and jingling her keys, going from the granary to the cellar and from there to the shop, and old Tsybukin looked at her good-humouredly while his eyes glowed, and at such moments he regretted she had not been married to his elder son instead of to the younger one, who was deaf, and who evidently knew very little about female beauty.

The old man had always an inclination for family life, and he loved his family more than anything on earth, especially his elder son, the detective, and his daughter-in-law. Aksinya had no sooner married the deaf son than she began to display an extraordinary gift for business, and knew who could be allowed to run up a bill and who could not: she kept the keys and would not trust them even to her husband; she kept the accounts by means of the reckoning beads, looked at the horses' teeth like a peasant, and was always laughing or shouting; and whatever she did or said the old man was simply delighted and muttered:

" Well done, daughter-in-law ! You are a smart wench !"

He was a widower, but a year after his son's marriage he could not resist getting married himself. A girl was found for him, living twenty miles from Ukleevo, called Varvara Nikolaevna, no longer quite young, but good-looking, comely, and belonging to a decent family. As soon as she was installed into the upper-storey room everything in the house seemed to brighten up as though new glass had been put into all the windows. The lamps gleamed before the ikons, the tables were covered with snow-white cloths, flowers with red buds made their appearance in the windows and in the front garden, and at dinner, instead of eating from a single bowl, each person had a separate plate set for him. Varvara Nikolaevna had a pleasant, friendly smile, and it seemed as though the whole house were smiling, too. Beggars and pilgrims, male and female, began to come into the yard, a thing which had never happened in the past; the plaintive sing-song voices of the Ukleevo peasant women and the apologetic coughs of weak, seedy-looking men, who had been dismissed from the factory for drunkenness were heard under the windows. Varvara helped them with money, with bread, with old clothes, and afterwards, when she felt more at home, began taking things out of the shop. One day the deaf man saw her take four ounces of tea and that disturbed him.

" Here, mother's taken four ounces of tea," he informed his father afterwards; "where is that to be entered ?"

The old man made no reply but stood still and thought a moment, moving his eyebrows, and then went upstairs to his wife.

IN THE RAVINE

" Varvarushka, if you want anything out of the shop," he said affectionately, " take it, my dear. Take it and welcome; don't hesitate."

And the next day the deaf man, running across the yard, called to her:

" If there is anything you want, mother, take it."

There was something new, something gay and light-hearted in her giving of alms, just as there was in the lamps before the ikons and in the red flowers. When at Carnival or at the church festival, which lasted for three days, they sold the peasants tainted salt meat, smelling so strong it was hard to stand near the tub of it, and took scythes, caps, and their wives' kerchiefs in pledge from the drunken men; when the factory hands stupefied with bad vodka lay rolling in the mud, and sin seemed to hover thick like a fog in the air, then it was a relief to think that up there in the house there was a gentle, neatly dressed woman who had nothing to do with salt meat or vodka; her charity had in those burdensome, murky days the effect of a safety valve in a machine.

The days in Tsybukin's house were spent in business cares. Before the sun had risen in the morning Aksinya was panting and puffing as she washed in the outer room, and the samovar was boiling in the kitchen with a hum that boded no good. Old Grigory Petrovitch, dressed in a long black coat, cotton breeches and shiny top boots, looking a dapper little figure, walked about the rooms, tapping with his little heels like the father-in-law in a well-known song. The shop was opened.

When it was daylight a racing droshky was brought up to the front door and the old man got jauntily on to it, pulling his big cap down to his ears; and, looking at him, no one would have said he was fifty-six. His wife and daughter-in-law saw him off, and at such times when he had on a good, clean coat, and had in the droshky a huge black horse that had cost three hundred roubles, the old man did not like the peasants to come up to him with their complaints and petitions; he hated the peasants and disdained them, and if he saw some peasants waiting at the gate, he would shout angrily:

" Why are you standing there ? Go further off."

Or if it were a beggar, he would say:

" God will provide !"

He used to drive off on business; his wife, in a dark dress and a black apron, tidied the rooms or helped in the kitchen. Aksinya attended to the shop, and from the yard could be heard the clink of bottles and of money, her laughter and loud talk, and the anger of customers whom she had offended; and at the same time it could be seen that the secret sale of vodka was already going on in the shop. The deaf man sat in the shop, too, or walked about the street bare-headed, with his hands in his pockets looking absent-mindedly now at the huts, now at the sky over-head. Six times a day they had tea; four times a day they sat down to meals; and in the evening they counted over their takings, put them down, went to bed, and slept soundly.

IN THE RAVINE

All the three cotton factories in Ukleevo and the houses of the factory owners — Hrymin Seniors, Hrymin Juniors, and Kostukov—were on a telephone. The telephone was laid on in the local court, too, but it soon ceased to work as bugs and beetles bred there. The elder of the rural district had had little education and wrote every word in the official documents in capitals. But when the telephone was spoiled he said:

" Yes, now we shall be badly off without a telephone."

The Hrymin Seniors were continually at law with the Juniors, and sometimes the Juniors quarrelled among themselves and began going to law, and their factory did not work for a month or two till they were reconciled again, and this was an entertainment for the people of Ukleevo, as there was a great deal of talk and gossip on the occasion of each quarrel. On holidays Kostukov and the Juniors used to get up races, used to dash about Ukleevo and run over calves. Aksinya, rustling her starched petticoats, used to promenade in a low-necked dress up and down the street near her shop; the Juniors used to snatch her up and carry her off as though by force. Then old Tsybukin would drive out to show his new horse and take Varvara with him.

In the evening, after the races, when people were going to bed, an expensive concertina was played in the Juniors' yard and, if it were a moonlight night, those sounds sent a thrill of delight to the heart, and Ukleevo no longer seemed a wretched hole.

II.

The elder son Anisim came home very rarely, only on great holidays, but he often sent by a returning villager presents and letters written in very good writing by some other hand, always on a sheet of foolscap in the form of a petition. The letters were full of expressions that Anisim never made use of in conversation: "Dear papa and mamma, I send you a pound of flower tea for the satisfaction of your physical needs."

At the bottom of every letter was scratched, as though with a broken pen: "Anisim Tsybukin," and again in the same excellent hand: "Agent."

The letters were read aloud several times, and the old father, touched, red with emotion, would say:

"Here he did not care to stay at home, he has gone in for an intellectual line. Well, let him! Every man to his own job!"

It happened just before Carnival there was a heavy storm of rain mixed with hail; the old man and Varvara went to the window to look at it, and lo and behold! Anisim drove up in a sledge from the station. He was quite unexpected. He came indoors, looking anxious and troubled about something, and he remained the same all the time; there was something free and easy in his manner. He was in no haste to go away, it seemed as though he had been dismissed from the service. Varvara was pleased at his arrival; she looked at him with a sly expression, sighed, and shook her head.

" How is this, my friends ? " she said. " Tut,
tut, the lad's in his twenty-eighth year, and he is
still leading a gay bachelor life; tut, tut, tut. . . "

From the other room her soft, even speech
sounded like tut, tut, tut. She began whispering
with her husband and Aksinya, and their faces
wore the same sly and mysterious expression as
though they were conspirators.

It was decided to marry Anisim.

" Oh, tut, tut . . . the younger brother has
been married long ago," said Varvara, " and you
are still without a helpmate like a cock at a fair.
What is the meaning of it ? Tut, tut, you will
be married, please God, then as you choose—you
will go into the service and your wife will remain
here at home to help us. There is no order in
your life, young man, and I see you have forgotten
how to live properly. Tut, tut, it's the same
trouble with all you townspeople."

When the Tsybukins married, the most handsome girls were chosen as brides for them as rich
men. For Anisim, too, they found a handsome
one. He was himself of an uninteresting and
inconspicuous appearance; of a feeble, sickly
build and short stature; he had full, puffy cheeks
which looked as though he were blowing them
out; his eyes looked with a keen, unblinking stare;
his beard was red and scanty, and when he was
thinking he always put it into his mouth and bit
it; moreover he often drank too much, and that
was noticeable from his face and his walk. But
when he was informed that they had found a very
beautiful bride for him, he said:

" Oh well, I am not a fright myself. All of us Tsybukins are handsome, I may say."

The village of Torguevo was near the town. Half of it had lately been incorporated into the town, the other half remained a village. In the first—the town half—there was a widow living in her own little house; she had a sister living with her who was quite poor and went out to work by the day, and this sister had a daughter called Lipa, a girl who went out to work, too. People in Torguevo were already talking about Lipa's good looks, but her terrible poverty put everyone off; people opined that some widower or elderly man would marry her regardless of her poverty, or would perhaps take her to himself without marriage, and that her mother would get enough to eat living with her. Varvara heard about Lipa from the matchmakers, and she drove over to Torguevo.

Then a visit of inspection was arranged at the aunt's, with lunch and wine all in due order, and Lipa wore a new pink dress made on purpose for this occasion, and a crimson ribbon like a flame gleamed in her hair. She was pale-faced, thin, and frail, with soft, delicate features sunburnt from working in the open air; a shy, mournful smile always hovered about her face, and there was a childlike look in her eyes, trustful and curious.

She was young, quite a little girl, her bosom still scarcely perceptible, but she could be married because she had reached the legal age. She really was beautiful, and the only thing that might be thought unattractive was her big masculine hands which hung idle now like two big claws.

"There is no dowry—and we don't think much of that," said Tsybukin to the aunt. "We took a wife from a poor family for our son Stepan, too, and now we can't say too much for her. In house and in business alike she has hands of gold."

Lipa stood in the doorway and looked as though she would say: "Do with me as you will, I trust you," while her mother Praskovya the work-woman hid herself in the kitchen numb with shyness. At one time in her youth a merchant whose floors she was scrubbing stamped at her in a rage; she went chill with terror and there always was a feeling of fear at the bottom of her heart. When she was frightened her arms and legs trembled and her cheeks twitched. Sitting in the kitchen she tried to hear what the visitors were saying, and she kept crossing herself, pressing her fingers to her forehead, and gazing at the ikons. Anisim, slightly drunk, opened the door into the kitchen and said in a free-and-easy way:

"Why are you sitting in here, precious mamma? We are dull without you."

And Praskovya, overcome with timidity, pressing her hands to her lean, wasted bosom, said:

"Oh, not at all. . . . It's very kind of you."

After the visit of inspection the wedding day was fixed. Then Anisim walked about the rooms at home whistling, or suddenly thinking of something, would fall to brooding and would look at the floor fixedly, silently, as though he would probe to the depths of the earth. He expressed neither pleasure that he was to be married, married so soon, on Low Sunday, nor a desire to see his bride, but simply went on whistling. And it was evident he was only getting married because his father and stepmother wished him to, and because it was the custom in the village to marry the son in order to have a woman to help in the house. When he went away he seemed in no haste, and behaved altogether not as he had done on previous visits—was particularly free and easy, and talked inappropriately.

III.

In the village Shikalovo lived two dressmakers, sisters, belonging to the Flagellant sect. The new clothes for the wedding were ordered from them, and they often came to try them on, and stayed a long while drinking tea. They were making Varvara a brown dress with black lace and bugles on it, and Aksinya a light green dress with a yellow front, with a train. When the dressmakers had finished their work Tsybukin paid them not in money but in goods from the shop, and they went away depressed, carrying parcels of tallow candles and tins of sardines which they did not in the least need, and when they got out of the village into the open country they sat down on a hillock and cried.

Anisim arrived three days before the wedding, rigged out in new clothes from top to toe. He had dazzling india-rubber goloshes, and instead of a cravat wore a red cord with little balls on it, and over his shoulder he had hung an overcoat, also new, without putting his arms into the sleeves.

After crossing himself sedately before the ikon, he greeted his father and gave him ten silver roubles and ten half-roubles; to Varvara he gave as much, and to Aksinya twenty quarter-roubles. The chief charm of the present lay in the fact that all the coins, as though carefully matched, were new and glittered in the sun. Trying to seem grave and sedate he pursed up his face and puffed out his cheeks, and he smelt of spirits. Probably he had visited the refreshment bar at every station. And again there was a free-and-easiness about the man—something superfluous and out of place. Then Anisim had lunch and drank tea with the old man, and Varvara turned the new coins over in her hands and inquired about villagers who had gone to live in the town.

"They are all right, thank God, they get on quite well," said Anisim. "Only something has happened to Ivan Yegorov: his old wife Sofya Nikiforovna is dead. From consumption. They ordered the memorial dinner for the peace of her soul at the confectioner's at two and a half roubles a head. And there was real wine. Those who were peasants from our village—they paid two and a half roubles for them, too. They ate nothing, as though a peasant would understand sauce!"

"Two and a half," said his father, shaking his head.

"Well, it's not like the country there, you go into a restaurant to have a snack of something, you ask for one thing and another, others join till there is a party of us, one has a drink—and before you know where you are it is daylight and you've three or four roubles each to pay. And when one is with Samorodov he likes to have coffee with brandy in it after everything, and brandy is sixty kopecks for a little glass."

"And he is making it all up," said the old man enthusiastically; "he is making it all up, lying!"

"I am always with Samorodov now. It is Samorodov who writes my letters to you. He writes splendidly. And if I were to tell you, mamma," Anisim went on gaily, addressing Varvara, "the sort of fellow that Samorodov is, you would not believe me. We call him Muhtar because he is black like an Armenian. I can see through him, I know all his affairs like the five fingers of my hand, and he feels that, and he always follows me about, we are regular inseparables. He seems not to like it in a way, but he can't get on without me. Where I go he goes. I have a correct, trustworthy eye, mamma. One sees a peasant selling a shirt in the market place. 'Stay, that shirt's stolen.' And really it turns out it is so: the shirt was a stolen one."

"What do you tell from?" asked Varvara.

"Not from anything, I have just an eye for it. I know nothing about the shirt, only for some reason I seem drawn to it: it's stolen, and that's all I can say. Among us detectives it's come to their saying, 'Oh, Anisim has gone to shoot snipe!' That means looking for stolen goods.

Yes. . . . Anybody can steal, but it is another thing to keep! The earth is wide, but there is nowhere to hide stolen goods."

" In our village a ram and two ewes were carried off last week." said Varvara, and she heaved a sigh, " and there is no one to try and find them. . . . Oh, tut, tut. . . ."

" Well, I might have a try. I don't mind."

The day of the wedding arrived. It was a cool but bright, cheerful April day. People were driving about Ukleevo from early morning with pairs or teams of three horses decked with many-coloured ribbons on their yokes and manes, with a jingle of bells. The rooks, disturbed by this activity, were cawing noisily in the willows, and the starlings sang their loudest unceasingly as though rejoicing that there was a wedding at the Tsybukins'.

Indoors the tables were already covered with long fish, smoked hams, stuffed fowls, boxes of sprats, pickled savouries of various sorts, and a number of bottles of vodka and wine; there was a smell of smoked sausage and of sour tinned lobster. Old Tsybukin walked about near the tables, tapping with his heels and sharpening the knives against each other. They kept calling Varvara and asking for things, and she was constantly with a distracted face running breathlessly into the kitchen, where the man cook from Kostukov's and the woman cook from Hrymin Juniors' had been at work since early morning. Aksinya, with her hair curled, in her stays without her dress on, in new creaky boots, flew about the yard like a whirlwind showing glimpses of her bare knees and bosom.

It was noisy, there was a sound of scolding and oaths; passers-by stopped at the wide-open gates, and in everything there was a feeling that something extraordinary was happening.

" They have gone for the bride !"

The bells began jingling and died away far beyond the village. . . . Between two and three o'clock people ran up: again there was a jingling of bells: they were bringing the bride ! The church was full, the candelabra were lighted, the chòir were singing from music books as old Tsybukin had wished it. The glare of the lights and the bright coloured dresses dazzled Lipa; she felt as though the singers with their loud voices were hitting her on the head with a hammer. Her boots and the stays, which she had put on for the first time in her life, pinched her, and her face looked as though she had only just come to herself after fainting; she gazed about without understanding. Anisim, in his black coat with a red cord instead of a tie, stared at the same spot lost in thought, and when the singers shouted loudly he hurriedly crossed himself. He felt touched and disposed to weep. This church was familiar to him from earliest childhood; at one time his dead mother used to bring him here to take the sacrament; at one time he used to sing in the choir; every ikon he remembered so well, every corner. Here he was being married, he had to take a wife for the sake of doing the proper thing, but he was not thinking of that now, he had forgotten his wedding completely. Tears dimmed his eyes so that he could not see the ikons, he felt heavy at heart; he prayed and besought God that the misfortunes that threatened him, that were ready to burst upon him to-morrow, if not to-day, might somehow pass him by as storm-clouds in time of drought pass over the village without yielding one drop of rain. And so many sins were heaped up in the past, so many sins, all getting away from them or setting them right was so beyond hope that it seemed incongruous even to ask forgiveness. But he did ask forgiveness, and even gave a loud sob, but no one took any notice of that, since they all supposed he had had a drop too much.

There was a sound of a fretful childish wail:
" Take me away, mamma darling !"
" Quiet there !" cried the priest.

When they returned from the church people ran after them; there were crowds, too, round the shop, round the gates, and in the yard under the windows. The peasant women came in to sing songs of congratulation to them. The young couple had scarcely crossed the threshold when the singers, who were already standing in the outer room with their music books, broke into a loud chant at the top of their voices; a band ordered expressly from the town began playing. Foaming Don wine was brought in tall wine-glasses, and Elizarov, a carpenter who did jobs by contract, a tall, gaunt old man with eyebrows so bushy that his eyes could scarcely be seen, said, addressing the happy pair:

" Anisim and you, my child, love one another, live in God's way, little children, and the Heavenly Mother will not abandon you."

He leaned his face on the old father's shoulder and gave a sob.

" Grigory Petrovitch, let us weep, let us weep with joy !" he said in a thin voice, and then at once burst out laughing in a loud bass guffaw. " Ho-ho-ho ! This is a fine daughter-in-law for you too ! Everything is in its place in her; all runs smoothly, no creaking, the mechanism works well, lots of screws in it."

He was a native of the Yegoryevsky district, but had worked in the factories in Ukleevo and the neighbourhood from his youth up, and had made it his home. He had been a familiar figure for years as old and gaunt and lanky as now, and for years he had been nicknamed " Crutch." Perhaps because he had been for forty years occupied in repairing the factory machinery he judged everybody and everything by its soundness or its need of repair. And before sitting down to the table he tried several chairs to see whether they were solid, and he touched the smoked fish also.

After the Don wine, they all sat down to the table. The visitors talked, moving their chairs. The singers were singing in the outer room. The band was playing, and at the same time the peasant women in the yard were singing their songs all in chorus—and there was an awful, wild medley of sounds which made one giddy.

Crutch turned round in his chair and prodded

94

his neighbours with his elbows, prevented people from talking, and laughed and cried alternately.

" Little children, little children, little children," he muttered rapidly. " Aksinya my dear, Varvara darling, we will live all in peace and harmony, my dear little axes. . . ."

He drank little and was now only drunk from one glass of English bitters. The revolting bitters, made from nobody knows what, intoxicated everyone who drank it as though it had stunned them. Their tongues began to falter.

The local clergy, the clerks from the factories with their wives, the tradesmen and tavern-keepers from the other villages were present. The clerk and the elder of the rural district who had served together for fourteen years, and who had during all that time never signed a single document for anybody nor let a single person out of the local court without deceiving or insulting him, were sitting now side by side, both fat and well-fed, and it seemed as though they were so saturated in injustice and falsehood that even the skin of their faces were somehow peculiar, fraudulent. The clerk's wife, a thin woman with a squint, had brought all her children with her, and like a bird of prey looked aslant at the plates and snatched anything she could get hold of to put in her own or her children's pockets.

Lipa sat as though turned to stone, still with the same expression as in church. Anisim had not said a single word to her since he had made her acquaintance, so that he did not yet know the sound of her voice; and now, sitting beside her, he remained mute and went on drinking bitters, and when he got drunk he began talking to the aunt who was sitting opposite:

" I have a friend called Samorodov. A peculiar man. He is by rank an honorary citizen, and he can talk. But I know him through and through, auntie, and he feels it. Pray join me in drinking to the health of Samorodov, auntie !"

Varvara, worn out and distracted, walked round the table pressing the guests to eat, and was evidently pleased that there were so many dishes and that everything was so lavish—no one could disparage them now. The sun set, but the dinner went on: the guests were beyond knowing what they were eating or drinking, it was impossible to distinguish what was said, and only from time to time when the band subsided some peasant woman could be heard shouting:

" They have sucked the blood out of us, the Herods; a pest on them !"

In the evening they danced to the band. The Hrymin Juniors came, bringing their wine, and one of them, when dancing a quadrille, held a bottle in each hand and a wineglass in his mouth, and that made everyone laugh. In the middle of the quadrille they suddenly crooked their knees and danced in a squatting position; Aksinya in green flew by like a flash, stirring up a wind with her train. Someone trod on her flounce and Crutch shouted:

" Aie, they have torn off the panel ! Children !"

Aksinya had naïve grey eyes which rarely blinked, and a naïve smile played continually on her face. And in those unblinking eyes, and in that little head on the long neck, and in her slenderness there was something snake-like; all in green but for the yellow on her bosom, she looked with a smile on her face as a viper looks out of the young rye in the spring at the passers-by, stretching itself and lifting its head. The Hrymins were free in their behaviour to her, and it was very noticeable that she was on intimate terms with the elder of them. But her deaf husband saw nothing, he did not look at her; he sat with his legs crossed and ate nuts, cracking them so loudly that it sounded like pistol shots.

But, behold, old Tsybukin himself walked into the middle of the room and waved his handkerchief as a sign that he, too, wanted to dance the Russian dance, and all over the house and from the crowd in the yard rose a roar of approbation:

" *He*'s going to dance ! *He* himself !"

Varvara danced, but the old man only waved his handkerchief and kicked up his heels, but the people in the yard, propped against one another, peeping in at the windows, were in raptures, and for the moment forgave him everything—his wealth and the wrongs he had done them.

" Well done, Grigory Petrovitch !" was heard in the crowd. " That's right, do your best ! You can still play your part ! Ha-ha !"

It was kept up till late, till two o'clock in the morning. Anisim, staggering, went to take leave of the singers and bandsmen, and gave each of them a new half-rouble. His father, who was not staggering but still seemed to be standing

on one leg, saw his guests off, and said to each
of them:

" The wedding has cost two thousand."

As the party was breaking up, someone took
the Shikalovo innkeeper's good coat instead of his
own old one, and Anisim suddenly flew into a rage
and began shouting:

" Stop, I'll find it at once; I know who stole
it, stop."

He ran out into the street and pursued someone.
He was caught, brought back home and shoved,
drunken, red with anger, and wet, into the room
where the aunt was undressing Lipa, and was
locked in.

IV.

Five days had passed. Anisim, who was preparing to go, went upstairs to say good-bye to
Varvara. All the lamps were burning before the
ikons, there was a smell of incense, while she
sat at the window knitting a stocking of red
wool.

" You have not stayed with us long," she said.
" You've been dull, I dare say. Oh, tut, tut. . . .
We live comfortably; we have plenty of everything.
We celebrated your wedding properly, in good
style; your father says it came to two thousand.
In fact we live like merchants, only it's dreary.
We treat the people very badly. My heart aches,
my dear; how we treat them, my goodness!
Whether we exchange a horse or buy something
or hire a labourer—it's cheating in everything.

Cheating and cheating. The Lenten oil in the shop is bitter, rancid, the people have pitch that is better. But surely, tell me pray, couldn't we sell good oil ?"

" Every man to his job, mamma."

" But you know we all have to die ? Oy, oy, really you ought to talk to your father . . . !"

" Why, you should talk to him yourself."

" Well, well, I did put in my word, but he said just what you do: ' Every man to his own job.' Do you suppose in the next world they'll consider what job you have been put to ? God's judgment is just."

" Of course no one will consider," said Anisim, and he heaved a sigh. " There is no God, anyway, you know, mamma, so what considering can there be ?"

Varvara looked at him with surprise, burst out laughing, and clasped her hands. Perhaps because she was so genuinely surprised at his words and looked at him as though he were a queer person, he was confused.

" Perhaps there is a God, only there is no faith. When I was being married I was not myself. Just as you may take an egg from under a hen and there is a chicken chirping in it, so my conscience was beginning to chirp in me, and while I was being married I thought all the time there was a God ! But when I left the church it was nothing. And indeed, how can I tell whether there is a God or not ? We are not taught right from childhood, and while the babe is still at his mother's breast he is only taught ' every man to his own job.' Father does not believe in God, either. You were saying that Guntorev had some sheep stolen. . . . I have found them; it was a peasant at Shikalovo stole them; he stole them, but father's got the fleeces . . . so that's all his faith amounts to."

Anisim winked and wagged his head.

"The elder does not believe in God, either," he went on. "And the clerk, and the deacon, too. And as for their going to church and keeping the fasts, that is simply to prevent people talking ill of them, and in case it really may be true that there will be a Day of Judgment. Nowadays people say that the end of the world has come because people have grown weaker, do not honour their parents, and so on. All that is nonsense. My idea, mamma, is that all our trouble is because there is so little conscience in people. I see through things, mamma, and I understand. If a man has a stolen shirt I see it. A man sits in a tavern and you fancy he is drinking tea and no more, but to me the tea is neither here nor there; I see further, he has no conscience. You can go about the whole day and not meet one man with a conscience. And the whole reason is that they don't know whether there is a God or not. . . . Well, good-bye, mamma, keep alive and well, don't remember evil against me."

Anisim bowed down at Varvara's feet.

"I thank you for everything, mamma," he said. "You are a great gain to our family. You are a very ladylike woman, and I am very pleased with you."

Much moved, Anisim went out, but returned again and said:

" Samorodov has got me mixed up in something: I shall either make my fortune or come to grief. If anything happens, then you must comfort my father, mamma."

" Oh nonsense, don't you worry, tut, tut, tut . . . God is merciful. And Anisim, you should be affectionate to your wife, instead of giving each other sulky looks as you do; you might smile at least."

" Yes, she is rather a queer one," said Anisim, and he gave a sigh. " She does not understand anything, she never speaks. She is very young, let her grow up."

A tall, sleek white stallion was already standing at the front door, harnessed to the chaise.

Old Tsybukin jumped in jauntily with a run and took the reins. Anisim kissed Varvara, Aksinya, and his brother. On the steps Lipa, too, was standing; she was standing motionless, looking away, and it seemed as though she had not come to see him off but just by chance for some unknown reason. Anisim went up to her and just touched her cheek with his lips.

" Good-bye," he said.

And without looking at him she gave a strange smile; her face began to quiver, and everyone for some reason felt sorry for her. Anisim, too, leaped into the chaise with a bound and put his arms jauntily akimbo, for he considered himself a good-looking fellow.

When they drove up out of the ravine Anisim

kept looking back towards the village. It was a warm, bright day. The cattle were being driven out for the first time, and the peasant girls and women were walking by the herd in their holiday dresses. The dun-coloured bull bellowed, glad to be free, and pawed the ground with his fore-feet. On all sides, above and below, the larks were singing. Anisim looked round at the elegant white church—it had only lately been white-washed—and he thought how he had been praying in it five days before; he looked round at the school with its green roof, at the little river in which he used once to bathe and catch fish, and there was a stir of joy in his heart, and he wished that walls might rise up from the ground and prevent him from going further, and that he might be left with nothing but the past.

At the station they went to the refreshment room and drank a glass of sherry each. His father felt in his pocket for his purse to pay.

" I will stand treat," said Anisim. The old man, touched and delighted, slapped him on the shoulder, and winked to the waiter as much as to say, " See what a fine son I have got."

" You ought to stay at home in the business, Anisim," he said; " you would be worth any price to me ! I would shower gold on you from head to foot, my son."

" It can't be done, papa."

The sherry was sour and smelt of sealing-wax, but they had another glass.

When old Tsybukin returned home from the station, for the first moment he did not recognize

his younger daughter-in-law. As soon as her
husband had driven out of the yard, Lipa was
transformed and suddenly brightened up. Wearing a threadbare old petticoat, with her feet bare
and her sleeves tucked up to the shoulders, she
was scrubbing the stairs in the entry and singing
in a silvery little voice, and when she brought
out a big tub of dirty water and looked up at
the sun with her childlike smile it seemed as
though she, too, were a lark.

An old labourer who was passing by the door
shook his head and cleared his throat.

"Yes, indeed, your daughters-in-law, Grigory
Petrovitch, are a blessing from God," he said.
"Not women, but treasures!"

V.

On Friday, the 8th of July, Elizarov, nicknamed Crutch, and Lipa were returning from the
village of Kazanskoe, where they had been to a
service on the occasion of a church holiday in
the honour of the Holy Mother of Kazan. A
good distance after them walked Lipa's mother
Praskovya, who always fell behind, as she was ill
and short of breath. It was drawing towards
evening.

"A-a-a . . ." said Crutch, wondering as he
listened to Lipa. "A-a! . . . We-ell!"

"I am very fond of jam, Ilya Makaritch," said
Lipa. "I sit down in my little corner and drink
tea and eat jam. Or I drink it with Varvara

103

Nikolaevna, and she tells some story full of feeling. We have a lot of jam—four jars. 'Have some, Lipa; eat as much as you like.'"

"A-a-a, four jars!"

"They live very well. We have white bread with our tea; and meat, too, as much as one wants. They live very well, only I am frightened with them, Ilya Makaritch. Oh, oh, how frightened I am!"

"Why are you frightened, child?" asked Crutch, and he looked back to see how far Praskovya was behind.

"To begin with, when the wedding had been celebrated I was afraid of Anisim Grigoritch. Anisim Grigoritch did nothing, he didn't ill-treat me, only when he comes near me a cold shiver runs all over me, through all my bones. And I did not sleep one night, I trembled all over and kept praying to God. And now I am afraid of Aksinya, Ilya Makaritch. It's not that she does anything, she is always laughing, but sometimes she glances at the window, and her eyes are so fierce and there is a gleam of green in them—like the eyes of the sheep in the shed. The Hrymin Juniors are leading her astray: 'Your old man,' they tell her, 'has a bit of land at Butyokino, a hundred and twenty acres,' they say, 'and there is sand and water there, so you, Aksinya,' they say, 'build a brickyard there and we will go shares in it.' Bricks now are twenty roubles the thousand, it's a profitable business. Yesterday at dinner Aksinya said to my father-in-law: 'I want to build a brickyard at Butyokino; I'm

going into business on my own account.' She
laughed as she said it. And Grigory Petrovitch's
face darkened, one could see he did not like it.
' As long as I live,' he said, ' the family must not
break up, we must go on altogether.' She gave
a look and gritted her teeth. . . . Fritters were
served, she would not eat them."

" A-a-a ! . . ." Crutch was surprised.

" And tell me, if you please, when does she
sleep ?" said Lipa. " She sleeps for half an hour,
then jumps up and keeps walking and walking
about to see whether the peasants have not set
fire to something, have not stolen something. . . .
I am frightened with her, Ilya Makaritch. And
the Hrymin Juniors did not go to bed after the
wedding, but drove to the town to go to law
with each other ; and folks do say it is all on account
of Aksinya. Two of the brothers have promised
to build her a brickyard, but the third is offended,
and the factory has been at a standstill for a
month, and my uncle Prohor is without work and
goes about from house to house getting crusts.
' Hadn't you better go working on the land or
sawing up wood, meanwhile, uncle ?' I tell him ;
' why disgrace yourself ?' ' I've got out of the
way of it,' he says ; ' I don't know how to do any
sort of peasant's work now, Lipinka.' . . ."

They stopped to rest and wait for Praskovya
near a copse of young aspen-trees. Elizarov had
long been a contractor in a small way, but he
kept no horses, going on foot all over the district
with nothing but a little bag in which there was
bread and onions, and stalking along with big

strides, swinging his arms. And it was difficult to walk with him.

At the entrance to the copse stood a milestone. Elizarov touched it; read it. Praskovya reached them out of breath. Her wrinkled and always scared-looking face was beaming with happiness; she had been at church to-day like anyone else, then she had been to the fair and there had drunk pear cider. For her this was unusual, and it even seemed to her now that she had lived for her own pleasure that day for the first time in her life. After resting they all three walked on side by side. The sun had already set, and its beams filtered through the copse, casting a light on the trunks of the trees. There was a faint sound of voices ahead. The Ukleevo girls had long before pushed on ahead but had lingered in the copse, probably gathering mushrooms.

" Hey, wenches !" cried Elizarov. " Hey, my beauties !"

There was a sound of laughter in response.

" Crutch is coming ! Crutch ! The old horse-radish."

And the echo laughed, too. And then the copse was left behind. The tops of the factory chimneys came into view. The cross on the belfry glittered: this was the village: " the one at which the deacon ate all the caviare at the funeral." Now they were almost home; they only had to go down into the big ravine. Lipa and Praskovya, who had been walking bare-footed, sat down on the grass to put on their boots; Elizar sat down with them. If they looked down from above Ukleevo looked beautiful and peaceful with its willow-trees, its white church, and its little river, and the only blot on the picture was the roof of the factories, painted for the sake of cheapness a gloomy ashen grey. On the slope on the further side they could see the rye—some in stacks and sheaves here and there as though strewn about by the storm, and some freshly cut lying in swathes; the oats, too, were ripe and glistened now in the sun like mother-of-pearl. It was harvest-time. To-day was a holiday, to-morrow they would harvest the rye and carry the hay, and then Sunday a holiday again; every day there were mutterings of distant thunder. It was misty and looked like rain, and, gazing now at the fields, everyone thought, God grant we get the harvest in in time; and everyone felt gay and joyful and anxious at heart.

" Mowers ask a high price nowadays," said Praskovya. " One rouble and forty kopecks a day."

People kept coming and coming from the fair at Kazanskoe: peasant women, factory workers in new caps, beggars, children. . . . Here a cart would drive by stirring up the dust and behind it would run an unsold horse, and it seemed glad it had not been sold; then a cow was led along by the horns, resisting stubbornly; then a cart again, and in it drunken peasants swinging their legs. An old woman led a little boy in a big cap and big boots; the boy was tired out with the heat and the heavy boots which prevented his bending his legs at the knees, but yet blew un-

VI.

14

ceasingly with all his might at a tin trumpet. They had gone down the slope and turned into the street, but the trumpet could still be heard.

"'Our factory owners don't seem quite themselves . . .'" said Elizarov. "There's trouble. Kostukov is angry with me. 'Too many boards have gone on the cornices.' 'Too many? As many have gone on it as were needed, Vassily Danilitch; I don't eat them with my porridge.' 'How can you speak to me like that?' said he, 'you good-for-nothing blockhead! Don't forget yourself! It was I made you a contractor.' 'That's nothing so wonderful,' said I. 'Even before I was a contractor I used to have tea every day.' 'You are a rascal . . .' he said. I said nothing. 'We are rascals in this world,' thought I, 'and you will be rascals in the next. . . .' Ha-ha-ha! The next day he was softer. 'Don't you bear malice against me for my words, Makaritch,' he said. 'If I said too much,' says he, 'what of it? I am a merchant of the first guild, your superior—you ought to hold your tongue.' 'You,' said I, 'are a merchant of the first guild and I am a carpenter, that's correct. And Saint Joseph was a carpenter, too. Ours is a righteous calling and pleasing to God, and if you are pleased to be my superior you are very welcome to it, Vassily Danilitch.' And later on, after that conversation I mean, I thought: 'Which was the superior? A merchant of the first guild or a carpenter?' The carpenter must be, my child!"

Crutch thought a minute and added:

" Yes, that's how it is, child. He who works, he who is patient is the superior."

By now the sun had set and a thick mist as white as milk was rising over the river, in the church enclosure, and in the open spaces round the factories. Now when the darkness was coming on rapidly, when lights were twinkling below, and when it seemed as though the mist were hiding a fathomless abyss, Lipa and her mother who were born in poverty and prepared to live so till the end, giving up to others everything except their frightened, gentle souls, may have fancied for a minute perhaps that in the vast mysterious world, among the endless series of lives, they, too, counted for something, and they, too, were superior to someone; they liked sitting here at the top, they smiled happily and forgot that they must go down below again all the same.

At last they went home again. The mowers were sitting on the ground at the gates near the shop. As a rule the Ukleevo peasants did not go to Tsybukin's to work, and they had to hire strangers, and now in the darkness it seemed as though there were men sitting there with long black beards. The shop was open, and through the doorway they could see the deaf man playing draughts with a boy. The mowers were singing softly, scarcely audibly, or loudly demanding their wages for the previous day, but they were not paid for fear they should go away before to-morrow. Old Tsybukin, with his coat off, was sitting in his waistcoat with Aksinya under the birch-tree, drinking tea; a lamp was burning on the table.

"I say, grandfather," a mower called from outside the gates, as though taunting him, "pay us half anyway! Hey, grandfather."

And at once there was the sound of laughter, and then again they sang hardly audibly. . . . Crutch, too, sat down to have some tea.

"We have been at the fair, you know," he began telling them. "We have had a walk, a very nice walk, my children, praise the Lord. But an unfortunate thing happened: Sashka the blacksmith bought some tobacco and gave the shopman half a rouble to be sure. And the half rouble was a false one"—Crutch went on, and he meant to speak in a whisper, but he spoke in a smothered, husky voice which was audible to everyone. "The half-rouble turned out to be a bad one. He was asked where he got it. 'Anisim Tsybukin gave it me,' he said. 'When I went to his wedding,' he said. They called the police inspector, took the man away. . . . Look out, Grigory Petrovitch, that nothing comes of it, no talk. . . ."

"Gra-ndfather!" the same voice called tauntingly outside the gates. "Gra-andfather!"

A silence followed.

"Ah, little children, little children, little children . . ." Crutch muttered rapidly, and he got up. He was overcome with drowsiness. "Well, thank you for the tea, for the sugar, little children. It is time to sleep. I am like a bit of rotten timber nowadays, my beams are crumbling

under me.   Ho-ho-ho !   I suppose it's time I was
dead."

And he gave a gulp.   Old Tsybukin did not
finish his tea but sat on a little, pondering; and
his face looked as though he were listening to the
footsteps of Crutch, who was far away down the
street.

" Sashka the blacksmith told a lie, I expect,"
said Aksinya, guessing his thoughts.

He went into the house and came back a little
later with a parcel; he opened it, and there was
the gleam of roubles—perfectly new coins.   He
took one, tried it with his teeth, flung it on the
tray; then flung down another.

" The roubles really are false . . ." he said,
looking at Aksinya and seeming perplexed.
" These are those Anisim brought, his present.
Take them, daughter," he whispered, and thrust
the parcel into her hands.   " Take them and
throw them into the well . . . confound them !
And mind there is no talk about it.   Harm might
come of it. . . .   Take away the samovar, put
out the light."

Lipa and her mother sitting in the barn saw
the lights go out one after the other; only overhead in Varvara's room there were blue and red
lamps gleaming, and a feeling of peace, content,
and happy ignorance seemed to float down from
there.   Praskovya could never get used to her
daughter's being married to a rich man, and
when she came she huddled timidly in the outer
room with a deprecating smile on her face, and
tea and sugar were sent out to her.   And Lipa,

too, could not get used to it either, and after her husband had gone away she did not sleep in her bed, but lay down anywhere to sleep, in the kitchen or the barn, and every day she scrubbed the floor or washed the clothes, and felt as though she were hired by the day. And now, on coming back from the service, they drank tea in the kitchen with the cook, then they went into the barn and lay down on the ground between the sledge and the wall. It was dark here and smelt of harness. The lights went out about the house, then they could hear the deaf man shutting up the shop, the mowers settling themselves about the yard to sleep. In the distance at the Hrymin Juniors' they were playing on the expensive concertina. . . . Praskovya and Lipa began to go to sleep.

And when they were awakened by somebody's steps it was bright moonlight; at the entrance of the barn stood Aksinya with her bedding in her arms.

"Maybe it's a bit cooler here," she said; then she came in and lay down almost in the doorway so that the moonlight fell full upon her.

She did not sleep, but breathed heavily, tossing from side to side with the heat, throwing off almost all the bedclothes. And in the magic moonlight what a beautiful, what a proud animal she was! A little time passed, and then steps were heard again: the old father, white all over, appeared in the doorway.

"Aksinya," he called, "are you here?"

"Well?" she responded angrily.

"I told you just now to throw the money into the well, have you done so ?"

"What next, throwing property into the water ! I gave them to the mowers. . . ."

"Oh my God !" cried the old man, dumbfoundered and alarmed. "Oh my God ! you wicked woman. . . ."

He flung up his hands and went out, and he kept saying something as he went away. And a little later Aksinya sat up and sighed heavily with annoyance, then got up and, gathering up her bedclothes in her arms, went out.

"Why did you marry me into this family, mother ?" said Lipa.

"One has to be married, daughter. It was not us who ordained it."

And a feeling of inconsolable woe was ready to take possession of them. But it seemed to them that someone was looking down from the height of the heavens, out of the blue from where the stars were seeing everything that was going on in Ukleevo, watching over them. And however great was wickedness, still the night was calm and beautiful, and still in God's world there is and will be truth and justice as calm and beautiful, and everything on earth is only waiting to be made one with truth and justice, even as the moonlight is blended with the night.

And both, huddling close to one another, fell asleep comforted.

VI.

News had come long before that Anisim had been put in prison for coining and passing bad money. Months passed, more than half a year passed, the long winter was over, spring had begun, and everyone in the house and the village had grown used to the fact that Anisim was in prison. And when anyone passed by the house or the shop at night he would remember that Anisim was in prison; and when they rang at the churchyard for some reason, that, too, reminded them that he was in prison awaiting trial.

It seemed as though a shadow had fallen upon the house. The house looked darker, the roof was rustier, the heavy, iron-bound door into the shop, which was painted green, was covered with cracks, or, as the deaf man expressed it, "blisters"; and old Tsybukin seemed to have grown dingy, too. He had given up cutting his hair and beard, and looked shaggy. He no longer sprang jauntily into his chaise, nor shouted to beggars: "God will provide!" His strength was on the wane, and that was evident in everything. People were less afraid of him now, and the police officer drew up a formal charge against him in the shop though he received his regular bribe as before; and three times the old man was called up to the town to be tried for illicit dealing in spirits, and the case was continually adjourned owing to the non-appearance of witnesses, and old Tsybukin was worn out with worry.

He often went to see his son, hired somebody, handed in a petition to somebody else, presented a holy banner to some church. He presented the governor of the prison in which Anisim was confined with a silver glass stand with a long spoon and the inscription: "The soul knows its right measure."

"There is no one to look after things for us," said Varvara. "Tut, tut. . . . You ought to ask someone of the gentlefolks, they would write to the head officials. . . . At least they might let him out on bail! Why wear the poor fellow out?"

She, too, was grieved, but had grown stouter and whiter; she lighted the lamps before the ikons as before, and saw that everything in the house was clean, and regaled the guests with jam and apple cheese. The deaf man and Aksinya looked after the shop. A new project was in progress—a brickyard in Butyokino—and Aksinya went there almost every day in the chaise. She drove herself, and when she met acquaintances she stretched out her neck like a snake out of the young rye, and smiled naïvely and enigmatically. Lipa spent her time playing with the baby which had been born to her before Lent. It was a tiny, thin, pitiful little baby, and it was strange that it should cry and gaze about and be considered a human being, and even be called Nikifor. He lay in his swinging cradle, and Lipa would walk away towards the door and say, bowing to him:

"Good-day, Nikifor Anisimitch!"

And she would rush at him and kiss him. Then

she would walk away to the door, bow again, and say:

"Good-day, Nikifor Anisimitch!"

And he kicked up his little red legs, and his crying was mixed with laughter like the carpenter Elizarov's.

At last the day of the trial was fixed. Tsybukin went away five days before. Then they heard that the peasants called as witnesses had been fetched; their old workman who had received a notice to appear went too.

The trial was on a Thursday. But Sunday had passed, and Tsybukin was still not back, and there was no news. Towards the evening on Tuesday Varvara was sitting at the open window, listening for her husband to come. In the next room Lipa was playing with her baby. She was tossing him up in her arms and saying enthusiastically:

"You will grow up ever so big, ever so big. You will be a peasant, we shall go out to work together! We shall go out to work together!"

"Come, come," said Varvara, offended. "Go out to work, what an idea, you silly girl! He will be a merchant . . .!"

Lipa sang softly, but a minute later she forgot and again:

"You will grow ever so big, ever so big. You will be a peasant, we'll go out to work together."

"There she is at it again!"

Lipa, with Nikifor in her arms, stood still in the doorway and asked:

"Why do I love him so much, mamma? Why do I feel so sorry for him?" she went on in a quivering voice, and her eyes glistened with tears. " Who is he ? What is he like ? As light as a little feather, as a little crumb, but I love him; I love him like a real person. Here he can do nothing, he can't talk, and yet I know what he wants with his little eyes."

Varvara was listening; the sound of the evening train coming in to the station reached her. Had her husband come ? She did not hear and she did not heed what Lipa was saying, she had no idea how the time passed, but only trembled all over— not from dread, but intense curiosity. She saw a cart full of peasants roll quickly by with a rattle. It was the witnesses coming back from the station. When the cart passed the shop the old workman jumped out and walked into the yard. She could hear him being greeted in the yard and being asked some questions. . . .

" Deprivation of rights and all his property," he said loudly; " and six years' penal servitude in Siberia."

She could see Aksinya come out of the shop by the back way; she had just been selling kerosene, and in one hand held a bottle and in the other a can, and in her mouth she had some silver coins.

" Where is father ?" she asked, lisping.

" At the station," answered the labourer. " ' When it gets a little darker,' he said, ' then I shall come.' "

And when it became known all through the household that Anisim was sentenced to penal servitude, the cook in the kitchen suddenly broke into a wail as though at a funeral, imagining that this was demanded by the proprieties:

" There is no one to care for us now you have gone, Anisim Grigoritch, our bright falcon. . . ."

The dogs began barking in alarm. Varvara ran to the window, and rushing about in distress, shouted to the cook with all her might, straining her voice:

" Sto-op, Stepanida, sto-op ! Don't harrow us, for Christ's sake !"

They forgot to set the samovar, they could think of nothing. Only Lipa could not make out what it was all about and went on playing with her baby.

When the old father arrived from the station they asked him no questions. He greeted them and walked through all the rooms in silence; he had no supper.

" There was no one to see about things . . ." Varvara began when they were alone. " I said you should have asked some of the gentry, you would not heed me at the time. . . . A petition would . . ."

" I saw to things," said her husband with a wave of his hand. " When Anisim was condemned I went to the gentleman who was defending him. ' It's no use now,' he said, ' it's too late '; and Anisim said the same; it's too late. But all the same as I came out of the court I made an agreement with a lawyer, I paid him something in advance. I'll wait a week and then I will go again. It is as God wills."

Again the old man walked through all the

rooms, and when he went back to Varvara he said:

" I must be ill. My head's in a sort of . . . fog. My thoughts are in a maze."

He closed the door that Lipa might not hear, and went on softly:

" I am unhappy about my money. Do you remember on Low Sunday before his wedding Anisim's bringing me some new roubles and half-roubles? One parcel I put away at the time, but the others I mixed with my own money. When my uncle Dmitri Filatitch—the kingdom of heaven be his—was alive, he used constantly to go journeys to Moscow and to the Crimea to buy goods. He had a wife, and this same wife, when he was away buying goods, used to take up with other men. She had half a dozen children. And when uncle was in his cups he would laugh and say: ' I never can make out,' he used to say, ' which are my children and which are other people's.' An easy-going disposition, to be sure; and so I now can't distinguish which are genuine roubles and which are false ones. And it seems to me that they are all false."

" Nonsense, God bless you."

" I take a ticket at the station, I give the man three roubles, and I keep fancying they are false. And I am frightened. I must be ill."

" There's no denying it, we are all in God's hands. . . . Oh dear, dear . . ." said Varvara, and she shook her head. " You ought to think about this, Grigory Petrovitch: you never know, anything may happen, you are not a young man.

See they don't wrong your grandchild when you are dead and gone. Oy, I am afraid they will be unfair to Nikifor! He has as good as no father, his mother's young and foolish . . . you ought to secure something for him, poor little boy, at least the land, Butyokino, Grigory Petrovitch, really! Think it over!" Varvara went on persuading him. "The pretty boy, one is sorry for him! You go to-morrow and make out a deed; why put it off?"

"I'd forgotten about my grandson," said Tsybukin. "I must go and have a look at him. So you say the boy is all right? Well, let him grow up, please God."

He opened the door and, crooking his finger, beckoned to Lipa. She went up to him with the baby in her arms.

"If there is anything you want, Lipinka, you ask for it," he said. "And eat anything you like, we don't grudge it, so long as it does you good. . . ." He made the sign of the cross over the baby. "And take care of my grandchild. My son is gone, but my grandson is left."

Tears rolled down his cheeks; he gave a sob and went away. Soon afterwards he went to bed and slept soundly after seven sleepless nights.

VII.

Old Tsybukin went to the town for a short time. Someone told Aksinya that he had gone to the notary to make his will and that he was leaving Butyokino, the very place where she had set up a brickyard, to Nikifor, his grandson. She was informed of this in the morning when old Tsybukin and Varvara were sitting near the steps under the birch-tree, drinking their tea. She closed the shop in the front and at the back, gathered together all the keys she had, and flung them at her father-in-law's feet.

"I am not going on working for you," she began in a loud voice, and suddenly broke into sobs. "It seems I am not your daughter-in-law, but a servant! Everybody's jeering and saying, 'See what a servant the Tsybukins have got hold of!' I did not come to you for wages! I am not a beggar, I am not a slave, I have a father and mother."

She did not wipe away her tears, she fixed upon her father-in-law eyes full of tears, vindictive, squinting with wrath; her face and neck were red and tense, and she was shouting at the top of her voice.

"I don't mean to go on being a slave!" she went on. "I am worn out. When it is work, when it is sitting in the shop day in and day out, scurrying out at night for vodka—then it is my share, but when it is giving away the land then it is for that convict's wife and her imp. She is mistress here, and I am her servant. Give her everything, the convict's wife, and may it choke her; I am going home! Find yourselves some other fool, you damned Herods!"

Tsybukin had never in his life scolded or punished his children, and had never dreamed that one of his family could speak to him rudely or behave disrespectfully; and now he was very much frightened; he ran into the house and there hid behind the cupboard. And Varvara was so much flustered that she could not get up from her seat, and only waved her hands before her as though she were warding off a bee.

" Oh Holy Saints ! what's the meaning of it ?" she muttered in horror. " What is she shouting ? Oh, dear, dear ! . . . People will hear ! Hush. Oh, hush !"

" He has given Butyokino to the convict's wife," Aksinya went on bawling. " Give her everything now, I don't want anything from you ! Let me alone ! You are all a gang of thieves here ! I have seen my fill of it, I have had enough ! You have robbed folks coming in and going out; you have robbed old and young alike, you brigands ! And who has been selling vodka without a licence ? And false money ? You've filled boxes full of false coins, and now I am no more use !"

A crowd had by now collected at the open gate and was staring into the yard.

" Let the people look," bawled Aksinya. " I will shame you all ! You shall burn with shame ! You shall grovel at my feet. Hey ! Stepan," she called to the deaf man, " let us go home this minute ! Let us go to my father and mother; I don't want to live with convicts. Get ready !"

Clothes were hanging on lines stretched across the yard; she snatched off her petticoats and blouses still wet and flung them into the deaf

man's arms. Then in her fury she dashed about
the yard by the linen, tore down all of it, and
what was not hers she threw on the ground and
trampled upon.

" Holy Saints, take her away," moaned Varvara. " What a woman ! Give her Butyokino !
Give it her, for the Lord's sake !"

" Well ! Wha-at a woman !" people were
saying at the gate. " She's a wo-oman ! She's
going it—something like !"

Aksinya ran into the kitchen where washing
was going on. Lipa was washing alone, the cook
had gone to the river to rinse the clothes. Steam
was rising from the trough and from the caldron
on the side of the stove, and the kitchen was thick
and stifling from the steam. On the floor was a
heap of unwashed clothes, and Nikifor, kicking up
his little red legs, had been put down on a bench
near them so that if he fell he should not hurt himself. Just as Aksinya went in Lipa took the former's
chemise out of the heap and put it in the trough,
and was just stretching out her hand to a big ladle
of boiling water which was standing on the table.

" Give it here," said Aksinya, looking at her
with hatred, and snatching the chemise out of
the trough; " it is not your business to touch my
linen ! You are a convict's wife, and ought to
know your place and who you are."

Lipa gazed at her, taken aback, and did not
understand, but suddenly she caught the look
Aksinya turned upon the child, and at once she
understood and went numb all over.

" You've taken my land, so here you are !"

123

Saying this Aksinya snatched up the ladle with the boiling water and flung it over Nikifor.

After this there was heard a scream such as had never been heard before in Ukleevo, and no one would have believed that a little weak creature like Lipa could scream like that. And it was suddenly silent in the yard.

Aksinya walked into the house with her old naïve smile. . . . The deaf man kept moving about the yard with his arms full of linen, then he began hanging it up again, in silence, without haste. And until the cook came back from the river no one ventured to go into the kitchen and see what was there.

VIII.

Nikifor was taken to the district hospital, and towards evening he died there. Lipa did not wait for them to come for her, but wrapped the dead baby in its little quilt and carried it home.

The hospital, a new one recently built, with big windows, stood high up on a hill; it was glittering from the setting sun and looked as though it were on fire from inside. There was a little village below. Lipa went down along the road, and before reaching the village sat down by a pond. A woman brought a horse down to drink and the horse did not drink.

" What more do you want ? " said the woman to it softly. " What do you want ? "

A boy in a red shirt, sitting at the water's edge, was washing his father's boots. And not another soul was in sight either in the village or on the hill.

" It's not drinking," said Lipa, looking at the horse.

Then the woman with the horse and the boy with the boots walked away, and there was no one left at all. The sun went to bed wrapped in cloth of gold and purple, and long clouds, red and lilac, stretched across the sky, guarded its slumbers. Somewhere far away a bittern cried, a hollow, melancholy sound like a cow shut up in a barn. The cry of that mysterious bird was heard every spring, but no one knew what it was like or where it lived. At the top of the hill by the hospital, in the bushes close to the pond, and in the fields the nightingales were trilling. The cuckoo kept reckoning someone's years and losing count and beginning again. In the pond the frogs called angrily to one another, straining themselves to bursting, and one could even make out the words: " That's what you are ! That's what you are !" What a noise there was ! It seemed as though all these creatures were singing and shouting so that no one might sleep on that spring night, so that all, even the angry frogs, might appreciate and enjoy every minute: life is given only once.

A silver half-moon was shining in the sky; there were many stars. Lipa had no idea how long she sat by the pond, but when she got up and walked on everybody was asleep in the little village, and there was not a single light. It was probably about nine miles' walk home, but she had not the strength, she had not the power to think how to go: the moon gleamed now in front, now on the right, and the same cuckoo kept calling in a voice grown husky, with a chuckle as though gibing at her: " Oy, look out, you'll lose your way !" Lipa walked rapidly; she lost the kerchief from her head . . . she looked at the sky and wondered where her baby's soul was now: was it following her, or floating aloft yonder among the stars and thinking nothing now of his mother ? Oh, how lonely it was in the open country at night, in the midst of that singing when one cannot sing oneself; in the midst of the incessant cries of joy when one cannot oneself be joyful, when the moon, which cares not whether it is spring or winter, whether men are alive or dead, looks down as lonely, too. . . . When there is grief in the heart it is hard to be without people. If only her mother, Praskovya, had been with her, or Crutch, or the cook, or some peasant !

" Boo-oo !" cried the bittern. " Boo-oo !"

And suddenly she heard clearly the sound of human speech:

" Put the horses in, Vavila !"

By the wayside a camp fire was burning ahead of her: the flames had died down, there were only red embers. She could hear the horses munching In the darkness she could see the outlines of two carts, one with a barrel, the other, a lower one with sacks in it, and the figures of two men; one was leading a horse to put it into the shafts, the other was standing motionless by the fire with his hands behind his back. A dog growled by the carts. The one who was leading the horse stopped and said:

" It seems as though someone were coming along the road."

" Sharik, be quiet !" the other called to the dog.

And from the voice one could tell that the second was an old man. Lipa stopped and said:

" God help you."

The old man went up to her and answered not immediately:

" Good-evening !"

" Your dog does not bite, grandfather ?"

" No, come along, he won't touch you."

" I have been at the hospital," said Lipa after a pause. " My little son died there. Here I am carrying him home."

It must have been unpleasant for the old man to hear this, for he moved away and said hurriedly:

" Never mind, my dear. It's God's will. You are very slow, lad," he added, addressing his companion; " look alive !"

" Your yoke's nowhere," said the young man; ' it is not to be seen."

" You are a regular Vavila."

The old man picked up an ember, blew on it—only his eyes and nose were lighted up then, when they had found the yoke, he went with the light to Lipa and looked at her, and his look expressed compassion and tenderness.

" You are a mother," he said; " every mother grieves for her child."

And he sighed and shook his head as he said it. Vavila threw something on the fire, stamped on it—and at once it was very dark; the vision vanished, and as before there were only the fields, the sky with the stars, and the noise of the birds hindering each other from sleep. And the land-rail called, it seemed, in the very place where the fire had been.

But a minute passed, and again she could see the two carts and the old man and lanky Vavila. The carts creaked as they went out on the road.

" Are you holy men ?" Lipa asked the old man.

" No. We are from Firsanovo."

" You looked at me just now and my heart was softened. And the young man is so gentle. I thought you must be holy men."

" Are you going far ?"

" To Ukleevo."

" Get in, we will give you a lift,as far as Kuz-menki, then you go straight on and we turn off to the left."

Vavila got into the cart with the barrel and the old man and Lipa got into the other. They moved at a walking pace, Vavila in front.

" My baby was in torment all day," said Lipa. " He looked at me with his little eyes and said nothing; he wanted to speak and could not. Holy Father, Queen of Heaven ! In my grief I kept falling down on the floor. I stood up and fell down by the bedside. And tell me, grandfather, why a little thing should be tormented before his death ? When a grown-up person, a man or woman, are in torment their sins are forgiven, but why a little thing, when he has no sins ? Why ?"

" Who can tell ?" answered the old man.

They drove on for half an hour in silence.

"We can't know everything, how and wherefore," said the old man. "It is ordained for the bird to have not four wings but two because it is able to fly with two; and so it is ordained for man not to know everything but only a half or a quarter. As much as he needs to know so as to live, so much he knows."

"It is better for me to go on foot, grandfather. Now my heart is all of a tremble."

"Never mind, sit still."

The old man yawned and made the sign of the cross over his mouth.

"Never mind," he repeated. "Yours is not the worst of sorrows. Life is long, there will be good and bad to come, there will be everything. Great is mother Russia," he said, and looked round on each side of him. "I have been all over Russia, and I have seen everything in her, and you may believe my words, my dear. There will be good and there will be bad. I went as a delegate from my village to Siberia, and I have been to the Amur River and the Altai Mountains and I settled in Siberia; I worked the land there, then I was homesick for mother Russia and I came back to my native village. We came back to Russia on foot; and I remember we went on a steamer, and I was thin as thin, all in rags, barefoot, freezing with cold, and gnawing a crust, and a gentleman who was on the steamer—the kingdom of heaven be his if he is dead—looked at me pitifully, and the tears came into his eyes. 'Ah,' he said, 'your bread is black, your days are black. . . .' And when I got home, as the saying is, there was neither stick nor stall; I had a wife, but I left her behind in Siberia, she was buried there. So I am living as a day labourer. And yet I tell you: since then I have had good as well as bad. Here I do not want to die, my dear, I would be glad to live another twenty years; so there has been more of the good. And great is our mother Russia !" and again he gazed to each side and looked round.

"Grandfather," Lipa asked, "when anyone dies, how many days does his soul walk the earth?"

"Who can tell ! Ask Vavila here, he has been to school. Now they teach them everything. Vavila !" the old man called to him.

"Yes !"

"Vavila, when anyone dies, how long does his soul walk the earth ?"

Vavila stopped the horse and only then answered:

"Nine days. My uncle Kirilla died and his soul lived in our hut thirteen days after."

"How do you know ?"

"For thirteen days there was a knocking in the stove."

"Well, that's all right. Go on," said the old man, and it could be seen that he did not believe a word of all that.

Near Kuzmenki the cart turned into the high road while Lipa went straight on. It was by now getting light. As she went down into the ravine the Ukleevo huts and the church were hidden in fog. It was cold, and it seemed to her that the same cuckoo was calling still.

When Lipa reached home the cattle had not yet been driven out; everyone was asleep. She sat down on the steps and waited. The old man was the first to come out; he understood all that had happened from the first glance at her, and for a long time he could not articulate a word, but only moved his lips without a sound.

"Ech, Lipa," he said, "you did not take care of my grandchild. . . ."

Varvara was awakened. She clasped her hands and broke into sobs, and immediately began laying out the baby.

"And he was a pretty child . . ." she said. "Oh dear, dear. . . . You only had the one child. and you did not take care enough of him, you silly girl. . . ."

There was a requiem service in the morning and the evening. The funeral took place the next day, and after it the guests and the priests ate a great deal, and with such greed that one might have thought that they had not tasted food for a long time. Lipa waited at t ble, and the priest, lifting his fork on which there was a salted mushroom, said to her:

"Don't grieve for the babe. For of such is the kingdom of heaven."

And only when they had all separated Lipa realized fully that there was no Nikifor and never would be, she realized it and broke into sobs. And she did not know what room to go into to sob, for she felt that now that her child was dead there was no place for her in the house, that she had no reason to be here, that she was in the way; and the others felt it, too.

" Now what are you bellowing for ?" Aksinya shouted, suddenly appearing in the doorway; in honour of the funeral she was dressed all in new clothes and had powdered her face. " Shut up !"

Lipa tried to stop but could not, and sobbed louder than ever.

" Do you hear ?" shouted Aksinya, and she stamped her foot in violent anger. " Who is it I am speaking to ? Go out of the yard and don't set foot here again, you convict's wife. Get away."

" There, there, there," the old man put in fussily. " Aksinya, don't make such an outcry, my girl. . . . She is crying, it is only natural . . . her child is dead. . . ."

" ' It's only natural,' " Aksinya mimicked him. " Let her stay the night here, and don't let me see a trace of her here to-morrow ! ' It's only natural !' . . ." she mimicked him again, and, laughing, she went into the shop.

Early next morning Lipa went off to her mother at Torguevo.

IX.

At the present time the steps and the front door of the shop have been repainted and are as bright as though they were new, there are gay geraniums in the windows as of old, and what happened in Tsybukin's house and yard three years ago is almost forgotten.

IN THE RAVINE

Grigory Petrovitch is looked upon as the master as he was in old days, but in reality everything has passed into Aksinya's hands; she buys and sells, and nothing can be done without her consent. The brickyard is working well; and as bricks are wanted for the railway the price has gone up to twenty-four roubles a thousand; peasant women and girls cart the bricks to the station and load them up in the trucks and earn a quarter-rouble a day for the work.

Aksinya has gone into partnership with the Hrymin Juniors, and their factory is now called Hrymin Juniors and Co. They have opened a tavern near the station, and now the expensive concertina is played not at the factory but at the tavern, and the head of the post office often goes there, and he, too, is engaged in some sort of traffic, and the stationmaster, too. Hrymin Juniors have presented the deaf man Stepan with a gold watch, and he is constantly taking it out of his pocket and putting it to his ear.

People say of Aksinya that she has become a person of power; and it is true that when she drives in the morning to her brickyard, handsome and happy, with the naïve smile on her face, and afterwards when she is giving orders there, one is aware of great power in her. Everyone is afraid of her in the house and in the village and in the brickyard. When she goes to the post the head of the postal department jumps up and says to her:

" I humbly beg you to be seated, Aksinya Abramovna !"

A certain landowner, middle-aged but foppish, in a tunic of fine cloth and patent leather high boots, sold her a horse, and was so carried away by talking to her that he knocked down the price to meet her wishes. He held her hand a long time and, looking into her merry, sly, naïve eyes, said:

" For a woman like you, Aksinya Abramovna, I should be ready to do anything you please. Only say when we can meet where no one will interfere with us ?"

" Why, when you please."

And since then the elderly fop drives up to the shop almost every day to drink beer. And the beer is horrid, bitter as wormwood. The landowner shakes his head, but he drinks it.

Old Tsybukin does not have anything to do with the business now at all. He does not keep any money because he cannot distinguish between the good and the false, but he is silent, he says nothing of this weakness. He has become forgetful, and if they don't give him food he does not ask for it. They have grown used to having dinner without him, and Varvara often says:

" He went to bed again yesterday without any supper."

And she says it unconcernedly because she is used to it. For some reason, summer and winter alike, he wears a fur coat, and only in very hot weather he does not go out but sits at home. As a rule putting on his fur coat, wrapping it round him and turning up his collar, he walks about the village, along the road to the station, or sits from morning till night on the seat near the church gates. He sits there without stirring. Passers-by bow to him, but he does not respond, for as of old he dislikes the peasants. If he is asked a question he answers quite rationally and politely, but briefly.

There is a rumour going about in the village that his daughter-in-law turns him out of the house and gives him nothing to eat, and that he is fed by charity; some are glad, others are sorry for him.

Varvara has grown even fatter and whiter, and as before she is active in good works, and Aksinya does not interfere with her.

There is so much jam now that they have not time to eat it before the fresh fruit comes in; it goes sugary, and Varvara almost sheds tears, not knowing what to do with it.

They have begun to forget about Anisim. A letter has come from him written in verse on a big sheet of paper as though it were a petition, all in the same splendid handwriting. Evidently his friend Samorodov was sharing his punishment. Under the verses in an ugly, scarcely legible handwriting there was a single line: " I am ill here all the time; I am wretched, for Christ's sake help me !"

Towards evening—it was a fine autumn day— old Tsybukin was sitting near the church gates, with the collar of his fur coat turned up and nothing of him could be seen but his nose and the peak of his cap. At the other end of the long seat was sitting Elizarov the contractor, and beside him Yakov the school watchman, a tooth-less old man of seventy. Crutch and the watch-man were talking.

"Children ought to give food and drink to the old. . . . Honour thy father and mother . . ." Yakov was saying with irritation, "while she, this daughter-in-law, has turned her father-in-law out of his own house; the old man has neither food nor drink, where is he to go? He has not had a morsel for these three days."

"Three days!" said Crutch, amazed.

"Here he sits and does not say a word. He has grown feeble. And why be silent? He ought to prosecute her, they wouldn't flatter her in the police court."

"Wouldn't flatter whom?" asked Crutch, not hearing.

"What?"

"The woman's all right, she does her best. In their line of business they can't get on without that . . . without sin, I mean. . . ."

"From his own house," Yakov went on with irritation. "Save up and buy your own house, then turn people out of it! She is a nice one, to be sure! A pla-ague!"

Tsybukin listened and did not stir.

"Whether it is your own house or others' it makes no difference so long as it is warm and the women don't scold . . ." said Crutch, and he laughed. "When I was young I was very fond of my Nastasya. She was a quiet woman. And she used to be always at it: 'Buy a house, Makar-itch! Buy a house, Makaritch! Buy a house,

Makaritch !' She was dying and yet she kept on saying, 'Buy yourself a racing droshky, Makaritch, that you may not have to walk.' And I bought her nothing but gingerbread."

" Her husband's deaf and stupid," Yakov went on, not hearing Crutch; " a regular fool, just like a goose. He can't understand anything. Hit a goose on the head with a stick and even then it does not understand."

Crutch got up to go home to the factory. Yakov also got up, and both of them went off together, still talking. When they had gone fifty paces old Tsybukin got up, too, and walked after them, stepping uncertainly as though on slippery ice.

The village was already plunged in the dusk of evening and the sun only gleamed on the upper part of the road which ran wriggling like a snake up the slope. Old women were coming back from the woods and children with them; they were bringing baskets of mushrooms. Peasant women and girls came in a crowd from the station where they had been loading the trucks with bricks, and their noses and their cheeks under their eyes were covered with red brick-dust. They were singing. Ahead of them all was Lipa singing in a high voice, with her eyes turned upwards to the sky, breaking into trills as though triumphant and ecstatic that at last the day was over and she could rest. In the crowd was her mother Praskovya, who was walking with a bundle in her arms and breathless as usual.

" Good-evening, Makaritch !" cried Lipa, seeing Crutch. " Good-evening, darling !"

" Good-evening, Lipinka," cried Crutch delighted. " Dear girls and women, love the rich carpenter ! Ho-ho ! My little children, my little children. (Crutch gave a gulp.) My dear little axes !"

Crutch and Yakov went on further and could still be heard talking. Then after them the crowd was met by old Tsybukin and there was a sudden hush. Lipa and Praskovya had dropped a little behind, and when the old man was on a level with them Lipa bowed down low and said:

" Good-evening, Grigory Petrovitch."

Her mother, too, bowed down. The old man stopped and, saying nothing, looked at the two in silence; his lips were quivering and his eyes full of tears. Lipa took out of her mother's bundle a piece of savoury turnover and gave it him. He took it and began eating.

The sun had by now set; its glow died away on the road above. It grew dark and cool. Lipa and Praskovya walked on and for some time they kept crossing themselves.

1900

138

SLEEPY

NIGHT. Varka, the little nurse, a girl of thirteen, is rocking the cradle in which the baby is lying, and humming hardly audibly :

> " Hush-a-bye, my baby wee,
> While I sing a song for thee."

A little green lamp is burning before the ikon ; there is a string stretched from one end of the room to the other, on which baby-clothes and a pair of big black trousers are hanging.   There is a big patch of green on the ceiling from the ikon lamp, and the baby-clothes and the trousers throw long shadows on the stove, on the cradle, and on Varka. . . .   When the lamp begins to flicker, the green patch and the shadows come to life, and are set in motion, as though by the wind.   It is stuffy.   There is a smell of cabbage soup, and of the inside of a boot-shop.

The baby is crying.   For a long while he has been hoarse and exhausted with crying ; but he still goes on screaming, and there is no knowing when he will stop.   And Varka is sleepy.   Her eyes are glued together, her head droops, her neck aches.   She cannot move her eyelids or her lips, and she feels as though her face is dried and wooden, as though her head has become as small as the head of a pin.

" Hush-a-bye, my baby wee," she hums, " while I cook the groats for thee. . . ."

A cricket is churring in the stove. Through the door in the next room the master and the apprentice Afanasy are snoring. . . . The cradle creaks plaintively, Varka murmurs—and it all blends into that soothing music of the night to which it is so sweet to listen, when one is lying in bed. Now that music is merely irritating and oppressive, because it goads her to sleep, and she must not sleep ; if Varka—God forbid !—should fall asleep, her master and mistress would beat her.

The lamp flickers. The patch of green and the shadows are set in motion, forcing themselves on Varka's fixed, half-open eyes, and in her half slumbering brain are fashioned into misty visions. She sees dark clouds chasing one another over the sky, and screaming like the baby. But then the wind blows, the clouds are gone, and Varka sees a broad high road covered with liquid mud ; along the high road stretch files of wagons, while people with wallets on their backs are trudging along and shadows flit backwards and forwards ; on both sides she can see forests through the cold harsh mist. All at once the people with their wallets and their shadows fall on the ground in the liquid mud. " What is that for ? " Varka asks. " To sleep, to sleep ! " they answer her. And they fall sound asleep, and sleep sweetly, while crows and magpies sit on the telegraph wires, scream like the baby, and try to wake them.

" Hush-a-bye, my baby wee, and I will sing a song to thee," murmurs Varka, and now she sees herself in a dark stuffy hut.

Her dead father, Yefim Stepanov, is tossing from side to side on the floor. She does not see him, but she hears him moaning and rolling on the floor from pain. " His guts have burst," as he says ; the pain is so violent that he cannot utter a single word, and can only draw in his breath and clack his teeth like the rattling of a drum :

" Boo—boo—boo—boo. . . ."

Her mother, Pelageya, has run to the master's house to say that Yefim is dying. She has been gone a long time, and ought to be back. Varka lies awake on the stove, and hears her father's " boo—boo—boo." And then she hears someone has driven up to the hut. It is a young doctor from the town, who has been sent from the big house where he is staying on a visit. The doctor comes into the hut ; he cannot be seen in the darkness, but he can be heard coughing and rattling the door.

" Light a candle," he says.

" Boo—boo—boo," answers Yefim.

Pelageya rushes to the stove and begins looking for the broken pot with the matches. A minute passes in silence. The doctor, feeling in his pocket, lights a match.

" In a minute, sir, in a minute," says Pelageya. She rushes out of the hut, and soon afterwards comes back with a bit of candle.

Yefim's cheeks are rosy and his eyes are shining, and there is a peculiar keenness in his glance, as though he were seeing right through the hut and the doctor.

"Come, what is it? What are you thinking about?" says the doctor, bending down to him. "Aha! have you had this long?"

"What? Dying, your honour, my hour has come. . . . I am not to stay among the living. . ."

"Don't talk nonsense! We will cure you!"

"That's as you please, your honour, we humbly thank you, only we understand. . . . Since death has come, there it is."

The doctor spends a quarter of an hour over Yefim, then he gets up and says:

"I can do nothing. You must go into the hospital, there they will operate on you. Go at once. . . . You must go! It's rather late, they will all be asleep in the hospital, but that doesn't matter, I will give you a note. Do you hear?"

"Kind sir, but what can he go in?" says Pelageya. "We have no horse."

"Never mind. I'll ask your master, he'll let you have a horse."

The doctor goes away, the candle goes out, and again there is the sound of "boo—boo—boo." Half an hour later someone drives up to the hut. A cart has been sent to take Yefim to the hospital. He gets ready and goes. . . .

But now it is a clear bright morning. Pelageya is not at home; she has gone to the hospital to find what is being done to Yefim. Somewhere there is a baby crying, and Varka hears someone singing with her own voice:

" Hush-a-bye, my baby wee, I will sing a song to thee."

Pelageya comes back ; she crosses herself and whispers :

" They put him to rights in the night, but towards morning he gave up his soul to God. . . . The Kingdom of Heaven be his and peace everlasting. . . . They say he was taken too late. . . . He ought to have gone sooner. . . ."

Varka goes out into the road and cries there, but all at once someone hits her on the back of her head so hard that her forehead knocks against a birch tree. She raises her eyes, and sees facing her, her master, the shoemaker.

" What are you about, you scabby slut ? " he says. " The child is crying, and you are asleep ! "

He gives her a sharp slap behind the ear, and she shakes her head, rocks the cradle, and murmurs her song. The green patch and the shadows from the trousers and the baby-clothes move up and down, nod to her, and soon take possession of her brain again. Again she sees the high road covered with liquid mud. The people with wallets on their backs and the shadows have lain down and are fast asleep. Looking at them, Varka has a passionate longing for sleep ; she would lie down with enjoyment, but her mother Pelageya is walking beside her, hurrying her on. They are hastening together to the town to find situations.

" Give alms, for Christ's sake ! " her mother begs of the people they meet. " Show us the Divine Mercy, kind-hearted gentlefolk ! "

" Give the baby here ! " a familiar voice answers.

" Give the baby here ! " the same voice repeats, this time harshly and angrily. " Are you asleep, you wretched girl ? "

Varka jumps up, and looking round grasps what is the matter : there is no high road, no Pelageya, no people meeting them, there is only her mistress, who has come to feed the baby, and is standing in the middle of the room. While the stout, broad-shouldered woman nurses the child and soothes it, Varka stands looking at her and waiting till she has done. And outside the windows the air is already turning blue, the shadows and the green patch on the ceiling are visibly growing pale, it will soon be morning.

" Take him," says her mistress, buttoning up her chemise over her bosom ; " he is crying. He must be bewitched."

Varka takes the baby, puts him in the cradle, and begins rocking it again. The green patch and the shadows gradually disappear, and now there is nothing to force itself on her eyes and cloud her brain. But she is as sleepy as before, fearfully sleepy ! Varka lays her head on the edge of the cradle, and rocks her whole body to overcome her sleepiness, but yet her eyes are glued together, and her head is heavy.

" Varka, heat the stove ! " she hears the master's voice through the door.

So it is time to get up and set to work. Varka leaves the cradle, and runs to the shed for firewood. She is glad. When one moves and runs about, one is not so sleepy as when one is sitting down. She brings the wood, heats the stove, and feels that her wooden face is getting supple again, and that her thoughts are growing clearer.

" Varka, set the samovar ! " shouts her mistress.

Varka splits a piece of wood, but has scarcely time to light the splinters and put them in the samovar, when she hears a fresh order :

" Varka, clean the master's goloshes ! "

She sits down on the floor, cleans the goloshes, and thinks how nice it would be to put her head into a big deep golosh, and have a little nap in it. . . . And all at once the golosh grows, swells, fills up the whole room. Varka drops the brush, but at once shakes her head, opens her eyes wide, and tries to look at things so that they may not grow big and move before her eyes.

" Varka, wash the steps outside ; I am ashamed for the customers to see them ! "

Varka washes the steps, sweeps and dusts the rooms, then heats another stove and runs to the shop. There is a great deal of work : she hasn't one minute free.

But nothing is so hard as standing in the same place at the kitchen table peeling potatoes. Her head droops over the table, the potatoes dance before her eyes, the knife tumbles out of her hand while her fat, angry mistress is moving about near her with her sleeves tucked up, talking so loud that it makes a ringing in Varka's ears. It is agonising, too, to wait at dinner, to wash, to sew, there are minutes when she longs to flop on to the floor regardless of everything, and to sleep.

The day passes. Seeing the windows getting

dark, Varka presses her temples that feel as though they were made of wood, and smiles, though she does not know why. The dusk of evening caresses her eyes that will hardly keep open, and promises her sound sleep soon. In the evening visitors come.

" Varka, set the samovar ! " shouts her mistress.

The samovar is a little one, and before the visitors have drunk all the tea they want, she has to heat it five times. After tea Varka stands for a whole hour on the same spot, looking at the visitors, and waiting for orders.

" Varka, run and buy three bottles of beer ! "

She starts off, and tries to run as quickly as she can, to drive away sleep.

" Varka, fetch some vodka ! Varka, where's the corkscrew ? Varka, clean a herring ! "

But now, at last, the visitors have gone ; the lights are put out, the master and mistress go to bed.

" Varka, rock the baby ! " she hears the last order.

The cricket churrs in the stove ; the green patch on the ceiling and the shadows from the trousers and the baby-clothes force themselves on Varka's half-opened eyes again, wink at her and cloud her mind.

" Hush-a-bye, my baby wee," she murmurs, " and I will sing a song to thee."

And the baby screams, and is worn out with screaming. Again Varka sees the muddy high road, the people with wallets, her mother Pelageya, her father Yefim. She understands everything, she recognises everyone, but through her half sleep she cannot understand the force which binds her, hand and foot, weighs upon her, and prevents her from living. She looks round, searches for that force that she may escape from it, but she cannot find it. At last, tired to death, she does her very utmost, strains her eyes, looks up at the flickering green patch, and listening, to the screaming, finds the foe who will not let her live.

That foe is the baby.

She laughs. It seems strange to her that she has failed to grasp such a simple thing before. The green patch, the shadows, and the cricket seem to laugh and wonder too.

The hallucination takes possession of Varka. She gets up from her stool, and with a broad smile on her face and wide unblinking eyes, she walks up and down the room. She feels pleased and tickled at the thought that she will be rid directly of the baby that binds her hand and foot. . . . Kill the baby and then sleep, sleep, sleep. . . .

Laughing and winking and shaking her fingers at the green patch, Varka steals up to the cradle and bends over the baby. When she has strangled him, she quickly lies down on the floor, laughs with delight that she can sleep, and in a minute is sleeping as sound as the dead.

1888

IONITCH

I.

WHEN visitors to the provincial town S—— complained of the dreariness and monotony of life, the inhabitants of the town, as though defending themselves, declared that it was very nice in S——, that there was a library, a theatre, a club; that they had balls; and, finally, that there were clever, agreeable, and interesting families with whom one could make acquaintance. And they used to point to the family of the Turkins as the most highly cultivated and talented.

This family lived in their own house in the principal street, near the Governor's. Ivan Petrovitch Turkin himself—a stout, handsome, dark man with whiskers—used to get up amateur performances for benevolent objects, and used to take the part of an elderly general and cough very amusingly. He knew a number of anecdotes, charades, proverbs, and was fond of being humorous and witty, and he always wore an expression from which it was impossible to tell whether he were joking or in earnest. His wife, Vera Iosifovna —a thin, nice-looking lady who wore a pince-nez —used to write novels and stories, and was very

148

fond of reading them aloud to her visitors. The daughter, Ekaterina Ivanovna, a young girl, used to play on the piano. In short, every member of the family had a special talent. The Turkins welcomed visitors, and good-humouredly displayed their talents with genuine simplicity. Their stone house was roomy and cool in summer; half of the windows looked into a shady old garden, where nightingales used to sing in the spring. When there were visitors in the house, there was a clatter of knives in the kitchen and a smell of fried onions in the yard—and that was always a sure sign of a plentiful and savoury supper to follow.

And as soon as Dmitri Ionitch Startsev was appointed the district doctor, and took up his abode at Dyalizh, six miles from S——, he, too, was told that as a cultivated man it was essential for him to make the acquaintance of the Turkins. In the winter he was introduced to Ivan Petrovitch in the street; they talked about the weather, about the theatre, about the cholera; an invitation followed. On a holiday in the spring—it was Ascension Day—after seeing his patients, Startsev set off for town in search of a little recreation and to make some purchases. He walked in a leisurely way (he had not yet set up his carriage), humming all the time:

"' Before I'd drunk the tears from life's goblet. . . .'"

In town he dined, went for a walk in the gardens, then Ivan Petrovitch's invitation came into his mind, as it were of itself, and he decided to call on the Turkins and see what sort of people they were.

"How do you do, if you please?" said Ivan Petrovitch, meeting him on the steps. "Delighted, delighted to see such an agreeable visitor. Come along; I will introduce you to my better half. I tell him, Verotchka," he went on, as he presented the doctor to his wife—"I tell him that he has no human right to sit at home in a hospital; he ought to devote his leisure to society. Oughtn't he, darling?"

"Sit here," said Vera Iosifovna, making her visitor sit down beside her. "You can dance attendance on me. My husband is jealous—he is an Othello; but we will try and behave so well that he will notice nothing."

"Ah, you spoilt chicken!" Ivan Petrovitch muttered tenderly, and he kissed her on the forehead. "You have come just in the nick of time," he said, addressing the doctor again. "My better half has written a 'hugeous' novel, and she is going to read it aloud to-day."

"Petit Jean," said Vera Iosifovna to her husband, "dites que l'on nous donne du thé."

Startsev was introduced to Ekaterina Ivanovna, a girl of eighteen, very much like her mother, thin and pretty. Her expression was still childish and her figure was soft and slim; and her developed girlish bosom, healthy and beautiful, was suggestive of spring, real spring.

Then they drank tea with jam, honey, and sweetmeats, and with very nice cakes, which melted in the mouth. As the evening came on, other visitors gradually arrived, and Ivan Petrovitch fixed his laughing eyes on each of them and said:

" How do you do, if you please ?"

Then they all sat down in the drawing-room with very serious faces, and Vera Iosifovna read her novel. It began like this: " The frost was intense. . . ." The windows were wide open; from the kitchen came the clatter of knives and the smell of fried onions. . . . It was comfortable in the soft deep arm-chair; the lights had such a friendly twinkle in the twilight of the drawing-room, and at the moment on a summer evening when sounds of voices and laughter floated in from the street and whiffs of lilac from the yard, it was difficult to grasp that the frost was intense, and that the setting sun was lighting with its chilly rays a solitary wayfarer on the snowy plain. Vera Iosifovna read how a beautiful young countess founded a school, a hospital, a library, in her village, and fell in love with a wandering artist; she read of what never happens in real life, and yet it was pleasant to listen—it was comfortable, and such agreeable, serene thoughts kept coming into the mind, one had no desire to get up.

" Not badsome . . ." Ivan Petrovitch said softly.

And one of the visitors hearing, with his thoughts far away, said hardly audibly:

" Yes . . . truly. . . ."

One hour passed, another. In the town gardens close by a band was playing and a chorus was singing. When Vera Iosifovna shut her manuscript book, the company was silent for five minutes, listening to " Lutchina " being sung by the chorus, and the song gave what was not in the novel and is in real life.

" Do you publish your stories in magazines ?" Startsev asked Vera Iosifovna.

" No," she answered. " I never publish. I write it and put it away in my cupboard. Why publish ?" she explained. " We have enough to live on."

And for some reason everyone sighed.

" And now, Kitten, you play something," Ivan Petrovitch said to his daughter.

The lid of the piano was raised and the music lying ready was opened. Ekaterina Ivanovna sat down and banged on the piano with both hands, and then banged again with all her might, and then again and again; her shoulders and bosom shook. She obstinately banged on the same notes, and it sounded as if she would not leave off until she had hammered the keys into the piano. The drawing-room was filled with the din; everything was resounding; the floor, the ceiling, the furniture. . . . Ekaterina Ivanovna was playing a difficult passage, interesting simply on account of its difficulty, long and monotonous, and Startsev, listening, pictured stones dropping down a steep hill and going on dropping, and he wished they would leave off dropping; and at the same time Ekaterina Ivanovna, rosy from the violent exercise, strong and vigorous, with a lock of hair falling over her forehead, attracted him very much. After the winter spent at Dyalizh among patients and peasants, to sit in a drawing-room, to watch this young, elegant, and, in all probability, pure creature, and to listen to these noisy, tedious but still cultured sounds, was so pleasant, so novel. . . .

" Well, Kitten, you have played as never before," said Ivan Petrovitch, with tears in his eyes, when his daughter had finished and stood up. " Die, Denis; you won't write anything better."

All flocked round her, congratulated her, expressed astonishment, declared that it was long since they had heard such music, and she listened in silence with a faint smile, and her whole figure was expressive of triumph.

" Splendid, superb !"

" Splendid," said Startsev, too, carried away by the general enthusiasm. " Where have you studied ?" he asked Ekaterina Ivanovna. " At the Conservatoire ?"

" No, I am only preparing for the Conservatoire, and till now have been working with Madame Zavlovsky."

" Have you finished at the high school here ?"

" Oh no," Vera Iosifovna answered for her. " We have teachers for her at home; there might be bad influences at the high school or a boarding school, you know. While a young girl is growing up, she ought to be under no influence but her mother's."

" All the same, I'm going to the Conservatoire," siad Ekaterina Ivanovna.

" No. Kitten loves her mamma. Kitten won't grieve papa and mamma."

" No, I'm going, I'm going," said Ekaterina Ivanovna, with playful caprice, stamping her foot.

And at supper it was Ivan Petrovitch who displayed his talents. Laughing only with his eyes, he told anecdotes, made epigrams, asked ridiculous riddles and answered them himself, talking the whole time in his extraordinary language, evolved in the course of prolonged practice in witticism and evidently now become a habit: " Badsome," " Hugeous," " Thank you most dumbly," and so on.

But that was not all. When the guests, replete and satisfied, trooped into the hall, looking for their coats and sticks, there bustled about them the footman Pavlusha, or, as he was called in the family, Pava—a lad of fourteen with shaven head and chubby cheeks.

" Come, Pava, perform !" Ivan Petrovitch said to him.

Pava struck an attitude, flung up his arm, and said in a tragic tone: " Unhappy woman, die !"

And everyone roared with laughter.

" It's entertaining," thought Startsev, as he went out into the street.

He went to a restaurant and drank some beer, then set off to walk home to Dyalizh; he walked all the way singing:

" ' Thy voice to me so languid and caressing. . . .' "

On going to bed, he felt not the slightest fatigue after the six miles' walk. On the contrary, he felt as though he could with pleasure have walked another twenty.

"Not badsome," he thought, and laughed as he fell asleep.

II.

Startsev kept meaning to go to the Turkins' again, but there was a great deal of work in the hospital, and he was unable to find free time. In this way more than a year passed in work and solitude. But one day a letter in a light blue envelope was brought him from the town. . . .

Vera Iosifovna had been suffering for some time from migraine, but now since Kitten frightened her every day by saying that she was going away to the Conservatoire, the attacks began to be more frequent. All the doctors of the town had been at the Turkins'; at last it was the district doctor's turn. Vera Iosifovna wrote him a touching letter in which she begged him to come and relieve her °sufferings. Startsev went, and after that he began to be often, very often at the Turkins'. . . . He really did something for Vera Iosifovna, and she was already telling all her visitors that he was a wonderful and exceptional doctor. But it was not for the sake of her migraine that he visited the Turkins now. . . .

It was a holiday. Ekaterina Ivanovna finished her long, wearisome exercises on the piano. Then they sat a long time in the dining-room, drinking tea, and Ivan Petrovitch told some amusing story. Then there was a ring and he had to go into the hall to welcome a guest; Startsev took advantage of the momentary commotion, and whispered to Ekaterina Ivanovna in great agitation:

" For God's sake, I entreat you, don't torment me; let us go into the garden !"

She shrugged her shoulders, as though perplexed and not knowing what he wanted of her, but she got up and went.

" You play the piano for three or four hours," he said, following her; " then you sit with your mother, and there is no possibility of speaking to you. Give me a quarter of an hour at least, I beseech you."

Autumn was approaching, and it was quiet and melancholy in the old garden; the dark leaves lay thick in the walks. It was already beginning to get dark early.

" I haven't seen you for a whole week," Startsev went on, " and if you only knew what suffering it is ! Let us sit down. Listen to me."

They had a favourite place in the garden: a seat under an old spreading maple. And now they sat down on this seat.

" What do you want ?" said Ekaterina Ivanovna drily, in a matter-of-fact tone.

" I have not seen you for a whole week; I have not heard you for so long. I long passionately; I thirst for your voice. Speak."

She fascinated him by her freshness, the naïve expression of her eyes and cheeks. Even in the way her dress hung on her, he saw something

extraordinarily charming, touching in its simplicity
and naïve grace; and at the same time, in spite of
this naïveté, she seemed to him intelligent and
developed beyond her years. He could talk with
her about literature, about art, about anything he
liked; could complain to her of life, of people,
though it sometimes happened in the middle of
serious conversation she would laugh inappropriately or run away into the house. Like almost all
girls of her neighbourhood, she had read a great
deal (as a rule, people read very little in S——,
and at the lending library they said if it were not
for the girls and the young Jews, they might as
well shut up the library). This afforded Startsev
infinite delight; he used to ask her eagerly every
time what she had been reading the last few days,
and listened enthralled while she told him.

" What have you been reading this week since
I saw you last ?" he asked now. " Do please tell
me."

" I have been reading Pisemsky."

" What exactly ?"

" ' A Thousand Souls,' " answered Kitten.
" And what a funny name Pisemsky had—Alexey
Feofilaktitch !"

" Where are you going ?" cried Startsev in
horror, as she suddenly got up and walked towards
the house. " I must talk to you; I want to
explain myself. . . . Stay with me just five
minutes, I supplicate you !"

She stopped as though she wanted to say something, then awkwardly thrust a note into his hand,
ran home and sat down to the piano again.

"Be in the cemetery," Startsev read, "at eleven o'clock to-night, near the tomb of Demetti."

"Well, that's not at all clever," he thought, coming to himself. "Why the cemetery? What for?"

It was clear: Kitten was playing a prank. Who would seriously dream of making an appointment at night in the cemetery far out of the town, when it might have been arranged in the street or in the town gardens? And was it in keeping with him—a district doctor, an intelligent, staid man—to be sighing, receiving notes, to hang about cemeteries; to do silly things that even schoolboys think ridiculous nowadays? What would this romance lead to? What would his colleagues say when they heard of it? Such were Startsev's reflections as he wandered round the tables at the club, and at half-past ten he suddenly set off for the cemetery.

By now he had his own pair of horses, and a coachman called Panteleimon, in a velvet waistcoat. The moon was shining. It was still warm, warm as it is in autumn. Dogs were howling in the suburb near the slaughter-house. Startsev left his horses in one of the side-streets at the end of the town, and walked on foot to the cemetery.

"We all have our oddities," he thought. "Kitten is odd, too; and—who knows?—perhaps she is not joking, perhaps she will come;" and he abandoned himself to this faint, vain hope, and it intoxicated him.

He walked for half a mile through the fields; the cemetery showed as a dark streak in the

distance, like a forest or a big garden. The wall
of white stone came into sight, the gate. . . . In
the moonlight he could read on the gate: " The
hour cometh." Startsev went in at the little gate,
and before anything else he saw the white crosses
and monuments on both sides of the broad avenue,
and the black shadows of them and the poplars;
and for a long way round it was all white and
black, and the slumbering trees bowed their
branches over the white stones. It seemed as
though it were lighter here than in the fields; the
maple-leaves stood out sharply like paws on the
yellow sand of the avenue and on the stones, and
the inscriptions on the tombs could be clearly
read. For the first moments Startsev was struck
now by what he saw for the first time in his life,
and what he would probably never see again; a
world not like anything else, a world in which the
moonlight was as soft and beautiful, as though
slumbering here in its cradle, where there was no
life, none whatever; but in every dark poplar, in
every tomb, there was felt the presence of a
mystery that promised a life peaceful, beautiful,
eternal. The stones and faded flowers, together
with the autumn scent of the leaves, all told of
forgiveness, melancholy, and peace.

All was silence around; the stars looked down
from the sky in the profound stillness, and Startsev's footsteps sounded loud and out of place, and
only when the church clock began striking and
he imagined himself dead, buried there for ever,
he felt as though someone were looking at him,
and for a moment he thought that it was not

peace and tranquillity, but stifled despair, the dumb dreariness of non-existence. . . .

Demetti's tomb was in the form of a shrine with an angel at the top. The Italian opera had once visited S—— and one of the singers had died; she had been buried here, and this monument put up to her. No one in the town remembered her, but the lamp at the entrance reflected the moonlight, and looked as though it were burning.

There was no one, and, indeed, who would come here at midnight? But Startsev waited, and as though the moonlight warmed his passion, he waited passionately, and, in imagination, pictured kisses and embraces. He sat near the monument for half an hour, then paced up and down the side avenues, with his hat in his hand, waiting and thinking of the many women and girls buried in these tombs who had been beautiful and fascinating, who had loved, at night burned with passion, yielding themselves to caresses. How wickedly Mother Nature jested at man's expense, after all! How humiliating it was to recognize it!

Startsev thought this, and at the same time he wanted to cry out that he wanted love, that he was eager for it at all costs. To his eyes they were not slabs of marble, but fair white bodies in the moonlight; he saw shapes hiding bashfully in the shadows of the trees, felt their warmth, and the languor was oppressive. . . .

And as though a curtain were lowered, the moon went behind a cloud, and suddenly all was darkness. Startsev could scarcely find the gate—by now it was as dark as it is on an autumn night.

Then he wandered about for an hour and a half, looking for the side-street in which he had left his horses.

"I am tired; I can scarcely stand on my legs," he said to Panteleimon.

And settling himself with relief in his carriage, he thought: "Och! I ought not to get fat!"

III.

The following evening he went to the Turkins' to make an offer. But it turned out to be an inconvenient moment, as Ekaterina Ivanovna was in her own room having her hair done by a hairdresser. She was getting ready to go to a dance at the club.

He had to sit a long time again in the dining-room drinking tea. Ivan Petrovitch, seeing that his visitor was bored and preoccupied, drew some notes out of his waistcoat pocket, read a funny letter from a German steward, saying that all the ironmongery was ruined and the plasticity was peeling off the walls.

"I expect they will give a decent dowry," thought Startsev, listening absent-mindedly.

After a sleepless night, he found himself in a state of stupefaction, as though he had been given something sweet and soporific to drink; there was fog in his soul, but joy and warmth, and at the same time a sort of cold, heavy fragment of his brain was reflecting:

"Stop before it is too late! Is she the match for you? She is spoilt, whimsical, sleeps till two o'clock in the afternoon, while you are a deacon's son, a district doctor. . . ."

" What of it ?" he thought. " I don't care."

" Besides, if you marry her," the fragment went on, " then her relations will make you give up the district work and live in the town."

" After all," he thought, " if it must be the town, the town it must be. They will give a dowry; we can establish ourselves suitably."

At last Ekaterina Ivanovna came in, dressed for the ball, with a low neck, looking fresh and pretty; and Startsev admired her so much, and went into such ecstasies, that he could say nothing, but simply stared at her and laughed.

She began saying good-bye, and he—he had no reason for staying now—got up, saying that it was time for him to go home; his patients were waiting for him.

" Well, there's no help for that," said Ivan Petrovitch. " Go, and you might take Kitten to the club on the way."

It was spotting with rain; it was very dark, and they could only tell where the horses were by Panteleimon's husky cough. The hood of the carriage was put up.

" I stand upright; you lie down right; he lies all right," said Ivan Petrovitch as he put his daughter into the carriage.

They drove off.

" I was at the cemetery yesterday," Startsev began. " How ungenerous and merciless it was on your part ! . . ."

" You went to the cemetery ?"

" Yes, I went there and waited almost till two o'clock. I suffered . . ."

" Well, suffer, if you cannot understand a joke."

Ekaterina Ivanovna, pleased at having so cleverly taken in a man who was in love with her, and at being the object of such intense love, burst out laughing and suddenly uttered a shriek of terror, for, at that very minute, the horses turned sharply in at the gate of the club, and the carriage almost tilted over. Startsev put his arm round Ekaterina Ivanovna's waist; in her fright she nestled up to him, and he could not restrain himself, and passionately kissed her on the lips and on the chin, and hugged her more tightly.

" That's enough," she said drily.

And a minute later she was not in the carriage, and a policeman near the lighted entrance of the club shouted in a detestable voice to Panteleimon:

" What are you stopping for, you crow ? Drive on."

Startsev drove home, but soon afterwards returned. Attired in another man's dress suit and a stiff white tie which kept sawing at his neck and trying to slip away from the collar, he was sitting at midnight in the club drawing-room, and was saying with enthusiasm to Ekaterina Ivanovna:

" Ah, how little people know who have never loved ! It seems to me that no one has ever yet written of love truly, and I doubt whether this tender, joyful, agonizing feeling can be described, and anyone who has once experienced it would not attempt to put it into words. What is the use of preliminaries and introductions? What is the use of unnecessary fine words? My love is immeasurable. I beg, I beseech you," Startsev brought out at last, " be my wife !"

" Dmitri Ionitch," said Ekaterina Ivanovna, with a very grave face, after a moment's thought —" Dmitri Ionitch, I am very grateful to you for the honour. I respect you, but . . ." she got up and continued standing, " but, forgive me, I cannot be your wife. Let us talk seriously. Dmitri Ionitch, you know I love art beyond everything in life. I adore music; I love it frantically; I have dedicated my whole life to it. I want to be an artist; I want fame, success, freedom, and you want me to go on living in this town, to go on living this empty, useless life, which has become insufferable to me. To become a wife—oh no, forgive me ! One must strive towards a lofty, glorious goal, and married life would put me in bondage for ever. Dmitri Ionitch " (she faintly smiled as she pronounced his name; she thought of " Alexey Feofilaktitch ") —" Dmitri Ionitch, you are a good, clever, honourable man; you are better than anyone. . . ." Tears came into her eyes. " I feel for you with my whole heart, but . . . but you will understand. . . ."

And she turned away and went out of the drawing-room to prevent herself from crying.

Startsev's heart left off throbbing uneasily. Going out of the club into the street, he first of all tore off the stiff tie and drew a deep breath. He was a little ashamed and his vanity was wounded—he had not expected a refusal—and could not believe that all his dreams, his hopes and yearnings, had led him up to such a stupid end, just as in some little play at an amateur performance, and he was sorry for his feeling, for that love of his, so sorry that he felt as though he could have burst into sobs or have belaboured Panteleimon's broad back with his umbrella with all his might.

For three days he could not get on with anything, he could not eat nor sleep; but when the news reached him that Ekaterina Ivanovna had gone away to Moscow to enter the Conservatoire, he grew calmer and lived as before.

Afterwards, remembering sometimes how he had wandered about the cemetery or how he had driven all over the town to get a dress suit, he stretched lazily and said:

" What a lot of trouble, though !"

IV.

Four years had passed. Startsev already had a large practice in the town. Every morning he hurriedly saw his patients at Dyalizh, then he drove in to see his town patients. By now he drove, not with a pair, but with a team of three with bells on them, and he returned home late at night. He had grown broader and stouter, and was not very fond of walking, as he was somewhat asthmatic. And Panteleimon had grown stout, too, and the broader he grew, the more mournfully he sighed and complained of his hard luck: he was sick of driving!

Startsev used to visit various households and met many people, but did not become intimate with anyone. The inhabitants irritated him by their conversation, their views of life, and even their appearance. Experience taught him by degrees that while he played cards or lunched with one of these people, the man was a peaceable, friendly, and even intelligent human being; that as soon as one talked of anything not eatable, for instance, of politics or science, he would be completely at a loss, or would expound a philosophy so stupid and ill-natured that there was nothing else to do but wave one's hand in despair and go away. Even when Startsev tried to talk to liberal citizens, saying, for instance, that humanity, thank God, was progressing, and that one day it would be possible to dispense with passports and capital punishment, the liberal citizen would look at him askance and ask him mistrustfully: " Then anyone could murder anyone he chose in the open street?" And when, at tea or supper, Startsev observed in company that one should work, and that one ought not to live without working, everyone took this as a reproach, and began to get angry and argue aggressively. With all that, the inhabitants did nothing, absolutely nothing, and took no interest in anything, and it was quite impossible to think of anything to say. And Startsev avoided conversation, and confined himself to eating and playing *vint* ; and when there was a family festivity in some household and he was invited to a meal, then he sat and ate in silence, looking at his plate. And everything that was said at the time was uninteresting, unjust, and stupid; he felt irritated and disturbed, but held his tongue, and, because he sat glumly silent and looked at his plate, he was nicknamed in the town " the haughty Pole," though he never had been a Pole.

All such entertainments as theatres and concerts he declined, but he played *vint* every evening for three hours with enjoyment. He had another diversion to which he took imperceptibly, little by little: in the evening he would take out of his pockets the notes he had gained by his practice, and sometimes there were stuffed in his pockets notes—yellow and green, and smelling of scent and vinegar and incense and fish oil—up to the value of seventy roubles; and when they amounted to some hundreds he took them to the Mutual Credit Bank and deposited the money there to his account.

He was only twice at the Turkins' in the course of the four years after Ekaterina Ivanovna had gone away, on each occasion at the invitation of Vera Iosifovna, who was still undergoing treatment for migraine. Every summer Ekaterina Ivanovna came to stay with her parents, but he did not once see her; it somehow never happened.

But now four years had passed. One still warm morning a letter was brought to the hospital. Vera Iosifovna wrote to Dmitri Ionitch that she was missing him very much, and begged him to come and see them, and to relieve her sufferings;

and, by the way, it was her birthday. Below was a postscript: "I join in mother's request. —K."

Startsev considered, and in the evening he went to the Turkins'.

"How do you do, if you please?" Ivan Petrovitch met him, smiling with his eyes only. "Bongjour."

Vera Iosifovna, white-haired and looking much older, shook Startsev's hand, sighed affectedly, and said:

"You don't care to pay attentions to me, doctor. You never come and see us; I am too old for you. But now someone young has come; perhaps she will be more fortunate."

And Kitten? She had grown thinner, paler, had grown handsomer and more graceful; but now she was Ekaterina Ivanovna, not Kitten; she had lost the freshness and look of childish naïveté. And in her expression and manners there was something new—guilty and diffident, as though she did not feel herself at home here in the Turkins' house.

"How many summers, how many winters!" she said, giving Startsev her hand, and he could see that her heart was beating with excitement; and looking at him intently and curiously, she went on: "How much stouter you are! You look sunburnt and more manly, but on the whole you have changed very little."

Now, too, he thought her attractive, very attractive, but there was something lacking in her, or else something superfluous—he could not himself have said exactly what it was, but something prevented him from feeling as before. He did not like her pallor, her new expression, her faint smile, her voice, and soon afterwards he disliked her clothes, too, the low chair in which she was sitting; he disliked something in the past when he had almost married her. He thought of his love, of the dreams and the hopes which had troubled him four years before—and he felt awkward.

They had tea with cakes. Then Vera Iosifovna read aloud a novel; she read of things that never happen in real life, and Startsev listened, looked at her handsome grey head, and waited for her to finish.

" People are not stupid because they can't write novels, but because they can't conceal it when they do," he thought.

" Not badsome," said Ivan Petrovitch.

Then Ekaterina Ivanovna played long and noisily on the piano, and when she finished she was profusely thanked and warmly praised.

" It's a good thing I did not marry her," thought Startsev.

She looked at him, and evidently expected him to ask her to go into the garden, but he remained silent.

" Let us have a talk," she said, going up to him. " How are you getting on ? What are you doing ? How are things ? I have been thinking about you all these days," she went on nervously. " I wanted to write to you, wanted to come myself to see you at Dyalizh. I quite made up my mind to go, but afterwards I thought better of it. God knows what your attitude is towards me now; I have been looking forward to seeing you to-day with such emotion. For goodness' sake let us go into the garden."

They went into the garden and sat down on the seat under the old maple, just as they had done four years before. It was dark.

" How are you getting on ?" asked Ekaterina Ivanovna.

" Oh, all right; I am jogging along," answered Startsev.

And he could think of nothing more. They were silent.

" I feel so excited !" said Ekaterina Ivanovna, and she hid her face in her hands. " But don't pay attention to it. I am so happy to be at home; I am so glad to see everyone. I can't get used to it. So many memories ! I thought we should talk without stopping till morning."

Now he saw her face near, her shining eyes, and in the darkness she looked younger than in the room, and even her old childish expression seemed to have come back to her. And indeed she was looking at him with naïve curiosity, as though she wanted to get a closer view and understanding of the man who had loved her so ardently, with such tenderness, and so unsuccessfully; her eyes thanked him for that love. And he remembered all that had been, every minute detail; how he had wandered about the cemetery, how he had returned home in the morning exhausted, and he suddenly felt sad and regretted the past. A warmth began glowing in his heart.

" Do you remember how I took you to the dance at the club ?" he asked. " It was dark and rainy then. . . ."

The warmth was glowing now in his heart, and he longed to talk, to rail at life. . . .

" Ech !" he said with a sigh. " You ask how I am living. How do we live here ? Why, not at all. We grow old, we grow stout, we grow slack. Day after day passes; life slips by without colour, without impressions, without thoughts. . . . In the daytime working for gain, and in the evening the club, the company of card-players, alcoholic, raucous-voiced gentlemen whom I can't endure. What is there nice in it ?"

" Well, you have work—a noble object in life. You used to be so fond of talking of your hospital. I was such a queer girl then; I imagined myself such a great pianist. Nowadays all young ladies play the piano, and I played, too, like everybody else, and there was nothing special about me. I am just such a pianist as my mother is an authoress. And of course I didn't understand you then, but afterwards in Moscow I often thought of you. I thought of no one but you. What happiness to be a district doctor; to help the suffering; to be serving the people ! What happiness !" Ekaterina Ivanovna repeated with enthusiasm. " When I thought of you in Moscow, you seemed to me so ideal, so lofty. . . ."

Startsev thought of the notes he used to take out of his pockets in the evening with such pleasure, and the glow in his heart was quenched.

He got up to go into the house. She took his arm.

" You are the best man I've known in my life,"
she went on. " We will see each other and talk,
won't we ? Promise me. I am not a pianist; I
am not in error about myself now, and I will
not play before you or talk of music."

When they had gone into the house, and when
Startsev saw in the lamplight her face, and her
sad, grateful, searching eyes fixed upon him, he
felt uneasy and thought again:

" It's a good thing I did not marry her then."

He began taking leave.

" You have no human right to go before supper,"
said Ivan Petrovitch as he saw him off. " It's
extremely perpendicular on your part. Well now,
perform !" he added, addressing Pava in the hall.

Pava, no longer a boy, but a young man with
moustaches, threw himself into an attitude, flung
up his arm, and said in a tragic voice:

" Unhappy woman, die !"

All this irritated Startsev. Getting into his
carriage, and looking at the dark house and
garden which had once been so precious and so
dear, he thought of everything at once—Vera
Iosifovna's novels and Kitten's noisy playing, and
Ivan Petrovitch's jokes and Pava's tragic postur-
ing, and thought if the most talented people in the
town were so futile, what must the town be ?

Three days later Pava brought a letter from
Ekaterina Ivanovna:

" You don't come and see us—why ?" she wrote
to him. " I am afraid that you have changed
towards us. I am afraid, and I am terrified at

the very thought of it. Reassure me; come and tell me that everything is well.

"I must talk to you.—Your E. I."

He read this letter, thought a moment, and said to Pava:

"Tell them, my good fellow, that I can't come to-day; I am very busy. Say I will come in three days or so."

But three days passed, a week passed; he still did not go. Happening once to drive past the Turkins' house, he thought he must go in, if only for a moment, but on second thoughts . . . did not go in.

And he never went to the Turkins' again.

V.

Several more years have passed. Startsev has grown stouter still, has grown corpulent, breathes heavily, and already walks with his head thrown back. When stout and red in the face, he drives with his bells and his team of three horses, and Panteleimon, also stout and red in the face with his thick beefy neck, sits on the box, holding his arms stiffly out before him as though they were made of wood, and shouts to those he meets: "Keep to the ri-i-ight!" it is an impressive picture; one might think it was not a mortal, but some heathen deity in his chariot. He has an immense practice in the town, no time to breathe, and already has an estate and two houses in the town, and he is looking out for a third more profitable; and when at the Mutual Credit Bank he is told of a house that is for sale, he goes to the house without ceremony, and, marching through all the rooms, regardless of half-dressed women and children who gaze at him in amazement and alarm, he prods at the doors with his stick, and says:

" Is that the study ? Is that a bedroom ? And what's here ?"

And as he does so he breathes heavily and wipes the sweat from his brow.

He has a great deal to do, but still he does not give up his work as district doctor; he is greedy for gain, and he tries to be in all places at once. At Dyalizh and in the town he is called simply " Ionitch ": " Where is Ionitch off to ?" or " Should not we call in Ionitch to a consultation ?"

Probably because his throat is covered with rolls of fat, his voice has changed; it has become thin and sharp. His temper has changed, too: he has grown ill-humoured and irritable. When he sees his patients he is usually out of temper; he impatiently taps the floor with his stick, and shouts in his disagreeable voice:

" Be so good as to confine yourself to answering my questions ! Don't talk so much !"

He is solitary. He leads a dreary life; nothing interests him.

During all the years he had lived at Dyalizh his love for Kitten had been his one joy, and probably his last. In the evenings he plays *vint* at the club, and then sits alone at a big table and has supper. Ivan, the oldest and most respectable of the waiters, serves him, hands him Lafitte No. 17, and everyone at the club—the members of the committee, the cook and waiters—know what he likes and what he doesn't like, do their very utmost to satisfy him, or else he is sure to fly into a rage and bang on the floor with his stick.

As he eats his supper, he turns round from time to time and puts in his spoke in some conversation:

" What are you talking about ? Eh ? Whom ?"

And when at a neighbouring table there is talk of the Turkins, he asks:

"What Turkins are you speaking of ? Do you mean the people whose daughter plays on the piano ?"

That is all that can be said about him.

And the Turkins ? Ivan Petrovitch has grown no older; he is not changed in the least, and still makes jokes and tells anecdotes as of old. Vera Iosifovna still reads her novels aloud to her visitors with eagerness and touching simplicity. And Kitten plays the piano for four hours every day. She has grown visibly older, is constantly ailing, and every autumn goes to the Crimea with her mother. When Ivan Petrovitch sees them off at the station, he wipes his tears as the train starts, and shouts:

" Good-bye, if you please."

And he waves his handkerchief.

1898

AT CHRISTMAS TIME

I.

" WHAT shall I write ?" said Yegor, and he dipped his pen in the ink.

Vasilisa had not seen her daughter for four years. Her daughter Yefimya had gone after her wedding to Petersburg, had sent them two letters. and since then seemed to vanish out of their lives; there had been no sight nor sound of her. And whether the old woman were milking her cow at dawn, or heating her stove, or dozing at night, she was always thinking of one and the same thing—what was happening to Yefimya, whether she were alive out yonder. She ought to have sent a letter, but the old father could not write, and there was no one to write.

But now Christmas had come, and Vasilisa could not bear it any longer, and went to the tavern to Yegor, the brother of the innkeeper's wife, who had sat in the tavern doing nothing ever since he came back from the army; people said that he could write letters very well if he were properly paid. Vasilisa talked to the cook at the tavern, then to the mistress of the house, then to Yegor himself. They agreed upon fifteen kopecks.

And now—it happened on the second day of the holidays, in the tavern kitchen—Yegor was sitting at the table, holding the pen in his hand. Vasilisa was standing before him, pondering with an expression of anxiety and woe on her face. Pyotr, her husband, a very thin old man with a brownish bald patch, had come with her; he stood looking straight before him like a blind man. On the stove a piece of pork was being braised in a saucepan; it was spurting and hissing, and seemed to be actually saying: "Flu-flu-flu." It was stifling.

"What am I to write?" Yegor asked again.

"What?" asked Vasilisa, looking at him angrily and suspiciously. "Don't worry me! You are not writing for nothing; no fear, you'll be paid for it. Come, write: 'To our dear son-in-law, Andrey Hrisanfitch, and to our only beloved daughter, Yefimya Petrovna, with our love we send a low bow and our parental blessing abiding for ever.'"

"Written; fire away."

"'And we wish them a happy Christmas; we are alive and well, and I wish you the same, please the Lord . . . the Heavenly King.'"

Vasilisa pondered and exchanged glances with the old man.

"'And I wish you the same, please the Lord . . . the Heavenly King,'" she repeated, beginning to cry.

She could say nothing more. And yet before, when she lay awake thinking at night, it had seemed to her that she could not get all she had to say into a dozen letters. Since the time when her daughter had gone away with her husband much water had flowed into the sea, the old people had lived feeling bereaved, and sighed heavily at night as though they had buried their daughter. And how many events had occurred in the village since then, how many marriages and deaths ! How long the winters had been ! How long the nights !

" It's hot," said Yegor, unbuttoning his waist-coat. " It must be seventy degrees. What more ?" he asked.

The old people were silent.

" What does your son-in-law do in Petersburg ?" asked Yegor.

" He was a soldier, my good friend," the old man answered in a weak voice. " He left the service at the same time as you did. He was a soldier, and now, to be sure, he is at Petersburg at a hydropathic establishment. The doctor treats the sick with water. So he, to be sure, is house-porter at the doctor's."

" Here it is written down," said the old woman, taking a letter out of her pocket. " We got it from Yefimya, goodness knows when. Maybe they are no longer in this world."

Yegor thought a little and began writing rapidly:

" At the present time "—he wrote—" since your destiny through your own doing allotted you to the Military Career, we counsel you to look into the Code of Disciplinary Offences and Funda-mental Laws of the War Office, and you will see in that law the Civilization of the Officials of the War Office."

He wrote and kept reading aloud what was written, while Vasilisa considered what she ought to write: how great had been their want the year before, how their corn had not lasted even till Christmas, how they had to sell their cow. She ought to ask for money, ought to write that the old father was often ailing and would soon no doubt give up his soul to God . . . but how to express this in words ? What must be said first and what afterwards ?

" Take note," Yegor went on writing, " in volume five of the Army Regulations soldier is a common noun and a proper one, a soldier of the first rank is called a general, and of the last a private. . . ."

The old man stirred his lips and said softly:

" It would be all right to have a look at the grandchildren."

" What grandchildren ?" asked the old woman, and she looked angrily at him; " perhaps there are none."

" Well, but perhaps there are. Who knows ?"

" And thereby you can judge," Yegor hurried on, " what is the enemy without and what is the enemy within. The foremost of our enemies within is Bacchus." The pen squeaked, executing upon the paper flourishes like fish-hooks. Yegor hastened and read over every line several times. He sat on a stool sprawling his broad feet under the table, well-fed, bursting with health, with a coarse animal face and a red bull neck. He was vulgarity itself: coarse, conceited, invincible, proud of having been born and bred in a pot-house; and Vasilisa quite understood the vulgarity, but could not express it in words, and could only look angrily and suspiciously at Yegor. Her head was beginning to ache, and her thoughts were in confusion from the sound of his voice and his unintelligible words, from the heat and the stuffiness, and she said nothing and thought nothing, but simply waited for him to finish scribbling. But the old man looked with full confidence. He believed in his old woman who had brought him there, and in Yegor; and when he had mentioned the hydropathic establishment it could be seen that he believed in the establishment and the healing efficacy of water.

Having finished the letter, Yegor got up and read the whole of it through from the beginning. The old man did not understand, but he nodded his head trustfully.

" That's all right; it is smooth . . ." he said. " God give you health. That's all right. . . ."

They laid on the table three five-kopeck pieces and went out of the tavern; the old man looked immovably straight before him as though he were blind, and perfect trustfulness was written on his face; but as Vasilisa came out of the tavern she waved angrily at the dog, and said angrily:

" Ugh, the plague."

The old woman did not sleep all night; she was disturbed by thoughts, and at daybreak she got up, said her prayers, and went to the station to send off the letter.

It was between eight and nine miles to the station.

II.

Dr. B. O. Mozelweiser's hydropathic establishment worked on New Year's Day exactly as on ordinary days; the only difference was that the porter, Andrey Hrisanfitch, had on a uniform with new braiding, his boots had an extra polish, and he greeted every visitor with " A Happy New Year to you !"

It was the morning; Andrey Hrisanfitch was standing at the door, reading the newspaper. Just at ten o'clock there arrived a general, one of the habitual visitors, and directly after him the postman; Andrey Hrisanfitch helped the general off with his great-coat, and said:

" A Happy New Year to your Excellency !"

" Thank you, my good fellow; the same to you."

And at the top of the stairs the general asked, nodding towards the door (he asked the same question every day and always forgot the answer):

" And what is there in that room ?"

" The massage room, your Excellency."

When the general's steps had died away Andrey Hrisanfitch looked at the post that had come, and found one addressed to himself. He tore it open, read several lines, then, looking at the newspaper, he walked without haste to his own room, which was downstairs close by at the end of the passage.

His wife Yefimya was sitting on the bed, feeding her baby; another child, the eldest, was standing by, laying its curly head on her knee; a third was asleep on the bed.

Going into the room, Andrey gave his wife the letter and said:

" From the country, I suppose."

Then he walked out again without taking his eyes from the paper. He could hear Yefimya with a shaking voice reading the first lines. She read them and could read no more; these lines were enough for her. She burst into tears, and hugging her eldest child, kissing him, she began saying— and it was hard to say whether she were laughing or crying:

" It's from granny, from grandfather," she said. " From the country. . . . The Heavenly Mother, Saints and Martyrs ! The snow lies heaped up under the roofs now . . . the trees are as white as white. The boys slide on little sledges . . . and dear old bald grandfather is on the stove . . . and there is a little yellow dog. . . . My own darlings !"

Andrey Hrisanfitch, hearing this, recalled that his wife had on three or four occasions given him letters and asked him to send them to the country, but some important business had always prevented him; he had not sent them, and the letters somehow got lost.

" And little hares run about in the fields," Yefimya went on chanting, kissing her boy and shedding tears. " Grandfather is kind and gentle; granny is good, too—kind-hearted. They are warm-hearted in the country, they are God-fearing . . . and there is a little church in the village; the peasants sing in the choir. Queen of Heaven, Holy Mother and Defender, take us away from here!"

Andrey Hrisanfitch returned to his room to smoke a little till there was another ring at the door, and Yefimya ceased speaking, subsided, and wiped her eyes, though her lips were still quivering. She was very much frightened of him—oh, how frightened of him! She trembled and was reduced to terror by the ound of his steps, by the look in his eyes, and dared not utter a word in his presence.

Andrey Hrisanfitch lighted a cigarette, but at that very moment there was a ring from upstairs. He put out his cigarette, and, assuming a very grave face, hastened to his front door.

The general was coming downstairs, fresh and rosy from his bath.

" And what is there in that room?" he asked, pointing to a door.

Andrey Hrisanfitch put his hands down swiftly to the seams of his trousers, and pronounced oudly:

" Charcot douche, your Excellency!"

1900

MY LIFE

THE STORY OF A PROVINCIAL

I.

THE Superintendent said to me: " I only keep you out of regard for your worthy father; but for that you would have been sent flying long ago." I replied to him: " You flatter me too much, your Excellency, in assuming that I am capable of flying." And then I heard him say: " Take that gentleman away; he gets upon my nerves."

Two days later I was dismissed. And in this way I have, during the years I have been regarded as grown up, lost nine situations, to the great mortification of my father, the architect of our town. I have served in various departments, but all these nine jobs have been as alike as one drop of water is to another: I had to sit, write, listen to rude or stupid observations, and go on doing so till I was dismissed.

When I came in to my father he was sitting buried in a low arm-chair with his eyes closed. His dry, emaciated face, with a shade of dark blue where it was shaved (he looked like an old Catholic organist), expressed meekness and resignation.

Without responding to my greeting or opening his eyes, he said:

" If my dear wife and your mother were living, your life would have been a source of continual distress to her. I see the Divine Providence in her premature death. I beg you, unhappy boy," he continued, opening his eyes, " tell me: what am I to do with you ?"

In the past when I was younger my friends and relations had known what to do with me: some of them used to advise me to volunteer for the army, others to get a job in a pharmacy, and others in the telegraph department; now that I am over twenty-five, that grey hairs are beginning to show on my temples, and that I have been already in the army, and in a pharmacy, and in the telegraph department, it would seem that all earthly possibilities have been exhausted, and people have given up advising me, and merely sigh or shake their heads.

" What do you think about yourself ?" my father went on. " By the time they are your age, young men have a secure social position, while look at you: you are a proletarian, a beggar, a burden on your father !"

And as usual he proceeded to declare that the young people of to-day were on the road to perdition through infidelity, materialism, and self-conceit, and that amateur theatricals ought to be prohibited, because they seduced young people from religion and their duties.

" To-morrow we shall go together, and you shall apologize to the superintendent, and promise him to work conscientiously," he said in conclusion. "You ought not to remain one single day with no regular position in society."

"I beg you to listen to me," I said sullenly, expecting nothing good from this conversation. "What you call a position in society is the privilege of capital and education. Those who have neither wealth nor education earn their daily bread by manual labour, and I see no grounds for my being an exception."

"When you begin talking about manual labour it is always stupid and vulgar!" said my father with irritation. "Understand, you dense fellow —understand, you addle-pate, that besides coarse physical strength you have the divine spirit, a spark of the holy fire, which distinguishes you in the most striking way from the ass or the reptile, and brings you nearer to the Deity! This fire is the fruit of the efforts of the best of mankind during thousands of years. Your great-grand-father Poloznev, the general, fought at Borodino; your grandfather was a poet, an orator, and a Marshal of Nobility; your uncle is a schoolmaster; and lastly, I, your father, am an architect! All the Poloznevs have guarded the sacred fire for you to put it out!"

"One must be just," I said. "Millions of people put up with manual labour."

"And let them put up with it! They don't know how to do anything else! Anybody, even the most abject fool or criminal, is capable of manual labour; such labour is the distinguishing mark of the slave and the barbarian, while the holy fire is vouchsafed only to a few!"

To continue this conversation was unprofitable. My father worshipped himself, and nothing was convincing to him but what he said himself. Besides, I knew perfectly well that the disdain with which he talked of physical toil was founded not so much on reverence for the sacred fire as on a secret dread that I should become a workman, and should set the whole town talking about me; what was worse, all my contemporaries had long ago taken their degrees and were getting on well, and the son of the manager of the State Bank was already a collegiate assessor, while I, his only son, was nothing! To continue the conversation was unprofitable and unpleasant, but I still sat on and feebly retorted, hoping that I might at last be understood. The whole question, of course, was clear and simple, and only concerned with the means of my earning my living; but the simplicity of it was not seen, and I was talked to in mawkishly rounded phrases of Borodino, of the sacred fire, of my uncle a forgotten poet, who had once written poor and artificial verses; I was rudely called an addle-pate and a dense fellow. And how I longed to be understood! In spite of everything, I loved my father and my sister and it had been my habit from childhood to consult them—a habit so deeply rooted that I doubt whether I could ever have got rid of it; whether I were in the right or the wrong, I was in constant dread of wounding them, constantly afraid that my father's thin neck

187

would turn crimson and that he would have a stroke.

" To sit in a stuffy room," I began, " to copy, to compete with a typewriter, is shameful and humiliating for a man of my age. What can the sacred fire have to do with it ?"

" It's intellectual work, anyway," said my father. " But that's enough; let us cut short this conversation, and in any case I warn you: if you don't go back to your work again, but follow your contemptible propensities, then my daughter and I will banish you from our hearts. I shall strike you out of my will, I swear by the living God !"

With perfect sincerity to prove the purity of the motives by which I wanted to be guided in all my doings, I said:

" The question of inheritance does not seem very important to me. I shall renounce it all beforehand."

For some reason or other, quite to my surprise, these words were deeply resented by my father. He turned crimson.

" Don't dare to talk to me like that, stupid !" he shouted in a thin, shrill voice. " Wastrel !" and with a rapid, skilful, and habitual movement he slapped me twice in the face. " You are forgetting yourself."

When my father beat me as a child I had to stand up straight, with my hands held stiffly to my trouser seams, and look him straight in the face. And now when he hit me I was utterly overwhelmed, and, as though I were still a child, drew myself up and tried to look him in the face. My father was old and very thin, but his delicate muscles must have been as strong as leather, for his blows hurt a good deal.

I staggered back into the passage, and there he snatched up his umbrella, and with it hit me several times on the head and shoulders; at that moment my sister opened the drawing-room door to find out what the noise was, but at once turned away with a look of horror and pity without uttering a word in my defence.

My determination not to return to the Government office, but to begin a new life of toil, was not to be shaken. All that was left for me to do was to fix upon the special employment, and there was no particular difficulty about that, as it seemed to me that I was very strong and fitted for the very heaviest labour. I was faced with a monotonous life of toil in the midst of hunger, coarseness, and stench, continually preoccupied with earning my daily bread. And—who knows?— as I returned from my work along Great Dvoryansky Street, I might very likely envy Dolzhikov the engineer, who lived by intellectual work, but, at the moment, thinking over all my future hardships made me lighthearted. At times I had dreamed of spiritual activity, imagining myself a teacher, a doctor, or a writer, but these dreams remained dreams. The taste for intellectual pleasures—for the theatre, for instance, and for reading—was a passion with me, but whether I had any ability for intellectual work I don't know. At school I had had an unconquerable aversion for Greek, so that I was only in the fourth class when they had to take me from school. For a long while I had coaches preparing me for the fifth class. Then I served in various Government offices, spending the greater part of the day in complete idleness, and I was told that was intellectual work. My activity in the scholastic and official sphere had required neither mental application nor talent, nor special qualifications, nor creative impulse; it was mechanical. Such intellectual work I put on a lower level than physical toil; I despise it, and I don't think that for one moment it could serve as a justification for an idle, careless life, as it is indeed nothing but a sham, one of the forms of that same idleness. Real intellectual work I have in all probability never known.

Evening came on. We lived in Great Dvoryansky Street; it was the principal street in the town, and in the absence of decent public gardens our *beau monde* used to use it as a promenade in the evenings. This charming street did to some extent take the place of a public garden, as on each side of it there was a row of poplars which smelt sweet, particularly after rain, and acacias, tall bushes of lilac, wild-cherries and apple-trees hung over the fences and palings. The May twilight, the tender young greenery with its shifting shades, the scent of the lilac, the buzzing of the insects, the stillness, the warmth—how fresh and marvellous it all is, though spring is repeated every year ! I stood at the garden gate and watched the passers-by. With most of them

I had grown up and at one time played pranks; now they might have been disconcerted by my being near them, for I was poorly and unfashionably dressed, and they used to say of my very narrow trousers and huge, clumsy boots that they were like sticks of macaroni stuck in boats. Besides, I had a bad reputation in the town because I had no decent social position, and used often to play billiards in cheap taverns, and also, perhaps, because I had on two occasions been hauled up before an officer of the police, though I had done nothing whatever to account for this.

In the big house opposite someone was playing the piano at Dolzhikov's. It was beginning to get dark, and stars were twinkling in the sky. Here my father, in an old top-hat with wide upturned brim, walked slowly by with my sister on his arm, bowing in response to greetings.

" Look up," he said to my sister, pointing to the sky with the same umbrella with which he had beaten me that afternoon. " Look up at the sky! Even the tiniest stars are all worlds! How insignificant is man in comparison with the universe !"

And he said this in a tone that suggested that it was particularly agreeable and flattering to him that he was so insignificant. How absolutely devoid of talent and imagination he was ! Sad to say, he was the only architect in the town, and in the fifteen to twenty years that I could remember not one single decent house had been built in it. When any one asked him to plan a house, he usually drew first the reception hall and drawing-room; just as in old days the boarding-school misses always started from the stove when they danced, so his artistic ideas could only begin and develop from the hall and drawing-room. To them he tacked on a dining-room, a nursery, a study, linking the rooms together with doors, and so they all inevitably turned into passages, and every one of them had two or even three unnecessary doors. His imagination must have been lacking in clearness, extremely muddled, curtailed. As though feeling that something was lacking, he invariably had recourse to all sorts of outbuildings, planting one beside another; and I can see now the narrow entries, the poky little passages, the crooked staircases leading to half-landings where one could not stand upright, and where, instead of a floor, there were three huge steps like the shelves of a bath-house; and the kitchen was invariably in the basement with a brick floor and vaulted ceilings. The front of the house had a harsh, stubborn expression; the lines of it were stiff and timid; the roof was low-pitched and, as it were, squashed down; and the fat, well-fed-looking chimneys were invariably crowned by wire caps with squeaking black cowls. And for some reason all these houses, built by my father exactly like one another, vaguely reminded me of his top-hat and the back of his head, stiff and stubborn-looking. In the course of years they have grown used in the town to the poverty of my father's imagination. It has taken root and become our local style.

This same style my father had brought into my sister's life also, beginning with christening her Kleopatra (just as he had named me Misail). When she was a little girl he scared her by references to the stars, to the sages of ancient times, to our ancestors, and discoursed at length on the nature of life and duty; and now, when she was twenty-six, he kept up the same habits, allowing her to walk arm in arm with no one but himself, and imagining for some reason that sooner or later a suitable young man would be sure to appear, and to desire to enter into matrimony with her from respect for his personal qualities. She adored my father, feared him, and believed in his exceptional intelligence.

It was quite dark, and gradually the street grew empty. The music had ceased in the house opposite; the gate was thrown wide open, and a team with three horses trotted frolicking along our street with a soft tinkle of little bells. That was the engineer going for a drive with his daughter. It was bedtime.

I had my own room in the house, but I lived in a shed in the yard, under the same roof as a brick barn which had been built some time or other, probably to keep harness in; great hooks were driven into the wall. Now it was not wanted, and for the last thirty years my father had stowed away in it his newspapers, which for some reason he had bound in half-yearly volumes and allowed nobody to touch. Living here, I was less liable to be seen by my father and his visitors, and I fancied that if I did not live in a real room, and

G

did not go into the house every day to dinner, my father's words that I was a burden upon him did not sound so offensive.

My sister was waiting for me. Unseen by my father, she had brought me some supper: not a very large slice of cold veal and a piece of bread. In our house such sayings as: " A penny saved is a penny gained," and " Take care of the pence and the pounds will take care of themselves," and so on, were frequently repeated, and my sister, weighed down by these vulgar maxims, did her utmost to cut down the expenses, and so we fared badly. Putting the plate on the table, she sat down on my bed and began to cry.

" Misail," she said, " what a way to treat us !"

She did not cover her face; her tears dropped on her bosom and hands, and there was a look of distress on her face. She fell back on the pillow, and abandoned herself to her tears, sobbing and quivering all over.

" You have left the service again . . ." she articulated. " Oh, how awful it is !"

" But do understand, sister, do understand . . ." I said, and I was overcome with despair because she was crying.

As ill-luck would have it, the kerosene in my little lamp was exhausted; it began to smoke, and was on the point of going out, and the old hooks on the walls looked down sullenly, and their shadows flickered.

" Have mercy on us," said my sister, sitting up. " Father is in terrible distress and I am ill; I shall go out of my mind. What will become of you ?"

she said, sobbing and stretching out her arms to me. " I beg you, I implore you, for our dear mother's sake, I beg you to go back to the office !"

" I can't, Kleopatra !" I said, feeling that a little more and I should give way. " I cannot !"

" Why not ?" my sister went on. " Why not ? Well, if you can't get on with the Head, look out for another post. Why shouldn't you get a situation on the railway, for instance ? I have just been talking to Anyuta Blagovo; she declares they would take you on the railway-line, and even promised to try and get a post for you. For God's sake, Misail, think a little ! Think a little, I implore you."

We talked a little longer and I gave way. I said that the thought of a job on the railway that was being constructed had never occurred to me, and that if she liked I was ready to try it.

She smiled joyfully through her tears and squeezed my hand, and then went on crying because she could not stop, while I went to the kitchen for some kerosene.

II.

Among the devoted supporters of amateur theatricals, concerts, and *tableaux vivants* for charitable objects, the Azhogins, who lived in their own house in Great Dvoryansky Street, took a foremost place; they always provided the room, and took upon themselves all the troublesome arrangements and the expenses. They were a family of wealthy landowners who had an estate of some

nine thousand acres in the district and a capital
house, but they did not care for the country, and
lived winter and summer alike in the town. The
family consisted of the mother, a tall, spare, refined
lady, with short hair, a short jacket, and a flat-
looking skirt in the English fashion, and three
daughters who, when they were spoken of, were
called not by their names but simply: the eldest,
the middle, and the youngest. They all had ugly
sharp chins, and were short-sighted and round-
shouldered. They were dressed like their mother,
they lisped disagreeably, and yet, in spite of that,
infallibly took part in every performance and
were continually doing something with a charitable object—acting, reciting, singing. They were
very serious and never smiled, and even in a
musical comedy they played without the faintest
trace of gaiety, with a businesslike air, as though
they were engaged in bookkeeping.

I loved our theatricals, especially the numerous,
noisy, and rather incoherent rehearsals, after
which they always gave a supper. In the choice
of the plays and the distribution of the parts I
had no hand at all. The post assigned to me lay
behind the scenes. I painted the scenes, copied
out the parts, prompted, made up the actors'
faces; and I was entrusted, too, with various stage
effects such as thunder, the singing of nightingales,
and so on. Since I had no proper social position
and no decent clothes, at the rehearsals I held
aloof from the rest in the shadows of the wings and
maintained a shy silence.

I painted the scenes at the Azhogins' either in

the barn or in the yard. I was assisted by Andrey Ivanov, a house painter, or, as he called himself, a contractor for all kinds of house decoration, a tall, very thin, pale man of fifty, with a hollow chest, with sunken temples, with blue rings round his eyes, rather terrible to look at in fact. He was afflicted with some internal malady, and every autumn and spring people said that he wouldn't recover, but after being laid up for a while he would get up and say afterwards with surprise: " I have escaped dying again."

In the town he was called Radish, and they declared that this was his real name. He was as fond of the theatre as I was, and as soon as rumours reached him that a performance was being got up he threw aside all his work and went to the Azhogins' to paint scenes.

The day after my talk with my sister, I was working at the Azhogins' from morning till night. The rehearsal was fixed for seven o'clock in the evening, and an hour before it began all the amateurs were gathered together in the hall, and the eldest, the middle, and the youngest Azhogins were pacing about the stage, reading from manuscript books. Radish, in a long rusty-red overcoat and a scarf muffled round his neck, already stood leaning with his head against the wall, gazing with a devout expression at the stage. Madame Azhogin went up first to one and then to another guest, saying something agreeable to each. She had a way of gazing into one's face, and speaking softly as though telling a secret.

" It must be difficult to paint scenery," she said softly, coming up to me. " I was just talking to Madame Mufke about superstitions when I saw you come in. My goodness, my whole life I have been waging war against superstitions ! To convince the servants what nonsense all their terrors are, I always light three candles, and begin all my important undertakings on the thirteenth of the month."

Dolzhikov's daughter came in, a plump, fair beauty, dressed, as people said, in everything from Paris. She did not act, but a chair was set for her on the stage at the rehearsals, and the performances never began till she had appeared in the front row, dazzling and astounding everyone with her fine clothes. As a product of the capital she was allowed to make remarks during the rehearsals; and she did so with a sweet indulgent smile, and one could see that she looked upon our performance as a childish amusement. It was said she had studied singing at the Petersburg Conservatoire, and even sang for a whole winter in a private opera. I thought her very charming, and I usually watched her through the rehearsals and performances without taking my eyes off her.

I had just picked up the manuscript book to begin prompting when my sister suddenly made her appearance. Without taking off her cloak or hat, she came up to me and said:

" Come along, I beg you."

I went with her. Anyuta Blagovo, also in her hat and wearing a dark veil, was standing behind the scenes at the door. She was the daughter of the Assistant President of the Court, who had held that office in our town almost ever since the establishment of the circuit court. Since she was tall and had a good figure, her assistance was considered indispensable for *tableaux vivants*, and when she represented a fairy or something like Glory her face burned with shame; but she took no part in dramatic performances, and came to the rehearsals only for a moment on some special errand, and did not go into the hall. Now, too, it was evident that she had only looked in for a minute.

" My father was speaking about you," she said drily, blushing and not looking at me. " Dolzhikov has promised you a post on the railway-line. Apply to him to-morrow; he will be at home."

I bowed and thanked her for the trouble she had taken.

" And you can give up this," she said, indicating the exercise book.

My sister and she went up to Madame Azhogin and for two minutes they were whispering with her looking towards me; they were consulting about something.

" Yes, indeed," said Madame Azhogin, softly coming up to me and looking intently into my face. " Yes, indeed, if this distracts you from serious pursuits "—she took the manuscript book from my hands—" you can hand it over to someone else; don't distress yourself, my friend, go home, and good luck to you."

I said good-bye to her, and went away overcome

with confusion. As I went down 'the stairs I saw my sister and Anyuta Blagovo going away; they were hastening along, talking eagerly about something, probably about my going into the railway service. My sister had never been at a rehearsal before, and now she was most likely conscience-stricken, and afraid her father might find out that, without his permission, she had been to the Azhogins' !

I went to Dolzhikov's next day between twelve and one. The footman conducted me into a very beautiful room, which was the engineer's drawing-room and, at the same time, his working study. Everything here was soft and elegant, and, for a man so unaccustomed to luxury as I was, it seemed strange. There were costly rugs, huge arm-chairs, bronzes, pictures, gold and plush frames; among the photographs scattered about the walls there were very beautiful women, clever, lovely faces, easy attitudes; from the drawing-room there was a door leading straight into the garden on to a verandah: one could see lilac-trees; one could see a table laid for lunch, a number of bottles, a bouquet of roses; there was a fragrance of spring and expensive cigars, a fragrance of happiness—and everything seemed as though it would say: " Here is a man who has lived and laboured, and has attained at last the happiness possible on earth." The engineer's daughter was sitting at the writing-table, reading a newspaper.

" You have come to see my father ?" she asked. " He is having a shower bath; he will be here directly. Please sit down and wait."

I sat down.

" I believe you live opposite ?" she questioned me, after a brief silence.

" Yes."

" I am so bored that I watch you every day out of the window; you must excuse me," she went on, looking at the newspaper, " and I often see your sister; she always has such a look of kindness and concentration."

Dolzhikov came in. He was rubbing his neck with a towel.

" Papa, Monsieur Poloznev," said his daughter.

" Yes, yes, Blagovo was telling me," he turned briskly to me without giving me his hand. " But listen, what can I give you ? What sort of posts have I got ? You are a queer set of people !" he went on aloud in a tone as though he were giving me a lecture. " A score of you keep coming to me every day; you imagine I am the head of a department ! I am constructing a railway-line, my friends; I have employment for heavy labour: I need mechanics, smiths, navvies, carpenters, well-sinkers, and none of you can do anything but sit and write ! You are all clerks."

And he seemed to me to have the same air of happiness as his rugs and easy chairs. He was stout and healthy, ruddy-cheeked and broad-chested, in a print cotton shirt and full trousers like a toy china sledge-driver. He had a curly, round beard—and not a single grey hair—a hooked nose, and clear, dark, guileless eyes.

" What can you do ?" he went on. " There is nothing you can do ! I am an engineer. I am a man of an assured position, but before they gave me a railway-line I was for years in harness; I have been a practical mechanic. For two years I worked in Belgium as an oiler. You can judge for yourself, my dear fellow, what kind of work can I offer you ?"

"Of course that is so . . ." I muttered in extreme confusion, unable to face his clear, guileless eyes.

"Can you work the telegraph, any way ?" he asked, after a moment's thought.

"Yes, I have been a telegraph clerk."

"Hm ! Well, we will see then. Meanwhile, go to Dubetchnya. I have got a fellow there, but he is a wretched creature."

"And what will my duties consist of ?" I asked.

"We shall see. Go there; meanwhile I will make arrangements. Only please don't get drunk, and don't worry me with requests of any sort, or I shall send you packing."

He turned away from me without even a nod.

I bowed to him and his daughter who was reading a newspaper, and went away. My heart felt so heavy, that when my sister began asking me how the engineer had received me, I could not utter a single word.

I got up early in the morning, at sunrise, to go to Dubetchnya. There was not a soul in our Great Dvoryansky Street; everyone was asleep, and my footsteps rang out with a solitary, hollow sound. The poplars, covered with dew, filled the air with soft fragrance. I was sad, and did

not want to go away from the town. I was fond
of my native town. It seemed to be so beautiful
and so snug ! I loved the fresh greenery, the still,
sunny morning, the chiming of our bells; but the
people with whom I lived in this town were boring,
alien to me, sometimes even repulsive. I did not
like them nor understand them.

I did not understand what these sixty-five
thousand people lived for and by. I knew that
Kimry lived by boots, that Tula made samovars
and guns, that Odessa was a sea-port, but what
our town was, and what it did, I did not know.
Great Dvoryansky Street and the two other
smartest streets lived on the interest of capital,
or on salaries received by officials from the public
treasury; but what the other eight streets, which
ran parallel for over two miles and vanished beyond
the hills, lived upon, was always an insoluble
riddle to me. And the way these people lived one
is ashamed to describe ! No garden, no theatre,
no decent band; the public library and the club
library were only visited by Jewish youths, so that
the magazines and new books lay for months uncut;
rich and well-educated people slept in close, stuffy
bedrooms, on wooden bedsteads infested with
bugs; their children were kept in revoltingly dirty
rooms called nurseries, and the servants, even the
old and respected ones, slept on the floor in the
kitchen, covered with rags. On ordinary days the
houses smelt of beetroot soup, and on fast days
of sturgeon cooked in sunflower oil. The food was
not good, and the drinking water was unwholesome. In the town council, at the governor's, at

the head priest's, on all sides in private houses, people had been saying for years and years that our town had not a good and cheap water-supply, and that it was necessary to obtain a loan of two hundred thousand from the Treasury for laying on water; very rich people, of whom three dozen could have been counted up in our town, and who at times lost whole estates at cards, drank the polluted water too, and talked all their lives with great excitement of a loan for the water-supply—and I did not understand that; it seemed to me it would have been simpler to take the two hundred thousand out of their own pockets and lay it out on that object.

I did not know one honest man in the town. My father took bribes, and imagined that they were given him out of respect for his moral qualities; at the high school, in order to be moved up rapidly from class to class, the boys went to board with their teachers, who charged them exorbitant sums; the wife of the military commander took bribes from the recruits when they were called up before the board and even deigned to accept refreshments from them, and on one occasion could not get up from her knees in church because she was drunk; the doctors took bribes, too, when the recruits came up for examination, and the town doctor and the veterinary surgeon levied a regular tax on the butchers' shops and the restaurants; at the district school they did a trade in certificates, qualifying for partial exemption from military service; the higher clergy took bribes from the humbler priests and from the church elders; at the Municipal, the Artisans', and all the other Boards every petitioner was pursued by a shout: " Don't forget your thanks !" and the petitioner would turn back to give sixpence or a shilling. And those who did not take bribes, such as the higher officials of the Department of Justice, were haughty, offered two fingers instead of shaking hands, were distinguished by the frigidity and narrowness of their judgments, spent a great deal of time over cards, drank to excess, married heiresses, and undoubtedly had a pernicious corrupting influence on those around them. It was only the girls who had still the fresh fragrance of moral purity; most of them had higher impulses, pure and honest hearts; but they had no understanding of life, and believed that bribes were given out of respect for moral qualities, and after they were married grew old quickly, let themselves go completely, and sank hopelessly in the mire of vulgar, petty, bourgeois existence.

III.

A railway-line was being constructed in our neighbourhood. On the eve of feast days the streets were thronged with ragged fellows whom the townspeople called " navvies," and of whom they were afraid. And more than once I had seen one of these tatterdemalions with a bloodstained countenance being led to the police station, while a samovar or some linen, wet from the wash, was carried behind by way of material evidence. The navvies usually congregated about the taverns and the market-place; they drank, ate, and used bad language, and pursued with shrill whistles every woman of light behaviour who passed by. To entertain this hungry rabble our shopkeepers made cats and dogs drunk with vodka, or tied an old kerosene can to a dog's tail; a hue and cry was raised, and the dog dashed along the street, jingling the can, squealing with terror; it fancied some monster was close upon its heels; it would run far out of the town into the open country and there sink exhausted. There were in the town several dogs who went about trembling, with their tails between their legs; and people said this diversion had been too much for them, and had driven them mad.

A station was being built four miles from the town. It was said that the engineers asked for a bribe of fifty thousand roubles for bringing the line right up to the town, but the town council would only consent to give forty thousand; they could not come to an agreement over the difference, and now the townspeople regretted it, as they had to make a road to the station and that, it was reckoned, would cost more. The sleepers and rails had been laid throughout the whole length of the line, and trains ran up and down it, bringing building materials and labourers, and further progress was only delayed on account of the bridges which Dolzhikov was building, and some of the stations were not yet finished.

Dubetchnya, as our first station was called, was a little under twelve miles from the town. I walked. The cornfields, bathed in the morning sunshine were bright green. It was a flat, cheerful country, and in the distance there were the distinct outlines of the station, of ancient barrows, and far-away homesteads. . . . How nice it was out there in the open ! And how I longed to be filled with the sense of freedom, if only for that one morning, that I might not think of what was being done in the town, not think of my needs, not feel hungry ! Nothing has so marred my existence as an acute feeling of hunger, which made images of buckwheat porridge, rissoles, and baked fish mingle strangely with my best thoughts. Here I was standing alone in the open country, gazing upward at a lark which hovered in the air at the same spot, trilling as though in hysterics, and meanwhile I was thinking: " How nice it would be to eat a piece of bread and butter !" Or I would sit down by the roadside to rest, and shut my eyes to listen to the delicious sounds of May, and what haunted me was the smell of hot potatoes. Though I was tall and strongly built, I had as a rule to eat little, and so the predominant sensation throughout the day was hunger, and perhaps that was why I knew so well how it is that such multitudes of people toil merely for their daily bread, and can talk of nothing but things to eat.

At Dubetchnya they were plastering the inside of the station, and building a wooden upper storey to the pumping shed. It was hot; there was a smell of lime, and the workmen sauntered listlessly between the heaps of shavings and mortar rubble. The pointsman lay asleep near his sentry box, and the sun was blazing full on his face. There was not a single tree. The telegraph wire hummed faintly and hawks were perching on it here and there. I, wandering, too, among the heaps of rubbish, and not knowing what to do, recalled how the engineer, in answer to my question what my duties would consist in, had said: " We shall see when you are there " ; but what could one see in that wilderness ?

The plasterers spoke of the foreman, and of a certain Fyodot Vasilyev. I did not understand, and gradually I was overcome by depression— the physical depression in which one is conscious of one's arms and legs and huge body, and does not know what to do with them or where to put them.

After I had been walking about for at least a couple of hours, I noticed that there were telegraph poles running off to the right from the station, and that they ended a mile or a mile and a half away at a white stone wall. The workmen told me the office was there, and at last I reflected that that was where I ought to go.

It was a very old manor house, deserted long ago. The wall round it, of porous white stone, was mouldering and had fallen away in places, and the lodge, the blank wall of which looked out on the open country, had a rusty roof with patches of tin-plate gleaming here and there on it. Within the gates could be seen a spacious courtyard overgrown with rough weeds, and an old manor house with sunblinds on the windows, and a high roof red with rust. Two lodges, exactly alike,

stood one on each side of the house to right
and to left: one had its windows nailed up
with boards; near the other, of which the
windows were open, there was washing on the
line, and there were calves moving about. The
last of the telegraph poles stood in the courtyard,
and the wire from it ran to the window of the
lodge, of which the blank wall looked out into
the open country. The door stood open; I went
in. By the telegraph apparatus a gentleman with
a curly dark head, wearing a reefer coat made of
sailcloth, was sitting at a table; he glanced at me
morosely from under his brows, but immediately
smiled and said:

"Hullo, Better-than-nothing!"

It was Ivan Tcheprakov, an old schoolfellow
of mine, who had been expelled from the second
class for smoking. We used at one time, during
autumn, to catch goldfinches, finches, and linnets
together, and to sell them in the market early in
the morning, while our parents were still in their
beds. We watched for flocks of migrating
starlings and shot at them with small shot,
then we picked up those that were wounded, and
some of them died in our hands in terrible agonies
(I remember to this day how they moaned in the
cage at night); those that recovered we sold,
and swore with the utmost effrontery that they
were all cocks. On one occasion at the market
I had only one starling left, which I had offered
to purchasers in vain, till at last I sold it for a
farthing. "Anyway, it's better than nothing,"
I said to comfort myself, as I put the farthing in

my pocket, and from that day the street urchins and the schoolboys called after me: " Better-than-nothing; " and to this day the street boys and the shopkeepers mock at me with the nickname, though no one remembers how it arose.

Tcheprakov was not of robust constitution: he was narrow-chested, round-shouldered, and long-legged. He wore a silk cord for a tie, had no trace of a waistcoat, and his boots were worse than mine, with the heels trodden down on one side. He stared, hardly even blinking, with a strained expression, as though he were just going to catch something, and he was always in a fuss.

" You wait a minute," he would say fussily. " You listen. . . . Whatever was I talking about ?"

We got into conversation. I learned that the estate on which I now was had until recently been the property of the Tcheprakovs, and had only the autumn before passed into the possession of Dolzhikov, who considered it more profitable to put his money into land than to keep it in notes, and had already bought up three good-sized mortgaged estates in our neighbourhood. At the sale Tcheprakov's mother had reserved for herself the right to live for the next two years in one of the lodges at the side, and had obtained a post for her son in the office.

" I should think he could buy !" Tcheprakov said of the engineer. " See what he fleeces out of the contractors alone ! He fleeces everyone !"

Then he took me to dinner, deciding fussily that I should live with him in the lodge, and have my meals from his mother.

" She is a bit stingy," he said, " but she won't charge you much."

It was very cramped in the little rooms in which his mother lived; they were all, even the passage and the entry, piled up with furniture which had been brought from the big house after the sale; and the furniture was all old-fashioned mahogany. Madame Tcheprakov, a very stout middle-aged lady with slanting Chinese eyes, was sitting in a big arm-chair by the window, knitting a stocking. She received me ceremoniously.

" This is Poloznev, mamma," Tcheprakov introduced me. " He is going to serve here."

" Are you a nobleman ?" she asked in a strange, disagreeable voice: it seemed to me to sound as though fat were bubbling in her throat.

" Yes," I answered.

" Sit down."

The dinner was a poor one. Nothing was served but pies filled with bitter curd, and milk soup. Elena Nikiforovna, who presided, kept blinking in a queer way, first with one eye and then with the other. She talked, she ate, but yet there was something deathly about her whole figure, and one almost fancied the faint smell of a corpse. There was only a glimmer of life in her, a glimmer of consciousness that she had been a lady who had once had her own serfs, that she was the widow of a general whom the servants had to address as " your Excellency "; and when these feeble relics of life flickered up in her for an instant she would say to her son:

" Jean, you are not holding your knife properly !"

Or she would say to me, drawing a deep breath, with the mincing air of a hostess trying to entertain a visitor:

" You know we have sold our estate. Of course, it is a pity, we are used to the place, but Dolzhikov has promised to make Jean stationmaster of Dubetchnya, so we shall not have to go away; we shall live here at the station, and that is just the same as being on our own property ! The engineer is so nice ! Don't you think he is very handsome ?"

Until recently the Tcheprakovs had lived in a wealthy style, but since the death of the general everything had been changed. Elena Nikiforovna had taken to quarrelling with the neighbours, to going to law, and to not paying her bailiffs or her labourers; she was in constant terror of being robbed, and in some ten years Dubetchnya had become unrecognizable.

Behind the great house was an old garden which had already run wild, and was overgrown with rough weeds and bushes. I walked up and down the verandah, which was still solid and beautiful; through the glass doors one could see a room with parquetted floor, probably the drawing-room; an old-fashioned piano and pictures in deep mahogany frames—there was nothing else. In the old flower-beds all that remained were peonies and poppies, which lifted their white and bright red heads above the grass. Young maples and elms, already nibbled by the cows, grew beside the paths, drawn up and hindering each other's growth. The garden was thickly overgrown and seemed impassable, but this was only near the house where there stood poplars, fir-trees, and old lime-trees, all of the same age, relics of the former avenues. Further on, beyond them the garden had been cleared for the sake of hay, and here it was not moist and stuffy, and there were no spiders' webs in one's mouth and eyes. A light breeze was blowing. The further one went the more open it was, and here in the open space were cherries, plums, and spreading apple-trees, disfigured by props and by canker; and pear-trees so tall that one could not believe they were pear-trees. This part of the garden was let to some shopkeepers of the town, and it was protected from thieves and starlings by a feeble-minded peasant who lived in a shanty in it.

The garden, growing more and more open, till it became definitely a meadow, sloped down to the river, which was overgrown with green weeds and osiers. Near the milldam was the millpond, deep and full of fish; a little mill with a thatched roof was working away with a wrathful sound, and frogs croaked furiously. Circles passed from time to time over the smooth, mirror-like water, and the water-lilies trembled, stirred by the lively fish. On the further side of the river was the little village Dubetchnya. The still, blue millpond was alluring with its promise of coolness and peace. And now all this—the millpond and the mill and the snug-looking banks—belonged to the engineer !

And so my new work began. I received and

forwarded telegrams, wrote various reports, and
made fair copies of the notes of requirements,
the complaints, and the reports sent to the office
by the illiterate foremen and workmen. But for
the greater part of the day I did nothing but walk
about the room waiting for telegrams, or made a
boy sit in the lodge while I went for a walk in the
garden, until the boy ran to tell me that there
was a tapping at the operating machine. I had
dinner at Madame Tcheprakov's. Meat we had
very rarely: our dishes were all made of milk,
and Wednesdays and Fridays were fast days, and on
those days we had pink plates which were called
Lenten plates. Madame Tcheprakov was continually blinking—it was her invariable habit, and
I always felt ill at ease in her presence.

As there was not enough work in the lodge for
one, Tcheprakov did nothing, but simply dozed,
or went with his gun to shoot ducks on the millpond.
In the evenings he drank too much in the village
or the station, and before going to bed stared in the
looking-glass and said: " Hullo, Ivan Tcheprakov."

When he was drunk he was very pale, and kept
rubbing his hands and laughing with a sound like
a neigh: " hee-hee-hee !" By way of bravado he
used to strip and run about the country naked.
He used to eat flies and say they were rather sour.

IV.

One day, after dinner, he ran breathless into the
lodge and said: " Go along, your sister has come."
I went out, and there I found a hired brake

from the town standing before the entrance of the great house. My sister had come in it with Anyuta Blagovo and a gentleman in a military tunic. Going up closer I recognized the latter : it was the brother of Anyuta Blagovo, the army doctor.

" We have come to you for a picnic," he said; " is that all right ?"

My sister and Anyuta wanted to ask how I was getting on here, but both were silent, and simply gazed at me. I was silent too. They saw that I did not like the place, and tears came into my sister's eyes, while Anyuta Blagovo turned crimson.

We went into the garden. The doctor walked ahead of us all and said enthusiastically:

" What air ! Holy Mother, what air !"

In appearance he was still a student. And he walked and talked like a student, and the expression of his grey eyes was as keen, honest, and frank as a nice student's. Beside his tall and handsome sister he looked frail and thin; and his beard was thin too, and his voice, too, was a thin but rather agreeable tenor. He was serving in a regiment somewhere, and had come home to his people for a holiday, and said he was going in the autumn to Petersburg for his examination as a doctor of medicine. He was already a family man, with a wife and three children; he had married very young, in his second year at the University, and now people in the town said he was unhappy in his family life and was not living with his wife.

" What time is it ?" my sister asked uneasily. " We must get back in good time. Papa let me

215

come to see my brother on condition I was back at six."

" Oh, bother your papa !" sighed the doctor.

I set the samovar. We put down a carpet before the verandah of the great house and had our tea there, and the doctor knelt down, drank out of his saucer, and declared that he now knew what bliss was. Then Tcheprakov came with the key and opened the glass door, and we all went into the house. There it was half dark and mysterious, and smelt of mushrooms, and our footsteps had a hollow sound as though there were cellars under the floor. The doctor stopped and touched the keys of the piano, and it responded faintly with a husky, quivering, but melodious chord; he tried his voice and sang a song, frowning and tapping impatiently with his foot when some note was mute. My sister did not talk about going home, but walked about the rooms and kept saying :

" How happy I am ! How happy I am !"

There was a note of astonishment in her voice, as though it seemed to her incredible that she, too, could feel light-hearted. It was the first time in my life I had seen her so happy. She actually looked prettier. In profile she did not look nice; her nose and mouth seemed to stick out and had an expression as though she were pouting, but she had beautiful dark eyes, a pale, very delicate complexion, and a touching expression of goodness and melancholy, and when she talked she seemed charming and even beautiful. We both, she and I, took after our mother, were broad shouldered, strongly built, and capable of endurance, but her pallor was a sign of ill-health; she often had a cough, and I sometimes caught in her face that look one sees in people who are seriously ill, but for some reason conceal the fact. There was something naïve and childish in her gaiety now, as though the joy that had been suppressed and smothered in our childhood by harsh education had now suddenly awakened in her soul and had found a free outlet.

But when evening came on and the horses were brought round, my sister sank into silence and looked thin and shrunken, and she got into the brake as though she were going to the scaffold.

When they had all gone, and the sound had died away . . . I remembered that Anyuta Blagovo had not said a word to me all day.

" She is a wonderful girl !" I thought. " Wonderful girl !"

St. Peter's fast came, and we had nothing but Lenten dishes every day. I was weighed down by physical depression due to idleness and my unsettled position, and dissatisfied with myself. Listless and hungry, I lounged about the garden and only waited for a suitable mood to go away.

Towards evening one day, when Radish was sitting in the lodge, Dolzhikov, very sunburnt and grey with dust, walked in unexpectedly. He had been spending three days on his land, and had come now to Dubetchnya by the steamer, and walked to us from the station. While waiting for the carriage, which was to come for him from the town, he walked round the grounds with his bailiff, giving orders in a loud voice, then sat for a whole hour in our lodge, writing letters. While he was there telegrams came for him, and he him-self tapped off the answers. We three stood in silence at attention.

" What a muddle !" he said, glancing con-temptuously at a record book. " In a fortnight I am transferring the office to the station, and I don't know what I am to do with you, my friends."

" I do my best, your honour," said Tcheprakov.

" To be sure, I see how you do your best. The only thing you can do is to take your salary," the engineer went on, looking at me; " you keep relying on patronage to *faire la carrière* as quickly and as easily as possible. Well, I don't care for patronage. No one took any trouble on my behalf. Before they gave me a railway contract I went about as a mechanic and worked in Belgium as an oiler. And you, Panteley, what are you doing here ?" he asked, turning to Radish. " Drinking with them ?"

He, for some reason, always called humble people Panteley, and such as me and Tcheprakov he despised, and called them drunkards, beasts, and rabble to their face. Altogether he was cruel to humble subordinates, and used to fine them and turn them off coldly without explanations.

At last the horses came for him. As he said good-bye he promised to turn us all off in a fort-night; he called his bailiff a blockhead; and then, lolling at ease in his carriage, drove back to the town.

"Andrey Ivanitch," I said to Radish, "take me on as a workman."

"Oh, all right!"

And we set off together in the direction of the town. When the station and the big house with its buildings were left behind I asked: "Andrey Ivanitch, why did you come to Dubetchnya this evening?"

"In the first place my fellows are working on the line, and in the second place I came to pay the general's lady my interest. Last year I borrowed fifty roubles from her, and I pay her now a rouble a month interest."

The painter stopped and took me by the button.

"Misail Alexeyitch, our angel," he went on. "The way I look at it is that if any man, gentle or simple, takes even the smallest interest, he is doing evil. There cannot be truth and justice in such a man."

Radish, lean, pale, dreadful-looking, shut his eyes, shook his head, and, in the tone of a philosopher, pronounced:

"Lice consume the grass, rust consumes the iron, and lying the soul. Lord, have mercy upon us sinners."

V.

Radish was not practical, and was not at all good at forming an estimate; he took more work than he could get through, and when calculating he was agitated, lost his head, and so was almost always out of pocket over his jobs. He undertook painting, glazing, paperhanging, and even tiling roofs, and I can remember his running about for three days to find tilers for the sake of a paltry job. He was a first-rate workman; he sometimes earned as much as ten roubles a day; and if it had not been for the desire at all costs to be a master, and to be called a contractor, he would probably have had plenty of money.

He was paid by the job, but he paid me and the other workmen by the day, from one and twopence to two shillings a day. When it was fine and dry we did all kinds of outside work, chiefly painting roofs. When I was new to the work it made my feet burn as though I were walking on hot bricks, and when I put on felt boots they were hotter than ever. But this was only at first; later on I got used to it, and everything went swimmingly. I was living now among people to whom labour was obligatory, inevitable, and who worked like cart-horses, often with no idea of the moral significance of labour, and, indeed, never using the word "labour" in conversation at all. Beside them I, too, felt like a cart-horse, growing more and more imbued with the feeling of the obligatory and inevitable character of what I was doing, and this made my life easier, setting me free from all doubt and uncertainty.

At first everything interested me, everything was new, as though I had been born again. I could sleep on the ground and go about barefoot, and that was extremely pleasant; I could stand in a crowd of the common people and be no constraint to anyone, and when a cab horse fell down in the street I ran to help it up without being afraid of soiling my clothes. And the best of it all was, I was living on my own account and no burden to anyone!

Painting roofs, especially with our own oil and colours, was regarded as a particularly profitable job, and so this rough, dull work was not disdained, even by such good workmen as Radish. In short breeches, and wasted, purple-looking legs, he used to go about the roofs, looking like a stork, and I used to hear him, as he plied his brush, breathing heavily and saying: " Woe, woe to us sinners !"

He walked about the roofs as freely as though he were upon the ground. In spite of his being ill and pale as a corpse, his agility was extraordinary : he used to paint the domes and cupolas of the churches without scaffolding, like a young man, with only the help of a ladder and a rope, and it was rather horrible when standing on a height far from the earth; he would draw himself up erect, and for some unknown reason pronounce :

" Lice consume grass, rust consumes iron, and lying the soul !"

Or, thinking about something, would answer his thoughts aloud :

" Anything may happen ! Anything may happen !"

When I went home from my work, all the people who were sitting on benches by the gates, all the shopmen and boys and their employers, made sneering and spiteful remarks after me, and this upset me at first and seemed to be simply monstrous.

" Better-than-nothing !" I heard on all sides.
" House painter !   Yellow ochre !"

And none behaved so ungraciously to me as
those who had only lately been humble people
themselves, and had earned their bread by hard
manual labour.   In the streets full of shops I was
once passing an ironmonger's when water was
thrown over me as though by accident, and on one
occasion someone darted out with a stick at me,
while a fishmonger, a grey-headed old man, barred
my way and said, looking at me angrily:

" I am not sorry for you, you fool !   It's your
father I am sorry for."

And my acquaintances were for some reason
overcome with embarrassment when they met me.
Some of them looked upon me as a queer fish and a
comic fool; others were sorry for me; others did not
know what attitude to take up to me, and it was
difficult to make them out.   One day I met
Anyuta Blagovo in a side street near Great
Dvoryansky Street.   I was going to work, and
was carrying two long brushes and a pail of paint.
Recognizing me Anyuta flushed crimson.

" Please do not bow to me in the street," she
said nervously, harshly, and in a shaking voice,
without offering me her hand, and tears suddenly
gleamed in her eyes.   " If to your mind all this
is necessary, so be it . . . so be it, but I beg you
not to meet me !"

I no longer lived in Great Dvoryansky Street,
but in the suburb with my old nurse Karpovna,
a good-natured but gloomy old woman, who
always foreboded some harm, was afraid of all

dreams, and even in the bees and wasps that flew into her room saw omens of evil, and the fact that I had become a workman, to her thinking, boded nothing good.

"Your life is ruined," she would say, mournfully shaking her head, "ruined."

Her adopted son Prokofy, a huge, uncouth, red-headed fellow of thirty, with bristling moustaches, a butcher by trade, lived in the little house with her. When he met me in the passage he would make way for me in respectful silence, and if he was drunk he would salute me with all five fingers at once. He used to have supper in the evening, and through the partition wall of boards I could hear him clear his throat and sigh as he drank off glass after glass.

"Mamma," he would call in an undertone.

"Well," Karpovna, who was passionately devoted to her adopted son, would respond: "What is it, sonny?"

"I can show you a testimony of my affection, mamma. All this earthly life I will cherish you in your declining years in this vale of tears, and when you die I will bury you at my expense; I have said it, and you can believe it."

I got up every morning before sunrise, and went to bed early. We house painters ate a great deal and slept soundly; the only thing amiss was that my heart used to beat violently at night. I did not quarrel with my mates. Violent abuse, desperate oaths, and wishes such as, "Blast your eyes," or "Cholera take you," never ceased all day, but, nevertheless, we lived on very friendly terms.

The other fellows suspected me of being some sort of religious sectary, and made good-natured jokes at my expense, saying that even my own father had disowned me, and thereupon would add that they rarely went into the temple of God themselves, and that many of them had not been to confession for ten years. They justified this laxity on their part by saying that a painter among men was like a jackdaw among birds.

The men had a good opinion of me, and treated me with respect; it was evident that my not drinking, not smoking, but leading a quiet, steady life pleased them very much. It was only an unpleasant shock to them that I took no hand in stealing oil, and did not go with them to ask for tips from people on whose property we were working. Stealing oil and paints from those who employed them was a house painter's custom, and was not regarded as theft, and it was remarkable that even so upright a man as Radish would always carry away a little white lead and oil as he went home from work. And even the most respectable old fellows, who owned the houses in which they lived in the suburb, were not ashamed to ask for a tip, and it made me feel vexed and ashamed to see the men go in a body to congratulate some nonentity on the commencement or the completion of the job, and thank him with degrading servility when they had received a few coppers.

With people on whose work they were engaged they behaved like wily courtiers, and almost every day I was reminded of Shakespeare's Polonius.

" I fancy it is going to rain," the man whose house was being painted would say, looking at the sky.

" It is, there is not a doubt it is," the painters would agree.

" I don't think it is a rain-cloud, though. Perhaps it won't rain after all."

" No, it won't, your honour ! I am sure it won't."

But their attitude to their patrons behind their backs was usually one of irony, and when they saw, for instance, a gentleman sitting in the verandah reading a newspaper, they would observe:

" He reads the paper, but I daresay he has nothing to eat."

I never went home to see my own people. When I came back from work I often found waiting for me little notes, brief and anxious, in which my sister wrote to me about my father; that he had been particularly preoccupied at dinner and had eaten nothing, or that he had been giddy and staggering, or that he had locked himself in his room and had not come out for a long time. Such items of news troubled me; I could not sleep, and at times even walked up and down Great Dvoryansky Street at night by our house, looking in at the dark windows and trying to guess whether everything was well at home. On Sundays my sister came to see me, but came in secret, as though it were not to see me but our nurse. And if she came in to see me she was very pale, with tear-stained eyes, and she began crying at once.

" Our father will never live through this," she

would say. " If anything should happen to him
—God grant it may not—your conscience will
torment you all your life. It's awful, Misail; for
our mother's sake I beseech you: reform your
ways."

" My darling sister," I would say, " how can
I reform my ways if I am convinced that I am
acting in accordance with my conscience ? Do
understand !"

" I know you are acting on your conscience, but
perhaps it could be done differently, somehow,
so as not to wound anybody."

" Ah, holy Saints !" the old woman sighed
through the door. " Your life is ruined ! There
will be trouble, my dears, there will be trouble !"

VI.

One Sunday Dr. Blagovo turned up unexpectedly. He was wearing a military tunic over
a silk shirt and high boots of patent leather.

" I have come to see you," he began, shaking
my hand heartily like a student. " I am hearing
about you every day, and I have been meaning
to come and have a heart-to-heart talk, as they
say. The boredom in the town is awful, there is
not a living soul, no one to say a word to. It's
hot, Holy Mother," he went on, taking off his
tunic and sitting in his silk shirt. " My dear
fellow, let me talk to you."

I was dull myself, and had for a long time been
craving for the society of someone not a house
painter. I was genuinely glad to see him.

" I'll begin by saying," he said, sitting down on my bed, " that I sympathize with you from the bottom of my heart, and deeply respect the life you are leading. They don't understand you here in the town, and, indeed, there is no one to understand, seeing that, as you know, they are all, with very few exceptions, regular Gogolesque pig faces here. But I saw what you were at once that time at the picnic. You are a noble soul, an honest, high-minded man ! I respect you, and feel it a great honour to shake hands with you!" he went on enthusiastically. " To have made such a complete and violent change of life as you have done, you must have passed through a complicated spiritual crisis, and to continue this manner of life now, and to keep up to the high standard of your convictions continually, must be a strain on your mind and heart from day to day. Now to begin our talk, tell me, don't you consider that if you had spent your strength of will, this strained activity, all these powers on something else, for instance, on gradually becoming a great scientist, or artist, your life would have been broader and deeper and would have been more productive ?"

We talked, and when we got upon manual labour I expressed this idea: that what is wanted is that the strong should not enslave the weak, that the minority should not be a parasite on the majority, nor a vampire for ever sucking its vital sap; that is, all, without exception, strong and weak, rich and poor, should take part equally in the struggle for existence, each one on his own

account, and that there was no better means for
equalizing things in that way than manual labour,
in the form of universal service, compulsory for
all.　　　　　　　　　　　　　　　　　　　•

"Then do you think everyone without exception
ought to engage in manual labour?" asked the
doctor.

"Yes."

"And don't you think that if everyone, including
the best men, the thinkers and great scientists,
taking part in the struggle for existence, each on
his own account, are going to waste their time
breaking stones and painting roofs, may not that
threaten a grave danger to progress?"

"Where is the danger?" I asked. "Why,
progress is in deeds of love, in fulfilling the moral
law; if you don't enslave anyone, if you don't
oppress anyone, what further progress do you
want?"

"But, excuse me," Blagovo suddenly fired up,
rising to his feet. "But, excuse me! If a snail in
its shell busies itself over perfecting its own
personality and muddles about with the moral
law, do you call that progress?"

"Why muddles?" I said, offended. "If you
don't force your neighbour to feed and clothe you,
to transport you from place to place and defend
you from your enemies, surely in the midst of
a life entirely resting on slavery, that is progress,
isn't it? To my mind it is the most important
progress, and perhaps the only one possible and
necessary for man."

"The limits of universal world progress are in

228

infinity, and to talk of some 'possible' progress limited by our needs and temporary theories is, excuse my saying so, positively strange."

" If the limits of progress are in infinity as you say, it follows that its aims are not definite," I said. " To live without knowing definitely what you are living for !"

" So be it ! But that 'not knowing' is not so dull as your 'knowing.' I am going up a ladder which is called progress, civilization, culture; I go on and up without knowing definitely where I am going, but really it is worth living for the sake of that delightful ladder; while you know what you are living for, you live for the sake of some people's not enslaving others, that the artist and the man who rubs his paints may dine equally well. But you know that's the petty, bourgeois, kitchen, grey side of life, and surely it is revolting to live for that alone ? If some insects do enslave others, bother them, let them devour each other ! We need not think about them. You know they will die and decay just the same, however zealously you rescue them from slavery. We must think of that great millennium which awaits humanity in the remote future."

Blagovo argued warmly with me, but at the same time one could see he was troubled by some irrelevant idea.

" I suppose your sister is not coming ?" he said, looking at his watch. " She was at our house yesterday, and said she would be seeing you to-day. You keep saying slavery, slavery . . ." he went on. " But you know that is a special question, and all such questions are solved by humanity gradually."

We began talking of doing things gradually. I said that " the question of doing good or evil every one settles for himself, without waiting till humanity settles it by the way of gradual development. Moreover, this gradual process has more than one aspect. Side by side with the gradual development of human ideas the gradual growth of ideas of another order is observed. Serfdom is no more, but the capitalist system is growing. And in the very heyday of emancipating ideas, just as in the days of Baty, the majority feeds, clothes, and defends the minority while remaining hungry, inadequately clad, and defenceless. Such an order of things can be made to fit in finely with any tendencies and currents of thought you like, because the art of enslaving is also gradually being cultivated. We no longer flog our servants in the stable, but we give to slavery refined forms, at least, we succeed in finding a justification for it in each particular case. Ideas are ideas with us, but if now, at the end of the nineteenth century, it were possible to lay the burden of the most unpleasant of our physiological functions upon the working class, we should certainly do so, and afterwards, of course, justify ourselves by saying that if the best people, the thinkers and great scientists, were to waste their precious time on these functions, progress might be menaced with great danger."

But at this point my sister arrived. Seeing the doctor she was fluttered and troubled, and began saying immediately that it was time for her to go home to her father.

"Kleopatra Alexyevna," said Blagovo earnestly, pressing both hands to his heart, "what will happen to your father if you spend half an hour or so with your brother and me ?"

He was frank, and knew how to communicate his liveliness to others. After a moment's thought, my sister laughed, and all at once became suddenly gay as she had been at the picnic. We went out into the country, and lying in the grass went on with our talk, and looked towards the town where all the windows facing west were like glittering gold because the sun was setting.

After that, whenever my sister was coming to see me Blagovo turned up too, and they always greeted each other as though their meeting in my room was accidental. My sister listened while the doctor and I argued, and at such times her expression was joyfully enthusiastic, full of tenderness and curiosity, and it seemed to me that a new world she had never dreamed of before, and which she was now striving to fathom, was gradually opening before her eyes. When the doctor was not there she was quiet and sad, and now if she sometimes shed tears as she sat on my bed it was for reasons of which she did not speak.

In August Radish ordered us to be ready to go to the railway-line. Two days before we were "banished" from the town my father came to see me. He sat down and in a leisurely way, without looking at me, wiped his red face, then took out of his pocket our town *Messenger*, and deliberately, with emphasis on each word, read out the news that the son of the branch manager of the State Bank, a young man of my age, had been appointed head of a Department in the Exchequer.

" And now look at you," he said, folding up the newspaper, " a beggar, in rags, good for nothing ! Even working-class people and peasants obtain education in order to become men, while you, a Poloznev, with ancestors of rank and distinction, aspire to the gutter ! But I have not come here to talk to you; I have washed my hands of you—" he added in a stifled voice, getting up. " I have come to find out where your sister is, you worthless fellow. She left home after dinner, and here it is nearly eight and she is not back. She has taken to going out frequently, without telling me; she is less dutiful—and I see in it your evil and degrading influence. Where is she ?"

In his hand he had the umbrella I knew so well, and I was already flustered and drew myself up like a schoolboy, expecting my father to begin hitting me with it, but he noticed my glance at the umbrella and most likely that restrained him.

" Live as you please !" he said. " I shall not give you my blessing !"

" Holy Saints !" my nurse muttered behind the door. " You poor, unlucky child ! Ah, my heart bodes ill !"

I worked on the railway-line. It rained without stopping all August; it was damp and cold; they had not carried the corn in the fields, and on big farms where the wheat had been cut by machines it lay not in sheaves but in heaps, and

I remember how those luckless heaps of wheat turned blacker every day and the grain was sprouting in them. It was hard to work; the pouring rain spoiled everything we managed to do. We were not allowed to live or to sleep in the railway buildings, and we took refuge in the damp and filthy mud huts in which the navvies had lived during the summer, and I could not sleep at night for the cold and the woodlice crawling on my face and hands. And when we worked near the bridges the navvies used to come in the evenings in a gang, simply in order to beat the painters—it was a form of sport to them. They used to beat us, to steal our brushes. And to annoy us and rouse us to fight they used to spoil our work; they would, for instance, smear over the signal boxes with green paint. To complete our troubles, Radish took to paying us very irregularly. All the painting work on the line was given out to a contractor; he gave it out to another; and this subcontractor gave it to Radish after subtracting twenty per cent. for himself. The job was not a profitable one in itself, and the rain made it worse; time was wasted; we could not work while Radish was obliged to pay the fellows by the day. The hungry painters almost came to beating him, called him a cheat, a blood-sucker, a Judas, while he, poor fellow, sighed, lifted up his hand to Heaven in despair, and was continually going to Madame Tcheprakov for money.

VII.

Autumn came on, rainy, dark, and muddy. The season of unemployment set in, and I used to sit at home out of work for three days at a stretch, or did various little jobs, not in the painting line. For instance, I wheeled earth, earning about fourpence a day by it. Dr. Blagovo had gone away to Petersburg. My sister had given up coming to see me. Radish was laid up at home ill, expecting death from day to day.

And my mood was autumnal too. Perhaps because, having become a workman, I saw our town life only from the seamy side, it was my lot almost every day to make discoveries which reduced me almost to despair. Those of my fellow-citizens, about whom I had no opinion before, or who had externally appeared perfectly decent, turned out now to be base, cruel people, capable of any dirty action. We common people were deceived, cheated, and kept waiting for hours together in the cold entry or the kitchen; we were insulted and treated with the utmost rudeness. In the autumn I papered the reading-room and two other rooms at the club; I was paid a penny three-farthings the piece, but had to sign a receipt at the rate of twopence halfpenny, and when I refused to do so, a gentleman of benevolent appearance in gold-rimmed spectacles, who must have been one of the club committee e, said to me:

"If you say much more, you blackguard, I'll pound your face into a jelly!"

And when the flunkey whispered to him what I was, the son of Poloznev the architect, he became embarrassed, turned crimson, but immediately recovered himself and said: " Devil take him."

In the shops they palmed off on us workmen putrid meat, musty flour, and tea that had been used and dried again; the police hustled us in church, the assistants and nurses in the hospital plundered us, and if we were too poor to give them a bribe they revenged themselves by bringing us food in dirty vessels. In the post-office the pettiest official considered he had a right to treat us like animals, and to shout with coarse insolence: " You wait !" " Where are you shoving to ?" Even the housedogs were unfriendly to us, and fell upon us with peculiar viciousness. But the thing that struck me most of all in my new position was the complete lack of justice, what is defined by the peasants in the words: " They have forgotten God." Rarely did a day pass without swindling. We were swindled by the merchants who sold us oil, by the contractors and the workmen and the people who employed us. I need not say that there could never be a question of our rights, and we always had to ask for the money we earned as though it were a charity, and to stand waiting for it at the back door, cap in hand.

I was papering a room at the Club next to the reading-room; in the evening, when I was just getting ready to go, the daughter of Dolzhikov, the engineer, walked into the room with a bundle of books under her arm.

235

I bowed to her.

"Oh, how do you do!" she said, recognizing me at once, and holding out her hand. "I'm very glad to see you."

She smiled and looked with curiosity and wonder at my smock, my pail of paste, the paper stretched on the floor; I was embarrassed, and she, too, felt awkward.

"You must excuse my looking at you like this," she said. "I have been told so much about you. Especially by Dr. Blagovo; he is simply in love with you. And I have made the acquaintance of your sister too; a sweet, dear girl, but I can never persuade her that there is nothing awful about your adopting the simple life. On the contrary, you have become the most interesting man in the town."

She looked again at the pail of paste and the wallpaper, and went on:

"I asked Dr. Blagovo to make me better acquainted with you, but apparently he forgot, or had not time. Anyway, we are acquainted all the same, and if you would come and see me quite simply I should be extremely indebted to you. I so long to have a talk. I am a simple person," she added, holding out her hand to me, "and I hope that you will feel no constraint with me. My father is not here, he is in Petersburg."

She went off into the reading-room, rustling her skirts, while I went home, and for a long time could not get to sleep.

That cheerless autumn some kind soul, evidently wishing to alleviate my existence, sent me from time to time tea and lemons, or biscuits, or roast game. Karpovna told me that they were always brought by a soldier, and from whom they came she did not know; and the soldier used to enquire whether I was well, and whether I dined every day, and whether I had warm clothing. When the frosts began I was presented in the same way in my absence with a soft knitted scarf brought by the soldier. There was a faint elusive smell of scent about it, and I guessed who my good fairy was. The scarf smelt of lilies-of-the-valley, the favourite scent of Anyuta Blagovo.

Towards winter there was more work and it was more cheerful. Radish recovered, and we worked together in the cemetery church, where we were putting the ground-work on the ikon-stand before gilding. It was a clean, quiet job, and, as our fellows used to say, profitable. One could get through a lot of work in a day, and the time passed quickly, imperceptibly. There was no swearing, no laughter, no loud talk. The place itself compelled one to quietness and decent behaviour, and disposed one to quiet, serious thoughts. Absorbed in our work we stood or sat motionless like statues; there was a deathly silence in keeping with the cemetery, so that if a tool fell, or a flame spluttered in the lamp, the noise of such sounds rang out abrupt and resonant, and made us look round. After a long silence we would hear a buzzing like the swarming of bees: it was the requiem of a baby being chanted slowly in subdued voices in the porch; or an artist, painting a dove with stars round it on a cupola would begin softly whistling, and recollecting himself with a start would at once relapse into silence; or Radish, answering his thoughts, would say with a sigh: " Anything is possible ! Anything is possible !" or a slow disconsolate bell would begin ringing over our heads, and the painters would observe that it must be for the funeral of some wealthy person. . . .

My days I spent in this stillness in the twilight of the church, and in the long evenings I played billiards or went to the theatre in the gallery wearing the new trousers I had bought out of my own earnings. Concerts and performances had already begun at the Azhogins'; Radish used to paint the scenes alone now. He used to tell me the plot of the plays and describe the *tableaux vivants* which he witnessed. I listened to him with envy. I felt greatly drawn to the rehearsals, but I could not bring myself to go to the Azhogins'.

A week before Christmas Dr. Blagovo arrived. And again we argued and played billiards in the evenings. When he played he used to take off his coat and unbutton his shirt over his chest, and for some reason tried altogether to assume the air of a desperate rake. He did not drink much, but made a great uproar about it, and had a special faculty for getting through twenty roubles in an evening at such a poor cheap tavern as the *Volga*.

My sister began coming to see me again; they both expressed surprise every time on seeing each other, but from her joyful, guilty face it was evident that these meetings were not accidental. One evening, when we were playing billiards, the doctor said to me:

" I say, why don't you go and see Miss Dolzhikov? You don't know Mariya Viktorovna; she is a clever creature, a charmer, a simple, good-natured soul."

I described how her father had received me in the spring.

" Nonsense !" laughed the doctor, " the engineer's one thing and she's another. Really, my dear fellow, you mustn't be nasty to her; go and see her sometimes. For instance, let's go and see her to-morrow evening. What do you say ?"

He persuaded me. The next evening I put on my new serge trousers, and in some agitation I set off to Miss Dolzhikov's. The footman did not seem so haughty and terrible, nor the furniture so gorgeous, as on that morning when I had come to ask a favour. Mariya Viktorovna was expecting me, and she received me like an old acquaintance, shaking hands with me in a friendly way. She was wearing a grey cloth dress with full sleeves, and had her hair done in the style which we used to call " dogs' ears," when it came into fashion in the town a year before. The hair was combed down over the ears, and this made Mariya Viktorovna's face look broader, and she seemed to me this time very much like her father, whose face was broad and red, with something in its expression like a sledge-driver. She was handsome and elegant, but not youthful looking; she looked thirty, though in reality she was not more than twenty-five.

" Dear Doctor, how grateful I am to him," she
said, making me sit down. " If it hadn't been
for him you wouldn't have come to see me. I am
bored to death ! My father has gone away and
left me alone, and I don't know what to do with
myself in this town."

Then she began asking me where I was working
now, how much I earned, where I lived.

" Do you spend on yourself nothing but what
you earn ?" she asked.

" No."

" Happy man !" she sighed. " All the evil
in life, it seems to me, comes from idleness, boredom,
and spiritual emptiness, and all that is inevitable
when one is accustomed to living at other people's
expense. Don't think I am showing off, I tell
you truthfully: it is not interesting or pleasant
to be rich. ' Make to yourselves friends of the
mammon of unrighteousness ' is said, because there
is not and cannot be a mammon that's righteous."

She looked round at the furniture with a grave,
cold expression, as though she wanted to count it
over, and went on:

" Comfort and luxury have a magical power;
little by little they draw into their clutches even
strong-willed people. At one time father and I
lived simply, not in a rich style, but now you
see how ! It is something monstrous," she said,
shrugging her shoulders; " we spend up to twenty
thousand a year ! In the provinces !"

" One comes to look at comfort and luxury as the
invariable privilege of capital and education,"
I said, " and it seems to me that the comforts of

240

life may be combined with any sort of labour, even the hardest and dirtiest. Your father is rich, and yet he says himself that it has been his lot to be a mechanic and an oiler."

She smiled and shook her head doubtfully: "My father sometimes eats bread dipped in kvass," she said. "It's a fancy, a whim!"

At that moment there was a ring and she got up.

"The rich and well-educated ought to work like everyone else," she said, "and if there is comfort it ought to be equal for all. There ought not to be any privileges. But that's enough philosophizing. Tell me something amusing. Tell me about the painters. What are they like? Funny?"

The doctor came in; I began telling them about the painters, but, being unaccustomed to talking, I was constrained, and described them like an ethnologist, gravely and tediously. The doctor, too, told us some anecdotes of working men: he staggered about, shed tears, dropped on his knees, and, even, mimicking a drunkard, lay on the floor; it was as good as a play, and Mariya Viktorovna laughed till she cried as she looked at him. Then he played on the piano and sang in his thin, pleasant tenor, while Mariya Viktorovna stood by and picked out what he was to sing, and corrected him when he made a mistake.

"I've heard that you sing, too?" I enquired.

"Sing, too!" cried the doctor in horror. "She sings exquisitely, a perfect artist, and you talk of her ' singing too '! What an idea!"

"I did study in earnest at one time," she said,

answering my question, " but now I have given it up."

Sitting on a low stool she told us of her life in Petersburg, and mimicked some celebrated singers, imitating their voice and manner of singing. She made a sketch of the doctor in her album, then of me; she did not draw well, but both the portraits were like us. She laughed, and was full of mischief and charming grimaces, and this suited her better than talking about the mammon of unrighteousness, and it seemed to me that she had been talking just before about wealth and luxury, not in earnest, but in imitation of someone. She was a superb comic actress. I mentally compared her with our young ladies, and even the handsome, dignified Anyuta Blagovo could not stand comparison with her; the difference was immense, like the difference between a beautiful, cultivated rose and a wild briar.

We had supper together, the three of us. The doctor and Mariya Viktorovna drank red wine, champagne, and coffee with brandy in it; they clinked glasses and drank to friendship, to enlightenment, to progress, to liberty, and they did not get drunk but only flushed, and were continually, for no reason, laughing till they cried. So as not to be tiresome I drank claret too.

" Talented, richly endowed natures," said Miss Dolzhikov, " know how to live, and go their own way; mediocre people, like myself for instance, know nothing and can do nothing of themselves; there is nothing left for them but to discern some

242

deep social movement, and to float where they are carried by it."

" How can one discern what doesn't exist ?" asked the doctor.

" We think so because we don't see it."

" Is that so ? The social movements are the invention of the new literature. There are none among us."

An argument began.

" There are no deep social movements among us and never have been," the doctor declared loudly. " There is no end to what the new literature has invented ! It has invented intellectual workers in the country, and you may search through all our villages and find at the most some lout in a reefer jacket or a black frock-coat who will make four mistakes in spelling a word of three letters. Cultured life has not yet begun among us. There's the same savagery, the same uniform boorishness, the same triviality, as five hundred years ago. Movements, currents there have been, but it has all been petty, paltry, bent upon vulgar and mercenary interests—and one cannot see anything important in them. If you think you have discerned a deep social movement, and in following it you devote yourself to tasks in the modern taste, such as the emancipation of insects from slavery or abstinence from beef rissoles, I congratulate you, Madam. We must study, and study, and study, and we must wait a bit with our deep, social movements; we are not mature enough for them yet; and to tell the truth, we don't know anything about them."

243

"You don't know anything about them, but I do," said Mariya Viktorovna. "Goodness, how tiresome you are to-day!"

"Our duty is to study and to study, to try to accumulate as much knowledge as possible, for genuine social movements arise where there is knowledge; and the happiness of mankind in the future lies only in knowledge. I drink to science!"

"There is no doubt about one thing: one must organize one's life somehow differently," said Mariya Viktorovna, after a moment's silence and thought. "Life, such as it has been hitherto, is not worth having. Don't let us talk about it."

As we came away from her the cathedral clock struck two.

"Did you like her?" asked the doctor; "she's nice, isn't she?"

On Christmas day we dined with Mariya Viktorovna, and all through the holidays we went to see her almost every day. There was never anyone there but ourselves, and she was right when she said that she had no friends in the town but the doctor and me. We spent our time for the most part in conversation; sometimes the doctor brought some book or magazine and read aloud to us. In reality he was the first well-educated man I had met in my life: I cannot judge whether he knew a great deal, but he always displayed his knowledge as though he wanted other people to share it. When he talked about anything relating to medicine he was not like any one of the doctors in our town, but made a fresh, peculiar impression upon me, and I fancied that if he liked he might have become a real man of science. And he was perhaps the only person who had a real influence upon me at that time. Seeing him, and reading the books he gave me, I began little by little to feel a thirst for the knowledge which would have given significance to my cheerless labour. It seemed strange to me, for instance, that I had not known till then that the whole world was made up of sixty elements, I had not known what oil was, what paints were, and that I could have got on without knowing these things. My acquaintance with the doctor elevated me morally too. I was continually arguing with him and, though I usually remained of my own opinion, yet, thanks to him, I began to perceive that everything was not clear to me, and I began trying to work out as far as I could definite convictions in myself, that the dictates of conscience might be definite, and that there might be nothing vague in my mind. Yet, though he was the most cultivated and best man in the town, he was nevertheless far from perfection. In his manners, in his habit of turning every conversation into an argument, in his pleasant tenor, even in his friendliness, there was something coarse, like a divinity student, and when he took off his coat and sat in his silk shirt, or flung a tip to a waiter in the restaurant, I always fancied that culture might be all very well, but the Tatar was fermenting in him still.

At Epiphany he went back to Petersburg. He went off in the morning, and after dinner my sister came in. Without taking off her fur coat and her cap she sat down in silence, very pale, and kept her eyes fixed on the same spot. She was chilled by the frost and one could see that she was upset by it.

" You must have caught cold," I said.

Her eyes filled with tears; she got up and went out to Karpovna without saying a word to me, as though I had hurt her feelings. And a little later I heard her saying, in a tone of bitter reproach:

" Nurse, what have I been living for till now ? What ? Tell me, haven't I wasted my youth ? All the best years of my life to know nothing but keeping accounts, pouring out tea, counting the halfpence, entertaining visitors, and thinking there was nothing better in the world ! Nurse, do understand, I have the cravings of a human being, and I want to live, and they have turned me into something like a housekeeper. It's horrible, horrible !"

She flung her keys towards the door, and they fell with a jingle into my room. They were the keys of the sideboard, of the kitchen cupboard, of the cellar, and of the tea-caddy, the keys which my mother used to carry.

" Oh, merciful heavens !" cried the old woman in horror. " Holy Saints above !"

Before going home my sister came into my room to pick up the keys, and said:

" You must forgive me. Something queer has happened to me lately."

VIII.

On returning home late one evening from Mariya Viktorovna's I found waiting in my room a young police inspector in a new uniform; he was sitting at my table, looking through my books.

"At last," he said, getting up and stretching himself. "This is the third time I have been to you. The Governor commands you to present yourself before him at nine o'clock in the morning. Without fail."

He took from me a signed statement that I would act upon his Excellency's command, and went away. This late visit of the police inspector and unexpected invitation to the Governor's had an overwhelmingly oppressive effect upon me. From my earliest childhood I have felt terror-stricken in the presence of gendarmes, policemen, and law court officials, and now I was tormented by uneasiness, as though I were really guilty in some way. And I could not get to sleep. My nurse and Prokofy were also upset and could not sleep. My nurse had earache too; she moaned, and several times began crying with pain. Hearing that I was awake, Prokofy came into my room with a lamp and sat down at the table.

"You ought to have a drink of pepper cordial," he said, after a moment's thought. "If one does have a drink in this vale of tears it does no harm. And if Mamma were to pour a little pepper cordial in her ear it would do her a lot of good."

Between two and three he was going to the

slaughter-house for the meat. I knew I should not sleep till morning now, and to get through the time till nine o'clock I went with him. We walked with a lantern, while his boy Nikolka, aged thirteen, with blue patches on his cheeks from frostbites, a regular young brigand to judge by his expression, drove after us in the sledge, urging on the horse in a husky voice.

" I suppose they will punish you at the Governor's," Prokofy said to me on the way. " There are rules of the trade for governors, and rules for the higher clergy, and rules for the officers, and rules for the doctors, and every class has its rules. But you haven't kept to your rules, and you can't be allowed."

The slaughter-house was behind the cemetery, and till then I had only seen it in the distance. It consisted of three gloomy barns, surrounded by a grey fence, and when the wind blew from that quarter on hot days in summer, it brought a stifling stench from them. Now going into the yard in the dark I did not see the barns; I kept coming across horses and sledges, some empty, some loaded up with meat. Men were walking about with lanterns, swearing in a disgusting way. Prokofy and Nikolka swore just as revoltingly, and the air was in a continual uproar with swearing, coughing, and the neighing of horses.

There was a smell of dead bodies and of dung. It was thawing, the snow was changing into mud; and in the darkness it seemed to me that I was walking through pools of blood.

Having piled up the sledges full of meat we

set off to the butcher's shop in the market. It began to get light. Cooks with baskets and elderly ladies in mantles came along one after another, Prokofy, with a chopper in his hand, in a white apron spattered with blood, swore fearful oaths, crossed himself at the church, shouted aloud for the whole market to hear, that he was giving away the meat at cost price and even at a loss to himself. He gave short weight and short change, the cooks saw that, but, deafened by his shouts, did not protest, and only called him a hangman. Brandishing and bringing down his terrible chopper he threw himself into picturesque attitudes, and each time uttered the sound " Geck " with a ferocious expression, and I was afraid he really would chop off somebody's head or hand.

I spent all the morning in the butcher's shop, and when at last I went to the Governor's, my overcoat smelt of meat and blood. My state of mind was as though I were being sent spear in hand to meet a bear. I remember the tall staircase with a striped carpet on it, and the young official, with shiny buttons, who mutely motioned me to the door with both hands, and ran to announce me. I went into a hall luxuriously but frigidly and tastelessly furnished, and the high, narrow mirrors in the spaces between the walls, and the bright yellow window curtains, struck the eye particularly unpleasantly. One could see that the governors were changed, but the furniture remained the same. Again the young official motioned me with both hands to the door, and I went up to a big green table at which a military

general, with the Order of Vladimir on his breast,
was standing.

"Mr. Poloznev, I have asked you to come," he
began, holding a letter in his hand, and opening
his mouth wide like a round "o," "I have asked
you to come here to inform you of this. Your
highly respected father has appealed by letter
and by word of mouth to the Marshal of the
Nobility begging him to summon you, and to lay
before you the inconsistency of your behaviour
with the rank of the nobility to which you have
the honour to belong. His Excellency Alexandr
Pavlovitch, justly supposing that your conduct
might serve as a bad example, and considering
that mere persuasion on his part would not be
sufficient, but that official intervention in earnest
was essential, presents me here in this letter with
his views in regard to you, which I share."

He said this, quietly, respectfully, standing
erect, as though I were his superior officer and
looking at me with no trace of severity. His face
looked worn and wizened, and was all wrinkles;
there were bags under his eyes; his hair was dyed;
and it was impossible to tell from his appearance
how old he was—forty or sixty.

"I trust," he went on, "that you appreciate
the delicacy of our honoured Alexandr Pavlovitch,
who has addressed himself to me not officially,
but privately. I, too, have asked you to come
here unofficially, and I am speaking to you, not
as a Governor, but from a sincere regard for your
father. And so I beg you either to alter your
line of conduct and return to duties in keeping

with your rank, or to avoid setting a bad example,
remove to another district where you are not
known, and where you can follow any occupation
you please. In the other case, I shall be forced
to take extreme measures."

He stood for half a minute in silence, looking at
me with his mouth open.

" Are you a vegetarian ?" he asked.

" No, your Excellency, I eat meat."

He sat down and drew some papers towards
him. I bowed and went out.

It was not worth while now to go to work
before dinner. I went home to sleep, but could
not sleep from an unpleasant, sickly feeling, induced
by the slaughter-house and my conversation with
the Governor, and when the evening came I went,
gloomy and out of sorts, to Mariya Viktorovna.
I told her how I had been at the Governor's,
while she stared at me in perplexity as though
she did not believe it, then suddenly began
laughing gaily, loudly, irrepressibly, as only good-
natured, laughter-loving people can.

" If only one could tell that in Petersburg !"
she brought out, almost falling over with laughter,
and propping herself against the table. " If one
could tell that in Petersburg !"

IX.

Now we used to see each other often, sometimes
twice a day. She used to come to the cemetery
almost every day after dinner, and read the epitaphs
on the crosses and tombstones while she waited

for me. Sometimes she would come into the church, and, standing by me, would look on while I worked. The stillness, the naïve work of the painters and gilders, Radish's sage reflections, and the fact that I did not differ externally from the other workmen, and worked just as they did in my waistcoat with no socks on, and that I was addressed familiarly by them—all this was new to her and touched her. One day a workman, who was painting a dove on the ceiling, called out to me in her presence:

" Misail, hand me up the white paint."

I took him the white paint, and afterwards, when I let myself down by the frail scaffolding, she looked at me, touched to tears and smiling.

" What a dear you are !" she said.

I remembered from my childhood how a green parrot, belonging to one of the rich men of the town, had escaped from its cage, and how for quite a month afterwards the beautiful bird had haunted the town, flying from garden to garden, homeless and solitary. Mariya Viktorovna reminded me of that bird.

" There is positively nowhere for me to go now but the cemetery," she said to me with a laugh. " The town has become disgustingly dull. At the Azhogins' they are still reciting, singing, lisping. I have grown to detest them of late; your sister is an unsociable creature; Mademoiselle Blagovo hates me for some reason. I don't care for the theatre. Tell me where am I to go ?"

When I went to see her I smelt of paint and turpentine, and my hands were stained—and she liked that; she wanted me to come to her in my ordinary working clothes; but in her drawing-room those clothes made me feel awkward. I felt embarrassed, as though I were in uniform, so I always put on my new serge trousers when I went to her. And she did not like that.

"You must own you are not quite at home in your new character," she said to me one day. "Your workman's dress does not feel natural to you; you are awkward in it. Tell me, isn't that because you haven't a firm conviction, and are not satisfied? The very kind of work you have chosen—your painting—surely it does not satisfy you, does it?" she asked, laughing. "I know paint makes things look nicer and last longer, but those things belong to rich people who live in towns, and after all they are luxuries. Besides, you have often said yourself that everybody ought to get his bread by the work of his own hands, yet you get money and not bread. Why shouldn't you keep to the literal sense of your words? You ought to be getting bread, that is, you ought to be ploughing, sowing, reaping, threshing, or doing something which has a direct connection with agriculture, for instance, looking after cows, digging, building huts of logs. . . ."

She opened a pretty cupboard that stood near her writing-table, and said:

"I am saying all this to you because I want to let you into my secret. *Voilà!* This is my agricultural library. Here I have fields, kitchen garden and orchard, and cattleyard and beehives. I read them greedily, and have already learnt all the theory to the tiniest detail. My dream, my darling wish, is to go to our Dubetchnya as soon as March is here. It's marvellous there, exquisite, isn't it ? The first year I shall have a look round and get into things, and the year after I shall begin to work properly myself, putting my back into it as they say. My father has promised to give me Dubetchnya, and I shall do exactly what I like with it.'

Flushed, excited to tears, and laughing, she dreamed aloud how she would live at Dubetchnya, and what an interesting life it would be ! I envied her. March was near, the days were growing longer and longer, and on bright sunny days water dripped from the roofs at midday, and there was a fragrance of spring; I, too, longed for the country.

And when she said that she should move to Dubetchnya, I realized vividly that I should remain in the town alone, and I felt that I envied her with her cupboard of books and her agriculture. I knew nothing of work on the land, and did not like it, and I should have liked to have told her that work on the land was slavish toil, but I remembered that something similar had been said more than once by my father, and I held my tongue.

Lent began. Viktor Ivanitch, whose existence I had begun to forget, arrived from Petersburg. He arrived unexpectedly, without even a telegram to say he was coming. When I went in, as usual, in the evening, he was walking about the drawing-room, telling some story, with his face freshly washed and shaven, looking ten years younger: his daughter was kneeling on the floor, taking out of his trunks boxes, bottles, and books, and handing them to Pavel the footman. I involuntarily drew back a step when I saw the engineer, but he held out both hands to me and said, smiling, showing his strong white teeth that looked like a sledge-driver's:

" Here he is, here he is ! Very glad to see you, Mr. House-painter ! ·Masha has told me all about it; she has been singing your praises. I quite understand and approve," he went on, taking my arm. " To be a good workman is ever so much more honest and more sensible than wasting govern-ment paper and wearing a cockade on your head. I myself worked in Belgium with these very hands and then spent two years as a mechanic. . . ."

He was wearing a short reefer jacket and indoor slippers; he walked like a man with the gout, rolling slightly from side to side and rubbing his hands. Humming something he softly purred and hugged himself with satisfaction at being at home again at last, and able to have his beloved shower bath.

" There is no disputing," he said to me at supper, " there is no disputing; you are all nice and charming people, but for some reason, as soon as you take to manual labour, or go in for saving the peasants, in the long run it all comes to no more than being a dissenter. Aren't you a dissenter ? Here you don't take vodka. What's the meaning of that if it is not being a dissenter ?"

To satisfy him I drank some vodka and I drank

some wine, too. We tasted the cheese, the sausage, the pâtés, the pickles, and the savouries of all sorts that the engineer had brought with him, and the wine that had come in his absence from abroad. The wine was first-rate. For some reason the engineer got wine and cigars from abroad without paying duty; the caviare and the dried sturgeon someone sent him for nothing; he did not pay rent for his flat as the owner of the house provided the kerosene for the line; and altogether he and his daughter produced on me the impression that all the best in the world was at their service, and provided for them for nothing.

I went on going to see them, but not with the same eagerness. The engineer made me feel constrained, and in his presence I did not feel free. I could not face his clear, guileless eyes, his reflections wearied and sickened me; I was sickened, too, by the memory that so lately I had been in the employment of this red-faced, well-fed man, and that he had been brutally rude to me. It is true that he put his arm round my waist, slapped me on the shoulder in a friendly way, approved my manner of life, but I felt that, as before, he despised my insignificance, and only put up with me to please his daughter, and I couldn't now laugh and talk as I liked, and I behaved unsociably and kept expecting that in another minute he would address me as Panteley as he did his footman Pavel. How my pride as a provincial and a working man was revolted. I, a proletarian, a house painter, went every day to rich people who were alien to me, and whom the whole town regarded as though they were foreigners, and every day I drank costly wines with them and ate unusual dainties—my conscience refused to be reconciled to it! On my way to the house I sullenly avoided meeting people, and looked at them from under my brows as though I really were a dissenter, and when I was going home from the engineer's I was ashamed of my well-fed condition.

Above all I was afraid of being carried away. Whether I was walking along the street, or working, or talking to the other fellows, I was all the time thinking of one thing only, of going in the evening to see Mariya Viktorovna and was picturing her voice, her laugh, her movements. When I was getting ready to go to her I always spent a long time before my nurse's warped looking-glass, as I fastened my tie; my serge trousers were detestable in my eyes, and I suffered torments, and at the same time despised myself for being so trivial. When she called to me out of the other room that she was not dressed and asked me to wait, I listened to her dressing; it agitated me, I felt as though the ground were giving way under my feet. And when I saw a woman's figure in the street, even at a distance, I invariably compared it. It seemed to me that all our girls and women were vulgar, that they were absurdly dressed, and did not know how to hold themselves; and these comparisons aroused a feeling of pride in me: Mariya Viktorovna was the best of them all! And I dreamed of her and myself at night.

One evening at supper with the engineer we ate a whole lobster. As I was going home afterwards

I remembered that the engineer twice called me
" My dear fellow " at supper, and I reflected that
they treated me very kindly in that house, as they
might an unfortunate big dog who had been
kicked out by its owners, that they were amusing
themselves with me, and that when they were
tired of me they would turn me out like a dog. I
felt ashamed and wounded, wounded to the point
of tears as though I had been insulted, and looking
up at the sky I took a vow to put an end to all this.

The next day I did not go to the Dolzhikovs'.
Late in the evening, when it was quite dark and
raining, I walked along Great Dvoryansky Street,
looking up at the windows. Everyone was asleep
at the Azhogins', and the only light was in one
of the furthest windows. It was Madame
Azhogin in her own room, sewing by the light
of three candles, imagining that she was combating
superstition. Our house was in darkness, but
at the Dolzhikovs', on the contrary, the windows
were lighted up, but one could distinguish nothing
through the flowers and the curtains. I kept
walking up and down the street; the cold March
rain drenched me through. I heard my father
come home from the club; he stood knocking at
the gate. A minute later a light appeared at
the window, and I saw my sister, who was hastening
down with a lamp, while with the other hand she
was twisting her thick hair together as she went.
Then my father walked about the drawing-room,
talking and rubbing his hands, while my sister
sat in a low chair, thinking and not listening
to what he said.

But then they went away; the light went out. . . . I glanced round at the engineer's, and there, too, all was darkness now. In the dark and the rain I felt hopelessly alone, abandoned to the whims of destiny; I felt that all my doings, my desires, and everything I had thought and said till then were trivial in comparison with my loneliness, in comparison with my present suffering, and the suffering that lay before me in the future. Alas, the thoughts and doings of living creatures are not nearly so significant as their sufferings ! And without clearly realizing what I was doing, I pulled at the bell of the Dolzhikovs' gate, broke it, and ran along the street like some naughty boy, with a feeling of terror in my heart, expecting every moment that they would come out and recognize me. When I stopped at the end of the street to take breath I could hear nothing but the sound of the rain, and somewhere in the distance a watchman striking on a sheet of iron.

For a whole week I did not go to the Dolzhikovs'. My serge trousers were sold. There was nothing doing in the painting trade. I knew the pangs of hunger again, and earned from twopence to fourpence a day, where I could, by heavy and unpleasant work. Struggling up to my knees in the cold mud, straining my chest, I tried to stifle my memories, and, as it were, to punish myself for the cheeses and preserves with which I had been regaled at the engineer's. But all the same, as soon as I lay in bed, wet and hungry, my sinful imagination immediately began to paint exquisite, seductive pictures, and with amazement I acknowledged to myself that I was in love, passionately in love, and I fell into a sound, heavy sleep, feeling that hard labour only made my body stronger and younger.

One evening snow began falling most inappropriately, and the wind blew from the north as though winter had come back again. When I returned from work that evening I found Mariya Viktorovna in my room. She was sitting in her fur coat, and had both hands in her muff.

" Why don't you come to see me ?" she asked, raising her clear, clever eyes, and I was utterly confused with delight and stood stiffly upright before her, as I used to stand facing my father when he was going to beat me; she looked into my face and I could see from her eyes that she understood why I was confused.

" Why don't you come to see me ?" she repeated. " If you don't want to come, you see, I have come to you."

She got up and came close to me.

" Don't desert me," she said, and her eyes filled with tears. " I am alone, utterly alone."

She began crying; and, hiding her face in her muff, articulated:

" Alone ! My life is hard, very hard, and in all the world I have no one but you. Don't desert me !"

Looking for a handkerchief to wipe her tears she smiled; we were silent for some time, then I put my arms round her and kissed her, scratching my cheek till it bled with her hatpin as I did it.

260

And we began talking to each other as though we had been on the closest terms for ages and ages.

X.

Two days later she sent me to Dubetchnya and I was unutterably delighted to go. As I walked towards the station and afterwards, as I was sitting in the train, I kept laughing from no apparent cause, and people looked at me as though I were drunk. Snow was falling, and there were still frosts in the mornings, but the roads were already dark-coloured and rooks hovered over them, cawing.

At first I had intended to fit up an abode for us two, Masha and me, in the lodge at the side opposite Madame Tcheprakov's lodge, but it appeared that the doves and the ducks had been living there for a long time, and it was impossible to clean it without destroying a great number of nests. There was nothing for it but to live in the comfortless rooms of the big house with the sunblinds. The peasants called the house the palace; there were more than twenty rooms in it, and the only furniture was a piano and a child's arm-chair lying in the attic. And if Masha had brought all her furniture from the town we should even then have been unable to get rid of the impression of immense emptiness and cold. I picked out three small rooms with windows looking into the garden, and worked from early morning till night, setting them to rights, putting in new panes, papering the walls, filling up the holes and chinks in the floors. It was easy, pleasant work. I was continually running to the river to see whether the ice were not going; I kept fancying that starlings were flying. And at night, thinking of Masha, I listened with an unutterably sweet feeling, with clutching delight to the noise of the rats and the wind droning and knocking above the ceiling. It seemed as though some old house spirit were coughing in the attic.

The snow was deep; a great deal had fallen even at the end of March, but it melted quickly, as, though by magic, and the spring floods passed in a tumultuous rush, so that by the beginning of April the starlings were already noisy, and yellow butterflies were flying in the garden. It was exquisite weather. Every day, towards evening, I used to walk to the town to meet Masha, and what a delight it was to walk with bare feet along the gradually drying, still soft road. Half-way I used to sit down and look towards the town, not venturing to go near it. The sight of it troubled me. I kept wondering how the people I knew would behave to me when they heard of my love. What would my father say ? What troubled me particularly was the thought that my life was more complicated, and that I had completely lost all power to set it right, and that, like a balloon, it was bearing me away, God knows whither. I no longer considered the problem how to earn my daily bread, how to live, but thought about—I really don't know what.

Masha used to come in a carriage; I used to get

in with her, and we drove to Dubetchnya, feeling light-hearted and free. Or, after waiting till the sun had set, I would go back dissatisfied and dreary, wondering why Masha had not come; at the gate or in the garden I would be met by a sweet, unexpected apparition—it was she! It would turn out that she had come by rail, and had walked from the station. What a festival it was! In a simple woollen dress with a kerchief on her head, with a modest sunshade, but laced in, slender, in expensive foreign boots—it was a talented actress playing the part of a little workgirl. We looked round our domain and decided which should be her room, and which mine, where we would have our avenue, our kitchen garden, our beehives.

We already had hens, ducks, and geese, which we loved because they were ours. We had, all ready for sowing, oats, clover, timothy grass, buckwheat, and vegetable seeds, and we always looked at all these stores and discussed at length the crop we might get; and everything Masha said to me seemed extraordinarily clever, and fine. This was the happiest time of my life.

Soon after St. Thomas's week we were married at our parish church in the village of Kurilovka, two miles from Dubetchnya. Masha wanted everything to be done quietly; at her wish our " best men " were peasant lads, the sacristan sang alone, and we came back from the church in a small, jolting chaise which she drove herself. Our only guest from the town was my sister Kleopatra, to whom Masha sent a note three days before the wedding. My sister came in a white dress and

wore gloves. During the wedding she cried
quietly from joy and tenderness. Her expression
was motherly and infinitely kind. She was intoxicated with our happiness, and smiled as though
she were absorbing a sweet delirium, and, looking
at her during our wedding, I realized that for her
there was nothing in the world higher than love,
earthly love, and that she was dreaming of it
secretly, timidly, but continually and passionately.
She embraced and kissed Masha, and, not knowing
how to express her rapture, said to her of me: " He
is good ! He is very good !"

Before she went away she changed into her
ordinary dress, and drew me into the garden to talk
to me alone.

" Father is very much hurt," she said, " that
you have written nothing to him. You ought to
have asked for his blessing. But in reality he is very
much pleased. He says that this marriage will
raise you in the eyes of all society, and that under
the influence of Mariya Viktorovna you will begin
to take a more serious view of life. We talk of
nothing but you in the evenings now, and yesterday
he actually used the expression: ' Our Misail.'
That pleased me. It seems as though he had some
plan in his mind, and I fancy he wants to set you
an example of magnanimity and be the first to
speak of reconciliation. It is very possible he
may come here to see you in a day or two."

She hurriedly made the sign of the cross over me
several times and said:

" Well, God be with you. Be happy. Anyuta
Blagovo is a very clever girl; she says about your

marriage that God is sending you a fresh ordeal. To be sure—married life does not bring only joy but suffering too. That's bound to be so."

Masha and I walked a couple of miles to see her on her way; we walked back slowly and in silence, as though we were resting. Masha held my hand, my heart felt light, and I had no inclination to talk about love; we had become closer and more akin now that we were married, and we felt that nothing now could separate us.

" Your sister is a nice creature," said Masha, " but it seems as though she had been tormented for years. Your father must be a terrible man."

I began telling her how my sister and I had been brought up, and what a senseless torture our childhood had really been. When she heard how my father had so lately beaten me, she shuddered and drew closer to me.

" Don't tell me any more," she said. " It's horrible !"

Now she never left me. We lived together in the three rooms in the big house, and in the evenings we bolted the door which led to the empty part of the house, as though someone were living there whom we did not know, and were afraid of. I got up early, at dawn, and immediately set to work of some sort. I mended the carts, made paths in the garden, dug the flower beds, painted the roof of the house. When the time came to sow the oats I tried to plough the ground over again, to harrow and to sow, and I did it all conscientiously, keeping up with our labourer; I was worn out, the rain and the cold wind made my face and feet burn for hours afterwards. I dreamed of ploughed land at night. But field labour did not attract me. I did not understand farming, and I did not care for it; it was perhaps because my forefathers had not been tillers of the soil, and the very blood that flowed in my veins was purely of the city. I loved nature tenderly; I loved the fields and meadows and kitchen gardens, but the peasant who turned up the soil with his plough and urged on his pitiful horse, wet and tattered, with his craning neck, was to me the expression of coarse, savage, ugly force, and every time I looked at his uncouth movements I involuntarily began thinking of the legendary life of the remote past, before men knew the use of fire. The fierce bull that ran with the peasants' herd, and the horses, when they dashed about the village, stamping their hoofs, moved me to fear, and everything rather big, strong, and angry, whether it was the ram with its horns, the gander, or the yard-dog, seemed to me the expression of the same coarse, savage force. This mood was particularly strong in me in bad weather, when heavy clouds were hanging over the black ploughed land. Above all, when I was ploughing or sowing, and two or three people stood looking how I was doing it, I had not the feeling that this work was inevitable and obligatory, and it seemed to me that I was amusing myself. I preferred doing something in the yard, and there was nothing I liked so much as painting the roof.

I used to walk through the garden and the meadow to our mill. It was let to a peasant of Kurilovka called Stepan, a handsome, dark fellow with a thick black beard, who looked very strong. He did not like the miller's work, and looked upon it as dreary and unprofitable, and only lived at the mill in order not to live at home. He was a leather-worker, and was always surrounded by a pleasant smell of tar and leather. He was not fond of talking, he was listless and sluggish, and was always sitting in the doorway or on the river bank, humming "oo-loo-loo." His wife and mother-in-law, both white-faced, languid, and meek, used sometimes to come from Kurilovka to see him; they made low bows to him and addressed him formally, "Stepan Petrovitch," while he went on sitting on the river bank, softly humming "oo-loo-loo," without responding by word or movement to their bows. One hour and then a second would pass in silence. His mother-in-law and wife, after whispering together, would get up and gaze at him for some time, expecting him to look round; then they would make a low bow, and in sugary, chanting voices, say:

"Good-bye, Stepan Petrovitch!"

And they would go away. After that Stepan, picking up the parcel they had left, containing cracknels or a shirt, would heave a sigh and say, winking in their direction:

"The female sex!"

The mill with two sets of millstones worked day and night. I used to help Stepan; I liked the work, and when he went off I was glad to stay and take his place.

XI.

After bright warm weather came a spell of wet; all May it rained and was cold. The sound of the millwheels and of the rain disposed one to indolence and slumber. The floor trembled, there was a smell of flour, and that, too, induced drowsiness. My wife in a short fur-lined jacket, and in men's high golosh boots, would make her appearance twice a day, and she always said the same thing:

" And this is called summer! Worse than it was in October !"

We used to have tea and make the porridge together, or we would sit for hours at a stretch without speaking, waiting for the rain to stop. Once, when Stepan had gone off to the fair, Masha stayed all night at the mill. When we got up we could not tell what time it was, as the rainclouds covered the whole sky; but sleepy cocks were crowing at Dubetchnya, and landrails were calling in the meadows; it was still very, very early. . . . My wife and I went down to the millpond and drew out the net which Stepan had thrown in over night in our presence. A big pike was struggling in it, and a cray-fish was twisting about, clawing upwards with its pincers.

" Let them go," said Masha. " Let them be happy too."

Because we got up so early and afterwards did nothing, that day seemed very long, the longest day in my life. Towards evening Stepan came back and I went home.

" Your father came to-day," said Masha.

" Where is he ?" I asked.

" He has gone away. I would not see him."

Seeing that I remained standing and silent, that I was sorry for my father, she said:

" One must be consistent. I would not see him, and sent word to him not to trouble to come and see us again."

A minute later I was out at the gate and walking to the town to explain things to my father. It was muddy, slippery, cold. For the first time since my marriage I felt suddenly sad, and in my brain, exhausted by that long grey day, there was stirring the thought that perhaps I was not living as I ought. I was worn out; little by little I was overcome by despondency and indolence, I did not want to move or think, and after going on a little I gave it up with a wave of my hand and turned back.

The engineer in a leather overcoat with a hood was standing in the middle of the yard.

" Where's the furniture ? There used to be lovely furniture in the Empire style: there used to be pictures, there used to be vases, while now you could play ball in it ! I bought the place with the furniture. The devil take her !"

Moisey, a thin pock-marked fellow of twenty-five, with insolent little eyes, who was in the service of the general's widow, stood near him crumpling up his cap in his hands; one of his cheeks was bigger than the other, as though he had lain too long on it.

" Your honour was graciously pleased to buy

the place without the furniture," he brought out irresolutely, " I remember."

" Hold your tongue !" shouted the engineer; he turned crimson and shook with anger . . . and the echo in the garden loudly repeated his shout.

XII.

When I was doing anything in the garden or the yard, Moisey would stand beside me, and folding his arms behind his back he would stand lazily and impudently staring at me with his little eyes. And this irritated me to such a degree that I threw up my work and went away.

From Stepan we heard that Moisey was Madame Tcheprakov's lover. I noticed that when people came to her to borrow money they addressed themselves first to Moisey, and once I saw a peasant, black from head to foot—he must have been a coalheaver—bow down at Moisey's feet. Sometimes, after a little whispering, he gave out money himself, without consulting his mistress, from which I concluded that he did a little business on his own account.

He used to shoot in our garden under our windows, carried off victuals from our cellar, borrowed our horses without asking permission, and we were indignant and began to feel as though Dubetchnya were not ours, and Masha would say, turning pale:

" Can we really have to go on living with these reptiles another eighteen months ?"

Madame Tcheprakov's son, Ivan, was serving

as a guard on our railway-line. He had grown much thinner and feebler during the winter, so that a single glass was enough to make him drunk, and he shivered out of the sunshine. He wore the guard's uniform with aversion and was ashamed of it, but considered his post a good one, as he could steal the candles and sell them. My new position excited in him a mixed feeling of wonder, envy, and a vague hope that something of the same sort might happen to him. He used to watch Masha with ecstatic eyes, ask me what I had for dinner now, and his lean and ugly face wore a sad and sweetish expression, and he moved his fingers as though he were feeling my happiness with them.

"Listen, Better-than-nothing," he said fussily, relighting his cigarette at every instant; there was always a litter where he stood, for he wasted dozens of matches, lighting one cigarette. "Listen, my life now is the nastiest possible. The worst of it is any subaltern can shout: ' Hi, there, guard !' I have overheard all sorts of things in the train, my boy, and do you know, I have learned that life's a beastly thing ! My mother has been the ruin of me ! A doctor in the train told me that if parents are immoral, their children are drunkards or criminals. Think of that !"

Once he came into the yard, staggering; his eyes gazed about blankly, his breathing was laboured; he laughed and cried and babbled as though in a high fever, and the only words I could catch in his muddled talk were, " My mother ! Where's my mother ?" which he uttered with a wail like a child who has lost his mother in a crowd. I led him into our garden and laid him down under a tree, and Masha and I took turns to sit by him all that day and all night. He was very sick, and Masha looked with aversion at his pale, wet face, and said:

" Is it possible these reptiles will go on living another year and a half in our yard ? It's awful ! It's awful !"

And how many mortifications the peasants caused us ! How many bitter disappointments in those early days in the spring months, when we so longed to be happy. My wife built a school. I drew a plan of a school for sixty boys, and the Zemstvo Board approved of it, but advised us to build the school at Kurilovka the big village which was only two miles from us. Moreover, the school at Kurilovka in which children—from four villages, our Dubetchnya being one of the number—were taught, was old and too small, and the floor was scarcely safe to walk upon. At the end of March, at Masha's wish, she was appointed guardian of the Kurilovka school, and at the beginning of April we three times summoned the village assembly, and tried to persuade the peasants that their school was old and overcrowded, and that it was essential to build a new one. A member of the Zemstvo Board and the Inspector of Peasant Schools came, and they, too, tried to persuade them. After each meeting the peasants surrounded us, begging for a bucket of vodka; we were hot in the crowd; we were soon exhausted, and returned home dissatisfied and a little ill at ease.

In the end the peasants set apart a plot of ground for the school, and were obliged to bring all the building material from the town with their own horses. And the very first Sunday after the spring corn was sown carts set off from Kurilovka and Dubetchnya to fetch bricks for the foundations. They set off as soon as it was light, and came back late in the evening; the peasants were drunk, and said that they were worn out.

As ill-luck would have it, the rain and the cold persisted all through May. The road was in an awful state: it was deep in mud. The carts usually drove into our yard when they came back from the town—and what a horrible ordeal it was. A pot-bellied horse would appear at the gate, setting its front legs wide apart; it would stumble forward before coming into the yard; a beam, nine yards long, wet and slimy-looking, crept in on a waggon. Beside it, muffled up against the rain, strode a peasant with the skirts of his coat tucked up in his belt, not looking where he was going, but stepping through the puddles. Another cart would appear with boards, then a third with a beam, a fourth . . . and the space before our house was gradually crowded up with horses, beams, and planks. Men and women, with their heads muffled and their skirts tucked up, would stare angrily at our windows, make an uproar, and clamour for the mistress to come out to them; coarse oaths were audible. Meanwhile Moisey stood at one side, and we fancied he was enjoying our discomfiture.

"We are not going to cart any more," the

peasants would shout. " We are worn out ! Let her go and get the stuff herself."

Masha, pale and flustered, expecting every minute that they would break into the house, would send them out a half-pail of vodka; after that the noise would subside and the long beams, one after another, would crawl slowly out of the yard.

When I was setting off to see the building my wife was worried and said:

" The peasants are spiteful; I only hope they won't do you a mischief. Wait a minute, I'll come with you."

We drove to Kurilovka together, and there the carpenters asked us for a drink. The framework of the house was ready. It was time to lay the foundation, but the masons had not come; this caused delay, and the carpenters complained. And when at last the masons did come, it appeared that there was no sand; it had been somehow overlooked that it would be needed. Taking advantage of our helpless position, the peasants demanded thirty kopecks for each cartload, though the distance from the building to the river where they got the sand was less than a quarter of a mile, and more than five hundred cartloads were found to be necessary. There was no end to the misunderstandings, swearing, and importunity; my wife was indignant, and the foreman of the masons, Tit Petrov, an old man of seventy, took her by the arm, and said:

" You look here ! You look here ! You only bring me the sand; I set ten men on at once, and in two days it will be done ! You look here !"

But they brought the sand and two days passed, and four, and a week, and instead of the promised foundations there was still a yawning hole.

" It's enough to drive one out of one's senses," said my wife, in distress. " What people ! What people !"

In the midst of these disorderly doings the engineer arrived; he brought with him parcels of wine and savouries, and after a prolonged meal lay down for a nap in the verandah and snored so loudly that the labourers shook their heads and said: " Well !"

Masha was not pleased at his coming, she did not trust him, though at the same time she asked his advice. When, after sleeping too long after dinner, he got up in a bad humour and said unpleasant things about our management of the place, or expressed regret that he had bought Dubetchnya, which had already been a loss to him, poor Masha's face wore an expression of misery. She would complain to him, and he would yawn and say that the peasants ought to be flogged.

He called our marriage and our life a farce, and said it was a caprice, a whim.

" She has done something of the sort before," he said about Masha. " She once fancied herself a great opera singer and left me; I was looking for her for two months, and, my dear soul, I spent a thousand roubles on telegrams alone."

He no longer called me a dissenter or Mr. Painter, and did not as in the past express approval of my living like a workman, but said:

" You are a strange person ! You are not a

normal person! I won't venture to prophesy, but you will come to a bad end!"

And Masha slept badly at night, and was always sitting at our bedroom window thinking. There was no laughter at supper now, no charming grimaces. I was wretched and, when it rained, every drop that fell seemed to pierce my heart, like small shot, and I felt ready to fall on my knees before Masha and apologize for the weather. When the peasants made a noise in the yard I felt guilty also. For hours at a time I sat still in one place, thinking of nothing but what a splendid person Masha was, what a wonderful person. I loved her passionately, and I was fascinated by everything she did, everything she said. She had a bent for quiet studious pursuits; she was fond of reading for hours together, of studying. Although her knowledge of farming was only from books she surprised us all by what she knew; and every piece of advice she gave was of value; not one was ever thrown away; and, with all that, what nobility, what taste, what graciousness, that graciousness which is only found in well-educated people.

To this woman, with her sound, practical intelligence, the disorderly surroundings with petty cares and sordid anxieties in which we were living now were an agony: I saw that and could not sleep at night; my brain worked feverishly and I had a lump in my throat. I rushed about not knowing what to do.

I galloped to the town and brought Masha books, newspapers, sweets, flowers; with Stepan

I caught fish, wading for hours up to my neck in the cold water in the rain to catch eel-pout to vary our fare; I demeaned myself to beg the peasants not to make a noise; I plied them with vodka, bought them off, made all sorts of promises. And how many other foolish things I did !

At last the rain ceased, the earth dried. One would get up at four o'clock in the morning; one would go out into the garden—where there was dew sparkling on the flowers, the twitter of birds, the hum of insects, not one cloud in the sky; and the garden, the meadows, and the river were so lovely, yet there were memories of the peasants, of their carts, of the engineer. Masha and I drove out together in the racing droshky to the fields to look at the oats. She used to drive, I sat behind; her shoulders were raised and the wind played with her hair.

" Keep to the right !" she shouted to those she met.

" You are like a sledge-driver," I said to her one day.

" Maybe ! Why, my grandfather, the engineer's father, was a sledge-driver. Didn't you know that ?" she asked, turning to me, and at once she mimicked the way sledge-drivers shout and sing.

" And thank God for that," I thought as I listened to her. " Thank God."

And again memories of the peasants, of the carts, of the engineer. . . .

XIII.

Dr. Blagovo arrived on his bicycle. My sister began coming often. Again there were conversations about manual labour, about progress, about a mysterious millennium awaiting mankind in the remote future. The doctor did not like our farm-work, because it interfered with arguments, and said that ploughing, reaping, grazing calves were unworthy of a free man, and all these coarse forms of the struggle for existence men would in time relegate to animals and machines, while they would devote themselves exclusively to scientific investigation. My sister kept begging them to let her go home earlier, and if she stayed on till late in the evening, or spent the night with us, there would be no end to the agitation.

"Good Heavens, what a baby you are still!" said Masha reproachfully. "It is positively absurd."

"Yes, it is absurd," my sister agreed, "I know it's absurd; but what is to be done if I haven't the strength to get over it? I keep feeling as though I were doing wrong."

At haymaking I ached all over from the unaccustomed labour; in the evening, sitting on the verandah and talking with the others, I suddenly dropped asleep, and they laughed aloud at me. They waked me up and made me sit down to supper; I was overpowered with drowsiness, and I saw the lights, the faces, and the plates as it were in a dream, heard the voices, but did not understand them. And getting up early in the morning, I took up the scythe at once, or went to the building and worked hard all day.

When I remained at home on holidays I noticed that my sister and Masha were concealing something from me, and even seemed to be avoiding me. My wife was tender to me as before, but she had thoughts of her own apart, which she did not share with me. There was no doubt that her exasperation with the peasants was growing, the life was becoming more and more distasteful to her, and yet she did not complain to me. She talked to the doctor now more readily than she did to me, and I did not understand why it was so.

It was the custom in our province at haymaking and harvest time for the labourers to come to the manor house in the evening and be regaled with vodka; even young girls drank a glass. We did not keep up this practice; the mowers and the peasant women stood about in our yard till late in the evening expecting vodka, and then departed abusing us. And all the time Masha frowned grimly and said nothing, or murmured to the doctor with exasperation: " Savages ! Petchenyegs !"

In the country newcomers are met ungraciously, almost with hostility, as they are at school. And we were received in this way. At first we were looked upon as stupid, silly people, who had bought an estate simply because we did not know what to do with our money. We were laughed at. The peasants grazed their cattle in our wood and even in our garden; they drove away our cows and horses to the village, and then demanded money for the damage done by them. They came in whole companies into our yard, and loudly clamoured that at the mowing we had cut some piece of land that did not belong to us; and as we did not yet know the boundaries of our estate very accurately, we took their word for it and paid damages. Afterwards it turned out that there had been no mistake at the mowing. They barked the lime-trees in our wood. One of the Dubetchnya peasants, a regular shark, who did a trade in vodka without a licence, bribed our labourers, and in collaboration with them cheated us in a most treacherous way. They took the new wheels off our cart and replaced them with old ones, stole our ploughing harness and actually sold them to us, and so on. But what was most mortifying of all was what happened at the building; the peasant women stole by night boards, bricks, tiles, pieces of iron. The village elder with witnesses made a search in their huts; the village meeting fined them two roubles each, and afterwards this money was spent on drink by the whole commune.

When Masha heard about this, she would say to the doctor or my sister, indignantly:

" What beasts ! It's awful ! awful !"

And I heard her more than once express regret that she had ever taken it into her head to build the school.

" You must understand," the doctor tried to persuade her, " that if you build this school and do good in general, it's not for the sake of the peasants, but in the name of culture, in the name of the future; and the worse the peasants are the more reason for building the school. Understand that !"

But there was a lack of conviction in his voice, and it seemed to me that both he and Masha hated the peasants.

Masha often went to the mill, taking my sister with her, and they both said, laughing, that they went to have a look at Stepan, he was so handsome. Stepan, it appeared, was torpid and taciturn only with men; in feminine society his manners were free and easy, and he talked incessantly. One day, going down to the river to bathe, I accidentally overheard a conversation. Masha and Kleopatra, both in white dresses, were sitting on the bank in the spreading shade of a willow, and Stepan was standing by them with his hands behind his back, and was saying:

" Are peasants men ? They are not men, but, asking your pardon, wild beasts, impostors. What life has a peasant ? Nothing but eating and drinking; all he cares for is victuals to be cheaper and swilling liquor at the tavern like a fool; and there's no conversation, no manners, no formality, nothing but ignorance ! He lives in filth, his wife lives in filth, and his children live in filth. What he stands up in, he lies down to sleep in; he picks the potatoes out of the soup with his fingers; he drinks kvass with a cockroach in it, and doesn't bother to blow it away !"

" It's their poverty, of course," my sister put in.

"Poverty? There is want to be sure, there's different sorts of want, Madam. If a man is in prison, or let us say blind or crippled, that really is trouble I wouldn't wish anyone, but if a man's free and has all his senses, if he has his eyes and his hands and his strength and God, what more does he want? It's cockering themselves, and it's ignorance, Madam, it's not poverty. If you, let us suppose, good gentlefolk, by your education, wish out of kindness to help him he will drink away your money in his low way; or, what's worse, he will open a drinkshop, and with your money start robbing the people. You say poverty, but does the rich peasant live better? He, too, asking your pardon, lives like a swine: coarse, loud-mouthed, cudgel-headed, broader than he is long, fat, red-faced mug, I'd like to swing my fist and send him flying, the scoundrel. There's Larion, another rich one at Dubetchnya, and I bet he strips the bark off your trees as much as any poor one; and he is a foul-mouthed fellow; his children are the same, and when he has had a drop too much he'll topple with his nose in a puddle and sleep there. They are all a worthless lot, Madam. If you live in a village with them it is like hell. It has stuck in my teeth, that village has, and thank the Lord, the King of Heaven, I've plenty to eat and clothes to wear, I served out my time in the dragoons, I was village elder for three years, and now I am a free Cossack, I live where I like. I don't want to live in the village, and no one has the right to force me. They say—my wife. They say you are bound to live in your cottage with your wife. But why so? I am not her hired man."

"Tell me, Stepan, did you marry for love?" asked Masha.

"Love among us in the village!" answered Stepan, and he gave a laugh. "Properly speaking, Madam, if you care to know, this is my second marriage. I am not a Kurilovka man, I am from Zalegoshtcho, but afterwards I was taken into Kurilovka when I married. You see my father did not want to divide the land among us. There were five of us brothers. I took my leave and went to another village to live with my wife's family, but my first wife died when she was young."

"What did she die of?"

"Of foolishness. She used to cry and cry and cry for no reason, and so she pined away. She was always drinking some sort of herbs to make her better looking, and I suppose she damaged her inside. And my second wife is a Kurilovka woman too, there is nothing in her. She's a village woman, a peasant woman, and nothing more. I was taken in when they plighted me to her. I thought she was young and fair-skinned, and that they lived in a clean way. Her mother was just like a Flagellant and she drank coffee, and the chief thing, to be sure, they were clean in their ways. So I married her, and next day we sat down to dinner; I bade my mother-in-law give me a spoon, and she gives me a spoon, and I see her wipe it out with her finger. So much for you, thought I; nice sort of cleanliness yours is. I lived a year with them and then I went away. I might have married a girl from the town," he went on after a pause. " They say a wife is a helpmate to her husband. What do I want with a helpmate ? I help myself; I'd rather she talked to me, and not clack, clack, clack, but circumstantially, feelingly. What is life without good conversation ?"

Stepan suddenly paused, and at once there was the sound of his dreary, monotonous " oo-loo-loo-loo." This meant that he had seen me.

Masha used often to go to the mill, and evidently found pleasure in her conversations with Stepan. Stepan abused the peasants with such sincerity and conviction, and she was attracted to him Every time she came back from the mill the feeble-minded peasant, who looked after the garden, shouted at her:

" Wench Palashka ! Hullo, wench Palashka !" and he would bark like a dog: " Ga ! Ga !"

And she would stop and look at him attentively, as though in that idiot's barking she found an answer to her thoughts, and probably he attracted her in the same way as Stepan's abuse. At home some piece of news would await her, such, for instance, as that the geese from the village had ruined our cabbage in the garden, or that Larion had stolen the reins; and, shrugging her shoulders, she would say with a laugh:

" What do you expect of these people ?"

She was indignant, and there was rancour in her heart, and meanwhile I was growing used to the peasants, and I felt more and more drawn to them. For the most part they were nervous, irritable,

downtrodden people; they were people whose
imagination had been stifled, ignorant, with a
poor, dingy outlook on life, whose thoughts were
ever the same—of the grey earth, of grey days,
of black bread, people who cheated, but like birds
hiding nothing but their head behind the tree—
people who could not count. They would not
come to mow for us for twenty roubles, but they
came for half a pail of vodka, though for twenty
roubles they could have bought four pails. There
really was filth and drunkenness and foolishness
and deceit, but with all that one yet felt that
the life of the peasants rested on a firm, sound
foundation. However uncouth a wild animal
the peasant following the plough seemed, and
however he might stupefy himself with vodka,
still, looking at him more closely, one felt that there
was in him what was needed, something very important, which was lacking in Masha and in the
doctor, for instance, and that was that he believed
the chief thing on earth was truth and justice,
and that his salvation, and that of the whole people,
was only to be found in truth and justice, and so
more than anything in the world he loved just
dealing. I told my wife she saw the spots on the
glass, but not the glass itself; she said nothing
in reply, or hummed like Stepan " oo-loo-loo-loo."
When this good-hearted and clever woman turned
pale with indignation, and with a quiver in her
voice spoke to the doctor of the drunkenness and
dishonesty, it perplexed me, and I was struck by
the shortness of her memory. How could she
forget that her father the engineer drank too, and

drank heavily, and that the money with which Dubetchnya had been bought had been acquired by a whole series of shameless, impudent dishonesties? How could she forget it?

XIV.

My sister, too, was leading a life of her own which she carefully hid from me. She was often whispering with Masha. When I went up to her she seemed to shrink into herself, and there was a guilty, imploring look in her eyes; evidently there was something going on in her heart of which she was afraid or ashamed. So as to avoid meeting me in the garden, or being left alone with me, she always kept close to Masha, and I rarely had an opportunity of talking to her except at dinner.

One evening I was walking quietly through the garden on my way back from the building. It was beginning to get dark. Without noticing me, or hearing my step, my sister was walking near a spreading old apple-tree, absolutely noiselessly as though she were a phantom. She was dressed in black, and was walking rapidly backwards and forwards on the same track, looking at the ground. An apple fell from the tree; she started at the sound, stood still and pressed her hands to her temples. At that moment I went up to her.

In a rush of tender affection which suddenly flooded my heart, with tears in my eyes, suddenly remembering my mother and our childhood, I put my arm round her shoulders and kissed her.

"What is the matter?" I asked her. "You are unhappy; I have seen it for a long time. Tell me what's wrong?"

"I am frightened," she said, trembling.

"What is it?" I insisted. "For God's sake, be open!"

"I will, I will be open; I will tell you the whole truth. To hide it from you is so hard, so agonizing. Misail, I love . . ." she went on in a whisper, "I love him . . . I love him. . . . I am happy, but why am I so frightened?"

There was the sound of footsteps; between the trees appeared Dr. Blagovo in his silk shirt with his high top boots. Evidently they had arranged to meet near the apple-tree. Seeing him, she rushed impulsively towards him with a cry of pain, as though he were being taken from her.

"Vladimir! Vladimir!"

She clung to him and looked greedily into his face, and only then I noticed how pale and thin she had become of late. It was particularly noticeable from her lace collar which I had known for so long, and which now hung more loosely than ever before about her thin, long neck. The doctor was disconcerted, but at once recovered himself, and, stroking her hair, said:

"There, there. . . . Why so nervous? You see, I'm here."

We were silent, looking with embarrassment at each other, then we walked on, the three of us together, and I heard the doctor say to me:

"Civilized life has not yet begun among us. Old men console themselves by making out that

if there is nothing now, there was something in
the forties or the sixties; that's the old: you and
I are young; our brains have not yet been touched
by *marasmus senilis*; we cannot comfort ourselves
with such illusions. The beginning of Russia was
in 862, but the beginning of civilized Russia has
not come yet."

But I did not grasp the meaning of these reflections. It was somehow strange, I could not
believe it, that my sister was in love, that she was
walking and holding the arm of a stranger and
looking tenderly at him. My sister, this nervous,
frightened, crushed, fettered creature, loved a
man who was married and had children ! I felt
sorry for something, but what exactly I don't
know; the presence of the doctor was for some
reason distasteful to me now, and I could not
imagine what would come of this love of theirs.

XV.

Masha and I drove to Kurilovka to the dedication
of the school.

"Autumn, autumn, autumn, . . ." said Masha
softly, looking away. "Summer is over. There
are no birds and nothing is green but the willows."

Yes, summer was over. There were fine, warm
days, but it was fresh in the morning, and the
shepherds went out in their sheepskins already;
and in our garden the dew did not dry off the
asters all day long. There were plaintive sounds
all the time, and one could not make out whether
they came from the shutters creaking on their

rusty hinges, or from the flying cranes—and one's
heart felt light, and one was eager for life.

" The summer is over," said Masha. " Now
you and I can balance our accounts. We have
done a lot of work, a lot of thinking; we are the
better for it—all honour and glory to us—we
have succeeded in self-improvement; but have our
successes had any perceptible influence on the life
around us, have they brought any benefit to anyone
whatever ? No. Ignorance, physical uncleanli-
ness, drunkenness, an appallingly high infant
mortality, everything remains as it was, and no
one is the better for your having ploughed and
sown, and my having wasted money and read
books. Obviously we have been working only
for ourselves and have had advanced ideas only
for ourselves." Such reasonings perplexed me,
and I did not know what to think.

" We have been sincere from beginning to end,"
said I, " and if anyone is sincere he is right."

" Who disputes it ? We were right, but we
haven't succeeded in properly accomplishing what
we were right in. To begin with, our external
methods themselves—aren't they mistaken ? You
want to be of use to men, but by the very fact
of your buying an estate, from the very start you
cut yourself off from any possibility of doing
anything useful for them. Then if you work,
dress, eat like a peasant you sanctify, as it were,
by your authority, their heavy, clumsy dress,
their horrible huts, their stupid beards. . . . On
the other hand, if we suppose that you work for
long, long years, your whole life, that in the end

some practical results are obtained, yet what are they, your results, what can they do against such elemental forces as wholesale ignorance, hunger, cold, degeneration ? A drop in the ocean ! Other methods of struggle are needed, strong, bold, rapid ! If one really wants to be of use one must get out of the narrow circle of ordinary social work, and try to act direct upon the mass ! What is wanted, first of all, is a loud, energetic propaganda. Why is it that art—music, for instance—is so living, so popular, and in reality so powerful ? Because the musician or the singer affects thousands at once. Precious, precious art !" she went on, looking dreamily at the sky. " Art gives us wings and carries us far, far away ! Anyone who is sick of filth, of petty, mercenary interests, anyone who is revolted, wounded, and indignant, can find peace and satisfaction only in the beautiful."

When we drove into Kurilovka the weather was bright and joyous. Somewhere they were threshing; there was a smell of rye straw. A mountain ash was bright red behind the hurdle fences, and all the trees wherever one looked were ruddy or golden. They were ringing the bells, they were carrying the ikons to the school, and we could hear them sing: " Holy Mother, our Defender," and how limpid the air was, and how high the doves were flying.

The service was being held in the classroom. Then the peasants of Kurilovka brought Masha the ikon, and the peasants of Dubetchnya offered her a big loaf and a gilt salt cellar. And Masha broke into sobs.

" If anything has been said that shouldn't have been or anything done not to your liking, forgive us," said an old man, and he bowed down to her and to me.

As we drove home Masha kept looking round at the school; the green roof, which I had painted, and which was glistening in the sun, remained in sight for a long while. And I felt that the look Masha turned upon it now was one of farewell.

XVI.

In the evening she got ready to go to the town. Of late she had taken to going often to the town and staying the night there. In her absence I could not work, my hands felt weak and limp; our huge courtyard seemed a dreary, repulsive, empty hole. The garden was full of angry noises, and without her the house, the trees, the horses were no longer " ours."

I did not go out of the house, but went on sitting at her table beside her bookshelf with the books on land work, those old favourites no longer wanted and looking at me now so shamefacedly. For whole hours together, while it struck seven, eight, nine, while the autumn night, black as soot, came on outside, I kept examining her old glove, or the pen with which she always wrote, or her little scissors. I did nothing, and realized clearly that all I had done before, ploughing, mowing, chopping, had only been because she wished it. And if she had sent me to clean a deep well, where I had to stand up to my waist in deep water, I should have crawled into the well without considering whether it was necessary or not. And now when she was not near, Dubetchnya, with its ruins, its untidiness, its banging shutters, with its thieves by day and by night, seemed to me a chaos in which any work would be useless. Besides, what had I to work for here, why anxiety and thought about the future, if I felt that the earth was giving way under my feet, that I had played my part in Dubetchnya, and that the fate of the books on farming was awaiting me too? Oh, what misery it was at night, in hours of solitude, when I was listening every minute in alarm, as though I were expecting someone to shout that it was time for me to go away! I did not grieve for Dubetchnya. I grieved for my love which, too, was threatened with its autumn. What an immense happiness it is to love and be loved, and how awful to feel that one is slipping down from that high pinnacle!

Masha returned from the town towards the evening of the next day. She was displeased with something, but she concealed it, and only said, why was it all the window frames had been put in for the winter, it was enough to suffocate one. I took out two frames. We were not hungry, but we sat down to supper.

"Go and wash your hands," said my wife; "you smell of putty."

She had brought some new illustrated papers from the town, and we looked at them together after supper. There were supplements with fashion plates and patterns. Masha looked through them casually, and was putting them aside to examine them properly later on; but one dress, with a flat skirt as full as a bell and large sleeves, interested her, and she looked at it for a minute gravely and attentively.

" That's not bad," she said.

" Yes, that dress would suit you beautifully," I said, " beautifully."

And looking with emotion at the dress, admiring that patch of grey simply because she liked it, I went on tenderly:

" A charming, exquisite dress ! Splendid, glorious, Masha ! My precious Masha !"

And tears dropped on the fashion plate.

" Splendid Masha . . ." I muttered; " sweet, precious Masha. . . ."

She went to bed, while I sat another hour looking at the illustrations.

" It's a pity you took out the window frames," she said from the bedroom, " I am afraid it may be cold. Oh, dear, what a draught there is !"

I read something out of the column of odds and ends, a receipt for making cheap ink, and an account of the biggest diamond in the world. I came again upon the fashion plate of the dress she liked, and I imagined her at a ball, with a fan, with bare shoulders, brilliant, splendid, with a full understanding of painting, music, literature, and how small and how brief my part seemed !

Our meeting, our marriage, had been only one of the episodes of which there would be many more in the life of this vital, richly gifted woman. All the best in the world, as I have said already, was at her service, and she received it absolutely for nothing, and even ideas and the intellectual movement in vogue served simply for her recreation, giving variety to her life, and I was only the sledge-driver who drove her from one entertainment to another. Now she did not need me. She would take flight, and I should be left alone.

And as though in response to my thought, there came a despairing scream from the garden.

" He-e-elp !"

It was a shrill, womanish voice, and as though to mimic it the wind whistled in the chimney on the same shrill note. Half a minute passed, and again through the noise of the wind, but coming, it seemed, from the other end of the yard:

" He-e-elp !"

" Misail, do you hear ?" my wife asked me softly. " Do you hear ?"

She came out from the bedroom in her nightgown, with her hair down, and listened, looking at the dark window.

" Someone is being murdered," she said. " That is the last straw."

I took my gun and went out. It was very dark outside, the wind was high, and it was difficult to stand. I went to the gate and listened, the trees roared, the wind whistled and, probably at the feeble-minded peasant's, a dog howled lazily. Outside the gates the darkness was absolute, not a light on the railway-line. And near the lodge, which a year before had been the office, suddenly sounded a smothered scream:

" He-e-elp !"

" Who's there ?" I called.

There were two people struggling. One was thrusting the other out, while the other was resisting, and both were breathing heavily.

" Leave go," said one, and I recognized Ivan Tcheprakov; it was he who was shrieking in a shrill, womanish voice: "Let go, you damned brute, or I'll bite your hand off."

The other I recognized as Moisey. I separated them, and as I did so could not resist hitting Moisey two blows in the face. He fell down, then got up again, and I hit him once more.

" He tried to kill me," he muttered. " He was trying to get at his mamma's chest. . . . I want to lock him up in the lodge for security."

Tcheprakov was drunk and did not recognize me; he kept drawing deep breaths, as though he were just going to shout " help " again.

I left them and went back to the house; my wife was lying on her bed; she had dressed. I told her what had happened in the yard, and did not conceal the fact that I had hit Moisey.

" It's terrible to live in the country," she said. " And what a long night it is. Oh dear, if only it were over !"

" He-e-elp !" we heard again, a little later.

" I'll go and stop them," I said.

" No, let them bite each other's throats," she said with an expression of disgust.

She was looking up at the ceiling, listening, while I sat beside her, not daring to speak to her, feeling as though I were to blame for their shouting " help " in the yard and for the night's seeming so long.

We were silent, and I waited impatiently for a gleam of light at the window, and Masha looked all the time as though she had awakened from a trance and now was marvelling how she, so clever, and well-educated, so elegant, had come into this pitiful, provincial, empty hole among a crew of petty, insignificant people, and how she could have so far forgotten herself as ever to be attracted by one of these people, and for more than six months to have been his wife. It seemed to me that at that moment it did not matter to her whether it was I, or Moisey, or Tcheprakov; everything for her was merged in that savage drunken " help "—I and our marriage, and our work together, and the mud and slush of autumn, and when she sighed or moved into a more comfortable position I read in her face: " Oh, that morning would come quickly !"

In the morning she went away. I spent another three days at Dubetchnya expecting her, then I packed up all our things in one room, locked it, and walked to the town. It was already evening when I rang at the engineer's, and the street lamps were burning in Great Dvoryansky Street. Pavel told me there was no one at home; Viktor Ivanitch had gone to Petersburg, and Mariya Viktorovna was probably at the rehearsal at the Azhogins'. I remember with what emotion I went on to the Azhogins', how my heart throbbed and fluttered as I mounted the stairs, and stood waiting a long while on the landing at the top, not daring to enter that temple of the muses ! In the big room there were lighted candles everywhere, on a little table, on the piano, and on the stage, everywhere in threes; and the first performance was fixed for the thirteenth, and now the first rehearsal was on a Monday, an unlucky day. All part of the war against superstition! All the devotees of the scenic art were gathered together; the eldest, the middle, and the youngest sisters were walking about the stage, reading their parts in exercise books. Apart from all the rest stood Radish, motionless, with the side of his head pressed to the wall as he gazed with adoration at the stage, waiting for the rehearsal to begin. Everything as it used to be.

I was making my way to my hostess; I had to pay my respects to her, but suddenly everyone said, "Hush!" and waved me to step quietly. There was a silence. The lid of the piano was raised; a lady sat down at it screwing up her short-sighted eyes at the music, and my Masha walked up to the piano, in a low-necked dress, looking beautiful, but with a special, new sort of beauty not in the least like the Masha who used to come and meet me in the spring at the mill. She sang: "Why do I love the radiant night?"

It was the first time during our whole acquaintance that I had heard her sing. She had a fine, mellow, powerful voice, and while she sang I felt as though I were eating a ripe, sweet, fragrant melon. She ended, the audience applauded, and she smiled, very much pleased, making play with her eyes, turning over the music, smoothing her skirts, like a bird that has at last broken out of its cage and preens its wings in freedom. Her hair was arranged over her ears, and she had an unpleasant, defiant expression in her face, as though she wanted to throw down a challenge to us all, or to shout to us as she did to her horses: " Hey, there, my beauties !"

And she must at that moment have been very much like her grandfather the sledge-driver.

" You here too ?" she said, giving me her hand. " Did you hear me sing ? Well, what did you think of it ?" and without waiting for my answer she went on: " It's a very good thing you are here. I am going to-night to Petersburg for a short time. You'll let me go, won't you ?"

At midnight I went with her to the station. She embraced me affectionately, probably feeling grateful to me for not asking unnecessary questions, and she promised to write to me, and I held her hands a long time, and kissed them, hardly able to restrain my tears and not uttering a word.

And when she had gone I stood watching the retreating lights, caressing her in imagination and softly murmuring:

" My darling Masha, glorious Masha. . . ."

I spent the night at Karpovna's, and next morning I was at work with Radish, re-covering the furniture of a rich merchant who was marrying his daughter to a doctor.

XVII.

My sister came after dinner on Sunday and had tea with me.

" I read a great deal now," she said, showing

298

me the books which she had fetched from the public library on her way to me. "Thanks to your wife and to Vladimir, they have awakened me to self-realization. They have been my salvation; they have made me feel myself a human being. In old days I used to lie awake at night with worries of all sorts, thinking what a lot of sugar we had used in the week, or hoping the cucumbers would not be too salt. And now, too, I lie awake at night, but I have different thoughts. I am distressed that half my life has been passed in such a foolish, cowardly way. I despise my past; I am ashamed of it. And I look upon our father now as my enemy. Oh, how grateful I am to your wife ! And Vladimir ! He is such a wonderful person ! They have opened my eyes !"

"That's bad that you don't sleep at night," I said.

"Do you think I am ill ? Not at all. Vladimir sounded me, and said I was perfectly well. But health is not what matters, it is not so important. . . . Tell me: am I right ?"

She needed moral support, that was obvious. Masha had gone away. Dr. Blagovo was in Petersburg, and there was no one left in the town but me, to tell her she was right. She looked intently into my face, trying to read my secret thoughts, and if I were absorbed or silent in her presence she thought this was on her account, and was grieved. I always had to be on my guard, and when she asked me whether she was right I hastened to assure her that she was right, and that I had a deep respect for her.

" Do you know they have given me a part at the Azhogins'?" she went on. " I want to act on the stage, I want to live—in fact, I mean to drain the full cup. I have no talent, none, and the part is only ten lines, but still this is immeasurably finer and loftier than pouring out tea five times a day, and looking to see if the cook has eaten too much. Above all, let my father see I am capable of protest."

After tea she lay down on my bed, and lay for a little while with her eyes closed, looking very pale.

" What weakness," she said, getting up. " Vladimir says all city-bred women and girls are anæmic from doing nothing. What a clever man Vladimir is ! He is right, absolutely right. We must work !"

Two days later she came to the Azhogins' with her manuscript for the rehearsal. She was wearing a black dress with a string of coral round her neck, and a brooch that in the distance was like a pastry puff, and in her ears earrings sparkling with brilliants. When I looked at her I felt uncomfortable: I was struck by her lack of taste. That she had very inappropriately put on earrings and brilliants, and that she was strangely dressed, was remarked by other people too; I saw smiles on people's faces, and heard someone say with a laugh: " Kleopatra of Egypt."

She was trying to assume society manners, to be unconstrained and at her ease, and so seemed artificial and strange. She had lost simplicity and sweetness.

" I told father just now that I was going to the rehearsal," she began, coming up to me, " and he shouted that he would not give me his blessing, and actually almost struck me. Only fancy, I don't know my part," she said, looking at her manuscript. " I am sure to make a mess of it. So be it, the die is cast," she went on in intense excitement. " The die is cast. . . ."

It seemed to her that everyone was looking at her, and that all were amazed at the momentous step she had taken, that everyone was expecting something special of her, and it would have been impossible to convince her that no one was paying attention to people so petty and insignificant as she and I were.

She had nothing to do till the third act, and her part, that of a visitor, a provincial crony, consisted only in standing at the door as though listening, and then delivering a brief monologue. In the interval before her appearance, an hour and a half at least, while they were moving about on the stage reading their parts, drinking tea and arguing, she did not leave my side, and was all the time muttering her part and nervously crumpling up the manuscript. And imagining that everyone was looking at her and waiting for her appearance, with a trembling hand she smoothed back her hair and said to me:

" I shall certainly make a mess of it. . . . What a load on my heart, if only you knew ! I feel frightened, as though I were just going to be led to execution."

At last her turn came.

" Kleopatra Alexyevna, it's your cue !" said the stage manager.

She came forward into the middle of the stage with an expression of horror on her face, looking ugly and angular, and for half a minute stood as though in a trance, perfectly motionless, and only her big earrings shook in her ears.

" The first time you can read it," said someone.

It was clear to me that she was trembling, and trembling so much that she could not speak, and could not unfold her manuscript, and that she was incapable of acting her part; and I was already on the point of going to her and saying something, when she suddenly dropped on her knees in the middle of the stage and broke into loud sobs.

All was commotion and hubbub. I alone stood still, leaning against the side scene, overwhelmed by what had happened, not understanding and not knowing what to do. I saw them lift her up and lead her away. I saw Anyuta Blagovo come up to me; I had not seen her in the room before, and she seemed to háve sprung out of the earth. She was wearing her hat and veil, and, as always, had an air of having come only for a moment.

" I told her not to take a part," she said angrily, jerking out each word abruptly and turning crimson. " It's insanity ! You ought to have prevented her !"

Madame Azhogin, in a short jacket with short sleeves, with cigarette ash on her breast, looking thin and flat, came rapidly towards me.

" My dear, this is terrible," she brought out, wringing her hands, and, as her habit was, looking

intently into my face. "This is terrible! Your
sister is in a condition. . . . She is with child
Take her away, I implore you. . . ."

She was breathless with agitation, while on
one side stood her three daughters, exactly like
her, thin and flat, huddling together in a scared
way. They were alarmed, overwhelmed, as though
a convict had been caught in their house. What
a disgrace, how dreadful! And yet this estimable
family had spent its life waging war on superstition;
evidently they imagined that all the superstition
and error of humanity was limited to the three
candles, the thirteenth of the month, and to the
unluckiness of Monday!

"I beg you . . . I beg," repeated Madame
Azhogin, pursing up her lips in the shape of a
heart on the syllable "you." "I beg you take
her home."

XVIII.

A little later my sister and I were walking along
the street. I covered her with the skirts of my
coat; we hastened, choosing back streets where
there were no street lamps, avoiding passers-by;
it was as though we were running away. She
was no longer crying, but looked at me with dry
eyes. To Karpovna's, where I took her, it was
only twenty minutes' walk, and, strange to say, in
that short time we succeeded in thinking of our
whole life; we talked over everything, considered
our position, reflected. . . .

We decided we could not go on living in this
town, and that when I had earned a little money

we would move to some other place. In some houses everyone was asleep, in others they were playing cards; we hated these houses; we were afraid of them. We talked of the fanaticism, the coarseness of feeling, the insignificance of these respectable families, these amateurs of dramatic art whom we had so alarmed, and I kept asking in what way these stupid, cruel, lazy, and dishonest people were superior to the drunken and superstitious peasants of Kurilovka, or in what way they were better than animals, who in the same way are thrown into a panic when some incident disturbs the monotony of their life limited by their instincts. What would have happened to my sister now if she had been left to live at home ?

What moral agonies would she have experienced, talking with my father, meeting every day with acquaintances ? I imagined this to myself, and at once there came into my mind people, all people I knew, who had been slowly done to death by their nearest relations. I remembered the tortured dogs driven mad, the live sparrows plucked naked by boys and flung into the water, and a long, long series of obscure lingering miseries which I had looked on continually from early childhood in that town; and I could not understand what these sixty thousand people lived for, what they read the gospel for, why they prayed, why they read books and magazines. What good had they gained from all that had been said and written hitherto if they were still possessed by the same spiritual darkness and hatred of liberty, as they were a hundred and three hundred years ago ?

A master carpenter spends his whole life building houses in the town, and always, to the day of his death, calls a " gallery " a " galdery." So these sixty thousand people have been reading and hearing of truth, of justice, of mercy, of freedom for generations, and yet from morning till night, till the day of their death, they are lying, and tormenting each other, and they fear liberty and hate it as a deadly foe.

" And so my fate is decided," said my sister, as we arrived home. " After what has happened I cannot go back *there*. Heavens, how good that is ! My heart feels lighter."

She went to bed at once. Tears were glittering on her eyelashes, but her expression was happy; she fell into a sound sweet sleep, and one could see that her heart was lighter and that she was resting. It was a long, long time since she had slept like that.

And so we began our life together. She was always singing and saying that her life was very happy, and the books I brought her from the public library I took back unread, as now she could not read ; she wanted to do nothing but dream and talk of the future, mending my linen, or helping Karpovna near the stove; she was always singing, or talking of her Vladimir, of his cleverness, of his charming manners, of his kindness, of his extraordinary learning, and I assented to all she said, though by now I disliked her doctor. She wanted to work, to lead an independent life on her own account, and she used to say that she would become a school-teacher or a doctor's assistant as soon as her health would permit her, and would herself do the scrubbing and the washing. Already she was passionately devoted to her child; he was not yet born, but she knew already the colour of his eyes, what his hands would be like, and how he would laugh. She was fond of talking about education, and as her Vladimir was the best man in the world, all her discussion of education could be summed up in the question how to make the boy as fascinating as his father. There was no end to her talk, and everything she said made her intensely joyful. Sometimes I was delighted, too, though I could not have said why.

I suppose her dreaminess infected me. I, too, gave up reading, and did nothing but dream. In the evenings, in spite of my fatigue, I walked up and down the room, with my hands in my pockets, talking of Masha.

" What do you think ?" I would ask of my sister. " When will she come back ? I think she'll come back at Christmas, not later; what has she to do there ?"

" As she doesn't write to you, it's evident she will come back very soon."

" That's true," I assented, though I knew perfectly well that Masha would not return to our town.

I missed her fearfully, and could no longer deceive myself, and tried to get other people to deceive me. My sister was expecting her doctor, and I—Masha; and both of us talked incessantly, laughed ,and did not notice that we were preventing Karpovna from sleeping. She lay on the stove and kept muttering:

"The samovar hummed this morning, it did hum! Oh, it bodes no good, my dears, it bodes no good!"

No one ever came to see us but the postman, who brought my sister letters from the doctor, and Prokovy, who sometimes came in to see us in the evening, and after looking at my sister without speaking went away, and when he was in the kitchen said:

"Every class ought to remember its rules, and anyone, who is so proud that he won't understand that, will find it a vale of tears."

He was very fond of the phrase "a vale of tears." One day—it was in Christmas week, when I was walking by the bazaar—he called me into the butcher's shop, and not shaking hands with me, announced that he had to speak to me about something very important. His face was red from the frost and vodka; near him, behind the counter, stood Nikolka, with the expression of a brigand, holding a bloodstained knife in his hand.

"I desire to express my word to you," Prokovy began. "This incident cannot continue, because, as you understand yourself that for such a vale, people will say nothing good of you or of us. Mamma, through pity, cannot say something unpleasant to you, that your sister should move into another lodging on account of her condition, but I won't have it any more, because I can't approve of her behaviour."

I understood him, and I went out of the shop.

The same day my sister and I moved to Radish's. We had no money for a cab, and we walked on foot; I carried a parcel of our belongings on my back; my sister had nothing in her hands, but she gasped for breath and coughed, and kept asking whether we should get there soon.

XIX.

At last a letter came from Masha.

"Dear, good M. A." (she wrote), " our kind-gentle ' angel ' as the old painter calls you, fare, well; I am going with my father to America for the exhibition. In a few days I shall see the ocean—so far from Dubetchnya, it's dreadful to think ! It's far and unfathomable as the sky, and I long to be there in freedom. I am triumphant, I am mad, and you see how incoherent my letter is. Dear, good one, give me my freedom, make haste to break the thread, which still holds, binding you and me together. My meeting and knowing you was a ray from heaven that lighted up my existence; but my becoming your wife was a mistake, you understand that, and I am oppressed now by the consciousness of the mistake, and I beseech you, on my knees, my generous friend, quickly, quickly, before I start for the ocean, telegraph that you consent to correct our common mistake, to remove the solitary stone from my wings, and my father, who will undertake all the arrangements, promised me not to burden you too much with formalities. And so I am free to fly whither I will ? Yes ?

" Be happy, and God bless you; forgive me, a sinner.

" I am well, I am wasting money, doing all sorts of silly things, and I thank God every minute that such a bad woman as I has no children. I sing and have success, but it's not an infatuation; no, it's my haven, my cell to which I go for peace. King David had a ring with an inscription on it: ' All things pass.' When one is sad those words make one cheerful, and when one is cheerful it makes one sad. I have got myself a ring like that with Hebrew letters on it, and this talisman keeps me from infatuations. All things pass, life will pass, one wants nothing. Or at least one wants nothing but the sense of freedom, for when anyone is free, he wants nothing, nothing, nothing. Break the thread. A warm hug to you and your sister. Forgive and forget your M."

My sister used to lie down in one room, and Radish, who had been ill again and was now better, in another. Just at the moment when I received this letter my sister went softly into the painter's room, sat down beside him and began reading aloud. She read to him every day, Ostrovsky or Gogol, and he listened, staring at one point, not laughing, but shaking his head and muttering to himself from time to time:

"Anything may happen ! Anything may happen !"

If anything ugly or unseemly were depicted in the play he would say as though vindictively, thrusting his finger into the book:

" There it is, lying! That's what it does, lying does."

The plays fascinated him, both from their subjects and their moral, and from their skilful, complex construction, and he marvelled at " him," never calling the author by his name. How neatly *he* has put it all together.

This time my sister read softly only one page, and could read no more: her voice would not last out. Radish took her hand and, moving his parched lips, said, hardly audibly, in a husky voice:

" The soul of a righteous man is white and smooth as chalk, but the soul of a sinful man is like pumice stone. The soul of a righteous man is like clear oil, but the soul of a sinful man is gas tar. We must labour, we must sorrow, we must suffer sickness," he went on, " and he who does not labour and sorrow will not gain the Kingdom of Heaven. Woe, woe to them that are well fed, woe to the mighty, woe to the rich, woe to the moneylenders ! Not for them is the Kingdom of Heaven. Lice eat grass, rust eats iron . . ."

" And lying the soul," my sister added laughing.

I read the letter through once more. At that moment there walked into the kitchen a soldier who had been bringing us twice a week parcels of tea, French bread and game, which smelt of scent, from some unknown giver. I had no work. I had had to sit at home idle for whole days together, and probably whoever sent us the French bread knew that we were in want.

I heard my sister talking to the soldier and laughing gaily. Then, lying down, she ate some French bread and said to me:

"When you wouldn't go into the service, but became a house painter, Anyuta Blagovo and I knew from the beginning that you were right, but we were frightened to say so aloud. Tell me what force is it that hinders us from saying what one thinks? Take Anyuta Blagovo now, for instance. She loves you, she adores you, she knows you are right, she loves me too, like a sister, and knows that I am right, and I daresay in her soul envies me, but some force prevents her from coming to see us, she shuns us, she is afraid."

My sister crossed her arms over her breast, and said passionately:

"How she loves you, if only you knew! She has confessed her love to no one but me, and then very secretly in the dark. She led me into a dark avenue in the garden, and began whispering how precious you were to her. You will see, she'll never marry, because she loves you. Are you sorry for her?"

"Yes."

"It's she who has sent the bread. She is absurd really, what is the use of being so secret? I used to be absurd and foolish, but now I have got away from that and am afraid of nobody. I think and say aloud what I like, and am happy. When I lived at home I hadn't a conception of happiness, and now I wouldn't change with a queen."

Dr. Blagovo arrived. He had taken his doctor's

degree, and was now staying in our town with his father; he was taking a rest, and said that he would soon go back to Petersburg again. He wanted to study anti-toxins against typhus, and, I believe, cholera; he wanted to go abroad to perfect his training, and then to be appointed a professor. He had already left the army service, and wore a roomy serge reefer jacket, very full trousers, and magnificent neckties. My sister was in ecstasies over his scarf-pin, his studs, and the red silk handkerchief which he wore, I suppose from foppishness, sticking out of the breast pocket of his jacket. One day, having nothing to do, she and I counted up all the suits we remembered him wearing, and came to the conclusion that he had at least ten. It was clear that he still loved my sister as before, but he never once even in jest spoke of taking her with him to Petersburg or abroad, and I could not picture to myself clearly what would become of her if she remained alive and what would become of her child. She did nothing but dream endlessly, and never thought seriously of the future; she said he might go where he liked, and might abandon her even, so long as he was happy himself; that what had been was enough for her.

As a rule he used to sound her very carefully on his arrival, and used to insist on her taking milk and drops in his presence. It was the same on this occasion. He sounded her and made her drink a glass of milk, and there was a smell of creosote in our room afterwards.

" There's a good girl," he said, taking the glass

from her. " You mustn't talk too much now;
you've taken to chattering like a magpie of late.
Please hold your tongue."

She laughed. Then he came into Radish's room
where I was sitting and affectionately slapped me
on the shoulder.

" Well, how goes it, old man ?" he said, bending
down to the invalid.

" Your honour," said Radish, moving his lips
slowly, " your honour, I venture to submit. . . .
We all walk in the fear of God, we all have to die.
. . . Permit me to tell you the truth. . . . Your
honour, the Kingdom of Heaven will not be for
you !"

" There's no help for it," the doctor said jestingly; " there must be somebody in hell, you
know."

And all at once something happened with my
consciousness; as though I were in a dream, as
though I were standing on a winter night in the
slaughterhouse yard, and Prokofy beside me,
smelling of pepper cordial; I made an effort to
control myself, and rubbed my eyes, and at once
it seemed to me that I was going along the road to
the interview with the Governor. Nothing of the
sort had happened to me before, or has happened
to me since, and these strange memories that were
like dreams, I ascribed to over-exhaustion of my
nerves. I lived through the scene at the slaughter-
house, and the interview with the Governor, and at
the same time was dimly aware that it was not
real.

When I came to myself I saw that I was no

longer in the house, but in the street, and was standing with the doctor near a lamp-post.

" It's sad, it's sad," he was saying, and tears were trickling down his cheeks. " She is in good spirits, she's always laughing and hopeful, but her position's hopeless, dear boy. Your Radish hates me, and is always trying to make me feel that I have treated her badly. He is right from his standpoint, but I have my point of view too; and I shall never regret all that has happened. One must love; we ought all to love—oughtn't we ? There would be no life without love; anyone who fears and avoids love is not free."

Little by little he passed to other subjects, began talking of science, of his dissertation which had been liked in Petersburg. He was carried away by his subject, and no longer thought of my sister, nor of his grief, nor of me. Life was of absorbing interest to him. She has America and her ring with the inscription on it, I thought, while this fellow has his doctor's degree and a professor's chair to look forward to, and only my sister and I are left with the old things.

When I said good-bye to him, I went up to the lamp-post and read the letter once more. And I remembered, I remembered vividly how that spring morning she had come to me at the mill, lain down and covered herself with her jacket— she wanted to be like a simple peasant woman. And how, another time—it was in the morning also—we drew the net out of the water, and heavy drops of rain fell upon us from the river-side willows, and we laughed. . . .

It was dark in our house in Great Dvoryansky Street. I got over the fence and, as I used to do in the old days, went by the back way to the kitchen to borrow a lantern. There was no one in the kitchen. The samovar hissed near the stove, waiting for my father. "Who pours out my father's tea now?" I thought. Taking the lantern I went out to the shed, built myself up a bed of old newspapers and lay down. The hooks on the walls looked forbidding, as they used to of old, and their shadows flickered. It was cold. I felt that my sister would come in in a minute, and bring me supper, but at once I remembered that she was ill and was lying at Radish's, and it seemed to me strange that I should have climbed over the fence and be lying here in this unheated shed. My mind was in a maze, and I saw all sorts of absurd things.

There was a ring. A ring familiar from childhood: first the wire rustled against the wall, then a short plaintive ring in the kitchen. It was my father come back from the club. I got up and went into the kitchen. Axinya the cook clasped her hands on seeing me, and for some reason burst into tears.

"My own!" she said softly. "My precious! O Lord!"

And she began crumpling up her apron in her agitation. In the window there were standing jars of berries in vodka. I poured myself out a teacupful and greedily drank it off, for I was intensely thirsty. Axinya had quite recently scrubbed the table and benches, and there was that smell in the

315

kitchen which is found in bright, snug kitchens kept by tidy cooks. And that smell and the chirp of the cricket used to lure us as children into the kitchen, and put us in the mood for hearing fairy tales and playing at " Kings ". . . .

" Where's Kleopatra ?" Axinya asked softly, in a fluster, holding her breath; " and where is your cap, my dear ? Your wife, they say, has gone to Petersburg ?"

She had been our servant in our mother's time, and used once to give Kleopatra and me our baths, and to her we were still children who had to be talked to for their good. For a quarter of an hour or so she laid before me all the reflections which she had with the sagacity of an old servant been accumulating in the stillness of that kitchen, all the time since we had seen each other. She said that the doctor could be forced to marry Kleopatra ; he only needed to be thoroughly frightened; and that if an appeal were promptly written the bishop would annul the first marriage; that it would be a good thing for me to sell Dubetchnya without my wife's knowledge, and put the money in the bank in my own name; that if my sister and I were to bow down at my father's feet and ask him properly, he might perhaps forgive us; that we ought to have a service sung to the Queen of Heaven. . . .

" Come, go along, my dear, and speak to him," she said, when she heard my father's cough. " Go along, speak to him; bow down, your head won't drop off."

I went in. My father was sitting at the table

sketching a plan of a summer villa, with Gothic windows, and with a fat turret like a fireman's watch tower—something peculiarly stiff and tasteless. Going into the study I stood still where I could see this drawing. I did not know why I had gone in to my father, but I remember that when I saw his lean face, his red neck, and his shadow on the wall, I wanted to throw myself on his neck, and as Axinya had told me, bow down at his feet; but the sight of the summer villa with the Gothic windows, and the fat turret, restrained me.

" Good evening," I said.

He glanced at me, and at once dropped his eyes on his drawing.

" What do you want ?" he asked, after waiting a little.

" I have come to tell you my sister's very ill. She can't live very long," I added in a hollow voice.

" Well," sighed my father, taking off his spectacles, and laying them on the table. " What thou sowest that shalt thou reap. What thou sowest," he repeated, getting up from the table, " that shalt thou reap. I ask you to remember how you came to me two years ago, and on this very spot I begged you, I besought you to give up your errors; I reminded you of your duty, of your honour, of what you owed to your forefathers whose traditions we ought to preserve as sacred. Did you obey me ? You scorned my counsels, and obstinately persisted in clinging to your false ideas; worse still you drew your sister into the

317

path of error with you, and led her to lose her moral principles and sense of shame. Now you are both in a bad way. Well, as thou sowest, so shalt thou reap!"

As he said this he walked up and down the room. He probably imagined that I had come to him to confess my wrong doings, and he probably expected that I should begin begging him to forgive my sister and me. I was cold, I was shivering as though I were in a fever, and spoke with difficulty in a husky voice.

"And I beg you, too, to remember," I said, " on this very spot I besought you to understand me, to reflect, to decide with me how and for what we should live, and in answer you began talking about our forefathers, about my grandfather who wrote poems. One tells you now that your only daughter is hopelessly ill, and you go on again about your forefathers, your traditions. . . . And such frivolity in your old age, when death is close at hand and you haven't more than five or ten years left!"

"What have you come here for?" my father asked sternly, evidently offended at my reproaching him for his frivolity.

"I don't know. I love you, I am unutterably sorry that we are so far apart—so you see I have come. I love you still, but my sister has broken with you completely. She does not forgive you, and will never forgive you now. Your very name arouses her aversion for the past, for life."

"And who is to blame for it?" cried my father. "It's your fault, you scoundrel!"

"Well, suppose it is my fault," I said. "I admit I have been to blame in many things, but why is it that this life of yours, which you think binding upon us, too—why is it so dreary, so barren? How is it that in not one of these houses you have been building for the last thirty years has there been anyone from whom I might have learnt how to live, so as not to be to blame? There is not one honest man in the whole town! These houses of yours are nests of damnation, where mothers and daughters are made away with, where children are tortured. . . . My poor mother!" I went on in despair. "My poor sister! One has to stupefy oneself with vodka, with cards, with scandal; one must become a scoundrel, a hypocrite, or go on drawing plans for years and years, so as not to notice all the horrors that lie hidden in these houses. Our town has existed for hundreds of years, and all that time it has not produced one man of service to our country—not one. You have stifled in the germ everything in the least living and bright. It's a town of shopkeepers, publicans, counting-house clerks, canting hypocrites; it's a useless, unnecessary town, which not one soul would regret if it suddenly sank through the earth."

"I don't want to listen to you, you scoundrel!" said my father, and he took up his ruler from the table. "You are drunk. Don't dare come and see your father in such a state! I tell you for the last time, and you can repeat it to your depraved sister, that you'll get nothing from me, either of you. I have torn my disobedient

children out of my heart, and if they suffer for
their disobedience and obstinacy I do not pity
them. You can go whence you came. It has
pleased God to chastise me with you, but I will
bear the trial with resignation, and, like Job, I
will find consolation in my sufferings and in
unremitting labour. You must not cross my
threshold till you have mended your ways. I am
a just man, all I tell you is for your benefit, and if
you desire your own good you ought to remember
all your life what I say and have said to you. . . ."

I waved my hand in despair and went away.
I don't remember what happened afterwards, that
night and next day.

I am told that I walked about the streets bare-
headed, staggering, and singing aloud, while a
crowd of boys ran after me, shouting:

" Better-than-nothing !"

XX.

If I wanted to order a ring for myself, the
inscription I should choose would be: " Nothing
passes away." I believe that nothing passes
away without leaving a trace, and that every
step we take, however small, has significance
for our present and our future existence.

What I have been through has not been for
nothing. My great troubles, my patience, have
touched people's hearts, and now they don't
call me " Better-than-nothing," they don't laugh
at me, and when I walk by the shops they don't
throw water over me. They have grown used

320

to my being a workman, and see nothing strange in my carrying a pail of paint and putting in windows, though I am of noble rank; on the contrary, people are glad to give me orders, and I am now considered a first-rate workman, and the best foreman after Radish, who, though he has regained his health, and though, as before, he paints the cupola on the belfry without scaffolding, has no longer the force to control the workmen; instead of him I now run about the town looking for work, I engage the workmen and pay them, borrow money at a high rate of interest, and now that I myself am a contractor, I understand how it is that one may have to waste three days racing about the town in search of tilers on account of some twopenny-halfpenny job. People are civil to me, they address me politely, and in the houses where I work, they offer me tea, and send to enquire whether I wouldn't like dinner. Children and young girls often come and look at me with curiosity and compassion.

One day I was working in the Governor's garden, painting an arbour there to look like marble. The Governor, walking in the garden, came up to the arbour and, having nothing to do, entered into conversation with me, and I reminded him how he had once summoned me to an interview with him. He looked into my face intently for a minute, then made his mouth like a round " O," flung up his hands, and said: " I don't remember !"

I have grown older, have become silent, stern, and austere, I rarely laugh, and I am told that

I have grown like Radish, and that like him I bore the workmen by my useless exhortations.

Mariya Viktorovna, my former wife, is living now abroad, while her father is constructing a railway somewhere in the eastern provinces, and is buying estates there. Dr. Blagovo is also abroad. Dubetchnya has passed again into the possession of Madame Tcheprakov, who has bought it after forcing the engineer to knock the price down twenty per cent. Moisey goes about now in a bowler hat; he often drives into the town in a racing droshky on business of some sort, and stops near the bank. They say he has already bought up a mortgaged estate, and is constantly making enquiries at the bank about Dubetchnya, which he means to buy too. Poor Ivan Tcheprakov was for a long while out of work, staggering about the town and drinking. I tried to get him into our work, and for a time he painted roofs and put in window-panes in our company, and even got to like it, and stole oil, asked for tips, and drank like a regular painter. But he soon got sick of the work, and went back to Dubetchnya, and afterwards the workmen confessed to me that he had tried to persuade them to join him one night and murder Moisey and rob Madame Tcheprakov.

My father has greatly aged; he is very bent, and in the evenings walks up and down near his house. I never go to see him.

During an epidemic of cholera Prokofy doctored some of the shopkeepers with pepper cordial and pitch, and took money for doing so, and, as I learned from the newspapers, was flogged for

322

abusing the doctors as he sat in his shop. His shopboy Nikolka died of cholera. Karpovna is still alive and, as always, she loves and fears her Prokofy. When she sees me, she always shakes her head mournfully, and says with a sigh: " Your life is ruined."

On working days I am busy from morning till night. On holidays, in fine weather, I take my tiny niece (my sister reckoned on a boy, but the child is a girl) and walk in a leisurely way to the cemetery. There I stand or sit down, and stay a long time gazing at the grave that is so dear to me, and tell the child that her mother lies here.

Sometimes, by the graveside, I find Anyuta Blagovo. We greet each other and stand in silence, or talk of Kleopatra, of her child, of how sad life is in this world; then, going out of the cemetery, we walk along in silence and she slackens her pace on purpose to walk beside me a little longer. The little girl, joyous and happy, pulls at her hand, laughing and screwing up her eyes in the bright sunlight, and we stand still and join in caressing the dear child.

When we reach the town Anyuta Blagovo, agitated and flushing crimson, says good-bye to me and walks on alone, austere and respectable. . . . And no one who met her could, looking at her, imagine that she had just been walking beside me and even caressing the child.

1896

THE CHORUS GIRL

ONE day when she was younger and better-looking, and when her voice was stronger, Nikolay Petrovitch Kolpakov, her adorer, was sitting in the outer room in her summer villa. It was intolerably hot and stifling. Kolpakov, who had just dined and drunk a whole bottle of inferior port, felt ill-humoured and out of sorts. Both were bored and waiting for the heat of the day to be over in order to go for a walk.

All at once there was a sudden ring at the door. Kolpakov, who was sitting with his coat off, in his slippers, jumped up and looked inquiringly at Pasha.

" It must be the postman or one of the girls," said the singer.

Kolpakov did not mind being found by the postman or Pasha's lady friends, but by way of precaution gathered up his clothes and went into the next room, while Pasha ran to open the door. To her great surprise in the doorway stood, not the postman and not a girl friend, but an unknown woman, young and beautiful, who was dressed like a lady, and from all outward signs was one.

The stranger was pale and was breathing

324

heavily as though she had been running up a steep
flight of stairs.

" What is it ?" asked Pasha.

The lady did not at once answer. She took a
step forward, slowly looked about the room, and
sat down in a way that suggested that from fatigue,
or perhaps illness, she could not stand; then for
a long time her pale lips quivered as she tried in
vain to speak.

" Is my husband here ?" she asked at last,
raising to Pasha her big eyes with their red tear-
stained lids.

"Husband ?" whispered Pasha, and was suddenly
so frightened that her hands and feet turned cold.
" What husband ?" she repeated, beginning to
tremble.

" My husband, . . . Nikolay Petrovitch Kolpakov."

" N . . . no, madam. . . . I . . . I don't
know any husband."

A minute passed in silence. The stranger
several times passed her handkerchief over her
pale lips and held her breath to stop her inward
trembling, while Pasha stood before her motionless,
like a post, and looked at her with astonishment
and terror.

" So you say he is not here ?" the lady asked,
this time speaking with a firm voice and smiling
oddly.

" I . . . I don't know who it is you are asking
about."

" You are horrid, mean, vile . . ." the stranger
muttered, scanning Pasha with hatred and re-

pulsion. " Yes, yes . . . you are horrid. I am very, very glad that at last I can tell you so !"

Pasha felt that on this lady in black with the angry eyes and white slender fingers she produced the impression of something horrid and unseemly, and she felt ashamed of her chubby red cheeks, the pock-mark on her nose, and the fringe on her forehead, which never could be combed back. And it seemed to her that if she had been thin, and had had no powder on her face and no fringe on her forehead, then she could have disguised the fact that she was not " respectable," and she would not have felt so frightened and ashamed to stand facing this unknown, mysterious lady.

" Where is my husband ?" the lady went on. " Though I don't care whether he is here or not, but I ought to tell you that the money has been missed, and they are looking for Nikolay Petrovitch. . . . They mean to arrest him. That's your doing !"

The lady got up and walked about the room in great excitement. Pasha looked at her and was so frightened that she could not understand.

" He'll be found and arrested to-day," said the lady, and she gave a sob, and in that sound could be heard her resentment and vexation. " I know who has brought him to this awful position ! Low, horrid creature ! Loathsome, mercenary hussy !" The lady's lips worked and her nose wrinkled up with disgust. " I am helpless, do you hear, you low woman ? . . . I am helpless; you are stronger than I am, but there is One to defend me and my children ! God sees all ! He is just ! He will punish you for every tear I have shed, for all my sleepless nights! The time will come; you will think of me! . . ."

Silence followed again. The lady walked about the room and wrung her hands, while Pasha still gazed blankly at her in amazement, not understanding and expecting something terrible.

" I know nothing about it, madam," she said, and suddenly burst into tears.

" You are lying !" cried the lady, and her eyes flashed angrily at her. "I know all about it! I've known you a long time. I know that for the last month he has been spending every day with you !"

" Yes. What then ? What of it ? I have a great many visitors, but I don't force anyone to come. He is free to do as he likes."

" I tell you they have discovered that money is missing! He has embezzled money at the office! For the sake of such a . . . creature as you, for your sake he has actually committed a crime. Listen," said the lady in a resolute voice, stopping short, facing Pasha. "You can have no principles; you live simply to do harm—that's your object; but one can't imagine you have fallen so low that you have no trace of human feeling left! He has a wife, children. . . . If he is condemned and sent into exile we shall starve, the children and I. . . . Understand that ! And yet there is a chance of saving him and us from destitution and disgrace. If I take them nine hundred roubles to-day they will let him alone. Only nine hundred roubles !"

327

" What nine hundred roubles ?" Pasha asked softly. " I . . . I don't know. . . . I haven't taken it."

" I am not asking you for nine hundred roubles. . . . You have no money, and I don't want your money. I ask you for something else. . . . Men usually give expensive things to women like you. Only give me back the things my husband has given you !"

" Madam, he has never made me a present of anything ! " Pasha wailed, beginning to understand.

" Where is the money ? He has squandered his own and mine and other people's. . . . What has become of it all ? Listen, I beg you ! I was carried away by indignation and have said a lot of nasty things to you, but I apologize. You must hate me, I know, but if you are capable of sympathy, put yourself in my position ! I implore you to give me back the things !"

" H'm !" said Pasha, and she shrugged her shoulders. " I would with pleasure, but, God is my witness, he never made me a present of anything. Believe me, on my conscience. However, you are right, though," said the singer in confusion, " he did bring me two little things. Certainly I will give them back, if you wish it."

Pasha pulled out one of the drawers in the toilet-table and took out of it a hollow gold bracelet and a thin ring with a ruby in it.

" Here, madam !" she said, handing the visitor these articles.

The lady flushed and her face quivered. She was offended.

" What are you giving me ?" she said. " I am not asking for charity, but for what does not belong to you . . . what you have taken advantage of your position to squeeze out of my husband . . . that weak, unhappy man. . . . On Thursday, when I saw you with my husband at the harbour you were wearing expensive brooches and bracelets. So it's no use your playing the innocent lamb to me ! I ask you for the last time: will you give me the things, or not ?"

" You are a queer one, upon my word," said Pasha, beginning to feel offended. " I assure you that, except the bracelet and this little ring, I've never seen a thing from your Nikolay Petrovitch. He brings me nothing but sweet cakes."

" Sweet cakes !" laughed the stranger. " At home the children have nothing to eat, and here you have sweet cakes. You absolutely refuse to restore the presents ?"

Receiving no answer, the lady sat down and stared into space, pondering.

" What's to be done now ?" she said. " If I don't get nine hundred roubles, he is ruined, and the children and I are ruined, too. Shall I kill this low woman or go down on my knees to her ?"

The lady pressed her handkerchief to her face and broke into sobs.

" I beg you !" Pasha heard through the stranger's sobs. " You see you have plundered and ruined my husband. Save him. . . . You have no feeling for him, but the children . . . the children. . . . What have the children done ?"

Pasha imagined little children standing in

the street, crying with hunger, and she, too, sobbed.

" What can I do, madam ?" she said. " You say that I am a low woman and that I have ruined Nikolay Petrovitch, and I assure you . . . before God Almighty, I have had nothing from him whatever. . . . There is only one girl in our chorus who has a rich admirer; all the rest of us live from hand to mouth on bread and kvass. Nikolay Petrovitch is a highly educated, refined gentleman, so I've made him welcome. We are bound to make gentlemen welcome."

" I ask you for the things ! Give me the things ! I am crying. . . . I am humiliating myself. . . . If you like I will go down on my knees ! If you wish it !"

Pasha shrieked with horror and waved her hands. She felt that this pale, beautiful lady who expressed herself so grandly, as though she were on the stage, really might go down on her knees to her, simply from pride, from grandeur, to exalt herself and humiliate the chorus girl.

" Very well, I will give you things !" said Pasha, wiping her eyes and bustling about. " By all means. Only they are not from Nikolay Petrovitch. . . . I got these from other gentlemen. As you please. . . ."

Pasha pulled out the upper drawer of the chest, took out a diamond brooch, a coral necklace, some rings and bracelets, and gave them all to the lady.

" Take them if you like, only I've never had anything from your husband. Take them and grow rich," Pasha went on, offended at the threat to go down on her knees. "And if you are a lady . . . his lawful wife, you should keep him to yourself. I should think so! I did not ask him to come; he came of himself."

Through her tears the lady scrutinized the articles given her and said:

"This isn't everything. . . . There won't be five hundred roubles' worth here."

Pasha impulsively flung out of the chest a gold watch, a cigar-case and studs, and said, flinging up her hands:

"I've nothing else left. . . . You can search!"

The visitor gave a sigh, with trembling hands twisted the things up in her handkerchief, and went out without uttering a word, without even nodding her head.

The door from the next room opened and Kolpakov walked in. He was pale and kept shaking his head nervously, as though he had swallowed something very bitter; tears were glistening in his eyes.

"What presents did you make me?" Pasha asked, pouncing upon him. "When did you, allow me to ask you?"

"Presents . . . that's no matter!" said Kolpakov, and he tossed his head. "My God! She cried before you, she humbled herself. . . ."

"I am asking you, what presents did you make me?" Pasha cried.

"My God! She, a lady, so proud, so pure. . . . She was ready to go down on her knees to . . .

331

to this wench! And I've brought her to this! I've allowed it!"

He clutched his head in his hands and moaned.

"No, I shall never forgive myself for this! I shall never forgive myself! Get away from me . . . you low creature!" he cried with repulsion, backing away from Pasha, and thrusting her off with trembling hands. "She would have gone down on her knees, and . . . and to you! Oh, my God!"

He rapidly dressed, and pushing Pasha aside contemptuously, made for the door and went out.

Pasha lay down and began wailing aloud. She was already regretting her things which she had given away so impulsively, and her feelings were hurt. She remembered how three years ago a merchant had beaten her for no sort of reason, and she wailed more loudly than ever.

1892

332

THE NEW VILLA

I.

Two miles from the village of Obrutchanovo a huge bridge was being built. From the village, which stood up high on the steep river-bank, its trellis-like skeleton could be seen, and in foggy weather and on still winter days, when its delicate iron girders and all the scaffolding around was covered with hoar frost, it presented a picturesque and even fantastic spectacle. Kutcherov, the engineer who was building the bridge, a stout, broad-shouldered, bearded man in a soft crumpled cap, drove through the village in his racing droshky or his open carriage. Now and then on holidays navvies working on the bridge would come to the village; they begged for alms, laughed at the women, and sometimes carried off something. But that was rare; as a rule the days passed quietly and peacefully as though no bridge-building were going on, and only in the evening, when camp fires gleamed near the bridge, the wind faintly wafted the songs of the navvies. And by day there was sometimes the mournful clang of metal, don-don-don. . . .

It happened that the engineer's wife came to

see him. She was pleased with the river-banks
and the gorgeous view over the green valley with
trees, churches, flocks, and she began begging her
husband to buy a small piece of ground and to
build them a cottage on it. Her husband agreed.
They bought sixty acres of land, and on the high
bank in a field, where in earlier days the cows of
Obrutchanovo used to wander, they built a pretty
house of two storeys with a terrace and a verandah,
with a tower and a flagstaff on which a flag
fluttered on Sundays—they built it in about three
months, and then all the winter they were planting
big trees, and when spring came and everything
began to be green there were already avenues to
the new house, a gardener and two labourers in
white aprons were digging near it, there was a
little fountain, and a globe of looking-glass flashed
so brilliantly that it was painful to look at. The
house had already been named the New Villa.

On a bright, warm morning at the end of May
two horses were brought to Obrutchanovo to the
village blacksmith, Rodion Petrov. They came
from the New Villa. The horses were sleek,
graceful beasts, as white as snow, and strikingly
alike.

" Perfect swans !" said Rodion, gazing at them
with reverent admiration.

His wife Stepanida, his children and grandchildren came out into the street to look at them.
By degrees a crowd collected. The Lytchkovs,
father and son, both men with swollen faces and
entirely beardless, came up bare-headed. Kozov,
a tall, thin old man with a long, narrow beard,

came up leaning on a stick with a crook handle: he kept winking with his crafty eyes and smiling ironically as though he knew something.

"It's only that they are white; what is there in them?" he said. "Put mine on oats, and they will be just as sleek. They ought to be in a plough and with a whip, too. . . ."

The coachman simply looked at him with disdain, but did not utter a word. And afterwards, while they were blowing up the fire at the forge, the coachman talked while he smoked cigarettes. The peasants learned from him various details: his employers were wealthy people; his mistress, Elena Ivanovna, had till her marriage lived in Moscow in a poor way as a governess; she was kind-hearted, compassionate, and fond of helping the poor. On the new estate, he told them, they were not going to plough or to sow, but simply to live for their pleasure, live only to breathe the fresh air. When he had finished and led the horses back a crowd of boys followed him, the dogs barked, and Kozov, looking after him, winked sarcastically.

"Landowners, too-oo!" he said. "They have built a house and set up horses, but I bet they are nobodies—landowners, too-oo."

Kozov for some reason took a dislike from the first to the new house, to the white horses, and to the handsome, well-fed coachman. Kozov was a solitary man, a widower; he had a dreary life (he was prevented from working by a disease which he sometimes called a rupture and some-

335

times worms); he was maintained by his son, who worked at a confectioner's in Harkov and sent him money; and from early morning till evening he sauntered at leisure about the river or about the village; if he saw, for instance, a peasant carting a log, or fishing, he would say: "That log's dry wood—it is rotten," or, "They won't bite in weather like this." In times of drought he would declare that there would not be a drop of rain till the frost came; and when the rains came he would say that everything would rot in the fields, that everything was ruined. And as he said these things he would wink as though he knew something.

At the New Villa they burned Bengal lights and sent up fireworks in the evenings, and a sailing-boat with red lanterns floated by Obrutchanovo. One morning the engineer's wife, Elena Ivanovna, and her little daughter drove to the village in a carriage with yellow wheels and a pair of dark bay ponies; both mother and daughter were wearing broad-brimmed straw hats, bent down over their ears.

This was exactly at the time when they were carting manure, and the blacksmith Rodion, a tall, gaunt old man, bareheaded and barefooted, was standing near his dirty and repulsive-looking cart and, flustered, looked at the ponies, and it was evident by his face that he had never seen such little horses before.

"The Kutcherov lady has come!" was whispered around. "Look, the Kutcherov lady has come!"

THE NEW VILLA

Elena Ivanovna looked at the huts as though she were selecting one, and then stopped at the very poorest, at the windows of which there were so many children's heads—flaxen, red, and dark. Stepanida, Rodion's wife, a stout woman, came running out of the hut; her kerchief slipped off her grey head; she looked at the carriage facing the sun, and her face smiled and wrinkled up as though she were blind.

" This is for your children," said Elena Ivanovna, and she gave her three roubles.

Stepanida suddenly burst into tears and bowed down to the ground. Rodion, too, flopped to the ground, displaying his brownish bald head, and as he did so he almost caught his wife in the ribs with the fork. Elena Ivanovna was overcome with confusion and drove back.

II.

The Lytchkovs, father and son, caught in their meadows two cart-horses, a pony, and a broad-faced Aalhaus bull-calf, and with the help of red-headed Volodka, son of the blacksmith Rodion, drove them to the village. They called the village elder, collected witnesses, and went to look at the damage.

" All right, let 'em !" said Kozov, winking, " le-et 'em ! Let them get out of it if they can, the engineers ! Do you think there is no such thing as law ? All right ! Send for the police inspector, draw up a statement ! . . ."

" Draw up a statement," repeated Volodka.

" I don't want to let this pass !" shouted the younger Lytchkov. He shouted louder and louder, and his beardless face seemed to be more and more swollen. " They've set up a nice fashion ! Leave them free, and they will ruin all the meadows ! You've no sort of right to ill-treat people ! We are not serfs now !"

" We are not serfs now !" repeated Volodka.

" We got on all right without a bridge," said the elder Lytchkov gloomily; " we did not ask for it. What do we want a bridge for ? We don't want it !"

" Brothers, good Christians, we cannot leave it like this !"

" All right, let 'em !" said Kozov, winking. " Let them get out of it if they can ! Landowners, indeed !"

They went back to the village, and as they walked the younger Lytchkov beat himself on the breast with his fist and shouted all the way, and Volodka shouted, too, repeating his words. And meanwhile quite a crowd had gathered in the village round the thoroughbred bull-calf and the horses. The bull-calf was embarrassed and looked up from under his brows, but suddenly lowered his muzzle to the ground and took to his heels, kicking up his hind legs; Kozov was frightened and waved his stick at him, and they all burst out laughing. Then they locked up the beasts and waited.

In the evening the engineer sent five roubles for the damage, and the two horses, the pony and the bull-calf, without being fed or given water, returned home, their heads hanging with a guilty air as though they were convicted criminals.

On getting the five roubles the Lytchkovs, father and son, the village elder and Volodka, punted over the river in a boat and went to a hamlet on the other side where there was a tavern, and there had a long carousal. Their singing and the shouting of the younger Lytchkov could be heard from the village. Their women were uneasy and did not sleep all night. Rodion did not sleep either.

" It's a bad business," he said, sighing and turning from side to side. " The gentleman will be angry, and then there will be trouble. . . . They have insulted the gentleman. . . . Oh, they've insulted him. . . . It's a bad business. . . ."

It happened that the peasants, Rodion amongst them, went into their forest to divide the clearings for mowing, and as they were returning home they were met by the engineer. He was wearing a red cotton shirt and high boots; a setter dog with its long tongue hanging out, followed behind him.

" Good-day, brothers," he said.

The peasants stopped and took off their hats.

" I have long wanted to have a talk with you, friends," he went on. " This is what it is. Ever since the early spring your cattle have been in my copse and garden every day. Everything is trampled down; the pigs have rooted up the meadow, are ruining everything in the kitchen garden, and all the undergrowth in the copse is destroyed. There is no getting on with your herdsmen; one asks them civilly, and they are rude. Damage is done on my estate every day and I do nothing—I don't fine you or make a complaint; meanwhile you impounded my horses and my bull calf and exacted five roubles. Was that right? Is that neighbourly?" he went on, and his face was so soft and persuasive, and his expression was not forbidding. "Is that the way decent people behave? A week ago one of your people cut down two oak saplings in my copse. You have dug up the road to Eresnevo, and now I have to go two miles round. Why do you injure me at every step? What harm have I done you? For God's sake, tell me! My wife and I do our utmost to live with you in peace and harmony; we help the peasants as we can. My wife is a kind, warm-hearted woman; she never refuses you help. That is her dream—to be of use to you and your children. You reward us with evil for our good. You are unjust, my friends. Think of that. I ask you earnestly to think it over. We treat you humanely; repay us in the same coin."

He turned and went away. The peasants stood a little longer, put on their caps and walked away. Rodion, who always understood everything that was said to him in some peculiar way of his own, heaved a sigh and said:

"We must pay. 'Repay in coin, my friends' . . . he said."

They walked to the village in silence. On reaching home Rodion said his prayer, took off

his boots, and sat down on the bench beside his
wife. Stepanida and he always sat side by side
when they were at home, and always walked side
by side in the street; they ate and they drank
and they slept always together, and the older
they grew the more they loved one another. It
was hot and crowded in their hut, and there were
children everywhere—on the floors, in the windows,
on the stove. . . . In spite of her advanced
years Stepanida was still bearing children, and
now, looking at the crowd of children, it was hard
to distinguish which were Rodion's and which
were Volodka's. Volodka's wife, Lukerya, a
plain young woman with prominent eyes and a
nose like the beak of a bird, was kneading dough
in a tub; Volodka was sitting on the stove with
his legs hanging.

" On the road near Nikita's buckwheat . . .
the engineer with his dog . . ." Rodion began,
after a rest, scratching his ribs and his elbow.
" ' You must pay,' says he . . . ' coin,' says he.
. . . Coin or no coin, we shall have to collect ten
kopecks from every hut. We've offended the
gentleman very much. I am sorry for him. . . ."

" We've lived without a bridge," said Volodka,
not looking at anyone, " and we don't want one."

" What next; the bridge is a government
business."

" We don't want it."

" Your opinion is not asked. What is it to
you ?"

" ' Your opinion is not asked,' " Volodka
mimicked him. " We don't want to drive any-

341

where; what do we want with a bridge ? If we have to, we can cross by the boat."

Someone from the yard outside knocked at the window so violently that it seemed to shake the whole hut.

" Is Volodka at home ?" they heard the voice of the younger Lytchkov. " Volodka, come out, come along !"

Volodka jumped down off the stove and began looking for his cap.

" Don't go, Volodka," said Rodion diffidently. " Don't go with them, son. You are foolish, like a little child; they will teach you no good; don't go !"

" Don't go, son," said Stepanida, and she blinked as though about to shed tears. " I bet they are calling you to the tavern."

" 'To the tavern,' " Volodka mimicked.

" You'll come back drunk again, you currish Herod," said Lukerya, looking at him angrily. " Go along, go along, and may you burn up with vodka, you tailless Satan !"

" You hold your tongue," shouted Volodka.

" They've married me to a fool, they've ruined me, a luckless orphan, you red-headed drunkard . . ." wailed Lukerya, wiping her face with a hand covered with dough. " I wish I had never set eyes on you."

Volodka gave her a blow on the ear and went off.

THE NEW VILLA

III.

Elena Ivanovna and her little daughter visited the village on foot. They were out for a walk. It was a Sunday, and the peasant women and girls were walking up and down the street in their brightly-coloured dresses. Rodion and Stepanida, sitting side by side at their door, bowed and smiled to Elena Ivanovna and her little daughter as to acquaintances. From the windows more than a dozen children stared at them; their faces expressed amazement and curiosity, and they could be heard whispering:

" The Kutcherov lady has come! The Kutcherov lady !"

" Good-morning," said Elena Ivanovna, and she stopped; she paused, and then asked: " Well, how are you getting on ?"

" We get along all right, thank God," answered Rodion, speaking rapidly. " To be sure we get along."

" The life we lead !" smiled Stepanida. " You can see our poverty yourself, dear lady! The family is fourteen souls in all, and only two bread-winners. We are supposed to be blacksmiths, but when they bring us a horse to shoe we have no coal, nothing to buy it with. We are worried to death, lady," she went on, and laughed. " Oh, oh, we are worried to death."

Elena Ivanovna sat down at the entrance and, putting her arm round her little girl, pondered something, and judging from the little girl's expression, melancholy thoughts were straying through her mind, too; as she brooded she played with the sumptuous lace on the parasol she had taken out of her mother's hands.

" Poverty," said Rodion, " a great deal of anxiety—you see no end to it. Here, God sends no rain . . . our life is not easy, there is no denying it."

" You have a hard time in this life," said Elena Ivanovna, " but in the other world you will be happy."

Rodion did not understand her, and simply coughed into his clenched hand by way of reply. Stepanida said:

" Dear lady, the rich men will be all right in the next world, too. The rich put up candles, pay for services; the rich give to beggars, but what can the poor man do? He has no time to make the sign of the cross. He is the beggar of beggars himself; how can he think of his soul? And many sins come from poverty; from trouble we snarl at one another like dogs, we haven't a good word to say to one another, and all sorts of things happen, dear lady—God forbid ! It seems we have no luck in this world nor the next. All the luck has fallen to the rich."

She spoke gaily; she was evidently used to talking of her hard life. And Rodion smiled, too; he was pleased that his old woman was so clever, so ready of speech.

" It is only on the surface that the rich seem to be happy," said Elena Ivanovna. " Every man has his sorrow. Here my husband and I do

344

not live poorly, we have means, but are we happy ?
I am young, but I have had four children; my
children are always being ill. I am ill, too, and
constantly being doctored."

" And what is your illness ?" asked Rodion.

" A woman's complaint. I get no sleep; a
continual headache gives me no peace. Here I
am sitting and talking, but my head is bad, I am
weak all over, and I should prefer the hardest
labour to such a condition. My soul, too, is
troubled; I am in continual fear for my children,
my husband. Every family has its own trouble
of some sort; we have ours. I am not of noble
birth. My grandfather was a simple peasant, my
father was a tradesman in Moscow; he was a plain,
uneducated man, too, while my husband's parents
were wealthy and distinguished. They did not
want him to marry me, but he disobeyed them,
quarrelled with them, and they have not forgiven
us to this day. That worries my husband; it
troubles him and keeps him in constant agitation;
he loves his mother, loves her dearly. So I am
uneasy, too, my soul is in pain."

Peasants, men and women, were by now standing round Rodion's hut and listening. Kozov
came up, too, and stood twitching his long, narrow
beard. The Lytchkovs, father and son, drew
near.

" And say what you like, one cannot be happy
and satisfied if one does not feel in one's proper
place," Elena Ivanovna went on. " Each of you
has his strip of land, each of you works and knows
what he is working for; my husband builds bridges

—in short, everyone has his place, while I, I simply walk about. I have not my bit to work. I don't work, and feel as though I were an outsider. I am saying all this that you may not judge from outward appearances; if a man is expensively dressed and has means it does not prove that he is satisfied with his life."

She got up to go away and took her daughter by the hand.

" I like your place here very much," she said, and smiled, and from that faint, diffident smile one could tell how unwell she really was, how young and how pretty; she had a pale, thinnish face with dark eyebrows and fair hair. And the little girl was just such another as her mother: thin, fair, and slender. There was a fragrance of scent about them.

" I like the river and the forest and the village," Elena Ivanovna went on; " I could live here all my life, and I feel as though here I should get strong and find my place. I want to help you— I want to dreadfully—to be of use, to be a real friend to you. I know your need, and what I don't know I feel, my heart guesses. I am sick, feeble, and for me perhaps it is not possible to change my life as I would. But I have children, I will try to bring them up that they may be of use to you, may love you. I shall impress upon them continually that their life does not belong to them, but to you. Only I beg you earnestly, I beseech you, trust us, live in friendship with us. My husband is a kind, good man. Don't worry him, don't irritate him. He is sensitive to every trifle, and yesterday, for instance, your cattle were in our vegetable garden, and one of your people broke down the fence to the bee-hives, and such an attitude to us drives my husband to despair. I beg you," she went on in an imploring voice, and she clasped her hands on her bosom—" I beg you to treat us as good neighbours; let us live in peace ! There is a saying, you know, that even a bad peace is better than a good quarrel, and, ' Don't buy property, but buy neighbours.' I repeat, my husband is a kind man and good; if all goes well we promise to do everything in our power for you; we will mend the roads, we will build a school for your children. I promise you."

" Of course we thank you humbly, lady," said Lytchkov the father, looking at the ground; " you are educated people; it is for you to know best. Only, you see, Voronov, a rich peasant at Eresnevo, promised to build a school; he, too, said, ' I will do this for you,' ' I will do that for you,' and he only put up the framework and refused to go on. And then they made the peasants put the roof on and finish it; it cost them a thousand roubles. Voronov did not care; he only stroked his beard, but the peasants felt it a bit hard."

" That was a crow, but now there's a rook, too," said Kozov, and he winked.

There was the sound of laughter.

" We don't want a school," said Volodka sullenly. " Our children go to Petrovskoe, and they can go on going there; we don't want it."

Elena Ivanovna seemed suddenly intimidated; her face looked paler and thinner, she shrank into herself as though she had been touched with something coarse, and walked away without uttering another word. And she walked more and more quickly, without looking round.

" Lady," said Rodion, walking after her, " lady, wait a bit; hear what I would say to you."

He followed her without his cap, and spoke softly as though begging.

" Lady, wait and hear what I will say to you."

They had walked out of the village, and Elena Ivanovna stopped beside a cart in the shade of an old mountain ash.

" Don't be offended, lady," said Rodion. " What does it mean ? Have patience. Have patience for a couple of years. You will live here, you will have patience, and it will all come round. Our folks are good and peaceable; there's no harm in them; it's God's truth I'm telling you. Don't mind Kozov and the Lytchkovs, and don't mind Volodka. He's a fool; he listens to the first that speaks. The others are quiet folks; they are silent. Some would be glad, you know, to say a word from the heart and to stand up for themselves, but cannot. They have a heart and a conscience, but no tongue. Don't be offended . . . have patience. . . . What does it matter ?"

Elena Ivanovna looked at the broad, tranquil river, pondering, and tears flowed down her cheeks. And Rodion was troubled by those tears; he almost cried himself.

" Never mind . . ." he muttered. " Have

patience for a couple of years. You can have the school, you can have the roads, only not all at once. . . . If you went, let us say, to sow corn on that mound you would first have to weed it out, to pick out all the stones, and then to plough, and work and work . . . and with the people, you see, it is the same . . . you must work and work until you overcome them."

The crowd had moved away from Rodion's hut, and was coming along the street towards the mountain ash. They began singing songs and playing the concertina, and they kept coming closer and closer. . . .

"Mamma, let us go away from here," said the little girl, huddling up to her mother, pale and shaking all over; "let us go away, mamma!"

"Where?"

"To Moscow. . . . Let us go, mamma."

The child began crying.

Rodion was utterly overcome; his face broke into profuse perspiration; he took out of his pocket a little crooked cucumber, like a half-moon, covered with crumbs of rye bread, and began thrusting it into the little girl's hands.

"Come, come," he muttered, scowling severely; "take the little cucumber, eat it up. . . . You mustn't cry. Mamma will whip you. . . . She'll tell your father of you when you get home. Come, come. . . ."

They walked on, and he still followed behind them, wanting to say something friendly and persuasive to them. And seeing that they were both absorbed in their own thoughts and their

349

own griefs, and not noticing him, he stopped and, shading his eyes from the sun, looked after them for a long time till they disappeared into their copse.

IV.

The engineer seemed to grow irritable and petty, and in every trivial incident saw an act of robbery or outrage. His gate was kept bolted even by day, and at night two watchmen walked up and down the garden beating a board; and they gave up employing anyone from Obrut-chanovo as a labourer. As ill-luck would have it someone (either a peasant or one of the work-men) took the new wheels off the cart and re-placed them by old ones, then soon afterwards two bridles and a pair of pincers were carried off, and murmurs arose even in the village. People began to say that a search should be made at the Lytchkovs' and at Volodka's, and then the bridles and the pincers were found under the hedge in the engineer's garden; someone had thrown them down there.

It happened that the peasants were coming in a crowd out of the forest, and again they met the engineer on the road. He stopped, and without wishing them good-day he began, looking angrily first at one, then at another:

"I have begged you not to gather mushrooms in the park and near the yard, but to leave them for my wife and children, but your girls come before daybreak and there is not a mushroom left. . . . Whether one asks you or not it makes no difference. Entreaties, and friendliness, and persuasion I see are all useless."

He fixed his indignant eyes on Rodion and went on:

" My wife and I behaved to you as to human beings, as to our equals, and you ? But what's the use of talking ! It will end by our looking down upon you. There is nothing left !"

And making an effort to restrain his anger, not to say too much, he turned and went on.

On getting home Rodion said his prayer, took off his boots, and sat down beside his wife.

" Yes . . ." he began, with a sigh. " We were walking along just now, and Mr. Kutcherov met us. . . . Yes. . . . He saw the girls at day-break. . . . 'Why don't they bring mushrooms,' he said . . . 'to my wife and children ?' he said. . . . And then he looked at me and he said: ' I and my wife will look after you,' he said. I wanted to fall down at his feet, but I hadn't the courage. . . . God give him health. . . . God bless him ! . . ."

Stepanida crossed herself and sighed.

" They are kind, simple-hearted people," Rodion went on. " ' We shall look after you.' . . . He promised me that before everyone. In our old age . . . it wouldn't be a bad thing. . . . I should always pray for them. . . . Holy Mother, bless them. . . ."

The Feast of the Exaltation of the Cross, the fourteenth of September, was the festival of the village church. The Lytchkovs, father and son, went across the river early in the morning and returned to dinner drunk; they spent a long time going about the village, alternately singing and swearing; then they had a fight and went to the New Villa to complain. First Lytchkov the father went into the yard with a long ashen stick in his hands. He stopped irresolutely and took off his hat. Just at that moment the engineer and his family were sitting on the verandah, drinking tea.

"What do you want?" shouted the engineer.

"Your honour . . ." Lytchkov began, and burst into tears. "Show the Divine mercy, protect me . . . my son makes my life a misery . . . your honour. . . ."

Lytchkov the son walked up, too; he, too, was bareheaded and had a stick in his hand; he stopped and fixed his drunken, senseless eyes on the verandah.

"It is not my business to settle your affairs," said the engineer. "Go to the rural captain or the police officer."

"I have been everywhere. . . . I have lodged a petition . . ." said Lytchkov the father, and he sobbed. "Where can I go now? He can kill me now, it seems. He can do anything. Is that the way to treat a father? A father?"

He raised his stick and hit his son on the head; the son raised his stick and struck his father just on his bald patch such a blow that the stick bounced back. The father did not even flinch, but hit his son again and again on the head. And so they stood and kept hitting one another

352

on the head, and it looked not so much like a fight
as some sort of game. And peasants, men and
women, stood in a crowd at the gate and looked
into the garden, and the faces of all were grave.
They were the peasants who had come to greet
them for the holiday, but, seeing the Lytchkovs,
they were ashamed and did not go in.

The next morning Elena Ivanovna went with
the children to Moscow. And there was a rumour
that the engineer was selling his house. . . .

V.

The peasants had long ago grown used to the
sight of the bridge, and it was difficult to imagine
the river at that place without a bridge. The
heap of rubble left from the building of it had
long been overgrown with grass, the navvies were
forgotten, and instead of the strains of the
" Dubinushka " that they used to sing, the peasants
heard almost every hour the sounds of a passing
train.

The New Villa has long ago been sold; now it
belongs to a government clerk who comes here
from the town for the holidays with his family,
drinks tea on the terrace, and then goes back to
the town again. He wears a cockade on his cap;
he talks and clears his throat as though he were
a very important official, though he is only of
the rank of a collegiate secretary, and when the
peasants bow he makes no response.

In Obrutchanovo everyone has grown older;
Kozov is dead. In Rodion's hut there are even

more children. Volodka has grown a long red beard. They are still as poor as ever.

In the early spring the Obrutchanovo peasants were sawing wood near the station. And after work they were going home; they walked without haste one after the other. Broad saws curved over their shoulders; the sun was reflected in them. The nightingales were singing in the bushes on the bank, larks were trilling in the heavens. It was quiet at the New Villa; there was not a soul there, and only golden pigeons—golden because the sunlight was streaming upon them—were flying over the house. All of them—Rodion, the two Lytchkovs, and Volodka—thought of the white horses, the little ponies, the fireworks, the boat with the lanterns; they remembered how the engineer's wife, so beautiful and so grandly dressed, had come into the village and talked to them in such a friendly way. And it seemed as though all that had never been; it was all like a dream or a fairy-tale.

They trudged along, tired out, and mused as they went. . . . In their village, they mused, the people were good, quiet, sensible, fearing God, and Elena Ivanovna, too, was quiet, kind, and gentle; it made one sad to look at her, but why had they not got on together ? Why had they parted like enemies ? How was it that some mist had shrouded from their eyes what mattered most, and had let them see nothing but damage done by cattle, bridles, pincers, and all those trivial things which now, as they remembered them, seemed so nonsensical ? How was it that with the new owner they lived in peace, and yet had been on bad terms with the engineer?

And not knowing what answer to make to these questions they were all silent except Volodka, who muttered something.

" What is it?" Rodion asked.

" We lived without a bridge . . ." said Volodka gloomily. " We lived without a bridge, and did not ask for one . . . and we don't want it. . . ."

No one answered him, and they walked on in silence with drooping heads.

1899

THE TEACHER OF LITERATURE

I.

THERE was the thud of horses' hoofs on the wooden floor; they brought out of the stable the black horse, Count Nulin; then the white, Giant; then his sister Maika. They were all magnificent, expensive horses. Old Shelestov saddled Giant and said, addressing his daughter Masha:

" Well, Marie Godefroi, come, get on ! Hopla !"

Masha Shelestov was the youngest of the family; she was eighteen, but her family could not get used to thinking that she was not a little girl, and so they still called her Manya and Manyusa; and after there had been a circus in the town which she had eagerly visited, everyone began to call her Marie Godefroi.

" Hop-la !" she cried, mounting Giant. Her sister Varya got on Maika, Nikitin on Count Nulin, the officers on their horses, and the long picturesque cavalcade, with the officers in white tunics and the ladies in their riding habits, moved at a walking pace out of the yard.

Nikitin noticed that when they were mounting the horses and afterwards riding out into the street, Masha for some reason paid attention to no one but himself. She looked anxiously at him and at Count Nulin and said:

" You must hold him all the time on the curb, Sergey Vassilitch. Don't let him shy. He's pretending."

And either because her Giant was very friendly with Count Nulin, or perhaps by chance, she rode all the time beside Nikitin, as she had done the day before, and the day before that. And he looked at her graceful little figure sitting on the proud white beast, at her delicate profile, at the chimney-pot hat, which did not suit her at all and made her look older than her age—looked at her with joy, with tenderness, with rapture; listened to her, taking in little of what she said, and thought:

" I promise on my honour, I swear to God, I won't be afraid and I'll speak to her to-day."

It was seven o'clock in the evening—the time when the scent of white acacia and lilac. is so strong that the air and the very trees seem heavy with the fragrance. The band was already playing in the town gardens. The horses made a resounding thud on the pavement, on all sides there were sounds of laughter, talk, and the banging of gates. The soldiers they met saluted the officers, the schoolboys bowed to Nikitin, and all the people who were hurrying to the gardens to hear the band were pleased at the sight of the party. And how warm it was! How soft-looking were the clouds scattered carelessly about the sky, how kindly and comforting the shadows of the poplars and the acacias, which stretched across

357

the street and reached as far as the balconies and second storeys of the houses on the other side.

They rode on out of the town and set off at a trot along the highroad. Here there was no scent of lilac and acacia, no music of the band, but there was the fragrance of the fields, there was the green of young rye and wheat, the marmots were squeaking, the rooks were cawing. Wherever one looked it was green, with only here and there black patches of bare ground, and far away to the left in the cemetery a white streak of apple-blossom.

They passed the slaughter-houses, then the brewery, and overtook a military band hastening to the suburban gardens.

" Polyansky has a very fine horse, I don't deny that," Masha said to Nikitin, with a glance towards the officer who was riding beside Varya. " But it has blemishes. That white patch on its left leg ought not to be there, and, look, it tosses its head. You can't train it not to now; it will toss its head till the end of its days."

Masha was as passionate a lover of horses as her father. She felt a pang when she saw other people with fine horses, and was pleased when she saw defects in them. Nikitin knew nothing about horses; it made absolutely no difference to him whether he held his horse on the bridle or on the curb, whether he trotted or galloped; he only felt that his position was strained and unnatural, and that consequently the officers who knew how to sit in their saddles must please Masha more than he could. And he was jealous of the officers.

358

As they rode by the suburban gardens someone suggested their going in and getting some seltzer-water. They went in. There were no trees but oaks in the gardens; they had only just come into leaf, so that through the young foliage the whole garden could still be seen with its platform, little tables, and swings, and the crows' nests were visible, looking like big hats. The party dismounted near a table and asked for seltzer-water. People they knew, walking about the garden, came up to them. Among them the army doctor in high boots, and the conductor of the band, waiting for the musicians. The doctor must have taken Nikitin for a student, for he asked:

" Have you come for the summer holidays ?"

" No, I am here permanently," answered Nikitin. " I am a teacher at the school."

" You don't say so ?" said the doctor, with surprise. " So young and already a teacher ?"

" Young, indeed ! My goodness, I'm twenty-six !"

" You have a beard and moustache, but yet one would never guess you were more than twenty-two or twenty-three. How young-looking you are !"

" What a beast !" thought Nikitin. " He, too, takes me for a whipper-snapper !"

He disliked it extremely when people referred to his youth, especially in the presence of women or the schoolboys. Ever since he had come to the town as a master in the school he had detested his own youthful appearance. The schoolboys were not afraid of him, old people called him " young man," ladies preferred dancing with him to listening to his long arguments, and he would have given a great deal to be ten years older.

From the garden they went on to the Shelestovs' farm. There they stopped at the gate and asked the bailiff's wife, Praskovya, to bring some new milk. Nobody drank the milk; they all looked at one another, laughed, and galloped back. As they rode back the band was playing in the suburban garden; the sun was setting behind the cemetery, and half the sky was crimson from the sunset.

Masha again rode beside Nikitin. He wanted to tell her how passionately he loved her, but he was afraid he would be overheard by the officers and Varya, and he was silent. Masha was silent, too, and he felt why she was silent and why she was riding beside him, and was so happy that the earth, the sky, the lights of the town, the black outline of the brewery—all blended for him into something very pleasant and comforting, and it seemed to him as though Count Nulin were stepping on air and would climb up into the crimson sky.

They arrived home. The samovar was already boiling on the table, old Shelestov was sitting with his friends, officials in the Circuit Court, and as usual he was criticizing something.

" It's loutishness !" he said. " Loutishness and nothing more. Yes !"

Since Nikitin had been in love with Masha, everything at the Shelestovs' pleased him: the house, the garden, and the evening tea, and the wickerwork chairs, and the old nurse, and even the

word " loutishness," which the old man was fond
of using. The only thing he did not like was the
number of cats and dogs and the Egyptian pigeons,
who moaned disconsolately in a big cage in the
verandah. There were so many house-dogs and
yard-dogs that he had only learnt to recognize
two of them in the course of his acquaintance
with the Shelestovs: Mushka and Som. Mushka
was a little mangy dog with a shaggy face, spiteful
and spoiled. She hated Nikitin: when she saw
him she put her head on one side, showed her
teeth, and began: " Rrr . . . nga-nga-nga . . .
rrr . . . !" Then she would get under his chair,
and when he would try to drive her away she would
go off into piercing yaps, and the family would say:
" Don't be frightened. She doesn't bite. She is
a good dog."

Som was a tall black dog with long legs and a
tail as hard as a stick. At dinner and tea he
usually moved about under the table, and thumped
on people's boots and on the legs of the table
with his tail. He was a good-natured, stupid
dog, but Nikitin could not endure him because he
had the habit of putting his head on people's
knees at dinner and messing their trousers with
saliva. Nikitin had more than once tried to hit
him on his head with a knife-handle, to flip him
on the nose, had abused him, had complained of
him, but nothing saved his trousers.

After their ride the tea, jam, rusks, and butter
seemed very nice. They all drank their first glass
in silence and with great relish; over the second
they began an argument. It was always Varya

who started the arguments at tea; she was good-looking, handsomer than Masha, and was considered the cleverest and most cultured person in the house, and she behaved with dignity and severity, as an eldest daughter should who has taken the place of her dead mother in the house. As the mistress of the house, she felt herself entitled to wear a dressing-gown in the presence of her guests, and to call the officers by their surnames; she looked on Masha as a little girl, and talked to her as though she were a schoolmistress. She used to speak of herself as an old maid—so she was certain she would marry.

Every conversation, even about the weather, she invariably turned into an argument. She had a passion for catching at words, pouncing on contradictions, quibbling over phrases. You would begin talking to her, and she would stare at you and suddenly interrupt: "Excuse me, excuse me, Petrov, the other day you said the very opposite!"

Or she would smile ironically and say: "I notice, though, you begin to advocate the principles of the secret police. I congratulate you."

If you jested or made a pun, you would hear her voice at once: "That's stale," "That's pointless." If an officer ventured on a joke, she would make a contemptuous grimace and say, "An army joke!"

And she rolled the *r* so impressively that Mushka invariably answered from under a chair, "Rrr . . nga-nga-nga . . . !"

On this occasion at tea the argument began with Nikitin's mentioning the school examinations.

"Excuse me, Sergey Vassilitch," Varya interrupted him. "You say it's difficult for the boys. And whose fault is that, let me ask you? For instance, you set the boys in the eighth class an essay on 'Pushkin as a Psychologist.' To begin with, you shouldn't set such a difficult subject; and, secondly, Pushkin was not a psychologist. Shtchedrin now, or Dostoevsky let us say, is a different matter, but Pushkin is a great poet and nothing more."

"Shtchedrin is one thing, and Pushkin is another," Nikitin answered sulkily.

"I know you don't think much of Shtchedrin at the high school, but that's not the point. Tell me, in what sense is Pushkin a psychologist?"

"Why, do you mean to say he was not a psychologist? If you like, I'll give you examples."

And Nikitin recited several passages from "Onyegin" and then from "Boris Godunov."

"I see no psychology in that." Varya sighed. "The psychologist is the man who describes the recesses of the human soul, and that's fine poetry and nothing more."

"I know the sort of psychology you want," said Nikitin, offended. "You want someone to saw my finger with a blunt saw while I howl at the top of my voice—that's what you mean by psychology."

"That's poor! But still you haven't shown me in what sense Pushkin is a psychologist?"

When Nikitin had to argue against anything that seemed to him narrow, conventional, or something of that kind, he usually leaped up from his seat, clutched at his head with both hands, and began with a moan, running from one end of the room to another. And it was the same now: he jumped up, clutched his head in his hands, and with a moan walked round the table, then he sat down a little way off.

The officers took his part. Captain Polyansky began assuring Varya that Pushkin really was a psychologist, and to prove it quoted two lines from Lermontov; Lieutenant Gernet said that if Pushkin had not been a psychologist they would not have erected a monument to him in Moscow.

"That's loutishness!" was heard from the other end of the table. "I said as much to the governor: 'It's loutishness, your Excellency,' I said."

"I won't argue any more," cried Nikitin. "It's unending. . . . Enough! Ach, get away, you nasty dog!" he cried to Som, who laid his head and paw on his knee.

"Rrr . . . nga-nga-nga!" came from under the table.

"Admit that you are wrong!" cried Varya. "Own up!"

But some young ladies came in, and the argument dropped of itself. They all went into the drawing-room. Varya sat down at the piano and began playing dances. They danced first a waltz, then a polka, then a quadrille with a grand chain which Captain Polyansky led through all the rooms, then a waltz again.

During the dancing the old men sat in the drawing-room, smoking and looking at the young people. Among them was Shebaldin, the director of the municipal bank, who was famed for his love of literature and dramatic art. He had founded the local Musical and Dramatic Society, and took part in the performances himself, confining himself, for some reason, to playing comic footmen or to reading in a sing-song voice " The Woman who was a Sinner." His nickname in the town was " the Mummy," as he was tall, very lean and scraggy, and always had a solemn air and a fixed, lustreless eye. He was so devoted to the dramatic art that he even shaved his moustache and beard, and this made him still more like a mummy.

After the grand chain, he shuffled up to Nikitin sideways, coughed, and said:

" I had the pleasure of being present during the argument at tea. I fully share your opinion. We are of one mind, and it would be a great pleasure to me to talk to you. Have you read Lessing on the dramatic art of Hamburg ?"

" No, I haven't."

Shebaldin was horrified, and waved his hands as though he had burnt his fingers, and saying nothing more, staggered back from Nikitin. Shebaldin's appearance, his question, and his surprise, struck Nikitin as funny, but he thought none the less:

" It really is awkward. I am a teacher of literature, and to this day I've not read Lessing. I must read him."

Before supper the whole company, old and young, sat down to play " fate." They took two packs of cards: one pack was dealt round to the company, the other was laid on the table face downwards.

"The one who has this card in his hand," old Shelestov began solemnly, lifting the top card of the second pack, "is fated to go into the nursery and kiss nurse."

The pleasure of kissing the nurse fell to the lot of Shebaldin. They all crowded round him, took him to the nursery, and laughing and clapping their hands, made him kiss the nurse. There was a great uproar and shouting.

"Not so ardently!" cried Shelestov with tears of laughter. "Not so ardently!"

It was Nikitin's "fate" to hear the confessions of all. He sat on a chair in the middle of the drawing-room. A shawl was brought and put over his head. The first who came to confess to him was Varya.

"I know your sins," Nikitin began, looking in the darkness at her stern profile. "Tell me, madam, how do you explain your walking with Polyansky every day? Oh, it's not for nothing she walks with an hussar!"

"That's poor," said Varya, and walked away.

Then under the shawl he saw the shine of big motionless eyes, caught the lines of a dear profile in the dark, together with a familiar, precious fragrance which reminded Nikitin of Masha's room.

"Marie Godefroi," he said, and did not know his own voice, it was so soft and tender, "what are your sins?"

Masha screwed up her eyes and put out the tip

of her tongue at him, then she laughed and went away. And a minute later she was standing in the middle of the room, clapping her hands and crying:

" Supper, supper, supper !"

And they all streamed into the dining-room. At supper Varya had another argument, and this time with her father. Polyansky ate stolidly, drank red wine, and described to Nikitin how once in a winter campaign he had stood all night up to his knees in a bog; the enemy was so near that they were not allowed to speak or smoke, the night was cold and dark, a piercing wind was blowing. Nikitin listened and stole side-glances at Masha. She was gazing at him immovably, without blinking, as though she was pondering something or was lost in a reverie. . . . It was pleasure and agony to him both at once.

" Why does she look at me like that ?" was the question that fretted him. " It's awkward. People may notice it. Oh, how young, how naïve she is !"

The party broke up at midnight. When Nikitin went out at the gate, a window opened on the first-floor, and Masha showed herself at it.

" Sergey Vassilitch !" she called.

" What is it ?"

" I tell you what . . ." said Masha, evidently thinking of something to say. " I tell you what. . . . Polyansky said he would come in a day or two with his camera and take us all. We must meet here."

" Very well."

367

Masha vanished, the window was slammed, and someone immediately began playing the piano in the house.

"Well, it is a house !" thought Nikitin while he crossed the street. "A house in which there is no moaning except from Egyptian pigeons, and they only do it because they have no other means of expressing their joy !"

But the Shelestovs were not the only festive household. Nikitin had not gone two hundred paces before he heard the strains of a piano from another house. A little further he met a peasant playing the balalaika at the gate. In the gardens the band struck up a potpourri of Russian songs.

Nikitin lived nearly half a mile from the Shelestovs' in a flat of eight rooms at the rent of three hundred roubles a year, which he shared with his colleague Ippolit Ippolititch, a teacher of geography and history. When Nikitin went in this Ippolit Ippolititch, a snub-nosed, middle-aged man with a reddish beard, with a coarse, good-natured, unintellectual face like a workman's, was sitting at the table correcting his pupils' maps. He considered that the most important and necessary part of the study of geography was the drawing of maps, and of the study of history the learning of dates: he would sit for nights together correcting in blue pencil the maps drawn by the boys and girls he taught, or making chronological tables.

"What a lovely day it has been !" said Nikitin, going in to him. "I wonder at you—how can you sit indoors ?"

Ippolit Ippolititch was not a talkative person;

368

he either remained silent or talked of things which everybody knew already. Now what he answered was:

" Yes, very fine weather. It's May now; we soon shall have real summer. And summer's a very different thing from winter. In the winter you have to heat the stoves, but in summer you can keep warm without. In summer you have your window open at night and still are warm, and in winter you are cold even with the double frames in."

Nikitin had not sat at the table for more than one minute before he was bored.

" Good-night !" he said, getting up and yawning. " I wanted to tell you something romantic concerning myself, but you are—geography ! If one talks to you of love, you will ask one at once, ' What was the date of the Battle of Kalka ?' Confound you, with your battles and your capes in Siberia !"

" What are you cross about ?"

" Why, it is vexatious !"

And vexed that he had not spoken to Masha, and that he had no one to talk to of his love, he went to his study and lay down upon the sofa. It was dark and still in the study. Lying gazing into the darkness, Nikitin for some reason began thinking how in two or three years he would go to Petersburg, how Masha would see him off at the station and would cry; in Petersburg he would get a long letter from her in which she would entreat him to come home as quickly as possible. And he would write to her. . . . He would begin his letter like that: " My dear little rat !"

" Yes, my dear little rat !" he said, and he laughed.

He was lying in an uncomfortable position. He put his arms under his head and put his left leg over the back of the sofa. He felt more comfortable. Meanwhile a pale light was more and more perceptible at the windows, sleepy cocks crowed in the yard. Nikitin went on thinking how he would come back from Petersburg, how Masha would meet him at the station, and with a shriek of delight would fling herself on his neck; or, better still, he would cheat her and come home by stealth late at night: the cook would open the door, then he would go on tiptoe to the bedroom, undress noiselessly, and jump into bed ! And she would wake up and be overjoyed.

It was beginning to get quite light. By now there were no windows, no study. On the steps of the brewery by which they had ridden that day Masha was sitting, saying something. Then she took Nikitin by the arm and went with him to the suburban garden. There he saw the oaks and the crows' nests like hats. One of the nests rocked; out of it peeped Shebaldin, shouting loudly: " You have not read Lessing !"

Nikitin shuddered all over and opened his eyes. Ippolit Ippolititch was standing before the sofa, and, throwing back his head, was putting on his cravat.

" Get up; it's time for school," he said. " You shouldn't sleep in your clothes; it spoils your clothes. You should sleep in your bed, undressed."

And as usual he began slowly and emphatically saying what everybody knew.

Nikitin's first lesson was on Russian language in the second class. When at nine o'clock punctually he went into the classroom, he saw written on the blackboard two large letters—*M. S.* That, no doubt, meant Masha Shelestov.

"They've scented it out already, the rascals . . ." thought Nikitin. "How is it they know everything?"

The second lesson was in the fifth class. And there two letters, *M. S.*, were written on the blackboard; and when he went out of the classroom at the end of the lesson, he heard the shout behind him as though from a theatre gallery:

"Hurrah for Masha Shelestov!"

His head was heavy from sleeping in his clothes, his limbs were weighed down with inertia. The boys, who were expecting every day to break up before the examinations, did nothing, were restless, and so bored that they got into mischief. Nikitin, too, was restless, did not notice their pranks, and was continually going to the window. He could see the street brilliantly lighted up with the sun; above the houses the blue limpid sky, the birds, and far, far away, beyond the gardens and the houses, vast indefinite distance, the forests in the blue haze, the smoke from a passing train. . . .

Here two officers in white tunics, playing with their whips, passed in the street in the shade of the acacias. Here a lot of Jews, with grey beards, and caps on, drove past in a waggonette. . . . The governess walked by with the director's granddaughter. Som ran by in the company of two other dogs. . . . And then Varya, wearing a simple grey dress and red stockings, carrying the " Vyestnik Evropi " in her hand, passed by. She must have been to the town library. . . .

And it would be a long time before lessons were over at three o'clock ! And after school he could not go home nor to the Shelestovs', but must go to give a lesson at Wolf's. This Wolf, a wealthy Jew who had turned Lutheran, did not send his children to the high school, but had them taught at home by the high-school masters, and paid five roubles a lesson.

He was bored, bored, bored.

At three o'clock he went to Wolf's and spent there, as it seemed to him, an eternity. He left there at five o'clock, and before seven he had to be at the high school again to a meeting of the masters—to draw up the plan for the *viva voce* examination of the fourth and sixth classes.

When late in the evening he left the high school and went to the Shelestovs', his heart was beating and his face was flushed. A month before, even a week before, he had, every time that he made up his mind to speak to her, prepared a whole speech, with an introduction and a conclusion. Now he had not one word ready; everything was in a muddle in his head, and all he knew was that to-day he would *certainly* declare himself, and that it was utterly impossible to wait any longer.

" I will ask her to come to the garden," he thought; " we'll walk about a little and I'll speak."

There was not a soul in the hall; he went into

the dining-room and then into the drawing-room. . . . There was no one there either. He could hear Varya arguing with someone upstairs and the clink of the dressmaker's scissors in the nursery.

There was a little room in the house which had three names: the little room, the passage room, and the dark room. There was a big cupboard in it where they kept medicines, gunpowder, and their hunting gear. Leading from this room to the first floor was a narrow wooden staircase where cats were always asleep. There were two doors in it—one leading to the nursery, one to the drawing-room. When Nikitin went into this room to go upstairs, the door from the nursery opened and shut with such a bang that it made the stairs and the cupboard tremble; Masha, in a dark dress, ran in with a piece of blue material in her hand, and, not noticing Nikitin, darted towards the stairs.

" Stay . . ." said Nikitin, stopping her. " Good-evening, Godefroi. . . . Allow me. . . ."

He gasped, he did not know what to say; with one hand he held her hand and with the other the blue material. And she was half frightened, half surprised, and looked at him with big eyes.

" Allow me . . ." Nikitin went on, afraid she would go away. " There's something I must say to you. . . . Only . . . it's inconvenient here. I cannot, I am incapable. . . . Understand, Godefroi, I can't—that's all. . . ."

The blue material slipped on to the floor, and Nikitin took Masha by the other hand. She turned

373

pale, moved her lips, then stepped back from Nikitin and found herself in the corner between the wall and the cupboard.

" On my honour, I assure you . . ." he said softly. " Masha, on my honour. . . ."

She threw back her head and he kissed her lips, and that the kiss might last longer he put his fingers to her cheeks; and it somehow happened that he found himself in the corner between the cupboard and the wall, and she put her arms round his neck and pressed her head against his chin.

Then they both ran into the garden. The Shelestovs had a garden of nine acres. There were about twenty old maples and lime-trees in it; there was one fir-tree, and all the rest were fruit-trees: cherries, apples, pears, horse-chestnuts, silvery olive-trees. . . . There were heaps of flowers, too.

Nikitin and Masha ran along the avenues in silence, laughed, asked each other from time to time disconnected questions which they did not answer. A crescent moon was shining over the garden, and drowsy tulips and irises were stretching up from the dark grass in its faint light, as though entreating for words of love for them, too.

When Nikitin and Masha went back to the house, the officers and the young ladies were already assembled and dancing the mazurka. Again Polyansky led the grand chain through all the rooms, again after dancing they played " fate." Before supper, when the visitors had gone into the dining-room, Masha, left alone with Nikitin, pressed close to him and said:

" You must speak to papa and Varya yourself; I am ashamed."

After supper he talked to the old father. After listening to him, Shelestov thought a little and said:

" I am very grateful for the honour you do me and my daughter, but let me speak to you as a friend. I will speak to you, not as a father, but as one gentleman to another. Tell me, why do you want to be married so young ? Only peasants are married so young, and that, of course, is loutishness. But why should you ? Where's the satisfaction of putting on the fetters at your age ?"

" I am not young !" said Nikitin, offended. " I am in my twenty-seventh year."

" Papa, the farrier has come !" cried Varya from the other room.

And the conversation broke off. Varya, Masha, and Polyansky saw Nikitin home. When they reached his gate, Varya said:

" Why is it your mysterious Metropolit Metropolititch never shows himself anywhere ? He might come and see us."

The mysterious Ippolit Ippolititch was sitting on his bed, taking off his trousers, when Nikitin went in to him.

" Don't go to bed, my dear fellow," said Nikitin breathlessly. " Stop a minute; don't go to bed !"

Ippolit Ippolititch put on his trousers hurriedly and asked in a flutter:

375

" What is it ?"

" I am going to be married."

Nikitin sat down beside his companion, and looking at him wonderingly, as though surprised at himself, said:

" Only fancy, I am going to be married ! To Masha Shelestov ! I made an offer to-day."

" Well ? She seems a good sort of girl. Only she is very young."

" Yes, she is young," sighed Nikitin, and shrugged his shoulders with a careworn air. " Very, very young !"

" She was my pupil at the high school. I know her. She wasn't bad at geography, but she was no good at history. And she was inattentive in class, too."

Nikitin for some reason felt suddenly sorry for his companion, and longed to say something kind and comforting to him.

" My dear fellow, why don't you get married ?" he asked. " Why don't you marry Varya, for instance ? She is a splendid, first-rate girl ! It's true she is very fond of arguing, but a heart . . . what a heart ! She was just asking about you. Marry her, my dear boy ! Eh ?"

He knew perfectly well that Varya would not marry this dull, snub-nosed man, but still persuaded him to marry her—why ?

" Marriage is a serious step," said Ippolit Ippolititch after a moment's thought. " One has to look at it all round and weigh things thoroughly; it's not to be done rashly. Prudence is always a good thing, and especially in marriage, when a man, ceasing to be a bachelor, begins a new life."

And he talked of what everyone has known for ages. Nikitin did not stay to listen, said good-night, and went to his own room. He undressed quickly and quickly got into bed, in order to be able to think the sooner of his happiness, of Masha, of the future; he smiled, then suddenly recalled that he had not read Lessing.

" I must read him," he thought. " Though, after all, why should I ? Bother him !"

And exhausted by his happiness, he fell asleep at once and went on smiling till the morning.

He dreamed of the thud of horses' hoofs on a wooden floor; he dreamed of the black horse Count Nulin, then of the white Giant and its sister Maika, being led out of the stable.

II.

" It was very crowded and noisy in the church, and once someone cried out, and the head priest, who was marrying Masha and me, looked through his spectacles at the crowd, and said severely: ' Don't move about the church, and don't make a noise, but stand quietly and pray. You should have the fear of God in your hearts.'

" My best men were two of my colleagues, and Masha's best men were Captain Polyansky and Lieutenant Gernet. The bishop's choir sang superbly. The sputtering of the candles, the brilliant light, the gorgeous dresses, the officers, the numbers of gay, happy faces, and a special

377

ethereal look in Masha, everything together—the surroundings and the words of the wedding prayers—moved me to tears and filled me with triumph. I thought how my life had blossomed, how poetically it was shaping itself ! Two years ago I was still a student, I was living in cheap furnished rooms, without money, without relations, and, as I fancied then, with nothing to look forward to. Now I am a teacher in the high school in one of the best provincial towns, with a secure income, loved, spoiled. It is for my sake, I thought, this crowd is collected, for my sake three candelabra have been lighted, the deacon is booming, the choir is doing its best; and it's for my sake that this young creature, whom I soon shall call my wife, is so young, so elegant, and so joyful. I recalled our first meetings, our rides into the country, my declaration of love and the weather, which, as though expressly, was so exquisitely fine all the summer; and the happiness which at one time in my old rooms seemed to me possible only in novels and stories, I was now experiencing in reality—I was now, as it were, holding it in my hands.

" After the ceremony they all crowded in disorder round Masha and me, expressed their genuine pleasure, congratulated us and wished us joy. The brigadier-general, an old man of seventy, confined himself to congratulating Masha, and said to her in a squeaky, aged voice, so loud that it could be heard all over the church:

" ' I hope that even after you are married you may remain the rose you are now, my dear.'

378

" The officers, the director, and all the teachers smiled from politeness, and I was conscious of an agreeable artificial smile on my face, too. Dear Ippolit Ippolititch, the teacher of history and geography, who always says what everyone has heard before, pressed my hand warmly and said with feeling:

" ' Hitherto you have been unmarried and have lived alone, and now you are married and no longer single.'

" From the church we went to a two-storeyed house which I am receiving as part of the dowry Besides that house Masha is bringing me twenty thousand roubles, as well as a piece of waste land with a shanty on it, where I am told there are numbers of hens and ducks which are not looked after and are turning wild. When I got home from the church, I stretched myself at full length on the low sofa in my new study and began to smoke; I felt snug, cosy, and comfortable, as I never had in my life before. And meanwhile the wedding party were shouting ' Hurrah !' while a wretched band in the hall played flourishes and all sorts of trash. Varya, Masha's sister, ran into the study with a wineglass in her hand, and with a queer, strained expression, as though her mouth were full of water; apparently she had meant to go on further, but she suddenly burst out laughing and sobbing, and the wineglass crashed on the floor. We took her by the arms and led her away.

" ' Nobody can understand !' she muttered afterwards, lying on the old nurse's bed in a back

379

room. ' Nobody, nobody ! My God, nobody can understand !'

" But everyone understood very well that she was four years older than her sister Masha, and still unmarried, and that she was crying, not from envy, but from the melancholy consciousness that her time was passing, and perhaps had passed. When they danced the quadrille, she was back in the drawing-room with a tear-stained and heavily powdered face, and I saw Captain Polyansky holding a plate of ice before her while she ate it with a spoon.

" It is past five o'clock in the morning. I took up my diary to describe my complete and perfect happiness, and thought I would write a good six pages, and read it to-morrow to Masha ; but, strange to say, everything is muddled in my head and as misty as a dream, and I can remember vividly nothing but that episode with Varya, and I want to write, ' Poor Varya !' I could go on sitting here and writing ' Poor Varya !' By the way, the trees have begun rustling ; it will rain. The crows are cawing, and my Masha, who has just gone to sleep, has for some reason a sorrowful face."

For a long while afterwards Nikitin did not write his diary. At the beginning of August he had the school examinations, and after the fifteenth the classes began. As a rule he set off for school before nine in the morning, and before ten o'clock he was looking at his watch and pining for his Masha and his new house. In the lower forms he would set some boy to dictate, and while the boys were writing, would sit in the window

with his eyes shut, dreaming; whether he dreamed
of the future or recalled the past, everything
seemed to him equally delightful, like a fairy tale.
In the senior classes they were reading aloud
Gogol or Pushkin's prose works, and that made
him sleepy; people, trees, fields, horses, rose
before his imagination, and he would say with a
sigh, as though fascinated by the author:

" How lovely !"

At the midday recess Masha used to send him
lunch in a snow-white napkin, and he would eat
it slowly, with pauses, to prolong the enjoyment
of it; and Ippolit Ippolititch, whose lunch as a rule
consisted of nothing but bread, looked at him with
respect and envy, and gave expression to some
familiar fact, such as:

" Men cannot live without food."

After school Nikitin went straight to give his
private lessons, and when at last by six o'clock
he got home, he felt excited and anxious, as though
he had been away for a year. He would run
upstairs breathless, find Masha, throw his arms
round her, and kiss her and swear that he loved her,
that he could not live without her, declare that he
had missed her fearfully, and ask her in trepidation
how she was and why she looked so depressed.
Then they would dine together. After dinner
he would lie on the sofa in his study and smoke,
while she sat beside him and talked in a low
voice.

His happiest days now were Sundays and
holidays, when he was at home from morning till
evening. On those days he took part in the

naïve but extraordinarily pleasant life which
reminded him of a pastoral idyl. He was never
weary of watching how his sensible and practical
Masha was arranging her nest, and anxious to
show that he was of some use in the house, he would
do something useless—for instance, bring the chaise
out of the stable and look at it from every side.
Masha had installed a regular dairy with three
cows, and in her cellar she had many jugs of milk
and pots of sour cream, and she kept it all for
butter. Sometimes, by way of a joke, Nikitin
would ask her for a glass of milk, and she would
be quite upset because it was against her rules;
but he would laugh and throw his arms round her,
saying:

" There, there; I was joking, my darling ! I
was joking !"

Or he would laugh at her strictness when,
finding in the cupboard some stale bit of cheese or
sausage as hard as a stone, she would say seriously:

" They will eat that in the kitchen."

He would observe that such a scrap was only
fit for a mousetrap, and she would reply warmly
that men knew nothing about housekeeping, and
that it was just the same to the servants if you were
to send down a hundredweight of savouries to
the kitchen. He would agree, and embrace her
enthusiastically. Everything that was just in
what she said seemed to him extraordinary and
amazing; and what did not fit in with his convictions seemed to him naïve and touching.

Sometimes he was in a philosophical mood,
and he would begin to discuss some abstract

subject while she listened and looked at his face with curiosity.

"I am immensely happy with you, my joy," he used to say, playing with her fingers or plaiting and unplaiting her hair. "But I don't look upon this happiness of mine as something that has come to me by chance, as though it had dropped from heaven. This happiness is a perfectly natural, consistent, logical consequence. I believe that man is the creator of his own happiness, and now I am enjoying just what I have myself created. Yes, I speak without false modesty: I have created this happiness myself and I have a right to it. You know my past. My unhappy childhood, without father or mother; my depressing youth, poverty—all this was a struggle, all this was the path by which I made my way to happiness. . . ."

In October the school sustained a heavy loss: Ippolit Ippolititch was taken ill with erysipelas on the head and died. For two days before his death he was unconscious and delirious, but even in his delirium he said nothing that was not perfectly well known to everyone.

"The Volga flows into the Caspian Sea. . . . Horses eat oats and hay. . . ."

There were no lessons at the high school on the day of his funeral. His colleagues and pupils were the coffin-bearers, and the school choir sang all the way to the grave the anthem "Holy God." Three priests, two deacons, all his pupils and the staff of the boys' high school, and the bishop's choir in their best kaftans, took part in the procession

And passers-by who met the solemn procession crossed themselves and said:

" God grant us all such a death."

Returning home from the cemetery much moved, Nikitin got out his diary from the table and wrote:

" We have just consigned to the tomb Ippolit Ippolititch Ryzhitsky. Peace to your ashes, modest worker ! Masha, Varya, and all the women at the funeral, wept from genuine feeling, perhaps because they knew this uninteresting, humble man had never been loved by a woman. I wanted to say a warm word at my colleague's grave, but I was warned that this might displease the director, as he did not like our poor friend. I believe that this is the first day since my marriage that my heart has been heavy."

There was no other event of note in the scholastic year.

The winter was mild, with wet snow and no frost; on Epiphany Eve, for instance, the wind howled all night as though it were autumn, and water trickled off the roofs; and in the morning, at the ceremony of the blessing of the water, the police allowed no one to go on the river, because they said the ice was swelling up and looked dark. But in spite of bad weather Nikitin's life was as happy as in summer. And, indeed, he acquired another source of pleasure; he learned to play *vint*. Only one thing troubled him, moved him to anger, and seemed to prevent him from being perfectly happy: the cats and dogs which formed part of his wife's dowry The rooms, especially in the morning, always smelt like a menagerie, and nothing could destroy the odour; the cats frequently fought with the dogs. The spiteful beast Mushka was fed a dozen times a day; she still refused to recognize Nikitin and growled at him: " Rrr . . . nga-nga-nga !"

One night in Lent he was returning home from the club where he had been playing cards. It was dark, raining, and muddy. Nikitin had an unpleasant feeling at the bottom of his heart and could not account for it. He did not know whether it was because he had lost twelve roubles at cards, or whether because one of the players, when they were settling up, had said that of course Nikitin had pots of money, with obvious reference to his wife's portion. He did not regret the twelve roubles, and there was nothing offensive in what had been said; but, still, there was the unpleasant feeling. He did not even feel a desire to go home.

" Foo, how horrid !" he said, standing still at a lamp-post.

It occurred to him that he did not regret the twelve roubles because he got them for nothing. If he had been a working man he would have known the value of every farthing, and would not have been so careless whether he lost or won. And his good-fortune had all, he reflected, come to him by chance, for nothing, and really was as superfluous for him as medicine for the healthy. If, like the vast majority of people, he had been harassed by anxiety for his daily bread, had been struggling for existence, if his back and chest had ached from work, then supper, a warm snug home, and domestic happiness, would have been the necessity, the compensation, the crown of his life; as it was, all this had a strange, indefinite significance for him.

" Foo, how horrid !" he repeated, knowing perfectly well that these reflections were in themselves a bad sign.

When he got home Masha was in bed: she was breathing evenly and smiling, and was evidently sleeping with great enjoyment. Near her the white cat lay curled up, purring. While Nikitin lit the candle and lighted his cigarette, Masha woke up and greedily drank a glass of water.

" I ate too many sweets," she said, and laughed. " Have you been home ?" she asked after a pause. ": No."

Nikitin knew already that Captain Polyansky, on whom Varya had been building great hopes of late, was being transferred to one of the western provinces, and was already making his farewell visits in the town, and so it was depressing at his father-in-law's.

" Varya looked in this evening," said Masha, sitting up. "She did not say anything, but one could see from her face how wretched she is, poor darling ! I can't bear Polyansky. He is fat and bloated, and when he walks or dances his cheeks shake. . . . He is not a man I would choose. But, still, I did think he was a decent person."

" I think he is a decent person now," said Nikitin.

" Then why has he treated Varya so badly ?"

" Why badly ?" asked Nikitin, beginning to feel irritation against the white cat, who was stretching and arching its back. "As far as I know, he has made no proposal and has given her no promises."

"Then why was he so often at the house? If he didn't mean to marry her, he oughtn't to have come."

Nikitin put out the candle and got into bed. But he felt disinclined to lie down and to sleep. He felt as though his head were immense and empty as a barn, and that new, peculiar thoughts were wandering about in it like tall shadows. He thought that, apart from the soft light of the ikon lamp, that beamed upon their quiet domestic happiness, that apart from this little world in which he and this cat lived so peacefully and happily, there was another world. . . . And he had a passionate, poignant longing to be in that other world, to work himself at some factory or big workshop, to address big audiences, to write, to publish, to raise a stir, to exhaust himself, to suffer. . . . He wanted something that would engross him till he forgot himself, ceased to care for the personal happiness which yielded him only sensations so monotonous. And suddenly there rose vividly before his imagination the figure of Shebaldin with his clean-shaven face, saying to him with horror: " You haven't even read Lessing ! You are quite behind the times ! How you have gone to seed !"

Masha woke up and again drank some water. He glanced at her neck, at her plump shoulders and throat, and remembered the word the brigadier-general had used in church—" rose."

" Rose," he muttered, and laughed.

His laugh was answered by a sleepy growl from Mushka under the bed: " Rrr . . . nga-nga-nga . . . !"

A heavy anger sank like a cold weight on his heart, and he felt tempted to say something rude to Masha, and even to jump up and hit her; his heart began throbbing.

" So then," he asked, restraining himself, " since I went to your house, I was bound in duty to marry you ?"

" Of course. You know that very well."

" That's nice." And a minute later he repeated: " That's nice."

To relieve the throbbing of his heart, and to avoid saying too much, Nikitin went to his study and lay down on the sofa, without a pillow; then he lay on the floor on the carpet.

" What nonsense it is !" he said to reassure himself. " You are a teacher, you are working in the noblest of callings. . . . What need have you of any other world ? What rubbish !"

But almost immediately he told himself with conviction that he was not a real teacher, but simply a government employee, as commonplace and mediocre as the Czech who taught Greek. He had never had a vocation for teaching, he knew nothing of the theory of teaching, and never had been interested in the subject; he did not know how to treat children; he did not understand the significance of what he taught, and perhaps did not teach the right things. Poor Ippolit Ippolititch had been frankly stupid, and all the boys, as well as

388

his colleagues, knew what he was and what to expect from him; but he, Nikitin, like the Czech, knew how to conceal his stupidity and cleverly deceived everyone by pretending that, thank God, his teaching was a success. These new ideas frightened Nikitin; he rejected them, called them stupid, and believed that all this was due to his nerves, that he would laugh at himself.

And he did, in fact, by the morning laugh at himself and call himself an old woman; but it was clear to him that his peace of mind was lost, perhaps, for ever, and that in that little two-storey house happiness was henceforth impossible for him. He realized that the illusion had evaporated, and that a new life of unrest and clear sight was beginning which was incompatible with peace and personal happiness.

Next day, which was Sunday, he was at the school chapel, and there met his colleagues and the director. It seemed to him that they were entirely preoccupied with concealing their ignorance and discontent with life, and he, too, to conceal his uneasiness, smiled affably and talked of trivialities. Then he went to the station and saw the mail train come in and go out, and it was agreeable to him to be alone and not to have to talk to anyone.

At home he found Varya and his father-in-law, who had come to dinner. Varya's eyes were red with crying, and she complained of a headache, while Shelestov ate a great deal, saying that young men nowadays were unreliable, and that there was very little gentlemanly feeling among them.

" It's loutishness !" he said. " I shall tell him so to his face: ' It's loutishness, sir,' I shall say."

Nikitin smiled affably and helped Masha to look after their guests, but after dinner he went to his study and shut the door.

The March sun was shining brightly in at the windows and shedding its warm rays on the table. It was only the twentieth of the month, but already the cabmen were driving with wheels, and the starlings were noisy in the garden. It was just the weather in which Masha would come in, put one arm round his neck, tell him the horses were saddled or the chaise was at the door, and ask him what she should put on to keep warm. Spring was beginning as exquisitely as last spring, and it promised the same joys. . . . But Nikitin was thinking that it would be nice to take a holiday and go to Moscow, and stay at his old lodgings there. In the next room they were drinking coffee and talking of Captain Polyansky, while he tried not to listen and wrote in his diary: " Where am I, my God ? I am surrounded by vulgarity and vulgarity. Wearisome, insignificant people, pots of sour cream, jugs of milk, cockroaches, stupid women. . . . There is nothing more terrible, mortifying, and distressing than vulgarity. I must escape from here, I must escape to-day, or I shall go out of my mind !"

1894

THE WITCH

It was approaching nightfall. The sexton, Savély
Gykin, was lying in his huge bed in the hut adjoining the church. He was not asleep, though
it was his habit to go to sleep at the same time as
the hens. His coarse red hair peeped from under
one end of the greasy patchwork quilt, made up of
coloured rags, while his big unwashed feet stuck
out from the other. He was listening. His hut
adjoined the wall that encircled the church and the
solitary window in it looked out upon the open
country. And out there a regular battle was going
on. It was hard to say who was being wiped off
the face of the earth, and for the sake of whose
destruction nature was being churned up into
such a ferment; but, judging from the unceasing
malignant roar, someone was getting it very hot.
A victorious force was in full chase over the
fields, storming in the forest and on the church
roof, battering spitefully with its fists upon the
windows, raging and tearing, while something
vanquished was howling and wailing. . . . A
plaintive lament sobbed at the window, on the
roof, or in the stove. It sounded not like a call for
help, but like a cry of misery, a consciousness that
it was too late, that there was no salvation. The

snow drifts were covered with a thin coating of ice; tears quivered on them and on the trees; a dark slush of mud and melting snow flowed along the roads and paths. In short, it was thawing, but through the dark night the heavens failed to see it, and flung flakes of fresh snow upon the melting earth at a terrific rate. And the wind staggered like a drunkard. It would not let the snow settle on the ground, and whirled it round in the darkness at random.

Savély listened to all this din and frowned. The fact was that he knew, or at any rate suspected, what all this racket outside the window was tending to and whose handiwork it was.

"I know!" he muttered, shaking his finger menacingly under the bedclothes; "I know all about it."

On a stool by the window sat the sexton's wife, Raïssa Nilovna. A tin lamp standing on another stool, as though timid and distrustful of its powers, shed a dim and flickering light on her broad shoulders, on the handsome, tempting-looking contours of her person, and on her thick plait, which reached to the floor. She was making sacks out of coarse hempen stuff. Her hands moved nimbly, while her whole body, her eyes, her eyebrows, her full lips, her white neck were as still as though they were asleep, absorbed in the monotonous, mechanical toil. Only from time to time she raised her head to rest her weary neck, glanced for a moment towards the window, beyond which the snowstorm was raging, and bent again over her sacking. No desire, no joy, no grief, nothing was expressed by her handsome face with its turned-up nose and its dimples. So a beautiful fountain expresses nothing when it is not playing.

But at last she had finished a sack. She flung it aside, and, stretching luxuriously, rested her motionless, lack-lustre eyes on the window. The panes were swimming with drops like tears, and white with short-lived snowflakes which fell on the window, glanced at Raïssa, and melted. . . .

" Come to bed !" growled the sexton. Raïssa remained mute. But suddenly her eyelashes flickered and there was a gleam of attention in her eye. Savély, all the time watching her expression from under the quilt, put out his head and asked:

" What is it ?"

" Nothing. . . . I fancy someone's coming," she answered quietly.

The sexton flung the quilt off with his arms and legs, knelt up in bed, and looked blankly at his wife. The timid light of the lamp illuminated his hirsute, pock-marked countenance and glided over his rough matted hair.

" Do you hear ?" asked his wife.

Through the monotonous roar of the storm he caught a scarcely audible thin and jingling monotone like the shrill note of a gnat when it wants to settle on one's cheek and is angry at being prevented.

" It's the post," muttered Savély, squatting on his heels.

Two miles from the church ran the posting road.

In windy weather, when the wind was blowing from the road to the church, the inmates of the hut caught the sound of bells.

" Lord ! fancy people wanting to drive about in such weather," sighed Raïssa.

" It's government work. You've to go whether you like or not."

The murmur hung in the air and died away.

" It has driven by," said Savély, getting into bed.

But before he had time to cover himself up with the bedclothes he heard a distinct sound of the bell. The sexton looked anxiously at his wife, leapt out of bed and walked, waddling, to and fro by the stove. The bell went on ringing for a little, then died away again as though it had ceased.

" I don't hear it," said the sexton, stopping, and looking at his wife with his eyes screwed up.

But at that moment the wind rapped on the window and with it floated a shrill jingling note. Savély turned pale, cleared his throat, and flopped about the floor with his bare feet again.

" The postman is lost in the storm," he wheezed out, glancing malignantly at his wife. " Do you hear ? The postman has lost his way ! . . . I . . . I know ! Do you suppose I . . . don't understand ?" he muttered. " I know all about it, curse you !"

" What do you know ?" Raïssa asked quietly, keeping her eyes fixed on the window.

" I know that it's all your doing, you she-devil ! Your doing, damn you ! This snowstorm and the post going wrong, you've done it all—you !"

"You're mad, you silly," his wife answered calmly.

"I've been watching you for a long time past and I've seen it. From the first day I married you I noticed that you'd bitch's blood in you!"

"Tfoo!" said Raïssa, surprised, shrugging her shoulders and crossing herself. "Cross yourself, you fool!"

"A witch is a witch," Savély pronounced in a hollow, tearful voice, hurriedly blowing his nose on the hem of his shirt; "though you are my wife, though you are of a clerical family, I'd say what you are even at confession. . . . Why, God have mercy upon us! Last year on the Eve of the Prophet Daniel and the Three Young Men there was a snow-storm, and what happened then? The mechanic came in to warm himself. Then on St. Alexey's Day the ice broke on the river and the district policeman turned up, and he was chatting with you all night . . . the damned brute! And when he came out in the morning and I looked at him, he had rings under his eyes and his cheeks were hollow! Eh? During the August fast there were two storms and each time the huntsman turned up. I saw it all, damn him! Oh, she is redder than a crab now, aha!"

"You didn't see anything."

"Didn't I! And this winter before Christmas on the Day of the Ten Martyrs of Crete, when the storm lasted for a whole day and night—do you remember?—the marshal's clerk was lost, and turned up here, the hound. . . . Tfoo! To bg tempted by the clerk! It was worth upsettine

God's weather for him! A drivelling scribbler. not a foot from the ground, pimples all over his mug and his neck awry! If he were good-looking, anyway—but he, tfoo! he is as ugly as Satan!"

The sexton took breath, wiped his lips and listened. The bell was not to be heard, but the wind banged on the roof, and again there came a tinkle in the darkness.

"And it's the same thing now!" Savély went on. "It's not for nothing the postman is lost! Blast my eyes if the postman isn't looking for you! Oh, the devil is a good hand at his work; he is a fine one to help! He will turn him round and round and bring him here. I know, I see! You can't conceal it, you devil's bauble, you heathen wanton! As soon as the storm began I knew what you were up to."

"Here's a fool!" smiled his wife. "Why, do you suppose, you thick-head, that I make the storm?"

"H'm!... Grin away! Whether it's your doing or not, I only know that when your blood's on fire there's sure to be bad weather, and when there's bad weather there's bound to be some crazy fellow turning up here. It happens so every time! So it must be you!"

To be more impressive the sexton put his finger to his forehead, closed his left eye, and said in a sing-song voice:

"Oh, the madness! oh, the unclean Judas! If you really are a human being and not a witch, you ought to think what if he is not the mechanic, or the clerk, or the huntsman, but the devil in their form! Ah! You'd better think of that!"

396

"Why, you are stupid, Savély," said his wife, looking at him compassionately. "When father was alive and living here, all sorts of people used to come to him to be cured of the ague: from the village, and the hamlets, and the Armenian settlement. They came almost every day, and no one called them devils. But if anyone once a year comes in bad weather to warm himself, you wonder at it, you silly, and take all sorts of notions into your head at once."

His wife's logic touched Savély. He stood with his bare feet wide apart, bent his head, and pondered. He was not firmly convinced yet of the truth of his suspicions, and his wife's genuine and unconcerned tone quite disconcerted him. Yet after a moment's thought he wagged his head and said:

"It's not as though they were old men or bandy-legged cripples; it's always young men who want to come for the night. . . . Why is that? And if they only wanted to warm themselves—— But they are up to mischief. No, woman; there's no creature in this world as cunning as your female sort! Of real brains you've not an ounce, less than a starling; but for devilish slyness—oo-oo-oo! The Queen of Heaven protect us! There is the postman's bell! When the storm was only beginning I knew all that was in your mind. That's your witchery, you spider!"

"Why do you keep on at me, you heathen?" His wife lost her patience at last. "Why do you keep sticking to it like pitch?"

"I stick to it because if anything—God forbid—

happens to-night . . . do you hear ? . . . if anything happens to-night, I'll go straight off to-
morrow morning to Father Nikodim and tell him
all about it. 'Father Nikodim,' I shall say,
'graciously excuse me, but she is a witch.' 'Why
so ?' 'H'm ! do you want to know why ?
Certainly . . .' And I shall tell him. And woe
to you, woman ! Not only at the dread Seat of
Judgment, but in your earthly life you'll be
punished, too ! It's not for nothing there are
prayers in the breviary against your kind !"

Suddenly there was a knock at the window, so
loud and unusual that Savély turned pale and
almost dropped backwards with fright. His wife
jumped up, and she, too, turned pale.

" For God's sake, let us come in and get warm !"
they heard in a trembling deep bass. "Who lives
here ? For mercy's sake ! We've lost our way."

" Who are you ?" asked Raïssa, afraid to look
at the window.

" The post," answered a second voice.

" You've succeeded with your devil's tricks,"
said Savély with a wave of his hand. " No
mistake; I am right ! Well, you'd better look
out !"

The sexton jumped on to the bed in two skips,
stretched himself on the feather mattress, and
sniffing angrily, turned with his face to the wall.
Soon he felt a draught of cold air on his back.
The door creaked and the tall figure of a man,
plastered over with snow from head to foot,
appeared in the doorway. Behind him could be
seen a second figure as white.

THE WITCH

" Am I to bring in the bags ?" asked the second in a hoarse bass voice.

" You can't leave them there." Saying this, the first figure began untying his hood, but gave it up, and pulling it off impatiently with his cap, angrily flung it near the stove. Then taking off his greatcoat, he threw that down beside it, and, without saying good-evening, began pacing up and down the hut.

He was a fair-haired, young postman wearing a shabby uniform and black rusty-looking high boots. After warming himself by walking to and fro, he sat down at the table, stretched out his muddy feet towards the sacks and leaned his chin on his fist. His pale face, reddened in places by the cold, still bore vivid traces of the pain and terror he had just been through. Though distorted by anger and bearing traces of recent suffering, physical and moral, it was handsome in spite of the melting snow on the eyebrows, moustaches, and short beard.

" It's a dog's life !" muttered the postman, looking round the walls and seeming hardly able to believe that he was in the warmth. " We were nearly lost ! If it had not been for your light, I don't know what would have happened. Goodness only knows when it will all be over ! There's no end to this dog's life ! Where have we come ?" he asked, dropping his voice and raising his eyes to the sexton's wife.

" To the Gulyaevsky Hill on General Kalinovsky's estate," she answered, startled and blushing.

399

"Do you hear, Stepan?" The postman turned to the driver, who was wedged in the doorway with a huge mail-bag on his shoulders. "We've got to Gulyaevsky Hill."

"Yes . . . we're a long way out." Jerking out these words like a hoarse sigh, the driver went out and soon after returned with another bag, then went out once more and this time brought the postman's sword on a big belt, of the pattern of that long flat blade with which Judith is portrayed by the bedside of Holofernes in cheap woodcuts. Laying the bags along the wall, he went out into the outer room, sat down there and lighted his pipe.

"Perhaps you'd like some tea after your journey?" Raïssa inquired.

"How can we sit drinking tea?" said the postman, frowning. "We must make haste and get warm, and then set off, or we shall be late for the mail train. We'll stay ten minutes and then get on our way. Only be so good as to show us the way."

"What an infliction it is, this weather!" sighed Raïssa.

"H'm, yes. . . . Who may you be?"

"We? We live here, by the church. . . . We belong to the clergy. . . . There lies my husband. Savély, get up and say good-evening! This used to be a separate parish till eighteen months ago. Of course, when the gentry lived here there were more people, and it was worth while to have the services. But now the gentry have gone, and I need not tell you there's nothing

400

for the clergy to live on. The nearest village is Markovka, and that's over three miles away. Savély is on the retired list now, and has got the watchman's job; he has to look after the church. . . ."

And the postman was immediately informed that if Savély were to go to the General's lady and ask her for a letter to the bishop, he would be given a good berth. " But he doesn't go to the General's lady because he is lazy and afraid of people. We belong to the clergy all the same . . ." added Raïssa.

" What do you live on ?" asked the postman.

" There's a kitchen garden and a meadow belonging to the church. Only we don't get much from that," sighed Raïssa. " The old skinflint, Father Nikodim, from the next village celebrates here on St. Nicolas' Day in the winter and on St. Nicolas' Day in the summer, and for that he takes almost all the crops for himself. There's no one to stick up for us !"

" You are lying," Savély growled hoarsely. " Father Nikodim is a saintly soul, a luminary of the Church; and if he does take it, it's the regulation !"

" You've a cross one !" said the postman, with a grin. " Have you been married long ?"

" It was three years ago the last Sunday before Lent. My father was sexton here in the old days, and when the time came for him to die, he went to the Consistory and asked them to send some unmarried man to marry me that I might keep the place. So I married him."

" Aha, so you killed two birds with one stone !"
said the postman, looking at Savély's back.
" Got wife and job together."

Savély wriggled his leg impatiently and moved
closer to the wall. The postman moved away
from the table, stretched, and sat down on the
mail-bag. After a moment's thought he squeezed
the bags with his hands, shifted his sword to the
other side, and lay down with one foot touching
the floor.

" It's a dog's life," he muttered, putting his
hands behind his head and closing his eyes. " I
wouldn't wish a wild Tatar such a life."

Soon everything was still. Nothing was audible
except the sniffing of Savély and the slow, even
breathing of the sleeping postman, who uttered
a deep prolonged " h-h-h " at every breath.
From time to time there was a sound like a creaking wheel in his throat, and his twitching foot
rustled against the bag.

Savély fidgeted under the quilt and looked
round slowly. His wife was sitting on the stool,
and with her hands pressed against her cheeks
was gazing at the postman's face. Her face was
immovable, like the face of someone frightened
and astonished.

" Well, what are you gaping at ?" Savély
whispered angrily.

" What is it to you ? Lie down !" answered
his wife without taking her eyes off the flaxen
head.

Savély angrily puffed all the air out of his chest
and turned abruptly to the wall. Three minutes

later he turned over restlessly again, knelt up on the bed, and with his hands on the pillow looked askance at his wife. She was still sitting motionless, staring at the visitor. Her cheeks were pale and her eyes were glowing with a strange fire. The sexton cleared his throat, crawled on his stomach off the bed, and going up to the postman, put a handkerchief over his face.

" What's that for ?" asked his wife.

" To keep the light out of his eyes."

" Then put out the light !"

Savély looked distrustfully at his wife, put out his lips towards the lamp, but at once thought better of it and clasped his hands.

"Isn't that devilish cunning ?" he exclaimed. " Ah ! Is there any creature slyer than womenkind ?"

" Ah, you long-skirted devil !" hissed his wife, frowning with vexation. " You wait a bit !"

And settling herself more comfortably, she stared at the postman again.

It did not matter to her that his face was covered. She was not so much interested in his face as in his whole appearance, in the novelty of this man. His chest was broad and powerful, his hands were slender and well formed, and his graceful, muscular legs were much comelier than Savély's stumps. There could be no comparison, in fact.

" Though I am a long-skirted devil," Savély said after a brief interval, " they've no business to sleep here. . . . It's government work; we shall have to answer for keeping them. If you carry the letters, carry them, you can't go to sleep. . . . Hey! you!" Savély shouted into the outer room. "You, driver. . . . What's your name? Shall I show you the way? Get up; postmen mustn't sleep!"

And Savély, thoroughly roused, ran up to the postman and tugged him by the sleeve.

"Hey, your honour, if you must go, go; and if you don't, it's not the thing. . . . Sleeping won't do."

The postman jumped up, sat down, looked with blank eyes round the hut, and lay down again.

"But when are you going?" Savély pattered away. "That's what the post is for—to get there in good time, do you hear? I'll take you."

The postman opened his eyes. Warmed and relaxed by his first sweet sleep, and not yet quite awake, he saw as through a mist the white neck and the immovable, alluring eyes of the sexton's wife. He closed his eyes and smiled as though he had been dreaming it all.

"Come, how can you go in such weather!" he heard a soft feminine voice; "you ought to have a sound sleep and it would do you good!"

"And what about the post?" said Savély anxiously. "Who's going to take the post? Are you going to take it, pray, you?"

The postman opened his eyes again, looked at the play of the dimples on Raïssa's face, remembered where he was, and understood Savély. The thought that he had to go out into the cold darkness sent a chill shudder all down him, and he winced.

"I might sleep another five minutes," he said, yawning. "I shall be late, anyway. . . ."

"We might be just in time," came a voice from the outer room. "All days are not alike; the train may be late for a bit of luck."

The postman got up, and stretching lazily began putting on his coat.

Savély positively neighed with delight when he saw his visitors were getting ready to go.

"Give us a hand," the driver shouted to him as he lifted up a mail-bag.

The sexton ran out and helped him drag the post-bags into the yard. The postman began undoing the knot in his hood. The sexton's wife gazed into his eyes, and seemed trying to look right into his soul.

"You ought to have a cup of tea . . ." she said.

"I wouldn't say no . . . but, you see, they're getting ready," he assented. "We are late, anyway."

"Do stay," she whispered, dropping her eyes and touching him by the sleeve.

The postman got the knot undone at last and flung the hood over his elbow, hesitating. He felt it comfortable standing by Raïssa.

"What a . . . neck you've got! . . ." And he touched her neck with two fingers. Seeing that she did not resist, he stroked her neck and shoulders.

"I say, you are . . ."

"You'd better stay . . . have some tea."

"Where are you putting it?" The driver's

voice could be heard outside. "Lay it cross-ways."

"You'd better stay. . . . Hark how the wind howls."

And the postman, not yet quite awake, not yet quite able to shake off the intoxicating sleep of youth and fatigue, was suddenly overwhelmed by a desire for the sake of which mail-bags, postal trains . . . and all things in the world, are for-gotten. He glanced at the door in a frightened way, as though he wanted to escape or hide him-self, seized Raïssa round the waist, and was just bending over the lamp to put out the light, when he heard the tramp of boots in the outer room, and the driver appeared in the doorway. Savély peeped in over his shoulder. The postman dropped his hands quickly and stood still as though irresolute.

"It's all ready," said the driver. The postman stood still for a moment, resolutely threw up his head as though waking up completely, and followed the driver out. Raïssa was left alone.

"Come, get in and show us the way!" she heard.

One bell sounded languidly, then another, and the jingling notes in a long delicate chain floated away from the hut.

When little by little they had died away, Raïssa got up and nervously paced to and fro. At first she was pale, then she flushed all over. Her face was contorted with hate, her breathing was tremulous, her eyes gleamed with wild, savage anger, and, pacing up and down as in a cage, she looked like a tigress menaced with red-hot iron. For a moment she stood still and looked at her abode. Almost half of the room was filled up by the bed, which stretched the length of the whole wall and consisted of a dirty feather-bed, coarse grey pillows, a quilt, and nameless rags of various sorts. The bed was a shapeless ugly mass which suggested the shock of hair that always stood up on Savély's head whenever it occurred to him to oil it. From the bed to the door that led into the cold outer room stretched the dark stove surrounded by pots and hanging clouts. Everything, including the absent Savély himself, was dirty, greasy, and smutty to the last degree, so that it was strange to see a woman's white neck and delicate skin in such surroundings.

Raïssa ran up to the bed, stretched out her hands as though she wanted to fling it all about, stamp it underfoot, and tear it to shreds. But then, as though frightened by contact with the dirt, she leapt back and began pacing up and down again.

When Savély returned two hours later, worn out and covered with snow, she was undressed and in bed. Her eyes were closed, but from the slight tremor that ran over her face he guessed that she was not asleep. On his way home he had vowed inwardly to wait till next day and not to touch her, but he could not resist a biting taunt at her.

" Your witchery was all in vain: he's gone off," he said, grinning with malignant joy.

His wife remained mute, but her chin quivered. Savély undressed slowly, clambered over his wife, and lay down next to the wall.

"To-morrow I'll let Father Nikodim know what sort of wife you are!" he muttered, curling himself up.

Raïssa turned her face to him and her eyes gleamed.

"The job's enough for you, and you can look for a wife in the forest, blast you!" she said. "I am no wife for you, a clumsy lout, a slug-a-bed, God forgive me!"

"Come, come . . . go to sleep!"

"How miserable I am!" sobbed his wife. "If it weren't for you, I might have married a merchant or some gentleman! If it weren't for you, I should love my husband now! And you haven't been buried in the snow, you haven't been frozen on the highroad, you Herod!"

Raïssa cried for a long time. At last she drew a deep sigh and was still. The storm still raged without. Something wailed in the stove, in the chimney, outside the walls, and it seemed to Savély that the wailing was within him, in his ears. This evening had completely confirmed him in his suspicions about his wife. He no longer doubted that his wife, with the aid of the Evil One, controlled the winds and the post sledges. But to add to his grief, this mysteriousness, this supernatural, weird power gave the woman beside him a peculiar, incomprehensible charm of which he had not been conscious before. The fact that in his stupidity he unconsciously threw a poetic glamour over her made her seem, as it were, whiter, sleeker, more unapproachable.

"Witch!" he muttered indignantly. "Tfoo, horrid creature!"

THE WITCH

Yet, waiting till she was quiet and began breathing evenly, he touched her head with his finger . . . held her thick plait in his hand for a minute. She did not feel it. Then he grew bolder and stroked her neck.

" Leave off !" she shouted, and prodded him on the nose with her elbow with such violence that he saw stars before his eyes.

The pain in his nose was soon over, but the torture in his heart remained.

1886

409

AN ANONYMOUS STORY

I

THROUGH causes which it is not the time to go into
in detail, I had to enter the service of a Petersburg
official called Orlov, in the capacity of a footman.
He was about five and thirty, and was called
Georgy* Ivanitch.

I entered this Orlov's service on account of his
father, a prominent political man, whom I looked
upon as a serious enemy of my cause. I reckoned
that, living with the son, I should—from the
conversations I should hear, and from the letters
and papers I should find on the table—learn every
detail of the father's plans and intentions.

As a rule at eleven o'clock in the morning the
electric bell rang in my footman's quarters to let
me know that my master was awake. When I
went into the bedroom with his polished shoes
and brushed clothes, Georgy Ivanitch would be
sitting in his bed with a face that looked, not
drowsy, but rather exhausted by sleep, and he
would gaze off in one direction without any sign
of satisfaction at having waked. I helped him
to dress, and he let me do it with an air of reluct-

* Both *g*'s hard, as in " Gorgon " ; *e* like *ai* in *rain*.

ance without speaking or noticing my presence; then with his head wet with washing, smelling of fresh scent, he used to go into the dining-room to drink his coffee. He used to sit at the table, sipping his coffee and glancing through the newspapers, while the maid Polya and I stood respectfully at the door gazing at him. Two grown-up persons had to stand watching with the gravest attention a third drinking coffee and munching rusks. It was probably ludicrous and grotesque, but I saw nothing humiliating in having to stand near the door, though I was quite as well born and well educated as Orlov himself.

I was in the first stage of consumption, and was suffering from something else, possibly even more serious than consumption. I don't know whether it was the effect of my illness or of an incipient change in my philosophy of life of which I was not conscious at the time, but I was, day by day, more possessed by a passionate, irritating longing for ordinary everyday life. I yearned for mental tranquillity, health, fresh air, good food. I was becoming a dreamer, and, like a dreamer, I did not know exactly what I wanted. Sometimes I felt inclined to go into a monastery, to sit there for days together by the window and gaze at the trees and the fields; sometimes I fancied I would buy fifteen acres of land and settle down as a country gentleman; sometimes I inwardly vowed to take up science and become a professor at some provincial university. I was a retired navy lieutenant; I dreamed of the sea, of our squadron, and of the corvette in which I had made the cruise round the world. I longed to experience again the indescribable feeling when, walking in the tropical forest or looking at the sunset in the Bay of Bengal, one is thrilled with ecstasy and at the same time homesick. I dreamed of mountains, women, music, and, with the curiosity of a child, I looked into people's faces, listened to their voices. And when I stood at the door and watched Orlov sipping his coffee, I felt not a footman, but a man interested in everything in the world, even in Orlov.

In appearance Orlov was a typical Petersburger, with narrow shoulders, a long waist, sunken temples, eyes of an indefinite colour, and scanty, dingy-coloured hair, beard and moustaches. His face had a stale, unpleasant look, though it was studiously cared for. It was particularly unpleasant when he was asleep or lost in thought. It is not worth while describing a quite ordinary appearance; besides, Petersburg is not Spain, and a man's appearance is not of much consequence even in love affairs, and is only of value to a handsome footman or coachman. I have spoken of Orlov's face and hair only because there was something in his appearance worth mentioning. When Orlov took a newspaper or book, whatever it might be, or met people, whoever they might be, an ironical smile began to come into his eyes, and his whole countenance assumed an expression of light mockery in which there was no malice. Before reading or hearing anything he always had his irony in readiness, as a savage has his shield. It was an habitual irony, like some old liquor brewed years ago, and now it came into his face probably without any participation of his will, as it were by reflex action. But of that later.

Soon after midday he took his portfolio, full of papers, and drove to his office. He dined away from home and returned after eight o'clock. I used to light the lamp and candles in his study, and he would sit down in a low chair with his legs stretched out on another chair, and, reclining in that position, would begin reading. Almost every day he brought in new books with him or received parcels of them from the shops, and there were heaps of books in three languages, to say nothing of Russian, which he had read and thrown away, in the corners of my room and under my bed. He read with extraordinary rapidity. They say: "Tell me what you read, and I'll tell you who you are." That may be true, but it was absolutely impossible to judge of Orlov by what he read. It was a regular hotchpotch. Philosophy, French novels, political economy, finance, new poets, and publications of the firm *Posrednik**—and he read it all with the same rapidity and with the same ironical expression in his eyes.

After ten o'clock he carefully dressed, often in evening dress, very rarely in his *kammer-junker's* uniform, and went out, returning in the morning.

Our relations were quiet and peaceful, and we never had any misunderstanding. As a rule he did not notice my presence, and when he talked to me there was no expression of irony on his face

* *I.e.*, Tchertkov and others, publishers of Tolstoy, who issued good literature for peasants' reading.

—he evidently did not look upon me as a human being.

I only once saw him angry. One day—it was a week after I had entered his service—he came back from some dinner at nine o'clock; his face looked ill-humoured and exhausted. When I followed him into his study to light the candles, he said to me:

" There's a nasty smell in the flat."

" No, the air is fresh," I answered.

" I tell you, there's a bad smell," he answered irritably.

" I open the movable panes every day."

" Don't argue, blockhead !" he shouted.

I was offended, and was on the point of answering, and goodness knows how it would have ended if Polya, who knew her master better than I did, had not intervened.

" There really is a disagreeable smell," she said, raising her eyebrows. " What can it be from ? Stepan, open the pane in the drawing-room, and light the fire."

With much bustle and many exclamations, she went through all the rooms, rustling her skirts and squeezing the sprayer with a hissing sound. And Orlov was still out of humour; he was obviously restraining himself not to vent his ill-temper aloud. He was sitting at the table and rapidly writing a letter. After writing a few lines he snorted angrily and tore it up, then he began writing again.

" Damn them all !" he muttered. " They expect me to have an abnormal memory !"

At last the letter was written; he got up from the table and said, turning to me:

"Go to Znamensky Street and deliver this letter to Zinaida Fyodorovna Krasnovsky in person. But first ask the porter whether her husband—that is, Mr. Krasnovsky—has returned yet. If he has returned, don't deliver the letter, but come back. Wait a minute! . . . If she asks whether I have anyone here, tell her that there have been two gentlemen here since eight o'clock, writing something."

I drove to Znamensky Street. The porter told me that Mr. Krasnovsky had not yet come in, and I made my way up to the third storey. The door was opened by a tall, stout, drab-coloured flunkey with black whiskers, who in a sleepy, churlish, and apathetic voice, such as only flunkeys use in addressing other flunkeys, asked me what I wanted. Before I had time to answer, a lady dressed in black came hurriedly into the hall. She screwed up her eyes and looked at me.

"Is Zinaida Fyodorovna at home?" I asked.

"That is me," said the lady.

"A letter from Georgy Ivanitch."

She tore the letter open impatiently, and holding it in both hands, so that I saw her sparkling diamond rings, she began reading. I made out a pale face with soft lines, a prominent chin, and long dark lashes. From her appearance I should not have judged the lady to be more than five and twenty.

"Give him my thanks and my greetings," she said when she had finished the letter. "Is there anyone with Georgy Ivanitch?" she asked softly, joyfully, and as though ashamed of her mistrust.

"Two gentlemen," I answered. "They're writing something."

"Give him my greetings and thanks," she repeated, bending her head sideways, and, reading the letter as she walked, she went noiselessly out.

I saw few women at that time, and this lady of whom I had a passing glimpse made an impression on me. As I walked home I recalled her face and the delicate fragrance about her, and fell to dreaming. By the time I got home Orlov had gone out.

II.

And so my relations with my employer were quiet and peaceful, but still the unclean and degrading element which I so dreaded on becoming a footman was conspicuous and made itself felt every day. I did not get on with Polya. She was a well-fed and pampered hussy who adored Orlov because he was a gentleman and despised me because I was a footman. Probably, from the point of view of a real flunkey or cook, she was fascinating, with her red cheeks, her turned-up nose, her coquettish glances, and the plumpness, one might almost say fatness, of her person. She powdered her face, coloured her lips and eyebrows, laced herself in, and wore a bustle, and a bangle made of coins. She walked with little tripping steps; as she walked she swayed, or, as they say, wriggled her shoulders and back. The rustle of her skirts, the creaking of her stays, the jingle of her bangle and the vulgar smell of lip salve, toilet vinegar, and scent stolen from her master, aroused in me whilst I was doing the rooms with her in the morning a sensation as though I were taking part with her in some abomination.

Either because I did not steal as she did, or because I displayed no desire to become her lover, which she probably looked upon as an insult, or perhaps because she felt that I was a man of a different order, she hated me from the first day. My inexperience, my appearance—so unlike a flunkey—and my illness, seemed to her pitiful and excited her disgust. I had a bad cough at that time, and sometimes at night I prevented her from sleeping, as our rooms were only divided by a wooden partition, and every morning she said to me:

"Again you didn't let me sleep. You ought to be in hospital instead of in service."

She so genuinely believed that I was hardly a human being, but something infinitely below her, that, like the Roman matrons who were not ashamed to bathe before their slaves, she sometimes went about in my presence in nothing but her chemise.

Once when I was in a happy, dreamy mood, I asked her at dinner (we had soup and roast meat sent in from a restaurant every day):

"Polya, do you believe in God?"

"Why, of course!"

"Then," I went on, "you believe there will be a day of judgment, and that we shall have to answer to God for every evil action?"

She gave me no reply, but simply made a contemptuous grimace, and, looking that time at her cold eyes and over-fed expression, I realized that for her complete and finished personality no God, no conscience, no laws existed, and that if I had had to set fire to the house, to murder or to rob, I could not have hired a better accomplice.

In my novel surroundings I felt very uncomfortable for the first week at Orlov's before I got used to being addressed as " thou," and being constantly obliged to tell lies (saying " My master is not at home " when he was). In my flunkey's swallow-tail I felt as though I were in armour. But I grew accustomed to it in time. Like a genuine footman, I waited at table, tidied the rooms, ran and drove about on errands of all sorts. When Orlov did not want to keep an appointment with Zinaida Fyodorovna, or when he forgot that he had promised to go and see her, I drove to Znamensky Street, put a letter into her hands and told a lie. And the result of it all was quite different from what I had expected when I became a footman. Every day of this new life of mine was wasted for me and my cause, as Orlov never spoke of his father, nor did his visitors, and all I could learn of the statesman's doings was, as before, what I could glean from the newspapers or from correspondence with my comrades. The hundreds of notes and papers I used to find in the study and read had not the remotest connection with what I was looking for. Orlov was absolutely uninterested in his father's political work, and looked as though he had never heard of it, or as though his father had long been dead.

III.

Every Thursday we had visitors.

I ordered a piece of roast beef from the restaurant and telephoned to Eliseyev's to send us caviare, cheese, oysters, and so on. I bought playing-cards. Polya was busy all day getting ready the tea-things and the dinner service. To tell the truth, this spurt of activity came as a pleasant change in our idle life, and Thursdays were for us the most interesting days.

Only three visitors used to come. The most important and perhaps the most interesting was the one called Pekarsky—a tall, lean man of five and forty, with a long hooked nose, with a big black beard, and a bald patch on his head. His eyes were large and prominent, and his expression was grave and thoughtful like that of a Greek philosopher. He was on the board of management of some railway, and also had some post in a bank; he was a consulting lawyer in some important Government institution, and had business relations with a large number of private persons as a trustee, chairman of committees, and so on. He was of quite a low grade in the service, and modestly spoke of himself as a lawyer, but he had a vast influence.' A note or card from him was enough to make a celebrated doctor, a director of a railway, or a great dignitary see anyone without waiting; and it was said that through his protection one might obtain even a post of the Fourth Class, and get any sort of unpleasant business hushed up. He was looked upon as a very intelligent man, but his was a strange, peculiar intelligence. He was able to multiply 213 by 373 in his head instantaneously, or turn English pounds into German marks without help of pencil or paper; he understood finance and railway business thoroughly, and the machinery of Russian administration had no secrets for him; he was a most skilful pleader in civil suits, and it was not easy to get the better of him at law. But that exceptional intelligence could not grasp many things which are understood even by some stupid people. For instance, he was absolutely unable to understand why people are depressed, why they weep, shoot themselves, and even kill others; why they fret about things that do not affect them personally, and why they laugh when they read Gogol or Shtchedrin. . . . Everything abstract, everything belonging to the domain of thought and feeling, was to him boring and incomprehensible, like music to one who has no ear. He looked at people simply from the business point of view, and divided them into competent and incompetent. No other classification existed for him. Honesty and rectitude were only signs of competence. Drinking, gambling, and debauchery were permissible, but must not be allowed to interfere with business. Believing in God was rather stupid, but religion ought to be safeguarded, as the common people must have some principle to restrain them, otherwise they would not work. Punishment is only necessary as a deterrent. There was no need to go away for holidays, as it was just as nice in

town. And so on. He was a widower and had
no children, but lived on a large scale, as though
he had a family, and paid three thousand roubles
a year for his flat.

The second visitor, Kukushkin, an actual civil
councillor though a young man, was short, and
was conspicuous for his extremely unpleasant
appearance, which was due to the disproportion
between his fat, puffy body and his lean little face.
His lips were puckered up suavely, and his little
trimmed moustaches looked as though they had
been fixed on with glue. He was a man with the
manners of a lizard. He did not walk, but, as it
were, crept along with tiny steps, squirming and
sniggering, and when he laughed he showed his
teeth. He was a clerk on special commissions,
and did nothing, though he received a good salary,
especially in the summer, when special and lucra-
tive jobs were found for him. He was a man of
personal ambition, not only to the marrow of his
bones, but more fundamentally—to the last drop
of his blood; but even in his ambitions he was
petty and did not rely on himself, but was building
his career on the chance favour flung him by his
superiors. For the sake of obtaining some foreign
decoration, or for the sake of having his name
mentioned in the newspapers as having been
present at some special service in the company of
other great personages, he was ready to submit to
any kind of humiliation, to beg, to flatter, to
promise. He flattered Orlov and Pekarsky from
cowardice, because he thought they were powerful;
he flattered Polya and me because we were in the

service of a powerful man. Whenever I took off his fur coat he tittered and asked me: " Stepan, are you married ?" and then unseemly vulgarities followed—by way of showing me special attention. Kukushkin flattered Orlov's weaknesses, humoured his corrupted and blasé ways; to please him he affected malicious raillery and atheism, in his company criticized persons before whom in other places he would slavishly grovel. When at supper they talked of love and women, he pretended to be a subtle and perverse voluptuary. As a rule, one may say, Petersburg rakes are fond of talking of their abnormal tastes. Some young actual civil councillor is perfectly satisfied with the embraces of his cook or of some unhappy street-walker on the Nevsky Prospect, but to listen to him you would think he was contaminated by all the vices of East and West combined, that he was an honorary member of a dozen iniquitous secret societies and was already marked by the police. Kukushkin lied about himself in an unconscionable way, and they did not exactly disbelieve him, but paid little heed to his incredible stories.

The third guest was Gruzin, the son of a worthy and learned general; a man of Orlov's age, with long hair, short-sighted eyes, and gold spectacles. I remember his long white fingers, that looked like a pianist's; and, indeed, there was something of a musician, of a virtuoso, about his whole figure. The first violins in orchestras look just like that. He used to cough, suffered from migraine, and seemed altogether invalidish and delicate. Probably at home he was dressed and undressed

422

like a baby. He had finished at the College of
Jurisprudence, and had at first served in the
Department of Justice, then he was transferred
to the Senate; he left that, and through patronage
had received a post in the Department of Crown
Estates, and had soon afterwards given that up.
In my time he was serving in Orlov's department;
he was his head-clerk, but he said that he should
soon exchange into the Department of Justice
again. He took his duties and his shifting about
from one post to another with exceptional levity,
and when people talked before him seriously of
grades in the service, decorations, salaries, he
smiled good-naturedly and repeated Prutkov's
aphorism: " It's only in the Government service
you learn the truth." He had a little wife with
a wrinkled face, who was very jealous of him, and
five weedy-looking children. He was unfaithful
to his wife, he was only fond of his children when
he saw them, and on the whole was rather indifferent to his family, and made fun of them.
He and his family existed on credit, borrowing
wherever they could at every opportunity, even
from his superiors in the office and porters in
people's houses. His was a flabby nature; he was
so lazy that he did not care what became of himself, and drifted along heedless where or why he
was going. He went where he was taken. If he
was taken to some low haunt, he went; if wine
was set before him, he drank—if it were not put
before him, he abstained; if wives were abused in
his presence, he abused his wife, declaring she had
ruined his life—when wives were praised, he

praised his and said quite sincerely: " I am very fond of her, poor thing !" He had no fur coat and always wore a rug which smelt of the nursery. When at supper he rolled balls of bread and drank a great deal of red wine, absorbed in thought, strange to say, I used to feel almost certain that there was something in him of which perhaps he had a vague sense, though in the bustle and vulgarity of his daily life he had not time to understand and appreciate it. He played a little on the piano. Sometimes he would sit down at the piano, play a chord or two, and begin singing softly:

" What does the coming day bring to me ?"

But at once, as though afraid, he would get up and walk away from the piano.

The visitors usually arrived about ten o'clock. They played cards in Orlov's study, and Polya and I handed them tea. It was only on these occasions that I could gauge the full sweetness of a flunkey's life. Standing for four or five hours at the door, watching that no one's glass should be empty, changing the ash-trays, running to the table to pick up the chalk or a card when it was dropped, and, above all, standing, waiting, being attentive without venturing to speak, to cough, to smile—is harder, I assure you, is harder than the hardest of field labour. I have stood on watch at sea for four hours at a stretch on stormy winter nights, and to my thinking it is an infinitely easier duty.

They used to play cards till two, sometimes till

three o'clock at night, and then, stretching, they would go into the dining-room to supper, or, as Orlov said, for a snack of something. At supper there was conversation. It usually began by Orlov's speaking with laughing eyes of some acquaintance, of some book he had lately been reading, of a new appointment or Government scheme. Kukushkin, always ingratiating, would fall into his tone, and what followed was to me, in my mood at that time, a revolting exhibition. The irony of Orlov and his friends knew no bounds, and spared no one and nothing. If they spoke of religion, it was with irony; if they spoke of philosophy, of the significance and object of life—irony again; if anyone began about the peasantry, it was with irony.

There is in Petersburg a species of men whose speciality it is to jeer at every aspect of life; they cannot even pass by a starving man or a suicide without saying something vulgar. But Orlov and his friends did not jeer or make jokes, they talked ironically. They used to say that there was no God, and personality was completely lost at death; the immortals only existed in the French Academy. Real good did not and could not possibly exist, as its existence was conditional upon human perfection, which was a logical absurdity. Russia was a country as poor and dull as Persia. The intellectual class was hopeless; in Pekarsky's opinion the overwhelming majority in it were incompetent persons, good for nothing. The people were drunken, lazy, thievish, and degenerate. We had no science, our literature

was uncouth, our commerce rested on swindling—
" No selling without cheating." And everything
was in that style, and everything was a subject
for laughter.

Towards the end of supper the wine made them
more good-humoured, and they passed to more
lively conversation. They laughed over Gruzin's
family life, over Kukushkin's conquests, or at
Pekarsky, who had, they said, in his account book
one page headed *Charity* and another *Physiological
Necessities*. They said that no wife was faithful;
that there was no wife from whom one could not,
with practice, obtain caresses without leaving her
drawing-room while her husband was sitting in his
study close by; that girls in their teens were per-
verted and knew everything. Orlov had preserved
a letter of a schoolgirl of fourteen: on her way
home from school she had " hooked an officer on
the Nevsky," who had, it appears, taken her home
with him, and had only let her go late in the
evening; and she hastened to write about this to
her school friend to share her joy with her. They
maintained that there was not and never had
been such a thing as moral purity, and that
evidently it was unnecessary; mankind had so
far done very well without it. The harm done by
so-called vice was undoubtedly exaggerated.
Vices which are punished by our legal code had
not prevented Diogenes from being a philosopher
and a teacher. Cæsar and Cicero were profligates
and at the same time great men. Cato in his old
age married a young girl, and yet he was regarded
as a great ascetic and a pillar of morality.

At three or four o'clock the party broke up or they went off together out of town, or to Officers' Street, to the house of a certain Varvara Ossipovna, while I retired to my quarters, and was kept awake a long while by coughing and headache.

IV.

Three weeks after I entered Orlov's service—it was Sunday morning, I remember—somebody rang the bell. It was not yet eleven, and Orlov was still asleep. I went to open the door. You can imagine my astonishment when I found a lady in a veil standing at the door on the landing.

" Is Georgy Ivanitch up ?" she asked.

From her voice I recognized Zinaida Fyodorovna, to whom I had taken letters in Znamensky Street. I don't remember whether I had time or self-possession to answer her—I was taken aback at seeing her. And, indeed, she did not need my answer. In a flash she had darted by me, and, filling the hall with the fragrance of her perfume, which I remember to this day, she went on, and her footsteps died away. For at least half an hour afterwards I heard nothing. But again someone rang. This time it was a smartly dressed girl, who looked like a maid in a wealthy family, accompanied by our house porter. Both were out of breath, carrying two trunks and a dress-basket.

" These are for Zinaida Fyodorovna," said the girl.

And she went down without saying another word. All this was mysterious, and made Polya,

427

who had a deep admiration for the pranks of her betters, smile slyly to herself; she looked as though she would like to say, " So that's what we're up to," and she walked about the whole time on tiptoe. At last we heard footsteps; Zinaida Fyodorovna came quickly into the hall, and seeing me at the door of my room, said:

" Stepan, take Georgy Ivanitch his things."

When I went in to Orlov with his clothes and his boots, he was sitting on the bed with his feet on the bearskin rug. There was an air of embarrassment about his whole figure. He did not notice me, and my menial opinion did not interest him; he was evidently perturbed and embarrassed before himself, before his inner eye. He dressed, washed, and used his combs and brushes silently and deliberately, as though allowing himself time to think over his position and to reflect, and even from his back one could see he was troubled and dissatisfied with himself.

They drank coffee together. Zinaida Fyodorovna poured out coffee for herself and for Orlov, then she put her elbows on the table and laughed.

" I still can't believe it," she said. " When one has been a long while on one's travels and reaches a hotel at last, it's difficult to believe that one hasn't to go on. It is pleasant to breathe freely."

With the expression of a child who very much wants to be mischievous, she sighed with relief and laughed again.

" You will excuse me," said Orlov, nodding towards the coffee. " Reading at breakfast is a habit I can't get over. But I can do two things at once—read and listen."

" Read away. . . . You shall keep your habits and your freedom. But why do you look so solemn ? Are you always like that in the morning, or is it only to-day ? Aren't you glad ?"

" Yes, I am. But I must own I am a little overwhelmed."

" Why ? You had plenty of time to prepare yourself for my descent upon you. I've been threatening to come every day."

" Yes, but I didn't expect you to carry out your threat to-day."

" I didn't expect it myself, but that's all the better. It's all the better, my dear. It's best to have an aching tooth out and have done with it."

" Yes, of course."

" Oh, my dear," she said, closing her eyes, " all is well that ends well; but before this happy ending, what suffering there has been ! My laughing means nothing; I am glad, I am happy, but I feel more like crying than laughing. Yesterday I had to fight a regular battle," she went on in French. " God alone knows how wretched I was. But I laugh because I can't believe in it. I keep fancying that my sitting here drinking coffee with you is not real, but a dream."

Then, still speaking French, she described how she had broken with her husband the day before, and her eyes were alternately full of tears and of laughter while she gazed with rapture at Orlov. She told him her husband had long suspected her, but had avoided explanations; they had frequent

429

quarrels, and usually at the most heated moment he would suddenly subside into silence and depart to his study for fear that in his exasperation he might give utterance to his suspicions or she might herself begin to speak openly. And she had felt guilty, worthless, incapable of taking a bold and serious step, and that had made her hate herself and her husband more every day, and she had suffered the torments of hell. But the day before, when during a quarrel he had cried out in a tearful voice, " My God, when will it end ?" and had walked off to his study, she had run after him like a cat after a mouse, and, preventing him from shutting the door, she had cried that she hated him with her whole soul. Then he let her come into the study and she had told him everything, had confessed that she loved someone else, that that someone else was her real, most lawful husband, and that she thought it her true duty to go away to him that very day, whatever might happen, if she were to be shot for it.

" There's a very romantic streak in you," Orlov interrupted, keeping his eyes fixed on the newspaper.

She laughed and went on talking without touching her coffee. Her cheeks glowed and she was a little embarrassed by it, and she looked in confusion at Polya and me. From what she went on to say I learnt that her husband had answered her with threats, reproaches, and finally tears, and that it would have been more accurate to say that she, and not he, had been the attacking party.

"Yes, my dear, so long as I was worked up, everything went all right," she told Orlov; "but as night came on, my spirits sank. You don't believe in God, *George*, but I do believe a little, and I fear retribution. God requires of us patience, magnanimity, self-sacrifice, and here I am refusing to be patient and want to remodel my life to suit myself. Is that right? What if from the point of view of God it's wrong? At two o'clock in the night my husband came to me and said: 'You dare not go away. I'll fetch you back through the police and make a scandal.' And soon afterwards I saw him like a shadow at my door. 'Have mercy on me! Your elopement may injure me in the service.' Those words had a coarse effect upon me and made me feel stiff all over. I felt as though the retribution were beginning already; I began crying and trembling with terror. I felt as though the ceiling would fall upon me, that I should be dragged off to the police-station at once, that you would grow cold to me —all sorts of things, in fact! I thought I would go into a nunnery or become a nurse, and give up all thought of happiness, but then I remembered that you loved me, and that I had no right to dispose of myself without your knowledge; and everything in my mind was in a tangle—I was in despair and did not know what to do or think. But the sun rose and I grew happier. As soon as it was morning I dashed off to you. Ah, what I've been through, dear one! I haven't slept for two nights!"

She was tired out and excited. She was sleepy,

431

and at the same time she wanted to talk endlessly, to laugh and to cry, and to go to a restaurant to lunch that she might feel her freedom.

" You have a cosy flat, but I am afraid it may be small for the two of us," she said, walking rapidly through all the rooms when they had finished breakfast. " What room will you give me ? I like this one because it is next to your study."

At one o'clock she changed her dress in the room next to the study, which from that time she called hers, and she went off with Orlov to lunch. They dined, too, at a restaurant, and spent the long interval between lunch and dinner in shopping. Till late at night I was opening the door to messengers and errand-boys from the shops. They bought, among other things, a splendid pier-glass, a dressing-table, a bedstead, and a gorgeous tea service which we did not need. They bought a regular collection of copper saucepans, which we set in a row on the shelf in our cold, empty kitchen. As we were unpacking the tea service Polya's eyes gleamed, and she looked at me two or three times with hatred and fear that I, not she, would be the first to steal one of these charming cups. A lady's writing-table, very expensive and inconvenient, came too. It was evident that Zinaida Fyodorovna contemplated settling with us for good, and meant to make the flat her home.

She came back with Orlov between nine and ten. Full of the proud consciousness that she had done something bold and out of the common, passionately in love, and, as she imagined, passionately loved, exhausted, looking forward to a sweet sound sleep, Zinaida Fyodorovna was revelling in her new life. She squeezed her hands together in the excess of her joy, declared that everything was delightful, and swore that she would love Orlov for ever; and these vows, and the naïve, almost childish confidence that she too was deeply loved and would be loved for ever, made her at least five years younger. She talked charming nonsense and laughed at herself.

"There's no other blessing greater than freedom!" she said, forcing herself to say something serious and edifying. "How absurd it is when you think of it! We attach no value to our own opinion even when it is wise, but tremble before the opinion of all sorts of stupid people. Up to the last minute I was afraid of what other people would say, but as soon as I followed my own instinct and made up my mind to go my own way, my eyes were opened, I overcame my silly fears, and now I am happy and wish everyone could be as happy!"

But her thoughts immediately took another turn, and she began talking of another flat, of wallpapers, horses, a trip to Switzerland and Italy. Orlov was tired by the restaurants and the shops, and was still suffering from the same uneasiness that I had noticed in the morning. He smiled, but more from politeness than pleasure, and when she spoke of anything seriously, he agreed ironically: "Oh yes."

"Stepan, make haste and find us a good cook," she said to me.

"There's no need to be in a hurry over the kitchen arrangements," said Orlov, looking at me coldly. "We must first move into another flat."

We had never had cooking done at home nor kept horses, because, as he said, "he did not like disorder about him," and only put up with having Polya and me in his flat from necessity. The so-called domestic hearth with its everyday joys and its petty cares offended his taste as vulgarity; to be with child, or to have children and talk about them, was bad form, like a petty bourgeois. And I began to feel very curious to see how these two creatures would get on together in one flat— she, domestic and home-loving with her copper saucepans and her dreams of a good cook and horses; and he, fond of saying to his friends that a decent and orderly man's flat ought, like a warship, to have nothing in it superfluous—no women, no children, no rags, no kitchen utensils.

V.

Then I will tell you what happened the following Thursday. That day Zinaida Fyodorovna dined at Content's or Donon's. Orlov returned home alone, and Zinaida Fyodorovna, as I learnt afterwards, went to the Petersburg Side to spend with her old governess the time visitors were with us. Orlov did not care to show her to his friends. I realized that at breakfast, when he began assuring her that for the sake of her peace of mind it was essential to give up his Thursday evenings.

As usual the visitors arrived at almost the same time.

" Is your mistress at home, too ?" Kukushkin asked me in a whisper.

" No, sir," I answered.

He went in with a sly, oily look in his eyes, smiling mysteriously, rubbing his hands, which were cold from the frost.

" I have the honour to congratulate you," he said to Orlov, shaking all over with ingratiating, obsequious laughter. " May you increase and multiply like the cedars of Lebanon."

The visitors went into the bedroom, and were extremely jocose on the subject of a pair of feminine slippers, the rug that had been put down between the two beds, and a grey dressing-jacket that hung at the foot of the bedstead. They were amused that the obstinate man who despised all the commonplace details of love had been caught in feminine snares in such a simple and ordinary way.

" He who pointed the finger of scorn is bowing the knee in homage," Kukushkin repeated several times. He had, I may say in parenthesis, an unpleasant habit of adorning his conversation with texts in Church Slavonic. " Sh-sh !" he said as they went from the bedroom into the room next to the study. " Sh-sh ! Here Gretchen is dreaming of her Faust."

He went off into a peal of laughter as though he had said something very amusing. I watched Gruzin, expecting that his musical soul would not endure this laughter, but I was mistaken. His

thin, good-natured face beamed with pleasure.
When they sat down to play cards, he, lisping
and choking with laughter, said that all that
" dear *George* " wanted to complete his domestic
1elicity was a cherry-wood pipe and a guitar.
Pekarsky laughed sedately, but from his serious
expression one could see that Orlov's new love
affair was distasteful to him. He did not understand what had happened exactly.

" But how about the husband ?" he asked
in perplexity, after they had played three
rubbers.

" I don't know," answered Orlov.

Pekarsky combed his big beard with his fingers
and sank into thought, and he did not speak again
till supper-time. When they were seated at
supper, he began deliberately, drawling every
word :

" Altogether, excuse my saying so, I don't
understand either of you. You might love each
other and break the seventh commandment to
your hearts' content—that I understand. Yes,
that's comprehensible. But why make the husband a party to your secrets ? Was there any
need for that ?"

" But does it make any difference ?"

" Hm ! . . ." Pekarsky mused. " Well, then,
let me tell you this, my friend," he went on,
evidently thinking hard : " if I ever marry again
and you take it into your head to seduce my wife,
please do it so that I don't notice it. It's much
more honest to deceive a man than to break up
his family life and injure his reputation. I under-

stand.   You both imagine that in living together openly you are doing something exceptionally honourable and advanced, but I can't agree with that . . . what shall I call it ? . . . romantic attitude ?"

Orlov made no reply.   He was out of humour and disinclined to talk.   Pekarsky, still perplexed, drummed on the table with his fingers, thought a little, and said:

" I don't understand you, all the same.   You are not a student and she is not a dressmaker. You are both of you people with means.   I should have thought you might have arranged a separate flat for her."

" No, I couldn't.   Read Turgenev."

" Why should I read him ?   I have read him already."

" Turgenev teaches us in his novels that every exalted, noble-minded girl should follow the man she loves to the ends of the earth, and should serve his idea," said Orlov, screwing up his eyes ironically.   " The ends of the earth are poetic license; the earth and all its ends can be reduced to the flat of the man she loves. . . .   And so not to live in the same flat with the woman who loves you is to deny her her exalted vocation and to refuse to share her ideals.   Yes, my dear fellow, Turgenev wrote, and I have to suffer for it."

" What Turgenev has got to do with it I don't understand," said Gruzin softly, and he shrugged his shoulders.   " Do you remember, *George*, how in ' Three Meetings ' he is walking late in the evening somewhere in Italy, and suddenly hears,

'*Vieni pensando a me segretamente,*'" Gruzin
hummed. "It's fine."

"But she hasn't come to settle with you by
force," said Pekarsky. "It was your own wish."

"What next! Far from wishing it, I never
imagined that this would ever happen. When she
said she was coming to live with me, I thought it
was a charming joke on her part."

Everybody laughed.

"I couldn't have wished for such a thing," said
Orlov in the tone of a man compelled to justify
himself. "I am not a Turgenev hero, and if I
ever wanted to free Bulgaria I shouldn't need a
lady's company. I look upon love primarily as
a necessity of my physical nature, degrading and
antagonistic to my spirit; it must either be satisfied
with discretion or renounced altogether, otherwise
it will bring into one's life elements as unclean as
itself. For it to be an enjoyment and not a
torment, I try to make it beautiful and to surround
it with a mass of illusions. I should never go
and see a woman unless I were sure beforehand
that she would be beautiful and fascinating; and
I should never go unless I were in the mood.
And it is only in that way that we succeed in
deceiving one another, and fancying that we are
in love and happy. But can I wish for copper
saucepans and untidy hair, or like to be seen
myself when I am unwashed or out of humour?
Zinaida Fyodorovna in the simplicity of her heart
wants me to love what I have been shunning all
my life. She wants my flat to smell of cooking
and washing up; she wants all the fuss of moving

into another flat, of driving about with her own horses; she wants to count over my linen and to look after my health; she wants to meddle in my personal life at every instant, and to watch over every step; and at the same time she assures me genuinely that my habits and my freedom will be untouched. She is persuaded that, like a young couple, we shall very soon go for a honeymoon— that is, she wants to be with me all the time in trains and hotels, while I like to read on the journey and cannot endure talking in trains."

" You should give her a talking to," said Pekarsky.

" What ! Do you suppose she would understand me ? Why, we think so differently. In her opinion, to leave one's papa and mamma or one's husband for the sake of the man one loves is the height of civic virtue, while I look upon it as childish. To fall in love and run away with a man to her means beginning a new life, while to my mind it means nothing at all. Love and man constitute the chief interest of her life, and possibly it is the philosophy of the unconscious at work in her. Try and make her believe that love is only a simple physical need, like the need of food or clothes; that it doesn't mean the end of the world if wives and husbands are unsatisfactory; that a man may be a profligate and a libertine, and yet a man of honour and a genius; and that, on the other hand, one may abstain from the pleasures of love and at the same time be a stupid, vicious animal ! The civilized man of to-day, even among the lower classes—for instance, the French workman—spends ten *sous* on dinner, five *sous* on his wine, and five or ten *sous* on woman, and devotes his brain and nerves entirely to his work. But Zinaida Fyodorovna assigns to love not so many *sous*, but her whole soul. I might give her a talking to, but she would raise a wail in answer, and declare in all sincerity that I had ruined her, that she had nothing left to live for."

" Don't say anything to her," said Pekarsky, " but simply take a separate flat for her, that's all."

" That's easy to say. . . ."

There was a brief silence.

" But she is charming," said Kukushkin. " She is exquisite. Such women imagine that they will be in love for ever, and abandon themselves with tragic intensity."

" But one must keep a head on one's shoulders," said Orlov; " one must be reasonable. All experience gained from everyday life and handed down in innumerable novels and plays, uniformly confirms the fact that adultery and cohabitation of any sort between decent people never lasts longer than two or at most three years, however great the love may have been at the beginning. That she ought to know. And so all this business of moving, of saucepans, hopes of eternal love and harmony, are nothing but a desire to delude herself and me. She is charming and exquisite—who denies it ? But she has turned my life upside down; what I have regarded as trivial and nonsensical till now she has forced me to raise to the level of a serious problem; I serve an idol whom

I have never looked upon as God. She is charming —exquisite, but for some reason now when I am going home, I feel uneasy, as though I expected to meet with something inconvenient at home, such as workmen pulling the stove to pieces and blocking up the place with heaps of bricks. In fact, I am no longer giving up to love a *sou*, but part of my peace of mind and my nerves. And that's bad."

"And she doesn't hear this villain!" sighed Kukushkin. "My dear șir," he said theatrically, "I will relieve you from the burdensome obligation to love that adorable creature! I will wrest Zinaida Fyodorovna from you!"

"You may . . ." said Orlov carelessly.

For half a minute Kukushkin laughed a shrill little laugh, shaking all over, then he said:

"Look out; I am in earnest! Don't you play the Othello afterwards!"

They all began talking of Kukushkin's indefatigable energy in love affairs, how irresistible he was to women, and what a danger he was to husbands; and how the devil would roast him in the other world for his immorality in this. He screwed up his eyes and remained silent, and when the names of ladies of their acquaintance were mentioned, he held up his little finger—as though to say they mustn't give away other people's secrets.

Orlov suddenly looked at his watch.

His friends understood, and began to take their leave. I remember that Gruzin, who was a little drunk, was wearisomely long in getting off. He put on his coat, which was cut like children's coats in poor families, pulled up the collar, and began telling some long-winded story; then, seeing he was not listened to, he flung the rug that smelt of the nursery over one shoulder, and with a guilty and imploring face begged me to find his hat.

" *George*, my angel," he said tenderly. " Do as I ask you, dear boy; come out of town with us !"

" You can go, but I can't. I am in the position of a married man now."

" She is a dear, she won't be angry. My dear chief, come along ! It's glorious weather; there's snow and frost. . . . Upon my word, you want shaking up a bit; you are out of humour. I don't know what the devil is the matter with you. . . ."

Orlov stretched, yawned, and looked at Pekarsky.

" Are you going ?" he said, hesitating.

" I don't know. Perhaps."

" Shall I get drunk ? All right, I'll come," said Orlov after some hesitation. " Wait a minute; I'll get some money."

He went into the study, and Gruzin slouched in, too, dragging his rug after him. A minute later both came back into the hall. Gruzin, a little drunk and very pleased, was crumpling a ten-rouble note in his hands.

" We'll settle up to-morrow," he said. " And she is kind, she won't be cross. . . . She is my Lisotchka's godmother; I am fond of her, poor thing ! Ah, my dear fellow !" he laughed joyfully, and pressing his forehead on Pekarsky's back. "Ah, Pekarsky, my dear soul! Advocatissimus—as dry as a biscuit, but you bet he is fond of women. . . ."

"Fat ones," said Orlov, putting on his fur coat. "But let us get off, or we shall be meeting her on the doorstep."

"'*Vieni pensando a me segretamente,*'" hummed Gruzin.

At last they drove off: Orlov did not sleep at home, and returned next day at dinner-time.

VI.

Zinaida Fyodorovna had lost her gold watch, a present from her father. This loss surprised and alarmed her. She spent half a day going through the rooms, looking helplessly on all the tables and on all the windows. But the watch had disappeared completely.

Only three days afterwards Zinaida Fyodorovna, on coming in, left her purse in the hall. Luckily for me, on that occasion it was not I but Polya who helped her off with her coat. When the purse was missed, it could not be found in the hall.

"Strange," said Zinaida Fyodorovna in bewilderment. "I distinctly remember taking it out of my pocket to pay the cabman . . . and then I put it here near the looking-glass. It's very odd!"

I had not stolen it, but I felt as though I had stolen it and had been caught in the theft. Tears actually came into my eyes. When they were seated at dinner, Zinaida Fyodorovna said to Orlov in French:

"There seem to be spirits in the flat. I lost my purse in the hall to-day, and now, lo and behold, it is on my table. But it's not quite a disinterested trick of the spirits. They took out a gold coin and twenty roubles in notes."

"You are always losing something; first it's your watch and then it's your money . . ." said Orlov. "Why is it nothing of the sort ever happens to me ?"

A minute later Zinaida Fyodorovna had forgotten the trick played by the spirits, and was telling with a laugh how the week before she had ordered some notepaper and had forgotten to give her new address, and the shop had sent the paper to her old home at her husband's, who had to pay twelve roubles for it. And suddenly she turned her eyes on Polya and looked at her intently. She blushed as she did so, and was so confused that she began talking of something else.

When I took in the coffee to the study, Orlov was standing with his back to the fire and she was sitting in an arm-chair facing him.

"I am not in a bad temper at all," she was saying in French. "But I have been putting things together, and now I see it clearly. I can give you the day and the hour when she stole my watch. And the purse ? There can be no doubt about it. Oh !" she laughed as she took the coffee from me. "Now I understand why I am always losing my handkerchiefs and gloves. Whatever you say, I shall dismiss the magpie to-morrow and send Stepan for my Sofya. She is not a thief and has not got such a . . . repulsive appearance."

" You are out of humour. To-morrow you will feel differently, and will realize that you can't discharge people simply because you suspect them."

" It's not suspicion; it's certainty," said Zinaida Fyodorovna. " So long as I suspected that unhappy-faced, poor-looking valet of yours, I said nothing. It's too bad of you not to believe me, *George*."

" If we think differently about anything, it doesn't follow that I don't believe you. You may be right," said Orlov, turning round and flinging his cigarette-end into the fire, " but there is no need to be excited about it, anyway. In fact, I must say, I never expected my humble establishment would cause you so much serious worry and agitation. You've lost a gold coin: never mind—you may have a hundred of mine; but to change my habits, to pick up a new housemaid, to wait till she is used to the place—all that's a tedious, tiring business and does not suit me. Our present maid certainly is fat, and has, perhaps, a weakness for gloves and handkerchiefs, but she is perfectly well behaved, well trained, and does not shriek when Kukushkin pinches her."

" You mean that you can't part with her ? . . . Why don't you say so ?"

" Are you jealous ?"

" Yes, I am," said Zinaida Fyodorovna decidedly.

" Thank you."

" Yes, I am jealous," she repeated, and tears glistened in her eyes. " No, it's something worse . . . which I find it difficult to find a name for." She pressed her hands on her temples, and went on impulsively. " You men are so disgusting ! It's horrible !"

" I see nothing horrible about it."

" I've not seen it; I don't know; but they say that you men begin with housemaids as boys, and get so used to it that you feel no repugnance. I don't know, I don't know, but I have actually read . . . *George*, of course you are right," she said, going up to Orlov and changing to a caressing and imploring tone. " I really am out of humour to-day. But, you must understand, I can't help it. She disgusts me and I am afraid of her. It makes me miserable to see her."

" Surely you can rise above such paltriness ?" said Orlov, shrugging his shoulders in perplexity, and walking away from the fire. " Nothing could be simpler: take no notice of her, and then she won't disgust you, and you won't need to make a regular tragedy out of a trifle."

I went out of the study, and I don't know what answer Orlov received. Whatever it was, Polya remained. After that Zinaida Fyodorovna never applied to her for anything, and evidently tried to dispense with her services. When Polya handed her anything or even passed by her, jingling her bangle and rustling her skirts, she shuddered.

I believe that if Gruzin or Pekarsky had asked Orlov to dismiss Polya he would have done so without the slightest hesitation, without troubling about any explanations. He was easily persuaded, like all indifferent people. But in his relations with Zinaida Fyodorovna he displayed for some reason, even in trifles, an obstinacy which sometimes was almost irrational. I knew beforehand that if Zinaida Fyodorovna liked anything, it would be certain not to please Orlov. When on coming in from shopping she made haste to show him with pride some new purchase, he would glance at it and say coldly that the more unnecessary objects they had in the flat, the less airy it would be. It sometimes happened that after putting on his dress clothes to go out somewhere, and after saying good-bye to Zinaida Fyodorovna, he would suddenly change his mind and remain at home from sheer perversity. I used to think that he remained at home then simply in order to feel injured.

"Why are you staying?" said Zinaida Fyodorovna, with a show of vexation, though at the same time she was radiant with delight. "Why do you? You are not accustomed to spending your evenings at home, and I don't want you to alter your habits on my account. Do go out as usual, if you don't want me to feel guilty."

"No one is blaming you," said Orlov.

With the air of a victim he stretched himself in his easy-chair in the study, and shading his eyes with his hand, took up a book. But soon the book dropped from his hand, he turned heavily in his chair, and again screened his eyes as though from the sun. Now he felt annoyed that he had not gone out.

" May I come in ?" Zinaida Fyodorovna would say, coming irresolutely into the study. " Are you reading ? I felt dull by myself, and have come just for a minute . . . to have a peep at you."

I remember one evening she went in like that, irresolutely and inappropriately, and sank on the rug at Orlov's feet, and from her soft, timid movements one could see that she did not understand his mood and was afraid.

" You are always reading . . ." she said cajolingly, evidently wishing to flatter him. " Do you know, *George*, what is one of the secrets of your success ? You are very clever and well-read. What book have you there ?"

Orlov answered. A silence followed for some minutes which seemed to me very long. I was standing in the drawing-room, from which I could watch them, and was afraid of coughing.

" There is something I wanted to tell you," said Zinaida Fyodorovna, and she laughed; " shall I ? Very likely you'll laugh and say that I flatter myself. You know I want, I want horribly to believe that you are staying at home to-night for my sake . . . that we might spend the evening together. Yes ? May I think so ?"

" Do," he said, screening his eyes. " The really happy man is he who thinks not only of what is, but of what is not."

" That was a long sentence which I did not quite understand. You mean happy people live in their imagination. Yes, that's true. I love to sit in your study in the evening and let my

448

AN ANONYMOUS STORY

thoughts carry me far, far away. . . . It's
pleasant sometimes to dream. Let us dream
aloud, *George*."

" I've never been at a girls' boarding-school; I
never learnt the art."

" You are out of humour ?" said Zinaida
Fyodorovna, taking Orlov's hand. " Tell me
why. When you are like that, I'm afraid. I
don't know whether your head aches or whether
you are angry with me. . . ."

Again there was a silence lasting several long
minutes.

" Why have you changed ?" she said softly.
" Why are you never so tender or so gay as you
used to be at Znamensky Street ? I've been with
you almost a month, but it seems to me as though
we had not yet begun to live, and have not yet
talked of anything as we ought to. You always
answer me with jokes or else with a long cold
lecture like a teacher. And there is something
cold in your jokes. . . . Why have you given up
talking to me seriously ?"

" I always talk seriously."

" Well, then, let us talk. For God's sake,
George. . . . Shall we ?"

" Certainly, but about what ?"

" Let us talk of our life, of our future," said
Zinaida Fyodorovna dreamily. " I keep making
plans for our life, plans and plans—and I enjoy
doing it so ! *George*, I'll begin with the question,
when are you going to give up your post ?"

" What for ?" asked Orlov, taking his hand from
his forehead.

449   P

" With your views you cannot remain in the service. You are out of place there."

" My views ?" Orlov repeated. " My views ? In conviction and temperament I am an ordinary official, one of Shtchedrin's heroes. You take me for something different, I venture to assure you."

" Joking again, *George !*"

" Not in the least. The service does not satisfy me, perhaps; but, anyway, it is better for me than anything else. I am used to it, and in it I meet men of my own sort; I am in my place there and find it tolerable."

" You hate the service and it revolts you."

" Indeed ? If I resign my post, take to dreaming aloud and letting myself be carried away into another world, do you suppose that that world would be less hateful to me than the service ?"

" You are ready to libel yourself in order to contradict me." Zinaida Fyodorovna was offended and got up. " I am sorry I began this talk."

" Why are you angry ? I am not angry with you for not being an official. Everyone lives as he likes best."

" Why, do you live as you like best ? Are you free ? To spend your life writing documents that are opposed to your own ideas," Zinaida Fyodorovna went on, clasping her hands in despair: " to submit to authority, congratulate your superiors at the New Year, and then cards and nothing but cards: worst of all, to be working for a system which must be distasteful to you—no, *George*, no ! You should not make such horrid jokes. It's dreadful. You are a man of ideas, and you ought to be working for your ideas and nothing else."

" You really take me for quite a different person from what I am," sighed Orlov.

" Say simply that you don't want to talk to me. You dislike me, that's all," said Zinaida Fyodorovna through her tears.

" Look here, my dear," said Orlov admonishingly, sitting up in his chair. " You were pleased to observe yourself that I am a clever, well-read man, and to teach one who knows does nothing but harm. I know very well all the ideas, great and small, which you mean when you call me a man of ideas. So if I prefer the service and cards to those ideas, you may be sure I have good grounds for it. That's one thing. Secondly, you have, so far as I know, never been in the service, and can only have drawn your ideas of Government service from anecdotes and indifferent novels. So it would not be amiss for us to make a compact, once for all, not to talk of things we know already or of things about which we are not competent to speak."

" Why do you speak to me like that ?" said Zinaida Fyodorovna, stepping back as though in horror. " What for ? *George*, for God's sake, think what you are saying !"

Her voice quivered and broke; she was evidently trying to restrain her tears, but she suddenly broke into sobs.

" *George*, my darling, I am perishing !" she said in French, dropping down before Orlov, and

laying her head on his knees. " I am miserable,
I am exhausted. I can't bear it, I can't bear it.
. . . In my childhood my hateful, depraved step-
mother, then my husband, now you . . . you ! . . .
You meet my mad love with coldness and irony.
. . . And that horrible, insolent servant," she
went on, sobbing. " Yes, yes, I see: I am not
your wife nor your friend, but a woman you don't
respect because she has become your mistress. . . .
I shall kill myself !"

I had not expected that her words and her tears
would make such an impression on Orlov. He
flushed, moved uneasily in his chair, and instead
of irony, his face wore a look of stupid, school-
boyish dismay.

" My darling, you misunderstood me," he
muttered helplessly, touching her hair and her
shoulders. " Forgive me, I entreat you. I was
unjust . . . and I hate myself."

" I insult you with my whining and complaints.
. . . You are a true, generous . . . rare man—I
am conscious of it every minute; but I've been
horribly depressed for the last few days. . . ."

Zinaida Fyodorovna impulsively embraced Orlov
and kissed him on the cheek.

" Only please don't cry," he said.

" No, no. . . . I've had my cry, and now I
am better."

" As for the servant, she shall be gone to-
morrow," he said, still moving uneasily in his
chair.

" No, she must stay, *George !* Do you hear ?
I am not afraid of her now. . . . One must

rise above trifles and not imagine silly things. You are right! You are a wonderful, rare person!"

She soon left off crying. With tears glistening on her eyelashes, sitting on Orlov's knee, she told him in a low voice something touching, something like a reminiscence of childhood and youth. She stroked his face, kissed him, and carefully examined his hands with the rings on them and the charms on his watch-chain. She was carried away by what she was saying, and by being near the man she loved, and probably because her tears had cleared and refreshed her soul, there was a note of wonderful candour and sincerity in her voice. And Orlov played with her chestnut hair and kissed her hands, noiselessly pressing them to his lips.

Then they had tea in the study, and Zinaida Fyodorovna read aloud some letters. Soon after midnight they went to bed.

I had a fearful pain in my side that night, and could not get warm or go to sleep till morning. I could hear Orlov go from the bedroom into his study. After sitting there about an hour, he rang the bell. In my pain and exhaustion I forgot all the rules and conventions, and went to his study in my night attire, barefooted. Orlov, in his dressing-gown and cap, was standing in the doorway, waiting for me.

"When you are sent for you should come dressed," he said sternly. "Bring some fresh candles."

I was about to apologize, but suddenly broke

into a violent cough, and clutched at the side of the door to save myself from falling.

" Are you ill ?" said Orlov.

I believe it was the first time of our acquaintance that he addressed me not in the singular—goodness knows why. Most likely, in my night clothes and with my face distorted by coughing, I played my part poorly, and was very little like a flunkey.

" If you are ill, why do you take a place ?" he said.

" That I may not die of starvation," I answered.

" How disgusting it all is, really !" he said softly, going up to his table.

While hurriedly getting into my coat, I put up and lighted fresh candles. He was sitting at the table, with feet stretched out on a low chair, cutting a book.

I left him deeply engrossed, and the book did not drop out of his hands as it had done in the evening.

VII.

Now that I am writing these lines I am restrained by that dread of appearing sentimental and ridiculous, in which I have been trained from childhood; when I want to be affectionate or to say anything tender, I don't know how to be natural. And it is that dread, together with lack of practice, that prevents me from being able to express with perfect clearness what was passing in my soul at that time.

I was not in love with Zinaida Fyodorovna,

but in the ordinary human feeling I had for her, there was far more youth, freshness, and joyousness than in Orlov's love.

As I worked in the morning, cleaning boots or sweeping the rooms, I waited with a thrill at my heart for the moment when I should hear her voice and her footsteps. To stand watching her as she drank her coffee in the morning or ate her lunch, to hold her fur coat for her in the hall, and to put the goloshes on her little feet while she rested her hand on my shoulder; then to wait till the hall porter rang up for me, to meet her at the door, cold, and rosy, powdered with the snow, to listen to her brief exclamations about the frost or the cabman—if only you knew how much all that meant to me! I longed to be in love, to have a wife and child of my own. I wanted my future wife to have such just a face, such a voice. I dreamed of it at dinner, and in the street when I was sent on some errand, and when I lay awake at night. Orlov rejected with disgust children, cooking, copper saucepans, and feminine knick-knacks, and I gathered them all up, tenderly cherished them in my dreams, loved them, and begged them of destiny. I had visions of a wife, a nursery, a little house with garden paths. . . .

I knew that if I did love her I could never dare to hope for the miracle of her returning my love, but that reflection did not worry me. In my quiet, modest feeling akin to ordinary affection, there was no jealousy of Orlov or even envy of him, since I realized that for a wreck like me happiness was only to be found in dreams.

When Zinaida Fyodorovna sat up night after night for her *George*, looking immovably at a book of which she never turned a page, or when she shuddered and turned pale at Polya's crossing the room, I suffered with her, and the idea occurred to me to lance this festering wound as quickly as possible by letting her know what was said here at supper on Thursdays; but—how was it to be done? More and more often I saw her tears. For the first weeks she laughed and sang to herself, even when Orlov was not at home, but by the second month there was a mournful stillness in our flat broken only on Thursday evenings.

She flattered Orlov, and to wring from him a counterfeit smile or kiss, was ready to go on her knees to him, to fawn on him like a dog. Even when her heart was heaviest, she could not resist glancing into a looking-glass if she passed· one and straightening her hair. It seemed strange to me that she could still take an interest in clothes and go into ecstasies over her purchases. It did not seem in keeping with her genuine grief. She paid attention to the fashions and ordered expensive dresses. What for? On whose account? I particularly remember one dress which cost four hundred roubles. To give four hundred roubles for an unnecessary, useless dress while women for their hard day's work get only twenty kopecks a day without food, and the makers of Venice and Brussels lace are only paid half a franc a day on the supposition that they can earn the rest by immorality! And it seemed strange to me that Zinaida Fyodorovna was not conscious of it; it vexed me. But she had only to go out of the house for me to find excuses and explanations for everything, and to be waiting eagerly for the hall porter to ring for me.

She treated me as a flunkey, a being of a lower order. One may pat a dog, and yet not notice it; I was given orders and asked questions, but my presence was not observed. My master and mistress thought it unseemly to say more to me than is usually said to servants; if when waiting at dinner I had laughed or put in my word in the conversation, they would certainly have thought I was mad and have dismissed me. Zinaida Fyodorovna was favourably disposed to me, all the same. When she was sending me on some errand or explaining to me the working of a new lamp or anything of that sort, her face was extraordinarily kind, frank, and cordial, and her eyes looked me straight in the face. At such moments I always fancied she remembered with gratitude how I used to bring her letters to Znamensky Street. When she rang the bell, Polya, who considered me her favourite and hated me for it, used to say with a jeering smile:

" Go along, *your* mistress wants you."

Zinaida Fyodorovna considered me as a being of a lower order, and did not suspect that if anyone in the house were in a humiliating position it was she. She did not know that I, a footman, was unhappy on her account, and used to ask myself twenty times a day what was in store for her and how it would all end. Things were growing visibly worse day by day. After the evening on which they had talked of his official work, Orlov, who could not endure tears, unmistakably began to avoid conversation with her; whenever Zinaida Fyodorovna began to argue, or to beseech him, or seemed on the point of crying, he seized some plausible excuse for retreating to his study or going out. He more and more rarely slept at home, and still more rarely dined there: on Thursdays he was the one to suggest some expedition to his friends. Zinaida Fyodorovna was still dreaming of having the cooking done at home, of moving to a new flat, of travelling abroad, but her dreams remained dreams. Dinner was sent in from the restaurant. Orlov asked her not to broach the question of moving until after they had come back from abroad, and apropos of their foreign tour, declared that they could not go till his hair had grown long, as one could not go trailing from hotel to hotel and serving the idea without long hair.

To crown it all, in Orlov's absence, Kukushkin began calling at the flat in the evening. There was nothing exceptional in his behaviour, but I could never forget the conversation in which he had offered to cut Orlov out. He was regaled with tea and red wine, and he used to titter and, anxious to say something pleasant, would declare that a free union was superior in every respect to legal marriage, and that all decent people ought really to come to Zinaida Fyodorovna and fall at her feet.

VIII.

Christmas was spent drearily in vague anticipations of calamity. On New Year's Eve Orlov unexpectedly announced at breakfast that he was being sent to assist a senator who was on a revising commission in a certain province.

"I don't want to go, but I can't find an excuse to get off," he said with vexation. "I must go; there's nothing for it."

Such news instantly made Zinaida Fyodorovna's eyes look red.

"Is it for long?" she asked.

"Five days or so."

"I am glad, really, you are going," she said after a moment's thought. "It will be a change for you. You will fall in love with someone on the way, and tell me about it afterwards."

At every opportunity she tried to make Orlov feel that she did not restrict his liberty in any way, and that he could do exactly as he liked, and this artless, transparent strategy deceived no one, and only unnecessarily reminded Orlov that he was not free.

"I am going this evening," he said, and began reading the paper.

Zinaida Fyodorovna wanted to see him off at the station, but he dissuaded her, saying that he was not going to America, and not going to be away five years, but only five days—possibly less.

The parting took place between seven and eight.

459

He put one arm round her, and kissed her on the lips and on the forehead.

"Be a good girl, and don't be depressed while I am away," he said in a warm, affectionate tone which touched even me. "God keep you!"

She looked greedily into his face, to stamp his dear features on her memory, then she put her arms gracefully round his neck and laid her head on his breast.

"Forgive me our misunderstandings," she said in French. "Husband and wife cannot help quarrelling if they love each other, and I love you madly. Don't forget me. . . . Wire to me often and fully."

Orlov kissed her once more, and, without saying a word, went out in confusion. When he heard the click of the lock as the door closed, he stood still in the middle of the staircase in hesitation and glanced upwards. It seemed to me that if a sound had reached him at that moment from above, he would have turned back. But all was quiet. He straightened his coat and went downstairs irresolutely.

The sledges had been waiting a long while at the door. Orlov got into one, I got into the other with two portmanteaus. It was a hard frost and there were fires smoking at the cross-roads. The cold wind nipped my face and hands, and took my breath away as we drove rapidly along; and, closing my eyes, I thought what a splendid woman she was. How she loved him! Even useless rubbish is collected in the courtyards nowadays and used for some purpose, even broken glass is considered a useful commodity, but something so precious, so rare, as the love of a refined, young, intelligent, and good woman is utterly thrown away and wasted. One of the early sociologists regarded every evil passion as a force which might by judicious management be turned to good, while among us even a fine, noble passion springs up and dies away in impotence, turned to no account, misunderstood or vulgarized. Why is it?

The sledges stopped unexpectedly. I opened my eyes and I saw that we had come to a standstill in Sergievsky Street, near a big house where Pekarsky lived. Orlov got out of the sledge and vanished into the entry. Five minutes later Pekarsky's footman came out, bareheaded, and, angry with the frost, shouted to me:

"Are you deaf? Pay the cabmen and go up-stairs. You are wanted!"

At a complete loss, I went to the first storey. I had been to Pekarsky's flat before—that is, I had stood in the hall and looked into the drawing-room, and, after the damp, gloomy street, it always struck me by the brilliance of its picture-frames, its bronzes and expensive furniture. To-day in the midst of this splendour I saw Gruzin, Kukushkin, and, after a minute, Orlov.

"Look here, Stepan," he said, coming up to me. "I shall be staying here till Friday or Saturday. If any letters or telegrams come, you must bring them here every day. At home, of course you will say that I have gone, and send my greetings. Now you can go."

When I reached home Zinaida Fyodorovna was

lying on the sofa in the drawing-room, eating a pear. There was only one candle burning in the candelabra.

"Did you catch the train?" asked Zinaida Fyodorovna.

"Yes, madam. His honour sends his greetings."

I went into my room and I, too, lay down. I had nothing to do, and I did not want to read. I was not surprised and I was not indignant. I only racked my brains to think why this deception was necessary. It is only boys in their teens who deceive their mistresses like that. How was it that a man who had thought and read so much could not imagine anything more sensible? I must confess I had by no means a poor opinion of his intelligence. I believe if he had had to deceive his minister or any other influential person he would have put a great deal of skill and energy into doing so; but to deceive a woman, the first idea that occurred to him was evidently good enough. If it succeeded—well and good; if it did not, there would be no harm done—he could tell some other lie just as quickly and simply, with no mental effort.

At midnight when the people on the floor overhead were moving their chairs and shouting hurrah to welcome the New Year, Zinaida Fyodorovna rang for me from the room next to the study. Languid from lying down so long, she was sitting at the table, writing something on a scrap of paper.

"I must send a telegram," she said, with a smile. "Go to the station as quick as you can and ask them to send it after him."

Going out into the street, I read on the scrap of paper:

"May the New Year bring new happiness. Make haste and telegraph; I miss you dreadfully. It seems an eternity. I am only sorry I can't send a thousand kisses and my very heart by telegraph. Enjoy yourself, my darling.—ZINA."

I sent the telegram, and next morning I gave her the receipt.

IX.

The worst of it was that Orlov had thoughtlessly let Polya, too, into the secret of his deception, telling her to bring his shirts to Sergievsky Street. After that, she looked at Zinaida Fyodorovna with a malignant joy and hatred I could not understand, and was never tired of snorting with delight to herself in her own room and in the hall.

"She's outstayed her welcome; it's time she took herself off!" she would say with zest. "She ought to realize that herself. . . ."

She already divined by instinct that Zinaida Fyodorovna would not be with us much longer, and, not to let the chance slip, carried off everything she set her eyes on—smelling-bottles, tortoise-shell hairpins, handkerchiefs, shoes! On the day after New Year's Day, Zinaida Fyodorovna summoned me to her room and told me in a low voice that she missed her black dress. And then she walked through all the rooms, with a pale, frightened, and indignant face, talking to herself:

463

" It's too much ! It's beyond everything !
Why, it's unheard-of insolence !"

At dinner she tried to help herself to soup, but
could not—her hands were trembling. Her lips
were trembling, too. She looked helplessly at
the soup and at the little pies, waiting for the
trembling to pass off, and suddenly she could not
resist looking at Polya.

" You can go, Polya," she said. " Stepan is
enough by himself."

" I'll stay; I don't mind," answered Polya.

" There's no need for you to stay. You go
away altogether," Zinaida Fyodorovna went on,
getting up in great agitation. " You may look
out for another place. You can go at once."

" I can't go away without the master's orders.
He engaged me. It must be as he orders."

" You can take orders from me, too ! I am
mistress here !" said Zinaida Fyodorovna, and
she flushed crimson.

" You may be the mistress, but only the master
can dismiss me. It was he engaged me."

" You dare not stay here another minute !"
cried Zinaida Fyodorovna, and she struck the
plate with her knife. " You are a thief ! Do you
hear ?"

Zinaida Fyodorovna flung her dinner-napkin on
the table, and with a pitiful, suffering face, went
quickly out of the room. Loudly sobbing and
wailing something indistinct, Polya, too, went
away. The soup and the grouse got cold. And
for some reason all the restaurant dainties on the
table struck me as poor, thievish, like Polya.

464

Two pies on a plate had a particularly miserable and guilty air. " We shall be taken back to the restaurant to-day," they seemed to be saying, " and to-morrow we shall be put on the table again for some official or celebrated singer."

" She is a fine lady, indeed," I heard uttered in Polya's room. " I could have been a lady like that long ago, but I have some self-respect ! We'll see which of us will be the first to go !"

Zinaida Fyodorovna rang the bell. She was sitting in her room, in the corner, looking as though she had been put in the corner as a punishment.

" No telegram has come ?" she asked.

" No, madam."

" Ask the porter; perhaps there is a telegram. And don't leave the house," she called after me. " I am afraid to be left alone."

After that I had to run down almost every hour to ask the porter whether a telegram had come. I must own it was a dreadful time ! To avoid seeing Polya, Zinaida Fyodorovna dined and had tea in her own room; it was here that she slept, too, on a short sofa like a half-moon, and she made her own bed. For the first days I took the telegrams; but, getting no answer, she lost her faith in me and began telegraphing herself. Looking at her, I, too, began impatiently hoping for a telegram. I hoped he would contrive some deception, would make arrangements, for instance, that a telegram should be sent to her from some station. If he were too much engrossed with cards or had been attracted by some other woman, I thought that both Gruzin and Kukushkin would remind him of us. But our expectations were vain. Five times a day I would go in to Zinaida Fyodorovna, intending to tell her the truth, but her eyes looked piteous as a fawn's, her shoulders seemed to droop, her lips were moving, and I went away again without saying a word. Pity and sympathy seemed to rob me of all manliness. Polya, as cheerful and well satisfied with herself as though nothing had happened, was tidying the master's study and the bedroom, rummaging in the cupboards, and making the crockery jingle, and when she passed Zinaida Fyodorovna's door, she hummed something and coughed. She was pleased that her mistress was hiding from her. In the evening she would go out somewhere, and rang at two or three o'clock in the morning, and I had to open the door to her and listen to remarks about my cough. Immediately afterwards I would hear another ring; I would run to the room next to the study, and Zinaida Fyodorovna, putting her head out of the door, would ask, " Who was it rang ?" while she looked at my hands to see whether I had a telegram.

When at last on Saturday the bell rang below and she heard the familiar voice on the stairs, she was so delighted that she broke into sobs. She rushed to meet him, embraced him, kissed him on the breast and sleeves, said something one could not understand. The hall porter brought up the portmanteaus; Polya's cheerful voice was heard. It was as though someone had come home for the holidays.

" Why didn't you wire ?" asked Zinaida Fyodor-ovna, breathless with joy. " Why was it ? I have been in misery; I don't know how I've lived through it. . . . Oh, my God !"

" It was very simple ! I returned with the senator to Moscow the very first day, and didn't get your telegrams," said Orlov. " After dinner, my love, I'll give you a full account of my doings, but now I must sleep and sleep. . . . I am worn out with the journey."

It was evident that he had not slept all night; he had probably been playing cards and drinking freely. Zinaida Fyodorovna put him to bed, and we all walked about on tiptoe all that day. The dinner went off quite satisfactorily, but when they went into the study and had coffee the explanation began. Zinaida Fyodorovna began talking of something rapidly in a low voice; she spoke in French, and her words flowed like a stream. Then I heard a loud sigh from Orlov, and his voice.

" My God !" he said in French. " Have you really nothing fresher to tell me than this ever-lasting tale of your servant's misdeeds ?"

" But, my dear, she robbed me and said insulting things to me."

" But why is it she doesn't rob me or say insulting things to me ? Why is it I never notice the maids nor the porters nor the footmen ? My dear, you are simply capricious and refuse to know your own mind. . . . I really begin to suspect that you must be in a certain condition. When I offered to let her go, you insisted on her remaining, and now you want me to turn her away. I can be obstinate, too, in such cases. You want her to go, but I want her to remain. That's the only way to cure you of your nerves."

"Oh, very well, very well," said Zinaida Fyodorovna in alarm. "Let us say no more about that. . . . Let us put it off till to-morrow. . . . Now tell me about Moscow. . . . What is going on in Moscow?"

X.

After lunch next day—it was the seventh of January, St. John the Baptist's Day—Orlov put on his black dress coat and his decoration to go to visit his father and congratulate him on his name day. He had to go at two o'clock, and it was only half-past one when he had finished dressing. What was he to do for that half-hour? He walked about the drawing-room, declaiming some congratulatory verses which he had recited as a child to his father and mother.

Zinaida Fyodorovna, who was just going out to a dressmaker's or to the shops, was sitting, listening to him with a smile. I don't know how their conversation began, but when I took Orlov his gloves, he was standing before her with a capricious, beseeching face, saying:

"For God's sake, in the name of everything that's holy, don't talk of things that everybody knows! What an unfortunate gift our intellectual thoughtful ladies have for talking with enthusiasm and an air of profundity of things that every

468

schoolboy is sick to death of! Ah, if only you would exclude from our conjugal programme all these serious questions! How grateful I should be to you!"

"We women may not dare, it seems, to have views of our own."

"I give you full liberty to be as liberal as you like, and quote from any authors you choose, but make me one concession: don't hold forth in my presence on either of two subjects: the corruption of the upper classes and the evils of the marriage system. Do understand me, at last. The upper class is always abused in contrast with the world of tradesmen, priests, workmen and peasants, Sidors and Nikitas of all sorts. I detest both classes, but if I had honestly to choose between the two, I should, without hesitation, prefer the upper class, and there would be no falsity or affectation about it, since all my tastes are in that direction. Our world is trivial and empty, but at any rate we speak French decently, read something, and don't punch each other in the ribs even in our most violent quarrels, while the Sidors and the Nikitas and their worships in trade talk about 'being quite agreeable,' 'in a jiffy,' 'blast your eyes,' and display the utmost license of pot-house manners and the most degrading superstition."

"The peasant and the tradesman feed you."

"Yes, but what of it? That's not only to my discredit, but to theirs too. They feed me and take off their caps to me, so it seems they have not the intelligence and honesty to do otherwise. I don't blame or praise anyone: I only mean that the upper class and the lower are as bad as one another. My feelings and my intelligence are opposed to both, but my tastes lie more in the direction of the former. Well, now for the evils of marriage," Orlov went on, glancing at his watch. "It's high time for you to understand that there are no evils in the system itself; what is the matter is that you don't know yourselves what you want from marriage. What is it you want? In legal and illegal cohabitation, in every sort of union and cohabitation, good or bad, the underlying reality is the same. You ladies live for that underlying reality alone: for you it's everything; your existence would have no meaning for you without it. You want nothing but that, and you get it; but since you've taken to reading novels you are ashamed of it: you rush from pillar to post, you recklessly change your men, and to justify this turmoil you have begun talking of the evils of marriage. So long as you can't and won't renounce what underlies it all, your chief foe, your devil—so long as you serve that slavishly, what use is there in discussing the matter seriously? Everything you may say to me will be falsity and affectation. I shall not believe you."

I went to find out from the hall porter whether the sledge was at the door, and when I came back I found it had become a quarrel. As sailors say a squall had blown up.

"I see you want to shock me by your cynicism to-day," said Zinaida Fyodorovna, walking about the drawing-room in great emotion.

470

" It revolts me to listen to you. I am pure before God and man, and have nothing to repent of. I left my husband and came to you, and am proud of it. I swear, on my honour, I am proud of it !"

" Well, that's all right, then !"

" If you are a decent, honest man, you, too, ought to be proud of what I did. It raises you and me above thousands of people who would like to do as we have done, but do not venture through cowardice or petty prudence. But you are not a decent man. You are afraid of freedom, and you mock the promptings of genuine feeling, from fear that some ignoramus may suspect you of being sincere. You are afraid to show me to your friends; there's no greater infliction for you than to go about with me in the street. . . . Isn't that true ? Why haven't you introduced me to your father or your cousin all this time ? Why is it ? No, I am sick of it at last," cried Zinaida Fyodorovna, stamping. " I demand what is mine by right. You must present me to your father."

" If you want to know him, go and present yourself. He receives visitors every morning from ten till half-past."

" How base you are !" said Zinaida Fyodorovna, wringing her hands in despair. " Even if you are not sincere, and are not saying what you think, I might hate you for your cruelty. Oh, how base you are !"

" We keep going round and round and never reach the real point. The real point is that you made a mistake, and you won't acknowledge it aloud. You imagined that I was a hero, and that

471

I had some extraordinary ideas and ideals, and it has turned out that I am a most ordinary official, a card-player, and have no partiality for ideas of any sort. I am a worthy representative of the rotten world from which you have run away because you were revolted with its triviality and emptiness. Recognize it and be just: don't be indignant with me, but with yourself, as it is your mistake, and not mine."

" Yes, I admit I was mistaken."

" Well, that's all right, then. We've reached that point at last, thank God. Now hear something more, if you please: I can't rise to your level—I am too depraved; you can't descend to my level, either, for you are too exalted. So there is only one thing left to do. . . ."

" What ?" Zinaida Fyodorovna asked quickly, holding her breath and turning suddenly as white as a sheet of paper.

" To call logic to our aid. . . ."

" Georgy, why are you torturing me ?" Zinaida Fyodorovna said suddenly in Russian in a breaking voice. " What is it for? Think of my misery. . . ."

Orlov, afraid of tears, went quickly into his study, and I don't know why—whether it was that he wished to cause her extra pain, or whether he remembered it was usually done in such cases— he locked the door after him. She cried out and ran after him with a rustle of her skirt.

" What does this mean ?" she cried, knocking at his door. " What . . . what does this mean ?" she repeated in a shrill voice breaking with indignation. " Ah, so this is what you do ! Then let me tell you I hate you, I despise you ! Everything is over between us now."

I heard hysterical weeping mingled with laughter. Something small in the drawing-room fell off the table and was broken. Orlov went out into the hall by another door, and, looking round him nervously, he hurriedly put on his great-coat and went out.

Half an hour passed, an hour, and she was still weeping. I remembered that she had no father or mother, no relations, and here she was living between a man who hated her and Polya, who robbed her—and how desolate her life seemed to me ! I do not know why, but I went into the drawing-room to her. Weak and helpless, looking with her lovely hair like an embodiment of tenderness and grace, she was in anguish, as though she were ill; she was lying on a couch, hiding her face, and quivering all over.

" Madam, shouldn't I fetch a doctor ?" I asked gently.

" No, there's no need . . . it's nothing," she said, and she looked at me with her tear-stained eyes. " I have a little headache. . . . Thank you."

I went out, and in the evening she was writing letter after letter, and sent me out first to Pekarsky, then to Gruzin, then to Kukushkin, and finally anywhere I chose, if only I could find Orlov and give him the letter. Every time I came back with the letter she scolded me, entreated me, thrust money into my hand—as though she were in a fever. And all the night she did not sleep, but sat in the drawing-room, talking to herself.

Orlov returned to dinner next day, and they were reconciled.

The first Thursday afterwards Orlov complained to his friends of the intolerable life he led; he smoked a great deal, and said with irritation:

" It is no life at all; it's the rack. Tears, wailing, intellectual conversations, begging for forgiveness, again tears and wailing; and the long and the short of it is that I have no flat of my own now. I am wretched, and I make her wretched. Surely I haven't to live another month or two like this? How can I? But yet I may have to."

" Why don't you speak, then ?" said Pekarsky.

" I've tried, but I can't. One can boldly tell the truth, whatever it may be, to an independent, rational man; but in this case one has to do with a creature who has no will, no strength of character, and no logic. I cannot endure tears; they disarm me. When she cries, I am ready to swear eternal love and cry myself."

Pekarsky did not understand; he scratched his broad forehead in perplexity and said:

" You really had better take another flat for her. It's so simple !"

" She wants me, not the flat. But what's the good of talking ?" sighed Orlov. " I only hear endless conversations, but no way out of my position. It certainly is a case of ' being guilty without guilt.' I don't claim to be a mushroom, but it seems I've got to go into the basket. The last thing I've ever set out to be is a hero. I never could endure Turgenev's novels; and now, all of a sudden, as though to spite me, I've heroism forced upon me. I assure her on my honour that I'm not a hero at all, I adduce irrefutable proofs of the same, but she doesn't believe me. Why doesn't she believe me? I suppose I really must have something of the appearance of a hero."

"You go off on a tour of inspection in the provinces," said Kukushkin, laughing.

"Yes, that's the only thing left for me."

A week after this conversation Orlov announced that he was again ordered to attend the senator and the same evening he went off with his portmanteaus to Pekarsky.

XI.

An old man of sixty, in a long fur coat reaching to the ground, and a beaver cap, was standing at the door.

"Is Georgy Ivanitch at home?" he asked.

At first I thought it was one of the moneylenders, Gruzin's creditors, who sometimes used to come to Orlov for small payments on account; but when he came into the hall and flung open his coat, I saw the thick brows and the characteristically compressed lips which I knew so well from the photographs, and two rows of stars on the uniform. I recognized him: it was Orlov's father, the distinguished statesman.

I answered that Georgy Ivanitch was not at home. The old man pursed up his lips tightly and looked into space, reflecting, showing me his dried-up, toothless profile.

" I'll leave a note," he said; " show me in."

He left his goloshes in the hall, and, without taking off his long, heavy fur coat, went into the study. There he sat down before the table, and, before taking up the pen, for three minutes he pondered, shading his eyes with his hand as though from the sun—exactly as his son did when he was out of humour. His face was sad, thoughtful, with that look of resignation which I have only seen on the faces of the old and religious. I stood behind him, gazed at his bald head and at the hollow at the nape of his neck, and it was clear as daylight to me that this weak old man was now in my power. There was not a soul in the flat except my enemy and me. I had only to use a little physical violence, then snatch his watch to disguise the object of the crime, and to get off by the back way, and I should have gained infinitely more than I could have imagined possible when I took up the part of a footman. I thought that I could hardly get a better opportunity. But instead of acting, I looked quite unconcernedly, first at his bald patch and then at his fur, and calmly meditated on this man's relation to his only son, and on the fact that people spoiled by power and wealth probably don't want to die. . . .

" Have you been long in my son's service ?" he asked, writing a large hand on the paper.

" Three months, your High Excellency."

He finished the letter and stood up. I still had time. I urged myself on and clenched my fists, trying to wring out of my soul some trace of my former hatred; I recalled what a passionate, implacable, obstinate hate I had felt for him only a little while before. . . . But it is difficult to strike a match against a crumbling stone. The sad old face and the cold glitter of his stars roused in me nothing but petty, cheap, unnecessary thoughts of the transitoriness of everything earthly, of the nearness of death. . . .

" Good-day, brother," said the old man. He put on his cap and went out.

There could be no doubt about it: I had undergone a change; I had become different. To convince myself, I began to recall the past, but at once I felt uneasy, as though I had accidentally peeped into a dark, damp corner. I remembered my comrades and friends, and my first thought was how I should blush in confusion if ever I met any of them. What was I now ? What had I to think of and to do ? Where was I to go ? What was I living for ?

I could make nothing of it. I only knew one thing—that I must make haste to pack my things and be off. Before the old man's visit my position as a flunkey had a meaning; now it was absurd. Tears dropped into my open portmanteau; I felt insufferably sad; but how I longed to live ! I was ready to embrace and include in my short life every possibility open to man. I wanted to speak, to read, and to hammer in some big factory, and to stand on watch, and to plough. I yearned for the Nevsky Prospect, for the sea and the fields— for every place to which my imagination travelled.

When Zinaida Fyodorovna came in, I rushed to open the door for her, and with peculiar tenderness took off her fur coat. The last time !

We had two other visitors that day besides the old man. In the evening when it was quite dark, Gruzin came to fetch some papers for Orlov. He opened the table-drawer, took the necessary papers, and, rolling them up, told me to put them in the hall beside his cap while he went in to see Zinaida Fyodorovna. She was lying on the sofa in the drawing-room, with her arms behind her head. Five or six days had already passed since Orlov went on his tour of inspection, and no one knew when he would be back, but this time she did not send telegrams and did not expect them. She did not seem to notice the presence of Polya, who was still living with us. " So be it, then," was what I read on her passionless and very pale face. Like Orlov, she wanted to be unhappy out of obstinacy. To spite herself and everything in the world, she lay for days together on the sofa, desiring and expecting nothing but evil for herself. Probably she was picturing to herself Orlov's return and the inevitable quarrels with him; then his growing indifference to her, his infidelities; then how they would separate; and perhaps these agonizing thoughts gave her satisfaction. But what would she have said if she found out the actual truth ?

" I love you, Godmother," said Gruzin, greeting her and kissing her hand. " You are so kind ! And so dear *George* has gone away," he lied. " He has gone away, the rascal !"

He sat down with a sigh and tenderly stroked her hand.

"Let me spend an hour with you, my dear," he said. "I don't want to go home, and it's too early to go to the Birshovs'. The Birshovs are keeping their Katya's birthday to-day. She is a nice child!"

I brought him a glass of tea and a decanter of brandy. He slowly and with obvious reluctance drank the tea, and returning the glass to me, asked timidly:

"Can you give me . . . something to eat, my friend? I have had no dinner."

We had nothing in the flat. I went to the restaurant and brought him the ordinary rouble dinner.

"To your health, my dear," he said to Zinaida Fyodorovna, and he tossed off a glass of vodka. "My little girl, your godchild, sends you her love. Poor child! she's ricketty. Ah, children, children!" he sighed. "Whatever you may say, Godmother, it is nice to be a father. Dear *George* can't understand that feeling."

He drank some more. Pale and lean, with his dinner-napkin over his chest like a little pinafore, he ate greedily, and raising his eyebrows, kept looking guiltily, like a little boy, first at Zinaida Fyodorovna and then at me. It seemed as though he would have begun crying if I had not given him the grouse or the jelly. When he had satisfied his hunger he grew more lively, and began laughingly telling some story about the Birshov household, but perceiving that it was tiresome and that

479

Zinaida Fyodorovna was not laughing, he ceased. And there was a sudden feeling of dreariness. After he had finished his dinner they sat in the drawing-room by the light of a single lamp, and did not speak; it was painful to him to lie to her, and she wanted to ask him something, but could not make up her mind to. So passed half an hour. Gruzin glanced at his watch.

" I suppose it's time for me to go."

" No, stay a little. . . . We must have a talk."

Again they were silent. He sat down to the piano, struck one chord, then began playing, and sang softly, " What does the coming day bring me ?" but as usual he got up suddenly and tossed his head.

" Play something," Zinaida Fyodorovna asked him.

" What shall I play ?" he asked, shrugging his shoulders. " I have forgotten everything. I've given it up long ago."

Looking at the ceiling as though trying to remember, he played two pieces of Tchaikovsky with exquisite expression, with such warmth, such insight ! His face was just as usual—neither stupid nor intelligent—and it seemed to me a perfect marvel that a man whom I was accustomed to see in the midst of the most degrading, impure surroundings, was capable of such purity, of rising to a feeling so lofty, so far beyond my reach. Zinaida Fyodorovna's face glowed, and she walked about the drawing-room in emotion.

" Wait a bit, Godmother; if I can remember it,

I will play you something," he said; "I heard it played on the violoncello."

Beginning timidly and picking out the notes, and then gathering confidence, he played Saint-Saëns's "Swan Song." He played it through, and then played it a second time.

"It's nice, isn't it?" he said.

Moved by the music, Zinaida Fyodorovna stood beside him and asked:

"Tell me honestly, as a friend, what do you think about me?"

"What am I to say?" he said, raising his eyebrows. "I love you and think nothing but good of you. But if you wish that I should speak generally about the question that interests you," he went on, rubbing his sleeve near the elbow and frowning, "then, my dear, you know. . . . To follow freely the promptings of the heart does not always give good people happiness. To feel free and at the same time to be happy, it seems to me, one must not conceal from oneself that life is coarse, cruel, and merciless in its conservatism, and one must retaliate with what it deserves— that is, be as coarse and as merciless in one's striving for freedom. That's what I think."

"That's beyond me," said Zinaida Fyodorovna, with a mournful smile. "I am exhausted already. I am so exhausted that I wouldn't stir a finger for my own salvation."

"Go into a nunnery."

He said this in jest, but after he had said it, tears glistened in Zinaida Fyodorovna's eyes and then in his.

" Well," he said, " we've been sitting and sitting, and now we must go. Good-bye, dear Godmother. God give you health."

He kissed both her hands, and stroking them tenderly, said that he should certainly come to see her again in a day or two. In the hall, as he was putting on his overcoat, that was so like a child's pelisse, he fumbled long in his pockets to find a tip for me, but found nothing there.

" Good-bye, my dear fellow," he said sadly, and went away.

I shall never forget the feeling that this man left behind him.

Zinaida Fyodorovna still walked about the room in her excitement. That she was walking about and not still lying down was so much to the good. I wanted to take advantage of this mood to speak to her openly and then to go away, but I had hardly seen Gruzin out when I heard a ring. It was Kukushkin.

" Is Georgy Ivanitch at home ?" he said. "Has he come back ? You say no ? What a pity ! In that case, I'll go in and kiss your mistress's hand, and so away. Zinaida Fyodorovna, may I come in ?" he cried. " I want to kiss your hand. Excuse my being so late."

He was not long in the drawing-room, not more than ten minutes, but I felt as though he were staying a long while and would never go away. I bit my lips from indignation and annoyance, and already hated Zinaida Fyodorovna. " Why does she not turn him out ?" I thought indignantly, though it was evident that she was bored by his company.

When I held his fur coat for him he asked me, as a mark of special good-will, how I managed to get on without a wife.

" But I don't suppose you waste your time," he said, laughing. " I've no doubt Polya and you are as thick as thieves. . . . You rascal!"

In spite of my experience of life, I knew very little of mankind at that time, and it is very likely that I often exaggerated what was of little consequence and failed to observe what was important. It seemed to me it was not without motive that Kukushkin tittered and flattered me. Could it be that he was hoping that I, like a flunkey, would gossip in other kitchens and servants' quarters of his coming to see us in the evenings when Orlov was away, and staying with Zinaida Fyodorovna till late at night ? And when my tittle-tattle came to the ears of his acquaintance, he would drop his eyes in confusion and shake his little finger. And would not he, I thought, looking at his little honeyed face, this very evening at cards pretend and perhaps declare that he had already won Zinaida Fyodorovna from Orlov ?

That hatred which failed me at midday when the old father had come, took possession of me now. Kukushkin went away at last, and as I listened to the shuffle of his leather goloshes, I felt greatly tempted to fling after him, as a parting shot, some coarse word of abuse, but I restrained myself. And when the steps had died away on the stairs, I went back to the hall, and, hardly conscious of what I was doing, took up the roll

of papers that Gruzin had left behind, and ran
headlong downstairs. Without cap or overcoat,
I ran down into the street. It was not cold, but
big flakes of snow were falling and it was windy.

" Your Excellency !" I cried, catching up
Kukushkin. " Your Excellency !"

He stopped under a lamp-post and looked round
with surprise.

" Your Excellency !" I said, breathless, " your
Excellency !"

And not able to think of anything to say, I hit
him two or three times on the face with the roll
of paper. Completely at a loss, and hardly
wondering—I had so completely taken him by
surprise—he leaned his back against the lamp-
post and put up his hands to protect his face. At
that moment an army doctor passed, and saw
how I was beating the man, but he merely looked
at us in astonishment and went on.

I felt ashamed and I ran back to the house.

XII.

With my head wet from the snow, and gasping
for breath, I ran to my room, and immediately
flung off my swallow-tails, put on a reefer jacket
and an overcoat, and carried my portmanteau
out into the passage; I must get away ! But
before going I hurriedly sat down and began
writing to Orlov:

" I leave you my false passport," I began.
" I beg you to keep it as a memento, you false
man, you Petersburg official !"

"To steal into another man's house under a false name, to watch under the mask of a flunkey this person's intimate life, to hear everything, to see everything in order later on, unasked, to accuse a man of lying—all this, you will say, is on a level with theft. Yes, but I care nothing for fine feelings now. I have endured dozens of your dinners and suppers when you said and did what you liked, and I had to hear, to look on, and be silent. I don't want to make you a present of my silence. Besides, if there is not a living soul at hand who dares to tell you the truth without flattery, let your flunkey Stepan wash your magnificent countenance for you."

I did not like this beginning, but I did not care to alter it. Besides, what did it matter?

The big windows with their dark curtains, the bed, the crumpled dress coat on the floor, and my wet footprints, looked gloomy and forbidding. And there was a peculiar stillness.

Possibly because I had run out into the street without my cap and goloshes I was in a high fever. My face burned, my legs ached. . . . My heavy head drooped over the table, and there was that kind of division in my thought when every idea in the brain seemed dogged by its shadow.

"I am ill, weak, morally cast down," I went on; "I cannot write to you as I should like to. For the first moment I desired to insult and humiliate you, but now I do not feel that I have the right to do so. You and I have both fallen, and neither of us will ever rise up again; and even if my letter were eloquent, terrible, and passionate, it would still seem like beating on the lid of a coffin: however one knocks upon it, one will not wake up the dead ! No efforts could warm your accursed cold blood, and you know that better than I do. Why write ? But my mind and heart are burning, and I go on writing; for some reason I am moved as though this letter still might save you and me. I am so feverish that my thoughts are disconnected, and my pen scratches the paper without meaning; but the question I want to put to you stands before me as clear as though in letters of flame.

" Why I am prematurely weak and fallen is not hard to explain. Like Samson of old, I have taken the gates of Gaza on my shoulders to carry them to the top of the mountain, and only when I was exhausted, when youth and health were quenched in me for ever, I noticed that that burden was not for my shoulders, and that I had deceived myself. I have been, moreover, in cruel and continual pain. I have endured cold, hunger, illness, and loss of liberty. Of personal happiness I know and have known nothing. I have no home; my memories are bitter, and my conscience is often in dread of them. But why have you fallen — you ? What fatal, diabolical causes hindered your life from blossoming into full flower ? Why, almost before beginning life, were you in such haste to cast off the image and likeness of God, and to become a cowardly beast who backs and scares others because he is afraid himself ? You are afraid of life—as afraid of it as an Oriental who sits all day on a cushion smoking

486

his hookah. Yes, you read a great deal, and a European coat fits you well, but yet with what tender, purely Oriental, pasha-like care you protect yourself from hunger, cold, physical effort, from pain and uneasiness ! How early your soul has taken to its dressing-gown ! What a cowardly part you have played towards real life and nature, with which every healthy and normal man struggles ! How soft, how snug, how warm, how comfortable—and how bored you are ! Yes, it is deathly boredom, unrelieved by one ray of light, as in solitary confinement; but you try to hide from that enemy, too, you play cards eight hours out of twenty-four.

" And your irony ? Oh, but how well I understand it ! Free, bold, living thought is searching and dominating; for an indolent, sluggish mind it is intolerable. That it may not disturb your peace, like thousands of your contemporaries, you made haste in youth to put it under bar and bolt. Your ironical attitude to life, or whatever you like to call it, is your armour; and your thought, fettered and frightened, dare not leap over the fence you have put round it; and when you jeer at ideas which you pretend to know all about, you are like the deserter fleeing from the field of battle, and, to stifle his shame, sneering at war and at valour. Cynicism stifles pain. In some novel of Dostoevsky's an old man tramples underfoot the portrait of his dearly loved daughter because he had been unjust to her, and you vent your foul and vulgar jeers upon the ideas of goodness and truth because you have not the strength to follow them. You are frightened of every honest and truthful hint at your degradation, and you purposely surround yourself with people who do nothing but flatter your weaknesses. And you may well, you may well dread the sight of tears!

" By the way, your attitude to women. Shamelessness has been handed down to us in our flesh and blood, and we are trained to shamelessness; but that is what we are men for—to subdue the beast in us. When you reached manhood and *all* ideas became known to you, you could not have failed to see the truth; you knew it, but you did not follow it; you were afraid of it, and to deceive your conscience you began loudly assuring yourself that it was not you but woman that was to blame, that she was as degraded as your attitude to her. Your cold, scabrous anecdotes, your coarse laughter, all your innumerable theories concerning the underlying reality of marriage and the indefinite demands made upon it, concerning the ten *sous* the French workman pays his woman; your everlasting attacks on female logic, lying, weakness, and so on—doesn't it all look like a desire at all costs to force woman down into the mud that she may be on the same level as your attitude to her? You are a weak, unhappy, unpleasant person!"

Zinaida Fyodorovna began playing the piano in the drawing-room, trying to recall the song of Saint-Saëns that Gruzin had played. I went and lay on my bed, but remembering that it was time for me to go, I got up with an effort and with a heavy, burning head went to the table again.

" But this is the question," I went on. " Why are we worn out ? Why are we, at first so passionate, so bold, so noble, and so full of faith, complete bankrupts at thirty or thirty-five ? Why does one waste in consumption, another put a bullet through his brains, a third seek forgetfulness in vodka and cards, while the fourth tries to stifle his fear and misery by cynically trampling underfoot the pure image of his fair youth ? Why is it that, having once fallen, we do not try to rise up again, and, losing one thing, do not seek something else ? Why is it ?

" The thief hanging on the Cross could bring back the joy of life and the courage of confident hope, though perhaps he had not more than an hour to live. You have long years before you, and I shall probably not die so soon as one might suppose. What if by a miracle the present turned out to be a dream, a horrible nightmare, and we should wake up renewed, pure, strong, proud of our righteousness ? Sweet visions fire me, and I am almost breathless with emotion. I have a terrible longing to live. I long for our life to be holy, lofty, and majestic as the heavens above. Let us live ! The sun doesn't rise twice a day, and life is not given us again—clutch at what is left of your life and save it. . . ."

I did not write another word. I had a multitude of thoughts in my mind, but I could not connect them and get them on to paper. Without finishing the letter, I signed it with my name and rank, and went into the study. It was dark. I felt for the table and put the letter on it. I must have stumbled against the furniture in the dark and made a noise.

"Who is there?" I heard an alarmed voice in the drawing-room.

And the clock on the table softly struck one at the moment.

XIII.

For at least half a minute I fumbled at the door in the dark, feeling for the handle; then I slowly opened it and walked into the drawing-room. Zinaida Fyodorovna was lying on the couch, and raising herself on her elbow, she looked towards me. Unable to bring myself to speak, I walked slowly by, and she followed me with her eyes. I stood for a little time in the dining-room and then walked by her again, and she looked at me intently and with perplexity, even with alarm. At last I stood still and said with an effort:

"He is not coming back."

She quickly got on to her feet, and looked at me without understanding.

"He is not coming back," I repeated, and my heart beat violently. "He will not come back, for he has not left Petersburg. He is staying at Pekarsky's."

She understood and believed me—I saw that from her sudden pallor, and from the way she laid her arms upon her bosom in terror and entreaty. In one instant all that had happened of late flashed through her mind; she reflected, and with pitiless clarity she saw the whole truth.

But at the same time she remembered that I was a flunkey, a being of a lower order. . . . A casual stranger, with hair ruffled, with face flushed with fever, perhaps drunk, in a common overcoat, was coarsely intruding into her intimate life, and that offended her. She said to me sternly:

" It's not your business: go away."

" Oh, believe me !" I cried impetuously, holding out my hands to her. "I am not a footman; I am as free as you."

I mentioned my name, and, speaking very rapidly that she might not interrupt me or go away, explained to her who I was and why I was living there. This new discovery struck her more than the first. Till then she had hoped that her footman had lied or made a mistake or been silly, but now after my confession she had no doubts left. From the expression of her unhappy eyes and face, which suddenly lost its softness and beauty and looked old; I saw that she was insufferably miserable, and that the conversation would lead to no good; but I went on impetuously:

" The senator and the tour of inspection were invented to deceive you. In January, just as now, he did not go away, but stayed at Pekarsky's, and I saw him every day and took part in the deception. He was weary of you, he hated your presence here, he mocked at you. . . . If you could have heard how he and his friends here jeered at you and your love, you would not have remained here one minute ! Go away from here ! Go away."

" Well," she said in a shaking voice, and moved her hand over her hair. " Well, so be it."

Her eyes were full of tears, her lips were quivering, and her whole face was strikingly pale and distorted with anger. Orlov's coarse, petty lying revolted her and seemed to her contemptible, ridiculous: she smiled and I did not like that smile.

" Well," she repeated, passing her hand over her hair again, " so be it. He imagines that I shall die of humiliation, and instead of that I am . . . amused by it. There's no need for him to hide." She walked away from the piano and said, shrugging her shoulders: " There's no need. . . . It would have been simpler to have it out with me instead of keeping in hiding in other people's flats. I have eyes; I saw it myself long ago. . . . I was only waiting for him to come back to have things out once for all."

Then she sat down on a low chair by the table, and, leaning her head on the arm of the sofa, wept bitterly. In the drawing-room there was only one candle burning in the candelabra, and the chair where she was sitting was in darkness; but I saw how her head and shoulders were quivering, and how her hair, escaping from her combs, covered her neck, her face, her arms. . . . Her quiet, steady weeping, which was not hysterical but a woman's ordinary weeping, expressed a sense of insult, of wounded pride, of injury, and of something helpless, hopeless, which one could not set right and to which one could not get used. Her tears stirred an echo in my troubled and suffering heart; I forgot my illness and everything else in the world; I walked about the drawing-room and muttered distractedly:

" Is this life ? . . . Oh, one can't go on living like this, one can't. . . . Oh, it's madness, wickedness, not life."

" What humiliation !" she said through her tears. " To live together, to smile at me at the very time when I was burdensome to him, ridiculous in his eyes ! Oh, how humiliating !"

She lifted up her head, and looking at me with tear-stained eyes through her hair, wet with her tears, and pushing it back as it prevented her seeing me, she asked:

" They laughed at me ?"

" To these men you were laughable—you and your love and Turgenev; they said your head was full of him. And if we both die at once in despair, that will amuse them, too; they will make a funny anecdote of it and tell it at your requiem service. But why talk of them ?" I said impatiently. " We must get away from here—I cannot stay here one minute longer."

She began crying again, while I walked to the piano and sat down.

" What are we waiting for ?" I asked dejectedly. " It's two o'clock."

" I am not waiting for anything," she said. " I am utterly lost."

" Why do you talk like that ? We had better consider together what we are to do. Neither you nor I can stay here. Where do you intend to go ?"

493

Suddenly there was a ring at the bell. My heart stood still. Could it be Orlov, to whom perhaps Kukushkin had complained of me? How should we meet? I went to open the door. It was Polya. She came in shaking the snow off her pelisse, and went into her room without saying a word to me. When I went back to the drawing-room, Zinaida Fyodorovna, pale as death, was standing in the middle of the room, looking towards me with big eyes.

" Who was it ?" she asked softly.

" Polya," I answered.

She passed her hand over her hair and closed her eyes wearily.

" I will go away at once," she said. " Will you be kind and take me to the Petersburg Side ? What time is it now ?"

" A quarter to three."

XIV.

When, a little afterwards, we went out of the house, it was dark and deserted in the street. Wet snow was falling and a damp wind lashed in one's face. I remember it was the beginning of March; a thaw had set in, and for some days past the cabmen had been driving on wheels. Under the impression of the back stairs, of the cold, of the midnight darkness, and the porter in his sheepskin who had questioned us before letting us out of the gate, Zinaida Fyodorovna was utterly cast down and dispirited. When we got into the cab and the hood was put up, trembling all over, she began hurriedly saying how grateful she was to me.

"I do not doubt your good-will, but I am ashamed that you should be troubled," she muttered. "Oh, I understand, I understand. . . . When Gruzin was here to-day, I felt that he was lying and concealing something. Well, so be it., But I am ashamed, anyway, that you should be troubled."

She still had her doubts. To dispel them finally, I asked the cabman to drive through Sergievsky Street; stopping him at Pekarsky's door, I got out of the cab and rang. When the porter came to the door, I asked aloud, that Zinaida Fyodorovna might hear, whether Georgy Ivanitch was at home.

"Yes," was the answer, "he came in half an hour ago. He must be in bed by now. What do you want?"

Zinaida Fyodorovna could not refrain from putting her head out.

"Has Georgy Ivanitch been staying here long?" she asked.

"Going on for three weeks."

"And he's not been away?"

"No," answered the porter, looking at me with surprise.

"Tell him, early to-morrow," I said, "that his sister has arrived from Warsaw. Good-bye."

Then we drove on. The cab had no apron, the snow fell on us in big flakes, and the wind, especially on the Neva, pierced us through and through. I began to feel as though we had been driving for a long time, that for ages we had been suffering, and that for ages I had been listening to Zinaida Fyodorovna's shuddering breath. In semi-delirium, as though half asleep, I looked back upon my strange, incoherent life, and for some reason recalled a melodrama, "The Parisian Beggars," which I had seen once or twice in my childhood. And when to shake off that semi-delirium I peeped out from the hood and saw the dawn, all the images of the past, all my misty thoughts, for some reason, blended in me into one distinct, overpowering thought: everything was irrevocably over for Zinaida Fyodorovna and for me. This was as certain a conviction as though the cold blue sky contained a prophecy, but a minute later I was already thinking of something else and believed differently.

"What am I now?" said Zinaida Fyodorovna, in a voice husky with the cold and the damp. "Where am I to go? What am I to do? Gruzin told me to go into a nunnery. Oh, I would! I would change my dress, my face, my name, my thoughts . . . everything—everything, and would hide myself for ever. But they will not take me into a nunnery. I am with child."

"We will go abroad together to-morrow," I said.

"That's impossible. My husband won't give me a passport."

"I will take you without a passport."

The cabman stopped at a wooden house of two storeys, painted a dark colour. I rang. Taking from me her small light basket—the only luggage

we had brought with us—Zinaida Fyodorovna
gave a wry smile and said:

" These are my *bijoux*."

But she was so weak that she could not carry
these *bijoux*.

It was a long while before the door was opened.
After the third or fourth ring a light gleamed in
the windows, and there was a sound of steps,
coughing and whispering; at last the key grated
in the lock, and a stout peasant woman with a
frightened red face appeared at the door.   Some
distance behind her stood a thin little old woman
with short grey hair, carrying a candle in her
hand.   Zinaida Fyodorovna ran into the passage
and flung her arms round the old woman's
neck.

" Nina, I've been deceived," she sobbed loudly.
" I've been coarsely, foully deceived ! Nina,
Nina !"

I handed the basket to the peasant woman.
The door was closed, but still I heard her sobs
and the cry " Nina !"

I got into the cab and told the man to drive
slowly to the Nevsky Prospect.   I had to think of
a night's lodging for myself.

Next day towards evening I went to see
Zinaida Fyodorovna.   She was terribly changed.
There were no traces of tears on her pale, terribly
sunken face, and her expression was different.   I
don't know whether it was that I saw her now in
different surroundings, far from luxurious, and
that our relations were by now different, or perhaps that intense grief had already set its mark

497

upon her; she did not strike me as so elegant and well dressed as before. Her figure seemed smaller; there was an abruptness and excessive nervousness about her as though she were in a hurry, and there was not the same softness even in her smile. I was dressed in an expensive suit which I had bought during the day. She looked first of all at that suit and at the hat in my hand, then turned an impatient, searching glance upon my face as though studying it.

" Your transformation still seems to me a sort of miracle," she said. " Forgive me for looking at you with such curiosity. You are an extra-ordinary man, you know."

I told her again who I was, and why I was living at Orlov's, and I told her at greater length and in more detail than the day before. She listened with great attention, and said without letting me finish:

" Everything there is over for me. You know, I could not refrain from writing a letter. Here is the answer."

On the sheet which she gave me there was written in Orlov's hand:

" I am not going to justify myself. But you must own that it was your mistake, not mine. I wish you happiness, and beg you to make haste and forget.

" Yours sincerely,

" G. O.

" P.S.—I am sending on your things."

498

The trunks and baskets despatched by Orlov were standing in the passage, and my poor little portmanteau was there beside them.

" So . . ." Zinaida Fyodorovna began, but she did not finish.

We were silent. She took the note and held it for a couple of minutes before her eyes, and during that time her face wore the same haughty, contemptuous, proud, and harsh expression as the day before at the beginning of our explanation; tears came into her eyes—not timid, bitter tears, but proud, angry tears.

" Listen," she said, getting up abruptly and moving away to the window that I might not see her face. " I have made up my mind to go abroad with you to-morrow."

" I am very glad. I am ready to go to-day."

" Accept me as a recruit. Have you read Balzac ?" she asked suddenly, turning round. " Have you ? At the end of his novel ' Père Goriot ' the hero looks down upon Paris from the top of a hill and threatens the town: ' Now we shall settle our account,' and after this he begins a new life. So when I look out of the train window at Petersburg for the last time, I shall say, ' Now we shall settle our account ! ' "

Saying this, she smiled at her jest, and for some reason shuddered all over.

XV.

At Venice I had an attack of pleurisy. Probably
I had caught cold in the evening when we were
rowing from the station to the Hotel Bauer. I had
to take to my bed and stay there for a fortnight.
Every morning while I was ill Zinaida Fyodorovna
came from her room to drink coffee with me, and
afterwards read aloud to me French and Russian
books, of which we had bought a number at
Vienna. These books were either long, long
familiar to me or else had no interest for me, but
I had the sound of a sweet, kind voice beside me,
so that the meaning of all of them was summed
up for me in the one thing—I was not alone. She
would go out for a walk, come back in her light
grey dress, her light straw hat, gay, warmed by
the spring sun; and sitting by my bed, bending
low down over me, would tell me something about
Venice or read me those books—and I was happy.

At night I was cold, ill, and dreary, but by day
I revelled in life—I can find no better expression
for it. The brilliant warm sunshine beating in at
the open windows and at the door upon the
balcony, the shouts below, the splash of oars, the
tinkle of bells, the prolonged boom of the cannon
at midday, and the feeling of perfect, perfect
freedom, did wonders with me; I felt as though
I were growing strong, broad wings which were
bearing me God knows whither. And what charm,
what joy at times at the thought that another
life was so close to mine! that I was the servant,

500

the guardian, the friend, the indispensable fellow-
traveller of a creature, young, beautiful, wealthy,
but weak, lonely, and insulted ! It is pleasant
even to be ill when you know that there are people
who are looking forward to your convalescence
as to a holiday. One day I heard her whispering
behind the door with my doctor, and then she
came in to me with tear-stained eyes. It was a
bad sign, but I was touched, and there was a
wonderful lightness in my heart.

But at last they allowed me to go out on
the balcony. The sunshine and the breeze from
the sea caressed and fondled my sick body. I
looked down at the familiar gondolas, which glide
with feminine grace smoothly and majestically as
though they were alive, and felt all the luxury
of this original, fascinating civilization. There
was a smell of the sea. Someone was playing a
stringed instrument and two voices were singing.
How delightful it was ! How unlike it was to
that Petersburg night when the wet snow was
falling and beating so rudely on our faces. If
one looks straight across the canal, one sees the
sea, and on the wide expanse towards the horizon
the sun glittered on the water so dazzlingly that
it hurt one's eyes to look at it. My soul yearned
towards that lovely sea, which was so akin to
me and to which I had given up my youth. I
longed to live—to live—and nothing more.

A fortnight later I began walking freely. I
loved to sit in the sun, and to listen to the gon-
doliers without understanding them, and for
hours together to gaze at the little house where,

they said, Desdemona lived—a naïve, mournful little house with a demure expression, as light as lace, so light that it looked as though one could lift it from its place with one hand. I stood for a long time by the tomb of Canova, and could not take my eyes off the melancholy lion. And in the Palace of the Doges I was always drawn to the corner where the portrait of the unhappy Marino Faliero was painted over with black. "It is fine to be an artist, a poet, a dramatist," I thought, " but since that is not vouchsafed to me, if only I could go in for mysticism ! If only I had a grain of some faith to add to the unruffled peace and serenity that fills the soul !"

In the evening we ate oysters, drank wine, and went out in a gondola. I remember our black gondola swayed softly in the same place while the water faintly gurgled under it. Here and there the reflection of the stars and the lights on the bank quivered and trembled. Not far from us, in a gondola hung with coloured lanterns which were reflected in the water, there were people singing. The sounds of guitars, of violins, of mandolins, of men's and women's voices, were audible in the dark. Zinaida Fyodorovna, pale, with a grave, almost stern face, was sitting beside me, compressing her lips and clenching her hands. She was thinking about something; she did not stir an eyelash, nor hear me. Her face, her attitude, and her fixed, expressionless gaze, and her incredibly miserable, dreadful, and icy-cold memories, and around her the gondolas, the lights, the music, the song with its vigorous passionate cry

of " *Jam-mo !   Jam-mo !*"—what contrasts in life !
When she sat like that, with tightly clasped hands,
stony, mournful, I used to feel as though we were
both characters in some novel in the old-fashioned
style called " The Ill-fated," " The Abandoned,"
or something of the sort. Both of us: she—the
ill-fated, the abandoned; and I—the faithful,
devoted friend, the dreamer, and, if you like it,
a superfluous man, a failure capable of nothing but
coughing and dreaming, and perhaps sacrificing
myself. . . . But who and what needed my
sacrifices now ? And what had I to sacrifice,
indeed ?

When we came in in the evening we always
drank tea in her room and talked. We did not
shrink from touching on old, unhealed wounds—
on the contrary, for some reason I felt a positive
pleasure in telling her about my life at Orlov's,
or referring openly to relations which I knew
and which could not have been concealed from me.

" At moments I hated you," I said to her.
" When he was capricious, condescending, told
you lies, I marvelled how it was you did not see,
did not understand, when it was all so clear !
You kissed his hands, you knelt to him, you
flattered him. . . ."

" When I . . . kissed his hands and knelt to
him, I loved him . . . ," she said, blushing
crimson.

" Can it have been so difficult to see through
him ? A fine sphinx ! A sphinx indeed—a
kammer-junker ! I reproach you for nothing, God
forbid," I went on, feeling I was coarse, that I

had not the tact, the delicacy which are so essential when you have to do with a fellow-creature's soul; in early days before I knew her I had not noticed this defect in myself. " But how could you fail to see what he was ?" I went on, speaking more softly and more diffidently, however.

" You mean to say you despise my past, and you are right," she said, deeply stirred. " You belong to a special class of men who cannot be judged by ordinary standards; your moral requirements are exceptionally rigorous, and I understand you can't forgive things. I understand you, and if sometimes I say the opposite, it doesn't mean that I look at things differently from you; I speak the same old nonsense simply because I haven't had time yet to wear out my old clothes and prejudices. I, too, hate and despise my past, and Orlov and my love. . . . What was that love ? It's positively absurd now," she said, going to the window and looking down at the canal. " All this love only clouds the conscience and confuses the mind. The meaning of life is to be found only in one thing—fighting. To get one's heel on the vile head of the serpent and to crush it ! That's the meaning of life. In that alone or in nothing."

I told her long stories of my past, and described my really astounding adventures. But of the change that had taken place in me I did not say one word. She always listened to me with great attention, and at interesting places she rubbed her hands as though vexed that it had not yet been her lot to experience such adventures, such joys and terrors. Then she would suddenly fall to musing and retreat into herself, and I could see from her face that she was not attending to me.

I closed the windows that looked out on the canal and asked whether we should not have the fire lighted.

" No, never mind. I am not cold," she said, smiling listlessly. " I only feel weak. Do you know, I fancy I have grown much wiser lately. I have extraordinary, original ideas now. When I think of my past, of my life then . . . people in general, in fact, it is all summed up for me in the image of my stepmother. Coarse, insolent, soulless, false, depraved, and a morphia maniac too. My father, who was feeble and weak-willed, married my mother for her money and drove her into consumption; but his second wife, my stepmother, he loved passionately, insanely. . . . What I had to put up with ! But what is the use of talking ! And so, as I say, it is all summed up in her image. . . . And it vexes me that my stepmother is dead. I should like to meet her now !"

" Why ?"

" I don't know," she answered with a laugh and a graceful movement of her head. " Good-night. You must get well. As soon as you are well, we'll take up our work. . . . It's time to begin."

After I had said good-night and had my hand on the door-handle, she said:

" What do you think ? Is Polya still living there ?"

" Probably."

And I went off to my room. So we spent a whole month. One grey morning when we both stood at my window, looking at the clouds which were moving up from the sea, and at the darkening canal, expecting every minute that it would pour with rain, and when a thick, narrow streak of rain covered the sea as though with a muslin veil, we both felt suddenly dreary. The same day we both set off for Florence.

XVI.

It was autumn, at Nice. One morning when I went into her room she was sitting on a low chair, bent together and huddled up, with her legs crossed and her face hidden in her hands. She was weeping bitterly, with sobs, and her long, unbrushed hair fell on her knees. The impression of the exquisite marvellous sea which I had only just seen and of which I wanted to tell her, left me all at once, and my heart ached.

" What is it ?" I asked; she took one hand from her face and motioned me to go away. " What is it ?" I repeated, and for the first time during our acquaintance I kissed her hand.

" No, it's nothing, nothing," she said quickly. " Ah, it's nothing, nothing. . . . Go away. . . . You see, I am not dressed."

I went out overwhelmed. The calm and serene mood in which I had been for so long was poisoned by compassion. I had a passionate longing to fall at her feet, to entreat her not to weep in

It sometimes happened even that I did not see her for days together. I would knock timidly and guiltily at her door and get no answer; I would knock again—still silence. . . . I would stand near the door and listen; then the chambermaid would pass and say coldly, "*Madame est partie.*" Then I would walk about the passages of the hotel, walk and walk. . . . English people, full-bosomed ladies, waiters in swallow-tails. . . . And as I keep gazing at the long striped rug that stretches the whole length of the corridor, the idea occurs to me that I am playing in the life of this woman a strange, probably false part, and that it is beyond my power to alter that part. I run to my room and fall on my bed, and think and think, and can come to no conclusion; and all that is clear to me is that I want to live, and that the plainer and the colder and the harder her face grows, the nearer she is to me, and the more intensely and painfully I feel our kinship. Never mind " My good sir," never mind her light careless tone, never mind anything you like, only don't leave me, my treasure. I am afraid to be alone.

Then I go out into the corridor again, listen in a tremor. . . . I have no dinner; I don't notice the approach of evening. At last about eleven I hear the familiar footstep, and at the turn near the stairs Zinaida Fyodorovna comes into sight.

" Are you taking a walk ?" she would ask as she passes me. " You had better go out into the air. . . . Good-night !"

" But shall we not meet again to-day ?"

" I think it's late. But as you like."

" Tell me, where have you been ?" I would ask, following her into the room.

" Where ? To Monte Carlo." She took ten gold coins out of her pocket and said: " Look, my good sir; I have won. That's at roulette."

" Nonsense ! As though you would gamble !"

" Why not ? I am going again to-morrow."

I imagined her with a sick and morbid face, in her condition, tightly laced, standing near the gaming-table in a crowd of cocottes, of old women in their dotage who swarm round the gold like flies round the honey. I remembered she had gone off to Monte Carlo for some reason in secret from me.

" I don't believe you," I said one day. " You wouldn't go there."

" Don't agitate yourself. I can't lose much."

" It's not the question of what you lose," I said with annoyance. " Has it never occurred to you while you were playing there that the glitter of gold, all these women, young and old, the croupiers, all the surroundings—that it is all a vile, loathesome mockery at the toiler's labour, at his bloody sweat ?"

" If one doesn't play, what is one to do here ?" she asked. " The toiler's labour and his bloody sweat—all that eloquence you can put off till another time; but now, since you have begun, let me go on. Let me ask you bluntly, what is there for me to do here, and what am I to do ?"

" What are you to do ?" I said, shrugging my

shoulders. " That's a question that can't be answered straight off."

" I beg you to answer me honestly, Vladimir Ivanitch," she said, and her face looked angry. " Once I have brought myself to ask you this question, I am not going to listen to stock phrases. I am asking you," she went on, beating her hand on the table, as though marking time, " what ought I to do here ? And not only here at Nice, but in general ?"

I did not speak, but looked out of window to the sea. My heart was beating terribly.

" Vladimir Ivanitch," she said softly and breathlessly; it was hard for her to speak— " Vladimir Ivanitch, if you do not believe in the cause yourself, if you no longer think of going back to it, why . . . why did you drag me out of Petersburg ? Why did you make me promises, why did you rouse mad hopes ? Your convictions have changed; you have become a different man, and nobody blames you for it—our convictions are not always in our power. But . . . but, Vladimir Ivanitch, for God's sake, why are you not sincere ?" she went on softly, coming up to me. " All these months when I have been dreaming aloud, raving, going into raptures over my plans, remodelling my life on a new pattern, why didn't you tell me the truth ? Why were you silent or encouraged me by your stories, and behaved as though you were in complete sympathy with me ? Why was it ? Why was it necessary ?"

" It's difficult to acknowledge one's bankruptcy," I said, turning round, but not looking at her. "Yes, I have no faith; I am worn out, I have lost heart. . . . It is difficult to be truthful—very difficult, and I held my tongue. God forbid that anyone should have to go through what I have been through."

I felt that I was on the point of tears, and ceased speaking.

"Vladimir Ivanitch," she said, and took me by both hands, "you have been through so much and seen so much of life, you know more than I do; think seriously, and tell me, what am I to do? Teach me! If you haven't the strength to go forward yourself and take others with you, at least show me where to go. After all, I am a living, feeling, thinking being. To sink into a false position . . . to play an absurd part . . . is painful to me. I don't reproach you, I don't blame you; I only ask you."

Tea was brought in.

"Well?" said Zinaida Fyodorovna, giving me a glass. "What do you say to me?"

"There is more light in the world than you see through your window," I answered. "And there are other people besides me, Zinaida Fyodorovna."

"Then tell me who they are," she said eagerly. "That's all I ask of you."

"And I want to say, too," I went on, "one can serve an idea in more than one calling. If one has made a mistake and lost faith in one, one may find another. The world of ideas is large and cannot be exhausted."

"The world of ideas!" she said, and she looked

into my face sarcastically. "Then we had better leave off talking. What's the use ? . . ."

She flushed.

"The world of ideas !" she repeated. She threw her dinner-napkin aside, and an expression of indignation and contempt came into her face. "All your fine ideas, I see, lead up to one inevitable, essential step: I ought to become your mistress. That's what's wanted. To be taken up with ideas without being the mistress of an honourable, progressive man, is as good as not understanding the ideas. One has to begin with that . . . that is, with being your mistress, and the rest will come of itself."

"You are irritated, Zinaida Fyodorovna," I said.

"No, I am sincere !" she cried, breathing hard. "I am sincere !"

"You are sincere, perhaps, but you are in error, and it hurts me to hear you."

"I am in error ?" she laughed. "Anyone else might say that, but not you, my dear sir ! I may seem to you indelicate, cruel, but I don't care: you love me ? You love me, don't you ?"

I shrugged my shoulders.

"Yes, shrug your shoulders !" she went on sarcastically. "When you were ill I heard you in your delirium, and ever since these adoring eyes, these sighs, and edifying conversations about friendship, about spiritual kinship. . . . But the point is, why haven't you been sincere ? Why have you concealed what is and talked about what isn't ? Had you said from the beginning

513   R

what ideas exactly led you to drag me from Petersburg, I should have known. I should have poisoned myself then as I meant to, and there would have been none of this tedious farce. . . . But what's the use of talking !"

With a wave of the hand she sat down.

" You speak to me as though you suspected me of dishonourable intentions," I said, offended.

" Oh, very well. What's the use of talking ! I don't suspect you of intentions, but of having no intentions. If you had any, I should have known them by now. You had nothing but ideas and love. For the present—ideas and love, and in prospect—me as your mistress. That's in the order of things both in life and in novels. . . . Here you abused him," she said, and she slapped the table with her hand, " but one can't help agreeing with him. He has good reasons for despising these ideas."

" He does not despise ideas; he is afraid of them," I cried. " He is a coward and a liar."

" Oh, very well. He is a coward and a liar, and deceived me. And you ? Excuse my frankness; what are you ? He deceived me and left me to take my chance in Petersburg, and you have deceived me and abandoned me here. But he did not mix up ideas with his deceit, and you . . ."

" For goodness' sake, why are you saying this ?" I cried in horror, wringing my hands and going up to her quickly. " No, Zinaida Fyodorovna, this is cynicism. You must not be so despairing; listen to me," I went on, catching at a thought which flashed dimly upon me, and which seemed to me might still save us both. "Listen. I have passed through so many experiences in my time that my head goes round at the thought of them, and I have realized with my mind, with my racked soul, that man finds his true destiny in nothing if not in self-sacrificing love for his neighbour. It is towards that we must strive, and that is our destination! That is my faith!"

I wanted to go on to speak of mercy, of forgiveness, but there was an insincere note in my voice, and I was embarrassed.

"I want to live!" I said genuinely. "To live, to live! I want peace, tranquillity; I want warmth —this sea here—to have you near. Oh, how I wish I could rouse in you the same thirst for life! You spoke just now of love, but it would be enough for me to have you near, to hear your voice, to watch the look in your face . . . !"

She flushed crimson, and to hinder my speaking, said quickly:

"You love life, and I hate it. So our ways lie apart."

She poured herself out some tea, but did not touch it, went into the bedroom, and lay down.

"I imagine it is better to cut short this conversation," she said to me from within. "Everything is over for me, and I want nothing. . . . What more is there to say?"

"No, it's not all over!"

"Oh, very well! . . . I know! I am sick of it. . . . That's enough."

I got up, took a turn from one end of the room to the other, and went out into the corridor. When late at night I went to her door and listened, I distinctly heard her crying.

Next morning the waiter, handing me my clothes, informed me, with a smile, that the lady in number thirteen was confined. I dressed somehow, and almost fainting with terror ran to Zinaida Fyodorovna. In her room I found a doctor, a midwife, and an elderly Russian lady from Harkov, called Darya Mihailovna. There was a smell of ether. I had scarcely crossed the threshold when from the room where she was lying I heard a low, plaintive moan, and, as though it had been wafted me by the wind from Russia, I thought of Orlov, his irony, Polya, the Neva, the drifting snow, then the cab without an apron, the prediction I had read in the cold morning sky, and the despairing cry " Nina ! Nina !"

" Go in to her," said the lady.

I went in to see Zinaida Fyodorovna, feeling as though I were the father of the child. She was lying with her eyes closed, looking thin and pale, wearing a white cap edged with lace. I remember there were two expressions on her face: one— cold, indifferent, apathetic; the other—a look of childish helplessness given her by the white cap. She did not hear me come in, or heard, perhaps, but did not pay attention. I stood, looked at her, and waited.

But her face was contorted with pain; she opened her eyes and gazed at the ceiling, as

though wondering what was happening to her. . . .
There was a look of loathing on her face.

" It's horrible . . ." she whispered.

" Zinaida Fyodorovna." I spoke her name
softly. She looked at me indifferently, listlessly,
and closed her eyes. I stood there a little while,
then went away.

At night, Darya Mihailovna informed me that
the child, a girl, was born, but that the mother
was in a dangerous condition. Then I heard noise
and bustle in the passage. Darya Mihailovna
came to me again and with a face of despair,
wringing her hands, said:

" Oh, this is awful ! The doctor suspects that
she has taken poison ! Oh, how badly Russians
do behave here !"

And at twelve o'clock the next day Zinaida
Fyodorovna died.

XVIII.

Two years had passed. Circumstances had
changed; I had come to Petersburg again and
could live here openly. I was no longer afraid
of being and seeming sentimental, and gave
myself up entirely to the fatherly, or rather
idolatrous feeling roused in me by Sonya, Zinaida
Fyodorovna's child. I fed her with my own
hands, gave her her bath, put her to bed, never
took my eyes off her for nights together, and
screamed when it seemed to me that the nurse
was just going to drop her. My thirst for normal

ordinary life became stronger and more acute as time went on, but wider visions stopped short at Sonya, as though I had found in her at last just what I needed. I loved the child madly. In her I saw the continuation of my life, and it was not exactly that I fancied, but I felt, I almost believed, that when I had cast off at last my long, bony, bearded frame, I should go on living in those little blue eyes, that silky flaxen hair, those dimpled pink hands which stroked my face so lovingly and were clasped round my neck.

Sonya's future made me anxious. Orlov was her father; in her birth certificate she was called Krasnovsky, and the only person who knew of her existence, and took interest in her—that is, I—was at death's door. I had to think about her seriously.

The day after I arrived in Petersburg I went to see Orlov. The door was opened to me by a stout old fellow with red whiskers and no moustache, who looked like a German. Polya, who was tidying the drawing-room, did not recognize me, but Orlov knew me at once.

" Ah, Mr. Revolutionist !" he said, looking at me with curiosity, and laughing. " What fate has brought you ?"

He was not changed in the least: the same well-groomed, unpleasant face, the same irony. And a new book was lying on the table just as of old, with an ivory paper-knife thrust in it. He had evidently been reading before I came in. He made me sit down, offered me a cigar, and with a delicacy only found in well-bred people, concealing the unpleasant feeling aroused by my face and my wasted figure, observed casually that I was not in the least changed, and that he would have known me anywhere in spite of my having grown a beard. We talked of the weather, of Paris. To dispose as quickly as possible of the oppressive, inevitable question, which weighed upon him and me, he asked:

" Zinaida Fyodorovna is dead ?"

" Yes," I answered.

" In childbirth ?"

" Yes, in childbirth. The doctor suspected another cause of death, but . . . it is more comforting for you and for me to think that she died in childbirth."

He sighed decorously and was silent. The angel of silence passed over us, as they say.

" Yes. And here everything is as it used to be —no changes," he said briskly, seeing that I was looking about the room. " My father, as you know, has left the service and is living in retirement; I am still in the same department. Do you remember Pekarsky ? He is just the same as ever. Gruzin died of diphtheria a year ago. . . . Kukushkin is alive, and often speaks of you. By the way," said Orlov, dropping his eyes with an air of reserve, " when Kukushkin heard who you were, he began telling everyone you had attacked him and tried to murder him . . . and that he only just escaped with his life."

I did not speak.

" Old servants do not forget their masters. . . . It's very nice of you," said Orlov jocosely. " Will

you have some wine and some coffee, though?
I will tell them to make some."

" No, thank you. I have come to see you about
a very important matter, Georgy Ivanitch."

" I am not very fond of important matters, but
I shall be glad to be of service to you. What do
you want?"

" You see," I began, growing agitated, " I have
here with me Zinaida Fyodorovna's daughter. . . .
Hitherto I have brought her up, but, as you see,
before many days I shall be an empty sound.
I should like to die with the thought that she is
provided for."

Orlov coloured a little, frowned a little, and
took a cursory and sullen glance at me. He was
unpleasantly affected, not so much by the " important matter " as by my words about death,
about becoming an empty sound.

" Yes, it must be thought about," he said,
screening his eyes as though from the sun. " Thank
you. You say it's a girl?"

" Yes, a girl. A wonderful child !"

" Yes. Of course, it's not a lap-dog, but a
human being. I understand we must consider it
seriously. I am prepared to do my part, and am
very grateful to you."

He got up, walked about, biting his nails, and
stopped before a picture.

" We must think about it," he said in a hollow
voice, standing with his back to me. " I shall go
to Pekarsky's to-day and will ask him to go to
Krasnovsky's. I don't think he will make much
ado about consenting to take the child."

" But, excuse me, I don't see what Krasnovsky has got to do with it," I said, also getting up and walking to a picture at the other end of the room.

" But she bears his name, of course !" said Orlov.

" Yes, he may be legally obliged to accept the child—I don't know; but I came to you, Georgy Ivanitch, not to discuss the legal aspect."

" Yes, yes, you are right," he agreed briskly. " I believe I am talking nonsense. But don't excite yourself. We will decide the matter to our mutual satisfaction. If one thing won't do, we'll try another; and if that won't do, we'll try a third—one way or another this delicate question shall be settled. Pekarsky will arrange it all. Be so good as to leave me your address and I will let you know at once what we decide. Where are you living ?"

Orlov wrote down my address, sighed, and said with a smile:

" Oh, Lord, what a job it is to be the father of a little daughter ! But Pekarsky will arrange it all. He is a sensible man. Did you stay long in Paris ?"

" Two months."

We were silent. Orlov was evidently afraid I should begin talking of the child again, and to turn my attention in another direction, said:

" You have probably forgotten your letter by now. But I have kept it. I understand your mood at the time, and, I must own, I respect that letter. ' Damnable cold blood,' ' Asiatic,' ' coarse laugh '—that was charming and characteristic," he went on with an ironical smile. "And the fundamental thought is perhaps near the truth, though one might dispute the question endlessly. That is," he hesitated, "not dispute the thought itself, but your attitude to the question—your temperament, so to say. Yes, my life is abnormal, corrupted, of no use to anyone, and what prevents me from beginning a new life is cowardice—there you are quite right. But that you take it so much to heart, are troubled, and reduced to despair by it—that's irrational; there you are quite wrong."

"A living man cannot help being troubled and reduced to despair when he sees that he himself is going to ruin and others are going to ruin round him."

"Who doubts it! I am not advocating indifference; all I ask for is an objective attitude to life. The more objective, the less danger of falling into error. One must look into the root of things, and try to see in every phenomenon a cause of all the other causes. We have grown feeble, slack—degraded, in fact. Our generation is entirely composed of neurasthenics and whimperers; we do nothing but talk of fatigue and exhaustion. But the fault is neither yours nor mine; we are of too little consequence to affect the destiny of a whole generation. We must suppose for that larger, more general causes with a solid *raison d'être* from the biological point of view. We are neurasthenics, flabby, renegades, but perhaps it's necessary and of service for generations that will come after us. Not one hair falls from the head without the will of the Heavenly Father—in other words, nothing happens by chance in Nature and in human environment. Everything has its cause and is inevitable. And if so, why should we worry and write despairing letters?"

"That's all very well," I said, thinking a little. "I believe it will be easier and clearer for the generations to come; our experience will be at their service. But one wants to live apart from future generations and not only for their sake. Life is only given us once, and one wants to live it boldly, with full consciousness and beauty. One wants to play a striking, independent, noble part; one wants to make history so that those generations may not have the right to say of each of us that we were nonentities or worse. . . . I believe what is going on about us is inevitable and not without a purpose, but what have I to do with that inevitability? Why should my *ego* be lost?"

"Well, there's no help for it," sighed Orlov, getting up and, as it were, giving me to understand that our conversation was over.

I took my hat.

"We've only been sitting here half an hour, and how many questions we have settled, when you come to think of it!" said Orlov, seeing me into the hall. "So I will see to that matter. . . . I will see Pekarsky to-day. . . . Don't be uneasy."

He stood waiting while I put on my coat, and was obviously relieved at the feeling that I was going away.

523

"Georgy Ivanitch, give me back my letter," I said.

"Certainly."

He went to his study, and a minute later returned with the letter. I thanked him and went away.

The next day I got a letter from him. He congratulated me on the satisfactory settlement of the question. Pekarsky knew a lady, he wrote, who kept a school, something like a kindergarten, where she took quite little children. The lady could be entirely depended upon, but before concluding anything with her it would be as well to discuss the matter with Krasnovsky—it was a matter of form. He advised me to see Pekarsky at once and to take the birth certificate with me, if I had it. "Rest assured of the sincere respect and devotion of your humble servant. . . ."

I read this letter, and Sonya sat on the table and gazed at me attentively without blinking, as though she knew her fate was being decided.

1893

THE BEAUTIES

I.

I REMEMBER, when I was a high-school boy in the fifth or sixth class, I was driving with my grandfather from the village of Bolshoe Kryepkoe in the Don region to Rostov-on-the-Don. It was a sultry, languidly dreary day of August. Our eyes were glued together, and our mouths were parched from the heat and the dry burning wind which drove clouds of dust to meet us; one did not want to look or speak or think, and when our drowsy driver, a Little Russian called Karpo, swung his whip at the horses and lashed me on my cap, I did not protest or utter a sound, but only, rousing myself from half-slumber, gazed mildly and dejectedly into the distance to see whether there was a village visible through the dust. We stopped to feed the horses in a big Armenian village at a rich Armenian's whom my grandfather knew. Never in my life have I seen a greater caricature than that Armenian. Imagine a little shaven head with thick overhanging eyebrows, a beak of a nose, long grey moustaches, and a wide mouth with a long cherry-wood chibouk sticking out of it. This little head was clumsily attached to a lean hunchback carcase attired in a fantastic garb, a short red

525

jacket, and full bright blue trousers. This figure walked straddling its legs and shuffling with its slippers, spoke without taking the chibouk out of its mouth, and behaved with truly Armenian dignity, not smiling, but staring with wide-open eyes and trying to take as little notice as possible of its guests.

There was neither wind nor dust in the Armenian's rooms, but it was just as unpleasant, stifling, and dreary as in the steppe and on the road. I remember, dusty and exhausted by the heat, I sat in the corner on a green box. The unpainted wooden walls, the furniture, and the floors coloured with yellow ochre, smelt of dry wood baked by the sun. Wherever I looked there were flies and flies and flies . . . . Grandfather and the Armenian were talking about grazing, about manure, and about oats. . . . I knew that they would be a good hour getting the samovar; that grandfather would be not less than an hour drinking his tea, and then would lie down to sleep for two or three hours; that I should waste a quarter of the day waiting, after which there would be again the heat, the dust, the jolting cart. I heard the muttering of the two voices, and it began to seem to me that I had been seeing the Armenian, the cupboard with the crockery, the flies, the windows with the burning sun beating on them, for ages and ages, and should only cease to see them in the far-off future, and I was seized with hatred for the steppe, the sun, the flies. . . .

A Little Russian peasant woman in a kerchief brought in a tray of tea-things, then the samovar.

The Armenian went slowly out into the passage and shouted: " Mashya, come and pour out tea ! Where are you, Mashya ?"

Hurried footsteps were heard, and there came into the room a girl of sixteen in a simple cotton dress and a white kerchief. As she washed the crockery and poured out the tea, she was standing with her back to me, and all I could see was that she was of a slender figure, bare-footed, and that her little bare heels were covered by long trousers.

The Armenian invited me to have tea. Sitting down to the table, I glanced at the girl, who was handing me a glass of tea, and felt all at once as though a wind were blowing over my soul and blowing away all the impressions of the day with their dust and dreariness. I saw the bewitching features of the most beautiful face I have ever met in real life or in my dreams. Before me stood a beauty, and I recognized that at the first glance as I should have recognized lightning.

I am ready to swear that Masha—or, as her father called her, Mashya—was a real beauty, but I don't know how to prove it. It sometimes happens that clouds are huddled together in disorder on the horizon, and the sun hiding behind them colours them and the sky with tints of every possible shade — crimson, orange, gold, lilac, muddy pink; one cloud is like a monk, another like a fish, a third like a Turk in a turban. The glow of sunset enveloping a third of the sky gleams on the cross on the church, flashes on the windows of the manor house, is reflected in the river and the puddles, quivers on the trees; far, far away against the background of the sunset, a flock of wild ducks is flying homewards. . . . And the boy herding the cows, and the surveyor driving in his chaise over the dam, and the gentleman out for a walk, all gaze at the sunset, and every one of them thinks it terribly beautiful, but no one knows or can say in what its beauty lies.

I was not the only one to think the Armenian girl beautiful. My grandfather, an old man of seventy, gruff and indifferent to women and the beauties of nature, looked caressingly at Masha for a full minute, and asked:

" Is that your daughter, Avert Nazaritch ?"

" Yes, she is my daughter," answered the Armenian.

" A fine young lady," said my grandfather approvingly.

An artist would have called the Armenian girl's beauty classical and severe; it was just that beauty, the contemplation of which—God knows why !—inspires in one the conviction that one is seeing correct features; that hair, eyes, nose, mouth, neck, bosom, and every movement of the young body all go together in one complete harmonious accord in which nature has not blundered over the smallest line. You fancy for some reason that the ideally beautiful woman must have such a nose as Masha's, straight and slightly aquiline, just such great dark eyes, such long lashes, such a languid glance; you fancy that her black curly hair and eyebrows go with the soft white tint of her brow and cheeks as the green reeds go with the quiet stream.

Masha's white neck and her youthful bosom were not fully developed, but you fancy the sculptor would need a great creative genius to mould them. You gaze, and little by little the desire comes over you to say to Masha something extraordinarily pleasant, sincere, beautiful, as beautiful as she herself was.

At first I felt hurt and abashed that Masha took no notice of me, but was all the time looking down; it seemed to me as though a peculiar atmosphere, proud and happy, separated her from me and jealously screened her from my eyes.

"That's because I am covered with dust," I thought, " am sunburnt, and am still a boy."

But little by little I forgot myself, and gave myself up entirely to the consciousness of beauty. I thought no more now of the dreary steppe, of the dust, no longer heard the buzzing of the flies, no longer tasted the tea, and felt nothing except that a beautiful girl was standing only the other side of the table.

I felt this beauty rather strangely. It was not desire, nor ecstasy, nor enjoyment that Masha excited in me, but a painful though pleasant sadness. It was a sadness vague and undefined as a dream. For some reason I felt sorry for myself, for my grandfather and for the Armenian, even for the girl herself, and I had a feeling as though we all four had lost something important and essential to life which we should never find again. My grandfather, too, grew melancholy; he talked no more about manure or about oats, but sat silent, looking pensively at Masha.

After tea my grandfather lay down for a nap while I went out of the house into the porch. The house, like all the houses in the Armenian village, stood in the full sun; there was not a tree, not an awning, no shade. The Armenian's great court-yard, overgrown with goosefoot and wild mallows, was lively and full of gaiety in spite of the great heat. Threshing was going on behind one of the low hurdles which intersected the big yard here and there. Round a post stuck into the middle of the threshing-floor ran a dozen horses har-nessed side by side, so that they formed one long radius. A Little Russian in a long waistcoat and full trousers was walking beside them, crack-ing a whip and shouting in a tone that sounded as though he were jeering at the horses and showing off his power over them.

" A—a—a, you damned brutes ! . . . A—a—a, plague take you ! Are you frightened ?"

The horses, sorrel, white, and piebald, not under-standing why they were made to run round in one place and to crush the wheat straw, ran unwillingly, as though with effort, swinging their tails with an offended air. The wind raised up perfect clouds of golden chaff from under their hoofs and carried it away far beyond the hurdle. Near the tall fresh stacks peasant women were swarming with rakes, and carts were moving, and beyond the stacks in another yard another dozen similar horses were running round a post, and a similar Little Russian was cracking his whip and jeering at the horses.

The steps on which I was sitting were hot; on the

thin rails and here and there on the window-frames sap was oozing out of the wood from the heat; red ladybirds were huddling together in the streaks of shadow under the steps and under the shutters. The sun was baking me on my head, on my chest, and on my back, but I did not notice it, and was conscious only of the thud of bare feet on the uneven floor in the passage and in the rooms behind me. After clearing away the tea-things, Masha ran down the steps, fluttering the air as she passed, and like a bird flew into a little grimy outhouse— I suppose the kitchen—from which came the smell of roast mutton and the sound of angry talk in Armenian. She vanished into the dark doorway, and in her place there appeared on the threshold an old bent, red-faced Armenian woman wearing green trousers. The old woman was angry and was scolding someone. Soon afterwards Masha appeared in the doorway, flushed with the heat of the kitchen and carrying a big black loaf on her shoulder; swaying gracefully under the weight of the bread, she ran across the yard to the threshing-floor, darted over the hurdle, and, wrapt in a cloud of golden chaff, vanished behind the carts. The Little Russian who was driving the horses lowered his whip, sank into silence, and gazed for a minute in the direction of the carts. Then when the Armenian girl darted again by the horses and leaped over the hurdle, he followed her with his eyes, and shouted to the horses in a tone as though he were greatly disappointed:

" Plague take you, unclean devils !"

And all the while I was unceasingly hearing her

531

bare feet, and seeing how she walked across the yard with a grave, preoccupied face. She ran now down the steps, swishing the air about me, now into the kitchen, now to the threshing-floor, now through the gate, and I could hardly turn my head quickly enough to watch her.

And the oftener she fluttered by me with her beauty, the more acute became my sadness. I felt sorry both for her and for myself and for the Little Russian, who mournfully watched her every time she ran through the cloud of chaff to the carts. Whether it was envy of her beauty, or that I was regretting that the girl was not mine, and never would be, or that I was a stranger to her; or whether I vaguely felt that her rare beauty was accidental, unnecessary, and, like everything on earth, of short duration; or whether, perhaps, my sadness was that peculiar feeling which is excited in man by the contemplation of real beauty, God only knows.

The three hours of waiting passed unnoticed. It seemed to me that I had not had time to look properly at Masha when Karpo drove up to the river, bathed the horse, and began to put it in the shafts. The wet horse snorted with pleasure and kicked his hoofs against the shafts. Karpo shouted to it: " Ba—ack !" My grandfather woke up. Masha opened the creaking gates for us, we got into the chaise and drove out of the yard. We drove in silence as though we were angry with one another.

When, two or three hours later, Rostov and Nahitchevan appeared in the distance, Karpo, who had been silent the whole time, looked round quickly, and said:

"A fine wench, that at the Armenian's."

And he lashed his horses.

II.

Another time, after I had become a student, I was travelling by rail to the south. It was May. At one of the stations, I believe it was between Byelgorod and Harkov, I got out of the train to walk about the platform.

The shades of evening were already lying on the station garden, on the platform, and on the fields; the station screened off the sunset, but on the topmost clouds of smoke from the engine, which were tinged with rosy light, one could see the sun had not yet quite vanished.

As I walked up and down the platform I noticed that the greater number of the passengers were standing or walking near a second-class compartment, and that they looked as though some celebrated person were in that compartment. Among the curious whom I met near this compartment I saw, however, an artillery officer who had been my fellow-traveller, an intelligent, cordial, and sympathetic fellow—as people mostly are whom we meet on our travels by chance and with whom we are not long acquainted.

"What are you looking at there?" I asked.

He made no answer, but only indicated with his eyes a feminine figure. It was a young girl of seventeen or eighteen, wearing a Russian dress, with

533

her head bare and a little shawl flung carelessly on one shoulder; not a passenger, but I suppose a sister or daughter of the station-master. She was standing near the carriage window, talking to an elderly woman who was in the train. Before I had time to realize what I was seeing, I was suddenly overwhelmed by the feeling I had once experienced in the Armenian village.

The girl was remarkably beautiful, and that was unmistakable to me and to those who were looking at her as I was.

If one is to describe her appearance feature by feature, as the practice is, the only really lovely thing was her thick wavy fair hair, which hung loose with a black ribbon tied round her head; all the other features were either irregular or very ordinary. Either from a peculiar form of coquettishness, or from short-sightedness, her eyes were screwed up, her nose had an undecided tilt, her mouth was small, her profile was feebly and insipidly drawn, her shoulders were narrow and undeveloped for her age—and yet the girl made the impression of being really beautiful, and looking at her, I was able to feel convinced that the Russian face does not need strict regularity in order to be lovely; what is more, that if instead of her turn-up nose the girl had been given a different one, correct and plastically irreproachable like the Armenian girl's, I fancy her face would have lost all its charm from the change.

Standing at the window talking, the girl, shrugging at the evening damp, continually looking round at us, at one moment put her arms akimbo, at the next raised her hands to her head to straighten her hair, talked, laughed, while her face at one moment wore an expression of wonder, the next of horror, and I don't remember a moment when her face and body were at rest. The whole secret and magic of her beauty lay just in these tiny, infinitely elegant movements, in her smile, in the play of her face, in her rapid glances at us, in the combination of the subtle grace of her movements with her youth, her freshness, the purity of her soul that sounded in her laugh and voice, and with the weakness we love so much in children, in birds, in fawns, and in young trees.

It was that butterfly's beauty so in keeping with waltzing, darting about the garden, laughter and gaiety, and incongruous with serious thought, grief, and repose; and it seemed as though a gust of wind blowing over the platform, or a fall of rain, would be enough to wither the fragile body and scatter the capricious beauty like the pollen of a flower.

" So—o ! . . ." the officer muttered with a sigh when, after the second bell, we went back to our compartment.

And what that " So—o " meant I will not undertake to decide.

Perhaps he was sad, and did not want to go away from the beauty and the spring evening into the stuffy train; or perhaps he, like me, was unaccountably sorry for the beauty, for himself, and for me, and for all the passengers, who were listlessly and reluctantly sauntering back to their compartments. As we passed the station

535

window, at which a pale, red-haired telegraphist with upstanding curls and a faded, broad-cheeked face was sitting beside his apparatus, the officer heaved a sigh and said:

" I bet that telegraphist is in love with that pretty girl. To live out in the wilds under one roof with that ethereal creature and not fall in love is beyond the power of man. And what a calamity, my friend ! what an ironical fate, to be stooping, unkempt, grey, a decent fellow and not a fool, and to be in love with that pretty, stupid little girl who would never take a scrap of notice of you ! Or worse still: imagine that telegraphist is in love, and at the same time married, and that his wife is as stooping, as unkempt, and as decent a person as himself."

On the platform between our carriage and the next the guard was standing with his elbows on the railing, looking in the direction of the beautiful girl, and his battered, wrinkled, unpleasantly beefy face, exhausted by sleepless nights and the jolting of the train, wore a look of tenderness and of the deepest sadness, as though in that girl he saw happiness, his own youth, soberness, purity, wife, children; as though he were repenting and feeling in his whole being that that girl was not his, and that for him, with his premature old age, his un-couthness, and, his beefy face, the ordinary happi-ness of a man and a passenger was as far away as heaven. . . .

The third bell rang, the whistles sounded, and the train slowly moved off. First the guard, the station-master, then the garden, the beautiful girl with her exquisitely sly smile, passed before our windows. . . .

Putting my head out and looking back, I saw how, looking after the train, she walked along the platform by the window where the telegraph clerk was sitting, smoothed her hair, and ran into the garden. The station no longer screened off the sunset, the plain lay open before us, but the sun had already set and the smoke lay in black clouds over the green, velvety young corn. It was melancholy in the spring air, and in the darkening sky, and in the railway carriage.

The familiar figure of the guard came into the carriage, and he began lighting the candles.

1888

A TRANSGRESSION

A COLLEGIATE assessor called Miguev stopped at a telegraph-post in the course of his evening walk and heaved a deep sigh. A week before, as he was returning home from his evening walk, he had been overtaken at that very spot by his former house-maid, Agnia, who said to him viciously:

" Wait a bit ! I'll cook you such a crab that'll teach you to ruin innocent girls ! I'll leave the baby at your door, and I'll have the law of you, and I'll tell your wife, too. . . ."

And she demanded that he should put five thousand roubles into the bank in her name. Miguev remembered it, heaved a sigh, and once more reproached himself with heartfelt repentance for the momentary infatuation which had caused him so much worry and misery.

When he reached his bungalow, he sat down to rest on the doorstep. It was just ten o'clock, and a bit of the moon peeped out from behind the clouds. There was not a soul in the street nor near the bungalows; elderly summer visitors were already going to bed, while young ones were walking in the wood. Feeling in both his pockets for a match to light his cigarette, Miguev brought his elbow into contact with something soft. He looked

idly at his right elbow, and his face was instantly
contorted by a look of as much horror as though
he had seen a snake beside him. On the step at the
very door lay a bundle. Something oblong in
shape was wrapped up in something—judging by
the feel of it, a wadded quilt. One end of the
bundle was a little open, and the collegiate assessor,
putting in his hand, felt something damp and
warm. He leaped on to his feet in horror, and
looked about him like a criminal trying to escape
from his warders. . . .

"She has left it!" he muttered wrathfully
through his teeth, clenching his fists. "Here it
lies. . . . Here lies my transgression! O Lord!"

He was numb with terror, anger, and shame. . . .
What was he to do now? What would his wife
say if she found out? What would his colleagues
at the office say? His Excellency would be sure
to dig him in the ribs, guffaw, and say: "I congratulate you! . . . He-he-he! Though your
beard is grey, your heart is gay. . . . You are a
rogue, Semyon Erastovitch!" The whole colony
of summer visitors would know his secret now,
and probably the respectable mothers of families
would shut their doors to him. Such incidents
always get into the papers, and the humble name
of Miguev would be published all over Russia. . . .

The middle window of the bungalow was open,
and he could distinctly hear his wife, Anna Filippovna, laying the table for supper; in the yard close
to the gate Yermolay, the porter, was plaintively
strumming on the balalaika. The baby had only
to wake up and begin to cry, and the secret would

be discovered. Miguev was conscious of an over-whelming desire to make haste.

"Haste, haste! . . ." he muttered, "this minute, before anyone sees. I'll carry it away and lay it on somebody's doorstep. . . ."

Miguev took the bundle in one hand and quietly with a deliberate step to avoid awakening suspicion, went down the street. . . .

"A wonderfully nasty position!" he reflected, trying to assume an air of unconcern. "A colle-giate assessor walking down the street with a baby! Good heavens! if anyone sees me and understands the position, I am done for. . . . I'd better put it on this doorstep. . . . No, stay, the windows are open and perhaps someone is looking. Where shall I put it? I know! I'll take it to the mer-chant Myelkin's. . . . Merchants are rich people and tender-hearted; very likely they will say thank you and adopt it."

And Miguev made up his mind to take the baby to Myelkin's, although the merchant's villa was in the furthest street, close to the river.

"If only it does not begin screaming or wriggle out of the bundle," thought the collegiate assessor. "This is indeed a pleasant surprise! Here I am carrying a human being under my arm as though it were a portfolio. A human being, alive, with soul, with feelings like anyone else. . . . If by good luck the Myelkins adopt him, he may turn out somebody. . . . Maybe he will become a professor, a great general, an author. . . . Any-thing may happen! Now I am carrying it under my arm like a bundle of rubbish, and perhaps in thirty or forty years I may not dare to sit down in his presence. . . ."

As Miguev was walking along a narrow, deserted alley, beside a long row of fences, in the thick black shade of the lime-trees, it suddenly struck him that he was doing something very cruel and criminal.

" How mean it is really !" he thought. " So mean that one can't imagine anything meaner. . . . Why are we shifting this poor baby from door to door ? It's not its fault that it's been born. It's done us no harm. We are scoundrels. . . . We take our pleasure, and the innocent babies have to pay the penalty. Only to think of all this wretched business ! I've done wrong and the child has a cruel fate before it. If I lay it at the Myelkins' door, they'll send it to the foundling hospital, and there it will grow up among strangers, in mechanical routine, . . . no love, no petting, no spoiling. . . . And then he'll be apprenticed to a shoemaker, . . . he'll take to drink, will learn to use filthy language, will go hungry. A shoemaker ! and he the son of a collegiate assessor, of good family. . . . He is my flesh and blood. . . ."

Miguev came out of the shade of the lime-trees into the bright moonlight of the open road, and opening the bundle, he looked at the baby.

" Asleep !" he murmured. " You little rascal ! why, you've an aquiline nose like your father's. . . . He sleeps and doesn't feel that it's his own father looking at him ! . . . It's a drama, my boy. . . . Well, well, you must forgive me. Forgive me, old boy. . . . It seems it's your fate. . . ."

The collegiate assessor blinked and felt a spasm running down his cheeks. . . . He wrapped up the baby, put him under his arm, and strode on. All the way to the Myelkins' villa social questions were swarming in his brain and conscience was gnawing in his bosom.

"If I were a decent, honest man," he thought, "I should damn everything, go with this baby to Anna Filippovna, fall on my knees before her, and say: 'Forgive me! I have sinned! Torture me, but we won't ruin an innocent child. We have no children; let us adopt him!' She's a good sort, she'd consent. . . . And then my child would be with me. . . . Ech!"

He reached the Myelkins' villa and stood still hesitating. He imagined himself in the parlour at home, sitting reading the paper while a little boy with an aquiline nose played with the tassels of his dressing-gown. At the same time visions forced themselves on his brain of his winking colleagues, and of his Excellency digging him in the ribs and guffawing. . . . Besides the pricking of his conscience, there was something warm, sad, and tender in his heart. . . .

Cautiously the collegiate assessor laid the baby on the verandah step and waved his hand. Again he felt a spasm run over his face. . . .

"Forgive me, old fellow! I am a scoundrel," he muttered. "Don't remember evil against me!"

He stepped back, but immediately cleared his throat resolutely and said:

"Oh, come what will! Damn it all! I'll take him, and let people say what they like!"

542

Miguev took the baby and strode rapidly back.

"Let them say what they like," he thought. "I'll go at once, fall on my knees, and say: 'Anna Filippovna!' Anna is a good sort, she'll understand. . . . And we'll bring him up. . . . If it's a boy we'll call him Vladimir, and if it's a girl we'll call her Anna! Anyway, it will be a comfort in our old age."

And he did as he determined. Weeping and almost faint with shame and terror, full of hope and vague rapture, he went into his bungalow, went up to his wife, and fell on his knees before her. . . .

"Anna Filippovna!" he said with a sob, and he laid the baby on the floor. "Hear me before you punish. . . . I have sinned! This is my child. . . . You remember Agnia? Well, it was the devil drove me to it. . . ."

And, almost unconscious with shame and terror, he jumped up without waiting for an answer, and ran out into the open air as though he had received a thrashing. . . .

"I'll stay here outside till she calls me," he thought. "I'll give her time to recover, and to think it over. . . ."

The porter Yermolay passed him with his balalaika, glanced at him and shrugged his shoulders. A minute later he passed him again, and again he shrugged his shoulders.

"Here's a go! Did you ever!" he muttered, grinning. "Aksinya, the washerwoman, was here just now, Semyon Erastitch. The silly woman put her baby down on the steps here, and while she was indoors with me, someone took and carried off the baby. . . . Who'd have thought it !''

" What ? What are you saying ?" shouted Miguev at the top of his voice.

Yermolay, interpreting his master's wrath in his own fashion, scratched his head and heaved a sigh.

" I am sorry, Semyon Erastitch," he said, " but it's the summer holidays, . . . one can't get on without . . . without a woman, I mean. . . ."

And glancing at his master's eyes glaring at him with anger and astonishment, he cleared his throat guiltily and went on:

" It's a sin, of course, but there—what is one to do ? . . . You've forbidden us to have strangers in the house, I know, but we've none of our own now. When Agnia was here I had no women to see me, for I had one at home; but now, you can see for yourself, sir, . . . one can't help having strangers. In Agnia's time, of course, there was nothing irregular, because . . .''

" Be off, you scoundrel !" Miguev shouted at him, stamping, and he went back into the room.

Anna Filippovna, amazed and wrathful, was sitting as before, her tear-stained eyes fixed on the baby. . . .

" There ! there !" Miguev muttered with a pale face, twisting his lips into a smile. " It was a joke. . . . It's not my baby, . . . it's the washer-woman's : . . . I . . . I was joking. . . . Take it to the porter."

1887

GUSEV

I.

It was getting dark; it would soon be night.

Gusev, a discharged soldier, sat up in his hammock and said in an undertone:

" I say, Pavel Ivanitch. A soldier at Sutchan told me: while they were sailing a big fish came into collision with their ship and stove a hole in it."

The nondescript individual whom he was addressing, and whom everyone in the ship's hospital called Pavel Ivanitch, was silent, as though he had not heard.

And again a stillness followed. . . . The wind frolicked with the rigging, the screw throbbed, the waves lashed, the hammocks creaked, but the ear had long ago become accustomed to these sounds, and it seemed that everything around was asleep and silent. It was dreary. The three invalids—two soldiers and a sailor—who had been playing cards all the day were asleep and talking in their dreams.

It seemed as though the ship were beginning to rock. The hammock slowly rose and fell under Gusev, as though it were heaving a sigh, and this

545   s

was repeated once, twice, three times. . . . Something crashed on to the floor with a clang: it must have been a jug falling down.

" The wind has broken loose from its chain . . ." said Gusev, listening.

This time Pavel Ivanitch cleared his throat and answered irritably:

" One minute a vessel's running into a fish, the next, the wind's breaking loose from its chain. . . . Is the wind a beast that it can break loose from its chain ?"

" That's how christened folk talk."

" They are as ignorant as you are then. . . . They say all sorts of things. One must keep a head on one's shoulders and use one's reason. You are a senseless creature."

Pavel Ivanitch was subject to sea-sickness. When the sea was rough he was usually ill-humoured, and the merest trifle would make him irritable. And in Gusev's opinion there was absolutely nothing to be vexed about. What was there strange or wonderful, for instance, in the fish or in the wind's breaking loose from its chain ? Suppose the fish were as big as a mountain and its back were as hard as a sturgeon's: and in the same way, supposing that away yonder at the end of the world there stood great stone walls and the fierce winds were chained up to the walls . . . if they had not broken loose, why did they tear about all over the sea like maniacs, and struggle to escape like dogs ? If they were not chained up, what did become of them when it was calm ?

Gusev pondered for a long time about fishes as big as a mountain and stout, rusty chains, then he began to feel dull and thought of his native place to which he was returning after five years' service in the East. He pictured an immense pond covered with snow. . . . On one side of the pond the red-brick building of the potteries with a tall chimney and clouds of black smoke; on the other side—a village. . . . His brother Alexey comes out in a sledge from the fifth yard from the end; behind him sits his little son Vanka in big felt over-boots, and his little girl Akulka, also in big felt boots. Alexey has been drinking, Vanka is laughing, Akulka's face he could not see, she had muffled herself up.

"You never know, he'll get the children frozen . . ." thought Gusev. "Lord send them sense and judgment that they may honour their father and mother and not be wiser than their parents."

"They want re-soleing," a delirious sailor says in a bass voice. "Yes, yes!"

Gusev's thoughts break off, and instead of a pond there suddenly appears apropos of nothing a huge bull's head without eyes, and the horse and sledge are not driving along, but are whirling round and round in a cloud of smoke. But still he was glad he had seen his own folks. He held his breath from delight, shudders ran all over him, and his fingers twitched.

"The Lord let us meet again," he muttered feverishly, but he at once opened his eyes and sought in the darkness for water.

He drank and lay back, and again the sledge was moving, then again the bull's head without eyes, smoke, clouds. . . . And so on till daybreak.

II.

The first outline visible in the darkness was a blue circle—the little round window; then little by little Gusev could distinguish his neighbour in the next hammock, Pavel Ivanitch. The man slept sitting up, as he could not breathe lying down. His face was grey, his nose was long and sharp, his eyes looked huge from the terrible thinness of his face, his temples were sunken, his beard was skimpy, his hair was long. . . . Looking at him you could not make out of what class he was, whether he were a gentleman, a merchant, or a peasant. Judging from his expression and his long hair he might have been a hermit or a lay brother in a monastery—but if one listened to what he said it seemed that he could not be a monk. He was worn out by his cough and his illness and by the stifling heat. and breathed with difficulty, moving his parched lips. Noticing that Gusev was looking at him he turned his face towards him and said:

" I begin to guess. . . . Yes. . . . I understand it all perfectly now."

" What do you understand, Pavel Ivanitch ?"

" I'll tell you. . . . It has always seemed to me strange that terribly ill as you are you should be here in a steamer where it is so hot and stifling

548

and we are always being tossed up and down,
where, in fact, everything threatens you with
death; now it is all clear to me. . . . Yes. . . .
Your doctors put you on the steamer to get rid
of you. They get sick of looking after poor
brutes like you. . . . You don't pay them anything, they have a bother with you, and you
damage their records with your deaths—so, of
course, you are brutes! It's not difficult to get
rid of you. . . . All that is necessary is, in the
first place, to have no conscience or humanity;
and, secondly, to deceive the steamer authorities.
The first condition need hardly be considered, in
that respect we are artists; and one can always
succeed in the second with a little practice. In
a crowd of four hundred healthy soldiers and
sailors half a dozen sick ones are not conspicuous;
well, they drove you all on to the steamer, mixed
you with the healthy ones, hurriedly counted
you over, and in the confusion nothing amiss was
noticed, and when the steamer had started they
saw that there were paralytics and consumptives
in the last stage lying about on the deck. . . ."

Gusev did not understand Pavel Ivanitch; but
supposing he was being blamed, he said in self-
defence:

"I lay on the deck because I had not the
strength to stand; when we were unloaded from
the barge on to the ship I caught a fearful chill."

"It's revolting," Pavel Ivanitch went on.
"The worst of it is they know perfectly well that
you can't last out the long journey, and yet they
put you here. Supposing you get as far as the

Indian Ocean, what then ? It's horrible to think of it. . . . And that's their gratitude for your faithful, irreproachable service !"

Pavel Ivanitch's eyes looked angry; he frowned contemptuously and said, gasping:

" Those are the people who ought to be plucked in the newspapers till the feathers fly in all directions."

The two sick soldiers and the sailor were awake and already playing cards. The sailor was half reclining in his hammock, the soldiers were sitting near him on the floor in the most uncomfortable attitudes. One of the soldiers had his right arm in a sling, and the hand was swathed up in a regular bundle so that he held his cards under his right arm or in the crook of his elbow while he played with the left. The ship was rolling heavily. They could not stand up, nor drink tea, nor take their medicines.

" Were you an officer's servant ?" Pavel Ivanitch asked Gusev.

" Yes, an officer's servant."

" My God, my God !" said Pavel Ivanitch, and he shook his head mournfully. " To tear a man out of his home, drag him twelve thousand miles away, then to drive him into consumption and . . . and what is it all for, one wonders ? To turn him into a servant for some Captain Kopeikin or midshipman Dirka ! How logical !"

" It's not haid work, Pavel Ivanitch. You get up in the morning and clean the boots, get the samovar, sweep the rooms, and then you have nothing more to do. The lieutenant is all the day drawing plans, and if you like you can say your prayers, if you like you can read a book or go out into the street. God grant everyone such a life."

" Yes, very nice, the lieutenant draws plans all the day and you sit in the kitchen and pine for home. . . . Plans indeed ! . . . It is not plans that matter, but a human life . Life is not given twice, it must be treated mercifully."

" Of course, Pavel Ivanitch, a bad man gets no mercy anywhere, neither at home nor in the army, but if you live as you ought and obey orders, who has any need to insult you ? The officers are educated gentlemen, they understand. . . . In five years I was never once in prison, and I was never struck a blow, so help me God, but once."

" What for ?"

" For fighting. I have a heavy hand, Pavel Ivanitch. Four Chinamen came into our yard; they were bringing firewood or something, I don't remember. Well, I was bored and I knocked them about a bit, one's nose began bleeding, damn the fellow. . . . The lieutenant saw it through the little window, he was angry and gave me a box on the ear."

" Foolish, pitiful man . . ." whispered Pavel Ivanitch. " You don't understand anything."

He was utterly exhausted by the tossing of the ship and closed his eyes; his head alternately fell back and dropped forward on his breast. Several times he tried to lie down but nothing came of it; his difficulty in breathing prevented it.

" And what did you hit the four Chinamen for ?" he asked a little while afterwards.

" Oh, nothing. They came into the yard and I hit them."

And a stillness followed. . . . The card-players had been playing for two hours with enthusiasm and loud abuse of one another, but the motion of the ship overcame them, too; they threw aside the cards and lay down. Again Gusev saw the big pond, the brick building, the village. . . . Again the sledge was coming along, again Vanka was laughing and Akulka, silly little thing, threw open her fur coat and stuck her feet out, as much as to say: " Look, good people, my snowboots are not like Vanka's, they are new ones."

" Five years old, and she has no sense yet," Gusev muttered in delirium. " Instead of kicking your legs you had better come and get your soldier uncle a drink. I will give you something nice."

Then Andron with a flintlock gun on his shoulder was carrying a hare he had killed, and he was followed by the decrepit old Jew Isaitchik, who offers to barter the hare for a piece of soap; then the black calf in the shed, then Domna sewing at a shirt and crying about something, and then again the bull's head without eyes, black smoke. . . .

Overhead someone gave a loud shout, several sailors ran by, they seemed to be dragging something bulky over the deck, something fell with a crash. Again they ran by. . . . Had something gone wrong ? Gusev raised his head, listened, and saw that the two soldiers and the

sailor were playing cards again; Pavel Ivanitch
was sitting up moving his lips. It was stifling, one
hadn't strength to breathe, one was thirsty, the
water was warm, disgusting. The ship heaved as
much as ever.

Suddenly something strange happened to one
of the soldiers playing cards. . . . He called
hearts diamonds, got muddled in his score, and
dropped his cards, then with a frightened, foolish
smile looked round at all of them.

" I shan't be a minute, mates, I'll . . ." he
said, and lay down on the floor.

Everybody was amazed. They called to him,
he did not answer.

" Stepan, maybe you are feeling bad, eh ?" the
soldier with his arm in a sling asked him. " Perhaps we had better bring the priest, eh ?"

" Have a drink of water, Stepan . . ." said the
sailor. " Here, lad, drink."

" Why are you knocking the jug against his
teeth ?" said Gusev angrily. " Don't you see,
turnip head ?"

" What ?"

" What ?" Gusev repeated, mimicking him.
" There is no breath in him, he is dead ! That's
what ! What nonsensical people, Lord, have
mercy on us . . . !"

III.

The ship was not rocking and Pavel Ivanitch
was more cheerful. He was no longer ill-
humoured. His face had a boastful, defiant,

mocking expression. He looked as though he wanted to say: " Yes, in a minute I will tell you something that will make you split your sides with laughing." The little round window was open and a soft breeze was blowing on Pavel Ivanitch. There was a sound of voices, of the plash of oars in the water. . . . Just under the little window someone began droning in a high, unpleasant voice: no doubt it was a Chinaman singing.

" Here we are in the harbour," said Pavel Ivanitch, smiling ironically. " Only another month and we shall be in Russia. Well, worthy gentlemen and warriors ! I shall arrive at Odessa and from there go straight to Harkov. In Harkov I have a friend, a literary man. I shall go to him and say, ' Come, old man, put aside your horrid subjects, ladies' amours and the beauties of nature, and show up human depravity.' "

For a minute he pondered, then said:

" Gusev, do you know how I took them in ?"

" Took in whom, Pavel Ivanitch ?"

" Why, these fellows. . . . You know that on this steamer there is only a first-class and a third-class, and they only allow peasants—that is the riff-raff—to go in the third. If you have got on a reefer jacket and have the faintest resemblance to a gentleman or a bourgeois you must go first-class; if you please. You must fork out five hundred roubles if you die for it. Why, I ask, have you made such a rule ? Do you want to raise the prestige of educated Russians thereby ? Not a bit of it. We don't let you go third-class

simply because a decent person can't go third-
class: it is very horrible and disgusting. Yes,
indeed. I am very grateful for such solicitude
for decent people's welfare. But in any case,
whether it is nasty there or nice, five hundred
roubles I haven't got. I haven't pilfered government money, I haven't exploited the natives, I
haven't trafficked in contraband, I have flogged
no one to death, so judge whether I have the
right to travel first-class and even less to reckon
myself of the educated class? But you won't
catch them with logic. . . . One has to resort
to deception. I put on a workman's coat and
high boots, I assumed a drunken, servile mug and
went to the agents: 'Give us a little ticket, your
honour,' said I. . . ."

"Why, what class do you belong to?" asked
a sailor.

"Clerical. My father was an honest priest,
he always told the great ones of the world the
truth to their faces; and he had a great deal to
put up with in consequence."

Pavel Ivanitch was exhausted with talking and
gasped for breath, but still went on:

"Yes, I always tell people the truth to their
faces. I am not afraid of anyone or anything.
There is a vast difference between me and all of
you in that respect. You are in darkness, you
are blind, crushed; you see nothing and what
you do see you don't understand. . . . You are
told the wind breaks loose from its chain, that
you are beasts, Petchenyegs, and you believe it;
they punch you in the neck, you kiss their hands;

555

some animal in a sable-lined coat robs you and
then tips you fifteen kopecks and you: ' Let me
kiss your hand, sir.' You are pariahs, pitiful
people. . . . I am a different sort. My eyes are
open, I see it all as clearly as a hawk or an eagle
when it floats over the earth, and I understand it
all. I am a living protest. I see irresponsible
tyranny—I protest. I see cant and hypocrisy—
I protest. I see swine triumphant—I protest.
And I cannot be suppressed, no Spanish Inquisi-
tion can make me hold my tongue. No. . . .
Cut out my tongue and I would protest in dumb
show; shut me up in a cellar—I will shout from
it to be heard half a mile away, or I will starve
myself to death that they may have another
weight on their black consciences. Kill me and
I will haunt them with my ghost. All my acquaintances say to me: ' You are a most insufferable person, Pavel Ivanitch.' I am proud of such
a reputation. I have served three years in the
far East, and I shall be remembered there for a
hundred years: I had rows with everyone. My
friends write to me from Russia, ' Don't come
back,' but here I am going back to spite them . . .
yes. . . . That is life as I understand it. That
is what one can call life."

Gusev was looking at the little window and
was not listening. A boat was swaying on the
transparent, soft, turquoise water all bathed in
hot, dazzling sunshine. In it there were naked
Chinamen holding up cages with canaries and
calling out:

" It sings, it sings !"

Another boat knocked against the first; the steam cutter darted by. And then there came another boat with a fat Chinaman sitting in it, eating rice with little sticks.

Languidly the water heaved, languidly the white seagulls floated over it.

" I should like to give that fat fellow one in the neck," thought Gusev, gazing at the stout Chinaman, with a yawn.

He dozed off, and it seemed to him that all nature was dozing, too. Time flew swiftly by; imperceptibly the day passed, imperceptibly the darkness came on. . . . The steamer was no longer standing still, but moving on further.

IV.

Two days passed, Pavel Ivanitch lay down instead of sitting up; his eyes were closed, his nose seemed to have grown sharper.

" Pavel Ivanitch," Gusev called to him. " Hey, Pavel Ivanitch."

Pavel Ivanitch opened his eyes and moved his lips.

" Are you feeling bad ?"

" No . . . it's nothing . . ." answered Pavel Ivanitch, gasping. " Nothing; on the contrary . . . I am rather better. . . . You see I can lie down. . . . I am a little easier. . . ."

" Well, thank God for that, Pavel Ivanitch."

" When I compare myself with you I am sorry for you . . . poor fellow. My lungs are all right,

557

it is only a stomach cough. . . . I can stand hell, let alone the Red Sea. Besides I take a critical attitude to my illness and to the medicines they give me for it. While you . . . you are in darkness. . . . It's hard for you, very, very hard !"

The ship was not rolling, it was calm, but as hot and stifling as a bath-house; it was not only hard to speak but even hard to listen. Gusev hugged his knees, laid his head on them and thought of his home. Good heavens, what a relief it was to think of snow and cold in that stifling heat ! You drive in a sledge, all at once the horses take fright at something and bolt . . . Regardless of the road, the ditches, the ravines, they dash like mad things, right through the village, over the pond by the pottery works, out across the open fields. "Hold on," the pottery hands and the peasants shout, meeting them. "Hold on." But why ? Let the keen, cold wind beat in one's face and bite one's hands; let the lumps of snow, kicked up by the horses' hoofs, fall on one's cap, on one's back, down one's collar, on one's chest; let the runners ring on the snow, and the traces and the sledge be smashed, deuce take them one and all ! And how delightful when the sledge upsets and you go flying full tilt into a drift, face downwards in the snow, and then you get up white all over with icicles on your moustaches; no cap, no gloves, your belt undone. . . . People laugh, the dogs bark. . . .

Pavel Ivanitch half opened one eye, looked at Gusev with it, and asked softly:

" Gusev, did your commanding officer steal ?"

" Who can tell, Pavel Ivanitch ! We can't say, it didn't reach us."

And after that a long time passed in silence. Gusev brooded, muttered something in delirium, and kept drinking water; it was hard for him to talk and hard to listen, and he was afraid of being talked to. An hour passed, a second, a third; evening came on, then night, but he did not notice it. He still sat dreaming of the frost.

There was a sound as though someone came into the hospital, and voices were audible, but a few minutes passed and all was still again.

" The Kingdom of Heaven and eternal peace," said the soldier with his arm in a sling. " He was an uncomfortable man."

" What ?" asked Gusev. " Who ?"

" He is dead, they have just carried him up."

" Oh well," muttered Gusev, yawning, " the Kingdom of Heaven be his."

" What do you think ?" the soldier with his arm in a sling asked Gusev. " Will he be in the Kingdom of Heaven or not ?"

" Who is it you are talking about ?"

" Pavel Ivanitch."

" He will be . . . he suffered so long. And there is another thing, he belonged to the clergy, and the priests always have a lot of relations. Their prayers will save him."

The soldier with the sling sat down on a hammock near Gusev and said in an undertone:

" And you, Gusev, are not long for this world. You will never get to Russia."

"Did the doctor or his assistant say so?" asked Gusev.

"It isn't that they said so, but one can see it. . . . One can see directly when a man's going to die. You don't eat, you don't drink; it's dreadful to see how thin you've got. It's consumption, in fact. I say it, not to upset you, but because maybe you would like to have the sacrament and extreme unction. And if you have any money you had better give it to the senior officer."

"I haven't written home . . ." Gusev sighed. "I shall die and they won't know."

"They'll hear of it," the sick sailor brought out in a bass voice. "When you die they will put it down in the *Gazette*, at Odessa they will send in a report to the commanding officer there and he will send it to the parish or somewhere. . . ."

Gusev began to be uneasy after such a conversation and to feel a vague yearning. He drank water—it was not that; he dragged himself to the window and breathed the hot, moist air— it was not that; he tried to think of home, of the frost—it was not that. . . . At last it seemed to him one minute longer in the ward and he would certainly expire.

"It's stifling, mates . . ." he said. "I'll go on deck. Help me up, for Christ's sake."

"All right," assented the soldier with the sling. "I'll carry you, you can't walk, hold on to my neck."

Gusev put his arm round the soldier's neck, the latter put his unhurt arm round him and carried him up. On the deck sailors and time-expired soldiers were lying asleep side by side; there were so many of them it was difficult to pass.

"Stand down," the soldier with the sling said softly. "Follow me quietly, hold on to my shirt. . . ."

It was dark. There was no light on deck, nor on the masts, nor anywhere on the sea around. At the furthest end of the ship the man on watch was standing perfectly still like a statue, and it looked as though he were asleep. It seemed as though the steamer were abandoned to itself and were going at its own will.

"Now they will throw Pavel Ivanitch into the sea," said the soldier with the sling. "In a sack and then into the water."

"Yes, that's the rule."

"But it's better to lie at home in the earth. Anyway, your mother comes to the grave and weeps."

"Of course."

There was a smell of hay and of dung. There were oxen standing with drooping heads by the ship's rail. One, two, three; eight of them! And there was a little horse. Gusev put out his hand to stroke it, but it shook its head, showed its teeth, and tried to bite his sleeve.

"Damned brute . . ." said Gusev angrily.

The two of them, he and the soldier, threaded their way to the head of the ship, then stood at the rail and looked up and down. Overhead deep sky, bright stars, peace and stillness, exactly as at home in the village, below darkness and disorder. The tall waves were resounding, no one could tell why. Whichever wave you looked at each one was trying to rise higher than all the rest and to chase and crush the next one; after it a third as fierce and hideous flew noisily, with a glint of light on its white crest.

The sea has no sense and no pity. If the steamer had been smaller and not made of thick iron, the waves would have crushed it to pieces without the slightest compunction, and would have devoured all the people in it with no distinction of saints or sinners. The steamer had the same cruel and meaningless expression. This monster with its huge beak was dashing onwards, cutting millions of waves in its path; it had no fear of the darkness nor the wind, nor of space, nor of solitude, caring for nothing, and if the ocean had its people this monster would have crushed them, too, without distinction of saints or sinners.

" Where are we now ?" asked Gusev.

" I don't know. We must be in the ocean."

" There is no sight of land. . . ."

" No indeed ! They say we shan't see it for seven days."

The two soldiers watched the white foam with the phosphorus light on it and were silent, thinking. Gusev was the first to break the silence.

" There is nothing to be afraid of," he said, " only one is full of dread as though one were sitting in a dark forest; but if, for instance, they let a boat down on to the water this minute and an officer ordered me to go a hundred miles over the sea to catch fish, I'd go. Or, let's say, if a Christian were to fall into the water this minute, I'd go in after him. A German or a Chinaman I wouldn't save, but I'd go in after a Christian."

" And are you afraid to die ?"

" Yes. I am sorry for the folks at home. My brother at home, you know, isn't steady; he drinks, he beats his wife for nothing, he does not honour his parents. Everything will go to ruin without me, and father and my old mother will be begging their bread, I shouldn't wonder. But my legs won't bear me, brother, and it's hot here. Let's go to sleep."

V.

Gusev went back to the ward and got into his hammock. He was again tormented by a vague craving, and he could not make out what he wanted. There was an oppression on his chest, a throbbing in his head, his mouth was so dry that it was difficult for him to move his tongue. He dozed, and murmured in his sleep, and, worn out with nightmares, his cough, and the stifling heat, towards morning he fell into a sound sleep. He dreamed that they were just taking the bread out of the oven in the barracks and he climbed into the stove and had a steam bath in it, lashing himself with a bunch of birch twigs. He slept for two days, and at midday on the third two sailors came down and carried him out.

He was sewn up in sailcloth and to make him heavier they put with him two iron weights.

Sewn up in the sailcloth he looked like a carrot or a radish: broad at the head and narrow at the feet. . . . Before sunset they brought him up to the deck and put him on a plank; one end of the plank lay on the side of the ship, the other on a box, placed on a stool. Round him stood the soldiers and the officers with their caps off.

"Blessed be the Name of the Lord . . ." the priest began. "As it was in the beginning, is now, and ever shall be."

"Amen," chanted three sailors.

The soldiers and the officers crossed themselves and looked away at the waves. It was strange that a man should be sewn up in sailcloth and should soon be flying into the sea. Was it possible that such a thing might happen to anyone?

The priest strewed earth upon Gusev and bowed down. They sang "Eternal Memory."

The man on watch duty tilted up the end of the plank, Gusev slid off and flew head foremost, turned a somersault in the air and splashed into the sea. He was covered with foam and for a moment looked as though he were wrapped in lace, but the minute passed and he disappeared in the waves.

He went rapidly towards the bottom. Did he reach it? It was said to be three miles to the bottom. After sinking sixty or seventy feet, he began moving more and more slowly, swaying rhythmically, as though he were hesitating and, carried along by the current, moved more rapidly sideways than downwards.

Then he was met by a shoal of the fish called

harbour pilots. Seeing the dark body the fish stopped as though petrified, and suddenly turned round and disappeared. In less than a minute they flew back swift as an arrow to Gusev, and began zigzagging round him in the water.

After that another dark body appeared. It was a shark. It swam under Gusev with dignity and no show of interest, as though it did not notice him, and sank down upon its back, then it turned belly upwards, basking in the warm, transparent water and languidly opened its jaws with two rows of teeth. The harbour pilots are delighted, they stop to see what will come next. After playing a little with the body the shark nonchalantly puts its jaws under it, cautiously touches it with its teeth, and the sailcloth is rent its full length from head to foot; one of the weights falls out and frightens the harbour pilots, and striking the shark on the ribs goes rapidly to the bottom.

Overhead at this time the clouds are massed together on the side where the sun is setting; one cloud like a triumphal arch, another like a lion, a third like a pair of scissors. . . . From behind the clouds a broad, green shaft of light pierces through and stretches to the middle of the sky; a little later another, violet-coloured, lies beside it; next that, one of gold, then one rose-coloured. . . . The sky turns a soft lilac. Looking at this gorgeous, enchanted sky, at first the ocean scowls, but soon it, too, takes tender, joyous, passionate colours for which it is hard to find a name in human speech.

1890

A WOMAN'S KINGDOM

A WOMAN'S KINGDOM

I.

CHRISTMAS EVE.

HERE was a thick roll of notes. It came from the bailiff at the forest villa; he wrote that he was sending fifteen hundred roubles, which he had been awarded as damages, having won an appeal. Anna Akimovna disliked and feared such words as " awarded damages " and " won the suit." She knew that it was impossible to do without the law, but for some reason, whenever Nazaritch, the manager of the factory, or the bailiff of her villa in the country, both of whom frequently went to law, used to win lawsuits of some sort for her benefit, she always felt uneasy and as it were, ashamed. On this occasion, too, she felt uneasy and awkward, and wanted to put that fifteen hundred roubles further away that it might be out of her sight.

She thought with vexation that other girls of her age—she was in her twenty-sixth year—were now busy looking after their households, were weary and would sleep sound, and would wake up to-morrow morning in holiday mood; many of them had long been married and had children.

Only she, for some reason, was compelled to sit
like an old woman over these letters, to make
notes upon them, to write answers, then to do
nothing the whole evening till midnight, but wait
till she was sleepy; and to-morrow they would
all day long be coming with Christmas greetings
and asking for favours; and the day after to-morrow
there would certainly be some scandal at the
factory—someone would be beaten or would die
of drinking too much vodka, and she would be
fretted by pangs of conscience; and after the
holidays Nazaritch would turn off some twenty
of the workpeople for absence from work, and all
of the twenty would hang about at the front
door, without their caps on, and she would be
ashamed to go out to them, and they would be
driven away like dogs. And all her acquaintances
would say behind her back, and write to her in
anonymous letters, that she was a millionaire and
an exploiter—that she was devouring other men's
lives and sucking the blood of the workers.

Here there lay a heap of letters read through
and laid aside already. They were all begging
letters. They were from people who were hungry,
drunken, dragged down by large families, sick,
degraded, despised. . . . Anna Akimovna had
already noted on each letter, three roubles to be
paid to one, five to another; these letters would go
the same day to the office, and next the distribution
of assistance would take place, or, as the clerks
used to say, the beasts would be fed.

They would distribute also in small sums four
hundred and seventy roubles—the interest on a

sum bequeathed by the late Akim Ivanovitch for the relief of the poor and needy. There would be a hideous crush. From the gates to the doors of the office there would stretch a long file of strange people with brutal faces, in rags, numb with cold, hungry and already drunk, in husky voices calling down blessings upon Anna Akimovna, their benefactress, and her parents: those at the back would press upon those in front, and those in front would abuse them with bad language. The clerk would get tired of the noise, the swearing, and the sing-song whining and blessing; would fly out and give someone a box on the ear to the delight of all. And her own people, the factory hands, who received nothing at Christmas but their wages, and had already spent every farthing of it, would stand in the middle of the yard, looking on and laughing—some enviously, others ironically.

"Merchants, and still more their wives, are fonder of beggars than they are of their own workpeople," thought Anna Akimovna. "It's always so."

Her eye fell upon the roll of money. It would be nice to distribute that hateful, useless money among the workpeople to-morrow, but it did not do to give the workpeople anything for nothing, or they would demand it again next time. And what would be the good of fifteen hundred roubles when there were eighteen hundred workmen in the factory besides their wives and children? Or she might, perhaps, pick out one of the writers of those begging letters—some luckless man who had long ago lost all hope of anything better,

and give him the fifteen hundred. The money
would come upon the poor creature like a thunder-
clap, and perhaps for the first time in his life he
would feel happy. This idea struck Anna Akimovna as original and amusing, and it fascinated
her. She took one letter at random out of the
pile and read it. Some petty official called
Tchalikov had long been out of a situation, was
ill, and living in Gushtchin's Buildings; his wife
was in consumption, and he had five little girls.
Anna Akimovna knew well the four-storeyed
house, Gushtchin's Buildings, in which Tchalikov
lived. Oh, it was a horrid, foul, unhealthy house !

"Well, I will give it to that Tchalikov," she
decided. "I won't send it; I had better take it
myself to prevent unnecessary talk. Yes," she
reflected, as she put the fifteen hundred roubles in
her pocket, "and I'll have a look at them, and
perhaps I can do something for the little girls."

She felt light-hearted; she rang the bell and
ordered the horses to be brought round.

When she got into the sledge it was past six
o'clock in the evening. The windows in all the
blocks of buildings were brightly lighted up, and
that made the huge courtyard seem very dark:
at the gates, and at the far end of the yard near
the warehouses and the workpeople's barracks,
electric lamps were gleaming.

Anna Akimovna disliked and feared those huge
dark buildings, warehouses, and barracks where
the workmen lived. She had only once been in
the main building since her father's death. The
high ceilings with iron girders; the multitude of

huge, rapidly turning wheels, connecting straps and levers; the shrill hissing; the clank of steel; the rattle of the trolleys; the harsh puffing of steam; the faces—pale, crimson, or black with coal-dust; the shirts soaked with sweat; the gleam of steel, of copper, and of fire; the smell of oil and coal; and the draught, at times very hot and at times very cold—gave her an impression of hell. It seemed to her as though the wheels, the levers, and the hot hissing cylinders were trying to tear themselves away from their fastenings to crush the men, while the men, not hearing one another, ran about with anxious faces, and busied themselves about the machines, trying to stop their terrible movement. They showed Anna Akimovna something and respectfully explained it to her. She remembered how in the forge a piece of red-hot iron was pulled out of the furnace; and how an old man with a strap round his head, and another, a young man in a blue shirt with a chain on his breast, and an angry face, probably one of the foremen, struck the piece of iron with hammers; and how the golden sparks had been scattered in all directions; and how, a little afterwards, they had dragged out a huge piece of sheet-iron with a clang. The old man had stood erect and smiled, while the young man had wiped his face with his sleeve and explained something to her. And she remembered, too, how in another department an old man with one eye had been filing a piece of iron, and how the iron filings were scattered about; and how a red-haired man in black spectacles, with holes in his shirt, had been working at a lathe, making something out of a piece of steel: the lathe roared and hissed and squeaked, and Anna Akimovna felt sick at the sound, and it seemed as though they were boring into her ears. She looked, listened, did not understand, smiled graciously, and felt ashamed. To get hundreds of thousands of roubles from a business which one does not understand and cannot like—how strange it is !

And she had not once been in the workpeople's barracks. There, she was told, it was damp; there were bugs, debauchery, anarchy. It was an astonishing thing: a thousand roubles were spent annually on keeping the barracks in good order, yet, if she were to believe the anonymous letters, the condition of the workpeople was growing worse and worse every year.

" There was more order in my father's day," thought Anna Akimovna, as she drove out of the yard, " because he had been a workman himself. I know nothing about it and only do silly things."

She felt depressed again, and was no longer glad that she had come, and the thought of the ucky man upon whom fifteen hundred roubles would drop from heaven no longer struck her as original and amusing. To go to some Tchalikov or other, when at home a business worth a million was gradually going to pieces and being ruined, and the workpeople in the barracks were living worse than convicts, meant doing something silly and cheating her conscience. Along the highroad and across the fields near it, workpeople from the neighbouring cotton and paper factories were walking towards the lights of the town. There was the sound of talk and laughter in the frosty air. Anna Akimovna looked at the women and young people, and she suddenly felt a longing for a plain rough life among a crowd. She recalled vividly that far-away time when she used to be called Anyutka, when she was a little girl and used to lie under the same quilt with her mother, while a washerwoman who' lodged with them used to wash clothes in the next room; while through the thin walls there came from the neighbouring flats sounds of laughter, swearing, children's crying, the accordion, and the whirr of carpenters' lathes and sewing-machines; while her father, Akim Ivanovitch, who was clever at almost every craft, would be soldering something near the stove, or drawing or planing, taking no notice whatever of the noise and stuffiness. And she longed to wash, to iron, to run to the shop and the tavern as she used to do every day when she lived with her mother. She ought to have been a work-girl and not the factory owner! Her big house with its chandeliers and pictures; her footman Mishenka, with his glossy moustache and swallow-tail coat; the devout and dignified Varvarushka, and smooth-tongued Agafyushka; and the young people of both sexes who came almost every day to ask her for money, and with whom she always for some reason felt guilty; and the clerks, the doctors, and the ladies who were charitable at her expense, who flattered her and secretly despised her for her humble origin—how wearisome and alien it all was to her!

Here was the railway crossing and the city gate;
then came houses alternating with kitchen gardens;
and at last the broad street where stood the
renowned Gushtchin's Buildings. The street,
usually quiet, was now on Christmas Eve full of
life and movement. The eating-houses and beer-
shops were noisy. If someone who did not
belong to that quarter but lived in the centre of
the town had driven through the street now, he
would have noticed nothing but dirty, drunken,
and abusive people; but Anna Akimovna, who had
lived in those parts all her life, was constantly
recognizing in the crowd her own father or mother
or uncle. Her father was a soft fluid character,
a little fantastical, frivolous, and irresponsible.
He did not care for money, respectability, or power;
he used to say that a working man had no time
to keep the holy-days and go to church; and if it
had not been for his wife, he would probably
never have gone to confession, taken the sacrament or kept the fasts. While her uncle, Ivan
Ivanovitch, on the contrary, was like flint; in
everything relating to religion, politics, and morality, he was harsh and relentless, and kept a strict
watch, not only over himself, but also over all
his servants and acquaintances. God forbid that
one should go into his room without crossing
oneself before the ikon! The luxurious mansion
in which Anna Akimovna now lived he had always
kept locked up, and only opened it on great
holidays for important visitors, while he lived
himself in the office, in a little room covered with
ikons. He had leanings towards the Old Believers,

and was continually entertaining priests and bishops of the old ritual, though he had been christened, and married, and had buried his wife in accordance with the Orthodox rites. He disliked Akim, his only brother and his heir, for his frivolity, which he called simpleness and folly, and for his indifference to religion. He treated him as an inferior, kept him in the position of a workman, paid him sixteen roubles a month. Akim addressed his brother with formal respect, and on the days of asking forgiveness, he and his wife and daughter bowed down to the ground before him. But three years before his death Ivan Ivanovitch had drawn closer to his brother, forgave his shortcomings, and ordered him to get a governess for Anyutka.

There was a dark, deep, evil-smelling archway under Gushtchin's Buildings; there was a sound of men coughing near the walls. Leaving the sledge in the street, Anna Akimovna went in at the gate and there inquired how to get to No. 46 to see a clerk called Tchalikov. She was directed to the furthest door on the right in the third storey. And in the courtyard and near the outer door, and even on the stairs, there was still the same loathsome smell as under the archway. In Anna Akimovna's childhood, when her father was a simple workman, she used to live in a building like that, and afterwards, when their circumstances were different, she had often visited them in the character of a Lady Bountiful. The narrow stone staircase with its steep dirty steps, with landings at every storey; the greasy swinging lanterns; the stench; the troughs, pots, and rags on the landings near the doors

—all this had been familiar to her long ago. . . . One door was open, and within could be seen Jewish tailors in caps, sewing. Anna Akimovna met people on the stairs, but it never entered her head that people might be rude to her. She was no more afraid of peasants or workpeople, drunk or sober than of her acquaintances of the educated class.

There was no entry at No. 46; the door opened straight into the kitchen. As a rule the dwellings of workmen and mechanics smell of varnish, tar, hides, smoke, according to the occupation of the tenant; the dwellings of persons of noble or official class who have come to poverty may be known by a peculiar rancid, sour smell. This disgusting smell enveloped Anna Akimovna on all sides, and as yet she was only on the threshold. A man in a black coat, no doubt Tchalikov himself, was sitting in a corner at the table with his back to the door, and with him were five little girls. The eldest, a broad-faced thin girl with a comb in her hair, looked about fifteen, while the youngest, a chubby child with hair that stood up like a hedgehog, was not more than three. All the six were eating. Near the stove stood a very thin little woman with a yellow face, far gone in pregnancy. She was wearing a skirt and white blouse, and had an oven fork in her hand.

"I did not expect you to be so disobedient, Liza," the man was saying reproachfully. "Fie, fie, for shame! Do you want papa to whip you—eh?"

Seeing an unknown lady in the doorway, the thin woman started, and put down the fork.

"Vassily Nikititch!" she cried, after a pause, in a hollow voice, as though she could not believe her eyes.

The man looked round and jumped up. He was a flat-chested, bony man with narrow shoulders and sunken temples. His eyes were small and hollow with dark rings round them, he had a wide mouth, and a long nose like a bird's beak—a little bit bent to the right. His beard was parted in the middle, his moustache was shaven, and this made him look more like a hired footman than a government clerk.

' Does Mr. Tchalikov live here?" asked Anna Akimovna.

"Yes, madam," Tchalikov answered severely, but immediately recognizing Anna Akimovna, he cried: "Anna Akimovna!" and all at once he gasped and clasped his hands as though in terrible alarm. "Benefactress!"

With a moan he ran to her, grunting inarticulately as though he were paralyzed—there was cabbage on his beard and he smelt of vodka—pressed his forehead to her muff, and seemed as though he were in a swoon.

"Your hand, your holy hand!" he brought out breathlessly. "It's a dream, a glorious dream! Children, awaken me!"

He turned towards the table and said in a sobbing voice, shaking his fists:

"Providence has heard us! Our saviour, our angel, has come! We are saved! Children, down on your knees! on your knees!"

Madame Tchalikov and the little girls, except

the youngest one, began for some reason rapidly clearing the table.

" You wrote that your wife was very ill," said Anna Akimovna, and she felt ashamed and annoyed. " I am not going to give them the fifteen hundred," she thought.

" Here she is, my wife," said Tchalikov in a thin feminine voice, as though his tears had gone to his head. " Here she is, unhappy creature ! With one foot in the grave ! But we do not complain, madam. Better death than such a life. Better die, unhappy woman !"

" Why is he playing these antics ?" thought Anna Akimovna with annoyance. " One can see at once he is used to dealing with merchants."

" Speak to me like a human being," she said. " I don't care for farces."

" Yes, madam; five bereaved children round their mother's coffin with funeral candles—that's a farce ? Eh ?" said Tchalikov bitterly, and turned away.

" Hold your tongue," whispered his wife, and she pulled at his sleeve. " The place has not been tidied up, madam," she said, addressing Anna Akimovna; " please excuse it . . . you know what it is where there are children. A crowded hearth, but harmony."

" I am not going to give them the fifteen hundred," Anna Akimovna thought again.

And to escape as soon as possible from these people and from the sour smell, she brought out her purse and made up her mind to leave them twenty-five roubles, not more; but she suddenly

felt ashamed that she had come so far and disturbed
people for so little.

" If you give me paper and ink, I will write at
once to a doctor who is a friend of mine to come
and see you," she said, flushing red. " He is a
very good doctor. And I will leave you some
money for medicine."

Madame Tchalikov was hastening to wipe the
table.

" It's messy here! What are you doing?"
hissed Tchalikov, looking at her wrathfully.
" Take her to the lodger's room! I make bold
to ask you, madam, to step into the lodger's
room," he said, addressing Anna Akimovna.
" It's clean there."

"Osip Ilyitch told us not to go into his room!"
said one of the little girls, sternly.

But they had already led Anna Akimovna out
of the kitchen, through a narrow passage room
between two bedsteads: it was evident from the
arrangement of the beds that in one two slept
lengthwise, and in the other three slept across the
bed. In the lodger's room, that came next, it
really was clean. A neat-looking bed with a red
woollen quilt, a pillow in a white pillow-case,
even a slipper for the watch, a table covered with
a hempen cloth and on it, an inkstand of milky-
looking glass, pens, paper, photographs in frames—
everything as it ought to be; and another table for
rough work, on which lay tidily arranged a watchmaker's tools and watches taken to pieces. On
the walls hung hammers, pliers, awls, chisels,
nippers, and so on, and there were three hanging

578

clocks which were ticking; one was a big clock with thick weights, such as one sees in eating-houses.

As she sat down to write the letter, Anna Akimovna saw facing her on the table the photographs of her father and of herself. That surprised her.

" Who lives here with you ?" she asked.

" Our lodger, madam, Pimenov. He works in your factory."

" Oh, I thought he must be a watchmaker."

" He repairs watches privately, in his leisure hours. He is an amateur."

After a brief silence during which nothing could be heard but the ticking of the clocks and the scratching of the pen on the paper, Tchalikov heaved a sigh and said ironically, with indignation:

" It's a true saying: gentle birth and a grade in the service won't put a coat on your back. A cockade in your cap and a noble title, but nothing to eat. To my thinking, if anyone of humble class helps the poor he is much more of a gentleman than any Tchalikov who has sunk into poverty and vice."

To flatter Anna Akimovna, he uttered a few more disparaging phrases about his gentle birth, and it was evident that he was humbling himself because he considered himself superior to her. Meanwhile she had finished her letter and had sealed it up. The letter would be thrown away and the money would not be spent on medicine— that she knew, but she put twenty-five roubles on the table all the same, and after a moment's thought, added two more red notes. She saw the wasted, yellow hand of Madame Tchalikov, like the claw of a hen, dart out and clutch the money tight.

" You have graciously given this for medicine," said Tchalikov in a quivering voice, " but hold out a helping hand to me also . . . and the children !" he added with a sob. " My unhappy children ! I am not afraid for myself; it is for my daughters I fear ! It's the hydra of vice that I fear !"

Trying to open her purse, the catch of which had gone wrong, Anna Akimovna was confused and turned red. She felt ashamed that people should be standing before her, looking at her hands and waiting, and most likely at the bottom of their hearts laughing at her. At that instant someone came into the kitchen and stamped his feet, knocking the snow off.

" The lodger has come in," said Madame Tchalikov.

Anna Akimovna grew even more confused. She did not want anyone from the factory to find her in this ridiculous position. As ill-luck would have it, the lodger came in at the very moment when, having broken the catch at last, she was giving Tchalikov some notes, and Tchalikov, grunting as though he were paralyzed, was feeling about with his lips where he could kiss her. In the lodger she recognized the workman who had once clanked the sheet-iron before her in the forge, and had explained things to her. Evidently he had come in straight from the factory; his face looked dark and grimy, and on one cheek near his nose was a smudge of soot. His hands were perfectly black, and his unbelted shirt shone with oil and grease. He was a man of thirty, of medium height, with black hair and broad shoulders, and a look of great physical strength. At the first glance Anna Akimovna perceived that he must be a foreman, who must be receiving at least thirty-five roubles a month, and a stern, loud-voiced man who struck the workmen in the face; all this was evident from his manner of standing, from the attitude he involuntarily assumed at once on seeing a lady in his room, and most of all from the fact that he did not wear top-boots, that he had breast pockets, and a pointed, picturesquely clipped beard. Her father, Akim Ivanovitch, had been the brother of the factory owner, and yet he had been afraid of foremen like this lodger and had tried to win their favour.

"Excuse me for having come in here in your absence," said Anna Akimovna.

The workman looked at her in surprise, smiled in confusion and did not speak.

"You must speak a little louder, madam . . ." said Tchalikov softly. "When Mr. Pimenov comes home from the factory in the evenings he is a little hard of hearing."

But Anna Akimovna was by now relieved that there was nothing more for her to do here; she nodded to them and went rapidly out of the room. Pimenov went to see her out.

"Have you been long in our employment?" she asked in a loud voice, without turning to him.

"From nine years old. I entered the factory in your uncle's time."

" That's a long while ! My uncle and my father knew all the workpeople, and I know hardly any of them. I had seen you before, but I did not know your name was Pimenov."

Anna Akimovna felt a desire to justify herself before him, to pretend that she had just given the money not seriously, but as a joke.

" Oh, this poverty," she sighed. " We give charity on holidays and working days, and still there is no sense in it. I believe it is useless to help such people as this Tchalikov."

" Of course it is useless," he agreed. " However much you give him, he will drink it all away. And now the husband and wife will be snatching it from one another and fighting all night," he added with a laugh.

" Yes, one must admit that our philanthropy is useless, boring, and absurd. But still, you must agree, one can't sit with one's hands in one's lap; one must do something. What's to be done with the Tchalikovs, for instance ?"

She turned to Pimenov and stopped, expecting an answer from him; he, too, stopped and slowly, without speaking, shrugged his shoulders. Obviously he knew what to do with the Tchalikovs, but the treatment would have been so coarse and inhuman that he did not venture to put it into words. And the Tchalikovs were to him so utterly uninteresting and worthless, that a moment later he had forgotten them; looking into Anna Akimovna's eyes, he smiled with pleasure, and his face wore an expression as though he were dreaming about something very pleasant. Only, now standing close to him, Anna Akimovna saw from his face, and especially from his eyes, how exhausted and sleepy he was.

" Here, I ought to give him the fifteen hundred roubles !" she thought, but for some reason this idea seemed to her incongruous and insulting to Pimenov.

" I am sure you are aching all over after your work, and you come to the door with me," she said as they went down the stairs. " Go home."

But he did not catch her words. When they came out into the street, he ran on ahead, unfastened the cover of the sledge, and helping Anna Akimovna in, said:

" I wish you a happy Christmas !"

II.

CHRISTMAS MORNING.

" They have left off ringing ever so long ! It's dreadful; you won't be there before the service is over ! Get up !"

" Two horses are racing, racing . . ." said Anna Akimovna, and she woke up; before her, candle in hand, stood her maid, red-haired Masha. " Well, what is it ?"

" Service is over already," said Masha with despair. " I have called you three times ! Sleep till evening for me, but you told me yourself to call you !"

Anna Akimovna raised herself on her elbow and glanced towards the window. It was still quite dark outside, and only the lower edge of the window-frame was white with snow. She could hear a low, mellow chime of bells; it was not the parish church, but somewhere further away. The watch on the little table showed three minutes past six.

" Very well, Masha. . . . In three minutes . . ." said Anna Akimovna in an imploring voice, and she snuggled under the bed-clothes.

She imagined the snow at the front door, the sledge, the dark sky, the crowd in the church, and the smell of juniper, and she felt dread at the thought; but all the same, she made up her mind that she would get up at once and go to early service. And while she was warm in bed and struggling with sleep—which seems, as though to spite one, particularly sweet when one ought to get up—and while she had visions of an immense garden on a mountain and then Gushtchin's Buildings, she was worried all the time by the thought that she ought to get up that very minute and go to church.

But when she got up it was quite light, and it turned out to be half-past nine. There had been a heavy fall of snow in the night; the trees were clothed in white, and the air was particularly light, transparent, and tender, so that when Anna Akimovna looked out of the window her first impulse was to draw a deep, deep breath. And when she had washed, a relic of far-away childish feelings—joy that to-day was Christmas—suddenly stirred within her; after that she felt light-hearted, free and pure in soul, as though her soul, too, had been washed or plunged in the white snow. Masha came in, dressed up and tightly laced, and wished her a happy Christmas; then she spent a long time combing her mistress's hair and helping her to dress. The fragrance and feeling of the new, gorgeous, splendid dress, its faint rustle, and the smell of fresh scent, excited Anna Akimovna.

" Well, it's Christmas," she said gaily to Masha. " Now we will try our fortunes."

" Last year, I was to marry an old man. It turned up three times the same."

" Well, God is merciful."

" Well, Anna Akimovna, what I think is, rather than neither one thing nor the other, I'd marry an old man," said Masha mournfully, and she heaved a sigh. " I am turned twenty; it's no joke."

Everyone in the house knew that red-haired Masha was in love with Mishenka, the footman, and this genuine, passionate, hopeless love had already lasted three years.

" Come, don't talk nonsense," Anna Akimovna consoled her. " I am going on for thirty, but I am still meaning to marry a young man."

While his mistress was dressing, Mishenka, in a new swallow-tail and polished boots, walked about the hall and drawing-room and waited for her to come out, to wish her a happy Christmas. He had a peculiar walk, stepping softly and delicately; looking at his feet, his hands, and the bend of his head, it might be imagined that he was not simply walking, but learning to dance the first figure of the quadrille. In spite of his fine velvety moustache and handsome, rather flashy appearance, he was steady, prudent, and devout as an old man. He said his prayers, bowing down to the ground, and liked burning incense in his room. He respected people of wealth and rank and had a reverence for them; he despised poor people, and all who came to ask favours of any kind, with all the strength of his cleanly flunkey soul. Under his starched shirt he wore a flannel, winter and summer alike, being very careful of his health; his ears were plugged with cotton-wool.

When Anna Akimovna crossed the hall with Masha, he bent his head downwards a little and said in his agreeable, honeyed voice:

" I have the honour to congratulate you, Anna Akimovna, on the most solemn feast of the birth of our Lord."

Anna Akimovna gave him five roubles, while poor Masha was numb with ecstasy. His holiday get-up, his attitude, his voice, and what he said, impressed her by their beauty and elegance; as she followed her mistress she could think of nothing, could see nothing, she could only smile, first blissfully and then bitterly. The upper storey of the house was called the best or visitors' half, while the name of the business part—old people's or simply women's part—was given to the rooms on the lower storey where Aunt Tatyana Ivanovna kept house. In the upper part the gentry and educated visitors were entertained; in the lower storey, simpler folk and the aunt's personal friends. Handsome, plump, and healthy, still young and fresh, and feeling she had on a magnificent dress which seemed to her to diffuse a sort of radiance all about her, Anna Akimovna went down to the lower storey. Here she was met with reproaches for forgetting God now that she was so highly educated, for sleeping too late for the service, and for not coming downstairs to break the fast, and they all clasped their hands and exclaimed with perfect sincerity that she was lovely, wonderful; and she believed it, laughed, kissed them, gave one a rouble, another three or five according to their position. She liked being downstairs. Wherever one looked there were shrines, ikons, little lamps, portraits of ecclesiastical personages—the place smelt of monks; there was a rattle of knives in the kitchen, and already a smell of something savoury, exceedingly appetizing, was pervading all the rooms. The yellow-painted floors shone, and from the doors narrow rugs with bright blue stripes ran like little paths to the ikon corner, and the sunshine was simply pouring in at the windows.

In the dining-room some old women, strangers, were sitting; in Varvarushka's room, too, there were old women, and with them a deaf and dumb girl, who seemed abashed about something and kept saying, " Bli, bli ! . . ." Two skinny-looking little girls who had been brought out of the orphanage for Christmas came up to kiss Anna Akimovna's hand, and stood before her transfixed with admiration of her splendid dress; she noticed that one of the girls squinted, and in the midst of her light-hearted holiday mood she felt a sick pang at her heart at the thought that young men would despise the girl, and that she would never marry. In the cook Agafya's room, five huge peasants in new shirts were sitting round the samovar; these were not workmen from the factory, but relations of the cook. Seeing Anna Akimovna, all the peasants jumped up from their seats, and from regard for decorum, ceased munching though their mouths were full. The cook Stepan, in a white cap, with a knife in his hand, came into the room and gave her his greetings; porters in high felt boots came in, and they, too, offered their greetings. The water-carrier peeped in with icicles on his beard, but did not venture to come in.

Anna Akimovna walked through the rooms followed by her retinue—the aunt, Varvarushka, Nikandrovna, the sewing-maid Marfa Petrovna, and the downstairs Masha. Varvarushka—a tall, thin, slender woman, taller than anyone in the house, dressed all in black, smelling of cypress and coffee—crossed herself in each room before the ikon, bowing down from the waist. And whenever one looked at her one was reminded that she had already prepared her shroud and that lottery tickets were hidden away by her in the same box.

" Anyutinka, be merciful at Christmas," she said, opening the door into the kitchen. " Forgive him, bless the man ! Have done with it !"

The coachman Panteley, who had been dismissed for drunkenness in November, was on his knees in the middle of the kitchen. He was a good-natured man, but he used to be unruly when he was drunk, and could not go to sleep, but persisted in wandering about the buildings and shouting in a threatening voice, "I know all about it!" Now from his beefy and bloated face and from his bloodshot eyes it could be seen that he had been drinking continually from November till Christmas.

"Forgive me, Anna Akimovna," he brought out in a hoarse voice, striking his forehead on the floor and showing his bull-like neck.

"It was Auntie dismissed you; ask her."

"What about auntie?" said her aunt, walking into the kitchen, breathing heavily; she was very stout, and on her bosom one might have stood a tray of teacups and a samovar. "What about auntie now? You are mistress here, give your own orders; though these rascals might be all dead for all I care. Come, get up, you hog!" she shouted at Panteley, losing patience. "Get out of my sight! It's the last time I forgive you, but if you transgress again—don't ask for mercy!"

Then they went into the dining-room to coffee. But they had hardly sat down, when the downstairs Masha rushed headlong in, saying with horror, "The singers!" And ran back again. They heard someone blowing his nose, a low bass cough, and footsteps that sounded like horses' iron-shod hoofs tramping about the entry near the hall. For half a minute all was hushed. . . . The singers burst out so suddenly and loudly that everyone started. While they were singing, the priest from the almshouses with the deacon and the sexton arrived. Putting on the stole, the priest slowly said that when they were ringing for matins it was snowing and not cold, but that the frost was sharper towards morning, God bless it ! and now there must be twenty degrees of frost.

" Many people maintain, though, that winter is healthier than summer," said the deacon; then immediately assumed an austere expression and chanted after the priest. " Thy Birth, O Christ our Lord. . . ."

Soon the priest from the workmen's hospital came with the deacon, then the Sisters from the hospital, children from the orphanage, and then singing could be heard almost uninterruptedly. They sang, had lunch, and went away.

About twenty men from the factory came to offer their Christmas greetings. They were only the foremen, mechanicians, and their assistants, the pattern-makers, the accountant, and so on— all of good appearance, in new black coats. They were all first-rate men, as it were picked men; each one knew his value—that is, knew that if he lost his berth to-day, people would be glad to take him on at another factory. Evidently they liked Auntie, as they behaved freely in her presence and even smoked, and when they had all trooped in to have something to eat, the account-ant put his arm round her immense waist. They were free-and-easy, perhaps, partly also because Varvarushka, who under the old masters had wielded great power and had kept watch over the morals of the clerks, had now no authority what-ever in the house; and perhaps because many of them still remembered the time when Auntie Tatyana Ivanovna, whose brothers kept a strict hand over her, had been dressed like a simple peasant woman like Agafya, and when Anna Akimovna used to run about the yard near the factory buildings and everyone used to call her Anyutka.

The foremen ate, talked, and kept looking with amazement at Anna Akimovna, how she had grown up and how handsome she had become ! But this elegant girl, educated by governesses and teachers, was a stranger to them; they could not understand her, and they instinctively kept closer to " Auntie," who called them by their names, continually pressed them to eat and drink, and, clinking glasses with them, had already drunk two wine-glasses of rowanberry wine with them. Anna Akimovna was always afraid of their thinking her proud, an upstart, or a crow in peacock's feathers; and now while the foremen were crowding round the food, she did not leave the dining-room, but took part in the conversation. She asked Pimenov, her acquaintance of the previous day:

" Why have you so many clocks in your room ?"

" I mend clocks," he answered. " I take the work up between times, on holidays, or when I can't sleep."

" So if my watch goes wrong I can bring it to you to be repaired ?" Anna Akimovna asked, laughing.

" To be sure, I will do it with pleasure," said Pimenov, and there was an expression of tender devotion in his face, when, not herself knowing why, she unfastened her magnificent watch from its chain and handed it to him; he looked at it in silence and gave it back. "To be sure, I will do it with pleasure," he repeated. "I don't mend watches now. My eyes are weak, and the doctors have forbidden me to do fine work. But for you I can make an exception."

"Doctors talk nonsense," said the accountant. They all laughed. "Don't you believe them," he went on, flattered by the laughing; "last year a tooth flew out of a cylinder and hit old Kalmykov such a crack on the head that you could see his brains, and the doctor said he would die; but he is alive and working to this day, only he has taken to stammering since that mishap."

"Doctors do talk nonsense, they do, but not so much," sighed Auntie. "Pyotr Andreyitch, poor dear, lost his sight. Just like you, he used to work day in day out at the factory near the hot furnace, and he went blind. The eyes don't like heat. But what are we talking about?" she said, rousing herself. "Come and have a drink. My best wishes for Christmas, my dears. I never drink with anyone else, but I drink with you, sinful woman as I am. Please God!"

Anna Akimovna fancied that after yesterday Pimenov despised her as a philanthropist, but was fascinated by her as a woman. She looked at him and thought that he behaved very charmingly and was nicely dressed. It is true that the sleeves of his coat were not quite long enough, and the coat itself seemed short-waisted, and his trousers were not wide and fashionable, but his tie was tied carelessly and with taste and was not as gaudy as the others'. And he seemed to be a good-natured man, for he ate submissively whatever Auntie put on his plate. She remembered how black he had been the day before, and how sleepy, and the thought of it for some reason touched her.

When the men were preparing to go, Anna Akimovna put out her hand to Pimenov. She wanted to ask him to come in sometimes to see her, without ceremony, but she did not know how to—her tongue would not obey her; and that they might not think she was attracted by Pimenov, she shook hands with his companions, too.

Then the boys from the school of which she was a patroness came. They all had their heads closely cropped and all wore grey blouses of the same pattern. The teacher—a tall, beardless young man with patches of red on his face—was visibly agitated as he formed the boys into rows; the boys sang in tune, but with harsh, disagreeable voices. The manager of the factory, Nazaritch, a bald, sharp-eyed Old Believer, could never get on with the teachers, but the one who was now anxiously waving his hands he despised and hated, though he could not have said why. He behaved rudely and condescendingly to the young man, kept back his salary, meddled with the teaching, and had finally tried to dislodge him by appointing, a fortnight before Christmas, as porter to the school a drunken peasant, a distant relation of his wife's, who disobeyed the teacher and said rude things to him before the boys.

Anna Akimovna was aware of all this, but she could be of no help, for she was afraid of Nazaritch herself. Now she wanted at least to be very nice to the schoolmaster, to tell him she was very much pleased with him; but when after the singing he began apologizing for something in great confusion, and Auntie began to address him familiarly as she drew him without ceremony to the table, she felt, for some reason, bored and awkward, and giving orders that the children should be given sweets, went upstairs.

"In reality there is something cruel in these Christmas customs," she said a little while afterwards, as it were to herself, looking out of window at the boys, who were flocking from the house to the gates and shivering with cold, putting their coats on as they ran. "At Christmas one wants to rest, to sit at home with one's own people, and the poor boys, the teacher, and the clerks and foremen, are obliged for some reason to go through the frost, then to offer their greetings, show their respect, be put to confusion . . ."

Mishenka, who was standing at the door of the drawing-room and overheard this, said:

"It has not come from us, and it will not end with us. Of course, I am not an educated man, Anna Akimovna, but I do understand that the poor must always respect the rich. It is well said, 'God marks the rogue.' In prisons, night refuges, and pot-houses you never see any but the poor, while decent people, you may notice, are always rich. It has been said of the rich, 'Deep calls to deep.'"

" You always express yourself so tediously and incomprehensibly," said Anna Akimovna, and she walked to the other end of the big drawing-room.

It was only just past eleven. The stillness of the big room, only broken by the singing that floated up from below, made her yawn. The bronzes, the albums, and the pictures on the walls, representing a ship at sea, cows in a meadow, and views of the Rhine, were so absolutely stale that her eyes simply glided over them without observing them. The holiday mood was already growing tedious. As before, Anna Akimovna felt that she was beautiful, good-natured, and wonderful, but now it seemed to her that that was of no use to anyone; it seemed to her that she did not know for whom and for what she had put on this expensive dress, too, and, as always happened on all holidays, she began to be fretted by loneliness and the persistent thought that her beauty, her health, and her wealth, were a mere cheat, since she was not wanted, was of no use to anyone, and nobody loved her. She walked through all the rooms, humming and looking out of window; stopping in the drawing-room, she could not resist beginning to talk to Mishenka.

" I don't know what you think of yourself, Misha," she said, and heaved a sigh. " Really, God might punish you for it."

" What do you mean ?"

" You know what I mean. Excuse my meddling in your affairs. But it seems you are spoiling your own life out of obstinacy. You'll admit that it is high time you got married, and she is

an excellent and deserving girl. You will never
find anyone better. She's a beauty, clever,
gentle, and devoted. . . . And her appearance !
. . . If she belonged to our circle or a higher
one, people would be falling in love with her for
her red hair alone. See how beautifully her hair
goes with her complexion. Oh, goodness ! You
don't understand anything, and don't know what
you want," Anna Akimovna said bitterly, and
tears came into her eyes. " Poor girl, I am so
sorry for her ! I know you want a wife with
money, but I have told you already I will give
Masha a dowry."

Mishenka could not picture his future spouse
in his imagination except as a tall, plump, sub-
stantial, pious woman, stepping like a peacock,
and, for some reason, with a long shawl over her
shoulders; while Masha was thin, slender, tightly
laced, and walked with little steps, and, worst of
all, she was too fascinating and at times extremely
attractive to Mishenka, and that, in his opinion,
was incongruous with matrimony and only in
keeping with loose behaviour. When Anna Akimovna had promised to give Masha a dowry, he
had hesitated for a time; but once a poor student
in a brown overcoat over his uniform, coming with
a letter for Anna Akimovna, was fascinated by
Masha, and could not resist embracing her near
the hat-stand, and she had uttered a faint shriek;
Mishenka, standing on the stairs above, had seen
this, and from that time had begun to cherish a
feeling of disgust for Masha. A poor student !
Who knows, if she had been embraced by a rich

student or an officer the consequences might have been different.

" Why don't you wish it ?" Anna Akimovna asked. " What more do you want ?"

Mishenka was silent and looked at the arm-chair fixedly, and raised his eyebrows.

" Do you love someone else ?"

Silence. The red-haired Masha came in with letters and visiting cards on a tray. Guessing that they were talking about her, she blushed to tears.

" The postmen have come," she muttered. " And there is a clerk called Tchalikov waiting below. He says you told him to come to-day for something."

" What insolence !" said Anna Akimovna, moved to anger. " I gave him no orders. Tell him to take himself off; say I am not at home !"

A ring was heard. It was the priests from her parish. They were always shown into the aristocratic part of the house— that is, upstairs. After the priests, Nazaritch, the manager of the factory, came to pay his visit, and then the factory doctor; then Mishenka announced the inspector of the elementary schools. Visitors kept arriving.

When there was a moment free, Anna Akimovna sat down in a deep arm-chair in the drawing-room, and shutting her eyes, thought that her loneliness was quite natural because she had not married and never would marry. . . . But that was not her fault. Fate itself had flung her out of the simple working-class surroundings in which, if she could trust her memory, she had felt so snug and at home, into these immense rooms, where she could never think what to do with herself, and could not understand why so many people kept passing before her eyes. What was happening now seemed to her trivial, useless, since it did not and could not give her happiness for one minute.

"If I could fall in love," she thought, stretching; the very thought of this sent a rush of warmth to her heart. "And if I could escape from the factory . . ." she mused, imagining how the weight of those factory buildings, barracks, and schools would roll off her conscience, roll off her mind. . . . Then she remembered her father, and thought if he had lived longer he would certainly have married her to a working-man—to Pimenov, for instance. He would have told her to marry, and that would have been all about it. And it would have been a good thing; then the factory would have passed into capable hands.

She pictured his curly head, his bold profile, his delicate, ironical lips and the strength, the tremendous strength, in his shoulders, in his arms, in his chest, and the tenderness with which he had looked at her watch that day.

"Well," she said, "it would have been all right. . . . I would have married him."

"Anna Akimovna," said Mishenka, coming noiselessly into the drawing-room.

"How you frightened me!" she said, trembling all over. "What do you want?"

"Anna Akimovna," he said, laying his hand on his heart and raising his eyebrows, "you are my mistress and my benefactress, and no one but you can tell me what I ought to do about marriage, for you are as good as a mother to me. . . . But kindly forbid them to laugh and jeer at me downstairs. They won't let me pass without it."

" How do they jeer at you ?"

" They call me Mashenka's Mishenka."

" Pooh, what nonsense !" cried Anna Akimovna indignantly. " How stupid you all are ! What a stupid you are, Misha ! How sick I am of you ! I can't bear the sight of you."

III.

DINNER.

Just as the year before, the last to pay her visits were Krylin, an actual civil councillor, and Lysevitch, a well-known barrister. It was already dark when they arrived. Krylin, a man of sixty, with a wide mouth and with grey whiskers close to his ears, with a face like a lynx, was wearing a uniform with an Anna ribbon, and white trousers. He held Anna Akimovna's hand in both of his for a long while, looked intently in her face, moved his lips, and at last said, drawling upon one note:

" I used to respect your uncle . . . and your father, and enjoyed the privilege of their friendship. Now I feel it an agreeable duty, as you see, to present my Christmas wishes to their honoured heiress . . . in spite of my infirmities and the distance I have to come. . . . And I am very glad to see you in good health."

599

The lawyer Lysevitch, a tall, handsome fair man, with a slight sprinkling of grey on his temples and beard, was distinguished by exceptionally elegant manners; he walked with a swaying step, bowed as it were reluctantly, and shrugged his shoulders as he talked, and all this with an indolent grace, like a spoiled horse fresh from the stable. He was well fed, extremely healthy, and very well off; on one occasion he had won forty thousand roubles, but concealed the fact from his friends. He was fond of good fare, especially cheese, truffles, and grated radish with hemp oil; while in Paris he had eaten, so he said, baked but unwashed guts. He spoke smoothly, fluently, without hesitation, and only occasionally, for the sake of effect, permitted himself to hesitate and snap his fingers as if picking up a word. He had long ceased to believe in anything he had to say in the law courts, or perhaps he did believe in it, but attached no kind of significance to it; it had all so long been familiar, stale, ordinary. . . . He believed in nothing but what was original and unusual. A copy-book moral in an original form would move him to tears. Both his notebooks were filled with extraordinary expressions which he had read in various authors; and when he needed to look up any expression, he would search nervously in both books, and usually failed to find it. Anna Akimovna's father had in a good-humoured moment ostentatiously appointed him legal adviser in matters concerning the factory, and had assigned him a salary of twelve thousand roubles. The legal business of the factory had been confined to two or three trivial actions for recovering debts, which Lyse-vitch handed to his assistants.

Anna Akimovna knew that he had nothing to do at the factory, but she could not dismiss him—she had not the moral courage; and besides, she was used to him. He used to call himself her legal adviser, and his salary, which he invariably sent for on the first of the month punctually, he used to call "stern prose." Anna Akimovna knew that when, after her father's death, the timber of her forest was sold for railway sleepers, Lyse-vitch had made more than fifteen thousand out of the transaction, and had shared it with Naza-ritch. When first she found out they had cheated her she had wept bitterly, but afterwards she had grown used to it.

Wishing her a happy Christmas, and kissing both her hands, he looked her up and down, and frowned.

" You mustn't," he said with genuine disap-pointment. " I have told you, my dear, you mustn't " !

" What do you mean, Viktor Nikolaitch ?"

" I have told you you mustn't get fat. All your family have an unfortunate tendency to grow fat. You mustn't," he repeated in an imploring voice, and kissed her hand. " You are so handsome ! You are so splendid ! Here, your Excellency, let me introduce the one woman in the world whom I have ever seriously loved."

" There is nothing surprising in that. To know Anna Akimovna at your age and not to be in love with her, that would be impossible."

" I adore her," the lawyer continued with perfect sincerity, but with his usual indolent grace. " I love her, but not because I am a man and she is a woman. When I am with her I always feel as though she belongs to some third sex, and I to a fourth, and we float away together into the domain of the subtlest shades, and there we blend into the spectrum. Leconte de Lisle defines such relations better than anyone. He has a superb passage, a marvellous passage. . . ."

Lysevitch rummaged in one notebook, then in the other, and, not finding the quotation, subsided. They began talking of the weather, of the opera, of the arrival, expected shortly, of Duse. Anna Akimovna remembered that the year before Lysevitch and, she fancied, Krylin had dined with her, and now when they were getting ready to go away, she began with perfect sincerity pointing out to them in an imploring voice that as they had no more visits to pay, they ought to remain to dinner with her. After some hesitation the visitors agreed.

In addition to the family dinner, consisting of cabbage soup, sucking pig, goose with apples, and so on, a so-called " French " or " chef's " dinner used to be prepared in the kitchen on great holidays, in case any visitor in the upper storey wanted a meal. When they heard the clatter of crockery in the dining-room, Lysevitch began to betray a noticeable excitement; he rubbed his hands, shrugged his shoulders, screwed up his eyes, and described with feeling what dinners her father and uncle used to give at one time. and a marvellous *matelote* of turbots the cook here could make: it was not a *matelote*, but a veritable revelation! He was already gloating over the dinner, already eating it in imagination and enjoying it. When Anna Akimovna took his arm and led him to the dining-room, he tossed off a glass of vodka and put a piece of salmon in his mouth; he positively purred with pleasure. He munched loudly, disgustingly, emitting sounds from his nose, while his eyes grew oily and rapacious.

The *hors d'œuvres* were superb; among other things, there were fresh white mushrooms stewed in cream, and *sauce provençale* made of fried oysters and crayfish, strongly flavoured with some bitter pickles. The dinner, consisting of elaborate holiday dishes, was excellent, and so were the wines. Mishenka waited at table with enthusiasm. When he laid some new dish on the table and lifted the shining cover, or poured out the wine, he did it with the solemnity of a professor of black magic, and, looking at his face and his movements suggesting the first figure of a quadrille, the lawyer thought several times, " What a fool !"

After the third course Lysevitch said, turning to Anna Akimovna:

" The *fin de siècle* woman—I mean when she is young, and of course wealthy—must be independent, clever, elegant, intellectual, bold, and a little depraved. Depraved within limits, a little; for excess, you know, is wearisome. You ought not to vegetate, my dear; you ought not to live like everyone else, but to get the full savour of life, and a slight flavour of depravity is the sauce of life. Revel among flowers of intoxicating fragrance, breathe the perfume of musk, eat hashish, and best of all, love, love, love. . . . To begin with, in your place I would set up seven lovers—one for each day of the week; and one I would call Monday, one Tuesday, the third Wednesday, and so on, so that each might know his day."

This conversation troubled Anna Akimovna; she ate nothing and only drank a glass of wine.

" Let me speak at last," she said. " For myself personally, I can't conceive of love without family life. I am lonely, lonely as the moon in the sky, and a waning moon, too; and whatever you may say, I am convinced, I feel that this waning can only be restored by love in its ordinary sense. It seems to me that such love would define my duties, my work, make clear my conception of life. I want from love peace of soul, tranquillity; I want the very opposite of musk, and spiritualism, and *fin de siècle* . . . in short "—she grew embarrassed—" a husband and children."

" You want to be married ? Well, you can do that, too," Lysevitch assented. " You ought to have all experiences: marriage, and jealousy, and the sweetness of the first infidelity, and even children. . . . But make haste and live—make haste, my dear: time is passing; it won't wait."

" Yes, I'll go and get married !" she said, looking angrily at his well-fed, satisfied face. " I will marry in the simplest, most ordinary way and be radiant with happiness. And, would you believe it, I will marry some plain working man, some mechanic or draughtsman."

" There is no harm in that, either. The Duchess Josiana loved Gwinplin, and that was permissible for her because she was a grand duchess. Everything is permissible for you, too, because you are an exceptional woman: if, my dear, you want to love a negro or an Arab, don't scruple; send for a negro. Don't deny yourself anything. You ought to be as bold as your desires; don't fall short of them."

" Can it be so hard to understand me ?" Anna Akimovna asked with amazement, and her eyes were bright with tears. " Understand, I have an immense business on my hands—two thousand workmen, for whom I must answer before God. The men who work for me grow blind and deaf. I am afraid to go on like this; I am afraid ! I am wretched, and you have the cruelty to talk to me of negroes and . . . and you smile !" Anna Akimovna brought her fist down on the table. " To go on living the life I am living now, or to marry someone as idle and incompetent as myself, would be a crime. I can't go on living like this," she said hotly, " I cannot !"

" How handsome she is !" said Lysevitch, fascinated by her. " My God, how handsome she is ! But why are you angry, my dear ? Perhaps I am wrong; but surely you don't imagine that if, for the sake of ideas for which I have the deepest respect, you renounce the joys of life and lead a dreary existence, your workmen will be any the better for it ? Not a scrap ! No, frivolity, frivolity!" he said decisively. "It's essential for you; it's your duty to be frivolous and depraved! Ponder that, my dear, ponder it."

Anna Akimovna was glad she had spoken out, and her spirits rose. She was pleased she had spoken so well, and that her ideas were so fine and just, and she was already convinced that if Pimenov, for instance, loved her, she would marry him with pleasure.

Mishenka began to pour out champagne.

"You make me angry, Viktor Nikolaitch," she said, clinking glasses with the lawyer. "It seems to me you give advice and know nothing of life yourself. According to you, if a man be a mechanic or a draughtsman, he is bound to be a peasant and an ignoramus! But they are the cleverest people! Extraordinary people!"

"Your uncle and father . . . I knew them and respected them . . ." Krylin said, pausing for emphasis (he had been sitting upright as a post, and had been eating steadily the whole time), "were people of considerable intelligence and . . . of lofty spiritual qualities."

"Oh, to be sure, we know all about their qualities," the lawyer muttered, and asked permission to smoke.

When dinner was over Krylin was led away for a nap. Lysevitch finished his cigar, and, staggering from repletion, followed Anna Akimovna into her study. Cosy corners with photographs and fans on the walls, and the inevitable pink or pale blue lanterns in the middle of the ceiling, he did not like, as the expression of an insipid and un-original character; besides, the memory of certain of his love affairs of which he was now ashamed was associated with such lanterns. Anna Aki-movna's study with its bare walls and tasteless furniture pleased him exceedingly. It was snug and comfortable for him to sit on a Turkish divan and look at Anna Akimovna, who usually sat on the rug before the fire, clasping her knees and look-ing into the fire and thinking of something; and at such moments it seemed to him that her peasant Old Believer blood was stirring within her.

Every time after dinner when coffee and liqueurs were handed, he grew livelier and began telling her various bits of literary gossip. He spoke with eloquence and inspiration, and was carried away by his own stories; and she listened to him and thought every time that for such enjoyment it was worth paying not only twelve thousand, but three times that sum, and forgave him everything she disliked in him. He sometimes told her the story of some tale or novel he had been reading, and then two or three hours passed unnoticed like a minute. Now he began rather dolefully in a failing voice with his eyes shut.

" It's ages, my dear, since I have read anything," he said when she asked him to tell her something. " Though I do sometimes read Jules Verne."

" I was expecting you to tell me something new."

" H'm! . . . . new," Lysevitch muttered sleepily, and he settled himself further back in the corner of the sofa. " None of the new literature, my dear, is any use for you or me. Of course, it is bound to be such as it is, and to refuse to recognize it is to refuse to recognize—would mean refusing to recognize the natural order of things, and I do recognize it, but . . ." Lysevitch seemed to have fallen asleep. But a minute later his voice was heard again:

" All the new literature moans and howls like the autumn wind in the chimney. ' Ah, unhappy wretch ! Ah, your life may be likened to a prison ! Ah, how damp and dark it is in your prison ! Ah, you will certainly come to ruin, and there is no chance of escape for you !' That's very fine, but I should prefer a literature that would tell us how to escape from prison. Of all contemporary writers, however, I prefer Maupassant." Lysevitch opened his eyes. " A fine writer, a perfect writer !" Lysevitch shifted in his seat. " A wonderful artist ! A terrible, prodigious, supernatural artist !" Lysevitch got up from the sofa and raised his right arm. " Maupassant !" he said rapturously. " My dear, read Maupassant ! one page of his gives you more than all the riches of the earth ! Every line is a new horizon. The softest, tenderest impulses of the soul alternate with violent tempestuous sensations; your soul, as though under the weight of forty thousand atmospheres, is transformed into the most insignificant little bit of some great thing of an undefined rosy hue which I fancy, if one could put it on one's tongue, would yield a pungent voluptuous taste. What a fury of transitions, of motives, of melodies ! You rest peacefully on

the lilies and the roses, and suddenly a thought—
a terrible, splendid, irresistible thought—swoops
down upon you like a locomotive, and bathes you
in hot steam and deafens you with its whistle.
Read Maupassant, dear girl; I insist on it."

Lysevitch waved his arms and paced from
corner to corner in violent excitement.

"Yes, it is inconceivable," he pronounced, as
though in despair; "his last thing overwhelmed
me, intoxicated me! But I am afraid you will
not care for it. To be carried away by it you must
savour it, slowly suck the juice from each line,
drink it in. . . . You must drink it in ! . . ."

After a long introduction, containing many
words such as dæmonic sensuality, a network of
the most delicate nerves, simoom, crystal, and so
on, he began at last telling the story of the novel.
He did not tell the story so whimsically, but told
it in minute detail, quoting from memory whole
descriptions and conversations; the characters
of the novel fascinated him, and to describe them
he threw himself into attitudes, changed the
expression of his face and voice like a real actor.
He laughed with delight at one moment in a
deep bass, and at another, on a high shrill note,
clasped his hands and clutched at his head with
an expression which suggested that it was just
going to burst. Anna Akimovna listened enthralled, though she had already read the novel,
and it seemed to her ever so much finer and more
subtle in the lawyer's version than in the book
itself. He drew her attention to various subtleties,
and emphasized the felicitous expressions and the

profound thoughts, but she saw in it, only life, life, life and herself, as though she had been a character in the novel. Her spirits rose, and she, too, laughing and clasping her 'hands, thought that she could not go on living such a life, that there was no need to have a wretched life when one might have a splendid one. She remembered her words and thoughts at dinner, and was proud of them; and when Pimenov suddenly rose up in her imagination, she felt happy and longed for him to love her.

When he had finished the story, Lysevitch sat down on the sofa, exhausted.

" How splendid you are ! How handsome !" he began, a little while afterwards in a faint voice as if he were ill. " I am happy near you, dear girl, but why am I forty-two instead of thirty ? Your tastes and mine do not coincide: you ought to be depraved, and I have long passed that phase, and want a love as delicate and immaterial as a ray of sunshine—that is, from the point of view of a woman of your age, I am of no earthly use."

In his own words, he loved Turgenev, the singer of virginal love and purity, of youth, and of the melancholy Russian landscape; but he loved virginal love, not from knowledge but from hearsay, as something abstract, existing outside real life. Now he assured himself that he loved Anna Akimovna platonically, ideally, though he did not know what those words meant. But he felt comfortable, snug, warm. Anna Akimovna seemed to him enchanting, original, and he imagined that the pleasant sensation that was aroused in him by these surroundings was the very thing that was called platonic love.

He laid his cheek on her hand and said in the tone commonly used in coaxing little children:

" My precious, why have you punished me ?"

" How ? When ?"

" I have had no Christmas present from you."

Anna Akimovna had never heard before of their sending a Christmas box to the lawyer, and now she was at a loss how much to give him. But she must give him something, for he was expecting it, though he looked at her with eyes full of love.

" I suppose Nazaritch forgot it," she said, " but it is not too late to set it right."

She suddenly remembered the fifteen hundred she had received the day before, which was now lying in the toilet drawer in her bedroom. And when she brought that ungrateful money and gave it to the lawyer, and he put it in his coat pocket with indolent grace, the whole incident passed off charmingly and naturally. The sudden reminder of a Christmas box and this fifteen hundred was not unbecoming in Lysevitch.

" Merci," he said, and kissed her finger.

Krylin came in with blissful, sleepy face, but without his decorations.

Lysevitch and he stayed a little longer and drank a glass of tea each, and began to get ready to go. Anna Akimovna was a little embarrassed. . . . She had utterly forgotten in what department

Krylin served, and whether she had to give him money or not; and if she had to, whether to give it now or send it afterwards in an envelope.

"Where does he serve?" she whispered to Lysevitch.

"Goodness knows," muttered Lysevitch, yawning.

She reflected that if Krylin used to visit her father and her uncle and respected them, it was probably not for nothing: apparently he had been charitable at their expense, serving in some charitable institution. As she said good-bye she slipped three hundred roubles into his hand; he seemed taken aback, and looked at her for a minute in silence with his pewtery eyes, but then seemed to understand and said:

"The receipt, honoured Anna Akimovna, you can only receive on the New Year."

Lysevitch had become utterly limp and heavy, and he staggered when Mishenka put on his overcoat.

As he went downstairs he looked like a man in the last stage of exhaustion, and it was evident that he would drop asleep as soon as he got into his sledge.

"Your Excellency," he said languidly to Krylin, stopping in the middle of the staircase, "has it ever happened to you to experience a feeling as though some unseen force were drawing you out longer and longer? You are drawn out and turn into the finest wire. Subjectively this finds expression in a curious voluptuous feeling which is impossible to compare with anything."

Anna Akimovna, standing at the top of the stairs, saw each of them give Mishenka a note.

" Good-bye ! Come again !" she called to them, and ran into her bedroom.

She quickly threw off her dress, that she was weary of already, put on a dressing-gown, and ran downstairs; and as she ran downstairs she laughed and thumped with her feet like a schoolboy; she had a great desire for mischief.

IV.

EVENING.

Auntie, in a loose print blouse, Varvarushka and two old women, were sitting in the diningroom having supper. A big piece of salt meat, a ham, and various savouries, were lying on the table before them, and clouds of steam were rising from the meat, which looked particularly fat and appetizing. Wine was not served on the lower storey, but they made up for it with a great number of spirits and home-made liqueurs. Agafyushka, the fat, white-skinned, well-fed cook, was standing with her arms crossed in the doorway and talking to the old women, and the dishes were being handed by the downstairs Masha, a dark girl with a crimson ribbon in her hair. The old women had had enough to eat before the morning was over, and an hour before supper had had tea and buns, and so they were now eating with effort—as if it were, from a sense of duty.

" Oh, my girl !" sighed Auntie, as Anna Akimovna ran into the dining-room and sat down beside her. " You've frightened me to death !"

Everyone in the house was pleased when Anna Akimovna was in good spirits and played pranks; this always reminded them that the old men were dead and that the old women had no authority in the house, and anyone could do as he liked without any fear of being sharply called to account for it. Only the two old women glanced askance at Anna Akimovna with amazement: she was humming, and it was a sin to sing at table.

" Our mistress, our beauty, our picture," Agafyushka began chanting with sugary sweetness " Our precious jewel ! The people, the people that have come to-day to look at our queen. Lord, have mercy upon us ! Generals, and officers and gentlemen. . . . I kept looking out of window and counting and counting till I gave it up."

" I'd as soon they did not come at all," said Auntie; she looked sadly at her niece and added: " They only waste the time for my poor orphan girl."

Anna Akimovna felt hungry, as she had eaten nothing since the morning. They poured her out some very bitter liqueur; she drank it off, and tasted the salt meat with mustard, and thought it extraordinarily nice. Then the downstairs Masha brought in the turkey, the pickled apples and the gooseberries. And that pleased her, too. There was only one thing that was disagreeable: there was a draught of hot air from the tiled stove; it was stiflingly close and everyone's cheeks were burning. After supper the cloth was taken off and plates of peppermint biscuits, walnuts, and raisins were brought in.

" You sit down, too . . . no need to stand there !" said Auntie to the cook.·

Agafyushka sighed and sat down to the table; Masha set a wineglass of liqueur before her, too, and Anna Akimovna began to feel as though Agafyushka's white neck were giving out heat like the stove. They were all talking of how difficult it was nowadays to get married, and saying that in old days, if men did not court beauty, they paid attention to money, but now there was no making out what they wanted; and while hunchbacks and cripples used to be left old maids, nowadays men would not have even the beautiful and wealthy. Auntie began to set this down to immorality, and said that people had no fear of God, but she suddenly remembered that Ivan Ivanitch, her brother, and Varvarushka—both people of holy life—had feared God, but all the same had had children on the sly, and had sent them to the Foundling Asylum. She pulled herself up and changed the conversation, telling them about a suitor she had once had, a factory hand, and how she had loved him, but her brothers had forced her to marry a widower, an ikon-painter, who, thank God, had died two years after. The downstairs Masha sat down to the table, too, and told them with a mysterious air that for the last week some unknown man with a black moustache, in a great-coat with an astrachan collar, had made his appearance every morning in the yard, had stared at the windows of the big house, and had gone on further—to the buildings; the man was all right, nice-looking. . . .

All this conversation made Anna Akimovna suddenly long to be married—long intensely, painfully; she felt as though she would give half her life and all her fortune only to know that upstairs there was a man who was closer to her than anyone in the world, that he loved her warmly and was missing her; and the thought of such closeness, ecstatic and inexpressible in words, troubled her soul. And the instinct of youth and health flattered her with lying assurances that the real poetry of life was not over but still to come, and she believed it, and leaning back in her chair (her hair fell down as she did so), she began laughing, and, looking at her, the others laughed, too. And it was a long time before this causeless laughter died down in the dining-room.

She was informed that the Stinging Beetle had come. This was a pilgrim woman called Pasha or Spiridonovna—a thin little woman of fifty, in a black dress with a white kerchief, with keen eyes, sharp nose, and a sharp chin; she had sly, viperish eyes and she looked as though she could see right through everyone. Her lips were shaped like a heart. Her viperishness and hostility to everyone had earned her the nickname of the Stinging Beetle.

Going into the dining-room without looking at anyone, she made for the ikons and chanted in a high voice " Thy Holy Birth," then she sang, " The Virgin to-day gives birth to the Son," then " Christ is born," then she turned round and bent a piercing gaze upon all of them.

"A happy Christmas," she said, and she kissed Anna Akimovna on the shoulder. "It's all I could do, all I could do to get to you, my kind friends." She kissed Auntie on the shoulder. "I should have come to you this morning, but I went in to some good people to rest on the way. 'Stay, Spiridonovna, stay,' they said, and I did not notice that evening was coming on."

As she did not eat meat, they gave her salmon and caviare. She ate looking from under her eyelids at the company, and drank three glasses of vodka. When she had finished she said a prayer and bowed down to Anna Akimovna's feet.

They began to play a game of "kings," as they had done the year before, and the year before that, and all the servants in both storeys crowded in at the doors to watch the game. Anna Akimovna fancied she caught a glimpse once or twice of Mishenka, with a patronizing smile on his face, among the crowd of peasant men and women. The first to be king was Stinging Beetle, and Anna Akimovna as the soldier paid her tribute; and then Auntie was king and Anna Akimovna was peasant, which excited general delight, and Agafyushka was prince, and was quite abashed with pleasure. Another game was got up at the other end of the table—played by the two Mashas, Varvarushka, and the sewing-maid Marfa Petrovna, who was waked on purpose to play "kings," and whose face looked cross and sleepy.

While they were playing they talked of men, and of how difficult it was to get a good husband nowadays, and which state was to be preferred—that of an old maid or a widow.

" You are a handsome, healthy, sturdy lass," said Stinging Beetle to Anna Akimovna. " But I can't make out for whose sake you are holding back."

" What's to be done if nobody will have me ?"

" Or maybe you have taken a vow to remain a maid ?" Stinging Beetle went on, as though she did not hear. " Well, that's a good deed. . . . Remain one," she repeated, looking intently and maliciously at her cards. " All right, my dear, remain one. . . . Yes . . . only maids, these saintly maids, are not all alike." She heaved a sigh and played the king. " Oh no, my girl, they are not all alike ! Some really watch over themselves like nuns, and butter would not melt in their mouths; and if such a one does sin in an hour of weakness, she is worried to death, poor thing ! so it would be a sin to condemn her. While others will go dressed in black and sew their shroud, and yet love rich old men on the sly. Yes, y-es, my canary birds, some hussies will bewitch an old man and rule over him, my doves, rule over him and turn his head; and when they've saved up money and lottery tickets enough, they will bewitch him to his death."

Varvarushka's only response to these hints was to heave a sigh and look towards the ikons. There was an expression of Christian meekness on her countenance.

" I know a maid like that, my bitterest enemy," Stinging Beetle went on, looking round at everyone

618

in triumph; " she is always sighing, too, and looking at the ikons, the she-devil.   When she used to
rule in a certain old man's house, if one went to
her she would give one a crust, and bid one bow
down to the ikons while she would sing: ' In conception Thou dost abide a Virgin . . . !'   On
holidays she will give one a bite, and on working
days she will reproach one for it.   But nowadays
I will make merry over her !   I will make as merry
as I please, my jewel."

Varvarushka glanced at the ikons again and
crossed herself.

" But no one will have me, Spiridonovna,"
said Anna Akimovna to change the conversation.
" What's to be done ?"

" It's your own fault.   You keep waiting for
highly educated gentlemen, but you ought to
marry one of your own sort, a merchant."

" We don't want a merchant," said Auntie, all
in a flutter.   " Queen of Heaven, preserve us !
A gentleman will spend your money, but then he
will be kind to you, you poor little fool.   But a
merchant will be so strict that you won't feel at
home in your own house.   You'll be wanting to
fondle him and he will be counting his money,
and when you sit down to meals with him, he'll
grudge you every mouthful, though it's your own,
the lout ! . . .   Marry a gentleman."

They all talked at once, loudly interrupting
one another, and Auntie tapped on the table
with the nutcrackers and said, flushed and
angry:

" We won't have a merchant; we won't have

one! If you choose a merchant I shall go to an almshouse."

"Sh! . . . Sh! . . . Hush!" cried Stinging Beetle; when all were silent she screwed up one eye and said: "Do you know what, Annushka, my birdie . . .? There is no need for you to get married really like everyone else. You're rich and free, you are your own mistress; but yet, my child, it doesn't seem the right thing for you to be an old maid. I'll find you, you know, some trumpery and simple-witted man. You'll marry him for appearances and then have your fling, bonny lass! You can hand him five thousand or ten maybe, and pack him off where he came from, and you will be mistress in your own house—you can love whom you like and no one can say anything to you. And then you can love your highly educated gentlemen. You'll have a jolly time!" Stinging Beetle snapped her fingers and gave a whistle.

"It's sinful," said Auntie.

"Oh, sinful," laughed Stinging Beetle. "She is educated, she understands. To cut someone's throat or bewitch an old man—that's a sin, that's true; but to love some charming young friend is not a sin at all. And what is there in it, really? There's no sin in it at all! The old pilgrim women have invented all that to make fools of simple folk. I, too, say everywhere it's a sin; I don't know myself why it's a sin." Stinging Beetle emptied her glass and cleared her throat. "Have your fling, bonny lass," this time evidently addressing herself. "For thirty years, wenches,

I have thought of nothing but sins and been afraid, but now I see I have wasted my time, I've let it slip by like a ninny! Ah, I have been a fool, a fool!" She sighed. "A woman's time is short and every day is precious. You are handsome, Annushka, and very rich; but as soon as thirty-five or forty strikes for you your time is up. Don't listen to anyone, my girl; live, have your fling till you are forty, and then you will have time to pray forgiveness—there will be plenty of time to bow down and to sew your shroud. A candle to God and a poker to the devil! You can do both at once! Well, how is it to be? Will you make some little man happy?"

"I will," laughed Anna Akimovna. "I don't care now; I would marry a working man."

"Well, that would do all right! Oh, what a fine fellow you would choose then!" Stinging Beetle screwed up her eyes and shook her head. "O—o—oh!"

"I tell her myself," said Auntie, "it's no good waiting for a gentleman, so she had better marry, not a gentleman, but someone humbler; anyway we should have a man in the house to look after things. And there are lots of good men. She might have someone out of the factory. They are all sober, steady men. . . . ."

"I should think so," Stinging Beetle agreed. "They are capital fellows. If you like, Aunt, I will make a match for her with Vassily Lebedinsky?"

"Oh, Vasya's legs are so long," said Auntie seriously. "He is so lanky. He has no looks."

There was laughter in the crowd by the door.

" Well, Pimenov ? Would you like to marry Pimenov ?" Stinging Beetle asked Anna Akimovna.

" Very good. Make a match for me with Pimenov."

" Really ?"

" Yes, do !" Anna Akimovna said resolutely, and she struck her fist on the table. " On my honour, I will marry him."

" Really ?"

Anna Akimovna suddenly felt ashamed that her cheeks were burning and that everyone was looking at her; she flung the cards together on the table and ran out of the room. As she ran up the stairs and, reaching the upper storey, sat down to the piano in the drawing-room, a murmur of sound reached her from below like the roar of the sea; most likely they were talking of her and of Pimenov, and perhaps Stinging Beetle was taking advantage of her absence to insult Varvarushka and was putting no check on her language.

The lamp in the big room was the only light burning in the upper storey, and it sent a glimmer through the door into the dark drawing-room. It was between nine and ten, not later. Anna Akimovna played a waltz, then another, then a third; she went on playing without stopping. She looked into the dark corner beyond the piano, smiled, and inwardly called to it, and the idea occurred to her that she might drive off to the town to see someone, Lysevitch for instance, and tell him what was passing in her heart. She wanted to talk without ceasing, to laugh, to play the fool, but the dark corner was sullenly silent, and all round in all the rooms of the upper storey it was still and desolate.

She was fond of sentimental songs, but she had a harsh, untrained voice, and so she only played the accompaniment and sang hardly audibly, just above her breath. She sang in a whisper one song after another, for the most part about love, separation, and frustrated hopes, and she imagined how she would hold out her hands to him and say with entreaty, with tears, " Pimenov, take this burden from me !" And then, just as though her sins had been forgiven, there would be joy and comfort in her soul, and perhaps a free, happy life would begin. In an anguish of anticipation she leant over the keys, with a passionate longing for the change in her life to come at once without delay, and was terrified at the thought that her old life would go on for some time longer. Then she played again and sang hardly above her breath, and all was stillness about her. There was no noise coming from downstairs now, they must have gone to bed. It had struck ten some time before. A long, solitary, wearisome night was approaching.

Anna Akimovna walked through all the rooms, lay down for a while on the sofa, and read in her study the letters that had come that evening; there were twelve letters of Christmas greetings and three anonymous letters. In one of them some workman complained in a horrible, almost illegible handwriting that Lenten oil sold in the factory shop was rancid and smelt of paraffin; in another, someone respectfully informed her that over a purchase of iron Nazaritch had lately taken a bribe of a thousand roubles from someone; in a third she was abused for her inhumanity.

The excitement of Christmas was passing off, and to keep it up Anna Akimovna sat down at the piano again and softly played one of the new waltzes, then she remembered how cleverly and creditably she had spoken at dinner to-day. She looked round at the dark windows, at the walls with the pictures, at the faint light that came from the big room, and all at once she began suddenly crying, and she felt vexed that she was so lonely, and that she had no one to talk to and consult. To cheer herself she tried to picture Pimenov in her imagination, but it was unsuccessful.

It struck twelve. Mishenka, no longer wearing his swallowtail but in his reefer jacket, came in, and without speaking lighted two candles; then he went out and returned a minute later with a cup of tea on a tray.

"What are you laughing at?" she asked, noticing a smile on his face.

"I was downstairs and heard the jokes you were making about Pimenov . . ." he said, and put his hand before his laughing mouth. "If he were sat down to dinner to-day with Viktor Nikolaitch and the general, he'd have died of fright." Mishenka's shoulders were shaking with laughter. "He doesn't know even how to hold his fork, I bet."

The footman's laughter and words, his reefer jacket and moustache, gave Anna Akimovna a feeling of uncleanness. She shut her eyes to avoid seeing him, and, against her own will, imagined Pimenov dining with Lysevitch and Krylin, and his timid, unintellectual figure seemed to her pitiful and helpless, and she felt repelled by it. And only now, for the first time in the whole day, she realized clearly that all she had said and thought about Pimenov and marrying a workman was nonsense, folly, and wilfulness. To convince herself of the opposite, to overcome her repulsion, she tried to recall what she had said at dinner, but now she could not see anything in it: shame at her own thoughts and actions, and the fear that she had said something improper during the day, and disgust at her own lack of spirit, overwhelmed her completely. She took up a candle and, as rapidly as if someone were pursuing her, ran downstairs, woke Spiridonovna, and began assuring her she had been joking. Then she went to her bedroom. Red-haired Masha, who was dozing in an arm-chair near the bed, jumped up and began shaking up the pillows. Her face was exhausted and sleepy, and her magnificent hair had fallen on one side.

" Tchalikov came again this evening," she said, yawning, " but I did not dare to announce him; he was very drunk. He says he will come again to-morrow."

" What does he want with me ?" said Anna Akimovna, and she flung her comb on the floor. " I won't see him, I won't."

She made up her mind she had no one left in life but this Tchalikov, that he would never leave off persecuting her, and would remind her every day how uninteresting and absurd her life was. So all she was fit for was to help the poor. Oh, how stupid it was !

She lay down without undressing, and sobbed with shame and depression: what seemed to her most vexatious and stupid of all was that her dreams that day about Pimenov had been right, lofty, honourable, but at the same time she felt that Lysevitch and even Krylin were nearer to her than Pimenov and all the workpeople taken together. She thought that if the long day she had just spent could have been represented in a picture, all that had been bad and vulgar—as, for instance, the dinner, the lawyer's talk, the game of " kings "—would have been true, while her dreams and talk about Pimenov would have stood out from the whole as something false, as out of drawing; and she thought, too, that it was too late to dream of happiness, that everything was over for her, and it was impossible to go back to the life when she had slept under the same quilt with her mother, or to devise some new special sort of life.

Red-haired Masha was kneeling before the bed, gazing at her in mournful perplexity; then she, too, began crying, and laid her face against her mistress's arm, and without words it was clear why she was so wretched.

" We are fools !" said Anna Akimovna, laughing and crying. "We are fools ! Oh, what fools we are !"

MIRE

I.

GRACEFULLY swaying in the saddle, a young man wearing the snow-white tunic of an officer rode into the great yard of the vodka distillery belonging to the heirs of M. E. Rothstein. The sun smiled carelessly on the lieutenant's little stars, on the white trunks of the birch-trees, on the heaps of broken glass scattered here and there in the yard. The radiant, vigorous beauty of a summer day lay over everything, and nothing hindered the sappy young green leaves from dancing gaily and winking at the clear blue sky. Even the dirty and soot-begrimed appearance of the brick-sheds and the stifling fumes of the distillery did not spoil the general good impression. The lieutenant sprang gaily out of the saddle, handed over his horse to a man who ran up, and stroking with his finger his delicate black moustaches, went in at the front door. On the top step of the old but light and softly carpeted staircase he was met by a maidservant with a haughty, not very youthful face. The lieutenant gave her his card without speaking.

As she went through the rooms with the card, the maid could see on it the name "Alexandr

627

Grigoryevitch Sokolsky." A minute later she came back and told the lieutenant that her mistress could not see him, as she was not feeling quite well. Sokolsky looked at the ceiling and thrust out his lower lip.

"How vexatious!" he said. "Listen, my dear," he said eagerly. "Go and tell Susanna Moiseyevna that it is very necessary for me to speak to her —very. I will only keep her one minute. Ask her to excuse me."

The maid shrugged one shoulder and went off languidly to her mistress.

"Very well!" she sighed, returning after a brief interval. "Please walk in!"

The lieutenant went with her through five or six large, luxuriously furnished rooms and a corridor, and finally found himself in a large and lofty square room, in which from the first step he was impressed by the abundance of flowers and plants and the sweet, almost revoltingly heavy fragrance of jasmine. Flowers were trained to trellis-work along the walls, screening the windows, hung from the ceiling, and were wreathed over the corners, so that the room was more like a greenhouse than a place to live in. Tits, canaries, and goldfinches chirruped among the green leaves and fluttered against the window-panes.

"Forgive me for receiving you here," the lieutenant heard in a mellow feminine voice with a burr on the letter *r* which was not without charm. "Yesterday I had a sick headache, and I'm trying to keep still to prevent its coming on again. What do you want?"

628

MIRE

Exactly opposite the entrance, he saw sitting in a big low chair, such as old men use, a woman in an expensive Chinese dressing-gown, with her head wrapped up, leaning back on a pillow. Nothing could be seen behind the woollen shawl in which she was muffled but a pale, long, pointed, somewhat aquiline nose, and one large dark eye. Her ample dressing-gown concealed her figure, but judging from her beautiful hand, from her voice, her nose, and her eye, she might be twenty-six or twenty-eight.

"Forgive me for being so persistent . . ." began the lieutenant, clinking his spurs. "Allow me to introduce myself: Sokolsky! I come with a message from my cousin, your neighbour, Alexey Ivanovitch Kryukov, who . . ."

"I know!" interposed Susanna Moiseyevna. "I know Kryukov. Sit down; I don't like anything big standing before me."

"My cousin charges me to ask you a favour," the lieutenant went on, clinking his spurs once more and sitting down. "The fact is, your late father made a purchase of oats from my cousin last winter, and a small sum was left owing. The payment only becomes due next week, but my cousin begs you most particularly to pay him—if possible, to-day."

As the lieutenant talked, he stole side-glances about him.

"Surely I'm not in her bedroom?" he thought.

In one corner of the room, where the foliage was thickest and tallest, under a pink awning like a funeral canopy, stood a bed not yet made, with the bedclothes still in disorder. Close by on two armchairs lay heaps of crumpled feminine garments. Petticoats and sleeves with rumpled lace and flounces were trailing on the carpet, on which here and there lay bits of white tape, cigarette-ends, and the papers of caramels. . . . Under the bed the toes, pointed and square, of slippers of all kinds peeped out in a long row. · And it seemed to the lieutenant that the scent of the jasmine came not from the flowers, but from the bed and the slippers.

" And what is the sum owing ?" asked Susanna Moiseyevna.

" Two thousand three hundred."

" Oho !" said the Jewess, showing another large black eye. " And you call that—a small sum ! However, it's just the same paying it to-day or paying it in a week, but I've had so many payments to make in the last two months since my father's death. . . . Such a lot of stupid business, it makes my head go round ! A nice idea ! I want to go abroad, and they keep forcing me to attend to these silly things. Vodka, oats . . ." she muttered, half closing her eyes, " oats, bills, percentages, or, as my head-clerk says, ' precentage.' . . . It's awful. Yesterday I simply turned the excise officer out. He pesters me with his Tralles. I said to him: ' Go to the devil with your Tralles ! I can't see anyone !' He kissed my hand and went away. I tell you what: can't your cousin wait two or three months ?"

" A cruel question !" laughed the lieutenant. " My cousin can wait a year, but it's I who cannot wait! You see, it's on my own account I'm acting, I ought to tell you. At all costs I must have money, and by ill-luck my cousin hasn't a rouble to spare. I'm forced to ride about and collect debts. I've just been to see a peasant, our tenant; here I'm now calling on you; from here I shall go on to somewhere else, and keep on like that until I get together five thousand roubles. I need money awfully!"

"Nonsense! What does a young man want with money? Whims, mischief. Why, have you been going in for dissipation? Or losing at cards? Or are you getting married?"

"You've guessed!" laughed the lieutenant, and rising slightly from his seat, he clinked his spurs. "I really am going to be married."

Susanna Moiseyevna looked intently at her visitor, made a wry face, and sighed.

"I can't make out what possesses people to get married!" she said, looking about her for her pocket-handkerchief. "Life is so short, one has so little freedom, and they must put chains on themselves!"

"Everyone has his own way of looking at things. . . ."

"Yes, yes, of course; everyone has his own way of looking at things. . . . But, I say, are you really going to marry someone poor? Are you passionately in love? And why must you have five thousand? Why won't four do, or three?"

"What a tongue she has!" thought the lieutenant, and answered: "The difficulty is that an officer is not allowed by law to marry till he is twenty-eight; if you choose to marry, you have to leave the Service or else pay a deposit of five thousand."

"Ah, now I understand. Listen. You said just now that everyone has his own way of looking at things. . . . Perhaps your fiancée is someone special and remarkable, but . . . but I am utterly unable to understand how any decent man can live with a woman. I can't for the life of me understand it. I have lived, thank the Lord, twenty-seven years, and I have never yet seen an endurable woman. They're all affected minxes, immoral, liars. . . . The only ones I can put up with are cooks and housemaids, but so-called ladies I won't let come within shooting distance of me. But, thank God, they hate me and don't force themselves on me! If one of them wants money she sends her husband, but nothing will induce her to come herself, not from pride—no, but from cowardice; she's afraid of my making a scene. Oh, I understand their hatred very well! Rather! I openly display what they do their very utmost to conceal from God and man. How can they help hating me? No doubt you've heard bushels of scandal about me already. . . ."

"I've only arrived here so lately . . ."

"Tut, tut, tut! . . . I see from your eyes! But your brother's wife, surely she primed you for this expedition? Think of letting a young man come to see such an awful woman without warning him—how could she? Ha, ha! . . . But tell me, how is your brother? He's a fine fellow, such a handsome man! . . . I've seen

632

him several times at mass. Why do you look at me like that ? I very often go to church ! We all have the same God. To an educated person externals matter less than the idea. . . . That's so, isn't it ?"

" Yes, of course . . ." smiled the lieutenant.

" Yes, the idea. . . . But you are not a bit like your brother. You are handsome, too, but your brother is a great deal better-looking. There's wonderfully little likeness !"

" That's quite natural; he's not my brother, but my cousin."

" Ah, to be sure ! So you must have the money to-day ? Why to-day ?"

" My furlough is over in a few days."

" Well, what's to be done with you !" sighed Susanna Moiseyevna. " So be it. I'll give you the money, though I know you'll abuse me for it afterwards. You'll quarrel with your wife after you are married, and say: ' If that mangy Jewess hadn't given me the money, I should perhaps have been as free as a bird to-day !' Is your fiancée pretty ?"

" Oh yes. . . ."

" H'm ! . . . Anyway, better something, if it's only beauty, than nothing. Though however beautiful a woman is, it can never make up to her husband for her silliness."

" That's original !" laughed the lieutenant. " You are a woman yourself, and such a woman-hater !"

" A woman . . ." smiled Susanna. " It's not my fault that God has cast me into this mould, is it? I'm no more to blame for it than you are for having moustaches. The violin is not responsible for the choice of its case. I am very fond of myself, but when anyone reminds me that I am a woman, I begin to hate myself. Well, you can go away, and I'll dress. Wait for me in the drawing-room."

The lieutenant went out, and the first thing he did was to draw a deep breath, to get rid of the heavy scent of jasmine, which had begun to irritate his throat and to make him feel giddy.

"What a strange woman!" he thought, looking about him. "She talks fluently, but . . . far too much, and too freely. She must be neurotic."

The drawing-room, in which he was standing now, was richly furnished, and had pretensions to luxury and style. There were dark bronze dishes with patterns in relief, views of Nice and the Rhine on the tables, old-fashioned sconces, Japanese statuettes, but all this striving after luxury and style only emphasized the lack of taste which was glaringly apparent in the gilt cornices, the gaudy wall-paper, the bright velvet table-cloths, the common oleographs in heavy frames. The bad taste of the general effect was the more complete from the lack of finish and the overcrowding of the room, which gave one a feeling that something was lacking, and that a great deal should have been thrown away. It was evident that the furniture had not been bought all at once, but had been picked up at auctions and other favourable opportunities.

Heaven knows what taste the lieutenant could boast of, but even he noticed one characteristic peculiarity about the whole place, which no luxury or style could efface—a complete absence of all trace of womanly, careful hands, which, as we all know, give a warmth, poetry, and snugness to the furnishing of a room. There was a chilliness about it such as one finds in waiting-rooms at stations, in clubs, and foyers at the theatres.

There was scarcely anything in the room definitely Jewish, except, perhaps, a big picture of the meeting of Jacob and Esau. The lieutenant looked round about him, and, shrugging his shoulders, thought of his strange, new acquaintance, of her free-and-easy manners, and her way of talking. But then the door opened, and in the doorway appeared the lady herself, in a long black dress, so slim and tightly laced that her figure looked as though it had been turned in a lathe. Now the lieutenant saw not only the nose and eyes, but also a thin white face, a head black and as curly as lamb's-wool. She did not attract him, though she did not strike him as ugly. He had a prejudice against un-Russian faces in general, and he considered, too, that the lady's white face, the whiteness of which for some reason suggested the cloying scent of jasmine, did not go well with her little black curls and thick eyebrows; that her nose and ears were astoundingly white, as though they belonged to a corpse, or had been moulded out of transparent wax. When she smiled she showed pale gums as well as her teeth, and he did not like that either.

"Anæmic debility . . ." he thought; "she's probably as nervous as a turkey."

"Here I am! Come along!" she said, going on rapidly ahead of him and pulling off the yellow leaves from the plants as she passed.

"I'll give you the money directly, and if you like I'll give you some lunch. Two thousand three hundred roubles! After such a good stroke of business you'll have an appetite for your lunch. Do you like my rooms? The ladies about here declare that my rooms always smell of garlic. With that culinary gibe their stock of wit is exhausted. I hasten to assure you that I've no garlic, even in the cellar. And one day when a doctor came to see me who smelt of garlic, I asked him to take his hat and go and spread his fragrance elsewhere. There is no smell of garlic here, but the place does smell of drugs. My father lay paralyzed for a year and a half, and the whole house smelt of medicine. A year and a half! I was sorry to lose him, but I'm glad he's dead: he suffered so!"

She led the officer through two rooms similar to the drawing-room, through a large reception hall, and came to a stop in her study, where there was a lady's writing-table covered with little knick-knacks. On the carpet near it several books lay strewn about, opened and folded back. Through a small door leading from the study he saw a table laid for lunch.

Still chatting, Susanna took out of her pocket a bunch of little keys and unlocked an ingeniously made cupboard with a curved, sloping lid. When the lid was raised the cupboard emitted a plaintive note which made the lieutenant think of an Æolian harp. Susanna picked out another key and clicked another lock.

" I have underground passages here and secret doors," she said, taking out a small morocco portfolio. " It's a funny cupboard, isn't it ? And in this portfolio I have a quarter of my fortune. Look how podgy it is ! You won't strangle me, will you ?"

Susanna raised her eyes to the lieutenant and laughed good-naturedly. The lieutenant laughed too.

" She's rather jolly," he thought, watching the keys flashing between her fingers.

" Here it is," she said, picking out the key of the portfolio. " Now, Mr. Creditor, trot out the IOU. What a silly thing money is really ! How paltry it is, and yet how women love it ! I am a Jewess, you know, to the marrow of my bones. I am passionately fond of Shmuls and Yankels, but how I loathe that passion for gain in our Semitic blood. They hoard and they don't know what they are hoarding for. One ought to live and enjoy oneself, but they're afraid of spending an extra farthing. In that way I am more like an hussar than a Shmul. I don't like money to be kept long in one place. And altogether I fancy I'm not much like a Jewess. Does my accent give me away much, eh ?"

" What shall I say ?" mumbled the lieutenant. " You speak good Russian, but you do roll your *r*s."

Susanna laughed and put the little key in the lock of the portfolio. The lieutenant took out of his pocket a little roll of IOUs and laid them with a notebook on the table.

" Nothing betrays a Jew as much as his accent," Susanna went on, looking gaily at the lieutenant. " However much he twists himself into a Russian or a Frenchman, ask him to say ' feather ' and he will say ' fedder ' . . . but I pronounce it correctly: ' Feather ! feather ! feather !' "

Both laughed.

" By Jove, she's very jolly !" thought Sokolsky.

Susanna put the portfolio on a chair, took a step towards the lieutenant, and bringing her face close to his, went on gaily:

" Next to the Jews I love no people so much as the Russian and the French. I did not do much at school and I know no history, but it seems to me that the fate of the world lies in the hands of those two nations. I lived a long time abroad. . . . I spent six months in Madrid. . . . I've gazed my fill at the public, and the conclusion I've come to is that there are no decent peoples except the Russian and the French. Take the languages, for instance. . . . The German language is like the neighing of horses; as for the English . . . you can't imagine anything stupider. Fight—feet—foot ! Italian is only pleasant when they speak it slowly. If you listen to Italians gabbling you get the effect of the Jewish jargon. And the Poles ? Mercy on us ! There's no language so disgusting ! ' Nie pieprz, Pietrze, pieprzem wieprza, bo możesz przepieprzyé wieprza pieprzem.' That means: ' Don't pepper a sucking pig with pepper, Pyotr, or perhaps you'll over-pepper the sucking pig with pepper.' Ha, ha, ha!'"

Susanna Moiseyevna rolled her eyes and broke into such a pleasant, infectious laugh that the lieutenant, looking at her, went off into a loud and merry peal of laughter. She took the visitor by the button, and went on:

" You don't like Jews, of course . . . they've many faults, like all nations. I don't dispute that. But are the Jews to blame for it? No, it's not the Jews who are to blame, but the Jewish women! They are narrow-minded, greedy; there's no sort of poetry about them, they're dull. . . . You have never lived with a Jewess, so you don't know how charming it is!" Susanna Moiseyevna pronounced the last words with deliberate emphasis and with no eagerness or laughter. She paused as though frightened at her own openness, and her face was suddenly distorted in a strange, unaccountable way. Her eyes stared at the lieutenant without blinking, her lips parted and showed clenched teeth. Her whole face, her throat, and even her bosom, seemed quivering with a spiteful, catlike expression. Still keeping her eyes fixed on her visitor, she rapidly bent to one side, and swiftly, like a cat, snatched something from the table. All this was the work of a few seconds. Watching her movements, the lieutenant saw five fingers crumple up his IOUs and caught a glimpse of the white rustling paper as it disappeared in her clenched fist. Such an extraordinary transition from good-

natured laughter to crime so appalled him that
he turned pale and stepped back. . . .

And she, still keeping her frightened, searching
eyes upon him, felt along her hip with her clenched
fist for her pocket. Her fist struggled convulsively
for the pocket, like a fish in the net, and could not
find the opening. In another moment the IOUs
would have vanished in the recesses of her feminine
garments, but at that point the lieutenant uttered
a faint cry, and, moved more by instinct than
reflection, seized the Jewess by her arm above the
clenched fist. Showing her teeth more than ever,
she struggled with all her might and pulled her
hand away. Then Sokolsky put his right arm
firmly round her waist, and the other round her
chest, and a struggle followed. Afraid of out-
raging her sex or hurting her, he tried only to
prevent her moving, and to get hold of the fist
with the IOUs; but she wriggled like an eel in
his arms with her supple, flexible body, struck
him in the chest with her elbows, and scratched
him, so that he could not help touching her all
over, and was forced to hurt her and disregard
her modesty.

" How unusual this is ! How strange !" he
thought, utterly amazed, hardly able to believe
his senses, and feeling rather sick from the scent
of jasmine.

In silence, breathing heavily, stumbling against
the furniture, they moved about the room.
Susanna was carried away by the struggle. She
flushed, closed her eyes, and forgetting herself,
once even pressed her face against the face of

the lieutenant, so that there was a sweetish taste left on his lips. At last he caught hold of her clenched hand. . . . Forcing it open, and not finding the papers in it, he let go the Jewess. With flushed faces and dishevelled hair, they looked at one another, breathing hard. The spiteful, cat-like expression on the Jewess's face was gradually replaced by a good-natured smile. She burst out laughing, and turning on one foot, went towards the room where lunch was ready. The lieutenant moved slowly after her. She sat down to the table, and, still flushed and breathing hard, tossed off half a glass of port.

" Listen "—the lieutenant broke the silence—" I hope you are joking ?"

" Not a bit of it," she answered, thrusting a piece of bread into her mouth.

" H'm ! . . . How do you wish me to take all this ?"

" As you choose. Sit down and have lunch !"

" But . . . it's dishonest !"

" Perhaps. But don't trouble to give me a sermon; I have my own way of looking at things."

" Won't you give them back ?"

" Of course not ! If you were a poor un-fortunate man, with nothing to eat, then it would be a different matter. But—he wants to get married !"

" It's not my money, you know; it's my cousin's !"

" And what does your cousin want with money ? To get fashionable clothes for his wife ? But I really don't care whether your *belle-sœur* has dresses or not."

The lieutenant had ceased to remember that he was in a strange house with an unknown lady, and did not trouble himself with decorum. He strode up and down the room, scowled and nervously fingered his waistcoat. The fact that the Jewess had lowered herself in his eyes by her dishonest action made him feel bolder and more free-and-easy.

"The devil knows what to make of it!" he muttered. "Listen. I shan't go away from here until I get the IOUs!"

"Ah, so much the better," laughed Susanna. "If you stay here for good, it will make it livelier for me."

Excited by the struggle, the lieutenant looked at Susanna's laughing, insolent face, at her munching mouth, at her heaving bosom, and grew bolder and more audacious. Instead of thinking about the IOUs he began for some reason recalling with a sort of relish his cousin's stories of the Jewess's romantic adventures, of her free way of life, and these reminiscences only provoked him to greater audacity. Impulsively he sat down beside the Jewess and thinking no more of the IOUs began to eat. . . .

"Will you have vodka or wine?" Susanna asked with a laugh. "So you will stay till you get the IOUs? Poor fellow! How many days and nights you will have to spend with me, waiting for those IOUs! Won't your fiancée have something to say about it?"

II.

Five hours had passed. The lieutenant's cousin, Alexey Ivanovitch Kryukov, was walking about the rooms of his country-house in his dressing-gown and slippers, and looking impatiently out of window. He was a tall, sturdy man, with a large black beard and a manly face; and as the Jewess had truly said, he was handsome, though he had reached the age when men are apt to grow too stout, puffy, and bald. By mind and temperament he was one of those natures in which the Russian intellectual classes are so rich: warm-hearted, good-natured, well-bred, having some knowledge of the arts and sciences, some faith, and the most chivalrous notions about honour, but indolent and lacking in depth. He was fond of good eating and drinking, was an ideal whist-player, was a connoisseur in women and horses, but in other things he was apathetic and sluggish as a seal, and to rouse him from his lethargy something extraordinary and quite revolting was needed, and then he would forget everything in the world and display intense activity; he would fume and talk of a duel, write a petition of seven pages to a Minister, gallop at breakneck speed about the district, call someone publicly " a scoundrel," would go to law, and so on.

" How is it our Sasha's not back yet ?" he kept asking his wife, glancing out of window. " Why, it's dinner-time !"

After waiting for the lieutenant till six o'clock,

they sat down to dinner. When supper-time came, however, Alexey Ivanovitch was listening to every footstep, to every sound of the door, and kept shrugging his shoulders.

"Strange!" he said. "The rascally dandy must have stayed on at the tenant's."

As he went to bed after supper, Kryukov made up his mind that the lieutenant was being entertained at the tenant's, where after a festive evening he was staying the night.

Alexandr Grigoryevitch only returned next morning. He looked extremely crumpled and confused.

"I want to speak to you alone . . ." he said mysteriously to his cousin.

They went into the study. The lieutenant shut the door, and he paced for a long time up and down before he began to speak.

"Something's happened, my dear fellow," he began, "that I don't know how to tell you about. You wouldn't believe it . . ."

And blushing, faltering, not looking at his cousin, he told what had happened with the IOUs. Kryukov, standing with his feet wide apart and his head bent, listened and frowned.

"Are you joking?" he asked.

"How the devil could I be joking? It's no joking matter!"

"I don't understand!" muttered Kryukov, turning crimson and flinging up his hands. "It's positively . . . immoral on your part. Before your very eyes a hussy is up to the devil knows what, a serious crime, plays a nasty trick, and you go and kiss her!"

644

" But I can't understand myself how it happened !" whispered the lieutenant, blinking guiltily. " Upon my honour, I don't understand it ! It's the first time in my life I've come across such a monster ! It's not her beauty that does for you, not her mind, but that . . . you understand . . . insolence, cynicism. . . ."

" Insolence, cynicism . . . it's unclean ! If you've such a longing for insolence and cynicism, you might have picked a sow out of the mire and have devoured her alive. It would have been cheaper, anyway ! Instead of two thousand three hundred !"

" You do express yourself elegantly !" said the lieutenant, frowning. " I'll pay you back the two thousand three hundred !"

" I know you'll pay it back, but it's not a question of money ! Damn the money ! What revolts me is your being such a limp rag . . . such filthy feebleness ! And engaged ! With a fiancée !"

" Don't speak of it . . ." said the lieutenant, blushing. " I loathe myself as it is. I should like to sink into the earth. It's sickening and vexatious that I shall have to bother my aunt for that five thousand. . . ."

Kryukov continued for some time longer expressing his indignation and grumbling, then, as he grew calmer, he sat down on the sofa and began to jeer at his cousin.

" You young officers !" he said with contemptuous irony. " Nice bridegrooms."

Suddenly he leapt up as though he had been

stung, stamped his foot, and ran about the study.

" No, I'm not going to leave it like that !" he said, shaking his fist. " I will have those IOUs, I will ! I'll give it her ! One doesn't beat women, but I'll break every bone in her body. . . . I'll pound her to a jelly ! I'm not a lieutenant ! You won't touch me with insolence or cynicism ! No-o-o, damn her ! Mishka !" he shouted, " run and tell them to get the racing droshky out for me !"

Kryukov dressed rapidly, and, without heeding the agitated lieutenant, got into the droshky, and with a wave of his hand resolutely raced off to Susanna Moiseyevna. For a long time the lieutenant gazed out of window at the clouds of dust that rolled after his cousin's droshky, stretched, yawned, and went to his own room. A quarter of an hour later he was sound asleep.

At six o'clock he was waked up and summoned to dinner.

" How nice this is of Alexey !" his cousin's wife greeted him in the dining-room. " He keeps us waiting for dinner."

" Do you mean to say he's not come back yet ?" yawned the lieutenant. " H'm ! . . . he's probably gone round to see the tenant."

But Alexey Ivanovitch was not back by supper either. His wife and Sokolsky decided that he was playing cards at the tenant's and would most likely stay the night there. What had happened was not what they had supposed, however.

Kryukov returned next morning, and without

greeting anyone, without a word, dashed into his study.

"Well?" whispered the lieutenant, gazing at him round-eyed.

Kryukov waved his hand and gave a snort.

"Why, what's the matter? What are you laughing at?"

Kryukov flopped on the sofa, thrust his head in the pillow, and shook with suppressed laughter. A minute later he got up, and looking at the surprised lieutenant, with his eyes full of tears from laughing, said:

"Close the door. Well . . . she *is* a fe-e-male, I beg to inform you!"

"Did you get the IOUs?"

Kryukov waved his hand and went off into a peal of laughter again.

"Well! she is a female!" he went on. "*Merci* for the acquaintance, my boy! She's a devil in petticoats. I arrived; I walked in like such an avenging Jove, you know, that I felt almost afraid of myself. . . . I frowned, I scowled, even clenched my fists to be more awe-inspiring. . . . 'Jokes don't pay with me, madam!' said I, and more in that style. And I threatened her with the law and with the Governor. To begin with she burst into tears, said she'd been joking with you, and even took me to the cupboard to give me the money. Then she began arguing that the future of Europe lies in the hands of the French and the Russians, swore at women. . . . Like you, I listened, fascinated, ass that I was. . . . She kept singing the praises of my beauty, patted me

647

on the arm near the shoulder, to see how strong I was, and . . . and as you see, I've only just got away from her! Ha, ha! She's enthusiastic about you!"

"You're a nice fellow!" laughed the lieutenant. "A married man! highly respected. . . . Well, aren't you ashamed? Disgusted? Joking apart, though, old man, you've got your Queen Tamara in your own neighbourhood. . . ."

"In my own neighbourhood! Why, you wouldn't find another such chameleon in the whole of Russia! I've never seen anything like it in my life, though I know a good bit about women, too. I have known regular devils in my time, but I never met anything like this. It is, as you say, by insolence and cynicism she gets over you. What is so attractive in her is the diabolical suddenness, the quick transitions, the swift shifting hues. . . . Brrr! And the IOU—phew! Write it off for lost. We are both great sinners, we'll go halves in our sin. I shall put down to you not two thousand three hundred, but half of it. Mind, tell my wife I was at the tenant's."

Kryukov and the lieutenant buried their heads in the pillows, and broke into laughter; they raised their heads, glanced at one another, and again subsided into their pillows.

"Engaged! A lieutenant!" Kryukov jeered.

"Married!" retorted Sokolsky. "Highly respected! Father of a family!"

At dinner they talked in veiled allusions, winked at one another, and, to the surprise of the others, were continually gushing with laughter into their dinner-napkins. After dinner, still in the best of spirits, they dressed up as Turks, and, running after one another with guns, played at soldiers with the children. In the evening they had a long argument. The lieutenant maintained that it was mean and contemptible to accept a dowry with your wife, even when there was passionate love on both sides. Kryukov thumped the table with his fists and declared that this was absurd, and that a husband who did not like his wife to have property of her own was an egoist and a despot. Both shouted, boiled over, did not understand each other, drank a good deal, and in the end, picking up the skirts of their dressing-gowns, went to their bedrooms. They soon fell asleep and slept soundly.

Life went on as before, even, sluggish and free from sorrow. The shadows lay on the earth, thunder pealed from the clouds, from time to time the wind moaned plaintively, as though to prove that nature, too, could lament, but nothing troubled the habitual tranquillity of these people. Of Susanna Moiseyevna and the IOUs they said nothing. Both of them felt, somehow, ashamed to speak of the incident aloud. Yet they remembered it and thought of it with pleasure, as of a curious farce, which life had unexpectedly and casually played upon them, and which it would be pleasant to recall in old age.

On the sixth or seventh day after his visit to the Jewess, Kryukov was sitting in his study in the morning writing a congratulatory letter to his aunt. Alexandr Grigoryevitch was walking to and fro near the table in silence. The lieutenant had slept badly that night; he woke up depressed, and now he felt bored. He paced up and down, thinking of the end of his furlough, of his fiancée, who was expecting him, of how people could live all their lives in the country without feeling bored. Standing at the window, for a long time he stared at the trees, smoked three cigarettes one after another, and suddenly turned to his cousin.

"I have a favour to ask you, Alyosha," he said. "Let me have a saddle-horse for the day. . . ."

Kryukov looked searchingly at him and continued his writing with a frown.

"You will, then?" asked the lieutenant.

Kryukov looked at him again, then deliberately drew out a drawer in the table, and taking out a thick roll of notes, gave it to his cousin.

"Here's five thousand . . ." he said. "Though it's not my money, yet, God bless you, it's all the same. I advise you to send for post-horses at once and go away. Yes, really!"

The lieutenant in his turn looked searchingly at Kryukov and laughed.

"You've guessed right, Alyosha," he said, reddening. "It was to her I meant to ride. Yesterday evening when the washerwoman gave me that damned tunic, the one I was wearing then, and it smelt of jasmine, why . . . I felt I must go!"

"You must go away."

"Yes, certainly. And my furlough's just over. I really will go to-day! Yes, by Jove! However

long one stays, one has to go in the end. . . .
I'm going!"

The post-horses were brought after dinner the
same day; the lieutenant said good-bye to the
Kryukovs and set off, followed by their good wishes.

Another week passed. It was a dull but hot
and heavy day. From early morning Kryukov
walked aimlessly about the house, looking out
of window, or turning over the leaves of albums,
though he was sick of the sight of them already.
When he came across his wife or children, he began
grumbling crossly. It seemed to him, for some
reason that day, that his children's manners were
revolting, that his wife did not know how to look
after the servants, that their expenditure was quite
disproportionate to their income. All this meant
that "the master" was out of humour.

After dinner, Kryukov, feeling dissatisfied with
the soup and the roast meat he had eaten, ordered
out his racing droshky. He drove slowly out of
the courtyard, drove at a walking pace for a
quarter of a mile, and stopped.

"Shall I . . . drive to her . . . that devil?"
he thought, looking at the leaden sky.

And Kryukov positively laughed, as though it
were the first time that day he had asked himself
that question. At once the load of boredom was
lifted from his heart, and there rose a gleam of
pleasure in his lazy eyes. He lashed the horse. . . .

All the way his imagination was picturing how
surprised the Jewess would be to see him, how he
would laugh and chat, and come home feeling
refreshed. . . .

" Once a month one needs something to brighten one up . . . something out of the common round," he thought, " something that would give the stagnant organism a good shaking up, a reaction . . . whether it's a drinking bout, or . . . Susanna. One can't get on without it."

It was getting dark when he drove into the yard of the vodka distillery. From the open windows of the owner's house came sounds of laughter and singing:

"'Brighter than lightning, more burning than flame. . . '"

sang a powerful, mellow bass voice.

" Aha ! she has visitors," thought Kryukov.

And he was annoyed that she had visitors.

" Shall I go back ?" he thought with his hand on the bell, but he rang all the same, and went up the familiar staircase. From the entry he glanced into the reception hall. There were about five men there—all landowners and officials of his acquaintance; one, a tall, thin gentleman, was sitting at the piano, singing, and striking the keys with his long, thin fingers. The others were listening and grinning with enjoyment. Kryukov looked himself up and down in the looking-glass, and was about to go into the hall, when Susanna Moiseyevna herself darted into the entry, in high spirits and wearing the same black dress. . . . Seeing Kryukov, she was petrified for an instant, then she uttered a little scream and beamed with delight.

" Is it you ?" she said, clutching his hand. " What a surprise !"

652

MIRE

" Here she is !" smiled Kryukov, putting his arm round her waist. " Well ! Does the destiny of Europe still lie in the hands of the French and the Russians ?"

" I'm so glad," laughed the Jewess, cautiously removing his arm. " Come, go into the hall; they're all friends there. . . . I'll go and tell them to bring you some tea. Your name's Alexey, isn't it ? Well, go in, I'll come directly. . . ."

She blew him a kiss and ran out of the entry, leaving behind her the same sickly smell of jasmine. Kryukov raised his head and walked into the hall. He was on terms of friendly intimacy with all the men in the room, but scarcely nodded to them; they, too, scarcely responded, as though the place in which they met were not quite decent, and as though they were in tacit agreement with one another that it was more suitable for them not to recognize one another.

From the hall Kryukov walked into the drawing-room, and from it into a second drawing-room. On the way he met three or four other guests, also men whom he knew, though they barely recognized him. Their faces were flushed with drink and merriment. Alexey Ivanovitch glanced furtively at them and marvelled that these men, respectable heads of families, who had known sorrow and privation, could demean themselves to such pitiful, cheap gaiety ! He shrugged his shoulders, smiled and walked on.

" There are places," he reflected, " where a sober man feels sick, and a drunken man rejoices.

653

I remember I never could go to the operetta or the gipsies when I was sober: wine makes a man more good-natured and reconciles him with vice. . . ."

Suddenly he stood still, petrified, and caught hold of the door-post with both hands. At the writing-table in Susanna's study was sitting Lieutenant Alexandr Grigoryevitch. He was discussing something in an undertone with a fat, flabby-looking Jew, and seeing his cousin, flushed crimson and looked down at an album.

The sense of decency was stirred in Kryukov and the blood rushed to his head. Overwhelmed with amazement, shame, and anger, he walked up to the table without a word. Sokolsky's head sank lower than ever. His face worked with an expression of agonizing shame.

"Ah, it's you, Alyosha!" he articulated, making a desperate effort to raise his eyes and to smile. "I called here to say good-bye, and, as you see. . . . But to-morrow I am certainly going."

"What can I say to him? What?" thought Alexey Ivanovitch. "How can I judge him since I'm here myself?"

And clearing his throat without uttering a word, he went out slowly.

"'Call her not heavenly, and leave her on earth. . . .'"

The bass was singing in the hall. A little while after, Kryukov's racing droshky was bumping along the dusty road.

EASTER EVE

I was standing on the bank of the River Goltva, waiting for the ferry-boat from the other side. At ordinary times the Goltva is a humble stream of moderate size, silent and pensive, gently glimmering from behind thick reeds; but now a regular lake lay stretched out before me. The waters of spring, running riot, had overflowed both banks and flooded both sides of the river for a long distance, submerging vegetable gardens, hayfields and marshes, so that it was no unusual thing to meet poplars and bushes sticking out above the surface of the water and looking in the darkness like grim solitary crags.

The weather seemed to me magnificent. It was dark, yet I could see the trees, the water and the people. . . . The world was lighted by the stars, which were scattered thickly all over the sky. I don't remember ever seeing so many stars. Literally one could not have put a finger in between them. There were some as big as a goose's egg, others tiny as hempseed. . . . They had come out for the festival procession, every one of them, little and big, washed, renewed and joyful, and every one of them was softly twinkling its beams. The sky was reflected in the water; the stars were bathing in its dark depths and trembling with the quivering eddies. The air was warm and still. . . . Here and there, far away on the further bank in the impenetrable darkness, several bright red lights were gleaming. . . .

A couple of paces from me I saw the dark silhouette of a peasant in a high hat, with a thick knotted stick in his hand.

" How long the ferry-boat is in coming !" I said.

" It is time it was here," the silhouette answered.

" You are waiting for the ferry-boat, too ?"

" No, I am not," yawned the peasant—" I am waiting for the illumination. I should have gone, but, to tell you the truth. I haven't the five kopecks for the ferry."

" I'll give you the five kopecks."

" No; I humbly thank you. . . . With that five kopecks put up a candle for me over there in the monastery. . . . That will be more interesting, and I will stand here. What can it mean, no ferry-boat, as though it had sunk in the water !"

The peasant went up to the water's edge, took the rope in his hands, and shouted: " Ieronim ! Ieron—im !"

As though in answer to his shout, the slow peal of a great bell floated across from the further bank. The note was deep and low, as from the thickest string of a double bass; it seemed as though the darkness itself had hoarsely uttered it. At once there was the sound of a cannon shot. It rolled away in the darkness and ended somewhere in the far distance behind me. The peasant took off his hat and crossed himself.

" Christ is risen," he said.

Before the vibrations of the first peal of the bell had time to die away in the air a second sounded, after it at once a third, and the darkness was filled with an unbroken quivering clamour. Near the red lights fresh lights flashed, and all began moving together and twinkling restlessly.

" Ieron—im !" we heard a hollow prolonged shout.

" They are shouting from the other bank," said the peasant, " so there is no ferry there either. Our Ieronim has gone to sleep."

The lights and the velvety chimes of the bell drew one towards them. . . . I was already beginning to lose patience and grow anxious, but behold at last, staring into the dark distance, I saw the outline of something very much like a gibbet. It was the long-expected ferry. It moved towards us with such deliberation that if it had not been that its lines grew gradually more definite, one might have supposed that it was standing still or moving to the other bank.

" Make haste ! Ieronim !" shouted my peasant. " The gentleman's tired of waiting !"

The ferry crawled to the bank, gave a lurch and stopped with a creak. A tall man in a monk's cassock and a conical cap stood on it, holding the rope.

" Why have you been so long ?" I asked, jumping upon the ferry.

" Forgive me, for Christ's sake," Ieronim answered gently. " Is there no one else ?"

" No one. . . ."

Ieronim took hold of the rope in both hands, bent himself to the figure of a mark of interrogation, and gasped. The ferry-boat creaked and gave a lurch. The outline of the peasant in the high hat began slowly retreating from me—so the ferry was moving off. Ieronim soon drew himself up and began working with one hand only. We were silent, gazing towards the bank to which we were floating. There the illumination for which the peasant was waiting had begun. At the water's edge barrels of tar were flaring like huge camp fires. Their reflections, crimson as the rising moon, crept to meet us in long broad streaks. The burning barrels lighted up their own smoke and the long shadows of men flitting about the fire; but further to one side and behind them from where the velvety chime floated there was still the same unbroken black gloom. All at once, cleaving the darkness, a rocket zigzagged in a golden ribbon up the sky; it described an arc and, as though broken to pieces against the sky, was scattered crackling into sparks. There was a roar from the bank like a far-away hurrah.

" How beautiful !" I said.

" Beautiful beyond words !" sighed Ieronim. " Such a night, sir ! Another time one would pay no attention to the fireworks, but to-day one rejoices in every vanity. Where do you come from ?"

I told him where I came from.

" To be sure . . . a joyful day to-day. . . ." Ieronim went on in a weak sighing tenor like the

voice of a convalescent. " The sky is rejoicing
and the earth and what is under the earth. All
the creatures are keeping holiday. Only tell me,
kind sir, why, even in the time of great rejoicing,
a man cannot forget his sorrows ?"

I fancied that this unexpected question was to
draw me into one of those endless religious conversations which bored and idle monks are so
fond of. I was not disposed to talk much, and
so I only asked:

" What sorrows have you, father ?"

" As a rule only the same as all men, kind sir,
but to-day a special sorrow has happened in the
monastery: at mass, during the reading of the
Bible, the monk and deacon Nikolay died."

" Well, it's God's will !" I said, falling into the
monastic tone. " We must all die. To my mind,
you ought to rejoice indeed. . . . They say if
anyone dies at Easter he goes straight to the
kingdom of heaven."

" That's true."

We sank into silence. The figure of the peasant
in the high hat melted into the lines of the bank.
The tar barrels were flaring up more and more.

" The Holy Scripture points clearly to the
vanity of sorrow, and so does reflection," said
Ieronim, breaking the silence; " but why does the
heart grieve and refuse to listen to reason ? Why
does one want to weep bitterly ?"

Ieronim shrugged his shoulders, turned to me
and said quickly:

" If I died, or anyone else, it would not be worth
notice, perhaps; but, you see, Nikolay is dead !

No one else but Nikolay! Indeed, it's hard to believe that he is no more! I stand here on my ferry-boat and every minute I keep fancying that he will lift up his voice from the bank. He always used to come to the bank and call to me that I might not be afraid on the ferry. He used to get up from his bed at night on purpose for that. He was a kind soul. My God! how kindly and gracious! Many a mother is not so good to her child as Nikolay was to me! Lord, save his soul!"

Ieronim took hold of the rope, but turned to me again at once.

"And such a lofty intelligence, your honour," he said in a vibrating voice. "Such a sweet and harmonious tongue! Just as they will sing immediately at early matins: 'Oh lovely! oh sweet is Thy Voice!' Besides all other human qualities, he had, too, an extraordinary gift!"

"What gift?" I asked.

The monk scrutinized me, and as though he had convinced himself that he could trust me with a secret, he laughed good-humouredly.

"He had a gift for writing hymns of praise," he said. "It was a marvel, sir; you couldn't call it anything else! You will be amazed if I tell you about it. Our Father Archimandrite comes from Moscow, the Father Sub-Prior studied at the Kazan academy, we have wise monks and elders, but, would you believe it, no one could write them; while Nikolay, a simple monk, a deacon, had not studied anywhere, and had not even any outer appearance of it, but he wrote them! A marvel! a real marvel!" Ieronim clasped his hands and, completely forgetting the rope, went on eagerly:

" The Father Sub-Prior has great difficulty in composing sermons; when he wrote the history of the monastery he worried all the brotherhood and drove a dozen times to town, while Nikolay wrote canticles ! Hymns of praise ! That's a very different thing from a sermon or a history !"

" Is it difficult to write them ?" I asked.

" There's great difficulty !" Ieronim wagged his head. " You can do nothing by wisdom and holiness if God has not given you the gift. The monks who don't understand argue that you only need to know the life of the saint for whom you are writing the hymn, and to make it harmonize with the other hymns of praise. But that's a mistake, sir. Of course, anyone who writes canticles must know the life of the saint to perfection, to the least trivial detail. To be sure, one must make them harmonize with the other canticles and know where to begin and what to write about. To give you an instance, the first response begins everywhere with ' the chosen ' or ' the elect.' . . . The first line must always begin with the ' angel.' In the canticle of praise to Jesus the Most Sweet, if you are interested in the subject, it begins like this: ' Of angels Creator and Lord of all powers !' In the canticle to the Holy Mother of God: ' Of angels the foremost sent down from on high,' to Nikolay, the Wonder-worker—' An angel in semblance, though in substance a man,' and so on. Everywhere you begin with the angel. Of course, it would be impossible without making them harmonize, but the lives of the saints and conformity with the others is not what matters; what matters is the beauty and sweetness of it. Everything must be harmonious, brief and complete. There must be in every line softness, graciousness and tenderness; not one word should be harsh or rough or unsuitable. It must be written so that the worshipper may rejoice at heart and weep, while his mind is stirred and he is thrown into a tremor. In the canticle to the Holy Mother are the words: ' Rejoice, O Thou too high for human thought to reach ! Rejoice, O Thou too deep for angels' eyes to fathom !' In another place in the same canticle: ' Rejoice, O tree that bearest the fair fruit of light that is the food of the faithful ! Rejoice, O tree of gracious spreading shade, under which there is shelter for multitudes !' "

Ieronim hid his face in his hands, as though frightened at something or overcome with shame, and shook his head.

" Tree that bearest the fair fruit of light . . . tree of gracious spreading shade. . . ." he muttered. " To think that a man should find words like those ! Such a power is a gift from God ! For brevity he packs many thoughts into one phrase, and how smooth and complete it all is ! ' Light-radiating torch to all that be . . .' comes in the canticle to Jesus the Most Sweet. ' Light-radiating !' There is no such word in conversation or in books, but you see he invented it, he found it in his mind ! Apart from the smoothness and grandeur of language, sir, every line must be beautified in every way; there must be flowers and lightning and wind and sun and all the objects

662

of the visible world. And every exclamation ought to be put so as to be smooth and easy for the ear. ' Rejoice, thou flower of heavenly growth !' comes in the hymn to Nikolay the Wonder-worker. It's not simply ' heavenly flower,' but ' flower of heavenly growth.' It's smoother so and sweet to the ear. That was just as Nikolay wrote it ! exactly like that ! I can't tell you how he used to write !"

" Well, in that case it is a pity he is dead," I said; " but let us get on, father, or we shall be late."

Ieronim started and ran to the rope; they were beginning to peal all the bells. Probably the procession was already going on near the monastery, for all the dark space behind the tar barrels was now dotted with moving lights.

" Did Nikolay print his hymns ?" I asked Ieronim.

" How could he print them ?" he sighed. " And, indeed, it would be strange to print them. What would be the object ? No one in the monastery takes any interest in them. They don't like them. They knew Nikolay wrote them, but they let it pass unnoticed. No one esteems new writings nowadays, sir !"

" Were they prejudiced against him ?"

" Yes, indeed. If Nikolay had been an elder perhaps the brethren would have been interested, but he wasn't forty, you know. There were some who laughed and even thought his writing a sin."

" What did he write them for ?"

" Chiefly for his own comfort. Of all the brotherhood, I was the only one who read his

663

hymns. I used to go to him in secret, that no one else might know of it, and he was glad that I took an interest in them. He would embrace me, stroke my head, speak to me in caressing words as to a little child. He would shut his cell, make me sit down beside him, and begin to read. . . ."

Ieronim left the rope and came up to me.

" We were dear friends in a way," he whispered, looking at me with shining eyes. " Where he went I would go. If I were not there he would miss me. And he cared more for me than for anyone, and all because I used to weep over his hymns. It makes me sad to remember. Now I feel just like an orphan or a widow. You know, in our monastery they are all good people, kind and pious, but . . . there is no one with softness and refinement, they are just like peasants. They all speak loudly, and tramp heavily when they walk; they are noisy, they clear their throats, but Nikolay always talked softly, caressingly, and if he noticed that anyone was asleep or praying he would slip by like a fly or a gnat. His face was tender, compassionate. . . ."

Ieronim heaved a deep sigh and took hold of the rope again. We were by now approaching the bank. We floated straight out of the darkness and stillness of the river into an enchanted realm, full of stifling smoke, crackling lights and uproar. By now one could distinctly see people moving near the tar barrels. The flickering of the lights gave a strange, almost fantastic, expression to their figures and red faces. From time to time one caught among the heads and faces a glimpse of a horse's head motionless as though cast in copper.

"They'll begin singing the Easter hymn directly, . . ." said Ieronim, "and Nikolay is gone; there is no one to appreciate it. . . . There was nothing written dearer to him than that hymn. He used to take in every word! You'll be there, sir, so notice what is sung; it takes your breath away!"

"Won't you be in church, then?"

"I can't; . . . I have to work the ferry. . . ."

"But won't they relieve you?"

"I don't know. . . . I ought to have been relieved at eight; but, as you see, they don't come! . . . And I must own I should have liked to be in the church. . . ."

"Are you a monk?"

"Yes . . . that is, I am a lay-brother."

The ferry ran into the bank and stopped. I thrust a five-kopeck piece into Ieronim's hand for taking me across, and jumped on land. Immediately a cart with a boy and a sleeping woman in it drove creaking onto the ferry. Ieronim, with a faint glow from the lights on his figure, pressed on the rope, bent down to it, and started the ferry back. . . .

I took a few steps through mud, but a little farther walked on a soft freshly trodden path. This path led to the dark monastery gates, that looked like a cavern through a cloud of smoke, through a disorderly crowd of people, unharnessed horses, carts and chaises. All this crowd was rattling, snorting, laughing, and the crimson light and wavering shadows from the smoke flickered over it all. . . . A perfect chaos! And in this hubbub the people yet found room to load a little cannon and to sell cakes. There was no less commotion on the other side of the wall in the monastery precincts, but there was more regard for decorum and order. Here there was a smell of juniper and incense. They talked loudly, but there was no sound of laughter or snorting. Near the tombstones and crosses people pressed close to one another with Easter cakes and bundles in their arms. Apparently many had come from a long distance for their cakes to be blessed and now were exhausted. Young lay brothers, making a metallic sound with their boots, ran busily along the iron slabs that paved the way from the monastery gates to the church door. They were busy and shouting on the belfry, too

"What a restless night!" I thought. "How nice!"

One was tempted to see the same unrest and sleeplessness in all nature, from the night darkness to the iron slabs, the crosses on the tombs and the trees under which the people were moving to and fro. But nowhere was the excitement and restlessness so marked as in the church. An unceasing struggle was going on in the entrance between the inflowing stream and the outflowing stream. Some were going in, others going out and soon coming back again to stand still for a little and begin moving again. People were scurrying from place to place, lounging about as though they were looking for something. The stream flowed from the entrance all round the church, disturbing even the front rows, where persons of weight and dignity were standing. There could be no thought of concentrated prayer. There were no prayers at all, but a sort of continuous, childishly irresponsible joy, seeking a pretext to break out and vent itself in some movement, even in senseless jostling and shoving.

The same unaccustomed movement is striking in the Easter service itself. The altar gates are flung wide open, thick clouds of incense float in the air near the candelabra; wherever one looks there are lights, the gleam and splutter of candles. . . . There is no reading; restless and lighthearted singing goes on to the end without ceasing. After each hymn the clergy change their vestments and come out to burn incense, which is repeated every ten minutes.

I had no sooner taken a place, when a wave rushed from in front and forced me back. A tall thick-set deacon walked before me with a long red candle; the grey-headed archimandrite in his golden mitre hurried after him with the censer. When they had vanished from sight the crowd squeezed me back to my former position. But ten minutes had not passed before a new wave burst on me, and again the deacon appeared. This time he was followed by the Father Sub-Prior, the man who, as Ieronim had told me, was writing the history of the monastery.

As I mingled with the crowd and caught the infection of the universal joyful excitement, I felt unbearably sore on Ieronim's account. Why did they not send someone to relieve him? Why could not someone of less feeling and less susceptibility go on the ferry? "Lift up thine eyes, O Sion, and look around," they sang in the choir, " for thy children have come to thee as to a beacon

667

of divine light from north and south, and from east and from the sea. . . ."

I looked at the faces; they all had a lively expression of triumph, but not one was listening to what was being sung and taking it in, and not one was "holding his breath." Why was not Ieronim released ? I could fancy Ieronim standing meekly somewhere by the wall, bending forward and hungrily drinking in the beauty of the holy phrase. All this that glided by the ears of people standing by me he would have eagerly drunk in with his delicately sensitive soul, and would have been spell-bound to ecstasy, to holding his breath, and there would not have been a man happier than he in all the church. Now he was plying to and fro over the dark river and grieving for his dead friend and brother.

The wave surged back. A stout smiling monk, playing with his rosary and looking round behind him, squeezed sideways by me, making way for a lady in a hat and velvet cloak. A monastery servant hurried after the lady, holding a chair over our heads.

I came out of the church. I wanted to have a look at the dead Nikolay, the unknown canticle writer. I walked about the monastery wall, where there was a row of cells, peeped into several windows, and, seeing nothing, came back again. I do not regret now that I did not see Nikolay; God knows, perhaps if I had seen him I should have lost the picture my imagination paints for me now. I imagine that lovable poetical figure, solitary and not understood, who went out at nights to call to Ieronim over the water, and filled his hymns with flowers, stars and sunbeams, as a pale timid man with soft, mild, melancholy features. His eyes must have shone, not only with intelligence, but with kindly tenderness and that hardly restrained childlike enthusiasm which I could hear in Ieronim's voice when he quoted to me passages from the hymns.

When we came out of church after mass it was no longer night. The morning was beginning. The stars had gone out and the sky was a morose greyish blue. The iron slabs, the tombstones and the buds on the trees were covered with dew. There was a sharp freshness in the air. Outside the precincts I did not find the same animated scene as I had beheld in the night. Horses and men looked exhausted, drowsy, scarcely moved, while nothing was left of the tar barrels but heaps of black ash. When anyone is exhausted and sleepy he fancies that nature, too, is in the same condition. It seemed to me that the trees and the young grass were asleep. It seemed as though even the bells were not pealing so loudly and gaily as at night. The restlessness was over, and of the excitement nothing was left but a pleasant weariness, a longing for sleep and warmth.

Now I could see both banks of the river; a faint mist hovered over it in shifting masses. There was a harsh cold breath from the water. When I jumped on to the ferry, a chaise and some two dozen men and women were standing on it already. The rope, wet and as I fancied drowsy, stretched far away across the broad river and in places disappeared in the white mist.

" Christ is risen ! Is there no one else ?" asked a soft voice.

I recognized the voice of Ieronim. There was no darkness now to hinder me from seeing the monk. He was a tall narrow-shouldered man of five-and-thirty, with large rounded features, with half-closed listless-looking eyes and an unkempt wedge-shaped beard. He had an extraordinarily sad and exhausted look.

" They have not relieved you yet ?" I asked in surprise.

" Me ?" he answered, turning to me his chilled and dewy face with a smile. " There is no one to take my place now till morning. They'll all be going to the Father Archimandrite's to break the fast directly."

With the help of a little peasant in a hat of reddish fur that looked like the little 'wooden tubs in which honey is sold, he threw his weight on the rope; they gasped simultaneously, and the ferry started.

We floated across, disturbing on the way the lazily rising mist. Everyone was silent. Ieronim worked mechanically with one hand. He slowly passed his mild lustreless eyes over us; then his glance rested on the rosy face of a young merchant's wife with black eyebrows, who was standing on the ferry beside me silently shrinking from the mist that wrapped her about. He did not take his eyes off her face all the way.

There was little that was masculine in that prolonged gaze. It seemed to me that Ieronim was looking in the woman's face for the soft and tender features of his dead friend.

A DREARY STORY

FROM THE NOTEBOOK OF AN OLD MAN

I.

THERE is in Russia an emeritus Professor Nikolay Stepanovitch, a chevalier and privy councillor; he has so many Russian and foreign decorations that when he has occasion to put them on the students nickname him " The Ikonstand." His acquaintances are of the most aristocratic; for the last twenty-five or thirty years, at any rate, there has not been one single distinguished man of learning in Russia with whom he has not been intimately acquainted. There is no one for him to make friends with nowadays; but if we turn to the past, the long list of his famous friends winds up with such names as Pirogov, Kavelin, and the poet Nekrasov, all of whom bestowed upon him a warm and sincere affection. He is a member of all the Russian and of three foreign universities. And so on, and so on. All that and a great deal more that might be said makes up what is called my " name."

That is my name as known to the public. In Russia it is known to every educated man, and abroad it is mentioned in the lecture-room with

671

the addition " honoured and distinguished." It
is one of those fortunate names to abuse which or
to take which in vain, in public or in print, is
considered a sign of bad taste. And that is as it
should be. You see, my name is closely associated
with the conception of a highly distinguished man
of great gifts and unquestionable usefulness. I
have the industry and power of endurance of a
camel, and that is important, and I have talent,
which is even more important. Moreover, while
I am on this subject, I am a well-educated, modest,
and honest fellow. I have never poked my nose
into literature or politics; I have never sought
popularity in polemics with the ignorant; I have
never made speeches either at public dinners or
at the funerals of my friends. . . . In fact, there
is no slur on my learned name, and there is no
complaint one can make against it. It is fortunate.

The bearer of that name, that is I, see myself
as a man of sixty-two, with a bald head, with false
teeth, and with an incurable tic douloureux. I
am myself as dingy and unsightly as my name is
brilliant and splendid. My head and my hands
tremble with weakness; my neck, as Turgenev says
of one of his heroines, is like the handle of a double
bass; my chest is hollow; my shoulders narrow;
when I talk or lecture, my mouth turns down at
one corner; when I smile, my whole face is covered
with aged-looking, deathly wrinkles. There is
nothing impressive about my pitiful figure; only,
perhaps, when I have an attack of tic douloureux
my face wears a peculiar expression, the sight of
which must have roused in everyone the grim and

impressive thought, "Evidently that man will soon die."

I still, as in the past, lecture fairly well; I can still, as in the past, hold the attention of my listeners for a couple of hours. My fervour, the literary skill of my exposition, and my humour, almost efface the defects of my voice, though it is harsh, dry, and monotonous as a praying beggar's. I write poorly. That bit of my brain which presides over the faculty of authorship refuses to work. My memory has grown weak; there is a lack of sequence in my ideas, and when I put them on paper it always seems to me that I have lost the instinct for their organic connection; my construction is monotonous; my language is poor and timid. Often I write what I do not mean; I have forgotten the beginning when I am writing the end. Often I forget ordinary words, and I always have to waste a great deal of energy in avoiding superfluous phrases and unnecessary parentheses in my letters, both unmistakable proofs of a decline in mental activity. And it is noteworthy that the simpler the letter the more painful the effort to write it. At a scientific article I feel far more intelligent and at ease than at a letter of congratulation or a minute of proceedings. Another point: I·find it easier to write German or English than to write Russian.

As regards my present manner of life, I must give a foremost place to the insomnia from which I have suffered of late. If I were asked what constituted the chief and fundamental feature of my existence now, I should answer, Insomnia.

As in the past, from habit I undress and go to bed
exactly at midnight. I fall asleep quickly, but
before two o'clock I wake up and feel as though
I had not slept at all. Sometimes I get out of
bed and light a lamp. For an hour or two I walk
up and down the room looking at the familiar
photographs and pictures. When I am weary of
walking about, I sit down to my table. I sit
motionless, thinking of nothing, conscious of no
inclination; if a book is lying before me, I mechanically move it closer and read it without any
interest—in that way not long ago I mechanically
read through in one night a whole novel, with the
strange title " The Song the Lark was Singing ";
or to occupy my attention I force myself to count
to a thousand; or I imagine the face of one of my
colleagues and begin trying to remember in what
year and under what circumstances he entered
the service. I like listening to sounds. Two
rooms away from me my daughter Liza says something rapidly in her sleep, or my wife crosses the
drawing-room with a candle and invariably drops
the matchbox; or a warped cupboard creaks; or
the burner of the lamp suddenly begins to
hum—and all these sounds, for some reason, excite
me

To lie awake at night means to be at every
moment conscious of being abnormal, and so I
look forward with impatience to the morning and
the day when I have a right to be awake. Many
wearisome hours pass before the cock crows in the
yard. He is my first bringer of good tidings. As
soon as he crows I know that within an hour the

porter will wake up below, and, coughing angrily, will go upstairs to fetch something. And then a pale light will begin gradually glimmering at the windows, voices will sound in th street. . . .

The day begins for me with the entrance of my wife. She comes in to me in her petticoat, before she has done her hair, but after she has washed, smelling of flower-scented eau-de-Cologne, looking as though she had come in by chance. Every time she says exactly the same thing: " Excuse me, I have just come for a minute. . . . Have you had a bad night again ?"

Then she puts out the lamp, sits down near the table, and begins talking. I am no prophet, but I know what she will talk about. Every morning it is exactly the same thing. Usually, after anxious inquiries concerning my health, she suddenly mentions our son who is an officer serving at Warsaw. After the twentieth of each month we send him fifty roubles, and that serves as the chief topic of our conversation.

" Of course it is difficult for us," my wife would sigh, " but until he is completely on his own feet it is our duty to help him. The boy is among strangers, his pay is small. . . . However, if you like, next month we won't send him fifty, but forty. What do you think ?"

Daily experience might have taught my wife that constantly talking of our expenses does not reduce them, but my wife refuses to learn by experience, and regularly every morning discusses our officer son, and tells me that bread, thank God, is cheaper, while sugar is a halfpenny dearer—

with a tone and an air as though she were communicating interesting news.

I listen, mechanically assent, and, probably because I have had a bad night, strange and inappropriate thoughts intrude themselves upon me. I gaze at my wife and wonder like a child. I ask myself in perplexity, is it possible that this old, very stout, ungainly woman, with her dull expression of petty anxiety and alarm about daily bread, with eyes dimmed by continual brooding over debts and money difficulties, who can talk of nothing but expenses and who smiles at nothing but things getting cheaper—is it possible that this woman is no other than the slender Varya whom I fell in love with so passionately for her fine, clear intelligence, for her pure soul, her beauty, and, as Othello his Desdemona, for her " sympathy " for my studies ? Could that woman be no other than the Varya who had once borne me a son ?

I look with strained attention into the face of this flabby, spiritless, clumsy old woman, seeking in her my Varya, but of her past self nothing is left but her anxiety over my health and her manner of calling my salary " our salary," and my cap " our cap." It is painful for me to look at her, and, to give her what little comfort I can, I let her say what she likes, and say nothing even when she passes unjust criticisms on other people or pitches into me for not having a private practice or not publishing textbooks.

Our conversation always ends in the same way. My wife suddenly remembers with dismay that I have not had my tea.

"What am I thinking about, sitting here?" she says, getting up. "The samovar has been on the table ever so long, and here I stay gossiping. My goodness! how forgetful I am growing!"

She goes out quickly, and stops in the doorway to say:

"We owe Yegor five months' wages. Did you know it? You mustn't let the servants' wages run on; how many times I have said it! It's much easier to pay ten roubles a month than fifty roubles every five months!"

As she goes out, she stops to say:

"The person I am sorriest for is our Liza. The girl studies at the Conservatoire, always mixes with people of good position, and goodness knows how she is dressed. Her fur coat is in such a state she is ashamed to show herself in the street. If she were somebody else's daughter it wouldn't matter, but of course everyone knows that her father is a distinguished professor a privy councillor."

And having reproached me with my rank and reputation, she goes away at last. That is how my day begins. It does not improve as it goes on.

As I am drinking my tea, my Liza comes in wearing her fur coat and her cap, with her music in her hand, already quite ready to go to the Conservatoire. She is two-and-twenty. She looks younger, is pretty, and rather like my wife in her young days. She kisses me tenderly on my forehead and on my hand, and says:

"Good-morning, papa; are you quite well?"

As a child she was very fond of ice-cream, and

I used often to take her to a confectioner's. Ice-cream was for her the type of everything delightful. If she wanted to praise me she would say: "You are as nice as cream, papa." We used to call one of her little fingers "pistachio ice," the next, "cream ice," the third "raspberry," and so on. Usually when she came in to say good-morning to me I used to sit her on my knee, kiss her little fingers, and say:

"Creamy ice . . . pistachio . . . lemon. . . ."

And now, from old habit, I kiss Liza's fingers and mutter: "Pistachio . . . cream . . . lemon . . ." but the effect is utterly different. I am cold as ice and I am ashamed. When my daughter comes in to me and touches my forehead with her lips I start as though a bee had stung me on the head, give a forced smile, and turn my face away. Ever since I have been suffering from sleeplessness, a question sticks in my brain like a nail. My daughter often sees me, an old man and a distinguished man, blush painfully at being in debt to my footman; she sees how often anxiety over petty debts forces me to lay aside my work and to walk up and down the room for hours together, thinking; but why is it she never comes to me in secret to whisper in my ear: "Father, here is my watch, here are my bracelets, my earrings, my dresses. . . . Pawn them all; you want money . . ."? How is it that, seeing how her mother and I are placed in a false position and do our utmost to hide our poverty from people, she does not give up her expensive pleasure of music lessons? I would not accept her watch nor her bracelets, nor the sacrifice of her lessons—God forbid! That isn't what I want.

I think at the same time of my son, the officer at Warsaw. He is a clever, honest, and sober fellow. But that is not enough for me. I think if I had an old father, and if I knew there were moments when he was put to shame by his poverty, I should give up my officer's commission to somebody else, and should go out to earn my living as a workman. Such thoughts about my children poison me. What is the use of them? It is only a narrow-minded or embittered man who can harbour evil thoughts about ordinary people because they are not heroes. But enough of that!

At a quarter to ten I have to go and give a lecture to my dear boys. I dress and walk along the road which I have known for thirty years, and which has its history for me. Here is the big grey house with the chemist's shop; at this point there used to stand a little house, and in it was a beershop; in that beershop I thought out my thesis and wrote my first love-letter to Varya. I wrote it in pencil, on a page headed " Historia morbi." Here there is a grocer's shop; at one time it was kept by a little Jew, who sold me cigarettes on credit; then by a fat peasant woman, who liked the students because " every one of them has a mother "; now there is a red-haired shopkeeper sitting in it, a very stolid man who drinks tea from a copper teapot. And here are the gloomy gates of the University, which have long needed doing up; I see the bored porter in his sheep-skin, the broom, the drifts of snow. . . .

On a boy coming fresh from the provinces and imagining that the temple of science must really be a temple, such gates cannot make a healthy impression. Altogether the dilapidated condition of the University buildings, the gloominess of the corridors, the griminess of the walls, the lack of light, the dejected aspect of the steps, the hat-stands and the benches, take a prominent position among predisposing causes in the history of Russian pessimism. . . . Here is our garden . . . I fancy it has grown neither better nor worse since I was a student. I don't like it. It would be far more sensible if there were tall pines and fine oaks growing here instead of sickly-looking lime-trees, yellow acacias, and skimpy pollard lilacs. The student, whose state of mind is in the majority of cases created by his surroundings, ought in the place where he is studying to see facing him at every turn nothing but what is lofty, strong, and elegant. . . . God preserve him from gaunt trees, broken windows, grey walls, and doors covered with torn American leather !

When I go to my own entrance the door is flung wide open, and I am met by my colleague, contemporary, and namesake, the porter Nikolay. As he lets me in he clears his throat and says:

" A frost, your Excellency !"

Or, if my great-coat is wet:

" Rain, your Excellency !"

Then he runs on ahead of me and opens all the doors on my way. In my study he carefully takes off my fur coat, and while doing so manages to tell me some bit of University news. Thanks to the close intimacy existing between all the University porters and beadles, he knows everything that goes on in the four faculties, in the office, in the rector's private room, in the library. What does he not know? When in an evil day a rector or a dean, for instance, retires, I hear him in conversation with the young porters mention the candidates for the post, explain that such a one would not be confirmed by the minister, that another would himself refuse to accept it, then drop into fantastic details concerning mysterious papers received in the office, secret conversations alleged to have taken place between the minister and the trustee, and so on. With the exception of these details, he almost always turns out to be right. His estimates of the candidates, though original, are very correct, too. If one wants to know in what year someone read his thesis, entered the service, retired, or died, then summon to your assistance the vast memory of that soldier, and he will not only tell you the year, the month and the day, but will furnish you also with the details that accompanied this or that event. Only one who loves can remember like that.

He is the guardian of the University traditions. From the porters who were his predecessors he has inherited many legends of University life, has added to that wealth much of his own gained during his time of service, and if you care to hear he will tell you many long and intimate stories. He can tell one about extraordinary sages who knew *everything*, about remarkable students who did not sleep for weeks, about numerous martyrs

681

and victims of science; with him good triumphs over evil, the weak always vanquishes the strong, the wise man the fool, the humble the proud, the young the old. There is no need to take all these fables and legends for sterling coin; but filter them, and you will have left what is wanted: our fine traditions and the names of real heroes, recognized as such by all.

In our society the knowledge of the learned world consists of anecdotes of the extraordinary absent-mindedness of certain old professors, and two or three witticisms variously ascribed to Gruber, to me, and to Babukin. For the educated public that is not much. If it loved science, learned men, and students, as Nikolay does, its literature would long ago have contained whole epics, records of sayings and doings such as, unfortunately, it cannot boast of now.

After telling me a piece of news, Nikolay assumes a severe expression, and conversation about business begins. If any outsider could at such times overhear Nikolay's free use of our terminology, he might perhaps imagine that he was a learned man disguised as a soldier. And, by the way, the rumours of the erudition of the University porters are greatly exaggerated. It is true that Nikolay knows more than a hundred Latin words, knows how to put the skeleton together, sometimes prepares the apparatus and amuses the students by some long, learned quotation, but the by no means complicated theory of the circulation of the blood, for instance, is as much a mystery to him now as it was twenty years ago.

682

A DREARY STORY

At the table in my study, bending low over some book or preparation, sits Pyotr Ignatyevitch, my demonstrator, a modest and industrious but by no means clever man of five-and-thirty, already bald and corpulent; he works from morning to night, reads a lot, remembers well everything he has read—and in that way he is not a man, but pure gold; in all else he is a carthorse or, in other words, a learned dullard. The carthorse characteristics that show his lack of talent are these: his outlook is narrow and sharply limited by his speciality; outside his special branch he is simple as a child.

"Fancy! what a misfortune! They say Skobelev is dead."

Nikolay crosses himself, but Pyotr Ignatyevitch turns to me and asks:

"What Skobelev is that?"

Another time—somewhat earlier—I told him that Professor Perov was dead. Good Pyotr Ignatyevitch asked:

"What did he lecture on?"

I believe if Patti had sung in his very ear, if a horde of Chinese had invaded Russia, if there had been an earthquake, he would not have stirred a limb, but screwing up his eye, would have gone on calmly looking through his microscope. What is he to Hecuba or Hecuba to him, in fact? I would give a good deal to see how this dry stick sleeps with his wife at night.

Another characteristic is his fanatical faith in the infallibility of science, and, above all, of everything written by the Germans. He believes in

himself, in his preparations; knows the object of
life, and knows nothing of the doubts and disappointments that turn the hair of talent grey.
He has a slavish reverence for authorities and a
complete lack of any desire for independent
thought. To change his convictions is difficult,
to argue with him impossible. How is one to
argue with a man who is firmly persuaded that
medicine is the finest of sciences, that doctors are
the best of men, and that the traditions of the
medical profession are superior to those of any
other? Of the evil past of medicine only one
tradition has been preserved—the white tie still
worn by doctors; for a learned—in fact, for any
educated man the only traditions that can exist are
those of the University as a whole, with no distinction between medicine, law, etc. But it would
be hard for Pyotr Ignatyevitch to accept these
facts, and he is ready to argue with you till the
day of judgment.

I have a clear picture in my mind of his future.
In the course of his life he will prepare many·
hundreds of chemicals of exceptional purity; he
will write a number of dry and very accurate
memoranda, will make some dozen conscientious
translations, but he won't do anything striking.
To do that one must have imagination, inventive-
ness, the gift of insight, and Pyotr Ignatyevitch
has nothing of the kind. In short, he is not a
master in science, but a journeyman.

Pyotr Ignatyevitch, Nikolay, and I, talk in
subdued tones. We are not quite ourselves.
There is always a peculiar feeling when one hears

through the doors a murmur as of the sea from the lecture-theatre. In the course of thirty years I have not grown accustomed to this feeling, and I experience it every morning. I nervously button up my coat, ask Nikolay unnecessary questions, lose my temper. . . . It is just as though I were frightened; it is not timidity, though, but something different which I can neither describe nor find a name for.

Quite unnecessarily, I look at my watch and say: " Well, it's time to go in."

And we march into the room in the following order: foremost goes Nikolay, with the chemicals and apparatus or with a chart; after him I come; and then the carthorse follows humbly, with hanging head; or, when necessary, a dead body is carried in first on a stretcher, followed by Nikolay, and so on. On my entrance the students all stand up, then they sit down, and the sound as of the sea is suddenly hushed. Stillness reigns.

I know what I am going to lecture about, but I don't know how I am going to lecture, where I am going to begin or with what I am going to end. I haven't a single sentence ready in my head. But I have only to look round the lecture-hall (it is built in the form of an amphitheatre) and utter the stereotyped phrase, " Last lecture we stopped at . . ." when sentences spring up from my soul in a long string, and I am carried away by my own eloquence. I speak with irresistible rapidity and passion, and it seems as though there were no force which could check the flow of my words. To lecture well—that is, with profit to the listeners and without boring them—one must have, besides talent, experience and a special knack; one must possess a clear conception of one's own powers, of the audience to which one is lecturing, and of the subject of one's lecture. Moreover, one must be a man who knows what he is doing; one must keep a sharp lookout, and not for one second lose sight of what lies before one.

A good conductor, interpreting the thought of the composer, does twenty things at once: reads the score, waves his baton, watches the singer, makes a motion sideways, first to the drum then to the wind-instruments, and so on. I do just the same when I lecture. Before me a hundred and fifty faces, all unlike one another; three hundred eyes all looking straight into my face. My object is to dominate this many-headed monster. If every moment as I lecture I have a clear vision of the degree of its attention and its power of comprehension, it is in my power. The other foe I have to overcome is in myself. It is the infinite variety of forms, phenomena, laws, and the multitude of ideas of my own and other people's conditioned by them. Every moment I must have the skill to snatch out of that vast mass of material what is most important and necessary, and, as rapidly as my words flow, clothe my thought in a form in which it can be grasped by the monster's intelligence, and may arouse its attention, and at the same time one must keep a sharp lookout that one's thoughts are conveyed, not just as they come, but in a certain order, essential for the correct composition of the picture I wish to sketch. Further, I endeavour to make my diction literary, my definitions brief and precise, my wording, as far as possible, simple and eloquent. Every minute I have to pull myself up and remember that I have only an hour and forty minutes at my disposal. In short, one has one's work cut out. At one and the same minute one has to play the part of savant and teacher and orator, and it's a bad thing if the orator gets the upper hand of the savant or of the teacher in one, or *vice versa*.

You lecture for a quarter of an hour, for half an hour, when you notice that the students are beginning to look at the ceiling, at Pyotr Ignatye-vitch; one is feeling for his handkerchief, another shifts in his seat, another smiles at his thoughts. . . . That means that their attention is flagging. Something must be done. Taking advantage of the first opportunity, I make some pun. A broad grin comes on to a hundred and fifty faces, the eyes shine brightly, the sound of the sea is audible for a brief moment. . . . I laugh too. Their attention is refreshed, and I can go on.

No kind of sport, no kind of game or diversion, has ever given me such enjoyment as lecturing. Only at lectures have I been able to abandon myself entirely to passion, and have understood that inspiration is not an invention of the poets, but exists in real life, and I imagine Hercules after the most piquant of his exploits felt just such voluptuous exhaustion as I experience after every lecture.

That was in old times. Now at lectures I feel

687

nothing but torture. Before half an hour is over
I am conscious of an overwhelming weakness in
my legs and my shoulders. I sit down in my
chair, but I am not accustomed to lecture sitting
down; a minute later I get up and go on standing,
then sit down again. There is a dryness in my
mouth, my voice grows husky, my head begins to
go round. . . . To conceal my condition from
my audience I continually drink water, cough,
often blow my nose as though I were hindered by
a cold, make puns inappropriately, and in the end
break off earlier than I ought to. But above all
I am ashamed.

My conscience and my intelligence tell me that
the very best thing I could do now would be to
deliver a farewell lecture to the boys, to say my
last word to them, to bless them, and give up my
post to a man younger and stronger than me.
But, God be my judge, I have not manly courage
enough to act according to my conscience.

Unfortunately, I am not a philosopher and not
a theologian. I know perfectly well that I cannot
live more than another six months; it might be
supposed that I ought now to be chiefly concerned
with the question of the shadowy life beyond the
grave, and the visions that will visit my slumbers
in the tomb. But for some reason my soul refuses
to recognize these questions, though my mind is
fully alive to their importance. Just as twenty,
thirty years ago, so now, on the threshold of
death, I am interested in nothing but science.
As I yield up my last breath I shall still believe
that science is the most important, the most

splendid, the most essential thing in the life of man; that it always has been and will be the highest manifestation of love, and that only by means of it will man conquer himself and nature. This faith is perhaps naïve and may rest on false assumptions, but it is not my fault that I believe that and nothing else; I cannot overcome in myself this belief.

But that is not the point. I only ask people to be indulgent to my weakness, and to realize that to tear from the lecture-theatre and his pupils a man who is more interested in the history of the development of the bone medulla than in the final object of creation would be equivalent to taking him and nailing him up in his coffin without waiting for him to be dead.

Sleeplessness and the consequent strain of combating increasing weakness leads to something strange in me. In the middle of my lecture tears suddenly rise in my throat, my eyes begin to smart, and I feel a passionate, hysterical desire to stretch out my hands before me and break into loud lamentation. I want to cry out in a loud voice that I, a famous man, have been sentenced by fate to the death penalty, that within some six months another man will be in control here in the lecture-theatre. I want to shriek that I am poisoned; new ideas such as I have not known before have poisoned the last days of my life, and are still stinging my brain like mosquitoes. And at that moment my position seems to me so awful that I want all my listeners to be horrified, to leap up from their seats and to rush in panic terror, with desperate screams, to the exit.

It is not easy to get through such moments.

II.

After my lecture I sit at home and work. I read journals and monographs, or prepare my next lecture; sometimes I write something. I work with interruptions, as I have from time to time to see visitors.

There is a ring at the bell. It is a colleague come to discuss some business matter with me. He comes in to me with his hat and his stick, and, holding out both these objects to me, says:

" Only for a minute ! Only for a minute ! Sit down, *collega !* Only a couple of words."

To begin with, we both try to show each other that we are extraordinarily polite and highly delighted to see each other. I make him sit down in an easy-chair, and he makes me sit down; as we do so, we cautiously pat each other on the back, touch each other's buttons, and it looks as though we were feeling each other and afraid of scorching our fingers. Both of us laugh, though we say nothing amusing. When we are seated we bow our heads towards each other and begin talking in subdued voices. However affection-ately disposed we may be to one another, we cannot help adorning our conversation with all sorts of Chinese mannerisms, such as " As you so justly observed," or " I have already had the honour to inform you "; we cannot help laughing if one of us makes a joke, however unsuccessfully. When we have finished with business my colleague gets up impulsively and, waving his hat in the direction of my work, begins to say good-bye. Again we paw one another and laugh. I see him into the hall; then I assist my colleague to put on his coat, while he does all he can to decline this high honour. Then when Yegor opens the door my colleague declares that I shall catch cold, while I make a show of being ready to go even into the street with him. And when at last I go back into my study my face still goes on smiling, I suppose from inertia.

A little later another ring at the bell. Somebody comes into the hall, and is a long time coughing and taking off his things. Yegor announces a student. I tell him to ask him in. A minute later a young man of agreeable appearance comes in. For the last year he and I have been on strained relations; he answers me disgracefully at the examinations, and I mark him one. Every year I have some seven such hopefuls whom, to express it in the students' slang, I " chivy " or " floor." Those of them who fail in their examination through incapacity or illness usually bear their cross patiently and do not haggle with me; those who come to the house and haggle with me are always youths of sanguine temperament, broad natures, whose failure at examinations spoils their appetites and hinders them from visiting the opera with their usual regularity. I let the first class off easily, but the second I chivy through a whole year.

" Sit down," I say to my visitor; " what have you to tell me ?"

" Excuse me, professor, for troubling you," he begins, hesitating, and not looking me in the face. " I would not have ventured to trouble you if it had not been . . . I have been up for your examination five times, and have been ploughed. . . . I beg you, be so good as to mark me for a pass, because . . ."

The argument which all the sluggards bring forward on their own behalf is always the same; they have passed well in all their subjects and have only come to grief in mine, and that is the more surprising because they have always been particularly interested in my subject and knew it so well; their failure has always been entirely owing to some incomprehensible misunderstanding.

" Excuse me, my friend," I say to the visitor; " I cannot mark you for a pass. Go and read up the lectures and come to me again. Then we shall see."

A pause. I feel an impulse to torment the student a little for liking beer and the opera better than science, and I say, with a sigh:

" To my mind, the best thing you can do now is to give up medicine altogether. If, with your abilities, you cannot succeed in passing the examination, it's evident that you have neither the desire nor the vocation for a doctor's calling."

The sanguine youth's face lengthens.

" Excuse me, professor," he laughs, " but that would be odd of me, to say the least of it. After studying for five years, all at once to give it up "

" Oh, well ! Better to have lost your five years
than have to spend the rest of your life in doing
work you do not care for."

But at once I feel sorry for him, and I hasten
to add:

" However, as you think best. And so read a
little more and come again."

" When ?" the idle youth asks in a hollow
voice.

" When you like. To-morrow if you like."

And in his good-natured eyes I read:

" I can come all right, but of course you will
plough me again, you beast !"

" Of course," I say, " you won't know more
science for going in for my examination another
fifteen times, but it is training your character,
and you must be thankful for that."

Silence follows. I get up and wait for my
visitor to go, but he stands and looks towards the
window, fingers his beard, and thinks. It grows
boring.

The sanguine youth's voice is pleasant and
mellow, his eyes are clever and ironical, his face
is genial, though a little bloated from frequent
indulgence in beer and overlong lying on the sofa;
he looks as though he could tell me a lot of interesting things about the opera, about his affairs
of the heart, and about comrades whom he likes.
Unluckily, it is not the thing to discuss these
subjects, or else I should have been glad to listen
to him.

" Professor, I give you my word of honour that
if you mark me for a pass I . . . I'll . . ." .

As soon as we reach the " word of honour " I wave my hands and sit down to the table. The student ponders a minute longer, and says dejectedly:

" In that case, good-bye. . . . I beg your pardon."

" Good-bye, my friend. Good luck to you."

He goes irresolutely into the hall, slowly puts on his outdoor things, and, going out into the street, probably ponders for some time longer; unable to think of anything, except " old devil," inwardly addressed to me, he goes into a wretched restaurant to dine and drink beer, and then home to bed. " Peace be to thy ashes, honest toiler."

A third ring at the bell. A young doctor, in a pair of new black trousers, gold spectacles, and of course a white tie, walks in. He introduces himself. I beg him to be seated, and ask what I can do for him. Not without emotion, the young devotee of science begins telling me that he has passed his examination as a doctor of medicine, and that he has now only to write his dissertation. He would like to work with me under my guidance, and he would be greatly obliged to me if I would give him a subject for his dissertation.

" Very glad to be of use to you, colleague," I say, " but just let us come to an understanding as to the meaning of a dissertation. That word is taken to mean a composition which is a product of independent creative effort. Is that not so ? A work written on another man's subject and under another man's guidance is called something different. . . ."

The doctor says nothing. I fly into a rage and jump up from my seat.

"Why is it you all come to me ?" I cry angrily. "Do I keep a shop ? I don't deal in subjects. For the thousand and oneth time I ask you all to leave me in peace ! Excuse my brutality, but I am quite sick of it !"

The doctor remains silent, but a faint flush is apparent on his cheek-bones. His face expresses a profound reverence for my fame and my learning, but from his eyes I can see he feels a contempt for my voice, my pitiful figure, and my nervous gesticulation. I impress him in my anger as a queer fish.

"I don't keep a shop," I go on angrily. "And it is a strange thing ! Why don't you want to be independent ? Why have you such a distaste for independence ?"

I say a great deal, but he still remains silent. By degrees I calm down, and of course give in. The doctor gets a subject from me for his theme not worth a halfpenny, writes under my supervision a dissertation of no use to anyone, with dignity defends it in a dreary discussion, and receives a degree of no use to him.

The rings at the bell may follow one another endlessly, but I will confine my description here to four of them. The bell rings for the fourth time, and I hear familiar footsteps, the rustle of a dress, a dear voice. . . .

Eighteen years ago a colleague of mine, an oculist, died leaving a little daughter Katya, a child of seven, and sixty thousand roubles. In his will he made me the child's guardian. Till she was ten years old Katya lived with us as one of the family, then she was sent to a boarding-school, and only spent the summer holidays with us. I never had time to look after her education. I only superintended it at leisure moments, and so I can say very little about her childhood.

The first thing I remember, and like so much in remembrance, is the extraordinary trustfulness with which she came into our house and let herself be treated by the doctors, a trustfulness which was always shining in her little face. She would sit somewhere out of the way, with her face tied up, invariably watching something with attention; whether she watched me writing or turning over the pages of a book, or watched my wife bustling about, or the cook scrubbing a potato in the kitchen, or the dog playing, her eyes invariably expressed the same thought—that is, " Everything that is done in this world is nice and sensible." She was curious, and very fond of talking to me. Sometimes she would sit at the table opposite me, watching my movements and asking questions. It interested her to know what I was reading, what I did at the University, whether I was not afraid of the dead bodies, what I did with my salary.

" Do the students fight at the University ?" she would ask.

" They do, dear."

" And do you make them go down on their knees ?"

" Yes, I do."

And she thought it funny that the students fought and I made them go down on their knees, and she laughed. She was a gentle, patient, good child. It happened not unfrequently that I saw something taken away from her, saw her punished without reason, or her curiosity repressed; at such times a look of sadness was mixed with the invariable expression of trustfulness on her face— that was all. I did not know how to take her part; only when I saw her sad I had an inclination to draw her to me and to commiserate her like some old nurse: " My poor little orphan one !"

I remember, too, that she was fond of fine clothes and of sprinkling herself with scent. In that respect she was like me. I, too, am fond of pretty clothes and nice scent.

I regret that I had not time nor inclination to watch over the rise and development of the passion which took complete possession of Katya when she was fourteen or fifteen. I mean her passionate love for the theatre. When she used to come from boarding-school and stay with us for the summer holidays, she talked of nothing with such pleasure and such warmth as of plays and actors. She bored us with her continual talk of the theatre. My wife and children would not listen to her. I was the only one who had not the courage to refuse to attend to her. When she had a longing to share her transports, she used to come into my study and say in an imploring tone:

" Nikolay Stepanitch, do let me talk to you about the theatre !"

I pointed to the clock, and said:

" I'll give you half an hour—begin."

Later on she used to bring with her dozens of portraits of actors and actresses which she worshipped; then she attempted several times to take part in private theatricals, and the upshot of it all was that when she left school she came to me and announced that she was born to be an actress.

I had never shared Katya's inclinations for the theatre. To my mind, if a play is good there is no need to trouble the actors in order that it may make the right impression; it is enough to read it. If the play is poor, no acting will make it good.

In my youth I often visited the theatre, and now my family takes a box twice a year and carries me off for a little distraction. Of course, that is not enough to give me the right to judge of the theatre. In my opinion the theatre has become no better than it was thirty or forty years ago. Just as in the past, I can never find a glass of clean water in the corridors or foyers of the theatre. Just as in the past, the attendants fine me twenty kopecks for my fur coat, though there is nothing reprehensible in wearing a warm coat in winter. As in the past, for no sort of reason, music is played in the intervals, which adds something new and uncalled-for to the impression made by the play. As in the past, men go in the intervals and drink spirits in the buffet. If no progress can be seen in trifles, I should look for it in vain in what is more important. When an actor wrapped from head to foot in stage traditions and conventions tries to recite a simple ordinary speech, " To be, or not to be,"

not simply, but invariably with the accompaniment
of hissing and convulsive movements all over his
body, or when he tries to convince me at all costs
that Tchatsky, who talks so much with fools and
is so fond of folly, is a very clever man, and that
" Woe from Wit " is not a dull play, the stage
gives me the same feeling of conventionality
which bored me so much forty years ago when I
was regaled with the classical howling and beating
on the breast. And every time I come out of
the theatre more conservative than I go in.

The sentimental and confiding public may be
persuaded that the stage, even in its present form,
is a school; but anyone who is familiar with a
school in its true sense will not be caught with
that bait. I cannot say what will happen in
fifty or a hundred years, but in its actual condition the theatre can serve only as an entertainment. But this entertainment is too costly to
be frequently enjoyed. It robs the state of
thousands of healthy and talented young men and
women, who, if they had not devoted themselves
to the theatre, might have been good doctors,
farmers, schoolmistresses, officers; it robs the
public of the evening hours—the best time for
intellectual work and social intercourse. I say
nothing of the waste of money and the moral
damage to the spectator when he sees murder,
fornication, or false witness unsuitably treated on
the stage.

Katya was of an entirely different opinion.
She assured me that the theatre, even in its
present condition, was superior to the lecture-hall,

to books, or to anything in the world. The stage was a power that united in itself all the arts, and actors were missionaries. No art nor science was capable of producing so strong and so certain an effect on the soul of man as the stage, and it was with good reason that an actor of medium quality enjoys greater popularity than the greatest savant or artist. And no sort of public service could provide such enjoyment and gratification as the theatre.

And one fine day Katya joined a troupe of actors, and went off, I believe to Ufa, taking away with her a good supply of money, a store of rainbow hopes, and the most aristocratic views of her work.

Her first letters on the journey were marvellous. I read them, and was simply amazed that those small sheets of paper could contain so much youth, purity of spirit, holy innocence, and at the same time subtle and apt judgments which would have done credit to a fine masculine intellect. It was more like a rapturous pæan of praise she sent me than a mere description of the Volga, the country, the towns she visited, her companions, her failures and successes; every sentence was fragrant with that confiding trustfulness I was accustomed to read in her face—and at the same time there were a great many grammatical mistakes, and there was scarcely any punctuation at all.

Before six months had passed I received a highly poetical and enthusiastic letter beginning with the words, " I have come to love . . ." This letter was accompanied by a photograph

representing a young man with a shaven face,
a wide-brimmed hat, and a plaid flung over his
shoulder. The letters that followed were as
splendid as before, but now commas and stops
made their appearance in them, the grammatical
mistakes disappeared, and there was a distinctly
masculine flavour about them. Katya began
writing to me how splendid it would be to build a
great theatre somewhere on the Volga, on a co-
operative system, and to attract to the enterprise
the rich merchants and the steamer owners; there
would be a great deal of money in it; there would
be vast audiences; the actors would play on co-
operative terms. . . . Possibly all this was really
excellent, but it seemed to me that such schemes
could only originate from a man's mind.

However that may have been, for a year and a
half everything seemed to go well: Katya was in
love, believed in her work, and was happy; but
then I began to notice in her letters unmistakable
signs of falling off. It began with Katya's com-
plaining of her companions—this was the first
and most ominous symptom; if a young scientific
or literary man begins his career with bitter complaints of scientific and literary men, it is a sure
sign that he is worn out and not fit for his work.
Katya wrote to me that her companions did not
attend the rehearsals and never knew their parts;
that one could see in every one of them an utter
disrespect for the public in the production of
absurd plays, and in their behaviour on the stage;
that for the benefit of the Actors' Fund, which
they only talked about, actresses of the serious

drama demeaned themselves by singing chan-
sonettes, while tragic actors sang comic songs
making fun of deceived husbands and the pregnant
condition of unfaithful wives, and so on. In
fact, it was amazing that all this had not yet
ruined the provincial stage, and that it could still
maintain itself on such a rotten and unsubstantial
footing.

In answer I wrote Katya a long and, I must
confess, a very boring letter. Among other things,
I wrote to her:

"I have more than once happened to converse
with old actors, very worthy men, who showed
a friendly disposition towards me; from my conversations with them I could understand that
their work was controlled not so much by their
own intelligence and free choice as by fashion and
the mood of the public. The best of them had
had to play in their day in tragedy, in operetta,
in Parisian farces, and in extravaganzas, and they
always seemed equally sure that they were on the
right path and that they were of use. So, as you
see, the cause of the evil must be sought, not in
the actors, but, more deeply, in the art itself and
in the attitude of the whole of society to it."

This letter of mine only irritated Katya. She
answered me:

"You and I are singing parts out of different
operas. I wrote to you, not of the worthy men
who showed a friendly disposition to you, but of a
band of knaves who have nothing worthy about
them. They are a horde of savages who have got on
the stage simply because no one would have taken

702

them elsewhere, and who call themselves artists simply because they are impudent. There are numbers of dull-witted creatures, drunkards, intriguing schemers and slanderers, but there not one person of talent among them. I cannot tell you how bitter it is to me that the art I love has fallen into the hands of people I detest; how bitter it is that the best men look on at evil from afar, not caring to come closer, and, instead of intervening, write ponderous commonplaces and utterly useless sermons. . . ." And so on, all in the same style.

A little time passed, and I got this letter: " I have been brutally deceived. I cannot go on living. Dispose of my money as you think best. I loved you as my father and my only friend. Good-bye."

It turned out that he, too, belonged to the a horde of savages." Later on, from certain isints, I gathered that there had been an attempt ht suicide. I believe Katya tried to poison her-'elf. I imagine that she must have been seriously 'll afterwards, as the next letter I got was from Yalta, where she had most probably been sent by the doctors. Her last letter contained a request to send her a thousand roubles to Yalta as quickly as possible, and ended with these words:

" Excuse the gloominess of this letter; yesterday I buried my child." After spending about a year in the Crimea, she returned home.

She had been about four years on her travels, and during those four years, I must confess, I had played a rather strange and unenviable part in regard to her. When in earlier days she had told me she was going on the stage, and then wrote to me of her love; when she was periodically overcome by extravagance, and I continually had to send her first one and then two thousand roubles; when she wrote to me of her intention of suicide, and then òf the death of her baby, every time I lost my head, and all my sympathy for her sufferings found no expression except that, after prolonged reflection, I wrote long, boring letters which I might just as well not have written. And yet I took a father's place with her and loved her like a daughter !

Now Katya is living less than half a mile off. She has taken a flat of five rooms, and has installed herself fairly comfortably and in the taste of the day. If anyone were to undertake to describe her surroundings, the most characteristic note in the picture would be indolence. For the indolent body there are soft lounges, soft stools; for indolent feet soft rugs; for indolent eyes faded, dingy, or flat colours; for the indolent soul the walls are hung with a number of cheap fans and trivial pictures, in which the originality of the execution is more conspicuous than the subject; and the room contains a multitude of little tables and shelves filled with utterly useless articles of no value, and shapeless rags in place of curtains. . . . All this, together with the dread of bright colours, of symmetry, and of empty space, bears witness not only to spiritual indolence, but also to a corruption of natural taste. For days together Katya lies on the lounge reading, prin-

cipally novels and stories. She only goes out of
the house once a day, in the afternoon, to see me.

I go on working while Katya sits silent not far
from me on the sofa, wrapping herself in her
shawl, as though she were cold. Either because I
find her sympathetic or because I was used to her
frequent visits when she was a little girl, her
presence does not prevent me from concentrating
my attention. From time to time I mechanically
ask her some question; she gives very brief replies;
or, to rest for a minute, I turn round and watch
her as she looks dreamily at some medical journal
or review. And at such moments I notice that her
face has lost the old look of confiding trustfulness.
Her expression now is cold, apathetic, and absent-
minded, like that of passengers who have had to
wait too long for a train. She is dressed, as in
old days, simply and beautifully, but carelessly;
her dress and her hair show visible traces of the
sofas and rocking-chairs in which she spends whole
days at a stretch. And she has lost the curiosity
she had in old days. She has ceased to ask me
questions now, as though she had experienced
everything in life and looked for nothing new
from it.

Towards four o'clock there begin to be sounds
of movement in the hall and in the drawing-room.
Liza has come back from the Conservatoire, and
has brought some girl-friends in with her. We
hear them playing on the piano, trying their
voices and laughing; in the dining-room Yegor is
laying the table, with the clatter of crockery.

" Good-bye," said Katya. " I won't go in and

see your people to-day. They must excuse me. I haven't time. Come and see me."

While I am seeing her to the door, she looks me up and down grimly, and says with vexation:

" You are getting thinner and thinner ! Why don't you consult a doctor ? I'll call at Sergey Fyodorovitch's and ask him to have a look at you."

" There's no need, Katya."

" I can't think where your people's eyes are ! They are a nice lot, I must say !"

She puts on her fur coat abruptly, and as she does so two or three hairpins drop unnoticed on the floor from her carelessly arranged hair. She is too lazy and in too great a hurry to do her hair up; she carelessly stuffs the falling curls under her hat, and goes away.

When I go into the dining-room my wife asks me:

" Was Katya with you just now ? Why didn't she come in to see us ? It's really strange . . ."

" Mamma," Liza says to her reproachfully, " let her alone, if she doesn't want to. We are not going down on our knees to her."

" It's very neglectful, anyway. To sit for three hours in the study without remembering our existence ! But of course she must do as she likes."

Varya and Liza both hate Katya. This hatred is beyond my comprehension, and probably one would have to be a woman in order to understand it. I am ready to stake my life that of the hundred and fifty young men I see every day in the lecture-

theatre, and of the hundred elderly ones I meet
every week, hardly one could be found capable
of understanding their hatred and aversion for
Katya's past—that is, for her having been a
mother without being a wife, and for her having
had an illegitimate child; and at the same time
I cannot recall one woman or girl of my acquaintance who would not consciously or unconsciously
harbour such feelings. And this is not because
woman is purer or more virtuous than man: why,
virtue and purity are not very different from vice
if they are not free from evil feeling. I attribute
this simply to the backwardness of woman. The
mournful feeling of compassion and the pang of
conscience experienced by a modern man at the
sight of suffering is, to my mind, far greater proof
of culture and moral elevation than hatred and
aversion. Woman is as tearful and as coarse in
her feelings now as she was in the Middle Ages,
and to my thinking those who advise that she
should be educated like a man, are quite right.

My wife also dislikes Katya for having been an
actress, for ingratitude, for pride, for eccentricity,
and for the numerous vices which one woman can
always find in another.

Besides my wife and daughter and me, there
are dining with us two or three of my daughter's
friends and Alexandr Adolfovitch Gnekker, her
admirer and suitor. He is a fair-haired young
man under thirty, of medium height, very stout
and broad-shouldered, with red whiskers near his
ears, and little waxed moustaches which make
his plump smooth face look like a toy. He is

dressed in a very short reefer jacket, a flowered waistcoat, breeches very full at the top and very narrow at the ankle, with a large check pattern on them, and yellow boots without heels. He has prominent eyes like a crab's, his cravat is like a crab's neck, and I even fancy there is a smell of crab-soup about the young man's whole person. He visits us every day, but no one in my family knows anything of his origin nor of the place of his education, nor of his means of livelihood. He neither plays nor sings, but has some connection with music and singing, sells somebody's pianos somewhere, is frequently at the Conservatoire, is acquainted with all the celebrities, and is a steward at the concerts; he criticizes music with great authority, and I have noticed that people are eager to agree with him.

Rich people always have dependents hanging about them; the arts and sciences have the same. I believe there is not an art nor a science in the world free from " foreign bodies " after the style of this Mr. Gnekker. I am not a musician, and possibly I am mistaken in regard to Mr. Gnekker, of whom, indeed, I know very little. But his air of authority and the dignity with which he takes his stand beside the piano when anyone is playing or singing strike me as very suspicious.

You may be ever so much of a gentleman and a privy councillor, but if you have a daughter you cannot be secure of immunity from that petty bourgeois atmosphere which is so often brought into your house and into your mood by the attentions of suitors, by matchmaking and marriage.

I can never reconcile myself, for instance, to the
expression of triumph on my wife's face every
time Gnekker is in our company, nor can I reconcile myself to the bottles of Lafitte, port, and
sherry which are only brought out on his account,
that he may see with his own eyes the liberal
and luxurious way in which we live. I cannot
tolerate the habit of spasmodic laughter Liza has
picked up at the Conservatoire, and her way of
screwing up her eyes whenever there are men in
the room. Above all, I cannot understand why
a creature utterly alien to my habits, my studies,
my whole manner of life, completely different
from the people I like, should come and see me
every day, and every day should dine with me.
My wife and my servants mysteriously whisper
that he is a suitor, but still I don't understand
his presence; it rouses in me the same wonder and
perplexity as if they were to set a Zulu beside me
at the table. And it seems strange to me, too,
that my daughter, whom I am used to thinking
of as a child, should love that cravat, those eyes,
those soft cheeks. . . .

In old days I used to like my dinner, or at
least was indifferent about it; now it excites in
me no feeling but weariness and irritation. Ever
since I became an " Excellency " and one of the
Deans of the Faculty my family has for some
reason found it necessary to make a complete
change in our menu and dining habits. Instead
of the simple dishes to which I was accustomed
when I was a student and when I was in practice,
now they feed me with a purée with little white

things like circles floating about in it, and kidneys stewed in madeira. My rank as a general and my fame have robbed me for ever of cabbage-soup and savoury pies, and goose with apple-sauce, and bream with boiled grain. They have robbed me of our maid-servant Agasha, a chatty and laughter-loving old woman, instead of whom Yegor, a dull-witted and conceited fellow with a white glove on his right hand, waits at dinner. The intervals between the courses are short, but they seem immensely long because there is nothing to occupy them. There is none of the gaiety of the old days, the spontaneous talk, the jokes, the laughter; there is nothing of mutual affection and the joy which used to animate the children, my wife, and me when in old days we met together at meals. For me, the celebrated man of science, dinner was a time of rest and reunion, and for my wife and children a fête—brief indeed, but bright and joyous—in which they knew that for half an hour I belonged, not to science, not to students, but to them alone. Our real exhilaration from one glass of wine is gone for ever, gone is Agasha, gone the bream with boiled grain, gone the uproar that greeted every little startling incident at dinner, such as the cat and dog fighting under the table, or Katya's bandage falling off her face into her soup-plate.

To describe our dinner nowadays is as un-interesting as to eat it. My wife's face wears a look of triumph and affected dignity, and her habitual expression of anxiety. She looks at our plates and says, " I see you don't care for the joint. Tell me; you don't like it, do you?" and I am obliged to answer: "There is no need for you to trouble, my dear; the meat is very nice." And she will say: "You always stand up for me, Nikolay Stepanovitch, and you never tell the truth. Why is Alexandr Adolfovitch eating so little?" And so on in the same style all through dinner. Liza laughs spasmodically and screws up her eyes. I watch them both, and it is only now at dinner that it becomes absolutely evident to me that the inner life of these two has slipped away out of my ken. I have a feeling as though I had once lived at home with a real wife and children and that now I am dining with visitors, in the house of a sham wife who is not the real one, and am looking at a Liza who is not the real Liza. A startling change has taken place in both of them; I have missed the long process by which that change was effected, and it is no wonder that I can make nothing of it. Why did that change take place? I don't know. Perhaps the whole trouble is that God has not given my wife and daughter the same strength of character as me. From childhood I have been accustomed to resisting external influences, and have steeled myself pretty thoroughly. Such catastrophes in life as fame, the rank of a general, the transition from comfort to living beyond our means, acquaintance with celebrities, etc., have scarcely affected me, and I have remained intact and unashamed; but on my wife and Liza, who have not been through the same hardening process and are weak, all this has fallen like an avalanche of snow, overwhelming them. Gnekker and the young ladies talk of fugues, of counterpoint, of singers and pianists, of Bach and Brahms, while my wife, afraid of their suspecting her of ignorance of music, smiles to them sympathetically and mutters: "That's exquisite . . . really! You don't say so! . . ." Gnekker eats with solid dignity, jests with solid dignity, and condescendingly listens to the remarks of the young ladies. From time to time he is moved to speak in bad French, and then, for some reason or other, he thinks it necessary to address me as " *Votre Excellence.*"

And I am glum. Evidently I am a constraint to them and they are a constraint to me. I have never in my earlier days had a close knowledge of class antagonism, but now I am tormented by something of that sort. I am on the lookout for nothing but bad qualities in Gnekker; I quickly find them, and am fretted at the thought that a man not of my circle is sitting here as my daughter's suitor. His presence has a bad influence on me in other ways, too. As a rule, when I am alone or in the society of people I like, I never think of my own achievements, or, if I do recall them, they seem to me as trivial as though I had only completed my studies yesterday; but in the presence of people like Gnekker my achievements in science seem to be a lofty mountain the top of which vanishes into the clouds, while at its foot Gnekkers are running about scarcely visible to the naked eye.

After dinner I go into my study and there smoke my pipe, the only one in the whole day, the sole relic of my old bad habit of smoking from morning till night. While I am smoking my wife comes in and sits down to talk to me. Just as in the morning, I know beforehand what our conversation is going to be about.

" I must talk to you seriously, Nikolay Stepanovitch," she begins. " I mean about Liza. . . . Why don't you pay attention to it ?"

" To what ?"

" You pretend to notice nothing. But that is not right. We can't shirk responsibility. . . . Gnekker has intentions in regard to Liza. . . . What do you say ?"

" That he is a bad man I can't say, because I don't know him, but that I don't like him I have told you a thousand times already."

" But you can't . . . you can't !"

She gets up and walks about in excitement.

" You can't take up that attitude to a serious step," she says. " When it is a question of our daughter's happiness we must lay aside all personal feeling. I know you do not like him. . . . Very good . . . if we refuse him now, if we break it all off, how can you be sure that Liza will not have a grievance against us all her life ? Suitors are not plentiful nowadays, goodness knows, and it may happen that no other match will turn up. . . . He is very much in love with Liza, and she seems to like him. . . . Of course, he has no settled position, but that can't be helped. Please God, in time he will get one. He is of good family and well off."

" Where did you learn that ?"

" He told us so. His father has a large house in Harkov and an estate in the neighbourhood. In short, Nikolay Stepanovitch, you absolutely must go to Harkov."

" What for ?"

" You will find out all about him there. . . . You know the professors there; they will help you. I would go myself, but I am a woman. I cannot. . . ."

" I am not going to Harkov," I say morosely.

My wife is frightened, and a look of intense suffering comes into her face.

" For God's sake, Nikolay Stepanovitch," she implores me, with tears in her voice—" for God's sake, take this burden off me ! I am so worried !"

It is painful for me to look at her.

" Very well, Varya," I say affectionately, " if you wish it, then certainly I will go to Harkov and do all you want."

She presses her handkerchief to her eyes and goes off to her room to cry, and I am left alone.

A little later lights are brought in. The armchair and the lamp-shade cast familiar shadows that have long grown wearisome on the walls and on the floor, and when I look at them I feel as though the night had come and with it my accursed sleeplessness. I lie on my bed, then get up and walk about the room, then lie down again. As a rule it is after dinner, at the approach of evening, that my nervous excitement reaches its highest pitch. For no reason I begin crying and burying my head in the pillow. At such times I am afraid that someone may come in; I am afraid of suddenly dying; I am ashamed of my tears, and altogether there is something insufferable in my soul. I feel that I can no longer bear the sight of my lamp, of my books, of the shadows on the floor. I cannot bear the sound of the voices coming from the drawing-room. Some force unseen, uncomprehended, is roughly thrusting me out of my flat. I leap up hurriedly, dress, and cautiously, that my family may not notice, slip out into the street. Where am I to go ?

The answer to that question has long been ready in my brain. To Katya.

III.

As a rule she is lying on the sofa or in a lounge-chair, reading. Seeing me, she raises her head languidly, sits up, and shakes hands.

" You are always lying down," I say, after pausing and taking breath. " That's not good for you. You ought to occupy yourself with something."

" What ?"

" I say you ought to occupy yourself in some way."

" With what ? A woman can be nothing but a simple workwoman or an actress."

" Well, if you can't be a workwoman, be an actress."

She says nothing.

" You ought to get married," I say, half in jest.

" There is no one to marry. There's no reason to, either."

715

' You can't live like this."

Without a husband ? Much that matters; I could have as many men as I like if I wanted to."

" That's ugly, Katya."

" What is ugly ?"

" Why, what you have just said."

Noticing that I am hurt and wishing to efface the disagreeable impression, Katya says:

" Let us go; come this way."

She takes me into a very snug little room, and says, pointing to the writing-table:

" Look . . . I have got that ready for you. You shall work here. Come here every day and bring your work with you. They only hinder you there at home. Will you work here ? Will you like to ?"

Not to wound her by refusing, I answer that I will work here, and that I like the room very much. Then we both sit down in the snug little room and begin talking.

The warm, snug surroundings and the presence of a sympathetic person does not, as in old days, arouse in me a feeling of pleasure, but an intense impulse to complain and grumble. I feel for some reason that if I lament and complain I shall feel better.

" Things are in a bad way with me, my dear—very bad. . . ."

" What is it ?"

" You see how it is, my dear; the best and holiest right of kings is the right of mercy. And I have always felt myself a king, since I have made unlimited use of that right. I have never

judged, I have been indulgent, I have readily
forgiven everyone, right and left. Where others
have protested and expressed indignation, I have
only advised and persuaded. All my life it has
been my endeavour that my society should not
be a burden to my family, to my students, to my
colleagues, to my servants. And I know that
this attitude to people has had a good influence
on all who have chanced to come into contact
with me. But now I am not a king. Something is
happening to me that is only excusable in a slave;
day and night my brain is haunted by evil thoughts,
and feelings such as I never knew before are
brooding in my soul. I am full of hatred, and
contempt, and indignation, and loathing, and
dread. I have become excessively severe, exact-
ing, irritable, ungracious, suspicious. Even things
that in old days would have provoked me only to
an unnecessary jest and a good-natured laugh
now arouse an oppressive feeling in me. My
reasoning, too, has undergone a change: in old
days I despised money; now I harbour an evil
feeling, not towards money, but towards the rich,
as though they were to blame: in old days I hated
violence and tyranny, but now I hate the men
who make use of violence, as though they were
alone to blame, and not all of us who do not know
how to educate each other. What is the meaning
of it ? If these new ideas and new feelings have
come from a change of convictions, what is that
change due to ? Can the world have grown worse
and I better, or was I blind before and indifferent ?
If this change is the result of a general decline of

physical and intellectual powers—I am ill, you know, and every day I am losing weight—my position is pitiable; it means that my new ideas are morbid and abnormal; I ought to be ashamed of them and think them of no consequence. . . ."

" Illness has nothing to do with it," Katya interrupts me; " it's simply that your eyes are opened, that's all. You have seen what in old days, for some reason, you refused to see. To my thinking, what you ought to do, first of all, is to break with your family for good, and go away."

" You are talking nonsense."

" You don't love them; why should you force your feelings ? Can you call them a family ? Nonentities ! If they died to-day, no one would notice their absence to-morrow."

Katya despises my wife and Liza as much as they hate her. One can hardly talk at this date of people's having a right to despise one another. But if one looks at it from Katya's standpoint and recognizes such a right, one can see she has as much right to despise my wife and Liza as they have to hate her.

" Nonentities," she goes on. " Have you had dinner to-day ? How was it they did not forget to tell you it was ready ? How is it they still remember your existence ? "

" Katya," I say sternly, " I beg you to be silent."

" You think I enjoy talking about them ? I should be glad not to know them at all. Listen, my dear: give it all up and go away. Go abroad. The sooner the better."

" What nonsense ! What about the University ? "

" The University, too. What is it to you ? There's no sense in it, anyway. You have been lecturing for thirty years, and where are your pupils ? Are many of them celebrated scientific men ? Count them up ! And to multiply the doctors who exploit ignorance and pile up hundreds of thousands for themselves, there is no need to be a good and talented man. You are not wanted."

" Good heavens ! how harsh you are ! " I cry in horror. " How harsh you are ! Be quiet or I will go away ! I don't know how to answer the harsh things you say ! "

The maid comes in and summons us to tea. At the samovar our conversation, thank God, changes. After having had my grumble out, I have a longing to give way to another weakness of old age, reminiscences. I tell Katya about my past, and to my great astonishment tell her incidents which, till then, I did not suspect of being still preserved in my memory, and she listens to me with tenderness, with pride, holding her breath. I am particularly fond of telling her how I was educated in a seminary and dreamed of going to the University.

" At times I used to walk about our seminary garden . . ." I would tell her. " If from some far-away tavern the wind floated sounds of a song and the squeaking of an accordion, or a sledge with bells dashed by the garden-fence, it was quite enough to send a rush of happiness, filling not only my heart, but even my stomach, my legs, my arms. . . . I would listen to the accordion or the bells dying away in the distance and imagine myself a doctor, and paint pictures, one better than another. And here, as you see, my dreams have come true. I have had more than I dared to dream of. For thirty years I have been the favourite professor, I have had splendid comrades, I have enjoyed fame and honour. I have loved, married from passionate love, have had children. In fact, looking back upon it, I see my whole life as a fine composition arranged with talent. Now all that is left to me is not to spoil the end. For that I must die like a man. If death is really a thing to dread, I must meet it as a teacher, a man of science, and a citizen of a Christian country ought to meet it, with courage and untroubled soul. But I am spoiling the end; I am sinking, I fly to you, I beg for help, and you tell me ' Sink; that is what you ought to do.' "

But here there comes a ring at the front-door. Katya and I recognize it, and say:

" It must be Mihail Fyodorovitch."

And a minute later my colleague, the philologist Mihail Fyodorovitch, a tall, well-built man of fifty, clean-shaven, with thick grey hair and black eyebrows, walks in. He is a good-natured man and an excellent comrade. He comes of a fortunate and talented old noble family which has played a prominent part in the history of literature and enlightenment. He is himself intelligent, talented, and very highly educated, but has his oddities. To a certain extent we are all odd and all queer fish, but in his oddities there is something exceptional, apt to cause anxiety among his acquaintances. I know a good many people for whom his oddities completely obscure his good qualities.

Coming in to us, he slowly takes off his gloves and says in his velvety bass:

" Good-evening. Are you having tea ? That's just right. It's diabolically cold."

Then he sits down to the table, takes a glass, and at once begins talking. What is most characteristic in his manner of talking is the continually jesting tone, a sort of mixture of philosophy and drollery as in Shakespeare's gravediggers. He is always talking about serious things, but he never speaks seriously. His judgments are always harsh and railing, but, thanks to his soft, even, jesting tone, the harshness and abuse do not jar upon the ear, and one soon grows used to them. Every evening he brings with him some five or six anecdotes from the University, and he usually begins with them when he sits down to table.

" Oh, Lord !" he sighs, twitching his black eyebrows ironically. " What comic people there are in the world !"

" Well ?" asks Katya.

" As I was coming from my lecture this morning I met that old idiot N. N—— on the stairs. . . . He was going along as usual, sticking out his chin like a horse, looking for someone to listen to his grumblings at his migraine, at his wife, and his students who won't attend his lectures. ' Oh,' I thought, ' he has seen me—I am done for now; it is all up. . . .' "

And so on in the same style. Or he will begin like this:

" I was yesterday at our friend Z. Z——'s public lecture. I wonder how it is our alma mater—don't speak of it after dark—dare display in public such noodles and patent dullards as that Z. Z——. Why, he is a European fool ! Upon my word, you could not find another like him all over Europe ! He lectures—can you imagine ?—as though he were sucking a sugarstick—sue, sue, sue; . . . he is in a nervous funk; he can hardly decipher his own manuscript; his poor little thoughts crawl along like a bishop on a bicycle, and, what's worse, you can never make out what he is trying to say. The deadly dulness is awful, the very flies expire. It can only be compared with the boredom in the assembly-hall at the yearly meeting when the traditional address is read—damn it !"

And at once an abrupt transition:

" Three years ago—Nikolay Stepanovitch here will remember it—I had to deliver that address. It was hot, stifling, my uniform cut me under the arms—it was deadly ! I read for half an hour, for an hour, for an hour and a half, for two hours. . . . ' Come,' I thought; ' thank God, there are only ten pages left !' And at the end there were four pages that there was no need to read, and I reckoned to leave them out. ' So there are only six really,' I thought; ' that is, only six pages left to read.' But, only fancy, I chanced to glance before me, and, sitting in the front row, side by side, were a general with a ribbon on his

722

breast and a bishop. The poor beggars were numb with boredom; they were staring with their eyes wide open to keep awake, and yet they were trying to put on an expression of attention and to pretend that they understood what I was saying and liked it. 'Well,' I thought, 'since you like it you shall have it! I'll pay you out;' so I just gave them those four pages too."

As is usual with ironical people, when he talks nothing in his face smiles but his eyes and eyebrows. At such times there is no trace of hatred or spite in his eyes, but a great deal of humour, and that peculiar fox-like slyness which is only to be noticed in very observant people. Since I am speaking about his eyes, I notice another peculiarity in them. When he takes a glass from Katya, or listens to her speaking, or looks after her as she goes out of the room for a moment, I notice in his eyes something gentle, beseeching, pure. . . .

The maid-servant takes away the samovar and puts on the table a large piece of cheese, some fruit, and a bottle of Crimean champagne—a rather poor wine of which Katya had grown fond in the Crimea. Mihail Fyodorovitch takes two packs of cards off the whatnot and begins to play patience. According to him, some varieties of patience require great concentration and attention, yet while he lays out the cards he does not leave off distracting his attention with talk. Katya watches his cards attentively, and more by gesture than by words helps him in his play. She drinks no more than a couple of wine-glasses of wine the whole evening; I drink four glasses, and the rest of the bottle falls to the share of Mihail Fyodorovitch, who can drink a great deal and never get drunk.

Over our patience we settle various questions, principally of the higher order, and what we care for most of all—that is, science and learning—is more roughly handled than anything.

" Science, thank God, has outlived its day," says Mihail Fyodorovitch emphatically. " Its song is sung. Yes, indeed. Mankind begins to feel impelled to replace it by something different. It has grown on the soil of superstition, been nourished by superstition, and is now just as much the quintessence of superstition as its defunct granddames, alchemy, metaphysics, and philosophy. And, after all, what has it given to mankind ? Why, the difference between the learned Europeans and the Chinese who have no science is trifling, purely external. The Chinese know nothing of science, but what have they lost thereby ?"

" Flies know nothing of science, either," I observe, " but what of that ?"

" There is no need to be angry, Nikolay Stepanovitch. I only say this here between ourselves. . . . I am more careful than you think, and I am not going to say this in public—God forbid ! The superstition exists in the multitude that the arts and sciences are superior to agriculture, commerce, superior to handicrafts. Our sect is maintained by that superstition, and it is not for you and me to destroy it. God forbid !"

After patience the younger generation comes in for a dressing too.

" Our audiences have degenerated," sighs Mihail Fyodorovitch. " Not to speak of ideals and all the rest of it, if only they were capable of work and rational thought ! In fact, it's a case of ' I look with mournful eyes on the young men of to-day.' "

" Yes; they have degenerated horribly," Katya agrees. " Tell me, have you had one man of distinction among them for the last five or ten years ?"

" I don't know how it is with the other professors, but I can't remember any among mine."

" I have seen in my day many of your students and young scientific men and many actors—well, I have never once been so fortunate as to meet—I won't say a hero or a man of talent, but even an interesting man. It's all the same grey mediocrity, puffed up with self-conceit."

All this talk of degeneration always affects me as though I had accidentally overheard offensive talk about my own daughter. It offends me that these charges are wholesale, and rest on such worn-out commonplaces, on such wordy vapourings as degeneration and absence of ideals, or on references to the splendours of the past. Every accusation, even if it is uttered in ladies' society, ought to be formulated with all possible definiteness, or it is not an accusation, but idle disparagement, unworthy of decent people.

I am an old man, I have been lecturing for thirty years, but I notice neither degeneration nor lack of ideals, and I don't find that the present is worse than the past. My porter Nikolay, whose experience of this subject has its value, says that the students of to-day are neither better nor worse than those of the past.

If I were asked what I don't like in my pupils of to-day, I should answer the question, not straight off and not at length, but with sufficient definiteness. I know their failings, and so have no need to resort to vague generalities. I don't like their smoking, using spirituous beverages, marrying late, and often being so irresponsible and careless that they will let one of their number be starving in their midst while they neglect to pay their subscriptions to the Students' Aid Society. They don't know modern languages, and they don't express themselves correctly in Russian; no longer ago than yesterday my colleague, the professor of hygiene, complained to me that he had to give twice as many lectures, because the students had a very poor knowledge of physics and were utterly ignorant of meteorology. They are readily carried away by the influence of the last new writers, even when they are not first-rate, but they take absolutely no interest in classics such as Shakespeare, Marcus Aurelius, Epictetus, or Pascal, and this inability to distinguish the great from the small betrays their ignorance of practical life more than anything. All difficult questions that have more or less a social character (for instance the migration question) they settle by studying monographs on the subject, but not by way of scientific investigation or experiment, though that method is at their disposal and is more in keeping with their calling. They gladly become ward-surgeons,

assistants, demonstrators, external teachers, and
are ready to fill such posts till they are forty,
though independence, a sense of freedom and
personal initiative, are no less necessary in science
than, for instance, in art or commerce. I have
pupils and listeners, but no successors and helpers,
and so I love them and am touched by them, but
am not proud of them. And so on, and so on. . . .

Such shortcomings, however numerous they
may be, can only give rise to a pessimistic or
fault-finding temper in a faint-hearted and timid
man. All these failings have a casual, transitory
character, and are completely dependent on
conditions of life; in some ten years they will
have disappeared or given place to other fresh
defects, which are all inevitable and will in their
turn alarm the faint-hearted. The students' sins
often vex me, but that vexation is nothing in
comparison with the joy I have been experiencing
now for the last thirty years when I talk to my
pupils, lecture to them, watch their relations,
and compare them with people not of their circle.

Mihail Fyodorovitch speaks evil of everything.
Katya listens, and neither of them notices into
what depths the apparently innocent diversion
of finding fault with their neighbours is gradually
drawing them. They are not conscious how by
degrees simple talk passes into malicious mockery
and jeering, and how they are both beginning
to drop into the habits and methods of slander.

" Killing types one meets with," says Mihail
Fyodorovitch. " I went yesterday to our friend
Yegor Petrovitch's, and there I found a studious

gentleman, one of your medicals in his third year,
I believe. Such a face! . . . in the Dobrolubov
style, the imprint of profound thought on his
brow; we got into talk. 'Such doings, young
man,' said I. 'I've read,' said I, 'that some
German—I've forgotten his name—has created
from the human brain a new kind of alkaloid,
idiotine.' What do you think? He believed it,
and there was positively an expression of respect
on his face, as though to say, 'See what we fellows
can do!' And the other day I went to the theatre.
I took my seat. In the next row directly in front
of me were sitting two men: one of 'us fellows'
and apparently a law student, the other a shaggy-
looking figure, a medical student. The latter was
as drunk as a cobbler. He did not look at the
stage at all. He was dozing with his nose on his
shirt-front. But as soon as an actor begins
loudly reciting a monologue, or simply raises his
voice, our friend starts, pokes his neighbour in the
ribs, and asks, 'What is he saying? Is it elevating?'
'Yes,' answers one of our fellows. 'B-r-r-ravo!'
roars the medical student. 'Elevating! Bravo!'
He had gone to the theatre, you see, the drunken
blockhead, not for the sake of art, the play, but
for elevation! He wanted noble sentiments."

Katya listens and laughs. She has a strange
laugh; she catches her breath in rhythmically
regular gasps, very much as though she were
playing the accordion, and nothing in her face
is laughing but her nostrils. I grow depressed
and don't know what to say. Beside myself, I
fire up, leap up from my seat, and cry:

" Do leave off ! Why are you sitting here like two toads, poisoning the air with your breath ? Give over !"

And without waiting for them to finish their gossip I prepare to go home. And, indeed, it is high time: it is past ten.

" I will stay a little longer" says Mihail Fyodorovitch. " Will you allow me, Ekaterina Vladimirovna ?"

" I will," answers Katya.

" *Bene !* In that case have up another little bottle."

They both accompany me with candles to the hall, and while I put on my fur coat, Mihail Fyodorovitch says:

" You have grown dreadfully thin and older looking, Nikolay Stepanovitch. What's the matter with you ? Are you ill ?"

" Yes; I am not very well."

" And you are not doing anything for it . . ." Katya puts in grimly.

" Why don't you ? You can't go on like that ! God helps those who help themselves, my dear fellow. Remember me to your wife and daughter, and make my apologies for not having been to see them. In a day or two, before I go abroad, I shall come to say good-bye. I shall be sure to. I am going away next week."

I come away from Katya, irritated and alarmed by what has been said about my being ill, and dissatisfied with myself. I ask myself whether I really ought not to consult one of my colleagues. And at once I imagine how my colleague, after listening to me, would walk away to the window without speaking, would think a moment, then would turn round to me and, trying to prevent my reading the truth in his face, would say in a careless tone: " So far I see nothing serious, but at the same time, *collega*, I advise you to lay aside your work. . . ." And that would deprive me of my last hope.

Who is without hope ? Now that I am diagnosing my illness and prescribing for myself, from time to time I hope that I am deceived by my own illness, that I am mistaken in regard to the albumen and the sugar I find, and in regard to my heart, and in regard to the swellings I have twice noticed in the mornings; when with the fervour of the hypochondriac I look through the textbooks of therapeutics and take a different medicine every day, I keep fancying that I shall hit upon something comforting. All that is petty.

Whether the sky is covered with clouds or the moon and the stars are shining, I turn my eyes towards it every evening and think that death is taking me soon. One would think that my thoughts at such times ought to be deep as the sky, brilliant, striking. . . . But no ! I think about myself, about my wife, about Liza, Gnekker, the students, people in general; my thoughts are evil, petty, I am insincere with myself, and at such times my theory of life may be expressed in the words the celebrated Araktcheev said in one of his intimate letters: " Nothing good can exist in the world without evil, and there is more evil than good." That is, everything is disgusting; there is nothing

to live for, and the sixty-two years I have already
lived must be reckoned as wasted. I catch myself
in these thoughts, and try to persuade myself that
they are accidental, temporary, and not deeply
rooted in me, but at once I think:

" If so, what drives me every evening to those
two toads ? "

And I vow to myself that I will never go to
Katya's again, though I know I shall go next
evening.

Ringing the bell at the door and going upstairs,
I feel that I have no family now and no desire
to bring it back again. It is clear that the new
Araktcheev thoughts are not casual, temporary
visitors, but have possession of my whole being,
With my conscience ill at ease, dejected, languid.
hardly able to move my limbs, feeling as though
tons were added to my weight, I get into bed and
quickly drop asleep.

And then—insomnia !

IV.

Summer comes on and life is changed.

One fine morning Liza comes in to me and says
in a jesting tone:

" Come, your Excellency ! We are ready."

My Excellency is conducted into the street, and
seated in a cab. As I go along, having nothing to
do, I read the signboards from right to left. The
word " Traktir " reads " Ritkart "; that would
just suit some baron's family: Baroness Ritkart.
Farther on I drive through fields, by the graveyard,

which makes absolutely no impression on me,
though I shall soon lie in it; then I drive by
forests and again by fields. There is nothing of
interest. After two hours of driving, my Excellency is conducted into the lower storey of a summer
villa and installed in a small, very cheerful little
room with light blue hangings.

At night there is sleeplessness as before, but in
the morning I do not put a good face upon it and
listen to my wife, but lie in bed. I do not sleep,
but lie in the drowsy, half-conscious condition
in which you know you are not asleep, but dreaming. At midday I get up and from habit sit down
at my table, but I do not work now; I amuse
myself with French books in yellow covers, sent
me by Katya. Of course, it would be more patriotic
to read Russian authors, but I must confess I
cherish no particular liking for them. With the
exception of two or three of the older writers,
all our literature of to-day strikes me as not being
literature, but a special sort of home industry,
which exists simply in order to be encouraged,
though people do not readily make use of its
products. The very best of these home products
cannot be called remarkable and cannot be
sincerely praised without qualification. I must say
the same of all the literary novelties I have read
during the last ten or fifteen years; not one of them
is remarkable, and not one of them can be praised
without a " but." Cleverness, a good tone, but
no talent; talent, a good tone, but no cleverness;
or talent, cleverness, but not a good tone.

I don't say the French books have talent,

cleverness, and a good tone. They don't satisfy me, either. But they are not so tedious as the Russian, and it is not unusual to find in them the chief element of artistic creation—the feeling of personal freedom which is lacking in the Russian authors. I don't remember one new book in which the author does not try from the first page to entangle himself in all sorts of conditions and contracts with his conscience. One is afraid to speak of the naked body; another ties himself up hand and foot in psychological analysis; a third must have a "warm attitude to man"; a fourth purposely scrawls whole descriptions of nature that he may not be suspected of writing with a purpose. . . . One is bent upon being middle-class in his work, another must be a nobleman, and so on. There is intentionalness, circumspection, and self-will, but they have neither the independence nor the manliness to write as they like, and therefore there is no creativeness.

All this applies to what is called belles-lettres.

As for serious treatises in Russian on sociology, for instance, on art, and so on, I do not read them simply from timidity. In my childhood and early youth I had for some reason a terror of doorkeepers and attendants at the theatre, and that terror has remained with me to this day. I am afraid of them even now. It is said that we are only afraid of what we do not understand. And, indeed, it is very difficult to understand why doorkeepers and theatre attendants are so dignified, haughty, and majestically rude. I feel exactly the same terror when I read serious articles.

Their extraordinary dignity, their bantering lordly tone, their familiar manner to foreign authors, their ability to split straws with dignity— all that is beyond my understanding; it is intimidating and utterly unlike the quiet, gentlemanly tone to which I am accustomed when I read the works of our medical and scientific writers. It oppresses me to read not only the articles written by serious Russians, but even works translated or edited by them. The pretentious, edifying tone of the preface; the redundancy of remarks made by the translator, which prevent me from concentrating my attention; the question marks and " sic " in parenthesis scattered all over the book or article by the liberal translator, are to my mind an outrage on the author and on my independence as a reader.

Once I was summoned as an expert to a circuit court; in an interval one of my fellow-experts drew my attention to the rudeness of the public prosecutor to the defendants, among whom there were two ladies of good education. I believe I did not exaggerate at all when I told him that the prosecutor's manner was no ruder than that of the authors of serious articles to one another. Their manners are, indeed, so rude that I cannot speak of them without distaste. They treat one another and the writers they criticize either with superfluous respect, at the sacrifice of their own dignity, or, on the contrary, with far more ruthlessness than I have shown in my notes and my thoughts in regard to my future son-in-law Gnekker. Accusations of irrationality, of evil intentions, and, indeed, of every sort of crime, form an habitual ornament of serious articles. And that, as young medical men are fond of saying in their monographs, is the *ultima ratio!* Such ways must infallibly have an effect on the morals of the younger generation of writers, and so I am not at all surprised that in the new works with which our literature has been enriched during the last ten or fifteen years the heroes drink too much vodka and the heroines are not over-chaste.

I read French books, and I look out of the window which is open; I can see the spikes of my garden-fence, two or three scraggy trees, and beyond the fence the road, the fields, and beyond them a broad stretch of pine-wood. Often I admire a boy and girl, both flaxen-headed and ragged, who clamber on the fence and laugh at my baldness. In their shining little eyes I read, "Go up, go up, thou baldhead!" They are almost the only people who care nothing for my celebrity or my rank.

Visitors do not come to me every day now. I will only mention the visits of Nikolay and Pyotr Ignatyevitch. Nikolay usually comes to me on holidays, with some pretext of business, though really to see me. He arrives very much exhilarated, a thing which never occurs to him in the winter.

"What have you to tell me?" I ask, going out to him in the hall.

"Your Excellency!" he says, pressing his hand to his heart and looking at me with the ecstasy of a lover—"your Excellency! God be my

735

witness! Strike me dead on the spot! *Gaudeamus egitur juventus!*"

And he greedily kisses me on the shoulder, on the sleeve, and on the buttons.

" Is everything going well ?" I ask him.

" Your Excellency ! So help me God ! . . ."

He persists in grovelling before me for no sort of reason, and soon bores me, so I send him away to the kitchen, where they give him dinner.

Pyotr Ignatyevitch comes to see me on holidays, too, with the special object of seeing me and sharing his thoughts with me. He usually sits down near my table, modest, neat, and reasonable, and does not venture to cross his legs or put his elbows on the table. All the time, in a soft, even, little voice, in rounded bookish phrases, he tells me various, to his mind, very interesting and piquant items of news which he has read in the magazines and journals. They are all alike and may be reduced to this type: " A Frenchman has made a discovery; someone else, a German, has denounced him, proving that the discovery was made in 1870 by some American; while a third person, also a German, trumps them both by proving they both had made fools of themselves, mistaking bubbles of air for dark pigment under the microscope. Even when he wants to amuse me, Pyotr Ignatyevitch tells me things in the same lengthy, circumstantial manner as though he were defending a thesis, enumerating in detail the literary sources from which he is deriving his narrative, doing his utmost to be accurate as to the date and number of the journals and the name of everyone concerned, invariably mentioning it in full—Jean Jacques Petit, never simply Petit. Sometimes he stays to dinner with us, and then during the whole of dinner-time he goes on telling me the same sort of piquant anecdotes, reducing everyone at table to a state of dejected boredom. If Gnekker and Liza begin talking before him of fugues and counterpoint, Brahms and Bach, he drops his eyes modestly, and is overcome with embarrassment; he is ashamed that such trivial subjects should be discussed before such serious people as him and me.

In my present state of mind five minutes of him is enough to sicken me as though I had been seeing and hearing him for an eternity. I hate the poor fellow. His soft, smooth voice and bookish language exhaust me, and his stories stupefy me. . . . He cherishes the best of feelings for me, and talks to me simply in order to give me pleasure, and I repay him by looking at him as though I wanted to hypnotize him, and think, " Go, go, go ! . . ." But he is not amenable to thought-suggestion, and sits on and on and on. . . .

While he is with me I can never shake off the thought, " It's possible when I die he will be appointed to succeed me," and my poor lecture-hall presents itself to me as an oasis in which the spring is dried up; and I am ungracious, silent, and surly with Pyotr Ignatyevitch, as though he were to blame for such thoughts, and not I myself. When he begins, as usual, praising up the German savants, instead of making fun of him good-humouredly, as I used to do, I mutter sullenly:

" Asses, your Germans ! . . ."

That is like the late Professor Nikita Krylov, who once, when he was bathing with Pirogov at Revel and vexed at the water being very cold, burst out with, " Scoundrels, these Germans !" I behave badly with Pyotr Ignatyevitch, and only when he is going away, and from the window I catch a glimpse of his grey hat behind the garden-fence, I want to call out and say, " Forgive me, my dear fellow !"

Dinner is even drearier than in the winter. Gnekker, whom now I hate and despise, dines with us almost every day. I used to endure his presence in silence, now I aim biting remarks at him which make my wife and daughter blush. Carried away by evil feeling, I often say things that are simply stupid, and I don't know why I say them. So on one occasion it happened that I stared a long time at Gnekker, and, *à propos* of nothing, I fired off:

" An eagle may perchance swoop down below a cock,
But never will the fowl soar upwards to the clouds. . . ."

And the most vexatious thing is that the fowl Gnekker shows himself much cleverer than the eagle professor. Knowing that my wife and daughter are on his side, he takes up the line of meeting my gibes with condescending silence, as though to say:

" The old chap is in his dotage; what's the use of talking to him ?"

Or he makes fun of me good-naturedly. It is wonderful how petty a man may become ! I am capable of dreaming all dinner-time of how Gnekker will turn out to be an adventurer, how my wife and Liza will come to see their mistake, and how I will taunt them—and such absurd thoughts at the time when I am standing with one foot in the grave !

There are now, too, misunderstandings of which in the old days I had no idea except from hearsay. Though I am ashamed of it, I will describe one that occurred the other day after dinner.

I was sitting in my room smoking a pipe; my wife came in as usual, sat down, and began saying what a good thing it would be for me to go to Harkov now while it is warm and I have free time, and there find out what sort of person our Gnekker is.

" Very good; I will go," I assented.

My wife, pleased with me, got up and was going to the door, but turned back and said:

" By the way, I have another favour to ask of you. I know you will be angry, but it is my duty to warn you. . . . Forgive my saying it, Nikolay Stepanovitch, but all our neighbours and acquaintances have begun talking about your being so often at Katya's. She is clever and well-educated; I don't deny that her company may be agreeable; but at your age and with your social position it seems strange that you should find pleasure in her society. . . . Besides, she has such a reputation that . . ."

All the blood suddenly rushed to my brain, my eyes flashed fire, I leaped up and, clutching at my head and stamping my feet, shouted in a voice unlike my own:

" Let me alone ! let me alone ! let me alone !"

Probably my face was terrible, my voice was strange, for my wife suddenly turned pale and began shrieking aloud in a despairing voice that was utterly unlike her own. Liza, Gnekker, then Yegor, came running in at our shouts. . . .

" Let me alone !" I cried; " let me alone ! Go away !".

My legs turned numb as though they had ceased to exist; I felt myself falling into someone's arms; for a little while I still heard weeping, then sank into a swoon which lasted two or three hours.

Now about Katya; she comes to see me every day towards evening, and of course neither the neighbours nor our acquaintances can avoid noticing it. She comes in for a minute and carries me off for a drive with her. She has her own horse and a new chaise bought this summer. Altogether she lives in an expensive style; she has taken a big detached villa with a large garden, and has brought all her town retinue with her—two maids, a coachman . . . I often ask her:

" Katya, what will you live on when you have spent your father's money ?"

" Then we shall see," she answers.

" That money, my dear, deserves to be treated more seriously. It was earned by a good man, by honest labour."

" You have told me that already. I know it."

At first we drive through the open country, then through the pine-wood which is visible from my window. Nature seems to me as beautiful as it always has been, though some evil spirit whispers

740

to me that these pines and fir trees, birds, and white
clouds on the sky, will not notice my absence
when in three or four months I am dead. Katya
loves driving, and she is pleased that it is fine
weather and that I am sitting beside her. She is
in good spirits and does not say harsh things.

" You are a very good man, Nikolay Stepanovitch," she says. " You are a rare specimen, and
there isn't an actor who would understand how to
play you. Me or Mihail Fyodorovitch, for instance, any poor actor could do, but not you.
And I envy you, I envy you horribly ! Do you
know what I stand for ? What ?"

She ponders for a minute, and then asks me :

" Nikolay Stepanovitch, I am a negative
phenomenon ! Yes ?"

" Yes," I answer.

" H'm ! what am I to do ?"

What answer was I to make her ? It is easy to
say " work," or " give your possessions to the
poor," or " know yourself," and because it is so
easy to say that, I don't know what to answer.

My colleagues when they teach therapeutics
advise " the individual study of each separate
case." One has but to obey this advice to gain
the conviction that the methods recommended
in the textbooks as the best and as providing
a safe basis for treatment turn out to be quite
unsuitable in individual cases. It is just the same
in moral ailments.

But I must make some answer, and I say :

" You have too much free time, my dear ; you
absolutely must take up some occupation. After

all, why shouldn't you be an actress again if it is your vocation?"

" I cannot!"

" Your tone and manner suggest that you are a victim. I don't like that, my dear; it is your own fault. Remember, you began with falling out with people and methods, but you have done nothing to make either better. You did not struggle with evil, but were cast down by it, and you are not the victim of the struggle, but of your own impotence. Well, of course you were young and inexperienced then; now it may all be different. Yes, really, go on the stage. You will work, you will serve a sacred art."

" Don't pretend, Nikolay Stepanovitch," Katya interrupts me. " Let us make a compact once for all; we will talk about actors, actresses, and authors, but we will let art alone. You are a splendid and rare person, but you don't know enough about art sincerely to think it sacred. You have no instinct or feeling for art. You have been hard at work all your life, and have not had time to acquire that feeling. Altogether . . . I don't like talk about art," she goes on nervously. " I don't like it! And, my goodness, how they have vulgarized it!"

" Who has vulgarized it?"

" They have vulgarized it by drunkenness, the newspapers by their familiar attitude, clever people by philosophy."

" Philosophy has nothing to do with it."

" Yes, it has. If anyone philosophizes about it, it shows he does not understand it."

742

To avoid bitterness I hasten to change the subject, and then sit a long time silent. Only when we are driving out of the wood and turning towards Katya's villa I go back to my former question, and say:

" You have still not answered me, why you don't want to go on the stage."

" Nikolay Stepanovitch, this is cruel !" she cries, and suddenly flushes all over. " You want me to tell you the truth aloud ? Very well, if · . . . if you like it ! I have no talent ! No talent and . . . and a great deal of vanity ! So there !"

After making this confession she turns her face away from me, and to hide the trembling of her hands tugs violently at the reins.

As we are driving towards her villa we see Mihail Fyodorovitch walking near the gate, impatiently awaiting us.

" That Mihail Fyodorovitch again !" says Katya with vexation. " Do rid me of him, please ! I am sick and tired of him . . . bother him !"

Mihail Fyodorovitch ought to have gone abroad long ago, but he puts off going from week to week. Of late there have been certain changes in him. He looks, as it were, sunken, has taken to drinking until he is tipsy, a thing which never used to happen to him, and his black eyebrows are beginning to turn grey. When our chaise stops at the gate he does not conceal his joy and his impatience. He fussily helps me and Katya out, hurriedly asks questions, laughs, rubs his hands, and that gentle, imploring, pure expression, which I used to notice

743

only in his eyes, is now suffused all over his face. He is glad and at the same time he is ashamed of his gladness, ashamed of his habit of spending every evening with Katya. And he thinks it necessary to explain his visit by some obvious absurdity such as: " I was driving by, and I thought I would just look in for a minute."

We all three go indoors; first we drink tea, then the familiar packs of cards, the big piece of cheese, the fruit, and the bottle of Crimean champagne are put upon the table. The subjects of our conversation are not new; they are just the same as in the winter. We fall foul of the University, the students, and literature and the theatre; the air grows thick and stifling with evil speaking, and poisoned by the breath, not of two toads as in the winter, but of three. Besides the velvety baritone laugh and the giggle like the gasp of a concertina, the maid who waits upon us hears an unpleasant cracked " He, he !" like the chuckle of a general in a vaudeville.

V.

There are terrible nights with thunder, lightning, rain, and wind, such as are called among the people " sparrow nights." There has been one such night in my personal life. . . .

I woke up after midnight and leaped suddenly out of bed. It seemed to me for some reason that I was just immediately going to die. Why did it seem so ? I had no sensation in my body that suggested my immediate death, but my soul was oppressed with terror, as though I had suddenly seen a vast menacing glow of fire.

I rapidly struck a light, drank some water straight out of the decanter, then hurried to the open window. The weather outside was magnificent. There was a smell of hay and some other very sweet scent. I could see the spikes of the fence, the gaunt, drowsy trees by the window, the road, the dark streak of woodland; there was a serene, very bright moon in the sky and not a single cloud, perfect stillness, not one leaf stirring. I felt that everything was looking at me and waiting for me to die. . . .

It was uncanny. I closed the window and ran to my bed. I felt for my pulse, and not finding it in my wrist, tried to find it in my temple, then in my chin, and again in my wrist, and everything I touched was cold and clammy with sweat. My breathing came more and more rapidly, my body was shivering, all my inside was in commotion; I had a sensation on my face and on my bald head as though they were covered with spiders' webs.

What should I do? Call my family? No; it would be no use. I could not imagine what my wife and Liza would do when they came in to me.

I hid my head under the pillow, closed my eyes, and waited and waited. . . . My spine was cold; it seemed to be drawn inwards, and I felt as though death were coming upon me stealthily from behind. . . .

" Kee-vee ! kee-vee !" I heard a sudden shriek

in the night's stillness, and did not know where it was—in my breast or in the street. " Kee-vee ! kee-vee !"

" My God, how terrible !" I would have drunk some more water, but by then it was fearful to open my eyes and I was afraid to raise my head. I was possessed by unaccountable animal terror, and I cannot understand why I was so frightened: was it that I wanted to live, or that some new unknown pain was in store for me ?

Upstairs, overhead, someone moaned or laughed. . . . I listened. Soon afterwards there was a sound of footsteps on the stairs. Someone came hurriedly down, then went up again. A minute later there was a sound of steps downstairs again; someone stopped near my door and listened.

" Who is there ?" I cried.

The door opened. I boldly opened my eyes, and saw my wife. Her face was pale and her eyes were tear-stained.

" You are not asleep, Nikolay Stepanovitch ?" she asked.

" What is it ?"

" For God's sake, go up and have a look at Liza; there is something the matter with her. . . ."

" Very good, with pleasure," I muttered, greatly relieved at not being alone. " Very good, this minute. . . ."

I followed my wife, heard what she said to me, and was too agitated to understand a word. Patches of light from her candle danced about the stairs, our long shadows trembled. My feet caught in the skirts of my dressing-gown; I gasped for breath, and felt as though something were pursuing me and trying to catch me from behind.

" I shall die on the spot, here on the staircase," I thought. " On the spot. . . ." But we passed the staircase, the dark corridor with the Italian windows, and went into Liza's room. She was sitting on the bed in her nightdress, with her bare feet hanging down, and she was moaning.

" Oh, my God ! Oh, my God !" she was muttering, screwing up her eyes at our candle. " I can't bear it."

" Liza, my child," I said, " what is it ?"

Seeing me, she began crying out, and flung herself on my neck.

" My kind papa ! . . ." she sobbed—" my dear, good papa . . . my darling, my pet, I don't know what is the matter with me. . . . I am miserable !"

She hugged me, kissed me, and babbled fond words I used to hear from her when she was a child.

" Calm yourself, my child. God be with you," I said. " There is no need to cry. I am miserable, too."

I tried to tuck her in; my wife gave her water, and we awkwardly stumbled by her bedside; my shoulder jostled against her shoulder, and meanwhile I was thinking how we used to give our children their bath together.

" Help her ! help her !" my wife implored me. " Do something !"

What could I do ? I could do nothing. There was some load on the girl's heart; but I did not understand, I knew nothing about it, and could only mutter:

" It's nothing, it's nothing; it will pass. Sleep, sleep !"

To make things worse, there was a sudden sound of dogs howling, at first subdued and uncertain, then loud, two dogs howling together. I had never attached significance to such omens as the howling of dogs or the shrieking of owls, but on that occasion it sent a pang to my heart, and I hastened to explain the howl to myself.

" It's nonsense," I thought, " the influence of one organism on another. The intensely strained condition of my nerves has infected my wife, Liza, the dog—that is all. . . . Such infection explains presentiments, forebodings. . . ."

When a little later I went back to my room to write a prescription for Liza, I no longer thought I should die at once, but only had such a weight, such a feeling of oppression in my soul that I felt actually sorry that I had not died on the spot. For a long time I stood motionless in the middle of the room, pondering what to prescribe for Liza. But the moans overhead ceased, and I decided to prescribe nothing, and yet I went on standing there. . . .

There was a deathlike stillness, such a stillness, as some author has expressed it, " it rang in one's ears." Time passed slowly; the streaks of moonlight on the window-sill did not shift their position, but seemed as though frozen. . . . It was still some time before dawn.

But the gate in the fence creaked, someone stole in and, breaking a twig from one of those scraggy trees, cautiously tapped on the window with it.

A DREARY STORY

" Nikolay Stepanovitch," I heard a whisper. " Nikolay Stepanovitch."

I opened the window, and fancied I was dreaming: under the window, huddled against the wall, stood a woman in a black dress, with the moonlight bright upon her, looking at me with great eyes. Her face was pale, stern, and weird-looking in the moonlight, like marble, her chin was quivering.

" It is I," she said—" I . . . . Katya."

In the moonlight all women's eyes look big and black, all people look taller and paler, and that was probably why I had not recognized her for the first minute.

" What is it ?"

" Forgive me !" she said. " I suddenly felt unbearably miserable . . . I couldn't stand it, so came here. There was a light in your window and . . . and I ventured to knock. . . . I beg your pardon. . . . Ah ! if you knew how miserable I am ! What are you doing just now ?"

" Nothing. . . . I can't sleep."

" I had a feeling that there was something wrong, but that is nonsense."

Her brows were lifted, her eyes shone with tears, and her whole face was lighted up with the familiar look of trustfulness which I had not seen for so long.

" Nikolay Stepanovitch," she said imploringly, stretching out both hands to me, " my precious friend, I beg you, I implore you. . . . If you don't despise my affection and respect for you, consent to what I ask of you."

" What is it ?"

749

" Take my money from me !"

" Come ! what an idea ! What do I want with your money ?"

" You'll go away somewhere for your health. . . . You ought to go for your health. Will you take it ? Yes ? Nikolay Stepanovitch darling, yes ?"

She looked greedily into my face and repeated: " Yes, you will take it ?"

" No, my dear, I won't take it . . ." I said. ' Thank you."

She turned her back upon me and bowed her head. Probably I refused her in a tone which made further conversation about money impossible.

" Go home to bed," I said. " We will see each other to-morrow."

" So you don't consider me your friend ?" she asked dejectedly.

" I don't say that. But your money would be no use to me now."

" I beg your pardon . . ." she said, dropping her voice a whole octave. " I understand you . . . to be indebted to a person like me . . . a retired actress. . . . But, good-bye. . . ."

And she went away so quickly that I had not time even to say good-bye.

VI.

I am in Harkov.

As it would be useless to contend against my present mood and, indeed, beyond my power, I have made up my mind that the last days of my life shall at least be irreproachable externally.

If I am unjust in regard to my wife and daughter, which I fully recognize, I will try and do as she wishes; since she wants me to go to Harkov, I go to Harkov. Besides, I have become of late so indifferent to everything that it is really all the same to me where I go, to Harkov, or to Paris, or to Berditchev.

I arrived here at midday, and have put up at the hotel not far from the cathedral. The train was jolting, there were draughts, and now I am sitting on my bed, holding my head and expecting tic douloureux. I ought to have gone to-day to see some professors of my acquaintance, but I have neither strength nor inclination.

The old corridor attendant comes in and asks whether I have brought my bed-linen. I detain him for five minutes, and put several questions to him about Gnekker, on whose account I have come here. The attendant turns out to be a native of Harkov; he knows the town like the fingers of his hand, but does not remember any household of the surname of Gnekker. I question him about the estate—the same answer.

The clock in the corridor strikes one, then two, then three. . . . These last months in which I am waiting for death seem much longer than the whole of my life. And I have never before been so ready to resign myself to the slowness of time as now. In the old days, when one sat in the station and waited for a train, or presided in an examination-room, a quarter of an hour would seem an eternity. Now I can sit all night on my bed without moving, and quite unconcernedly reflect that to-morrow will be followed by another night as long and colourless, and the day after to-morrow.

In the corridor it strikes five, six, seven. . . . It grows dark.

There is a dull pain in my cheek, the tic beginning. To occupy myself with thoughts, I go back to my old point of view, when I was not so indifferent, and ask myself why I, a distinguished man, a privy councillor, am sitting in this little hotel room, on this bed with the unfamiliar grey quilt. Why am I looking at that cheap tin washing-stand and listening to the whirr of the wretched clock in the corridor ? Is all this in keeping with my fame and my lofty position ? And I answer these questions with a jeer. I am amused by the naïveté with which I used in my youth to exaggerate the value of renown and of the exceptional position which celebrities are supposed to enjoy. I am famous, my name is pronounced with reverence, my portrait has been both in the *Niva* and in the *Illustrated News of the World* ; I have read my biography even in a German magazine. And what of all that ? Here I am sitting utterly alone in a strange town, on a strange bed, rubbing my aching cheek with my hand. . . . Domestic worries, the hard-heartedness of creditors, the rudeness of the railway servants, the inconveniences of the passport system, the expensive and unwholesome food in the refreshment-rooms, the general rudeness and coarseness in social intercourse—all this, and a great deal more which would take too long to reckon up, affects me as much as any working man who is famous only in his alley. In what way does my exceptional position find expression? Admitting that I am celebrated a thousand times over, that I am a hero of whom my country is proud. They publish bulletins of my illness in every paper, letters of sympathy come to me by post from my colleagues, my pupils, the general public; but all that does not prevent me from dying in a strange bed, in misery, in utter loneliness. Of course, no one is to blame for that; but I in my foolishness dislike my popularity. I feel as though it had cheated me.

At ten o'clock I fall asleep, and in spite of the tic I sleep soundly, and should have gone on sleeping if I had not been awakened. Soon after one came a sudden knock at the door.

" Who is there ?"

" A telegram."

" You might have waited till to-morrow," I say angrily, taking the telegram from the attendant. " Now I shall not get to sleep again."

" I am sorry. Your light was burning, so I thought you were not asleep."

I tear open the telegram and look first at the signature. From my wife.

" What does she want ?"

" Gnekker was secretly married to Liza yesterday. Return."

I read the telegram, and my dismay does not last long. I am dismayed, not by what Liza and Gnekker have done, but by the indifference with which I hear of their marriage. They say philosophers and the truly wise are indifferent. It is false: indifference is the paralysis of the soul; it is premature death.

I go to bed again, and begin trying to think of something to occupy my mind. What am I to think about ? I feel as though everything had been thought over already and there is nothing which could hold my attention now.

When daylight comes I sit up in bed with my arms round my knees, and to pass the time I try to know myself. " Know thyself " is excellent and useful advice; it is only a pity that the ancients never thought to indicate the means of following this precept.

When I have wanted to understand somebody or myself, I have considered, not the actions, in which everything is relative, but the desires.

" Tell me what you want, and I will tell you what manner of man you are."

And now I examine myself: what do I want ?

I want our wives, our children, our friends, our pupils, to love in us, not our fame, not the brand and not the label, but to love us as ordinary men. Anything else ? I should like to have had helpers and successors. Anything else ? I should like to wake up in a hundred years' time and to have just a peep out of one eye at what is happening in science. I should have liked to have lived another ten years. . . . What further ? Why, nothing further. I think and think, and can think of nothing more. And however much I might think, and however far my thoughts might travel, it is clear to me that there is nothing vital, nothing of great importance in my desires. In my passion for science, in my desire to live, in this sitting on a strange bed, and in this striving to know myself—in all the thoughts, feelings, and ideas I form about everything, there is no common bond to connect it all into one whole. Every feeling and every thought exists apart in me; and in all my criticisms of science, the theatre, literature, my pupils, and in all the pictures my imagination draws, even the most skilful analyst could not find what is called a general idea, or the god of a living man.

And if there is not that, then there is nothing.

In a state so poverty-stricken, a serious ailment, the fear of death, the influences of circumstance and men were enough to turn upside down and scatter in fragments all which I had once looked upon as my theory of life, and in which I had seen the meaning and joy of my existence. So there is nothing surprising in the fact that I have over-shadowed the last months of my life with thoughts and feelings only worthy of a slave and barbarian, and that now I am indifferent and take no heed of the dawn. When a man has not in him what is loftier and mightier than all external impressions, a bad cold is really enough to upset his equilibrium and make him begin to see an owl in every bird, to hear a dog howling in every sound. And all his pessimism or optimism with his thoughts great and small have at such times significance as symptoms and nothing more.

I am vanquished. If it is so, it is useless to

think, it is useless to talk. I will sit and wait in silence for what is to come.

In the morning the corridor attendant brings me tea and a copy of the local newspaper. Mechanically I read the advertisements on the first page, the leading article, the extracts from the newspapers and journals, the chronicle of events. . . . In the latter I find, among other things, the following paragraph: " Our distinguished savant, Professor Nikolay Stepanovitch So-and-so, arrived yesterday in Harkov, and is staying in the So-and-so Hotel."

Apparently, illustrious names are created to live on their own account, apart from those that bear them. Now my name is promenading tranquilly about Harkov; in another three months, printed in gold letters on my monument, it will shine bright as the sun itself, while I shall be already under the moss.

A light tap at the door. Somebody wants me.

" Who is there ? Come in."

The door opens, and I step back surprised and hurriedly wrap my dressing-gown round me. Before me stands Katya.

" How do you do ?" she says, breathless with running upstairs. " You didn't expect me ? I have come here, too. . . . I have come, too !"

She sits down and goes on, hesitating and not looking at me.

" Why don't you speak to me ? I have come, too . . . to-day. . . . I found out that you were in this hotel, and have come to you."

" Very glad to see you," I say, shrugging my shoulders, " but I am surprised. You seem to have dropped from the skies. What have you come for ?"

" Oh . . . I've simply come."

Silence. Suddenly she jumps up impulsively and comes to me.

" Nikolay Stepanovitch," she says, turning pale and pressing her hands on her bosom—" Nikolay Stepanovitch, I cannot go on living like this ! I cannot ! For God's sake, tell me quickly, this minute, what I am to do ! Tell me, what am I to do ?"

" What can I tell you ?" I ask in perplexity. " I can do nothing."

" Tell me, I beseech you," she goes on, breathing hard and trembling all over. " I swear that I cannot go on living like this. It's too much for me !"

She sinks on a chair and begins sobbing. She flings her head back, wrings her hands, taps with her feet; her hat falls off and hangs bobbing on its elastic; her hair is ruffled.

" Help me ! help me !" she implores me. " I cannot go on !"

She takes her handkerchief out of her travelling-bag, and with it pulls out several letters, which fall from her lap to the floor. I pick them up, and on one of them I recognize the handwriting of Mihail Fyodorovitch and accidentally read a bit of a word " passionat . . ."

" There is nothing I can tell you, Katya," I say.

" Help me !" she sobs, clutching at my hand and kissing it. " You are my father, you know, my only friend ! You are clever, educated; you have lived so long; you have been a teacher ! Tell me, what am I to do ?"

" Upon my word, Katya, I don't know. . . ."

I am utterly at a loss and confused, touched by her sobs, and hardly able to stand.

" Let us have lunch, Katya," I say, with a forced smile. " Give over crying."

And at once I add in a sinking voice:

" I shall soon be gone, Katya. . . ."

" Only one word, only one word !" she weeps, stretching out her hands to me.

" What am I to do ?"

" You are a queer girl, really . . ." I mutter. " I don't understand it ! So sensible, and all at once . . . crying your eyes out. . . ."

A silence follows. Katya straightens her hair, puts on her hat, then crumples up the letters and stuffs them in her bag—and all this deliberately, in silence. Her face, her bosom, and her gloves are wet with tears, but her expression now is cold and forbidding. . . . I look at her, and feel ashamed that I am happier than she. The absence of what my philosophic colleagues call a general idea I have detected in myself only just before death, in the decline of my days, while the soul of this poor girl has known and will know no refuge all her life, all her life !

" Let us have lunch, Katya," I say.

" No, thank you," she answers coldly.

Another minute passes in silence.

" I don't like Harkov," I say; " it's so grey here—such a grey town."

" Yes, perhaps. . . . It's ugly. I am here

not for long, passing through. I am going on
to-day."

" Where ?"

" To the Crimea . . . that is, to the Caucasus."

" Oh ! For long ?"

" I don't know."

Katya gets up, and, with a cold smile, holds
out her hand without looking at me.

I want to ask her, " Then, you won't be at my
funeral ?" but she does not look at me; her hand
is cold and, as it were, strange. I escort her to
the door in silence. She goes out, walks down the
long corridor without looking back; she knows
that I am looking after her, and most likely she
will look back at the turn.

No, she did not look back. I've seen her black
dress for the last time: her steps have died away.
Farewell, my treasure !

1889

AN INCIDENT

MORNING. Brilliant sunshine is piercing through the frozen lacework on the window-panes into the nursery. Vanya, a boy of six, with a cropped head and a nose like a button, and his sister Nina, a short, chubby, curly-headed girl of four, wake up and look crossly at each other through the bars of their cots.

" Oo-oo-oo ! naughty children ! " grumbles their nurse. " Good people have had their breakfast already, while you can't get your eyes open."

The sunbeams frolic over the rugs, the walls, and nurse's skirts, and seem inviting the children to join in their play, but they take no notice. They have woken up in a bad humour. Nina pouts, makes a grimace, and begins to whine :

" Brea-eakfast, nurse, breakfast ! "

Vanya knits his brows and ponders what to pitch upon to howl over. He has already begun screwing up his eyes and opening his mouth, but at that instant the voice of mamma reaches them from the drawing-room, saying: " Don't forget to give the cat her milk, she has a family now ! "

The children's puckered countenances grow smooth again as they look at each other in astonishment. Then both at once begin shouting, jump out of their cots, and filling the air with piercing shrieks, run barefoot, in their nightgowns, to the kitchen.

" The cat has puppies ! " they cry. " The cat has got puppies ! "

Under the bench in the kitchen there stands a small box, the one in which Stepan brings coal when he lights the fire. The cat is peeping out of the box. There is an expression of extreme exhaustion on her grey face ; her green eyes, with their narrow black pupils, have a languid, senti-mental look. . . . From her face it is clear that the only thing lacking to complete her happiness is the presence in the box of " him," the father of her children, to whom she had abandoned herself so recklessly ! She wants to mew, and opens her mouth wide, but nothing but a hiss comes from her throat ; the squealing of the kittens is audible.

The children squat on their heels before the box, and, motionless, holding their breath, gaze at the cat. . . . They are surprised, impressed, and do not hear nurse grumbling as she pursues them. The most genuine delight shines in the eyes of both.

Domestic animals play a scarcely noticed but undoubtedly beneficial part in the education and life of children. Which of us does not remember powerful but magnanimous dogs, lazy lapdogs, birds dying in captivity, dull-witted but haughty turkeys, mild old tabby cats, who forgave us when we trod on their tails for fun and caused them agonising pain ? I even fancy, sometimes, that the patience, the fidelity, the readiness to forgive, and the sincerity which are characteristic of our domestic animals have a far stronger and more definite effect on the mind of a child than the long exhortations of some dry, pale Karl Karlovitch, or the misty expositions of a governess, trying to prove to children that water is made up of hydrogen and oxygen.

" What little things ! " says Nina, opening her eyes wide and going off into a joyous laugh. " They are like mice ! "

" One, two, three," Vanya counts. " Three kittens. So there is one for you, one for me, and one for somebody else, too."

" Murrm . . . murrm . . ." purrs the mother, flattered by their attention. " Murrm."

After gazing at the kittens, the children take them from under the cat, and begin squeezing them in their hands, then, not satisfied with this, they put them in the skirts of their nightgowns, and run into the other rooms.

" Mamma, the cat has got pups ! " they shout.

Mamma is sitting in the drawing-room with some unknown gentleman. Seeing the children unwashed, undressed, with their nightgowns held up high, she is embarrassed, and looks at them severely.

" Let your nightgowns down, disgraceful children," she says. " Go out of the room, or I will punish you."

But the children do not notice either mamma's threats or the presence of a stranger. They put the kittens down on the carpet, and go off into deafening squeals. The mother walks round them, mewing imploringly. When, a little afterwards, the children are dragged off to the nursery, dressed, made to say their prayers, and given their breakfast, they are full of a passionate desire to get away from these prosaic duties as quickly as possible, and to run to the kitchen again.

Their habitual pursuits and games are thrown completely into the background.

The kittens throw everything into the shade by making their appearance in the world, and supply the great sensation of the day. If Nina or Vanya had been offered forty pounds of sweets or ten thousand kopecks for each kitten, they would have rejected such a barter without the slightest hesitation. In spite of the heated protests of the nurse and the cook, the children persist in sitting by the cat's box in the kitchen, busy with the kittens till dinner-time. Their faces are earnest and concentrated and express anxiety. They are worried not so much by the present as by the future of the kittens. They decide that one kitten shall remain at home with the old cat to be a comfort to her mother, while the second shall go to their summer villa, and the third shall live in the cellar, where there are ever so many rats.

" But why don't they look at us ? " Nina wondered. " Their eyes are blind like the beggars'."

Vanya, too, is perturbed by this question. He tries to open one kitten's eyes, and spends a long time puffing and breathing hard over it, but his operation is unsuccessful. They are a good deal troubled, too, by the circumstance that the kittens obstinately refuse the milk and the meat that is offered to them. Everything that is put before their little noses is eaten by their grey mamma.

" Let's build the kittens little houses," Vanya suggests. " They shall live in different houses, and the cat shall come and pay them visits. . . ."

Cardboard hat-boxes are put in the different corners of the kitchen and the kittens are installed in them. But this division turns out to be premature : the cat, still wearing an imploring and sentimental expression on her face, goes the round of all the hat-boxes, and carries off her children to their original position.

" The cat's their mother," observed Vanya, " but who is their father ? "

" Yes, who is their father ? " repeats Nina.

" They must have a father."

Vanya and Nina are a long time deciding who is to be the kittens' father, and, in the end, their choice falls on a big dark-red horse without a tail, which is lying in the store-cupboard under the stairs, together with other relics of toys that have outlived their day. They drag him up out of the store-cupboard and stand him by the box.

" Mind now ! " they admonish him, " stand here and see they behave themselves properly."

All this is said and done in the gravest way, with an expression of anxiety on their faces. Vanya and Nina refuse to recognise the existence of any world but the box of kittens. Their joy knows no bounds. But they have to pass through bitter, agonising moments, too.

Just before dinner, Vanya is sitting in his

father's study, gazing dreamily at the table. A
kitten is moving about by the lamp, on stamped
note paper. Vanya is watching its movements,
and thrusting first a pencil, then a match into its
little mouth. . . . All at once, as though he has
sprung out of the floor, his father is beside the
table.

" What's this ? " Vanya hears, in an angry voice.
" It's . . . it's the kitty, papa. . . ."

" I'll give it you ; look what you have done, you
naughty boy ! You've dirtied all my paper ! "

To Vanya's great surprise his papa does not
share his partiality for the kittens, and, instead of
being moved to enthusiasm and delight, he pulls
Vanya's ear and shouts :

" Stepan, take away this horrid thing."

At dinner, too, there is a scene. . . . During the
second course there is suddenly the sound of a
shrill mew. They begin to investigate its origin,
and discover a kitten under Nina's pinafore.

" Nina, leave the table ! " cries her father
angrily. " Throw the kittens in the cesspool !
I won't have the nasty things in the house ! . . ."

Vanya and Nina are horrified. Death in the
cesspool, apart from its cruelty, threatens to rob
the cat and the wooden horse of their children,
to lay waste the cat's box, to destroy their plans
for the future, that fair future in which one cat
will be a comfort to its old mother, another will
live in the country, while the third will catch rats
in the cellar. The children begin to cry and
entreat that the kittens may be spared. Their
father consents, but on the condition that the

children do not go into the kitchen and touch the kittens.

After dinner, Vanya and Nina slouch about the rooms, feeling depressed. The prohibition of visits to the kitchen has reduced them to dejection. They refuse sweets, are naughty, and are rude to their mother. When their uncle Petrusha comes in the evening, they draw him aside, and complain to him of their father, who wanted to throw the kittens into the cesspool.

" Uncle Petrusha, tell mamma to have the kittens taken to the nursery," the children beg their uncle, " do-o tell her."

" There, there . . . very well," says their uncle, waving them off. " All right."

Uncle Petrusha does not usually come alone. He is accompanied by Nero, a big black dog of Danish breed, with drooping ears, and a tail as hard as a stick. The dog is silent, morose, and full of a sense of his own dignity. He takes not the slightest notice of the children, and when he passes them hits them with his tail as though they were chairs. The children hate him from the bottom of their hearts, but on this occasion, practical considerations override sentiment.

" I say, Nina," says Vanya, opening his eyes wide. " Let Nero be their father, instead of the horse ! The horse is dead and he is alive, you see."

They are waiting the whole evening for the moment when papa will sit down to his cards and it will be possible to take Nero to the kitchen without being observed. . . . At last, papa sits down to cards, mamma is busy with the samovar and not noticing the children. . . .

The happy moment arrives.

" Come along ! " Vanya whispers to his sister.

But, at that moment, Stepan comes in and, with a snigger, announces :

" Nero has eaten the kittens, madam."

Nina and Vanya turn pale and look at Stepan with horror.

" He really has . . ." laughs the footman, " he went to the box and gobbled them up."

The children expect that all the people in the house will be aghast and fall upon the miscreant Nero. But they all sit calmly in their seats, and only express surprise at the appetite of the huge dog. Papa and mamma laugh. Nero walks about by the table, wags his tail, and licks his lips complacently . . . the cat is the only one who is uneasy. With her tail in the air she walks about the rooms, looking suspiciously at people and mewing plaintively.

" Children, it's past nine," cries mamma, " it's bedtime."

Vanya and Nina go to bed, shed tears, and spend a long time thinking about the injured cat, and the cruel, insolent, and unpunished Nero.

1886

767

AN ARTIST'S STORY

I

It was six or seven years ago when I was living in one of the districts of the province of T——, on the estate of a young landowner called Byelokurov, who used to get up very early, wear a peasant tunic, drink beer in the evenings, and continually complain to me that he never met with sympathy from anyone. He lived in the lodge in the garden, and I in the old seigniorial house, in a big room with columns, where there was no furniture except a wide sofa on which I used to sleep, and a table on which I used to lay out patience. There was always, even in still weather, a droning noise in the old Amos stoves, and in thunder-storms the whole house shook and seemed to be cracking into pieces; and it was rather terrifying, especially at night, when all the ten big windows were suddenly lit up by lightning.

Condemned by destiny to perpetual idleness, I did absolutely nothing. For hours together I gazed out of window at the sky, at the birds, at the avenue, read everything that was brought me by post, slept. Sometimes I went out of the house and wandered about till late in the evening.

AN ARTIST'S STORY

One day as I was returning home, I accidentally strayed into a place I did not know. The sun was already sinking, and the shades of evening lay across the flowering rye. Two rows of old, closely planted, very tall fir-trees stood like two dense walls forming a picturesque, gloomy avenue. I easily climbed over the fence and walked along the avenue, slipping over the fir-needles which lay two inches deep on the ground. It was still and dark, and only here and there on the high tree-tops the vivid golden light quivered and made rainbows in the spiders' webs. There was a strong, almost stifling smell of resin. Then I turned into a long avenue of limes. Here, too, all was desolation and age; last year's leaves rustled mournfully under my feet and in the twilight shadows lurked between the trees. From the old orchard on the right came the faint, reluctant note of the golden oriole, who must have been old too. But at last the limes ended. I walked by an old white house of two storeys with a terrace, and there suddenly opened before me a view of a courtyard, a large pond with a bathing-house, a group of green willows, and a village on the further bank, with a high, narrow belfry on which there glittered a cross reflecting the setting sun.

For a moment it breathed upon me the fascination of something near and very familiar, as though I had seen that landscape at some time in my childhood.

At the white stone gates which led from the yard to the fields, old-fashioned solid gates with lions on them, were standing two girls. One of them, the elder, a slim, pale, very handsome girl with a perfect haystack of chestnut hair and a little obstinate mouth, had a severe expression and scarcely took notice of me, while the other, who was still very young, not more than seventeen or eighteen, and was also slim and pale, with a large mouth and large eyes, looked at me with astonishment as I passed by, said something in English, and was overcome with embarrassment. And it seemed to me that these two charming faces, too, had long been familiar to me. And I returned home feeling as though I had had a delightful dream.

One morning soon afterwards, as Byelokurov and I were walking near the house, a carriage drove unexpectedly into the yard, rustling over the grass, and in it was sitting one of those girls. It was the elder one. She had come to ask for subscriptions for some villagers whose cottages had been burnt down. Speaking with great earnestness and precision, and not looking at us, she told us how many houses in the village of Siyanovo had been burnt, how many men, women, and children were left homeless, and what steps were proposed, to begin with, by the Relief Committee, of which she was now a member. After handing us the subscription list for our signatures, she put it away and immediately began to take leave of us.

"You have quite forgotten us, Pyotr Petrovitch," she said to Byelokurov as she shook hands with him. "Do come, and if Monsieur N. (she mentioned my name) cares to make the

acquaintance of admirers of his work, and will come and see us, mother and I will be delighted."
I bowed.

When she had gone Pyotr Petrovitch began to tell me about her. The girl was, he said, of good family, and her name was Lidia Voltchaninov, and the estate on which she lived with her mother and sister, like the village on the other side of the pond, was called Shelkovka. Her father had once held an important position in Moscow, and had died with the rank of a privy councillor. Although they had ample means, the Voltchaninovs lived on their estate summer and winter without going away. Lidia was a teacher in the Zemstvo school in her own village, and received a salary of twenty-five roubles a month. She spent nothing on herself but her salary, and was proud of earning her own living.

"An interesting family," said Byelokurov. "Let us go over one day. They will be delighted to see you."

One afternoon on a holiday we thought of the Voltchaninovs, and went to Shelkovka to see them. They—the mother and two daughters— were at home. The mother, Ekaterina Pavlovna, who at one time had been handsome, but now, asthmatic, depressed, vague, and over-feeble for her years, tried to entertain me with conversation about painting. Having heard from her daughter that I might come to Shelkovka, she had hurriedly recalled two or three of my landscapes which she had seen in exhibitions in Moscow, and now asked what I meant to express

by them. Lidia, or as they all called her, Lida,
talked more to Byelokurov than to me. Earnest
and unsmiling, she asked him why he was not on
the Zemstvo, and why he had not attended any
of its meetings.

" It's not right, Pyotr Petrovitch," she said
reproachfully. " It's not right. It's too bad."

" That's true, Lida—that's true," the mother
assented. " It isn't right."

" Our whole district is in the hands of Balagin,"
Lida went on, addressing me. " He is the chairman of the Zemstvo Board, and he has distributed
all the posts in the district among his nephews
and sons-in-law; and he does as he likes. He ought
to be opposed. The young men ought to make
a strong party, but you see what the young men
among us are like. It's a shame, Pyotr Petrovitch!"

The younger sister, Genya, was silent while
they were talking of the Zemstvo. She took no
part in serious conversation. She was not looked
upon as quite grown up by her family, and, like a
child, was always called by the nickname of Misuce,
because that was what she had called her English
governess when she was a child. She was all the
time looking at me with curiosity, and when I
glanced at the photographs in the album, she explained to me: " That's uncle . . . that's god-
father," moving her finger across the photograph.
As she did so she touched me with her shoulder
like a child, and I had a close view of her delicate,
undeveloped chest, her slender shoulders, her
plait, and her thin little body tightly drawn in
by her sash.

772

We played croquet and lawn tennis, we walked about the garden, drank tea, and then sat a long time over supper. After the huge empty room with columns, I felt, as it were, at home in this small snug house where there were no oleographs on the walls and where the servants were spoken to with civility. And everything seemed to me young and pure, thanks to the presence of Lida and Misuce, and there was an atmosphere of refinement over everything. At supper Lida talked to Byelokurov again of the Zemstvo, of Balagin, and of school libraries. She was an energetic, genuine girl, with convictions, and it was interesting to listen to her, though she talked a great deal and in a loud voice—perhaps because she was accustomed to talking at school. On the other hand, Pyotr Petrovitch, who had retained from his student days the habit of turning every conversation into an argument, was tedious, flat, long-winded, and unmistakably anxious to appear clever and advanced. Gesticulating, he upset a sauce-boat with his sleeve, making a huge pool on the tablecloth, but no one except me appeared to notice it.

It was dark and still as we went home.

" Good breeding is shown, not by not upsetting the sauce, but by not noticing it when somebody else does," said Byelokurov, with a sigh. " Yes, a splendid, intellectual family ! I've dropped out of all decent society; it's dreadful how I've dropped out of it ! It's all through work, work, work !"

He talked of how hard one had to work if one wanted to be a model farmer. And I thought what a heavy, sluggish fellow he was ! Whenever he talked of anything serious he articulated "Er-er" with intense effort, and worked just as he talked—slowly, always late and behind-hand. I had little faith in his business capacity if only from the fact that when I gave him letters to post he carried them about in his pocket for weeks together.

"The hardest thing of all," he muttered as he walked beside me—"the hardest thing of all is that, work as one may, one meets with no sympathy from anyone. No sympathy !"

II

I took to going to see the Voltchaninovs. As a rule I sat on the lower step of the terrace; I was fretted by dissatisfaction with myself; I was sorry at the thought of my life passing so rapidly and uninterestingly, and felt as though I would like to tear out of my breast the heart which had grown so heavy. And meanwhile I heard talk on the terrace, the rustling of dresses, the pages of a book being turned. I soon grew accustomed to the idea that during the day Lida received patients, gave out books, and often went into the village with a parasol and no hat, and in the evening talked aloud of the Zemstvo and schools. This slim, handsome, invariably austere girl, with her small well-cut mouth, always said dryly when the conversation turned on serious subjects:

' That's of no interest to you."

She did not like me. She disliked me because I was a landscape painter and did not in my pictures portray the privations of the peasants, and that, as she fancied, I was indifferent to what she put such faith in. I remember when I was travelling on the banks of Lake Baikal, I met a Buriat girl on horseback, wearing a shirt and trousers of blue Chinese canvas; I asked her if she would sell me her pipe. While we talked she looked contemptuously at my European face and hat, and in a moment she was bored with talking to me; she shouted to her horse and galloped on. And in just the same way Lida despised me as an alien. She never outwardly expressed her dislike for me, but I felt it, and sitting on the lower step of the terrace, I felt irritated, and said that doctoring peasants when one was not a doctor was deceiving them, and that it was easy to be benevolent when one had six thousand acres.

Meanwhile her sister Misuce had no cares, and spent her life in complete idleness just as I did. When she got up in the morning she immediately took up a book and sat down to read on the terrace in a deep arm-chair, with her feet hardly touching the ground, or hid herself with her book in the lime avenue, or walked out into the fields. She spent the whole day reading, poring greedily over her book, and only from the tired, dazed look in her eyes and the extreme paleness of her face one could divine how this continual reading exhausted her brain. When I arrived she would flush a little, leave her book, and looking into my face with her big eyes, would tell me eagerly of

775

anything that had happened—for instance, that
the chimney had been on fire in the servants' hall,
or that one of the men had caught a huge fish
in the pond. On ordinary days she usually went
about in a light blouse and a dark blue skirt. We
went for walks together, picked cherries for making
jam, went out in the boat. When she jumped
up to reach a cherry or sculled in the boat, her
thin, weak arms showed through her transparent
sleeves. Or I painted a sketch, and she stood
beside me watching rapturously.

One Sunday at the end of July I came to the
Voltchaninovs about nine o'clock in the morning.
I walked about the park, keeping a good distance
from the house, looking for white mushrooms,
of which there was a great number that summer,
and noting their position so as to come and pick
them afterwards with Genya. There was a warm
breeze. I saw Genya and her mother both in
light holiday dresses coming home from church,
Genya holding her hat in the wind. Afterwards
I heard them having tea on the terrace.

For a careless person like me, trying to find
justification for my perpetual idleness, those
holiday mornings in our country-houses in the
summer have always had a particular charm.
When the green garden, still wet with dew, is all
sparkling in the sun and looks radiant with happiness, when there is a scent of mignonette and
oleander near the house, when the young people
have just come back from church and are having
breakfast in the garden, all so charmingly dressed
and gay, and one knows that all these healthy,

well-fed, handsome people are going to do nothing the whole long day, one wishes that all life were like that. Now, too, I had the same thought, and walked about the garden prepared to walk about like that, aimless and unoccupied, the whole day, the whole summer.

Genya came out with a basket; she had a look in her face as though she knew she would find me in the garden, or had a presentiment of it. We gathered mushrooms and talked, and when she asked a question she walked a little ahead so as to see my face.

" A miracle happened in the village yesterday," she said. " The lame woman Pelagea has been ill the whole year. No doctors or medicines did her any good; but yesterday an old woman came and whispered something over her, and her illness passed away."

" That's nothing much," I said. " You mustn't look for miracles only among sick people and old women. Isn't health a miracle ? And life itself ? Whatever is beyond understanding is a miracle."

" And aren't you afraid of what is beyond understanding ?"

" No. Phenomena I don't understand I face boldly, and am not overwhelmed by them. I am above them. Man ought to recognize himself as superior to lions, tigers, stars, superior to everything in nature, even what seems miraculous and is beyond his understanding, or else he is not a man, but a mouse afraid of everything."

Genya believed that as an artist I knew a very great deal, and could guess correctly what I did not know. She longed for me to initiate her into the domain of the Eternal and the Beautiful—into that higher world in which, as she imagined, I was quite at home. And she talked to me of God, of the eternal life, of the miraculous. And I, who could never admit that my self and my imagination would be lost for ever after death, answered: "Yes, men are immortal;" "Yes, there is eternal life in store for us." And she listened, believed, and did not ask for proofs.

As we were going home she stopped suddenly and said:

"Our Lida is a remarkable person—isn't she? I love her very dearly, and would be ready to give my life for her any minute. But tell me "— Genya touched my sleeve with her finger—" tell me, why do you always argue with her? Why are you irritated?"

"Because she is wrong."

Genya shook her head and tears came into her eyes.

"How incomprehensible that is!" she said.

At that minute Lida had just returned from somewhere, and standing with a whip in her hand, a slim, beautiful figure in the sunlight, at the steps, she was giving some orders to one of the men. Talking loudly, she hurriedly received two or three sick villagers; then with a busy and anxious face she walked about the rooms, opening one cupboard after another, and went upstairs. It was a long time before they could find her and call her to dinner, and she came in when we had finished our soup. All these tiny details I remember with tenderness, and that whole day I remember vividly, though nothing special happened. After dinner Genya lay in a long arm-chair reading, while I sat upon the bottom step of the terrace. We were silent. The whole sky was overcast with clouds, and it began to spot with fine rain. It was hot; the wind had dropped, and it seemed as though the day would never end. Ekaterina Pavlovna came out on the terrace, looking drowsy and carrying a fan.

" Oh, mother," said Genya, kissing her hand, " it's not good for you to sleep in the day."

They adored each other. When one went into the garden, the other would stand on the terrace, and, looking towards the trees, call " Aa—oo, Genya !" or " Mother, where are you ?" They always said their prayers together, and had the same faith; and they understood each other perfectly even when they did not speak. And their attitude to people was the same. Ekaterina Pavlovna, too, grew quickly used to me and fond of me, and when I did not come for two or three days, sent to ask if I were well. She, too, gazed at my sketches with enthusiasm, and with the same openness and readiness to chatter as Misuce, she told me what had happened, and confided to me her domestic secrets.

She had a perfect reverence for her elder daughter. Lida did not care for endearments, she talked only of serious matters; she lived her life apart, and to her mother and sister was as sacred and enigmatic a person as the admiral, always sitting in his cabin, is to the sailors.

" Our Lida is a remarkable person," the mother would often say. " Isn't she ?"

Now, too, while it was drizzling with rain, we talked of Lida.

" She is a remarkable girl," said her mother, and added in an undertone, like a conspirator, looking about her timidly: " You wouldn't easily find another like her; only, do you know, I am beginning to be a little uneasy. The school, the dispensary, books—all that's very good, but why go to extremes ? She is three-and-twenty, you know; it's time for her to think seriously of herself. With her books and her dispensary she will find life has slipped by without having noticed it. . . . She must be married."

Genya, pale from reading, with her hair disarranged, raised her head and said as it were to herself, looking at her mother:

" Mother, everything is in God's hands."

And again she buried herself in her book.

Byelokurov came in his tunic and embroidered shirt. We played croquet and tennis, then when it got dark, sat a long time over supper and talked again about schools, and about Balagin, who had the whole district under his thumb. As I went away from the Voltchaninovs that evening, I carried away the impression of a long, long idle day, with a melancholy consciousness that everything ends in this world, however long it may be.

Genya saw us out to the gate, and perhaps because she had been with me all day, from morning till night, I felt dull without her, and that all that charming family were near and dear to me,

and for the first time that summer I had a yearning
to paint.

"Tell me, why do you lead such a dreary
colourless life?" I asked Byelokurov as I went
home. "My life is dreary, difficult, and monotonous because I am an artist, a strange person.
From my earliest days I've been wrung by envy,
self-dissatisfaction, distrust in my work. I'm
always poor, I'm a wanderer, but you—you're
a healthy, normal man, a landowner, and a
gentleman. Why do you live in such an uninteresting way? Why do you get so little out
of life? Why haven't you, for instance, fallen
in love with Lida or Genya?"

"You forget that I love another woman,"
answered Byelokurov.

He was referring to Liubov Ivanovna, the lady
who shared the lodge with him. Every day I saw
this lady, very plump, rotund, and dignified, not
unlike a fat goose, walking about the garden,
in the Russian national dress and beads, always
carrying a parasol; and the servant was continually calling her in to dinner or to tea. Three years
before she had taken one of the lodges for a
summer holiday, and had settled down at Byelokurov's apparently for ever. She was ten years
older than he was, and kept a sharp hand over
him, so much so that he had to ask her permission
when he went out of the house. She often sobbed
in a deep masculine note, and then I used to send
word to her that if she did not leave off, I should
give up my rooms there; and she left off.

When we got home Byelokurov sat down on the

sofa and frowned thoughtfully, and I began walking up and down the room, conscious of a soft emotion as though I were in love. I wanted to talk about the Voltchaninovs.

" Lida could only fall in love with a member of the Zemstvo, as devoted to schools and hospitals as she is," I said. " Oh, for the sake of a girl like that one might not only go into the Zemstvo, but even wear out iron shoes, like the girl in the fairy tale. And Misuce ? What a sweet creature she is, that Misuce !"

Byelokurov, drawling out " Er—er," began a long-winded disquisition on the malady of the age—pessimism. He talked confidently, in a tone that suggested that I was opposing him. Hundreds of miles of desolate, monotonous, burnt-up steppe cannot induce such deep depression as one man when he sits and talks, and one does not know when he will go.

" It's not a question of pessimism or optimism," I said irritably; " it's simply that ninety-nine people out of a hundred have no sense."

Byelokurov took this as aimed at himself, was offended, and went away.

III

" The prince is staying at Malozyomovo, and he asks to be remembered to you," said Lida to her mother. She had just come in, and was taking off her gloves. " He gave me a great deal of interesting news. . . . He promised to raise the question of a medical relief centre at Malozyomovo again at the provincial assembly, but he says there is very little hope of it." And turning to me, she said: "Excuse me, I always forget that this cannot be interesting to you."

I felt irritated.

"Why not interesting to me?" I said, shrugging my shoulders. "You do not care to know my opinion, but I assure you the question has great interest for me."

"Yes?"

"Yes. In my opinion a medical relief centre at Malozyomovo is quite unnecessary."

My irritation infected her; she looked at me, screwing up her eyes, and asked:

"What is necessary? Landscapes?"

"Landscapes are not, either. Nothing is."

She finished taking off her gloves, and opened the newspaper, which had just been brought from the post. A minute later she said quietly, evidently restraining herself:

"Last week Anna died in childbirth, and if there had been a medical relief centre near, she would have lived. And I think even landscape painters ought to have some opinions on the subject."

"I have a very definite opinion on that subject, I assure you," I answered; and she screened herself with the newspaper, as though unwilling to listen to me. "To my mind, all these schools, dispensaries, libraries, medical relief centres, under present conditions, only serve to aggravate the bondage of the people. The peasants are fettered by a great chain, and you do not break the chain, but only add fresh links to it—that's my view of it."

She raised her eyes to me and smiled ironically, and I went on trying to formulate my leading idea.

" What matters is not that Anna died in child-birth, but that all these Annas, Mavras, Pelageas, toil from early morning till dark, fall, ill from working beyond their strength, all their lives tremble for their sick and hungry children, all their lives are being doctored, and in dread of death and disease, fade and grow old early, and die in filth and stench. Their children begin the same story over again as soon as they grow up, and so it goes on for hundreds of years and milliards of men live worse than beasts—in continual terror, for a mere crust of bread. The whole horror of their position lies in their never having time to think of their souls, of their image and semblance. Cold, hunger, animal terror, a burden of toil, like avalanches of snow, block for them every way to spiritual activity—that is, to what dis-tinguishes man from the brutes and what is the only thing which makes life worth living. You go to their help with hospitals and schools, but you don't free them from their fetters by that; on the contrary, you bind them in closer bonds, as, by introducing new prejudices, you increase the number of their wants, to say nothing of the fact that they've got to pay the Zemstvo for blisters and books, and so toil harder than ever."

" I am not going to argue with you," said Lida, putting down the paper. " I've heard all that before. I will only say one thing: one cannot sit with one's hands in one's lap. It's true that we are not saving humanity, and perhaps we make a great many mistakes; but we do what we can, and we are right. The highest and holiest task for a civilized being is to serve his neighbours, and we try to serve them as best we can. You don't like it, but one can't please everyone."

"That's true, Lida," said her mother—"that's true."

In Lida's presence she was always a little timid, and looked at her nervously as she talked, afraid of saying something superfluous or inopportune. And she never contradicted her, but always assented: "That's true, Lida—that's true."

"Teaching the peasants to read and write, books of wretched precepts and rhymes, and medical relief centres, cannot diminish either ignorance or the death-rate, just as the light from your windows cannot light up this huge garden," said I. "You give nothing. By meddling in these people's lives you only create new wants in them, and new demands on their labour."

"Ach! Good heavens! But one must do something!" said Lida with vexation, and from her tone one could see that she thought my arguments worthless and despised them.

"The people must be freed from hard physical labour," said I. "We must lighten their yoke, let them have time to breathe, that they may not spend all their lives at the stove, at the wash-tub, and in the fields, but may also have time to think of their souls, of God—may have time to develop their spiritual capacities. The highest vocation of man is spiritual activity—the perpetual search for truth and the meaning of life. Make coarse animal labour unnecessary for them, let them feel themselves free, and then you will see what a mockery these dispensaries and books are. Once a man recognizes his true vocation, he can only be satisfied by religion, science, and art, and not by these trifles."

" Free them from labour ?" laughed Lida. " But is that possible ?"

"Yes. Take upon yourself a share of their labour. If all of us, townspeople and country people, all without exception, would agree to divide between us the labour which mankind spends on the satisfaction of their physical needs, each of us would perhaps need to work only for two or three hours a day. Imagine that we all, rich and poor, work only for three hours a day, and the rest of our time is free. Imagine further that in order to depend even less upon our bodies and to labour less, we invent machines to replace our work, we try to cut down our needs to the minimum. We would harden ourselves and our children that they should not be afraid of hunger and cold, and that we shouldn't be continually trembling for their health like Anna, Mavra, and Pelagea. Imagine that we don't doctor ourselves, don't keep dispensaries, tobacco factories, distilleries—what a lot of free time would be left us after all ! All of us together would devote our leisure to science and art. Just as the peasants sometimes work, the whole community together mending the roads, so all of us, as a community, would search for truth and the meaning of life, and I am convinced that the truth would be discovered very quickly; man would escape from this continual, agonizing, oppressive dread of death, and even from death itself."

" You contradict yourself, though," said Lida. " You talk about science, and are yourself opposed to elementary education."

" Elementary education when a man has nothing to read but the signs on public-houses and sometimes books which he cannot understand —such education has existed among us since the times of Rurik; Gogol's Petrushka has been reading for ever so long, yet as the village was in the days of Rurik so it has remained. What is needed is not elementary education, but freedom for a wide development of spiritual capacities. What are wanted are not schools, but universities."

" You are opposed to medicine, too."

" Yes. It would be necessary only for the study of diseases as natural phenomena, and not for the cure of them. If one must cure, it should not be diseases, but the causes of them. Remove the principal cause—physical labour, and then there will be no disease. I don't believe in a science that cures disease," I went on excitedly. " When science and art are real, they aim not at temporary, private ends, but at eternal and universal—they seek for truth and the meaning of life, they seek for God, for the soul, and when they are tied down to the needs and evils of the day, to dispensaries and libraries, they only complicate and hamper life.

787

We have plenty of doctors, chemists, lawyers, plenty of people can read and write, but we are quite without biologists, mathematicians, philosophers, poets. The whole of our intelligence, the whole of our spiritual energy, is spent on satisfying temporary, passing needs. Scientific men, writers, artists, are hard at work; thanks to them, the conveniences of life are multiplied from day to day. Our physical demands increase, yet truth is still a long way off, and man still remains the most rapacious and dirty animal; everything is tending to the degeneration of the majority of mankind, and the loss for ever of all fitness for life. In such conditions an artist's work has no meaning, and the more talented he is, the stranger and the more unintelligible is his position, as when one looks into it, it is evident that he is working for the amusement of a rapacious and unclean animal, and is supporting the existing order. And I don't care to work and I won't work. . . . Nothing is any use; let the earth sink to perdition !"

" Misuce, go out of the room !" said Lida to her sister, apparently thinking my words pernicious to the young girl.

Genya looked mournfully at her mother and sister, and went out of the room.

" These are the charming things people say when they want to justify their indifference," said Lida. " It is easier to disapprove of schools and hospitals, than to teach or heal."

" That's true, Lida—that's true," the mother assented.

" You threaten to give up working," said Lida

"You evidently set a high value on your work. Let us give up arguing; we shall never agree, since I put the most imperfect dispensary or library of which you have just spoken so contemptuously on a higher level than any landscape." And turning at once to her mother, she began speaking in quite a different tone: "The prince is very much changed, and much thinner than when he was with us last. He is being sent to Vichy."

She told her mother about the prince in order to avoid talking to me. Her face glowed, and to hide her feeling she bent low over the table as though she were short-sighted, and made a show of reading the newspaper. My presence was disagreeable to her. I said good-bye and went home.

IV

It was quite still out of doors; the village on the further side of the pond was already asleep; there was not a light to be seen, and only the stars were faintly reflected in the pond. At the gate with the lions on it Genya was standing motionless, waiting to escort me.

"Everyone is asleep in the village," I said to her, trying to make out her face in the darkness, and I saw her mournful dark eyes fixed upon me. "The publican and the horse-stealers are asleep, while we, well-bred people, argue and irritate each other."

It was a melancholy August night—melancholy because there was already a feeling of autumn:

789

the moon was rising behind a purple cloud, and it shed a faint light upon the road and on the dark fields of winter corn by the sides. From time to time a star fell. Genya walked beside me along the road, and tried not to look at the sky, that she might not see the falling stars, which for some reason frightened her.

"I believe you are right," she said, shivering with the damp night air. "If people, all together, could devote themselves to spiritual ends, they would soon know everything."

"Of course. We are higher beings, and if we were really to recognize the whole force of human genius and lived only for higher ends, we should in the end become like gods. But that will never be—mankind will degenerate till no traces of genius remain."

When the gates were out of sight, Genya stopped and shook hands with me.

"Good-night," she said, shivering; she had nothing but her blouse over her shoulders and was shrinking with cold. "Come to-morrow."

I felt wretched at the thought of being left alone, irritated and dissatisfied with myself and other people; and I, too, tried not to look at the falling stars.

"Stay another minute," I said to her, "I entreat you."

I loved Genya. I must have loved her because she met me when I came and saw me off when I went away; because she looked at me tenderly and enthusiastically. How touchingly beautiful were her pale face, slender neck, slender arms, her weakness, her idleness, her reading. And intelligence? I suspected in her intelligence above the average. I was fascinated by the breadth of her views, perhaps because they were different from those of the stern, handsome Lida, who disliked me. Genya liked me, because I was an artist. I had conquered her heart by my talent, and had a passionate desire to paint for her sake alone; and I dreamed of her as of my little queen who with me would possess those trees, those fields, the mists, the dawn, the exquisite and beautiful scenery in the midst of which I had felt myself hopelessly solitary and useless.

"Stay another minute," I begged her. "I beseech you."

I took off my overcoat and put it over her chilly shoulders; afraid of looking ugly and absurd in a man's overcoat, she laughed, threw it off, and at that instant I put my arms round her and covered her face, shoulders, and hands with kisses.

"Till to-morrow ' she whispered, and softly, as though afraid of breaking upon the silence of the night, she embraced me. "We have no secrets from one another. I must tell my mother and my sister at once. . . . It's so dreadful! Mother is all right; mother likes you—but Lida!"

She ran to the gates.

"Good-bye!" she called.

And then for two minutes I heard her running. I did not want to go home, and I had nothing to go for. I stood still for a little time hesitating, and made my way slowly back, to look once more

at the house in which she lived, the sweet, simple
old house, which seemed to be watching me from
the windows of its upper storey, and understanding
all about it. I walked by the terrace, sat on the
seat by the tennis ground, in the dark under the
old elm-tree, and looked from there at the house.
In the windows of the top storey where Misuce slept
there appeared a bright light, which changed to
a soft green—they had covered the lamp with
the shade. Shadows began to move. . . . I was
full of tenderness, peace, and satisfaction with
myself—satisfaction at having been able to be
carried away by my feelings and having fallen in
love, and at the same time I felt uncomfortable
at the thought that only a few steps away from
me, in one of the rooms of that house there was
Lida, who disliked and perhaps hated me. I
went on sitting there wondering whether Genya
would come out; I listened and fancied I heard
voices talking upstairs.

About an hour passed. The green light went
out, and the shadows were no longer visible. The
moon was standing high above the house, and
lighting up the sleeping garden and the paths;
the dahlias and the roses in front of the house
could be seen distinctly, and looked all the same
colour. It began to grow very cold. I went out
of the garden, picked up my coat on the road,
and slowly sauntered home.

When next day after dinner I went to the
Voltchaninovs, the glass door into the garden
was wide open. I sat down on the terrace,
expecting Genya every minute, to appear from

behind the flower-beds on the lawn, or from one of the avenues, or that I should hear her voice from the house. Then I walked into the drawing-room, the dining-room. There was not a soul to be seen. From the dining-room I walked along the long corridor to the hall and back. In this corridor there were several doors, and through one of them I heard the voice of Lida:

"'God . . . sent . . . a crow,'" she said in a loud, emphatic voice, probably dictating—"'God sent a crow a piece of cheese. . . . A crow . . . A piece of cheese. . . .' Who's there?" she called suddenly, hearing my steps.

"It's I."

"Ah! Excuse me, I cannot come out to you this minute; I'm giving Dasha her lesson."

"Is Ekaterina Pavlovna in the garden?"

"No, she went away with my sister this morning to our aunt in the province of Penza. And in the winter they will probably go abroad," she added after a pause. "'God sent . . . the crow . . . a piece . . . of cheese. . . .' Have you written it?"

I went into the hall, and stared vacantly at the pond and the village, and the sound reached me of "A piece of cheese. . . . God sent the crow a piece of cheese."

And I went back by the way I had come here for the first time—first from the yard into the garden past the house, then into the avenue of lime-trees. . . . At this point I was overtaken by a small boy who gave me a note:

"I told my sister everything and she insists

on my parting from you," I read. "I could not wound her by disobeying. God will give you happiness. Forgive me. If only you knew how bitterly my mother and I are crying!"

Then there was the dark fir avenue, the broken-down fence. . . . On the field where then the rye was in flower and the corncrakes were calling, now there were cows and hobbled horses. On the slopes there were bright green patches of winter corn. A sober workaday feeling came over me and I felt ashamed of all I had said at the Voltchaninovs', and felt bored with life as I had been before. When I got home, I packed and set off that evening for Petersburg.

*   *   *   *   *

I never saw the Voltchaninovs again. Not long ago, on my way to the Crimea, I met Byelokurov in the train. As before, he was wearing a jerkin and an embroidered shirt, and when I asked how he was, he replied that, God be praised, he was well. We began talking. He had sold his old estate and bought another smaller one, in the name of Liubov Ivanovna. He could tell me little about the Voltchaninovs. Lida, he said, was still living in Shelkovka and teaching in the school; she had by degrees succeeded in gathering round her a circle of people sympathetic to her who made a strong party, and at the last election had turned out Balagin, who had till then had the whole district under his thumb. About Genya he only told me that she did not live at home, and that he did not know where she was.

AN ARTIST'S STORY

I am beginning to forget the old house, and only
sometimes when I am painting or reading I
suddenly, apropos of nothing, remember the green
light in the window, the sound of my footsteps as
I walked home through the fields in the night,
with my heart full of love, rubbing my hands in
the cold. And still more rarely, at moments
when I am sad and depressed by loneliness, I
have dim memories, and little by little I begin to
feel that she is thinking of me, too—that she is
waiting for me, and that we shall meet. . . .

Misuce, where are you ?

1896

A MISFORTUNE

SOFYA PETROVNA, the wife of Lubyantsev the notary, a handsome young woman of five-and-twenty, was walking slowly along a track that had been cleared in the wood, with Ilyin, a lawyer who was spending the summer in the neighbourhood. It was five o'clock in the evening. Feathery-white masses of cloud stood overhead; patches of bright blue sky peeped out between them. The clouds stood motionless, as though they had caught in the tops of the tall old pine-trees. It was still and sultry.

Further on, the track was crossed by a low railway embankment on which a sentinel with a gun was for some reason pacing up and down. Just beyond the embankment there was a large white church with six domes and a rusty roof.

" I did not expect to meet you here," said Sofya Petrovna, looking at the ground and prodding at the last year's leaves with the tip of her parasol, " and now I am glad we have met. I want to speak to you seriously and once for all. I beg you, Ivan Mihalovitch, if you really love and respect me, please make an end of this pursuit of me ! You follow me about like a shadow, you are continually looking at me not in a nice way, making love to me, writing me strange letters, and . . . and I don't know where it's all going to end ! Why, what can come of it ?"

Ilyin said nothing. Sofya Petrovna walked on a few steps and continued:

" And this complete transformation in you all came about in the course of two or three weeks, after five years' friendship. I don't know you, Ivan Mihalovitch !"

Sofya Petrovna stole a glance at her companion. Screwing up his eyes, he was looking intently at the fluffy clouds. His face looked angry, ill-humoured, and preoccupied, like that of a man in pain forced to listen to nonsense.

" I wonder you don't see it yourself," Madame Lubyantsev went on, shrugging her shoulders. " You ought to realize that it's not a very nice part you are playing. I am married; I love and respect my husband. . . . I have a daughter. . . . Can you think all that means nothing ? Besides, as an old friend you know my attitude to family life and my views as to the sanctity of marriage."

Ilyin cleared his throat angrily and heaved a sigh.

" Sanctity of marriage . . ." he muttered. " Oh, Lord !"

" Yes, yes. . . . I love my husband, I respect him; and in any case I value the peace of my home. I would rather let myself be killed than be a cause of unhappiness to Andrey and his daughter. . . . And I beg you, Ivan Mihalovitch, for God's sake, leave me in peace ! Let us be as good, true friends as we used to be, and give up these sighs and groans, which really don't suit you. It's settled and over! Not a word more about it. Let us talk of something else."

Sofya Petrovna again stole a glance at Ilyin's face. Ilyin was looking up; he was pale, and was angrily biting his quivering lips. She could not understand why he was angry and why he was indignant, but his pallor touched her.

"Don't be angry; let us be friends," she said affectionately. "Agreed? Here's my hand."

Ilyin took her plump little hand in both of his, squeezed it, and slowly raised it to his lips.

"I am not a schoolboy," he muttered. "I am not in the least tempted by friendship with the woman I love."

"Enough, enough! It's settled and done with. We have reached the seat; let us sit down."

Sofya Petrovna's soul was filled with a sweet sense of relief: the most difficult and delicate thing had been said, the painful question was settled and done with. Now she could breathe freely and look Ilyin straight in the face. She looked at him, and the egoistic feeling of the superiority of the woman over the man who loves her, agreeably flattered her. It pleased her to see this huge, strong man, with his manly, angry face and his big black beard—clever, cultivated, and, people said, talented—sit down obediently beside her and bow his head dejectedly. For two or three minutes they sat without speaking.

"Nothing is settled or done with," began Ilyin. "You repeat copy-book maxims to me. 'I love and respect my husband . . . the sanctity of marriage. . . .' I know all that without your help, and I could tell you more, too. I tell you truthfully and honestly that I consider the way I am behaving as criminal and immoral. What more can one say than that ? But what's the good of saying what everybody knows ? Instead of feeding nightingales with paltry words, you had much better tell me what I am to do."

" I've told you already—go away."

" As you know perfectly well, I have gone away five times, and every time I turned back on the way. I can show you my through tickets— I've kept them all. I have not will enough to run away from you ! I am struggling, I am struggling horribly; but what the devil am I good for if I have no backbone, if I am weak, cowardly ! I can't struggle with Nature ! Do you understand ? I cannot ! I run away from here, and she holds on to me and pulls me back. Contemptible, loathsome weakness !"

Ilyin flushed crimson, got up, and walked up and down by the seat.

" I feel as cross as a dog," he muttered, clenching his fists. " I hate and despise myself ! My God ! like some depraved schoolboy, I am making love to another man's wife, writing idiotic letters, degrading myself . . . ugh !"

Ilyin clutched at his head, grunted, and sat down.

" And then your insincerity !" he went on bitterly. " If you do dislike my disgusting behaviour, why have you come here ? What drew you here ? In my letters I only ask you for a direct, definite answer—yes or no; but instead of a direct answer, you contrive every day these 'chance' meetings with me and regale me with copy-book maxims!"

Madame Lubyantsev was frightened and flushed. She suddenly felt the awkwardness which a decent woman feels when she is accidentally discovered undressed.

"You seem to suspect I am playing with you," she muttered. "I have always given you a direct answer, and . . . only to-day I've begged you . . ."

"Ough! as though one begged in such cases! If you were to say straight out 'Get away,' I should have been gone long ago; but you've never said that. You've never once given me a direct answer. Strange indecision! Yes, indeed; either you are playing with me, or else . . ."

Ilyin leaned his head on his fists without finishing. Sofya Petrovna began going over in her own mind the way she had behaved from beginning to end. She remembered that not only in her actions, but even in her secret thoughts, she had always been opposed to Ilyin's love-making; but yet she felt there was a grain of truth in the lawyer's words. But not knowing exactly what the truth was, she could not find answers to make to Ilyin's complaint, however hard she thought. It was awkward to be silent, and, shrugging her shoulders, she said:

"So I am to blame, it appears."

"I don't blame you for your insincerity," sighed Ilyin. "I did not mean that when I spoke of it. . . . Your insincerity is natural and in the order of things. If people agreed together and suddenly became sincere, everything would go to the devil."

Sofya Petrovna was in no mood for philosophical reflections, but she was glad of a chance to change the conversation, and asked:

" But why ?"

" Because only savage women and animals are sincere. Once civilization has introduced a demand for such comforts as, for instance, feminine virtue, sincerity is out of place. . . ."

Ilyin jabbed his stick angrily into the sand. Madame Lubyantsev listened to him and liked his conversation, though a great deal of it she did not understand. What gratified her most was that she, an ordinary woman, was talked to by a talented man on " intellectual " subjects; it afforded her great pleasure, too, to watch the working of his mobile, young face, which was still pale and angry. She failed to understand a great deal that he said, but what was clear to her in his words was the attractive boldness with which the modern man without hesitation or doubt decides great questions and draws conclusive deductions.

She suddenly realized that she was admiring him, and was alarmed.

" Forgive me, but I don't understand," she said hurriedly. " What makes you talk of insincerity ? I repeat my request again: be my good, true friend; let me alone ! I beg you most earnestly !"

" Very good; I'll try again," sighed Ilyin. " Glad to do my best. . . . Only I doubt whether anything will come of my efforts. Either I shall put a bullet through my brains or take to drink

in an idiotic way. I shall come to a bad end!
There's a limit to everything — to struggles
with Nature, too. Tell me, how can one struggle
against madness? If you drink wine, how are
you to struggle against intoxication? What am
I to do if your image has grown into my soul,
and day and night stands persistently before my
eyes, like that pine there at this moment? Come,
tell me, what hard and difficult thing can I do to
get free from this abominable, miserable condition.
in which all my thoughts, desires, and dreams
are no longer my own, but belong to some demon
who has taken possession of me? I love you,
love you so much that I am completely thrown
out of gear; I've given up my work and all who
are dear to me; I've forgotten my God! I've
never been in love like this in my life."

Sofya Petrovna, who had not expected such
a turn to their conversation, drew away from
Ilyin and looked into his face in dismay. Tears
came into his eyes, his lips were quivering, and
there was an imploring. hungry expression in his
face.

"I love you!" he muttered, bringing his eyes
near her big, frightened eyes. "You are so
beautiful! I am in agony now, but I swear I
would sit here all my life, suffering and looking
in your eyes. But . . . be silent, I implore you!"

Sofya Petrovna, feeling utterly disconcerted,
tried to think as quickly as possible of something
to say to stop him. "I'll go away," she decided,
but before she had time to make a movement to
get up, Ilyin was on his knees before her. . . . He

was clasping her knees, gazing into her face and speaking passionately, hotly, eloquently. In her terror and confusion she did not hear his words; for some reason now, at this dangerous moment, while her knees were being agreeably squeezed and felt as though they were in a warm bath, she was trying, with a sort of angry spite, to interpret her own sensations. She was angry that instead of brimming over with protesting virtue, she was entirely overwhelmed with weakness, apathy, and emptiness, like a drunken man utterly reckless; only at the bottom of her soul a remote bit of herself was malignantly taunting her: "Why don't you go? Is this as it should be? Yes?"

Seeking for some explanation, she could not understand how it was she did not pull away the hand to which Ilyin was clinging like a leech, and why, like Ilyin, she hastily glanced to right and to left to see whether anyone was looking. The clouds and the pines stood motionless, looking at them severely, like old ushers seeing mischief, but bribed not to tell the school authorities. The sentry stood like a post on the embankment and seemed to be looking at the seat.

"Let him look," thought Sofya Petrovna.

"But . . . but listen," she said at last, with despair in her voice. "What can come of this? What will be the end of this?"

"I don't know, I don't know," he whispered, waving off the disagreeable questions.

They heard the hoarse, discordant whistle of the train. This cold, irrelevant sound from the everyday world of prose made Sofya Petrovna rouse herself.

" I can't stay . . . it's time I was at home," she said, getting up quickly. " The train is coming in. . . . Andrey is coming by it ! He will want his dinner."

Sofya Petrovna turned towards the embankment with a burning face. The engine slowly crawled by, then came the carriages. It was not the local train, as she had supposed, but a goods train. The trucks filed by against the background of the white church in a long string like the days of a man's life, and it seemed as though it would never end.

But at last the train passed, and the last carriage with the guard and a light in it had disappeared behind the trees. Sofya Petrovna turned round sharply, and without looking at Ilyin, walked rapidly back along the track. She had regained her self-possession. Crimson with shame, humiliated not by Ilyin—no, but by her own cowardice, by the shamelessness with which she, a chaste and high-principled woman, had allowed a man, not her husband, to hug her knees—she had only one thought now : to get home as quickly as possible to her villa, to her family. The lawyer could hardly keep pace with her. Turning from the clearing into a narrow path, she turned round and glanced at him so quickly that she saw nothing but the sand on his knees, and waved to him to drop behind.

Reaching home, Sofya Petrovna stood in the middle of her room for five minutes without moving, and looked first at the window and then at her writing-table.

"You low creature!" she said, upbraiding herself. "You low creature!"

To spite herself, she recalled in precise detail, keeping nothing back—she recalled that though all this time she had been opposed to Ilyin's love-making, something had impelled her to seek an interview with him; and what was more, when he was at her feet she had enjoyed it enormously. She recalled it all without sparing herself, and now, breathless with shame, she would have liked to slap herself in the face.

"Poor Andrey!" she said to herself, trying as she thought of her husband to put into her face as tender an expression as she could. "Varya, my poor little girl, doesn't know what a mother she has! Forgive me, my dear ones! I love you so much : . . so much!"

And anxious to prove to herself that she was still a good wife and mother, and that corruption had not yet touched that "sanctity of marriage" of which she had spoken to Ilyin, Sofya Petrovna ran to the kitchen and abused the cook for not having yet laid the table for Andrey Ilyitch. She tried to picture her husband's hungry and exhausted appearance, commiserated him aloud, and laid the table for him with her own hands, which she had never done before. Then she found her daughter Varya, picked her up in her arms and hugged her warmly; the child seemed to her cold and heavy, but she was unwilling to acknowledge this to herself, and she began explaining to the child how good, kind, and honourable her papa was.

But when Andrey Ilyitch arrived soon afterwards she hardly greeted him. The rush of false feeling had already passed off without proving anything to her, only irritating and exasperating her by its falsity. She was sitting by the window, feeling miserable and cross. It is only by being in trouble that people can understand how far from easy it is to be the master of one's feelings and thoughts. Sofya Petrovna said afterwards that there was a tangle within her which it was as difficult to unravel as to count a flock of sparrows rapidly flying by. From the fact that she was not over-joyed to see her husband, that she did not like his manner at dinner, she concluded all of a sudden that she was beginning to hate her husband.

Andrey Ilyitch, languid with hunger and exhaustion, fell upon the sausage while waiting for the soup to be brought in, and ate it greedily, munching noisily and moving his temples.

" My goodness !" thought Sofya Petrovna. " I love and respect him, but . . . why does he munch so repulsively ?"

The disorder in her thoughts was no less than the disorder in her feelings. Like all persons inexperienced in combating unpleasant ideas, Madame Lubyantsev did her utmost not to think of her trouble, and the harder she tried the more vividly Ilyin, the sand on his knees, the fluffy clouds, the train, stood out in her imagination.

" And why did I go there this afternoon like a fool ?" she thought, tormenting herself. " And am I really so weak that I cannot depend upon myself ?"

Fear magnifies danger. By the time Andrey Ilyitch was finishing the last course, she had firmly made up her mind to tell her husband everything and to flee from danger !

" I've something serious to say to you, Andrey," she began after dinner while her husband was taking off his coat and boots to lie down for a nap.

" Well ?"

" Let us leave this place !"

" H'm ! . . . Where shall we go ? It's too soon to go back to town."

" No ; for a tour or something of that sort. . . ."

" For a tour . . ." repeated the notary, stretching. " I dream of that myself, but where are we to get the money, and to whom am I to leave the office ?"

And thinking a little he added:

" Of course, you must be bored. Go by yourself if you like."

Sofya Petrovna agreed, but at once reflected that Ilyin would be delighted with the opportunity, and would go with her in the same train, in the same compartment. . . . She thought and looked at her husband, now satisfied but still languid. For some reason her eyes rested on his feet—miniature, almost feminine feet, clad in striped socks; there was a thread standing out at the tip of each sock.

Behind the blind a bumble-bee was beating itself against the window-pane and buzzing. Sofya Petrovna looked at the threads on the socks, listened to the bee, and pictured how she would set off. . . . *Vis-à-vis* Ilyin would sit, day and night, never taking his eyes off her, wrathful at his own weakness and pale with spiritual agony. He would call himself an immoral schoolboy, would abuse her, tear his hair, but when darkness came on and the passengers were asleep or got out at a station, he would seize the opportunity to kneel before her and embrace her knees as he had at the seat in the wood. . . .

She caught herself indulging in this day-dream.

" Listen. I won't go alone," she said. " You must come with me."

" Nonsense, Sofotchka !" sighed Lubyantsev. " One must be sensible and not want the impossible."

" You will come when you know all about it," thought Sofya Petrovna.

Making up her mind to go at all costs, she felt that she was out of danger. Little by little her ideas grew clearer; her spirits rose and she allowed herself to think about it all, feeling that however much she thought, however much she dreamed, she would go away. While her husband was asleep, the evening gradually came on. She sat in the drawing-room and played the piano. The greater liveliness out of doors, the sounds of music, but above all the thought that she was a sensible person, that she had surmounted her difficulties, completely restored her spirits. Other women, her appeased conscience told her, would probably have been carried off their feet in her position, and would have lost their balance, while she had almost died of shame, had been miserable, and was now running out of the danger which perhaps did not exist! She was so touched by her own virtue and determination that she even looked at herself two or three times in the looking-glass.

When it got dark, visitors arrived. The men sat down in the dining-room to play cards; the ladies remained in the drawing-room and the verandah. The last to arrive was Ilyin. He was gloomy, morose, and looked ill. He sat down in the corner of the sofa and did not move the whole evening. Usually good-humoured and talkative, this time he remained silent, frowned, and rubbed his eyebrows. When he had to answer some question, he gave a forced smile with his upper lip only, and answered jerkily and irritably. Four or five times he made some jest, but his jests sounded harsh and cutting. It seemed to Sofya Petrovna that he was on the verge of hysterics. Only now, sitting at the piano, she recognized fully for the first time that this unhappy man was in deadly earnest, that his soul was sick, and that he could find no rest. For her sake he was wasting the best days of his youth and his career, spending the last of his money on a summer villa, abandoning his mother and sisters, and, worst of all, wearing himself out in an agonizing struggle with himself. From mere common humanity he ought to be treated seriously.

She recognized all this clearly till it made her heart ache, and if at that moment she had gone up to him and said to him, "No," there would have been a force in her voice hard to disobey. But she did not go up to him and did not speak—indeed, never thought of doing so. The pettiness and egoism of youth had never been more patent in her than that evening. She realized that Ilyin was unhappy, and that he was sitting on the sofa as though he were on hot coals; she felt sorry for him, but at the same time the presence of a man who loved her to distraction, filled her soul with triumph and a sense of her own power. She felt her youth, her beauty, and her unassailable virtue, and, since she had decided to go away, gave herself full licence for that evening. She flirted, laughed incessantly, sang with peculiar feeling and gusto. Everything delighted and amused her. She was amused at the memory of what had happened at the seat in the wood, of the sentinel who had looked on. She was amused by her guests, by Ilyin's cutting jests, by the pin in his cravat, which she had never noticed before. There was a red snake with diamond eyes on the pin; this snake struck her as so amusing that she could have kissed it on the spot.

Sofya Petrovna sang nervously, with defiant recklessness as though half intoxicated, and she chose sad, mournful songs which dealt with wasted hopes, the past, old age, as though in mockery of another's grief. " ' And old age comes nearer and nearer ' . . ." she sang. And what was old age to her ?

" It seems as though there is something going wrong with me," she thought from time to time through her laughter and singing.

The party broke up at twelve o'clock. Ilyin

was the last to leave. Sofya Petrovna was still reckless enough to accompany him to the bottom step of the verandah. She wanted to tell him that she was going away with her husband, and to watch the effect this news would produce on him.

The moon was hidden behind the clouds, but it was light enough for Sofya Petrovna to see how the wind played with the skirts of his overcoat and with the awning of the verandah. She could see, too, how white Ilyin was, and how he twisted his upper lip in the effort to smile.

" Sonia, Sonitchka . . . my darling woman !" he muttered, preventing her from speaking. " My dear ! my sweet !"

In a rush of tenderness, with tears in his voice, he showered caressing words upon her, that grew tenderer and tenderer, and even called her " thou," as though she were his wife or mistress. Quite unexpectedly he put one arm round her waist and with the other hand took hold of her elbow.

" My precious ! my delight !" he whispered, kissing the nape of her neck; " be sincere; come to me at once !"

She slipped out of his arms and raised her head to give vent to her indignation and anger, but the indignation did not come off, and all her vaunted virtue and chastity was only sufficient to enable her to utter the phrase used by all ordinary women on such occasions:

" You must be mad."

" Come, let us go," Ilyin continued. " I felt just now, as well as at the seat in the wood, that you are as helpless as I am, Sonia. . . . You are in the same plight ! You love me and are fruitlessly trying to appease your conscience. . . ."

Seeing that she was moving away, he caught her by her lace cuff and said rapidly:

" If not to-day, then to-morrow you will have to give in ! Why, then, this waste of time ? My precious, darling Sonia, the sentence is passed; why put off the execution ? Why deceive yourself ?"

Sofya Petrovna tore herself from him and darted in at the door. Returning to the drawing-room, she mechanically shut the piano, looked for a long time at the music-stand, and sat down. She could not stand up nor think. All that was left of her excitement and recklessness was a fearful weakness, apathy, and dreariness. Her conscience whispered to her that she had behaved badly, foolishly, that evening, like some madcap girl—that she had just been embraced on the verandah, and still had an uneasy feeling in her waist and her elbow. There was not a soul in the drawing-room; there was only one candle burning. Madame Lubyantsev sat on the round stool before the piano, motionless, as though expecting something. And as though taking advantage of the darkness and her extreme lassitude, an oppressive, overpowering desire began to assail her. Like a boa-constrictor it gripped her limbs and her soul, and grew stronger every second, and no longer menaced her as it had done, but stood clear before her in all its nakedness.

She sat for half an hour without stirring, not restraining herself from thinking of Ilyin, then she

IV.   19

got up languidly and dragged herself to her bed-room. Andrey Ilyitch was already in bed. She sat down by the open window and gave herself up to desire. There was no " tangle " now in her head; all her thoughts and feelings were bent with one accord upon a single aim. She tried to struggle against it, but instantly gave it up. . . . She understood now how strong and relentless was the foe. Strength and fortitude were needed to combat him, and her birth, her education, and her life had given her nothing to fall back upon.

" Immoral wretch ! Low creature !" she nagged at herself for her weakness. " So that's what you're like !"

Her outraged sense of propriety was moved to such indignation by this weakness that she lavished upon herself every term of abuse she knew, and told herself many offensive and humiliating truths. So, for instance, she told herself that she never had been moral, that she had not come to grief before simply because she had had no oppor-tunity, that her inward conflict during that day had all been a farce. . . .

" And even if I have struggled," she thought, " what sort of struggle was it ? Even the woman who sells herself struggles before she brings herself to it, and yet she sells herself. A fine struggle ! Like milk, I've turned in a day ! In one day !"

She convicted herself of being tempted, not by feeling, not by Ilyin personally, but by sensations which awaited her . . . an idle lady, having her fling in the summer holidays, like so many !

" ' Like an unfledged bird when the mother has been slain,' " sang a husky tenor outside the window.

" If I am to go, it's time," thought Sofya Petrovna. Her heart suddenly began beating violently.

" Andrey !" she almost shrieked. " Listen ! we . . . we are going ? Yes ?"

" Yes, I've told you already: you go alone."

" But listen," she began. " If you don't go with me, you are in danger of losing me. I believe I am . . . in love already."

" With whom ?" asked Andrey Ilyitch.

" It can't make any difference to you who it is !" cried Sofya Petrovna.

Andrey Ilyitch sat up with his feet out of bed and looked wonderingly at his wife's dark figure.

" It's a fancy !" he yawned.

He did not believe her, but yet he was frightened. After thinking a little and asking his wife several unimportant questions, he delivered himself of his opinions on the family, on infidelity . . . spoke listlessly for about ten minutes and got into bed again. His moralizing produced no effect. There are a great many opinions in the world, and a good half of them are held by people who have never been in trouble !

In spite of the late hour, summer visitors were still walking outside. Sofya Petrovna put on a light cape, stood a little, thought a little. . . . She still had resolution enough to say to her sleeping husband:

A MISFORTUNE

" Are you asleep ? I am going for a walk. . . .
Will you come with me ?"

That was her last hope. Receiving no answer,
she went out. . . . It was fresh and windy.
She was conscious neither of the wind nor the
darkness, but went on and on. . . . An over-
mastering force drove her on, and it seemed as
though, if she had stopped, it would have pushed
her in the back.

" Immoral creature !" she muttered mechanically. " Low wretch !"

She was breathless, hot with shame, did not feel
her legs under her, but what drove her on was
stronger than shame, reason, or fear.

1886

HAPPINESS

A FLOCK of sheep was spending the night on the broad steppe road that is called the great highway. Two shepherds were guarding it. One, a toothless old man of eighty, with a tremulous face, was lying on his stomach at the very edge of the road, leaning his elbows on the dusty leaves of a plantain; the other, a young fellow with thick black eyebrows and no moustache, dressed in the coarse canvas of which cheap sacks are made, was lying on his back, with his arms under his head, looking upwards at the sky, where the stars were slumbering and the Milky Way lay stretched exactly above his face.

The shepherds were not alone. A couple of yards from them in the dusk that shrouded the road a horse made a patch of darkness, and, beside it, leaning against the saddle, stood a man in high boots and a short full-skirted jacket who looked like an overseer on some big estate. Judging from his upright and motionless figure, from his manners, and his behaviour to the shepherds and to his horse, he was a serious, reasonable man who knew his own value; even in the darkness signs could be detected in him of military carriage and of the majestically condescending expression gained by frequent intercourse with the gentry and their stewards.

The sheep were asleep. Against the grey background of the dawn, already beginning to cover the eastern part of the sky, the silhouettes of sheep that were not asleep could be seen here and there; they stood with drooping heads, thinking. Their thoughts, tedious and oppressive, called forth by images of nothing but the broad steppe and the sky, the days and the nights, probably weighed upon them themselves, crushing them into apathy; and, standing there as though rooted to the earth, they noticed neither the presence of a stranger nor the uneasiness of the dogs.

The drowsy, stagnant air was full of the monotonous noise inseparable from a summer night on the steppes; the grasshoppers chirruped incessantly; the quails called, and the young nightingales trilled languidly half a mile away in a ravine where a stream flowed and willows grew.

The overseer had halted to ask the shepherds for a light for his pipe. He lighted it in silence and smoked the whole pipe; then, still without uttering a word, stood with his elbow on the saddle, plunged in thought. The young shepherd took no notice of him, he still lay gazing at the sky while the old man slowly looked the overseer up and down and then asked:

" Why, aren't you Panteley from Makarov's estate ? "

" That's myself," answered the overseer.

" To be sure, I see it is. I didn't know you—

that is a sign you will be rich. Where has God brought you from?"

" From the Kovylyevsky fields."

" That's a good way. Are you letting the land on the part-crop system?"

" Part of it. Some like that, and some we are letting on lease, and some for raising melons and cucumbers. I have just come from the mill."

A big shaggy old sheep-dog of a dirty white colour with woolly tufts about its nose and eyes walked three times quietly round the horse, trying to seem unconcerned in the presence of strangers, then all at once dashed suddenly from behind at the overseer with an angry aged growl; the other dogs could not refrain from leaping up too.

" Lie down, you damned brute," cried the old man, raising himself on his elbow; " blast you, you devil's creature."

When the dogs were quiet again, the old man resumed his former attitude and said quietly:

" It was at Kovyli on Ascension Day that Yefim Zhmenya died. Don't speak of it in the dark, it is a sin to mention such people. He was a wicked old man. I dare say you have heard."

" No, I haven't."

" Yefim Zhmenya, the uncle of Styopka, the blacksmith. The whole district round knew him. Aye, he was a cursed old man, he was! I knew him for sixty years, ever since Tsar Alexander who beat the French was brought from Taganrog to Moscow. We went together to meet the dead Tsar, and in those days the great highway did not run to Bahmut, but from Esaulovka to

Gorodishtche, and where Kovyli is now, there were bustards' nests—there was a bustard's nest at every step. Even then I had noticed that Yefim had given his soul to damnation, and that the Evil One was in him. I have observed that if any man of the peasant class is apt to be silent, takes up with old women's jobs, and tries to live in solitude, there is no good in it, and Yefim from his youth up was always one to hold his tongue and look at you sideways, he always seemed to be sulky and bristling like a cock before a hen. To go to church or to the tavern or to lark in the street with the lads was not his fashion, he would rather sit alone or be whispering with old women. When he was still young he took jobs to look after the bees and the market gardens. Good folks would come to his market garden sometimes and his melons were whistling. One day he caught a pike, when folks were looking on, and it laughed aloud, ' Ho-ho-ho-ho !' "

" It does happen," said Panteley.

The young shepherd turned on his side and, lifting his black eyebrows, stared intently at the old man.

" Did you hear the melons whistling ?" he asked.

" Hear them I didn't, the Lord spared me," sighed the old man, " but folks told me so. It is no great wonder . . . the Evil One will begin whistling in a stone if he wants to. Before the Day of Freedom a rock was humming for three days and three nights in our parts. I heard it myself. The pike laughed because Yefim caught a devil instead of a pike."

The old man remembered something. He got up quickly on to his knees and, shrinking as though from the cold, nervously thrusting his hands into his sleeves, he muttered in a rapid, womanish gabble:

" Lord, save us, and have mercy upon us ! I was walking along the river bank one day to Novopavlovka. A storm was gathering, such a tempest it was, preserve us, Holy Mother, Queen of Heaven. . . . I was hurrying on as best I could, I looked, and beside the path between the thorn bushes—the thorn was in flower at the time—there was a white bullock coming along. I wondered whose bullock it was, and what the devil had sent it there for. It was coming along and swinging its tail and moo-oo-oo ! but would you believe it, friends, I overtake it, I come up close—and it's not a bullock, but Yefim—holy, holy, holy ! I make the sign of the cross while he stares at me and mutters, showing the whites of his eyes; wasn't I frightened ! We came alongside, I was afraid to say a word to him—the thunder was crashing, the sky was streaked with lightning, the willows were bent right down to the water—all at once. my friends, God strike me dead that I die impenitent, a hare ran across the path . . . it ran and stopped, and said like a man: ' Good-evening, peasants.' Lie down, you brute !" the old man cried to the shaggy dog, who was moving round the horse again. " Plague take you !"

" It does happen," said the overseer, still leaning on the saddle and not stirring; he said this in the hollow, toneless voice in which men speak when they are plunged in thought.

" It does happen," he repeated, in a tone of profundity and conviction.

" Ugh, he was a nasty old fellow," the old shepherd went on with somewhat less fervour. " Five years after the Freedom he was flogged by the commune at the office, so to show his spite he took and sent the throat illness upon all Kovyli. Folks died out of number, lots and lots of them, just as in cholera. . . ."

" How did he send the illness ?" asked the young shepherd after a brief silence.

" We all know how, there is no great cleverness needed where there is a will to it. Yefim murdered people with viper's fat. That is such a poison that folks will die from the mere smell of it, let alone the fat."

" That's true," Panteley agreed.

" The lads wanted to kill him at the time, but the old people would not let them. It would never have done to kill him; he knew the place where the treasure is hidden, and not another soul did know. The treasures about here are charmed so that you may find them and not see them, but he did see them. At times he would walk along the river bank or in the forest, and under the bushes and under the rocks there would be little flames, little flames . . . little flames as though from brimstone. I have seen them myself. Everyone expected that Yefim would show people the places or dig the treasure up himself, but he— as the saying is, like a dog in the manger—so he died without digging it up himself or showing other people."

The overseer lit a pipe, and for an instant lighted up his big moustaches and his sharp, stern-looking, and dignified nose. Little circles of light danced from his hands to his cap, raced over the saddle along the horse's back, and vanished in its mane near its ears.

"There are lots of hidden treasures in these parts," he said.

And slowly stretching, he looked round him, resting his eyes on the whitening east and added:

"There must be treasures."

"To be sure," sighed the old man, "one can see from every sign there are treasures, only there is no one to dig them, brother. No one knows the real places; besides, nowadays, you must remember, all the treasures are under a charm. To find them and see them you must have a talisman, and without a talisman you can do nothing, lad. Yefim had talismans, but there was no getting anything out of him, the bald devil. He kept them, so that no one could get them."

The young shepherd crept two paces nearer to the old man and, propping his head on his fists, fastened his fixed stare upon him. A childish expression of terror and curiosity gleamed in his dark eyes, and seemed in the twilight to stretch and flatten out the large features of his coarse young face. He was listening intently.

"It is even written in the Scriptures that there are lots of treasures hidden here," the old man went on; "it is so for sure . . . and no mistake about it. An old soldier of Novopavlovka was shown at Ivanovka a writing, and in this writing it was printed about the place of the treasure and even how many pounds of gold was in it and the sort of vessel it was in; they would have found the treasures long ago by that writing, only the treasure is under a spell, you can't get at it."

"Why can't you get at it, grandfather?" asked the young man.

"I suppose there is some reason, the soldier didn't say. It is under a spell . . . you need a talisman."

The old man spoke with warmth, as though he were pouring out his soul before the overseer. He talked through his nose and, being unaccustomed to talk much and rapidly, stuttered; and, conscious of his defects, he tried to adorn his speech with gesticulations of the hands and head and thin shoulders, and at every movement his hempen shirt crumpled into folds, slipped upwards and displayed his back, black with age and sunburn. He kept pulling it down, but it slipped up again at once. At last, as though driven out of all patience by the rebellious shirt, the old man leaped up and said bitterly:

"There is fortune, but what is the good of it if it is buried in the earth? It is just riches wasted with no profit to anyone, like chaff or sheep's dung, and yet there are riches there, lad, fortune enough for all the country round, but not a soul sees it! It will come to this, that the gentry will dig it up or the government will take it away. The gentry have begun digging the barrows. . . . They scented something! They are envious of the peasants' luck! The government, too, is looking after itself. It is written in the law that if any peasant finds the treasure he is to take it to the authorities! I dare say, wait till you get it! There is a brew but not for you!"

The old man laughed contemptuously and sat down on the ground. The overseer listened with attention and agreed, but from his silence and the expression of his figure it was evident that what the old man told him was not new to him, that he had thought it all over long ago, and knew much more than was known to the old shepherd.

" In my day, I must own, I did seek for fortune a dozen times," said the old man, scratching himself nervously. " I looked in the right places, but I must have come on treasures under a charm. My father looked for it, too, and my brother, too —but not a thing did they find, so they died without luck. A monk revealed to my brother Ilya—the Kingdom of Heaven be his—that in one place in the fortress of Taganrog there was a treasure under three stones, and that that treasure was under a charm, and in those days— it was, I remember, in the year '38—an Armenian used to live at Matvyeev Barrow who sold talismans. Ilya bought a talisman, took two other fellows with him, and went to Taganrog. Only when he got to the place in the fortress, brother, there was a soldier with a gun, standing at the very spot. . . ."

A sound suddenly broke on the still air, and floated in all directions over the steppe. Something in the distance gave a menacing bang, crashed against stone, and raced over the steppe, uttering, "Tah! tah! tah! tah!" When the sound had died away the old man looked inquiringly at Panteley, who stood motionless and unconcerned.

"It's a bucket broken away at the pits," said the young shepherd after a moment's thought.

It was by now getting light. The Milky Way had turned pale and gradually melted like snow, losing its outlines; the sky was becoming dull and dingy so that you could not make out whether it was clear or covered thickly with clouds, and only from the bright leaden streak in the east and from the stars that lingered here and there could one tell what was coming.

The first noiseless breeze of morning, cautiously stirring the spurges and the brown stalks of last year's grass, fluttered along the road.

The overseer roused himself from his thoughts and tossed his head. With both hands he shook the saddle, touched the girth and, as though he could not make up his mind to mount the horse, stood still again, hesitating.

"Yes," he said, "your elbow is near, but you can't bite it. There is fortune, but there is not the wit to find it."

And he turned facing the shepherds. His stern face looked sad and mocking, as though he were a disappointed man.

"Yes, so one dies without knowing what

happiness is like . . ." he said emphatically, lifting his left leg into the stirrup. " A younger man may live to see it, but it is time for us to lay aside all thought of it."

Stroking his long moustaches covered with dew, he seated himself heavily on the horse and screwed up his eyes, looking into the distance, as though he had forgotten something or left something unsaid. In the bluish distance where the furthest visible hillock melted into the mist nothing was stirring; the ancient barrows, once watch-mounds and tombs, which rose here and there above the horizon and the boundless steppe had a sullen and death-like look; there was a feeling of endless time and utter indifference to man in their immobility and silence; another thousand years would pass, myriads of men would die, while they would still stand as they had stood, with no regret for the dead nor interest in the living, and no soul would ever know why they stood there, and what secret of the steppes was hidden under them.

The rooks awakening, flew one after another in silence over the earth. No meaning was to be seen in the languid flight of those long-lived birds, nor in the morning which is repeated punctually every twenty-four hours, nor in the boundless expanse of the steppe.

The overseer smiled and said:

" What space, Lord, have mercy upon us ! You would have a hunt to find treasure in it ! Here," he went on, dropping his voice and making a serious face, " here there are two treasures buried for a certainty. The gentry don't know of them,

826

but the old peasants, particularly the soldiers, know all about them. Here, somewhere on that ridge [the overseer pointed with his whip] robbers one time attacked a caravan of gold; the gold was being taken from Petersburg to the Emperor Peter who was building a fleet at the time at Voronezh. The robbers killed the men with the caravan and buried the gold, but did not find it again afterwards. Another treasure was buried by our Cossacks of the Don. In the year '12 they carried off lots of plunder of all sorts from the French, goods and gold and silver. When they were going homewards they heard on the way that the government wanted to take away all the gold and silver from them. Rather than give up their plunder like that to the government for nothing, the brave fellows took and buried it, so that their children, anyway, might get it; but where they buried it no one knows."

" I have heard of those treasures," the old man muttered grimly.

" Yes . . ." Panteley pondered again. " So it is . . ."

A silence followed. The overseer looked dreamily into the distance, gave a laugh and pulled the rein, still with the same expression as though he had forgotten something or left something unsaid. The horse reluctantly started at a walking pace. After riding a hundred paces Panteley shook his head resolutely, roused himself from his thoughts and, lashing his horse, set off at a trot.

The shepherds were left alone.

"That was Panteley from Makarov's estate," said the old man. "He gets a hundred and fifty a year and provisions found, too. He is a man of education. . . ."

The sheep, waking up—there were about three thousand of them—began without zest to while away the time, nipping at the low, half-trampled grass. The sun had not yet risen, but by now all the barrows could be seen and, like a cloud in the distance, Saur's Grave with its peaked top. If one clambered up on that tomb one could see the plain from it, level and boundless as the sky, one could see villages, manor-houses, the settlements of the Germans and of the Molokani, and a long-sighted Kalmuck could even see the town and the railway-station. Only from there could one see that there was something else in the world besides the silent steppe and the ancient barrows, that there was another life that had nothing to do with buried treasure and the thoughts of sheep.

The old man felt beside him for his crook—a long stick with a hook at the upper end—and got up. He was silent and thoughtful. The young shepherd's face had not lost the look of childish terror and curiosity. He was still under the influence of what he had heard in the night, and impatiently awaiting fresh stories.

"Grandfather," he asked, getting up and taking his crook, "what did your brother Ilya do with the soldier?"

The old man did not hear the question. He looked absent-mindedly at the young man, and answered, mumbling with his lips:

"I keep thinking, Sanka, about that writing that was shown to that soldier at Ivanovka. I didn't tell Panteley—God be with him—but you know in that writing the place was marked out so that even a woman could find it. Do you know where it is? At Bogata Bylotchka at the spot, you know, where the ravine parts like a goose's foot into three little ravines; it is the middle one."

"Well, will you dig?"

"I will try my luck . . ."

"And, grandfather, what will you do with the treasure when you find it?"

"Do with it?" laughed the old man. "H'm! . . . If only I could find it then. . . . I would show them all. . . . H'm! . . . I should know what to do. . . ."

And the old man could not answer what he would do with the treasure if he found it. That question had presented itself to him that morning probably for the first time in his life, and judging from the expression of his face, indifferent and uncritical, it did not seem to him important and deserving of consideration. In Sanka's brain another puzzled question was stirring: why was it only old men searched for hidden treasure, and what was the use of earthly happiness to people who might die any day of old age? But Sanka could not put this perplexity into words, and the old man could scarcely have found an answer to it.

An immense crimson sun came into view surrounded by a faint haze. Broad streaks of light, still cold, bathing in the dewy grass, lengthening out with a joyous air as though to prove they were not weary of their task, began spreading over the earth. The silvery wormwood, the blue flowers of the pig's onion, the yellow mustard, the corn-flowers—all burst into gay colours, taking the sunlight for their own smile.

The old shepherd and Sanka parted and stood at the further sides of the flock. Both stood like posts, without moving, staring at the ground and thinking. The former was haunted by thoughts of fortune, the latter was pondering on what had been said in the night; what interested him was not the fortune itself, which he did not want and could not imagine, but the fantastic, fairy-tale character of human happiness.

A hundred sheep started and, in some inexplicable panic as at a signal, dashed away from the flock; and as though the thoughts of the sheep—tedious and oppressive—had for a moment infected Sanka also, he, too, dashed aside in the same inexplicable animal panic, but at once he recovered himself and shouted:

"You crazy creatures! You've gone mad, plague take you!"

When the sun, promising long hours of overwhelming heat, began to bake the earth, all living things that in the night had moved and uttered sounds were sunk in drowsiness. The old shepherd and Sanka stood with their crooks on opposite sides of the flock, stood without stirring, like fakirs at their prayers, absorbed in thought. They did not hee each other; each of them was living in his own life. The sheep were pondering, too.

THE DARLING

Olenka, the daughter of the retired collegiate assessor, Plemyanniakov, was sitting in her back porch, lost in thought. It was hot, the flies were persistent and teasing, and it was pleasant to reflect that it would soon be evening. Dark rain-clouds were gathering from the east, and bringing from time to time a breath of moisture in the air.

Kukin, who was the manager of an open-air theatre called the Tivoli, and who lived in the lodge, was standing in the middle of the garden looking at the sky.

"Again!" he observed despairingly. "It's going to rain again! Rain every day, as though to spite me! I might as well hang myself! It's ruin! Fearful losses every day."

He flung up his hands, and went on, addressing Olenka:

"There! that's the life we lead, Olga Semyonovna. It's enough to make one cry. One works and does one's utmost; one wears oneself out, getting no sleep at night, and racks one's brain what to do for the best. And then what happens? To begin with, one's public is ignorant, boorish. I give them the very best operetta, a dainty masque, first - rate music - hall artists. But do you suppose that's what they want! They don't understand anything of that sort. They want a clown; what they ask for is vulgarity. And then look at the weather! Almost every evening it rains. It started on the tenth of May, and it's kept it up all May and June. It's simply awful! The public doesn't come, but I've to pay the rent just the same, and pay the artists."

The next evening the clouds would gather again, and Kukin would say with an hysterical laugh:

"Well, rain away, then! Flood the garden, drown me! Damn my luck in this world and the next! Let the artists have me up! Send me to prison!—to Siberia!—the scaffold! Ha, ha, ha!"

And next day the same thing.

Olenka listened to Kukin with silent gravity, and sometimes tears came into her eyes. In the end his misfortunes touched her; she grew to love him. He was a small thin man, with a yellow face, and curls combed forward on his forehead. He spoke in a thin tenor; as he talked his mouth worked on one side, and there was always an expression of despair on his face; yet he aroused a deep and genuine affection in her. She was always fond of someone, and could not exist without loving. In earlier days she had loved her papa, who now sat in a darkened room, breathing with difficulty; she had loved her aunt who used to come every other year from Bryansk; and before that, when she was at school, she had loved her French master. She was a gentle, soft-hearted, compassionate girl, with mild, tender eyes and very good health. At the sight of her full rosy cheeks, her soft white neck with a little dark mole on it, and the kind, naïve smile, which came into her face when she listened to anything pleasant, men thought, " Yes, not half bad," and smiled too, while lady visitors could not refrain from seizing her hand in the middle of a conversation, exclaiming in a gush of delight, " You darling !"

The house in which she had lived from her birth upwards, and which was left her in her father's will, was at the extreme end of the town, not far from the Tivoli. In the evenings and at night she could hear the band playing, and the crackling and banging of fireworks, and it seemed to her that it was Kukin struggling with his destiny, storming the entrenchments of his chief foe, the indifferent public; there was a sweet thrill at her heart, she had no desire to sleep, and when he returned home at daybreak, she tapped softly at her bedroom window, and showing him only her face and one shoulder through the curtain, she gave him a friendly smile. . . .

He proposed to her, and they were married. And when he had a closer view of her neck and her plump, fine shoulders, he threw up his hands, and said:

" You darling !"

He was happy, but as it rained on the day and night of his wedding, his face still retained an expression of despair.

They got on very well together. She used to sit in his office, to look after things in the Tivoli, to put down the accounts and pay the wages. And her rosy cheeks, her sweet, naïve, radiant smile, were to be seen now at the office window, now in the refreshment bar or behind the scenes at the theatre. And already she used to say to her acquaintances that the theatre was the chief and most important thing in life, and that it was only through the drama that one could derive true enjoyment and become cultivated and humane.

"But do you suppose the public understands that ? " she used to say. "What they want is a clown. Yesterday we gave 'Faust Inside Out,' and almost all the boxes were empty; but if Vanitchka and I had been producing some vulgar thing, I assure you the theatre would have been packed. To-morrow Vanitchka and I are doing 'Orpheus in Hell.' Do come."

And what Kukin said about the theatre and the actors she repeated. Like him she despised the public for their ignorance and their indifference to art; she took part in the rehearsals, she corrected the actors, she kept an eye on the behaviour of the musicians, and when there was an unfavourable notice in the local paper, she shed tears, and then went to the editor's office to set things right.

The actors were fond of her and used to call her " Vanitchka and I," and " the darling "; she was sorry for them and used to lend them small sums of money, and if they deceived her, she used to shed a few tears in private, but did not complain to her husband.

They got on well in the winter too. They took the theatre in the town for the whole winter, and let it for short terms to a Little Russian company, or to a conjurer, or to a local dramatic society. Olenka grew stouter, and was always beaming with satisfaction, while Kukin grew thinner and yellower, and continually complained of their terrible losses, although he had not done badly all the winter. He used to cough at night, and she used to give him hot raspberry tea or lime-flower water, to rub him with eau-de-Cologne and to wrap him in her warm shawls.

" You're such a sweet pet ! " she used to say with perfect sincerity, stroking his hair. " You're such a pretty dear ! "

Towards Lent he went to Moscow to collect a new troupe, and without him she could not sleep, but sat all night at her window, looking at the stars, and she compared herself with the hens, who are awake all night and uneasy when the cock is not in the hen-house. Kukin was detained in Moscow, and wrote that he would be back at Easter, adding some instructions about the Tivoli. But on the Sunday before Easter, late in the evening, came a sudden ominous knock at the gate ; someone was hammering on the gate as though on a barrel—boom, boom, boom ! The drowsy cook went flopping with her bare feet through the puddles, as she ran to open the gate.

" Please open," said someone outside in a thick bass. " There is a telegram for you."

Olenka had received telegrams from her husband before, but this time for some reason she felt numb with terror. With shaking hands she opened the telegram and read as follows:

" Ivan Petrovitch died suddenly to-day. Awaiting immate instructions fufuneral Tuesday."

That was how it was written in the telegram—"fufuneral," and the utterly incomprehensible word "immate." It was signed by the stage manager of the operatic company.

" My darling !" sobbed Olenka. " Vanitchka, my precious, my darling ! Why did I ever meet you ! Why did I know you and love you ! Your poor heart-broken Olenka is all alone without you !"

Kukin's funeral took place on Tuesday in Moscow, Olenka returned home on Wednesday, and as soon as she got indoors she threw herself on her bed and sobbed so loudly that it could be heard next door, and in the street.

" Poor darling !" the neighbours said, as they crossed themselves. " Olga Semyonovna, poor darling ! How she does take on !"

Three months later Olenka was coming home from mass, melancholy and in deep mourning. It happened that one of her neighbours, Vassily Andreitch Pustovalov, returning home from church, walked back beside her. He was the manager at Babakayev's, the timber merchant's. He wore a straw hat, a white waistcoat, and a gold watch-chain, and looked more like a country gentleman than a man in trade.

" Everything happens as it is ordained, Olga Semyonovna," he said gravely, with a sympathetic note in his voice; " and if any of our dear ones die, it must be because it is the will of God, so we ought to have fortitude and bear it submissively."

After seeing Olenka to her gate, he said good-bye and went on. All day afterwards she heard his sedately dignified voice, and whenever she shut her eyes she saw his dark beard. She liked him very much. And apparently she had made an impression on him too, for not long afterwards an elderly lady, with whom she was only slightly acquainted, came to drink coffee with her, and as soon as she was seated at table began to talk about Pustovalov, saying that he was an excellent man whom one could thoroughly depend upon, and that any girl would be glad to marry him. Three days later Pustovalov came himself. He did not stay long, only about ten minutes, and he did not say much, but when he left, Olenka loved him—loved him so much that she lay awake all night in a perfect fever, and in the morning she sent for the elderly lady. The match was quickly arranged, and then came the wedding.

Pustovalov and Olenka got on very well together when they were married.

Usually he sat in the office till dinner-time, then he went out on business, while Olenka took his place, and sat in the office till evening, making up accounts and booking orders.

"Timber gets dearer every year; the price rises twenty per cent.," she would say to her customers and friends. "Only fancy we used to sell local timber, and now Vassitchka always has to go for wood to the Mogilev district. And the freight!" she would add, covering her cheeks with her hands in horror. "The freight!"

It seemed to her that she had been in the timber

trade for ages and ages, and that the most important and necessary thing in life was timber; and there was something intimate and touching to her in the very sound of words such as " baulk," " post," " beam," " pole," " scantling," " batten," " lath," " plank," etc.

At night when she was asleep she dreamed of perfect mountains of planks and boards, and long strings of waggons, carting timber somewhere far away. She dreamed that a whole regiment of six-inch beams forty feet high, standing on end, was marching upon the timber-yard; that logs, beams, and boards knocked together with the resounding crash of dry wood, kept falling and getting up again, piling themselves on each other. Olenka cried out in her sleep, and Pustovalov said to her tenderly: " Olenka, what's the matter, darling ? Cross yourself !"

Her husband's ideas were hers. If he thought the room was too hot, or that business was slack, she thought the same. Her husband did not care for entertainments, and on holidays he stayed at home. She did likewise.

"You are always at home or in the office," her friends said to her. "You should go to the theatre, darling, or to the circus."

"Vassitchka and I have no time to go to theatres," she would answer sedately. "We have no time for nonsense. What's the use of these theatres ?"

On Saturdays Pustovalov and she used to go to the evening service; on holidays to early mass, and they walked side by side with softened faces as they came home from church. There was a pleasant fragrance about them both, and her silk dress rustled agreeably. At home they drank tea, with fancy bread and jams of various kinds, and afterwards they ate pie. Every day at twelve o'clock there was a savoury smell of beet-root soup and of mutton or duck in their yard, and on fast-days of fish, and no one could pass the gate without feeling hungry. In the office the samovar was always boiling, and customers were regaled with tea and cracknels. Once a week the couple went to the baths and returned side by side, both red in the face.

" Yes, we have nothing to complain of, thank God," Olenka used to say to her acquaintances. " I wish everyone were as well off as Vassitchka and I."

When Pustovalov went away to buy wood in the Mogilev district, she missed him dreadfully, lay awake and cried. A young veterinary surgeon in the army, called Smirnin, to whom they had let their lodge, used sometimes to come in in the evening. He used to talk to her and play cards with her, and this entertained her in her husband's absence. She was particularly interested in what he told her of his home life. He was married and had a little boy, but was separated from his wife because she had been unfaithful to him, and now he hated her and used to send her forty roubles a month for the maintenance of their son. And hearing of all this, Olenka sighed and shook her head. She was sorry for him.

" Well, God keep you," she used to say to him

at parting, as she lighted him down the stairs with a candle. "Thank you for coming to cheer me up, and may the Mother of God give you health."

And she always expressed herself with the same sedateness and dignity, the same reasonableness, in imitation of her husband. As the veterinary surgeon was disappearing behind the door below, she would say:

"You know, Vladimir Platonitch, you'd better make it up with your wife. You should forgive her for the sake of your son. You may be sure the little fellow understands."

And when Pustovalov came back, she told him in a low voice about the veterinary surgeon and his unhappy home life, and both sighed and shook their heads and talked about the boy, who, no doubt, missed his father, and by some strange connection of ideas, they went up to the holy ikons, bowed to the ground before them and prayed that God would give them children.

And so the Pustovalovs lived for six years quietly and peaceably in love and complete harmony.

But behold! one winter day after drinking hot tea in the office, Vassily Andreitch went out into the yard without his cap on to see about sending off some timber, caught cold and was taken ill. He had the best doctors, but he grew worse and died after four months' illness. And Olenka was a widow once more.

"I've nobody, now you've left me, my darling," she sobbed, after her husband's funeral. "How

can I live without you, in wretchedness and misery !
Pity me, good people, all alone in the world !"

She went about dressed in black with long
" weepers," and gave up wearing hat and gloves
for good. She hardly ever went out, except to
church, or to her husband's grave, and led the life
of a nun. It was not till six months later that she
took off the weepers and opened the shutters of
the windows. She was sometimes seen in the
mornings, going with her cook to market for
provisions, but what went on in her house and
how she lived now could only be surmised. People
guessed, from seeing her drinking tea in her garden
with the veterinary surgeon, who read the newspaper aloud to her, and from the fact that, meeting
a lady she knew at the post-office, she said to her:

" There is no proper veterinary inspection in
our town, and that's the cause of all sorts of epi-
demics. One is always hearing of people's getting
infection from the milk supply, or catching diseases from horses and cows. The health of domestic animals ought to be as well cared for as
the health of human beings."

She repeated the veterinary surgeon's words, and
was of the same opinion as he about everything.
It was evident that she could not live a year
without some attachment, and had found new
happiness in the lodge. In anyone else this would
have been censured, but no one could think ill
of Olenka; everything she did was so natural.
Neither she nor the veterinary surgeon said anything to other people of the change in their rela·
tions, and tried, indeed, to conceal it, but without

DD*

success, for Olenka could not keep a secret. When he had visitors, men serving in his regiment, and she poured out tea or served the supper, she would begin talking of the cattle plague, of the foot and mouth disease, and of the municipal slaughter-houses. He was dreadfully embarrassed, and when the guests had gone, he would seize her by the hand and hiss angrily:

" I've asked you before not to talk about what you don't understand. When we veterinary surgeons are talking among ourselves, please don't put your word in. It's really annoying."

And she would look at him with astonishment and dismay, and ask him in alarm: " But, Voloditchka, what *am* I to talk about ?"

And with tears in her eyes she would embrace him, begging him not to be angry, and they were both happy.

But this happiness did not last long. The veterinary surgeon departed, departed for ever with his regiment, when it was transferred to a distant place—to Siberia, it may be. And Olenka was left alone.

Now she was absolutely alone. Her father had long been dead, and his arm-chair lay in the attic, covered with dust and lame of one leg. She got thinner and plainer, and when people met her in the street they did not look at her as they used to, and did not smile to her; evidently her best years were over and left behind, and now a new sort of life had begun for her, which did not bear thinking about. In the evening Olenka sat in the porch, and heard the band playing and the fireworks popping in the Tivoli, but now the sound stirred no response. She looked into her yard without interest, thought of nothing, wished for nothing, and afterwards, when night came on she went to bed and dreamed of her empty yard. She ate and drank as it were unwillingly.

And what was worst of all, she had no opinions of any sort. She saw the objects about her and understood what she saw, but could not form any opinion about them, and did not know what to talk about. And how awful it is not to have any opinions ! One sees a bottle, for instance, or the rain, or a peasant driving in his cart, but what the bottle is for, or the rain, or the peasant, and what is the meaning of it, one can't say, and could not even for a thousand roubles. When she had Kukin, or Pustovalov, or the veterinary surgeon, Olenka could explain everything, and give her opinion about anything you like, but now there was the same emptiness in her brain and in her heart as there was in her yard outside. And it was as harsh and as bitter as wormwood in the mouth.

Little by little the town grew in all directions. The road became a street, and where the Tivoli and the timber-yard had been, there were new turnings and houses. How rapidly time passes ! Olenka's house grew dingy, the roof got rusty, the shed sank on one side, and the whole yard was overgrown with docks and stinging-nettles. Olenka herself had grown plain and elderly; in summer she sat in the porch, and her soul, as before, was empty and dreary and full of bitterness. In winter she sat at her window and looked at the snow. When she caught the scent of spring, or heard the chime of the church bells, a sudden rush of memories from the past came over her, there was a tender ache in her heart, and her eyes brimmed over with tears; but this was only for a minute, and then came emptiness again and the sense of the futility of life. The black kitten, Briska, rubbed against her and purred softly, but Olenka was not touched by these feline caresses. That was not what she needed. She wanted a love that would absorb her whole being, her whole soul and reason—that would give her ideas and an object in life, and would warm her old blood. And she would shake the kitten off her skirt and say with vexation:

" Get along; I don't want you !"

And so it was, day after day and year after year, and no joy, and no opinions. Whatever Mavra, the cook, said she accepted.

One hot July day, towards evening, just as the cattle were being driven by, and the whole yard was full of dust, someone suddenly knocked at the gate. Olenka went to open it herself and was dumbfounded when she looked out: she saw Smirnin, the veterinary surgeon, grey-headed, and dressed as a civilian. She suddenly remembered everything. She could not help crying and letting her head fall on his breast without uttering a word, and in the violence of her feeling she did not notice how they both walked into the house and sat down to tea.

"My dear Vladimir Platonitch ! What fate has brought you ?" she muttered, trembling with joy.

" I want to settle here for good, Olga Semyonovna," he told her. " I have resigned my post,
and have come to settle down and try my luck on
my own account. Besides, it's time for my boy
to go to school. He's a big boy. I am reconciled
with my wife, you know."

" Where is she ? " asked Olenka.

" She's at the hotel with the boy, and I'm looking
for lodgings."

" Good gracious, my dear soul ! Lodgings !
Why not have my house ? Why shouldn't that
suit you ? Why, my goodness, I wouldn't take
any rent !" cried Olenka in a flutter, beginning to
cry again. " You live here, and the lodge will do
nicely for me. Oh dear ! how glad I am !"

Next day the roof was painted and the walls
were whitewashed, and Olenka, with her arms
akimbo, walked about the yard giving directions.
Her face was beaming with her old smile, and she
was brisk and alert as though she had waked from
a long sleep. The veterinary's wife arrived—a
thin, plain lady, with short hair and a peevish
expression. With her was her little Sasha, a boy
of ten, small for his age, blue-eyed, chubby, with
dimples in his cheeks. And scarcely had the boy
walked into the yard when he ran after the cat,
and at once there was the sound of his gay, joyous
laugh.

" Is that your puss, auntie ? " he asked Olenka.
" When she has little ones, do give us a kitten.
Mamma is awfully afraid of mice."

Olenka talked to him, and gave him tea. Her
heart warmed and there was a sweet ache in her

bosom, as though the boy had been her own child. And when he sat at the table in the evening, going over his lessons, she looked at him with deep tenderness and pity as she murmured to herself:

" You pretty pet ! . . . my precious ! . . . Such a fair little thing, and so clever."

" ' An island is a piece of land which is entirely surrounded by water,' " he read aloud.

" An island is a piece of land," she repeated, and this was the first opinion to which she gave utterance with positive conviction after so many years of silence and dearth of ideas.

Now she had opinions of her own, and at supper she talked to Sasha's parents, saying how difficult the lessons were at the high schools, but that yet the high school was better than a commercial one, since with a high school education all careers were open to one, such as being a doctor or an engineer.

Sasha began going to the high school. His mother departed to Harkov to her sister's and did not return; his father used to go off every day to inspect cattle, and would often be away from home for three days together, and it seemed to Olenka as though Sasha was entirely abandoned, that he was not wanted at home, that he was being starved, and she carried him off to her lodge and gave him a little room there.

And for six months Sasha had lived in the lodge with her. Every morning Olenka came into his bedroom and found him fast asleep, sleeping noiselessly with his hand under his cheek. She was sorry to wake him.

846

"Sashenka," she would say mournfully, "get up, darling. It's time for school."

He would get up, dress and say his prayers, and then sit down to breakfast, drink three glasses of tea, and eat two large cracknels and half a buttered roll. All this time he was hardly awake and a little ill-humoured in consequence.

"You don't quite know your fable, Sashenka," Olenka would say, looking at him as though he were about to set off on a long journey. "What a lot of trouble I have with you! You must work and do your best, darling, and obey your teachers."

"Oh, do leave me alone!" Sasha would say.

Then he would go down the street to school, a little figure, wearing a big cap and carrying a satchel on his shoulder. Olenka would follow him noiselessly.

"Sashenka!" she would call after him, and she would pop into his hand a date or a caramel. When he reached the street where the school was, he would feel ashamed of being followed by a tall, stout woman; he would turn round and say:

"You'd better go home, auntie. I can go the rest of the way alone."

She would stand still and look after him fixedly till he had disappeared at the school-gate.

Ah, how she loved him! Of her former attachments not one had been so deep; never had her soul surrendered to any feeling so spontaneously, so disinterestedly, and so joyously as now that her maternal instincts were aroused. For this little boy with the dimple in his cheek and the big school cap, she would have given her whole life, she would have given it with joy and tears of tenderness. Why? Who can tell why?

When she had seen the last of Sasha, she returned home, contented and serene, brimming over with love; her face, which had grown younger during the last six months, smiled and beamed; people meeting her looked at her with pleasure.

"Good-morning, Olga Semyonovna, darling. How are you, darling?"

"The lessons at the high school are very difficult now," she would relate at the market. "It's too much; in the first class yesterday they gave him a fable to learn by heart, and a Latin translation and a problem. You know it's too much for a little chap."

And she would begin talking about the teachers, the lessons, and the school books, saying just what Sasha said.

At three o'clock they had dinner together: in the evening they learned their lessons together and cried. When she put him to bed, she would stay a long time making the cross over him and murmuring a prayer; then she would go to bed and dream of that far-away misty future when Sasha would finish his studies and become a doctor or an engineer, would have a big house of his own with horses and a carriage, would get married and have children. . . . She would fall asleep still thinking of the same thing, and tears would run down her cheeks from her closed eyes, while the black cat lay purring beside her: "Mrr, mrr, mrr."

Suddenly there would come a loud knock at the gate.

THE DARLING

Olenka would wake up breathless with alarm, her heart throbbing. Half a minute later would come another knock.

"It must be a telegram from Harkov," she would think, beginning to tremble from head to foot. "Sasha's mother is sending for him from Harkov. . . . Oh, mercy on us!"

She was in despair. Her head, her hands, and her feet would turn chill, and she would feel that she was the most unhappy woman in the world. But another minute would pass, voices would be heard: it would turn out to be the veterinary surgeon coming home from the club.

"Well, thank God!" she would think.

And gradually the load in her heart would pass off, and she would feel at ease. She would go back to bed thinking of Sasha, who lay sound asleep in the next room, sometimes crying out in his sleep:

"I'll give it you! Get away! Shut up!"

1899

Printed by Lowe & Brydone, (Printers) Ltd.,
London, N.W.1.

ANTON TCHEHOV

Translated from the Russian by
Constance Garnett.

" Mrs. Garnett's translations from the Russian may
definitely be compared to the epoch-making translations
of the past—to North's Plutarch in the Elizabethan days,
to Schlegel's translation from Shakespeare at the latter
end of the German *Aufklärung* ; they have revealed a new
kingdom of the mind to us, and enabled us vicariously
to explore a whole vista of the human consciousness
that might otherwise have been unknown. . . . Other
writers lift us to the height of comprehension in their own
created worlds, but Tchehov seems to transmute the
common reality. The scales drop from our eyes while
we are looking at the reality itself, not at one refashioned
by the artist." J. MIDDLETON MURRY in the *Nation
and Athenaeum.*

THE TALES

Vol. x. THE HORSE-STEALERS, etc.

The Horse-Stealers : Ward No. 6 : The Petchenyeg : A Dead Body : A Happy Ending : The Looking-Glass : Old Age : Darkness : The Beggar : A Story without a Title : In Trouble : Frost : A Slander : Minds in Ferment : Gone Astray : An Avenger : The Jeune Premier : A Defenceless Creature : An Enigmatic Nature : A Happy Man : A Troublesome Visitor : An Actor's End.

Vol. xi. THE SCHOOLMASTER, etc.

The Schoolmaster : Enemies : The Examining Magistrate : Betrothed : From the Diary of a Violent-Tempered Man : In the Dark : A Play : A Mystery : Strong Impressions : Drunk : The Marshal's Widow : A Bad Business : In the Court : Boots : Joy : Ladies : A Peculiar Man : At the Barber's : An Inadvertence : The Album : Oh ! The Public : A Tripping Tongue : Overdoing It : The Orator : Malingerers : In the Graveyard : Hush ! : In an Hotel : In a Strange Land.

Vol. xii. THE COOK'S WEDDING, etc.

The Cook's Wedding : Sleepy : Children : The Runaway : Grisha : Oysters : Home : A Classical Student : Vanka : An Incident : A Day in the Country : Boys : Shrove-Tuesday : The Old House : In Passion Week : Whitebrow : Kashtanka : A Chameleon : The Dependents : Who was to Blame ? : The Bird Market : An Adventure : The Fish : Art : The Swedish Match.

Vol. xiii. LOVE, etc.

Love : Lights : A Story without an End : Mari d'Elle : A Living Chattel : The Doctor : Too Early ! : The Cossack : Aborigines : An Enquiry : Martyrs : The Lion and the Sun : A Daughter of Albion : Choristers : Nerves : A Work of Art : A Joke : A Country Cottage : A Blunder : Fat and Thin : The Death of a Government Clerk : A Pink Stocking : At a Summer Villa.

Pocket edition, St. Martin's Library. Leather, 5s. net each. Cloth, 3s. 6d. net each.

THE PLAYS

VOL. I. THE CHERRY ORCHARD AND OTHER PLAYS

The Cherry Orchard : Uncle Vanya : The Sea-Gull : The Bear : The Proposal.

VOL. II. THREE SISTERS, ETC.

Three Sisters : Ivanov : A Swan-Song : An Unwilling Martyr : The Anniversary : On the High Road : The Wedding.

Pocket edition, St. Martin's Library. Leather, 5s. net each. Cloth, 3s. 6d. net each.

LETTERS

LETTERS TO HIS FAMILY & FRIENDS

With a biographical sketch and 8 portraits. 12s. 6d. net.

LETTERS TO OLGA KNIPPER

With a biographical note by Olga Knipper, and a frontispiece. 15s. net.

THE WOOD DEMON

Translated by S. S. Koteliansky

The first version of ' Uncle Vanya '; a play. 5s. net.

∴

CHATTO & WINDUS : 97 & 99 ST. MARTIN'S LANE
LONDON, W.C.2